WAR AND PEACE
BOOK 1

Count Leo Nikolayevich Tolstoy was born on the family estate of Yasnaya Polyana in the province of Tula in 1828, into a family ennobled by Peter the Great. He was educated privately and then studied law and Oriental languages at Moscow and Kazan Universities. He returned to Yasnaya where he remained until 1851, after which he enlisted in the Army of the Caucasus. Here he began to see the problems of the Russian society structure, and a year later he started his autobiographical trilogy, *Child-hood, Boyhood* and *Youth*. He served in the Crimean War but retired from the Army after the fall of Sevastopol. Several years in St Petersburg society followed before he returned to Yasnaya and married Sophie Andreyevna Behrs in 1862. It was a very happy marriage and during the first fifteen years they had thirteen children.

War and Peace was begun in 1862 and finished seven years later. *Anna Karenina* was completed in two years, in 1877. After these two great novels, Tolstoy abandoned his beliefs and way of living for the simplicity of peasant life, and described the changeover in *Confession*, published in 1882. Several other books followed including *The Death of Ivan Ilyich* and *Resurrection*. Because of his new beliefs, family life became unbearable and in October 1910 Tolstoy escaped from home with Alexandra, his youngest daughter and only confidante. He became ill at a little railway station in central Russia and died in the stationmaster's room in early November.

WAR AND PEACE
BOOK 1

LEO TOLSTOY

RUPA

Published by
Rupa Publications India Pvt. Ltd 2016
7/16, Ansari Road, Daryaganj
New Delhi 110002

Sales centres:
Bengaluru Chennai
Hyderabad Jaipur Kathmandu
Kolkata Mumbai Prayagraj

Edition copyright © Rupa Publications India 2016

This is a work of fiction. Names, characters, places and incidents are either the product of the author's imagination or are used fictitiously, and any resemblance to any actual persons, living or dead, events or locales is entirely coincidental.

All rights reserved.
No part of this publication may be reproduced, transmitted, or stored in a retrieval system, in any form or by any means, electronic, mechanical, photocopying, recording or otherwise, without the prior permission of the publisher.

P-ISBN: 978-81-291-2413-5
E-ISBN: 978-93-5333-953-1

Third impression 2025

10 9 8 7 6 5 4 3

The moral right of the author has been asserted.

Printed in India

This book is sold subject to the condition that it shall not, by way of trade or otherwise, be lent, resold, hired out, or otherwise circulated, without the publisher's prior consent, in any form of binding or cover other than that in which it is published.

War and Peace
Book 1

The Chief Families in the novel and several important characters. The names most frequently used are in bold.

THE BEZUHOVS

Count Cyril **Bezuhov**
Pierre, his son, legitimised after his father's death, becomes Count Peter **Bezuhov**
Princess **Katish,** Pierre's cousin

THE ROSTOVS

Count Ilya Andreitch **Rostov**
Countess Nataly **Rostov,** his wife
Court **Nikolay** Rostov (**Nikolushka**), their elder son
Count Peter Rostov (**Petya**), their second son
Countess **Vera** Rostov, their elder daughter
Countess Nataly Rostov (**Natasha**), their younger daughter
Sonya, a poor member of the Rostov family circle
Berg, Alphonse Karlitch, an officer of German extraction, who marries Vera

THE BOLKONSKYAS

Prince Nikolay **Bolkonsky,** a retired General-in-Chief
Prince Andrey Bokonsky, his son
Princess Marya Bolkonsky, his daughter
Princess Elizabeth Bolkonsky (**Liza**), Andrey's wife
Tihon, Prince Nikolay's attendant
Alpatitch, his steward

THE KURAGINS

Prince Vassily Kuragin
Prince **Ippolit Kuragin**, his elder son
Prince **Anatole** Kuragin, his younger son
Princess **Ellen** Kuragin, his daughter, who marries Pierre

Princess **Anna Mihalovna** Drubetskoy
Prince **Boris** Drubetskoy, her son
Julie Karagin, an heiress who marries Boris
Anna Pavlovna Scherer, Maid of honour to the ex-Empress
Mariya Fyodorovna
Dolohov (Fedya), an officer and desperado
Marya Dmitryevna Ahrosimov (le terrible dragon)
Denison, Vaska, a hussar officer
Platon **Karataev**, a peasant

PART I

I

'WELL, Prince, Genoa and Lucca are now no more than private estates of the Bonaparte family. No, I warn you, that if you do not tell me we are at war, if you again allow yourself to palliate all the infamies and atrocities of this Antichrist (upon my word, I believe he is), I don't know you in future, you are no longer my friend, no longer my faithful slave, as you say. There, how do you do, how do you do? I see I'm scaring you, sit down and talk to me.'

These words were uttered in July 1805 by Anna Pavlovna Scherer, a distinguished lady of the court, and confidential maid-of-honour to the Empress Mariya Fyodorovna. It was her greeting to Prince Vassily, a man high in rank and office, who was the first to arrive at her *soirée*. Anna Pavlovna had been coughing for the last few days; she had an attack of *la grippe*, as she said—*grippe* was then a new word only used by a few people. In the notes she had sent round in the morning by a footman in red livery, she had written to all indiscriminately:

'If you have nothing better to do, count (or prince), and if the prospect of spending an evening with a poor invalid is not too alarming to you, I shall be charmed to see you at my house between 7 and 10. Annette Scherer.'

'Heavens! what a violent outburst!' the prince responded, not in the least disconcerted at such a reception. He was wearing an embroidered court uniform, stockings and slippers, and had stars on his breast, and a bright smile on his flat face.

He spoke in that elaborately choice French, in which our forefathers not only spoke but thought, and with those slow, patronising intonations peculiar to a man of importance who has grown old in court society. He went up to Anna Pavlovna, kissed her hand, presenting her with a view of his perfumed, shining bald head, and complacently settled himself on the sofa.

'First of all, tell me how you are, dear friend. Relieve a friend's anxiety,' he said, with no change of his voice and tone, in which indifference, and even irony, was perceptible through the veil of courtesy and sympathy.

'How can one be well when one is in moral suffering? How can one help being worried in these times, if one has any feeling?' said Anna Pavlovna. 'You'll spend the whole evening with me, I hope?'

'And the fête at the English ambassador's? Today is Wednesday. I must put in an appearance there,' said the prince. 'My daughter is coming to fetch me and take me there.'

'I thought today's fête had been put off. I confess that all these festivities and fireworks are beginning to pall.'

'If they had known that it was your wish, the fête would have been put off,' said the prince, from habit, like a wound-up clock, saying things he did not even wish to be believed.

'Don't tease me. Well, what has been decided in regard to the Novosiltzoff dispatch? You know everything.'

'What is there to tell?' said the prince in a tired, listless tone. 'What has been decided? It has been decided that Bonaparte has burnt his ships, and I think that we are about to burn ours.'

Prince Vassily always spoke languidly, like an actor repeating his part in an old play. Anna Pavlovna Scherer, in spite of her forty years, was on the contrary brimming over with excitement and impulsiveness. To be enthusiastic had become her pose in society, and at times even when she had, indeed, no inclination to be so, she was enthusiastic so as not to disappoint the expectations of those who knew her. The affected smile which played continually about Anna Pavlovna's face, out of keeping as it was with her faded looks, expressed a spoilt child's continual consciousness of a charming failing of which she had neither the wish nor the power to correct herself, which, indeed, she saw no need to correct.

In the midst of a conversation about politics, Anna Pavlovna became greatly excited.

'Ah, don't talk to me about Austria! I know nothing about it, perhaps, but Austria has never wanted, and doesn't want war. She is betraying us. Russia alone is to be the saviour of Europe. Our benefactor knows his lofty destiny, and will be true to it. That's the one thing I have faith in. Our good and sublime emperor has the greatest part in the world to play, and he is so virtuous and noble that God will not desert him, and he will fulfil his mission—to strangle the hydra of revolution, which is more horrible than ever now in the person of this murderer and miscreant.... Whom can we reckon on, I ask you? ... England with her commercial spirit will not comprehend and cannot comprehend all the loftiness of soul of the Emperor Alexander. She has refused to evacuate Malta. She tries to detect, she seeks a hidden motive in our actions. What have they said to Novosiltsov? Nothing. They didn't understand, they're incapable of understanding the self-sacrifice of our emperor, who desires nothing for himself, and everything for the good of humanity. And what have they promised? Nothing. What they have promised even won't come to anything! Prussia has declared that Bonaparte is invincible, and that all Europe can do nothing against him. ... And I don't believe a single word of what was said by Hardenberg or Haugwitz. That famous Prussian neutrality is a mere snare. I have no faith but in God and the lofty destiny of our adored emperor. He will save Europe!' She stopped short abruptly, with a smile of amusement at her own warmth.

'I imagine,' said the prince, smiling, 'that if you had been sent instead of our dear Wintsengerode, you would have carried the Prussian king's consent by storm,—you are so eloquent. Will you give me some tea?'

'In a moment. By the way,' she added, subsiding into calm again, 'there are two very interesting men to be here to-night, the vicomte de Mortemart; he is connected with the Montmorencies through the Rohans, one of the best families in France. He is one of the good emigrants, the real ones. Then Abbé Morio; you know that profound intellect? He has been received by the emperor. Do you know him?'

'Ah! I shall be delighted,' said the prince. 'Tell me,' he added, as though he had just recollected something, speaking with special nonchalance, though the question was the chief motive of his visit: 'is it true that the dowager empress desires the appointment of Baron Funke as first secretary to the Vienna legation? He is a poor creature, it appears, that baron.' Prince Vassily would have liked to see his son appointed to the post, which people were trying, through the Empress Mariya Fyodorovna, to obtain for the baron.

Anna Pavlovna almost closed her eyes to signify that neither she nor any one else could pass judgment on what the empress might be pleased or see fit to do.

'Baron Funke has been recommended to the empress-mother by her sister,' was all she said in a dry, mournful tone. When Anna Pavlovna spoke of the empress her countenance suddenly assumed a profound and genuine expression of devotion and respect, mingled with melancholy, and this happened whenever she mentioned in conversation her illustrious patroness. She said that her Imperial Majesty had been graciously pleased to show great esteem to Baron Funke, and again a shade of melancholy passed over her face. The prince preserved an indifferent silence. Anna Pavlovna, with the adroitness and quick tact of a courtier and a woman, felt an inclination to chastise the prince for his temerity in referring in such terms to a person recommended to the empress, and at the same time to console him.

'But about your own family,' she said, 'do you know that your daughter, since she has come out, charms everybody. People say she is as beautiful as the day.'

The prince bowed in token of respect and acknowledgment.

'I often think,' pursued Anna Pavlovna, moving up to the prince and smiling cordially to him, as though to mark that political and worldly conversation was over and now intimate talk was to begin: 'I often think how unfairly the blessings of life are sometimes apportioned. Why has fate given you two such splendid children—I don't include Anatole, your youngest—him I don't like' (she put in with a decision admitting of no appeal, raising her eyebrows)—'such charming children? And you really seem to appreciate them less than any one, and so you don't deserve them.'

And she smiled her ecstatic smile.

'What would you have? Lavater would have said that I have not the bump of paternity,' said the prince.

'Don't keep on joking. I wanted to talk to you seriously. Do you know I'm not pleased with your youngest son. Between ourselves' (her face took its mournful expression). 'people have been talking about him to her majesty and commiserating you . . .'

The prince did not answer, but looking at him significantly, she waited in silence for his answer. Prince Vassily frowned.

'What would you have me do?' he said at last. 'You know I have done everything for their education a father could do, and they have both turned out *des imbéciles*. Ippolit is at least a quiet fool, while Anatole's a fool that won't keep quiet, that's the only difference,' he said, with a smile, more unnatural and more animated than usual, bringing out with peculiar prominence something surprisingly brutal and unpleasant in the lines about his mouth.

'Why are children born to men like you? If you weren't a father, I could find no fault with you,' said Anna Pavlovna, raising her eyes pensively.

'I am your faithful slave and to you alone I can confess. My children are the bane of my existence. It's the cross I have to bear, that's how I explain it to myself. What would you have?' . . . He broke off with a gesture expressing his resignation to a cruel fate. Anna Pavlovna pondered a moment.

'Have you never thought of marrying your prodigal son Anatole? People say,' she said, 'that old maids have a mania for matchmaking. I have never been conscious of this failing before, but I have a little person in my mind, who is very unhappy with her father, a relation of ours, the young Princess Bolkonsky.'

Prince Vassily made no reply, but with the rapidity of reflection and memory characteristic of worldly people, he signified by a motion of the head that he had taken in and was considering what she said.

'No, do you know that that boy is costing me forty thousand roubles a year?' he said, evidently unable to restrain the gloomy current of his thoughts. He paused. 'What will it be in five years if this goes on? These are the advantages of being a father. ... Is she rich, your young princess?'

'Her father is very rich and miserly. He lives in the country. You know that notorious Prince Bolkonsky, retired under the late emperor, and nicknamed the "Prussian King". He's a very clever man, but eccentric and tedious. The poor little thing is as unhappy as possible. Her brother it is who has lately been married to Liza Meinen, an adjutant of Kutuzov's. He'll be here this evening.'

'Listen, dear Annette,' said the prince, suddenly taking his companion's hand, and for some reason bending it downwards. 'Arrange this matter for me and I am your faithful slave for ever and ever. She's of good family and well off. That's all I want.'

And with the freedom, familiarity, and grace that distinguished him, he took the maid-of-honour's hand, kissed it, and as he kissed it waved her hand, while he stretched forward in his low chair and gazed away into the distance.

'Wait,' said Anna Pavlovna, considering. 'I'll talk to Lise (the wife of young Bolkonsky) this very evening, and perhaps it can be arranged. I'll try my prentice hand as an old maid in your family.'

II

ANNA PAVLOVNA'S drawing-room gradually began to fill. The people of the highest distinction in Petersburg were there, people very different in ages and characters, but alike in the set in which they moved. The daughter of Prince Vassily, the beauty, Elena, came to fetch her father and go with him to the ambassador's fête. She was wearing a ball-dress with an imperial badge on it. The young Princess Bolkonsky was there, celebrated as the most seductive woman in Petersburg. She had been married the previous winter, and was not now going out into the great world on account of her interesting condition, but was still to be seen at small parties. Prince Ippolit, the son of Prince Vassily, came too with Mortemart, whom he introduced. The Abbé Morio was there too, and many others.

'Have you not yet seen, or not been introduced to *ma tante*?' Anna Pavlovna said to her guests as they arrived, and very seriously she led them up to a little old lady wearing tall bows, who had sailed in out of the next room as soon as the guests began to arrive. Anna Pavlovna mentioned their names, deliberately turning her eyes from the guest to *ma tante*, and then withdrew. All the guests performed the ceremony of greeting the aunt, who was unknown, uninteresting and unnecessary to every one. Anna Pavlovna with mournful, solemn sympathy, followed these greetings, silently approving them. *Ma tante* said to each person the same words about his health, her own health, and the health of her majesty, who was, thank God, better today. Every one, though from politeness showing no undue haste, moved away from the old lady with a sense of relief at a tiresome duty accomplished, and did not approach her again all the evening. The young Princess Bolkonsky had come with her work in a gold-embroidered velvet bag. Her pretty little upper lip, faintly darkened with down, was very short over her teeth, but was all the more charming when it was lifted, and still more charming when it was at times drawn down to meet the lower lip. As is always the case with perfectly charming women, her defect—the shortness of the lip and the half-opened mouth—seemed her peculiar, her characteristic beauty. Every one took delight in watching the pretty creature full of life and gaiety, so soon to be a mother, and so lightly bearing her burden. Old men and bored, depressed young men gazing at her felt as though they were becoming like her, by being with her and talking a little while to her. Any man who spoke to her, and at every word saw her bright little smile and shining white teeth, gleaming continually, imagined that he was being particularly successful this evening. And this each thought in turn.

The little princess, moving with a slight swing, walked with rapid little steps round the table with her work-bag in her hand, and gaily arranging the folds of her gown, sat down on a sofa near the silver samovar; it seemed as though everything she did was a festival for herself and all around her.

'I have brought my work,' she said, displaying her reticule, and addressing the company generally. 'Mind, Annette, don't play me a nasty trick,' she turned to the lady of the house; 'you wrote to me that it was quite a little gathering. See how I am got up.'

And she flung her arms open to show her elegant grey dress, trimmed with lace and girt a little below the bosom with a broad sash.

'Never mind, Lise, you will always be prettier than any one else,' answered Anna Pavlovna.

'You know my husband is deserting me,' she went on in just the same voice, addressing a general; 'he is going to get himself killed. Tell me what this nasty war is for,' she said to Prince Vassily, and without waiting for an answer she turned to Prince Vassily's daughter, the beautiful Ellen.

'How delightful this little princess is!' said Prince Vassily in an undertone to Anna Pavlovna.

Soon after the little princess, there walked in a massively built, stout young man in spectacles, with a cropped head, light breeches in the mode of the day, with a high lace ruffle and a ginger-coloured coat. This stout young man was the illegitimate son of a celebrated dandy of the days of Catherine, Count Bezuhov, who was now dying at Moscow. He had not yet entered any branch of the service; he had only just returned from abroad, where he had been educated, and this was his first appearance in society. Anna Pavlovna greeted him with a nod reserved for persons of the very lowest hierarchy in her drawing-room. But, in spite of this greeting, Anna Pavlovna's countenance showed signs on seeing Pierre of uneasiness and alarm, such as is shown at the sight of something too big and out of place. Though Pierre certainly was somewhat bigger than any of the other men in the room, this expression could only have reference to the clever, though shy, observant and natural look that distinguished him from every one else in the drawing-room.

'It is very kind of you, M. Pierre, to have come to see a poor invalid,' Anna Pavlovna said to him, exchanging anxious glances with her aunt, to whom she was conducting him.

Pierre murmured something unintelligible, and continued searching for something with his eyes. He smiled gleefully and delightedly, bowing to the little princess as though she were an intimate friend, and went up to the aunt. Anna Pavlovna's alarm was not without grounds, for Pierre walked away from the aunt without waiting to the end of her remarks about her majesty's health. Anna Pavlovna stopped him in dismay with the words: 'You don't know Abbé Morio? He's a very interesting man . . .' she said.

'Yes, I have heard of his scheme for perpetual peace, and it's very interesting, but hardly possible . . .'

'You think so?' said Anna Pavlovna in order to say something and to get away again to her duties as hostess, but Pierre committed the opposite incivility. Just now he had walked off without listening to the lady who was addressing him; now he detained by his talk a lady who wanted to get away from him. With head bent and legs planted wide apart, he began explaining to Anna Pavlovna why he considered the abbé's scheme chimerical.

'We will talk of it later,' said Anna Pavlovna, smiling.

And getting rid of this unmannerly young man she returned to her duties, keeping her eyes and ears open, ready to fly to the assistance at any point where the conversation was flagging. Just as the foreman of a spinning-mill settles the work-people in their places, walks up and down the works, and noting any stoppage or unusual creaking or too loud a whir in the spindles, goes up hurriedly, slackens the machinery and sets it going properly, so Anna Pavlovna, walking about her drawing-room, went up to any circle that was pausing or too loud in conversation and by a single word or change of position set the conversational machine going again in its regular, decorous way. But in the midst of these cares a special anxiety on Pierre's account could still be discerned in her. She kept an anxious watch on him as he went up to listen to what was being said near Mortemart, and walked away to another group where the abbé was talking. Pierre had been educated abroad, and this party at Anna Pavlovna's was the first at which he had been present in Russia. He knew all the intellectual lights of Petersburg gathered together here, and his eyes strayed about like a child's in a toy-shop. He was afraid at every moment of missing some intellectual conversation which he might have heard. Gazing at the self-confident and refined expressions of the personages assembled here, he was continually expecting something exceptionally clever. At last he moved up to Abbé Morio. The conversation seemed interesting, and he stood still waiting for an opportunity of expressing his own ideas, as young people are fond of doing.

III

ANNA PAVLOVNA'S *soirée* was in full swing. The spindles kept up their regular hum on all sides without pause. Except the aunt, beside whom was sitting no one but an elderly lady with a thin, careworn face, who seemed rather out of her element in this brilliant society, the company was broken up into three groups. In one of these, the more masculine, the centre was the abbé; in the other, the group of young people, the chief attractions were the beautiful Princess Ellen, Prince Vassily's daughter, and the little Princess Bolkonsky, with her rosy prettiness, too plump for her years. In the third group were Mortemart and Anna Pavlovna.

The vicomte was a pretty young gentleman with soft features and manners, who obviously regarded himself as a celebrity, but with good-breeding modestly allowed the company the benefit of his society. Anna Pavlovna unmistakably regarded him as the chief entertainment she was giving her guests. As a clever *maître d'hôtel* serves as something superlatively good the piece of beef which no one would have cared to eat seeing it in the dirty kitchen, Anna Pavlovna that evening served up to her guests—first, the vicomte and then the abbé, as something superlatively subtle. In Mortemart's group the talk turned at once on the execution of the duc d'Enghien. The vicomte said that the duc d'Enghien had been lost by his own magnanimity and that there were special reasons for Bonaparte's bitterness against him.

'Ah, come! Tell us about that, vicomte,' said Anna Pavlovna gleefully, feeling that the phrase had a peculiarly Louis Quinze note about it: '*Contez-nous cela, vicomte.*'

The vicomte bowed and smiled courteously in token of his readiness to obey. Anna Pavlovna made a circle round the vicomte and invited every one to hear his story.

'The vicomte was personally acquainted with his highness,' Anna Pavlovna whispered to one. 'The vicomte tells a story perfectly,' she said to another. 'How one sees the man of quality,' she said to a third, and the vicomte was presented to the company in the most elegant and advantageous light, like the roast-beef on the hot dish garnished with green parsley.

The vicomte was about to begin his narrative, and he smiled subtly.

'Come over here, *chère Hélène*,' said Anna Pavlovna to the young beauty who was sitting a little way off, the centre of another group.

Princess Ellen smiled. She got up with the same unchanging smile of the acknowledged beauty with which she had entered the drawing-room. Her white ball-dress adorned with ivy and moss rustled lightly; her white shoulders, glossy hair, and diamonds glittered, as she passed between the men who moved apart to make way for her. Not looking directly at any one, but smiling at every one, as it were courteously allowing to all the right to admire the beauty of her figure, her full shoulders, her bosom and back, which were extremely exposed in the mode of the day, she moved up to Anna Pavlovna, seeming to bring with her the brilliance of the ballroom. Ellen was so lovely that she was not merely free from the slightest shade of coquetry, she seemed on the contrary ashamed of the too evident, too violent and all-conquering influence of her beauty. She seemed to wish but to be unable to soften the effect of her beauty.

'What a beautiful woman!' every one said on seeing her. As though struck by something extraordinary, the vicomte shrugged his shoulders and dropped his eyes, when she seated herself near him and dazzled him too with the same unchanging smile.

'Madame, I doubt my abilities before such an audience,' he said, bowing with a smile.

The princess leaned her plump, bare arm on the table and did not find it necessary to say anything. She waited, smiling. During the vicomte's story she sat upright, looking from time to time at her beautiful, plump arm, which lay with its line changed by pressure on the table, then at her still lovelier bosom, on which she set straight her diamond necklace. Several times she settled the folds of her gown, and when the narrative made a sensation upon the audience, she glanced at Anna Pavlovna and at once assumed the expression she saw on the maid-of-honour's face, then she relapsed again into her unvarying smile. After Ellen the little princess too moved away from the tea-table.

'Wait for me, I will take my work,' she said. 'Come, what are you thinking of?' she said to Prince Ippolit. 'Bring me my reticule.'

The little princess, smiling and talking to every one, at once effected a change of position, and settling down again, gaily smoothed out her skirts.

'Now I'm comfortable,' she said, and begging the vicomte to begin, she took up her work. Prince Ippolit brought her reticule, moved to her side, and bending close over her chair, sat beside her.

Le charmant Hippolyte struck every one as extraordinarily like his sister, and, still more, as being, in spite of the likeness, strikingly ugly. His features were like his sister's, but in her, everything was radiant with joyous life, with the complacent, never-failing smile of youth and life and an extraordinary antique beauty of figure. The brother's face on the contrary was clouded over by imbecility and invariably wore a look of aggressive fretfulness, while he was thin and feebly built. His eyes, his nose, his mouth—everything was, as it were, puckered up in one vacant, bored grimace, while his arms and legs always fell into the most grotesque attitudes.

'It is not a ghost story,' he said, sitting down by the princess and hurriedly fixing his eyeglass in his eye, as though without that instrument he could not begin to speak.

'Why no, my dear fellow,' said the astonished vicomte, with a shrug.

'Because I detest ghost stories,' said Prince Ippolit in a tone which showed that he uttered the words before he was aware of their meaning.

From the self-confidence with which he spoke, no one could tell whether what he said was very clever or very stupid. He was dressed in a dark-green frock coat, breeches of the colour of the *cuisse de nymphe effrayée,* as he called it, stockings and slippers. The vicomte very charmingly related the anecdote then current, that the duc d'Enghien had secretly visited Paris for the sake of an interview with the actress, Mlle. Georges, and that there he met Bonaparte, who also enjoyed the favours of the celebrated actress, and that, meeting the duc, Napoleon had fallen into one of the fits to which he was subject and had been completely in the duc's power, how the duc had not taken advantage of it, and Bonaparte had in the sequel avenged this magnanimity by the duc's death.

The story was very charming and interesting, especially at the point when the rivals suddenly recognise each other and the ladies seemed to be greatly excited by it. *'Charmant!'* said Anna Pavlovna, looking inquiringly at the little princess. 'Charming!' whispered the little princess, sticking her needle into her work as an indication that the interest and charm of the story prevented her working. The vicomte appreciated this silent homage, and smiling gratefully, resumed his narrative. But meanwhile Anna Pavlovna, still keeping a watch on the dreadful young man, noticed that he was talking too loudly and too warmly with the abbé and hurried to the spot of danger. Pierre had in fact succeeded in getting into a political conversation with the abbé on the balance of power, and the abbé, evidently interested by the simplehearted fervour of the young man, was unfolding to him his cherished idea. Both were listening and talking too eagerly and naturally, and Anna Pavlovna did not like it.

'The means?—the balance of power in Europe and the rights of the people,' said the abbé. 'One powerful state like Russia—with the prestige of barbarism—need only take a disinterested stand at the head of the alliance that aims at securing the balance of power in Europe, and it would save the world!' 'How are you going to get such a balance of power?' Pierre was beginning; but at that moment Anna Pavlovna came up, and glancing severely at Pierre, asked the Italian how he was supporting the climate. The Italian's face changed instantly and assumed the look of offensive, affected sweetness, which was evidently its habitual expression in conversation with women. 'I am so enchanted by the wit and culture of the society—especially of the ladies—in which I have had the happiness to be received, that I have not yet had time to think of the climate,' he said. Not letting the abbé and Pierre slip out of her grasp, Anna Pavlovna, for greater convenience in watching them, made them join the bigger group.

At that moment another guest walked into the drawing-room. This was the young Prince Andrey Bolkonsky, the husband of the little princess. Prince Bolkonsky was a very handsome young man, of medium height, with clear, clean-cut features. Everything in his appearance, from his weary, bored expression to his slow, measured step, formed the most striking contrast to his lively little wife. Obviously all the people in the drawing-room were familiar figures to him, and more than that, he was unmistakably so sick of them that even to look at them and to listen to them was a weariness to him. Of all the wearisome faces the face of his pretty wife seemed to bore him most. With a grimace that distorted his handsome face he turned away from her. He kissed Anna Pavlovna's hand, and with half-closed eyelids scanned the whole company.

'You are enlisting for the war, prince?' said Anna Pavlovna.

'General Kutuzov has been kind enough to have me as an aide-de-camp,' said Bolkonsky.

'And Lise, your wife? —

'She is going into the country.'

'Isn't it too bad of you to rob us of your charming wife?'

'*André*,' said his wife, addressing her husband in exactly the same coquettish tone in which she spoke to outsiders, 'the vicomte has just told us such a story about Mlle. Georges and Bonaparte!'

Prince Andrey scowled and turned away. Pierre, who had kept his eyes joyfully and affectionately fixed on him ever since he came in, went up to him and took hold of his arm. Prince Andrey, without looking round, twisted his face into a grimace of annoyance at any one's touching him, but seeing Pierre's smiling face, he gave him a smile that was unexpectedly sweet and pleasant.

'Why, you! . . . And in such society too,' he said to Pierre.

'I knew you would be here,' answered Pierre. 'I'm coming to supper with you,' he added in an undertone, not to interrupt the vicomte who was still talking. 'Can I?'

'Oh no, impossible,' said Prince Andrey, laughing, with a squeeze of his hand giving Pierre to understand that there was no need to ask. He would have said something more, but at that instant Prince Vassily and his daughter got up and the two young men rose to make way for them.

'Pardon me, my dear vicomte,' said Prince Vassily in French, gently pulling him down by his sleeve to prevent him from getting up from his seat. 'This luckless fête at the ambassador's deprives me of a pleasure and interrupts you. I am very sorry to leave your enchanting party,' he said to Anna Pavlovna.

His daughter, Princess Ellen, lightly holding the folds of her gown, passed between the chairs, and the smile glowed more brightly than ever on her handsome face. Pierre looked with rapturous, almost frightened eyes at this beautiful creature as she passed them.

'Very lovely!' said Prince Andrey.

'Very,' said Pierre.

As he came up to them, Prince Vassily took Pierre by the arm, and addressing Anna Pavlovna:

'Get this bear into shape for me,' he said. 'Here he has been staying with me for a month, and this is the first time I have seen him in society. Nothing's so necessary for a young man as the society of clever women.'

IV

ANNA PAVLOVNA smiled and promised to look after Pierre, who was, she knew, related to Prince Vassily on his father's side. The elderly lady, who had been till then sitting by the aunt, got up hurriedly, and overtook Prince Vassily in the hall. All the affectation of interest she had assumed till now vanished. Her kindly, careworn face expressed nothing but anxiety and alarm.

'What have you to tell me, prince, of my Boris?' she said, catching him in the hall. 'I can't stay any longer in Petersburg. Tell me what news am I to take to my poor boy?'

Although Prince Vassily listened reluctantly and almost uncivilly to the elderly lady and even showed signs of impatience, she gave him an ingratiating and appealing smile, and to prevent his going away she took him by the arm. 'It is nothing for you to say a word to the Emperor, and he will be transferred at once to the Guards,' she implored.

'Believe me, I will do all I can, princess,' answered Prince Vassily; 'but it's not easy for me to petition the Emperor. I should advise you to apply to Rumyantsov, through Prince Galitsin; that would be the wisest course.'

The elderly lady was a Princess Drubetskoy, one of the best families in Russia; but she was poor, had been a long while out of society, and had lost touch with her former connections. She had come now to try and obtain the appointment of her only son to the Guards. It was simply in order to see Prince Vassily that she had invited herself and come to Anna Pavlovna's party, simply for that she had listened to the vicomte's story. She was dismayed at Prince Vassily's words; her once handsome face showed exasperation, but that lasted only one moment. She smiled again and grasped Prince Vassily's arm more tightly.

'Hear what I have to say, prince,' she said. 'I have never asked you a favour, and never will I ask one; I have never reminded you of my father's affection for you. But now, for God's sake, I beseech you, do this for my son, and I shall consider you my greatest benefactor,' she added hurriedly. 'No, don't be angry, but promise me. I have asked Galitsin; he has refused. Be as kind as you used to be,' she said, trying to smile, though there were tears in her eyes.

'Papa, we are late,' said Princess Ellen, turning her lovely head on her statuesque shoulders as she waited at the door.

But influence in the world is a capital, which must be carefully guarded if it is not to disappear. Prince Vassily knew this, and having once for all reflected that if he were to beg for all who begged him to do so, he would soon be unable to beg for himself, he rarely made use of his influence. In Princess Drubetskoy's case, however, he felt after her new appeal something akin to a conscience-prick. She had reminded him of the truth; for his first step upwards in the service he had been indebted to her father. Besides this, he saw from her manner that she was one of those women—especially mothers—who having once taken an idea into their heads will not give it up till their wishes are fulfilled, and till then are prepared for daily, hourly persistence, and even for scenes. This last consideration made him waver.

'Chère Anna Mihalovna,' he said, with his invariable familiarity and boredom in his voice, 'it's almost impossible for me to do what you wish; but to show you my devotion to you, and my reverence for your dear father's memory, I will do the impossible—your son shall be transferred to the Guards; here is my hand on it. Are you satisfied?'

'My dear prince, you are our benefactor. I expected nothing less indeed; I know how good you are —' He tried to get away. 'Wait a moment, one word. Once in the Guards ...' She hesitated. 'You are on friendly terms with Mihail Ilarionovitch Kutuzov, recommend Boris as his adjutant. Then my heart will be set at rest, then indeed ...'

Prince Vassily smiled. 'That I can't promise. You don't know how Kutuzov has been besieged ever since he has been appointed commander-in-chief. He told me himself that all the Moscow ladies were in league together to give him all their offspring as adjutants.'

'No, promise me; I can't let you off, kind, good friend, benefactor ...'

'Papa,' repeated the beauty in the same tone, 'we are late.'

'Come, au revoir, good-bye. You see how it is.'

'Tomorrow then you will speak to the emperor?'

'Certainly; but about Kutuzov I can't promise.'

'Yes; do promise, promise, Basile,' Anna Mihalovna said, pursuing him with the smile of a coquettish girl, once perhaps characteristic, but now utterly incongruous with her care-worn face. Evidently she had forgotten her age and from habit was bringing out every feminine resource. But as soon as he had gone out her face assumed once more the frigid, artificial expression it had worn all the evening. She went back to the group in which the vicomte was still talking, and again affected to be listening, waiting for the suitable moment to get away, now that her object had been attained.

'And what do you think of this latest farce of the coronation at Milan?' said Anna Pavlovna. 'And the new comedy of the people of Lucca and Genoa coming to present their petitions to Monsieur Buonaparte. Monsieur Buonaparte sitting on a throne and granting the petitions of nations! Adorable! Why, it is enough to drive one out of one's senses! It seems as though the whole world had lost its head.'

Prince Andrey smiled sarcastically, looking straight into Anna Pavlovna's face.

'God gives it me; let man beware of touching it,' he said (Bonaparte's words uttered at the coronation). 'They say that he was very fine as he spoke those words,' he added, and he repeated the same words in Italian: *'Dio mi la dona, gai a qui la tocca.'*

'I hope that at last,' pursued Anna Pavlovna, 'this has been the drop of water that will make the glass run over. The sovereigns cannot continue to endure this man who is a threat to everything.'

'The sovereigns! I am not speaking of Russia,' said the vicomte, deferentially and hopelessly. 'The sovereigns! ... Madame! What did they do for Louis the Sixteenth, for the queen, for Madame Elisabeth? Nothing,' he went on with more animation; 'and believe me, they are undergoing the punishment of their treason to the Bourbon cause. The sovereigns! ... They are sending ambassadors to congratulate the usurper.'

And with a scornful sigh he shifted his attitude again. Prince Ippolit, who had for a long time been staring through his eyeglass at the vicomte, at these words suddenly turned completely round, and bending over the little princess asked her for a needle, and began showing her the coat-of-arms of the Condé family, scratching it with the needle on the table. He explained the coat-of-arms with an air of gravity, as though the princess had asked him about it. 'Staff, gules; engrailed with gules of azure—house of Condé,' he said. The princess listened smiling.

'If Bonaparte remains another year on the throne of France,' resumed the vicomte, with the air of a man who, being better acquainted with the subject than any one else, pursues his own train of thought without listening to other people, 'things will have gone too far. By intrigue and violence, by exiles and executions, French society—I mean good society—will have been destroyed for ever and then ...'

He shrugged his shoulders, and made a despairing gesture with his hand. Pierre wanted to say something—the conversation interested him—but Anna Pavlovna, who was keeping her eye on him, interposed.

'And the Emperor Alexander,' she said with the pathetic note that always accompanied all her references to the imperial family, 'has declared his intention of leaving it to the French themselves to choose their own form of government. And I imagine there is no doubt that the whole nation, delivered from the usurper, would fling itself into the arms of its lawful king,' said Anna Pavlovna, trying to be agreeable to an *émigré* and loyalist.

'That's not certain,' said Prince Andrey. '*M. le vicomte* is quite right in supposing that things have gone too far by now. I imagine it would not be easy to return to the old régime.'

'As far as I could hear,' Pierre, blushing, again interposed in the conversation, 'almost all the nobility have gone over to Bonaparte.'

'That's what the Bonapartists assert,' said the vicomte without looking at Pierre. 'It's a difficult matter now to find out what public opinion is in France.'

'Bonaparte said so,' observed Prince Andrey with a sarcastic smile. It was evident that he did not like the vicomte, and that though he was not looking at him, he was directing his remarks against him.

'"I showed them the path of glory; they would not take it,"' he said after a brief pause, again quoting Napoleon's words. '"I opened my anterooms to them; they crowded in." ... I do not know in what degree he had a right to say so.'

'None!' retorted the vicomte. 'Since the duc's murder, even his warmest partisans have ceased to regard him as a hero. If indeed some people made a hero of him,' said the vicomte addressing Anna Pavlovna, 'since the duke's assassination there has been a martyr more in heaven, and a hero less on earth.'

Anna Pavlovna and the rest of the company hardly had time to smile their appreciation of the vicomte's words, when Pierre again broke into the conversation, and though Anna Pavlovna had a foreboding he would say something inappropriate, this time she was unable to stop him.

'The execution of the duc d'Enghien,' said Monsieur Pierre, 'was a political necessity, and I consider it a proof of greatness of soul that Napoleon did not hesitate to take the whole responsibility of it upon himself.'

'*Dieu! mon Dieu!*' moaned Anna Pavlovna, in a terrified whisper.

'What M. Pierre! you think assassination is greatness of soul,' said the little princess, smiling and moving her work nearer to her.

'Ah! no!' cried different voices.

'Capital!' Prince Ippolit said in English, and he began slapping his knee. The vicomte merely shrugged his shoulders.

Pierre looked solemnly over his spectacles at his audience.

'I say so,' he pursued desperately, 'because the Bourbons ran away from the Revolution, leaving the people to anarchy; and Napoleon alone was capable of understanding the Revolution, of overcoming it, and so for the public good he could not stop short at the life of one man.'

'Won't you come over to this table?' said Anna Pavlovna. But Pierre went on without answering her.

'Yes,' he said, getting more and more eager, 'Napoleon is great because he has towered above the Revolution, and subdued its evil tendencies, preserving all that was good—the equality of all citizens, and freedom of speech and of the press, and only to that end has he possessed himself of supreme power.'

'Yes, if on obtaining power he had surrendered it to the lawful king, instead of making use of it to commit murder,' said the vicomte, 'then I might have called him a great man.'

'He could not have done that. The people gave him power simply for him to rid them of the Bourbons, and that was just why the people believed him to be a great man. The Revolution was a grand fact,' pursued Monsieur Pierre, betraying by this desperate and irrelevantly provocative statement his extreme youth and desire to give full expression to everything.

'Revolution and regicide a grand fact? ... What next? ... but won't you come to this table?' repeated Anna Pavlovna.

'*Contrat social*,' said the vicomte with a bland smile.

'I'm not speaking of regicide. I'm speaking of the idea.'

'The idea of plunder, murder, and regicide!' an ironical voice put in.

'Those were extremes, of course; but the whole meaning of the Revolution did not lie in them, but in the rights of man, in emancipation from conventional ideas, in equality; and all these Napoleon has maintained in their full force.'

'Liberty and equality,' said the vicomte contemptuously, as though he had at last made up his mind to show this youth seriously all the folly of his assertions: 'all high-sounding words, which have long since been debased. Who does not love liberty and equality? Our Saviour indeed preached liberty and equality. Have men been any happier since the Revolution? On the contrary. We wanted liberty, but Bonaparte has crushed it.'

Prince Andrey looked with a smile first at Pierre, then at the vicomte, then at their hostess.

For the first minute Anna Pavlovna had, in spite of her social adroitness, been dismayed by Pierre's outbreak; but when she saw that the vicomte was not greatly discomposed by Pierre's sacrilegious utterances, and had convinced herself that it was impossible to suppress them, she rallied her forces and joined the vicomte in attacking the orator.

'*Mais, mon cher Monsieur Pierre*,' said Anna Pavlovna, 'what have you to say for a great man who was capable of executing the duc—or simply any human being—guiltless and untried?'

'I should like to ask,' said the vicomte, 'how *monsieur* would explain the 18th of Brumaire? Was not that treachery?'

'It was a juggling trick, not at all like a great man's way of acting.'

'And the wounded he killed in Africa?' said the little princess; 'that was awful!' And she shrugged her shoulders.

'He's a plebeian, whatever you may say,' said Prince Ippolit.

Monsieur Pierre did not know which to answer. He looked at them all and smiled. His smile was utterly unlike the half-smile of all the others. When he smiled, suddenly, instantaneously, his serious, even rather sullen, face vanished completely, and a quite different face appeared, childish, good-humoured, even rather stupid, that seemed to beg indulgence. The vicomte, who was seeing him for the first time, saw clearly that this Jacobin was by no means so formidable as his words. Every one was silent.

'How is he to answer every one at once?' said Prince Andrey. 'Besides, in the actions of a statesman, one must distinguish between his acts as a private person and as a general or an emperor. So it seems to me.'

'Yes, yes, of course,' put in Pierre, delighted at the assistance that had come to support him.

'One must admit,' pursued Prince Andrey, 'that Napoleon as a man was great at the bridge of Arcola, or in the hospital at Jaffa, when he gave his hand to the plague-stricken, but ... but there are other actions it would be hard to justify.'

Prince Andrey, who obviously wished to relieve the awkwardness of Pierre's position, got up to go, and made a sign to his wife.

Suddenly Prince Ippolit got up, and with a wave of his hands stopped every one, and motioning to them to be seated, began:

'Ah, I heard a Moscow story today; I must entertain you with it. You will excuse me, vicomte, I must tell it in Russian. If not, the point of the story will be lost.' And Prince Ippolit began speaking in Russian, using the sort of jargon Frenchmen speak after spending a year in Russia. Every one waited expectant; Prince Ippolit had so eagerly, so insistently called for the attention of all for his story.

'In Moscow there is a lady, *une dame*. And she is very stingy. She wanted to have two footmen behind her carriage. And very tall footmen. That was her taste. And she had a lady's maid, also very tall. She said ...'

Here Prince Ippolit paused and pondered, apparently collecting his ideas with difficulty.

'She said ... yes, she said: "Girl," to the lady's maid, "put on *livrée*, and get up behind the carriage, to pay calls."'

Here Prince Ippolit gave a loud guffaw, laughing long before any of his audience, which created an impression by no means flattering to him. Several persons, among them the elderly lady and Anna Pavlovna, did smile, however.

'She drove off. Suddenly there was a violent gust of wind. The girl lost her hat, and her long hair fell down ...'

At this point he could not restrain himself, and began laughing violently, articulating in the middle of a loud guffaw. 'And all the world knew ...'

There the anecdote ended. Though no one could understand why he had told it, and why he had insisted on telling it in Russian, still Anna Pavlovna and several other people appreciated the social breeding of Prince Ippolit in so agreeably putting a close to the disagreeable and ill-bred outbreak of Monsieur Pierre. The conversation after this episode broke up into small talk of no interest concerning the last and the approaching ball, the theatre, and where and when one would meet so-and-so again.

V

THANKING Anna Pavlovna for her *charmante soirée*, the guests began to take leave.

Pierre was clumsy, stout and uncommonly tall, with huge red hands; he did not, as they say, know how to come into a drawing-room and still less how to get out of one, that is, how to say something particularly agreeable on going away. Moreover, he was dreamy. He stood up, and picking up a three-cornered hat with the plume of a general in it instead of his own, he kept hold of it, pulling the feathers till the general asked him to restore it. But all his dreaminess and his inability to enter a drawing-room or talk properly in it were atoned for by his expression of good-nature, simplicity and modesty. Anna Pavlovna turned to him, and with Christian meekness signifying her forgiveness for his misbehaviour, she nodded to him and said:

'I hope I shall see you again, but I hope too you will change your opinions, my dear Monsieur Pierre.'

He made no answer, simply bowed and displayed to every one once more his smile, which said as plainly as words: 'Opinions or no opinions, you see what a nice, good-hearted fellow I am.' And Anna Pavlovna and every one else instinctively felt this. Prince Andrey had gone out into the hall and turning his shoulders to the footman who was ready to put his cloak on him, he listened indifferently to his wife's chatter with Prince Ippolit, who had also come out into the hall. Prince Ippolit stood close to the pretty princess, so soon to be a mother, and stared persistently straight at her through his eyeglass.

'Go in, Annette, you'll catch cold,' said the little princess, saying good-bye to Anna Pavlovna. 'It is settled,' she added in a low voice.

Anna Pavlovna had managed to have a few words with Liza about the match she was planning between Anatole and the sister-in-law of the little princess.

'I rely on you, my dear,' said Anna Pavlovna, also in an undertone; 'you write to her and tell me how the father will view the matter. *Au revoir!*' And she went back out of the hall.

Prince Ippolit went up to the little princess and, bending his face down close to her, began saying something to her in a half whisper.

Two footmen, one the princess's, the other his own, stood with shawl and redingote waiting till they should finish talking, and listened to their French prattle, incomprehensible to them, with faces that seemed to say that they understood what was being said but would not show it. The princess, as always, talked with a smile and listened laughing.

'I'm very glad I didn't go to the ambassador's,' Prince Ippolit was saying: 'such a bore. ... A delightful evening it has been, hasn't it? delightful.'

'They say the ball will be a very fine one,' answered the little princess, twitching up her downy little lip. 'All the pretty women are to be there.'

'Not all, since you won't be there; not all,' said Prince Ippolit, laughing gleefully; and snatching the shawl from the footman, shoving him aside as he did so, he began putting it on the little princess. Either from awkwardness or intentionally—no one could have said which—he did not remove his arms for a long while after the shawl had been put on, as it were holding the young woman in his embrace.

Gracefully, but still smiling, she moved away, turned round and glanced at her husband. Prince Andrey's eyes were closed: he seemed weary and drowsy.

'Are you ready?' he asked his wife, avoiding her eyes.

Prince Ippolit hurriedly put on his redingote, which in the latest mode hung down to his heels, and stumbling over it, ran out on to the steps after the princess, whom the footman was assisting into the carriage.

'*Princesse, au revoir,*' he shouted, his tongue tripping like his legs.

The princess, picking up her gown, seated herself in the darkness of the carriage; her husband was arranging his sabre; Prince Ippolit, under the pretence of assisting, was in every one's way.

'Allow me, sir,' Prince Andrey said in Russian drily and disagreeably to Prince Ippolit, who prevented his passing.

'I expect you, Pierre,' the same voice called in warm and friendly tones.

The postillion started at a trot, and the carriage rumbled away. Prince Ippolit gave vent to a short, jerky guffaw, as he stood on the steps waiting for the vicomte, whom he had promised to take home.

'Well, my dear fellow, your little princess is very good-looking, very good-looking,' said the vicomte, as he sat in the carriage with Ippolit. 'Very good-looking indeed;' he kissed his finger tips. 'And quite French.'

Ippolit snorted and laughed.

'And, do you know, you are a terrible fellow with that little innocent way of yours,' pursued the vicomte. 'I am sorry for the poor husband, that officer boy who gives himself the airs of a reigning prince.'

Ippolit guffawed again, and in the middle of a laugh articulated:

'And you said that the Russian ladies were not equal to the French ladies. You must know how to take them.'

Pierre, arriving first, went to Prince Andrey's study, like one of the household, and at once lay down on the sofa, as his habit was, and taking up the first book he came upon in the shelf (it was Cæsar's *Commentaries*) he propped himself on his elbow, and began reading it in the middle.

'What a shock you gave Mlle. Scherer! She'll be quite ill now,' Prince Andrey said, as he came into the study rubbing his small white hands.

Pierre rolled his whole person over so that the sofa creaked, turned his eager face to Prince Andrey, smiled and waved his hand to him.

'Oh, that abbé was very interesting, only he's got a wrong notion about it. ... To my thinking, perpetual peace is possible, but I don't know how to put it. ... Not by means of the balance of political power. ...'

Prince Andrey was obviously not interested in these abstract discussions.

'One can't always say all one thinks everywhere, *mon cher*. Come tell me, have you settled on anything at last? Are you going into the cavalry or the diplomatic service?' asked Prince Andrey, after a momentary pause.

Pierre sat on the sofa with his legs crossed under him.

'Can you believe it, I still don't know. I don't like either.'

'But you must decide on something; you know your father's expecting it.'

At ten years old Pierre had been sent with an abbé as tutor to be educated abroad, and there he remained till he was twenty. When he returned to Moscow, his father had dismissed the tutor and said to the young man: 'Now you go to Petersburg, look about you and make your choice. I agree to anything. Here is a letter to Prince Vassily and here is money. Write and tell me everything; I will help you in everything.' Pierre had been three months already choosing a career and had not yet made his choice. It was of this choice Prince Andrey spoke to him now. Pierre rubbed his forehead.

'But he must be a freemason,' he said, meaning the abbé he had seen that evening.

'That's all nonsense,' Prince Andrey pulled him up again; 'we'd better talk of serious things. Have you been to the horse guards?'

'No, I haven't; but this is what struck me and I wanted to talk to you about it. This war now is against Napoleon. If it were a war for freedom, I could have understood it, I would have been the first to go into the army; but to help England and Austria against the greatest man in the world—that's not right.'

Prince Andrey simply shrugged his shoulders at Pierre's childish words. He looked as though one really could not answer such absurdities. But in reality it was hard to find any other answer to this naïve question than the answer Prince Andrey made. 'If every one would only fight for his own convictions, there'd be no war,' he said.

'And a very good thing that would be too,' said Pierre.

Prince Andrey smiled ironically. 'Very likely it would be a good thing, but it will never come to pass ...'

'Well, what are you going to the war for?' asked Pierre.

'What for? I don't know. Because I have to. Besides, I'm going ...' he stopped. 'I'm going because the life I lead here, this life is—not to my taste!'

VI

THERE was the rustle of a woman's dress in the next room. Prince Andrey started up, as it were pulling himself together, and his face assumed the expression it had worn in Anna Pavlovna's drawing-room. Pierre dropped his legs down off the sofa. The princess came in. She had changed her gown, and was wearing a house dress as fresh and elegant as the other had been. Prince Andrey got up and courteously set a chair for her.

'Why is it, I often wonder,' she began in French as always, while she hurriedly and fussily settled herself in the low chair, 'why is it Annette never married? How stupid you gentlemen all are not to have married her. You must excuse me, but you really have no sense about women. What an argumentative person you are, Monsieur Pierre!'

'I'm still arguing with your husband; I can't make out why he wants to go to the war,' said Pierre, addressing the princess without any of the affectation so common in the attitude of a young man to a young woman.

The princess shivered. Clearly Pierre's words touched a tender spot.

'Ah, that's what I say,' she said. 'I can't understand, I simply can't understand why men can't get on without war. Why is it we women want nothing of the sort? we don't care for it. Come, you shall be the judge. I keep saying to him: here he is uncle's adjutant, a most brilliant position. He's so well known, so appreciated by every one. The other day at the Apraxins' I heard a lady ask: "So that is the famous Prince André? Upon my word!"' She laughed. 'He's asked everywhere. He could very easily be a flügel-adjutant. You know the Emperor has spoken very graciously to him. Annette and I were saying it would be quite easy to arrange it. What do you think?'

Pierre looked at Prince Andrey, and, noticing that his friend did not like this subject, made no reply.

'When are you starting?' he asked.

'Ah, don't talk to me about that going away; don't talk about it. I won't even hear it spoken of,' said the princess in just the capriciously playful tone in which she had talked to Ippolit at the *soirée*, a tone utterly incongruous in her own home circle, where Pierre was like one of the family. 'This evening when I thought all these relations so precious to me must be broken off.... And then, you know, André?' She looked significantly at her husband. 'I'm afraid! I'm afraid!' she whispered, twitching her shoulder. Her husband looked at her as though he were surprised to observe that there was some one in the room besides himself and Pierre, and with frigid courtesy he addressed an inquiry to his wife.

'What are you afraid of, Liza? I don't understand,' he said.

'See what egoists all men are; they are all, all egoists! Of his own accord, for his own whim, for no reason whatever, he is deserting me, shutting me up alone in the country.'

'With my father and sister, remember,' said Prince Andrey quietly.

'It's just the same as alone, without my friends. . . . And he doesn't expect me to be afraid.' Her tone was querulous now, her upper lip was lifted, giving her face not a joyous expression, but a wild-animal look, like a squirrel. She paused as though feeling it indecorous to speak of her condition before Pierre, though the whole gist of the matter lay in that.

'I still don't understand what you are afraid of,' Prince Andrey said deliberately, not taking his eyes off his wife. The princess flushed red, and waved her hands despairingly.

'No, André, I say you are so changed, so changed . . .'

'Your doctor's orders were that you were to go to bed earlier,' said Prince Andrey. 'It's time you were asleep.'

The princess said nothing, and suddenly her short, downy lip began to quiver; Prince Andrey got up and walked about the room, shrugging his shoulders.

Pierre looked over his spectacles in naïve wonder from him to the princess, and stirred uneasily as though he too meant to get up, but had changed his mind.

'What do I care if Monsieur Pierre is here,' the little princess said suddenly, her pretty face contorted into a tearful grimace; 'I have long wanted to say to you, Andrey, why are you so changed to me? What have I done to you? You go away to the war, you don't feel for me. Why is it?'

'Liza!' was all Prince Andrey said, but in that one word there was entreaty and menace, and, most of all, conviction that she would herself regret her words; but she went on hurriedly.

'You treat me as though I were ill, or a child. I see it all. You weren't like this six months ago.'

'Liza, I beg you to be silent,' said Prince Andrey, still more expressively.

Pierre, who had been growing more and more agitated during this conversation, got up and went to the princess. He seemed unable to endure the sight of her tears, and was ready to weep himself.

'Please don't distress yourself, princess. You only fancy that because . . . I assure you, I've felt so myself . . . because . . . through . . . Oh, excuse me, an outsider has no business . . . Oh, don't distress yourself . . . good-bye.'

Prince Andrey held his hand and stopped him.

'No, stay a little, Pierre. The princess is so good, she would not wish to deprive me of the pleasure of spending an evening with you.'

'No, he thinks of nothing but himself,' the princess declared, not attempting to check her tears of anger.

'Liza,' said Prince Andrey drily, raising his voice to a pitch that showed his patience was exhausted.

All at once the angry squirrel expression of the princess's lovely little face changed to an attractive look of terror that awakened sympathy. She glanced from under her brows with lovely eyes at her husband, and her face wore the timorous, deprecating look of a dog when it faintly but rapidly wags its tail in penitence.

'*Mon Dieu! mon Dieu!*' murmured the princess, and holding her gown with one hand, she went to her husband and kissed him on the forehead.

'Good-night, Liza,' said Prince Andrey, getting up and kissing her hand courteously, as though she were a stranger.

The friends were silent. Neither of them began to talk. Pierre looked at Prince Andrey; Prince Andrey rubbed his forehead with his small hand.

'Let us go and have supper,' he said with a sigh, getting up and going to the door.

They went into the elegantly, newly and richly furnished dining-room. Everything from the dinner-napkins to the silver, the china and the glass, wore that peculiar stamp of newness that is seen in the household belongings of newly married couples. In the middle of supper Prince Andrey leaned on his elbow, and like a man who has long had something on his mind, and suddenly resolves on giving it utterance, he began to speak with an expression of nervous irritation which Pierre had never seen in his friend before.

'Never, never marry, my dear fellow; that's my advice to you; don't marry till you have faced the fact that you have done all you're capable of doing, and till you cease to love the woman you have chosen, till you see her plainly, or else you will make a cruel mistake that can never be set right. Marry when you're old and good for nothing . . . Or else everything good and lofty in you will be done for. It will all be frittered away over trifles. Yes, yes, yes! Don't look at me with such surprise. If you expect anything of yourself in the future you will feel at every step that for you all is over, all is closed up except the drawing-room, where you will stand on the same level with the court lackey and the idiot . . . And why!' . . . He made a vigorous gesture.

Pierre took off his spectacles, which transformed his face, making it look even more good-natured, and looked wonderingly at his friend.

'My wife,' pursued Prince Andrey, 'is an excellent woman. She is one of those rare women with whom one can feel quite secure of one's honour; but, my God! what wouldn't I give now not to be married!. You are the first and the only person I say this to, because I like you.'

As Prince Andrey said this he was less than ever like the Bolkonsky who had sat lolling in Anna Pavlovna's drawing-room with half-closed eyelids, filtering French phrases through his teeth. His dry face was quivering with nervous excitement in every muscle; his eyes, which had seemed lustreless and lifeless, now gleamed with a full, vivid light. It seemed that the more lifeless he was at ordinary times, the more energetic he became at such moments of morbid irritability.

'You can't understand why I say this,' he went on. 'Why, the whole story of life lies in it. You talk of Bonaparte and his career,' he said, though Pierre had not talked of Bonaparte; 'you talk of Bonaparte, but Bonaparte when he was working his way up, going step by step straight to his aim, he was free; he had nothing except his aim and he attained it. But tie yourself up with a woman, and, like a chained convict, you lose all freedom. And all the hope and strength there is in you is only a drag on you, torturing you with regret. Drawing-rooms, gossip, balls, vanity, frivolity—that's the enchanted circle I can't get out of. I am setting off now to the war, the greatest war there has ever been, and I know nothing, and am good for nothing. I am very agreeable and sarcastic,' pursued Prince Andrey, 'and at Anna Pavlovna's every one listens to me. And this imbecile society without which my wife can't exist, and these women . . . If you only knew what these society women are, and indeed, women generally! My father's right. Egoism, vanity, silliness, triviality in everything—that's what women are when they show themselves as they really are. Looking at them in society, one fancies there's something in them, but there's nothing, nothing, nothing. No, don't marry, my dear fellow, don't marry!' Prince Andrey concluded.

'It seems absurd to me,' said Pierre, 'that *you, you* consider *yourself* a failure, your life wrecked. You have everything, everything before you. And *you* . . .'

He did not say *why you*, but his tone showed how highly he thought of his friend, and how much he expected of him in the future.

'How can he say that?' Pierre thought.

Pierre regarded Prince Andrey as a model of all perfection, because Prince Andrey possessed in the highest degree just that combination of qualities in which Pierre was deficient, and which might be most nearly expressed by the idea of strength of will. Pierre always marvelled at Prince Andrey's faculty for dealing with people of every sort with perfect composure, his exceptional memory, his wide knowledge (he had read everything, knew everything, had some notion of everything), and most of all at his capacity for working and learning. If Pierre were frequently struck in Andrey by his lack of capacity for dreaming and philosophising (to which Pierre was himself greatly given), he did not regard this as a defect but as a strong point. Even in the very warmest, friendliest, and simplest relations, flattery or praise is needed just as grease is needed to keep wheels going round.

'I am a man whose day is done,' said Prince Andrey. 'Why talk of me? let's talk about you,' he said after a brief pause, smiling at his own reassuring thoughts. The smile was instantly reflected on Pierre's face.

'Why, what is there to say about me?' said Pierre, letting his face relax into an easy-going, happy smile. 'What am I? I am a bastard.' And he suddenly flushed crimson. Apparently it was a great effort to him to say this. 'With no name, no fortune. . . . And after all, really . . .' He did not finish. 'Meanwhile, I'm free though and I'm content. Only I don't know in the least what to set about doing. I meant to ask your advice in earnest.'

Prince Andrey looked at him with kindly eyes. But in his eyes, friendly and kind as they were, there was yet a consciousness of his own superiority.

'You are dear to me just because you are the one live person in all our society. You're lucky. Choose what you will, that's all the same. You'll always be all right, but there's one thing: give up going about with the Kuragins and leading this sort of life. It's not the right thing for you at all; all this riotous living and dissipation and all . . .'

'What would you have, my dear fellow?' said Pierre, shrugging his shoulders; 'women, my dear fellow, women.'

'I can't understand it,' answered Andrey. 'Ladies, that's another matter, but Kuragin's women, women and wine, I can't understand!'

Pierre was living at Prince Vassily Kuragin's, and sharing in the dissipated mode of life of his son Anatole, the son whom they were proposing to marry to Prince Andrey's sister to reform him.

'Do you know what,' said Pierre, as though a happy thought had suddenly occurred to him; 'seriously, I have been thinking so for a long while. Leading this sort of life I can't decide on anything, or consider anything properly. My head aches and my money's all gone. He invited me tonight, but I won't go.'

'Give me your word of honour that you will give up going.'

'On my honour!'

It was past one o'clock when Pierre left his friend's house. It was a cloudless night, a typical Petersburg summer night. Pierre got into a hired coach, intending to drive home. But the nearer he got, the more he felt it impossible to go to bed on such a night, more like evening or morning. It was light enough to see a long way in the empty streets. On the way Pierre remembered that all the usual gambling set were to meet at Anatole Kuragin's that evening, after which there usually followed a drinking-bout, winding up with one of Pierre's favourite entertainments.

It would be jolly to go to Kuragin's, he thought. But he immediately recalled his promise to Prince Andrey not to go there again.

But, as so often happens with people of weak character, as it is called, he was at once overcome with such a passionate desire to enjoy once more this sort of dissipation which had become so familiar to him, that he determined to go. And the idea at once occurred to him that his promise was of no consequence, since he had already promised Prince Anatole to go before making the promise to Andrey. Finally he reflected that all such promises were merely relative matters, having no sort of precise significance, especially if one considered that tomorrow one might be dead or something so extraordinary might happen that the distinction between honourable and dishonourable would have ceased to exist. Such reflections often occurred to Pierre, completely nullifying all his resolutions and intentions. He went to Kuragin's.

Driving up to the steps of a big house in the Horse Guards' barracks, where Anatole lived, he ran up the lighted steps and the staircase and went in at an open door. There was no one in the ante-room; empty bottles, cloaks, and over-shoes were lying about in disorder: there was a strong smell of spirits; in the distance he heard talking and shouting.

The card-playing and the supper were over, but the party had not broken up. Pierre flung off his cloak, and went into the first room, where there were the remnants of supper, and a footman who, thinking himself unobserved, was emptying the half-full glasses on the sly. In the third room there was a great uproar of laughter, familiar voices shouting, and a bear growling. Eight young men were crowding eagerly about the open window. Three others were busy with a young bear, one of them dragging at its chain and frightening the others with it.

'I bet a hundred on Stevens!' cried one.

'Mind there's no holding him up!' shouted another.

'I'm for Dolohov!' shouted a third. 'Hold the stakes, Kuragin.'

'I say, let Mishka be, we're betting.'

'All at a go or the wager's lost!' cried a fourth.

'Yakov, give us a bottle, Yakov!' shouted Anatole himself, a tall, handsome fellow, standing in the middle of the room, in nothing but a thin shirt, open over his chest. 'Stop, gentlemen. Here he is, here's Petrusha, the dear fellow,' he turned to Pierre.

A man of medium height with bright blue eyes, especially remarkable from looking sober in the midst of the drunken uproar, shouted from the window: 'Come here. I'll explain the bets!' This was Dolohov, an officer of the Semenov regiment, a notorious gambler and duellist, who was living with Anatole. Pierre smiled, looking good-humouredly about him.

'I don't understand. What's the point?'

'Wait a minute, he's not drunk. A bottle here,' said Anatole; and taking a glass from the table he went up to Pierre.

'First of all, you must drink.'

Pierre began drinking off glass after glass, looking from under his brows at the drunken group, who had crowded about the window again, and listening to their talk. Anatole kept his glass filled and told him that Dolohov had made a bet with an Englishman, Stevens, a sailor who was staying here, that he, Dolohov, would drink a bottle of rum sitting in the third story window with his legs hanging down outside.

'Come, empty the bottle,' said Anatole, giving Pierre the last glass, 'or I won't let you go!'

'No, I don't want to,' said Pierre, shoving Anatole away; and he went up to the window.

Dolohov was holding the Englishman's hand and explaining distinctly the terms of the bet, addressing himself principally to Anatole and Pierre.

Dolohov was a man of medium height, with curly hair and clear blue eyes. He was five-and-twenty. Like all infantry officers he wore no moustache, so that his mouth, the most striking feature in his face, was not concealed. The lines of that mouth were extremely delicately chiselled. The upper lip closed vigorously in a sharp wedge-shape on the firm lower one, and at the corners the mouth always formed something like two smiles, one each side, and altogether, especially in conjunction with the resolute, insolent, shrewd look of his eyes, made such an impression that it was impossible to overlook his face. Dolohov was a man of small means and no connections. And yet though

Anatole was spending ten thousand a year, Dolohov lived with him and succeeded in so regulating the position that Anatole and all who knew them respected Dolohov more than Anatole. Dolohov played at every sort of game, and almost always won. However much he drank, his brain never lost its clearness. Both Kuragin and Dolohov were at that time notorious figures in the fast and dissipated world in Petersburg.

The bottle of rum was brought: the window-frame, which hindered any one sitting on the outside sill of the window, was being broken out by two footmen, obviously flurried and intimidated by the shouts and directions given by the gentlemen around them.

Anatole with his swaggering air came up to the window. He was longing to break something. He shoved the footmen aside and pulled at the frame, but the frame did not give. He smashed a pane.

'Now then, you're the strong man,' he turned to Pierre. Pierre took hold of the cross beam, tugged, and with a crash wrenched the oak frame out.

'All out, or they'll think I'm holding on,' said Dolohov.

'The Englishman's bragging ... it's a fine feat ... eh?' said Anatole.

'Fine,' said Pierre, looking at Dolohov, who with the bottle in his hand had gone up to the window, from which the light of the sky could be seen and the glow of morning and of evening melting into it. Dolohov jumped up on to the window, holding the bottle of rum in his hand. 'Listen!' he shouted, standing on the sill and facing the room. Every one was silent.

'I take a bet' (he spoke in French that the Englishman might hear him, and spoke it none too well) ... 'I take a bet for fifty imperials—like to make it a hundred?' he added, turning to the Englishman.

'No, fifty,' said the Englishman.

'Good, for fifty imperials, that I'll drink off a whole bottle of rum without taking it from my lips. I'll drink it sitting outside the window, here on this place' (he bent down and pointed to the sloping projection of the wall outside the window) ... 'and without holding on to anything. ... That right?'

'All right,' said the Englishman.

Anatole turned to the Englishman and taking him by the button of his coat, and looking down at him (the Englishman was a short man), he began repeating the terms of the wager in English.

'Wait a minute!' shouted Dolohov, striking the bottle on the window to call attention. 'Wait a minute, Kuragin; listen: if any one does the same thing, I'll pay him a hundred imperials. Do you understand?'

The Englishman nodded without making it plain whether he intended to take this new bet or not.

Anatole persisted in keeping hold of the Englishman, and although the latter, nodding, gave him to understand that he comprehended fully, Anatole translated Dolohov's words into English. A thin, youthful hussar, who had been losing at cards that evening, slipped up to the window, poked his head out and looked down.

'Oo! ... oo! ... oo!' he said, looking out of the window at the pavement below.

'Shut up!' cried Dolohov, and he pushed the officer away, so that, tripping over his spurs, he went skipping awkwardly into the room.

Setting the bottle on the window-sill, so as to have it within reach, Dolohov climbed slowly and carefully into the window. Lowering his legs over, with both hands spread open on the window-ledge, he tried the position, seated himself, let his hands go, moved a little to the right, and then to the left, and took the bottle. Anatole brought two candles, and set them on the window-ledge, so that it was quite light. Dolohov's back in his white shirt and his curly head were lighted up on both sides. All crowded round the window. The Englishman stood in front. Pierre smiled, and said nothing. One of the party, rather older than the rest, suddenly came forward with a scared and angry face, and tried to clutch Dolohov by his shirt.

'Gentlemen, this is idiocy; he'll be killed,' said this more sensible man.

Anatole stopped him.

'Don't touch him; you'll startle him and he'll be killed Eh? ... What then, eh?'

Dolohov turned, balancing himself, and again spreading his hands out.

'If any one takes hold of me again,' he said, letting his words drop one by one through his thin, tightly compressed lips, 'I'll throw him down from here. Now ...'

Saying 'now,' he turned again, let his hands drop, took the bottle and put it to his lips, bent his head back and held his disengaged hand upwards to keep his balance. One of the footmen who had begun clearing away the broken glass, stopped still in a stooping posture, his eyes fixed on the window and Dolohov's back. Anatole stood upright, with wide-open eyes. The Englishman stared from one side, pursing up his lips. The man who had tried to stop it, had retreated to the corner of the room, and lay on the sofa with his face to the wall. Pierre hid his face, and a smile strayed forgotten upon it, though it was full of terror and fear. All were silent. Pierre took his hands from his eyes; Dolohov was still sitting in the same position, only his head was so far bent back that his curls touched his shirt collar, and the hand with the bottle rose higher and higher, trembling with evident effort. Evidently the bottle was nearly empty, and so was tipped higher, throwing the head back. 'Why is it so long?' thought Pierre. It seemed to him that more than half an hour had passed. Suddenly Dolohov made a backward movement of the spine, and his arm trembled nervously; this was enough to displace his whole body as he sat on the sloping projection. He moved all over, and his arm and head trembled still more violently with the strain. One hand rose to clutch at the window-ledge, but it dropped again. Pierre shut his eyes once more, and said to himself that he would never open them again. Suddenly he was aware of a general stir about him. He glanced up, Dolohov was standing on the window-ledge, his face was pale and full of merriment.

'Empty!'

He tossed the bottle to the Englishman, who caught it neatly. Dolohov jumped down from the window. He smelt very strongly of rum.

'Capital! Bravo! That's something like a bet. You're a devil of a fellow!' came shouts from all sides.

The Englishman took out his purse and counted out the money. Dolohov frowned and did not speak. Pierre dashed up to the window.

'Gentlemen. Who'll take a bet with me? I'll do the same!' he shouted suddenly 'I don't care about betting; see here, tell them to give me a bottle. I'll do it. . . . Tell them to give it here.'

'Let him, let him!' said Dolohov, smiling.

'What, are you mad? No one would let you. Why, you turn giddy going downstairs,' various persons protested.

'I'll drink it; give me the bottle of rum,' roared Pierre, striking the table with a resolute, drunken gesture, and he climbed into the window. They clutched at his arms; but he was so strong that he shoved every one far away who came near him.

'No, there's no managing him like that,' said Anatole. 'Wait a bit, I'll get round him. . . . Listen, I'll take your bet, but for tomorrow, for we're all going on now to . . .'

'Yes, come along,' shouted Pierre, 'come along. . . . And take Mishka with us.' . . . And he caught hold of the bear, and embracing it and lifting it up, began waltzing round the room with it.

VII

PRINCE VASSILY kept the promise he had made at Anna Pavlovna's *soirée* to Princess Drubetskoy, who had petitioned him in favour of her only son Boris. His case had been laid before the emperor, and though it was not to be a precedent for others, he received a commission as sub-lieutenant in the Guards of the Semenovsky regiment. But the post of an adjutant or *attaché* in Kutuzov's service was not to be obtained for Boris by all Anna Mihalovna's efforts and entreaties. Shortly after the gathering at Anna Pavlovna's, Anna Mihalovna went back to Moscow, to her rich relatives the Rostovs, with whom she stayed in Moscow. It was with these relations that her adored Borinka, who had only recently entered a regiment of the line, and was now at once transferred to the Guards as a sub-lieutenant, had been educated from childhood and had lived for years. The Guards had already left Petersburg on the 10th of August, and her son, who was remaining in Moscow to get his equipment, was to overtake them on the road to Radzivilov.

The Rostovs were keeping the name-day of the mother and the younger daughter, both called Natalya. Ever since the morning, coaches with six horses had been incessantly driving to and from the Countess Rostov's big house in Povarsky, which was known to all Moscow. The countess and her handsome eldest daughter were sitting in the drawing-room with their visitors, who came in continual succession to present their congratulations to the elder lady.

The countess was a woman with a thin face of Oriental cast, forty-five years old, and obviously exhausted by child-bearing. She had had twelve children. The deliberate slowness of her movements and conversation, arising from weak health, gave her an air of dignity which inspired respect. Princess Anna Mihalovna Drubetskoy, as an intimate friend of the family, sat with them assisting in the work of receiving and entertaining their guests. The younger members of the family were in the back rooms, not seeing fit to take part in receiving visitors. The count met his visitors and escorted them to the door, inviting all of them to dinner.

'I am very, very grateful to you, *mon cher*' or '*ma chère*,' he said to every one without exception (making not the slightest distinction between persons of higher or of lower standing than his own), 'for myself and my two dear ones whose name-day we are keeping. Mind you come to dinner. I shall be offended if you don't, *mon cher*. I beg you most sincerely from all the family, my dear.' These words, invariably accompanied by the same expression on his full, good-humoured, clean-shaven face, and the same warm pressure of the hand, and repeated short bows, he said to all without exception or variation. When he had escorted one guest to the hall, the count returned to the gentleman or lady who was still in the drawing-room. Moving up a chair, and with the air of a man fond of society and at home in it, he would sit down, his legs jauntily apart, and his hands on his knees, and sway to and fro with dignity as he proffered surmises upon the weather, gave advice about health, sometimes in Russian, sometimes in very bad but complacent French. Then again he would get up, and with the air of a man weary but resolute in the performance of his duty, he would escort guests out, stroking up his grey hair over his bald patch, and again he would urge them to come to dinner. Sometimes on his way back from the hall, he would pass through the conservatory and the butler's room into a big room with a marble floor, where they were setting a table for eighty guests; and looking at the waiters who were bringing in the silver and china, setting out tables and unfolding damask tablecloths, he would call up Dmitry Vassilyevitch, a young man of good family, who performed the duties of a steward in his household, and would say: 'Now then, Mitenka, mind everything's right. That's it, that's it,' he would say, looking round with pleasure at the immense table opened out to its full extent; 'the great thing is the service. So, so.' . . . And he went off again with a sigh of satisfaction to the drawing-room.

'Marya Lvovna Karagin and her daughter,' the countess's huge footman announced in a deep bass at the drawing-room door. The countess thought a moment, and took a pinch from a golden snuff-box with her husband's portrait on it.

'I'm worn out with these callers,' she said; 'well, this is the last one I'll see. She's so affected. Show her up,' she said in a dejected tone, as though she were saying, 'Very well, finish me off entirely!'

A tall, stout, haughty-looking lady and her round-faced, smiling daughter walked with rustling skirts into the drawing-room.

'Dear countess, it is such a long time . . . she has been laid up, poor child . . . at the Razumovskys' ball, and the Countess Apraxin . . . I was so glad,' feminine voices chattered briskly, interrupting one another and mingling with the sound of rustling skirts and the scraping of chairs. Conversation began of the sort which is kept up just long enough for the caller to get up at the first pause, rustling her skirts and with a murmur of 'I am so charmed; mamma's health . . . and the Countess Apraxin . . .' walk out again with the same rustle to the hall to put on cloak or overcoat and drive away. The conversation touched on the chief items of news in the town, on the illness of the wealthy old Count Bezuhov, a man who had been renowned for his personal beauty in the days of Catherine, and on his illegitimate son, Pierre, who had behaved so improperly at a *soirée* at Anna Pavlovna's. 'I am very sorry for the poor count,' declared the visitor; 'his health in such a precarious state, and now this distress caused him by his son; it will be the death of him!'

'Why, what has happened?' asked the countess, as though she did not know what was meant, though she had heard about the cause of Count Bezuhov's distress fifteen times already.

'This is what comes of modern education! When he was abroad,' the visitor pursued, 'this young man was left to his own devices, and now in Petersburg, they say, he has been doing such atrocious things that he has been sent away under police escort.'

'Really!' said the countess.

'He has made a bad choice of his companions,' put in Princess Anna Mihalovna. 'Prince Vassily's son—he and a young man called Dolohov, they say—God only knows the dreadful things they've been doing. And both have suffered for it. Dolohov has been degraded to the rank of a common soldier, while Bezuhov's son has been banished to Moscow. As to Anatole Kuragin . . . his father managed to hush it up somehow. But he has been sent out of Petersburg too.'

'Why, what did they do?' asked the countess.

'They're perfect ruffians, especially Dolohov,' said the visitor. 'He's the son of Marya Ivanovna Dolohov, such a worthy woman, you know, but there! Only fancy, the three of them had got hold of a bear somewhere, put it in a carriage with them, and were taking it to some actress's. The police ran up to stop them. They took the police officer, tied him back to back to the bear, and dropped the bear into the Moika: the bear swam with the police officer on him.'

'A pretty figure he must have looked, *ma chère*,' cried the count, helpless with laughter.

'Ah, such a horror! What is there to laugh at in it, count?'

But the ladies could not help laughing at it themselves.

'It was all they could do to rescue the unlucky man,' the visitor went on. 'And that's the intellectual sort of amusement the son of Count Kirill Vladimirovitch Bezuhov indulges in!' she added. 'And people said he was so well educated and clever. That's how foreign education turns out. I hope no one will receive him here, in spite of his great wealth. They tried to introduce him to me. I gave an absolute refusal: I have daughters.'

'What makes you say the young man is so wealthy?' asked the countess, turning away from the girls, who at once looked as though they did not hear. 'He has none but illegitimate children. I believe that . . . Pierre too is illegitimate.'

The visitor waved her hand. 'He has a score of them, I suppose.'

Princess Anna Mihalovna interposed, obviously wishing to show her connections and intimate knowledge with every detail in society.

'This is how the matter stands,' she said meaningly, speaking in a half whisper. 'Count Kirill Vladimirovitch's reputation we all know. . . . He has lost count of his own children, indeed, but this Pierre was his favourite.'

'How handsome the old man was,' said the countess, 'only last year! A finer-looking man I have never seen.'

'Now he's very much altered,' said Anna Mihalovna. 'Well, I was just saying,' she went on, 'the direct heir to all the property is Prince Vassily through his wife, but the father is very fond of Pierre, has taken trouble over his education, and he has written to the Emperor . . . so that no one can tell, if he dies (he's so ill that it's expected any moment, and Lorrain has come from Petersburg), whom that immense property will come to, Pierre or Prince Vassily. Forty thousand serfs and millions of money. I know this for a fact, for Prince Vassily himself told me so. And indeed Kirill Vladimirovitch happens to be a third cousin of mine on my mother's side, and he's Boris's godfather too,' she added, apparently attaching no importance to this circumstance.

'Prince Vassily arrived in Moscow yesterday. He's coming on some inspection business, so I was told,' said the visitor.

'Yes, between ourselves,' said the princess, 'that's a pretext; he has come simply to see Prince Kirill Vladimirovitch, hearing he was in such a serious state.'

'But, really, *ma chère*, that was a capital piece of fun,' said the count; and seeing that the elder visitor did not hear him, he turned to the young ladies. 'A funny figure the police officer must have looked; I can just fancy him.'

And showing how the police officer waved his arms about, he went off again into his rich bass laugh, his sides shaking with mirth, as people do laugh who always eat and, still more, drink well. 'Then do, please, come to dinner with us,' he said.

VIII

A SILENCE followed. The countess looked at her guest, smiling affably, but still not disguising the fact that she would not take it at all amiss now if the guest were to get up and go. The daughter was already fingering at the folds of her gown and looking interrogatively at her mother, when suddenly they heard in the next room several girls and boys running to the door, and the grating sound of a chair knocked over and a girl of thirteen ran in, hiding something in her short muslin petticoat, and stopped short in the middle of the room. She had evidently bounded so far by mistake, unable to stop in her flight. At the same instant there appeared in the doorway a student with a crimson band on his collar, a young officer in the Guards, a girl of fifteen and a fat, rosy-cheeked boy in a child's smock.

The prince jumped up, and swaying from side to side, held his arms out wide round the little girl.

'Ah, here she is!' he cried, laughing. 'Our little darling on her fête day!'

'My dear, there is a time for everything,' said the countess, affecting severity. 'You're always spoiling her, *Elie*,' she added to her husband.

'*Bonjour, ma chere, je vous félicite*,' said the visitor. '*Quelle délicieuse enfant!*' she added, turning to her mother.

The dark-eyed little girl, plain, but full of life, with her wide mouth, her childish bare shoulders, which shrugged and panted in her bodice from her rapid motion, her black hair brushed back, her slender bare arms and little legs in lace-edged long drawers and open slippers, was at that charming stage when the girl is no longer a child, while the child is not yet a young girl. Wriggling away from her father, she ran up to her mother, and taking no notice whatever of her severe remarks, she hid her flushed face in her mother's lace kerchief and broke into laughter. As she laughed she uttered some incoherent phrases about the doll, which was poking out from her petticoat.

'Do you see? . . . My doll . . . Mimi . . . you see . . .' And Natasha could say no more, it all seemed to her so funny. She sank on her mother's lap, and went off into such a loud peal of laughter that every one, even the prim visitor, could not help laughing too.

'Come, run along, run along with your monstrosity!' said her mother, pushing her daughter off with a pretence of anger. 'This is my younger girl,' she said to the visitor. Natasha, pulling her face away from her mother's lace kerchief for a minute, peeped down at her through tears of laughter, and hid her face again.

The visitor, forced to admire this domestic scene, thought it suitable to take some part in it.

'Tell me, my dear,' she said, addressing Natasha, 'how did you come by your Mimi? Your daughter, I suppose?'

Natasha did not like the tone of condescension to childish things with which the visitor had spoken to her. She made no answer, but stared solemnly at her.

Meanwhile all of the younger generation, Boris, the officer, Anna Mihalovna's son; Nikolay, the student, the count's elder son; Sónya, the count's niece; and little Petya, his younger son, had all placed themselves about the drawing-room, and were obviously trying to restrain within the bounds of decorum the excitement and mirth which was brimming over in their faces. Clearly in the back part of the house, from which they had dashed out so impetuously, the conversation had been more amusing than the small-talk in the drawing-room of the scandal of the town, the weather, and Countess Apraxin. Now and then they glanced at one another and could hardly suppress their laughter.

The two young men, the student and the officer, friends from childhood, were of the same age, and both good-looking, but not like each other. Boris was a tall, fair-haired lad with delicate, regular features, and a look of composure on his handsome face. Nikolay was a curly-headed youth, not tall, with an open expression. On his upper lip there were already signs of a black moustache coming, and his whole face expressed impulsiveness and enthusiasm. Nikolay flushed red as he came into the drawing-room. He was unmistakably trying to find something to say, and unable to find anything. Boris, on the contrary, was at home immediately and talked easily and playfully of the doll Mimi, saying that he had known her as a young girl before her nose was broken, and she had grown older during the five years he remembered her, and how her head was cracked right across the skull. As he said this he looked at Natasha. Natasha turned away from him, glanced at her younger brother, who, with a scowl on his face, was shaking with noiseless laughter, and unable to restrain herself, she skipped up and flew out of the room as quickly as her swift little legs would carry her. Boris did not laugh.

'You were meaning to go out, mamma, weren't you? Do you want the carriage?' he said, addressing his mother with a smile.

'Yes, go along and tell them to get it ready,' she said, smiling. Boris walked slowly to the door and went after Natasha. The stout boy ran wrathfully after them, as though resenting the interruption of his pursuits.

IX

OF the young people, not reckoning the countess's elder daughter (who was four years older than her sister and behaved quite like a grown-up person) and the young lady visitor, there were left in the drawing-room Nikolay and Sonya, the niece. Sonya was a slender, miniature brunette, with soft eyes shaded by long lashes, thick black hair twisted in two coils round her head, and a skin of a somewhat sallow tint, particularly marked on her bare, thin, but shapely, muscular arms and neck. The smoothness of her movements, the softness and flexibility of her little limbs, and something of slyness and reserve in her manner, suggested a lovely half-grown kitten, which would one day be a charming cat. Apparently she thought it only proper to show an interest in the general conversation and to smile. But against her own will, her eyes turned under their thick, long lashes to her cousin, who was going away into the army, with such girlish, passionate adoration, that her smile could not for one moment impose upon any one, and it was clear that the kitten had only perched there to skip off more energetically than ever and to play with her cousin as soon as they could, like Boris and Natasha, get out of the drawing-room.

'Yes, *ma chère*,' said the old count, addressing the visitor and pointing to his Nikolay; 'here his friend Boris has received his commission as an officer, and he's so fond of him he doesn't want to be left behind, and is giving up the university and his poor old father to go into the army, *ma chère*. And there was a place all ready for him in the archives department, and all. Isn't that friendship now?' said the count interrogatively.

'But they do say that war has been declared, you know,' said the visitor.

'They've been saying so a long while,' said the count. 'They'll say so again and again, and so it will remain. There's friendship for you, *ma chère*!' he repeated. 'He's going into the hussars.'

The visitor, not knowing what to say, shook her head.

'It's not from friendship at all,' answered Nikolay, flushing hotly, and denying it as though it were some disgraceful imputation. 'Not friendship at all, but simply I feel drawn to the military service.'

He looked round at his cousin and the young lady visitor; both looked at him with a smile of approval.

'Schubert's dining with us tonight, the colonel of the Pavologradsky regiment of hussars. He has been here on leave, and is taking him with him. There's no help for it,' said the count, shrugging his shoulders and speaking playfully of what evidently was a source of much distress to him.

'I've told you already, papa,' said his son, 'that if you're unwilling to let me go, I'll stay. But I know I'm no good for anything except in the army. I'm not a diplomatist, or a government clerk. I'm not clever at disguising my feelings,' he said, glancing repeatedly with the coquetry of handsome youth at Sonya and the young lady.

The kitten, her eyes riveted on him, seemed on the point of breaking into frolic, and showing her cat-like nature.

'Well, well, it's all right!' said the old count; 'he always gets so hot. Bonaparte's turned all their heads; they're all dreaming of how he rose from a lieutenant to be an emperor. Well, and so may it turn out again, please God,' he added, not noticing the visitor's sarcastic smile.

While their elders began talking about Bonaparte, Julie, Madame Karagin's daughter, turned to young Rostov.

'What a pity you weren't at the Arharovs on Thursday. I was so dull without you,' she said, giving him a tender smile. The youth, highly flattered, moved with a coquettish smile nearer her, and entered into a conversation apart with the smiling Julie, entirely unaware that his unconscious smile had dealt a jealous stab to the heart of Sonya, who was flushing crimson and assuming a forced smile. In the middle of his talk with Julie he glanced round at her. Sonya gave him an intensely furious look, and, hardly able to restrain her tears, though there was still a constrained smile on her lips, she got up and went out of the room. All Nikolay's animation was gone. He waited for the first break in the conversation, and, with a face of distress, walked out of the room to look for Sonya.

'How all the young things wear their hearts on their sleeves!' said Anna Mihalovna, pointing to Nikolay's retreating figure. '*Cousinage, dangereux voisinage*,' she added.

'Yes,' said the countess, when the sunshine that had come into the drawing-room with the young people had vanished. She was, as it were, replying to a question which no one had put to her, but which was always in her thoughts: 'What miseries, what anxieties one has gone through for the happiness one has in them now! And even now one feels really more dread than joy over them. One's always in terror! At this age particularly when there are so many dangers both for girls and boys.'

'Everything depends on bringing up,' said the visitor.

'Yes, you are right,' the countess went on. 'So far I have been, thank God, my children's friend and have enjoyed their full confidence,' said the countess, repeating the error of so many parents, who imagine their children have no secrets from them. 'I know I shall always be first in my children's confidence, and that Nikolay, if, with his impulsive character, he does get into mischief (boys will be boys) it won't be like these Petersburg young gentlemen.'

'Yes, they're capital children, capital children,' assented the count, who always solved all perplexing questions by deciding that everything was capital. 'Fancy now, his taking it into his head to be an hussar! But what can one expect, *ma chère*!'

'What a sweet little thing your younger girl is!' said the visitor. 'Full of fun and mischief!'

'Yes, that she is,' said the count. 'She takes after me! And such a voice; though she's my daughter, it's the truth I'm telling you, she'll be a singer, another Salomini. We've engaged an Italian to give her lessons.'

'Isn't it too early? They say it injures the voice to train it at that age.'

'Oh, no! Too early!' said the count. 'Why, our mothers used to be married at twelve and thirteen.'

'Well, she's in love with Boris already! What do you say to that?' said the countess, smiling softly and looking at Boris's mother. And apparently in reply to the question that was always in her mind, she went on: 'Why, you know, if I were strict with her, if I were to forbid her . . . God knows what they might not be doing in secret' (the countess meant that they might kiss each other), 'but as it is I know every word she utters. She'll come to me this evening and tell me everything of herself. I spoil her, perhaps, but I really believe it's the best way. I brought my elder girl up more strictly.'

'Yes, I was brought up quite differently,' said the elder girl, the handsome young Countess Vera; and she smiled. But the smile did not improve Vera's face; on the contrary her face looked unnatural, and therefore unpleasing. Vera was good-looking; she was not stupid, was clever at her lessons, and well educated; she had a pleasant voice, and what she said was true and appropriate. But, strange to say, every one—both the visitor and the countess—looked at her, as though wondering why she had said it, and conscious of a certain awkwardness.

'People are always too clever with their elder children; they try to do something exceptional with them,' said the visitor.

'We won't conceal our errors, *ma chère*! My dear countess was too clever with Vera,' said the count. 'But what of it? she has turned out capitally all the same,' he added, with a wink of approval to Vera.

The guests got up and went away, promising to come to dinner.

'What manners! Staying on and on!' said the countess, when she had seen her guests out.

X

WHEN Natasha ran out of the drawing-room she only ran as far as the conservatory. There she stopped listening to the talk in the drawing-room, and waiting for Boris to come out. She was beginning to get impatient, and stamping her foot was almost ready to cry at his not coming at once, when she heard the young man's footsteps coming out discreetly, not too slowly nor too quickly. Natasha darted swiftly away and hid among the tubs of shrubs.

Boris stood still in the middle of the room, looked round him, brushed a speck of dirt off the sleeve of his uniform, and going up to the looking-glass examined his handsome face. Natasha, keeping quiet, peeped out of her hiding-place, waiting to see what he would do. He stood a little while before the glass, smiled at his reflection, and walked towards the other door. Natasha was on the point of calling to him, but she changed her mind. 'Let him look for me,' she said to herself. Boris had only just gone out, when at the other door Sonya came in, flushed and muttering something angrily through her tears. Natasha checked her first impulse to run out to her, and remained in her hiding-place, as it were under the invisible cap, looking on at what was going on in the world. She began to feel a peculiar novel sort of enjoyment in it. Sonya was murmuring something as she looked towards the drawing-room door. The door opened and Nikolay came in.

'Sonya! what is the matter? how can you?' said Nikolay, running up to her.

'Nothing, nothing, leave me alone!' Sonya was sobbing.

'No, I know what it is.'

'Very well, you do, so much the better then, and you can go back to her.'

'So-o-onya! one word! How can you torture me and yourself for a mere fancy?' said Nikolay, taking her hand. Sonya did not pull her hand away, and left off crying.

Natasha, not stirring and hardly breathing, looked with shining eyes from her hiding-place. 'What's coming now?' she thought.

'Sonya! I care for nothing in the whole world! You're everything to me,' said Nikolay. 'I'll prove it to you.'

'I don't like you to talk like that.'

'Well, I won't then; come, forgive me, Sonya.' He drew her to him and kissed her.

'Oh, that's nice,' thought Natasha, and when Sonya and Nikolay had gone out of the room she followed them and called Boris to her.

'Boris, come here,' she said with a sly and significant look. 'I've something I want to tell you. Here, here,' she said, and she led him into the conservatory, to the place where she had hidden between the tubs. Boris followed her, smiling.

'What is the *something*?' he inquired. She was a little embarrassed; she looked round her, and seeing her doll flung down on a tub she picked it up.

'Kiss the doll,' she said. Boris looked with observant, affectionate eyes at her eager face and made no answer. 'Don't you want to? Well, then come here,' she said, and went further in among the shrubs and tossed away the doll. 'Closer, closer!' she whispered. She caught hold of the young officer's arms above the cuff, and her flushed face had a look of solemnity and awe.

'Would you like to kiss me?' she whispered, hardly audibly, peeping up at him from under her eyelids, smiling and almost crying with excitement.

Boris reddened. 'How absurd you are!' he said, bending down to her, flushing redder still, but doing nothing, waiting what would come next. Suddenly she jumped on to a tub, so that as she stood she was taller than he, flung both arms round him so that her slender, bare arms clasped him above his neck, and flinging back her hair with a toss of her head, she kissed him just on his lips.

She slipped away among the flower-pots on the other side, and stood with hanging head.

'Natasha,' he said, 'you know I love you, but——'

'You're in love with me,' Natasha broke in.

'Yes I am, but, please, don't let us do like that . . . In another four years . . . Then I shall ask for your hand.' Natasha pondered a moment.

'Thirteen, fourteen, fifteen, sixteen . . .' she said, counting on her thin little fingers.

'Very well. Then it's settled?' And her excited face beamed with a smile of delight and relief.

'Settled!' said Boris.

'For ever?' said the little girl. 'Till death?' And taking his arm, with a happy face she walked quietly beside him into the next room.

XI

THE countess was so tired from seeing visitors that she gave orders that she would see no one else, and the doorkeeper was told to be sure and invite to dinner every one who should call with congratulations. The countess was longing for a *tête-à-tête* talk with the friend of her childhood, Anna Mihalovna, whom she had not seen properly since she had arrived from Petersburg. Anna Mihalovna, with her tear-worn and amiable face, moved closer up to the countess's easy-chair.

'With you I will be perfectly open,' said Anna Mihalovna. 'We haven't many old friends left. That's how it is I value your friendship so.'

Anna Mihalovna looked at Vera and stopped. The countess pressed her friend's hand.

'Vera,' said the countess to her eldest daughter, unmistakably not her favourite, 'how is it you have no notion about anything? Don't you feel that you're not wanted here? Go to your sister or . . .'

The handsome young countess smiled scornfully, apparently not in the least mortified.

'If you had told me, mamma, I would have gone away long ago,' she said, and went off towards her own room. But passing through the divan-room, she noticed two couples sitting symmetrically in the two windows. She stopped and smiled contemptuously at them. Sonya was sitting close beside Nikolay, who was copying out some verses for her, the first he had ever written. Boris and Natasha were sitting in the other window, and were silent when Vera came in. Sonya and Natasha looked at Vera with guilty, happy faces.

It was an amusing and touching sight to see these little girls in love, but the sight of them did not apparently arouse any agreeable feeling in Vera. 'How often have I asked you,' she said, 'not to take my things? you have a room of your own.' She took the inkstand away from Nikolay.

'One minute, one minute,' he said, dipping his pen in.

'You always manage to do things just at the wrong moment,' said Vera. 'First you burst into the drawing-room so that every one was ashamed of you.' Although or just because what she said was perfectly true, no one answered; all the four simply looked at one another. She lingered in the room with the inkstand in her hand. 'And what sort of secrets can you have at your age, Natasha and Boris, and you two!—it's all simply silly nonsense!'

'Well, what has it to do with you, Vera?' Natasha said in defence, speaking very gently. She was evidently more good-humoured and affectionate than usual that day with every one.

'It's very silly,' said Vera; 'I am ashamed of you. What sort of secret...'

'Every one has secrets. We don't interfere with you and Berg,' said Natasha, getting warmer.

'I should think you didn't interfere,' said Vera, 'because there could be no harm in any conduct of mine. But I shall tell mamma how you behave with Boris.'

'Natalya Ilyinishna behaves very well to me,' said Boris. 'I have nothing to complain of,' he said.

'Leave off, Boris, you're such a diplomatist' (the word *diplomatist* was much in use among the children in the special sense they attached to the word). 'It's tiresome, really,' said Natasha, in a mortified and shaking voice; 'why does she set upon me?'

'You'll never understand it,' she said, addressing Vera, 'because you've never cared for any one; you've no heart; you're simply Madame de Genlis' (this nickname, considered most offensive, had been given to Vera by Nikolay), 'and your greatest delight is in getting other people into trouble. You can flirt with Berg, as much as you like,' she said quickly.

'Well, I'm not likely to run after a young man before visitors....'

'Well, she has gained her object!' Nikolay put in; 'she has said something nasty to every one, and upset everybody. Let's go into the nursery.'

All four rose, like a flock of scared birds, and went out of the room.

'You've said nasty things to me, and I said nothing to any one,' said Vera.

'Madame de Genlis! Madame de Genlis!' cried laughing voices through the door.

The handsome girl who produced such an irritating and unpleasant effect on every one smiled; and, obviously unaffected by what had been said to her, she went up to the looking-glass and put her scarf and her hair tidy. Looking at her handsome face, she seemed to become colder and more composed than ever.

In the drawing-room the conversation was still going on.

'*Ah, chère,*' said the countess, 'in my life, too, everything is not rose-coloured. Do you suppose I don't see that, in the way we are going on, our fortune can't last long? And it's all the club and his good-nature. When we're in the country we have no rest from it,—it's nothing but theatricals, hunting parties, and God knows what. But we won't talk of me. Come, tell me how you managed it all. I often wonder at you, Annette, the way you go racing off alone, at your age, to Moscow, and to Petersburg, to all the ministers, and all the great people, and know how to get round them all too. I admire you, really! Well, how was it arranged? Why, I could never do it.'

'Ah, my dear!' answered Princess Anna Mihalovna, 'God grant that you never know what it is to be left a widow, with no one to support you, and a son whom you love to distraction. One learns how to do anything,' she said with some pride. 'My lawsuit trained me to it. If I want to see one of these great people, I write a note: "Princess so-and-so wishes to see so-and-so," and I go myself in a hired cab two or three times—four, if need be—till I get what I want. I don't mind what they think of me.'

'Well, tell me, then, whom did you interview for Borinka?' asked the countess. 'Here's your boy an officer in the Guards, while my Nikolinka's going as an ensign. There's no one to manage things for him. Whose help did you ask?'

'Prince Vassily's. He was so kind. Agreed to do everything immediately; put the case before the Emperor,' said Princess Anna Mihalovna enthusiastically, entirely forgetting all the humiliation she had been through to attain her object.

'And how is he? beginning to get old, Prince Vassily?' inquired the countess. 'I have never seen him since our theatricals at the Rumyantsovs', and I dare say he has forgotten me. He paid me attentions,' the countess recalled with a smile.

'He's just the same,' answered Anna Mihalovna,' so affable, brimming over. Greatness has not turned his head. "I am sorry I can do so little for you, Princess," he said to me; "I'm at your command." Yes, he's a splendid man, and very good to his relatives. But you know, Natalie, my love for my boy. I don't know what I would not do to make him happy. And my means are so scanty,' pursued Anna Mihalovna, dropping her voice mournfully, 'that now I am in a most awful position. My wretched lawsuit is eating up all I have, and making no progress. I have not, can you conceive it, literally, not sixpence in the world, and I don't know how to get Boris's equipment.' She took out her handkerchief and shed tears. 'I must have five hundred roubles, and I have only a twenty-five rouble note. I'm in such a position. . . . My one hope now is in Prince Kirill Vladimirovitch Bezuhov. If he will not come to the help of his godson—you know he is Boris's godfather—and allow him something for his maintenance, all my efforts will have been in vain; I shall have nothing to get his equipment with.'

The countess deliberated in tearful silence.

'I often think—perhaps it's a sinful thought,' said the princess—'but I often think: here is Prince Kirill Vladimirovitch Bezuhov living all alone ... that immense fortune ... and what is he living for? Life is a burden to him, while Boris is only just beginning life.'

'He will be sure to leave something to Boris,' said the countess.

'God knows, *chère amie!* These wealthy grand people are such egoists. But still I'm going to see him at once with Boris, and I will tell him plainly the state of the case. People may think what they choose of me, I really don't care, when my son's fate depends on it.' The princess got up. 'It's now two o'clock, and you dine at four. I shall have time to drive there and back.'

And with the air of a Petersburg lady, used to business, and knowing how to make use of every moment, Anna Mihalovna sent for her son, and with him went out into the hall.

'Good-bye, my dear,' she said to the countess, who accompanied her to the door. 'Wish me good-luck,' she added in a whisper unheard by her son.

'You're going to Prince Kirill Vladimirovitch's, *ma chère?* said the count, coming out of the dining-room into the hall. 'If he's better, invite Pierre to dine with us. He has been here; used to dance with the children. Be sure you invite him, *ma chère.* Now do come and look how Taras has surpassed himself today. He says Count Orlov never had such a dinner as we're going to have today.'

XII

'*Mon cher Boris,*' said Anna Mihalovna as the Countess Rostov's carriage drove along the street strewn with straw and into the wide courtyard of Count Kirill Vladimirovitch Bezuhov's house. '*Mon cher Boris,*' said the mother, putting her hand out from under her old mantle, and laying it on her son's hand with a timid, caressing movement, 'be nice, be attentive. Count Kirill Vladimirovitch is after all your godfather, and your future depends on him. Remember that, *mon cher*, be charming, as you know so well how to be....'

'If I knew anything would come of it but humiliation,' her son answered coldly. 'But I have promised, and I will do it for your sake.'

Although the carriage was standing at the entrance, the hall-porter, scanning the mother and son (they had not sent in their names, but had walked straight in through the glass doors between two rows of statues in niches), and looking significantly at the old mantle, inquired whom they wanted, the princesses or the count; and hearing that they wanted to see the count, said that his excellency was worse today, and his excellency could see no one.

'We may as well go away,' the son said in French.

'*Mon ami!*' said the mother in a voice of entreaty, again touching her son's hand, as though the contact might soothe or rouse him. Boris said no more, but without taking off his overcoat, looked inquiringly at his mother.

'My good man,' Anna Mihalovna said ingratiatingly, addressing the hall-porter, 'I know that Count Kirill Vladimirovitch is very ill . . . that is why I am here. . . . I am a relation. . . . I shall not disturb him, my good man. . . . I need only see Prince Vassily Sergyevitch; he's staying here, I know. Announce us, please.'

The hall-porter sullenly pulled the bell-rope that rang upstairs and turned away.

'Princess Drubetskoy to see Prince Vassily Sergyevitch,' he called to a footman in stockings, slippers and a frockcoat, who ran down from above, and looked down from the turn in the staircase.

The mother straightened out the folds of her dyed silk gown, looked at herself in the full-length Venetian looking-glass on the wall, and boldly walked up on the stair carpet in her shabby, shapeless shoes.

'My dear, you promised me,' she turned again to her son, rousing him by a touch on his arm. The son, with his eyes on the floor, walked submissively after her.

They went into a large room, from which a door led to the apartments that had been assigned to Prince Vassily.

At the moment when the mother and son reached the middle of the room and were about to ask their way of an old footman, who had darted out at their entrance, the bronze handle of one of the doors turned, and Prince Vassily, dressed in a house jacket of velvet, with one star, came out, accompanying a handsome, black-haired man. This man was the celebrated Petersburg doctor, Lorrain.

'It is positive, then?' said the Prince.

'Prince, *errare est humanum*,' answered the doctor, lisping, and pronouncing the Latin words with a French accent.

'Very well, very well . . .'

Perceiving Anna Mihalovna and her son, Prince Vassily dismissed the doctor with a bow, and in silence, with an air of inquiry, advanced to meet them. The son noticed how an expression of intense grief came at once into his mother's eyes, and he smiled slightly.

'Yes, in what distressing circumstances we were destined to meet again, prince. . . . Tell me how is our dear patient?' she said, apparently not observing the frigid, offensive glance that was fixed on her. Prince Vassily stared at her, then at Boris with a look of inquiry that amounted to perplexity. Boris bowed politely. Prince Vassily, without acknowledging his bow, turned away to Anna Mihalovna, and to her question he replied by a movement of the head and lips, indicative of the worst fears for the patient.

'Is it possible?' cried Anna Mihalovna. 'Ah, this is terrible! It is dreadful to think . . . This is my son,' she added, indicating Boris. 'He wanted to thank you in person.'

Boris once more made a polite bow.

'Believe me, prince, a mother's heart will never forget what you have done for us.'

'I am glad I have been able to do you any service, my dear Anna Mihalovna,' said Prince Vassily, pulling his lace frill straight, and in voice and manner manifesting here in Moscow, before Anna Mihalovna, who was under obligation to him, an even greater sense of his own dignity than in Petersburg at Anna Pavlovna's *soirée*.

'Try to do your duty in the service, and to be worthy of it,' he added, turning severely to him. 'I am glad . . . you are here on leave?' he asked in his expressionless voice.

'I am awaiting orders, your excellency, to join my new regiment,' answered Boris, showing no sign either of resentment at the prince's abrupt manner, nor of desire to get into conversation, but speaking with such respectful composure that the prince looked at him attentively.

'You are living with your mother?'

'I am living at Countess Rostov's,' said Boris, again adding: 'your excellency.'

'The Ilya Rostov, who married Natalie Shinshin,' said Anna Mihalovna.

'I know, I know,' said Prince Vassily in his monotonous voice. 'I have never been able to understand how Natalie Shinshin could make up her mind to marry that unlicked bear. A completely stupid and ridiculous person. And a gambler too, I am told.'

'But a very worthy man, Prince,' observed Anna Mihalovna, with a pathetic smile, as though she too recognised that Count Rostov deserved this criticism, but begged him not to be too hard on the poor old fellow. 'What do the doctors say?' asked the princess, after a brief pause, and again the expression of deep distress reappeared on her tear-worn face.

'There is little hope,' said the prince.

'And I was so longing to thank uncle once more for all his kindness to me and to Boris. He is his godson,' she added in a tone that suggested that Prince Vassily would be highly delighted to hear this fact.

Prince Vassily pondered and frowned. Anna Mihalovna saw he was afraid of finding in her a rival with claims on Count Bezuhov's will. She hastened to reassure him. 'If it were not for my genuine love and devotion for uncle,' she said, uttering the last word with peculiar assurance and carelessness, 'I know his character,—generous, upright; but with only the princesses about him. . . . They are young. . . .' She bent her head and added in a whisper: 'Has he performed his last duties, prince? How priceless are these last moments! He is as bad as he could be, it seems; it is absolutely necessary to prepare him, if he is so ill. We women, prince,' she smiled tenderly, 'always know how to say these things. I absolutely must see him. Hard as it will be for me, I am used to suffering.'

The prince evidently understood, and understood too, as he had at Anna Pavlovna's that it was no easy task to get rid of Anna Mihalovna.

'Would not this interview be trying for him, *chère* Anna Mihalovna,' he said. 'Let us wait till the evening; the doctors have predicted a crisis.'

'But waiting's out of the question, prince, at such a moment. Think, it is a question of saving his soul. Ah! how terrible, the duties of a Christian. . . .'

The door from the inner rooms opened, and one of the count's nieces entered with a cold and forbidding face, and a long waist strikingly out of proportion with the shortness of her legs.

Prince Vassily turned to her. 'Well, how is he?'

'Still the same. What can you expect with this noise? . . .' said the princess, scanning Anna Mihalovna, as a stranger.

'Ah, dear, I did not recognise you,' said Anna Mihalovna, with a delighted smile, and she ambled lightly up to the count's niece. 'I have just come, and I am at your service to help in nursing my uncle. I imagine what you have been suffering,' she added, sympathetically turning her eyes up.

The princess made no reply, she did not even smile, but walked straight away. Anna Mihalovna took off her gloves, and entrenched herself as it were in an armchair, inviting Prince Vassily to sit down beside her.

'Boris!' she said to her son, and she smiled at him, 'I am going in to the count, to poor uncle, and you can go to Pierre, *mon ami*, meanwhile, and don't forget to give him the Rostovs' invitation. They ask him to dinner. I suppose he won't go?' she said to the prince.

'On the contrary,' said the prince, visibly cast down, 'I should be very glad if you would take that young man off my hands. . . . He sticks on here. The count has not once asked for him.'

He shrugged his shoulders. A footman conducted the youth downstairs and up another staircase to the apartments of Pyotr Kirillovitch.

XIII

PIERRE had not succeeded in fixing upon a career in Petersburg, and really had been banished to Moscow for disorderly conduct. The story told about him at Count Rostov's was true. Pierre had assisted in tying the police officer to the bear. He had arrived a few days previously, stopping as he always did at his father's house. Though he had assumed that his story would be already known at Moscow, and that the ladies who were about his father, always unfavourably disposed to him, would profit by this opportunity of turning the count against him, he went on the day of his arrival to his father's part of the house. Going into the drawing-room, where the princesses usually sat, he greeted the ladies, two of whom were sitting at their embroidery frames, while one read aloud. There were three of them. The eldest, a trim, long-waisted, severe maiden-lady, the one who had come out to Anna Mihalovna, was reading. The younger ones, both rosy and pretty, were only to be distinguished by the fact that one of them had a little mole which made her much prettier. They were both working at their embroidery frames. Pierre was received like a man risen from the dead or stricken with plague. The eldest princess paused in her reading and stared at him in silence with dismay in her eyes. The second assumed precisely the same expression. The youngest, the one with the mole, who was of a mirthful and laughing disposition, bent over her frame, to conceal a smile, probably evoked by the amusing scene she foresaw coming. She pulled her embroidery wool out below, and bent down as though examining the pattern, hardly able to suppress her laughter.

'Good morning, cousin,' said Pierre. 'You don't know me?'

'I know you only too well, only too well.'

'How is the count? Can I see him?' Pierre asked, awkwardly as always, but not disconcerted.

'The count is suffering both physically and morally, and your only anxiety seems to be to occasion him as much suffering as possible.'

'Can I see the count?' repeated Pierre.

'Hm . . . if you want to kill him, to kill him outright, you can see him. Olga, go and see if uncle's broth is ready—it will soon be time for it,' she added, to show Pierre they were busy, and busy in seeing after his father's comfort, while he was obviously only busy in causing him discomfort.

Olga went out. Pierre stood still a moment, looked at the sisters and bowing said: 'Then I will go to my room. When I can see him, you will tell me.' He went away and heard the ringing but not loud laugh of the sister with the mole behind him.

The next day Prince Vassily had come and settled in the count's house. He sent for Pierre and said to him:

'My dear fellow, if you behave here as you did at Petersburg, you will come to a very bad end; that's all I have to say to you. The count is very, very ill; you must not see him.'

Since then Pierre had not been disturbed, and he spent the whole day alone in his room upstairs.

At the moment when Boris came in, Pierre was walking up and down his room, stopping now and then in the corners, making menacing gestures at the wall, as though thrusting some invisible enemy through with a lance, then he gazed sternly over his spectacles, then pacing up and down again, murmuring indistinct words, shrugging his shoulders and gesticulating.

'England's day is over!' he said, scowling and pointing at someone with his finger. 'Mr. Pitt, as a traitor to the nation and to the rights of man, is condemned . . .' he had not time to deliver Pitt's sentence, imagining himself at that moment Napoleon, and having in the person of his hero succeeded in the dangerous crossing of the Channel and in the conquest of London, when he saw a graceful, handsome young officer come in. He stood still. Pierre had seen Boris last as a boy of fourteen, and did not remember him in the least. But in spite of that he took his hand in his characteristically quick and warm-hearted manner, and smiled cordially at him.

'You remember me?' Boris said calmly with a pleasant smile. 'I have come with my mother to see the count, but it seems he is not quite well.'

'Yes, he is ill, it seems. People are always bothering him,' answered Pierre, trying to recall who this youth might be.

Boris perceived that Pierre did not know him, but did not think fit to make himself known, and without the slightest embarrassment looked him straight in the face.

'Count Rostov asks you to come to dinner with him today,' he said, after a rather long silence somewhat disconcerting for Pierre.

'Ah, Count Rostov,' began Pierre, delighted. 'So you are his son, Ilya? Can you believe it, for the first moment I did not recognise you.

Do you remember how we used to slide on the Sparrow Hills with Madame Jacquot . . . long ago?'

'You are mistaken,' said Boris, deliberately, with a bold and rather sarcastic smile. 'I am Boris, the son of Princess Anna Mihalovna Drubetskoy. It is the father of the Rostovs who is called Ilya, the son's Nikolay. And I don't know any Madame Jacquot.'

Pierre shook his hands and head, as though flies or bees were swarming upon him.

'Ah, how is it! I've mixed it all up. There are such a lot of relatives in Moscow! You are Boris . . . yes. Well, now, we have got it clear. Tell me, what do you think of the Boulogne expedition? Things will go badly with the English, you know, if Napoleon gets across the Channel. I believe that the expedition is very possible. If only Villeneuve doesn't make a mess of it!'

Boris knew nothing at all about the Boulogne expedition, and it was the first time he had heard of Villeneuve.

'Here in Moscow we are more interested in dinner parties and scandal than in politics,' he said in his self-possessed, sarcastic tone. 'I know nothing and think nothing about it. Moscow's more engrossed in scandal than anything,' he went on. 'Just now they are all talking about you and about the count.'

Pierre smiled his kindly smile, as though afraid for his companion's sake that he might say something he would regret. But Boris spoke distinctly, clearly and drily, looking straight into Pierre's face.

'There's nothing else to do in Moscow but talk scandal,' he went on. 'Every one's absorbed in the question whom the count will leave his fortune to, though perhaps he will outlive us all, as I sincerely hope he may.'

'Yes, all that's very horrid,' Pierre interposed, 'very horrid.' Pierre was still afraid this officer would inadvertently drop into some remark disconcerting for himself.

'And it must seem to you,' said Boris, flushing slightly, but not changing his voice or attitude, 'it must seem to you that every one's thinking of nothing but getting something from him.'

'That's just it,' thought Pierre.

'And that's just what I want to say to you to prevent misunderstandings, that you are very much mistaken if you reckon me and my mother among those people. We are very poor, but I—at least I speak for myself—just because your father is rich, I don't consider myself a relation of his, and neither I nor my mother would ever ask him for anything or take anything from him.'

It was a long while before Pierre understood, but, when he did understand, he jumped up from the sofa, seized Boris's hand with his characteristic quickness and awkwardness, and blushing far more than Boris, began speaking with a mixed sensation of shame and annoyance.

'Well, this is strange! Do you suppose I ... how you could think ... I know very well ...'

But Boris again interrupted him.

'I am glad I have told you everything frankly. Perhaps you dislike it: you must excuse me,' he said, trying to put Pierre at his ease instead of being put at his ease by him; 'but I hope I have not offended you. I make it a rule to say everything quite plainly.... Then what message am I to take? You will come to dinner at the Rostovs'?' And Boris, with an evident sense of having discharged an onerous duty, having extricated himself from an awkward position, and put somebody else into one, became perfectly pleasant again.

'No, let me tell you,' said Pierre, regaining his composure, 'you are a wonderful person. What you have just said was very fine, very fine. Of course you don't know me, it's so long since we've seen each other ... we were children.... You might suppose I should ... I understand, I quite understand. I shouldn't have done it, I shouldn't have had the courage, but it's splendid. I'm very glad I have made your acquaintance. A queer idea,' he added, pausing and smiling, 'you must have had of me.' He laughed. 'But what of it? Let us know each other better, please!' He pressed Boris's hand. 'Do you know I've not once seen the count. He has not sent for me... I am sorry for him, as a man ... But what can one do?'

'And so you think Napoleon will succeed in getting his army across?' Boris queried, smiling.

Pierre saw that Boris was trying to change the conversation, and so he began explaining the advantages and difficulties of the Boulogne expedition.

A footman came in to summon Boris to the princess. The princess was going. Pierre promised to come to dinner in order to see more of Boris, and pressed his hand warmly at parting, looking affectionately into his face over his spectacles.

When he had gone, Pierre walked for some time longer up and down his room, not thrusting at an unseen foe, but smiling at the recollection of that charming, intelligent, and resolute young man.

As so often happens with young people, especially if they are in a position of loneliness, he felt an unreasonable tenderness for this youth, and he firmly resolved to become friends with him.

Prince Vassily accompanied the princess to the hall. The princess was holding her handkerchief to her eyes, and her face was tearful.

'It is terrible, terrible!' she said; 'but whatever it costs me, I will do my duty. I will come to stay the night. He can't be left like this. Every minute is precious. I can't understand why his nieces put it off. Maybe God will help me to find a way to prepare him. Adieu, Prince, may God support you . . .'

'Adieu, my kind friend,' answered Prince Vassily, turning away from her.

'Oh, he is in an awful position!' said the mother to her son, when they were sitting in the carriage again. 'He scarcely knows any one.'

'I don't understand, mamma, what his attitude is as regards Pierre.'

'The will will make all that plain, my dear; our fate, too, hangs upon it . . .'

'But what makes you think he will leave us anything?'

'Oh, my dear! He is so rich, and we are so poor.'

'Well, that's hardly a sufficient reason, mamma.'

'Oh, my God, how ill he is, how ill he is!' cried his mother.

XIV

WHEN Anna Mihalovna had driven off with her son to Count Kirill Vladimirovitch Bezuhov's, Countess Rostov sat a long while alone, putting her handkerchief to her eyes. At last she rang the bell.

'What does it mean?' she said angrily to the maid, who had kept her waiting a few minutes; 'don't you care for my service, eh? I'll find you another place, if so.'

The countess was distressed at the troubles and degrading poverty of her friend, and so out of humour, which always found expression in such remarks to her servants.

'I'm very sorry,' said the maid.

'Ask the count to come to me.'

The count came waddling in to see his wife, looking, as usual, rather guilty.

'Well, little countess! What a *sauté* of woodcocks and Madeira we're to have, *ma chère*! I've tried it; I did well to give a thousand roubles for Taras. He's worth it!'

He sat down by his wife, setting his elbow jauntily on his knee, and ruffling up his grey hair. 'What are your commands, little countess?'

'It's this, my dear—why, what is this mess on you here?' she said, pointing to his waistcoat. 'It's the *sauté*, most likely,' she added, smiling. 'It's this, my dear, I want some money.' Her face became gloomy.

'Ah, little countess! . . .' And the count fidgeted about, pulling out his pocket-book.

'I want a great deal, count. I want five hundred roubles.' And taking out her cambric handkerchief she wiped her husband's waistcoat.

'This minute, this minute. Hey, who's there?' he shouted, as men only shout who are certain that those they call will run headlong at their summons. 'Send Mitenka to me!'

Mitenka, the young man of noble family who had been brought up in the count's house, and now had charge of all his money affairs, walked softly into the room.

'Here, my dear boy,' said the count to the young man, who came up respectfully. 'Bring me,' he thought a moment, 'yes, seven hundred roubles, yes. And mind, don't bring me such torn and dirty notes as last time; nice ones now, for the countess.'

'Yes, Mitenka, clean ones, please,' said the countess with a depressed sigh.

'Your excellency, when do you desire me to get the money?' said Mitenka. 'Your honour ought to know . . . But don't trouble,' he added, noticing that the count was beginning to breathe rapidly and heavily, which was always the sign of approaching anger. 'I was forgetting . . . This minute do you desire me to bring them?'

'Yes, yes, just so, bring them. Give them to the countess. What a treasure that Mitenka is,' added the count, smiling, when the young man had gone out. 'He doesn't know the meaning of impossible. That's a thing I can't bear. Everything's possible.'

'Ah, money, count, money, what a lot of sorrow it causes in the world!' said the countess. 'This money I am in great need of.'

'You are a terrible spendthrift, little countess, we all know,' said the count, and kissing his wife's hand he went away again to his own room.

When Anna Mihalovna came back from the Bezuhovs, the money was already on the countess's little table, all in new notes, under her pocket-handkerchief. Anna Mihalovna noticed that the countess was fluttered about something.

'Well, my dear?' queried the countess.

'Ah, he is in a terrible condition! One would not recognise him, he is so ill, so ill; I was there only a minute, and did not say two words.'

'Annette, for God's sake don't refuse me,' the countess said suddenly with a blush, which was strangely incongruous with her elderly, thin, and dignified face, taking the money from under her handkerchief. Anna Mihalovna instantly grasped the situation, and was already bending over to embrace the countess at the appropriate moment.

'This is for Boris, from me, for his equipment . . .'

Anna Mihalovna was already embracing her and weeping. The countess wept too. They wept because they were friends, and because they were soft-hearted, and that they, who had been friends in youth, should have to think of anything so base as money, and that their youth was over.... But the tears of both were sweet to them....

XV

COUNTESS ROSTOV, with her daughters and the greater number of the guests, was sitting in the drawing-room. The count led the gentlemen of the party to his room, calling their attention to his connoisseur's collection of Turkish pipes. Now and then he went out and inquired, had she come yet? They were waiting for Marya Dmitryevna Ahrosimov, known in society as *le terrible dragon*, a lady who owed her renown not to her wealth or her rank, but to her mental directness and her open, unconventional behaviour. Marya Dmitryevna was known to the imperial family; she was known to all Moscow and all Petersburg, and both cities, while they marvelled at her, laughed in their sleeves at her rudeness, and told good stories about her, nevertheless, all without exception respected and feared her.

In the count's room, full of smoke, there was talk of the war, which had been declared in a manifesto, and of the levies of troops. The manifesto no one had yet read, but every one knew of its appearance. The count was sitting on an ottoman with a man smoking and talking on each side of him. The count himself was neither smoking nor talking, but, with his head cocked first on one side and then on the other, gazed with evident satisfaction at the smokers, and listened to the argument he had got up between his two neighbours.

One of these two was a civilian with a thin, wrinkled, bilious, close-shaven face, a man past middle age, though dressed like the most fashionable young man. He sat with his leg up on the ottoman, as though he were at home, and with the amber mouthpiece in the side of his mouth, he smoked spasmodically, puckering up his face. This was an old bachelor, Shinshin, a cousin of the countess's, famed in Moscow drawing-rooms for his biting wit. He seemed supercilious in his manner to his companion, a fresh, rosy officer of the Guards, irreproachably washed and brushed and buttoned. He held his pipe in the middle of his mouth, and drawing in a little smoke, sent it coiling in rings out of his fine red lips. He was the Lieutenant Berg, an officer in the Semenovsky regiment with whom Boris was to go away, and about whom Natasha had taunted Vera, calling Berg her suitor. The count sat between these two listening intently to them. The count's favourite entertainment, next to playing boston, of which he was very fond, was that of listening to conversation, especially when he had succeeded in getting up a dispute between two talkative friends.

'Come, how is it, *mon très honorable* Alphonse Karlitch,' said Shinshin, chuckling, and using a combination of the most popular Russian colloquialisms and the most *recherchés* French expressions, which constituted the peculiarity of his phraseology. 'You reckon you'll get an income from the government, and you want to get a little something from your company too?'

'No, Pyotr Nikolaitch, I only want to show that in the cavalry the advantages are few as compared with the infantry. Consider my position now, for instance, Pyotr Nikolaitch.' Berg talked very precisely, serenely, and politely. All he said was always concerning himself. He always maintained a serene silence when any subject was discussed that had no direct bearing on himself. And he could be silent in that way for several hours at a time, neither experiencing nor causing the others the slightest embarrassment. But as soon as the conversation concerned him personally, he began to talk at length and with visible satisfaction.

'Consider my position, Pyotr Nikolaitch; if I were in the cavalry, I should get no more than two hundred roubles every four months, even at the rank of lieutenant, while as it is I get two hundred and thirty,' he explained with a beaming, friendly smile, looking at Shinshin and the count as though he had no doubt that his success would always be the chief goal of all other people's wishes. 'Besides that, Pyotr Nikolaitch, exchanging into the Guards, I'm so much nearer the front,' pursued Berg, 'and vacancies occur so much more frequently in the infantry guards. Then you can fancy how well I can manage on two hundred and thirty roubles. Why, I'm putting by and sending some off to my father too,' he pursued, letting off a ring of smoke.

'There is a balance. A German will thrash wheat out of the head of an axe, as the Russian proverb has it,' said Shinshin, shifting his pipe to the other side of his mouth and winking to the count.

The count chuckled. The other visitors seeing that Shinshin was talking came up to listen. Berg, without perceiving either their sneers or their lack of interest, proceeded to explain how by exchanging into the guards he had already gained a step in advance of his old comrades in the corps; how in war-time the commander of a company may so easily be killed, and he as next in command might very easily succeed him, and how every one in the regiment liked him, and how pleased his father was with him. Berg was unmistakably enjoying himself as he told all this, and seemed never to suspect that other people too might have their own interests. But all he said was so nice, so sedate, the naïveté of his youthful egoism was so undisguised, that he disarmed his listeners.

'Well, my good fellow, whether you're in the infantry or in the cavalry, you'll always get on all right, that I venture to predict,' said Shinshin, patting him on the shoulder, and setting his feet down off the ottoman. Berg smiled gleefully. The count and the guests after him went into the drawing-room.

It was that interval just before a dinner when the assembled guests do not care to enter on a lengthy conversation, expecting to be summoned to the dining-room; while they feel it incumbent on them to move about and not to be silent, so as to show that they are not impatient to sit down to table. The host and hostess look towards the door, and occasionally at one another. The guests try from these glances to divine whom or what they are waiting for; some important relation late in arriving, or some dish which is not ready.

Pierre arrived just at dinner-time, and awkwardly sat down in the middle of the drawing-room in the first easy-chair he came across, blocking up the way for every one. The countess tried to make him talk, but he looked naïvely round him over his spectacles as though he were looking for some one, and replied in monosyllables to all the countess's questions. He was in the way, and was the only person unaware of it. The greater number of the guests, knowing the story of the bear, looked inquisitively at this big, stout, inoffensive-looking person, puzzled to think how such a spiritless and staid young man could have played such a prank.

'You have only lately arrived?' the countess asked him.

'*Oui, madame.*'

'You have not seen my husband?'

'*Non, madame.*' He smiled very inappropriately.

'You have lately been in Paris, I believe? I suppose it's very interesting.'

'Very interesting.'

The countess exchanged glances with Anna Mihalovna. Anna Mihalovna saw that she was asked to undertake the young man, and sitting down by him she began talking of his father. But to her as to the countess he replied only in monosyllables. The other guests were all busily engaged together. 'The Razumovskys . . . It was very charming . . . You are so kind . . . Countess Apraxin . . .' rose in murmurs on all sides. The countess got up and went into the reception hall.

'Marya Dmitryevna?' her voice was heard asking from there.

'Herself,' a rough voice was heard in reply, and immediately after, Marya Dmitryevna walked into the room. All the girls and even the ladies, except the very old ones, got up. Marya Dmitryevna, a stout woman of fifty, stopped in the doorway, and holding her head with its grey curls erect, she looked down at the guests and as though tucking up her cuffs, she deliberately arranged the wide sleeves of her gown. Marya Dmitryevna always spoke Russian.

'Health and happiness to the lady whose name-day we are keeping and to her children,' she said in her loud, rich voice that dominated all other sounds. 'Well, you old sinner,' she turned to the count who was kissing her hand, 'I suppose you are tired of Moscow—nowhere to go out with the dogs? Well, my good man, what's to be done? these nestlings will grow up. . . .' She pointed to the girls. 'Willy-nilly, you must look out for young men for them.'

'Well, my Cossack?' (Marya Dmitryevna used to call Natasha a Cossack) she said, stroking the hand of Natasha, who came up to kiss her hand gaily without shyness. 'I know you're a wicked girl, but I like you.'

She took out of her huge reticule some amber earrings with drops, and giving them to Natasha, whose beaming birthday face flushed rosy red, she turned away immediately and addressed Pierre.

'Ay, ay! come here, sir!' she said in an intentionally quiet and gentle voice. 'Come here, sir . . .' And she tucked her sleeve up higher in an ominous manner.

Pierre went up, looking innocently at her over his spectacles.

'Come along, come along, sir! I was the only person that told your father the truth when he was in high favour, and in your case it is a sacred duty.' She paused. Every one was mutely expectant of what was to follow, feeling that this was merely a prelude. 'A pretty fellow, there's no denying! a pretty fellow! . . . His father is lying on his deathbed, and he's amusing himself, setting a police-constable astride on a bear! For shame, sir, for shame! You had better have gone to the war.'

She turned away and gave her hand to the count, who could hardly keep from laughing.

'Well, I suppose dinner's ready, eh?' said Marya Dmitryevna. The count led the way with Marya Dmitryevna, then followed the countess, taken in by a colonel of hussars, a person of importance, as Nikolay was to travel in his company to join the regiment; then Anna Mihalovna with Shinshin. Berg gave his arm to Vera, Julie Karagin walked in smiling with Nikolay. They were followed by a string of other couples, stretching right across the hall, and behind all, the children with their tutors and governesses trooped in, walking singly. There was a bustle among the waiters and a creaking of chairs; the orchestra began playing, as the guests took their places. Then the strains of the count's household band were succeeded by the clatter of knives and forks, the conversation of the guests, and the subdued tread of the waiters. The countess presided at one end of the table. On her right was Marya Dmitryevna; on her left Anna Mihalovna and the other ladies of the party. At the other end sat the count, with the colonel of hussars on his left, and on his right Shinshin and the other guests of the male sex. On one side of the large table sat the more grown-up of the young people: Vera beside Berg, Pierre beside Boris. On the other side were the children with their tutors and governesses. The count peeped from behind the crystal of the decanters and fruit-dishes at his wife and her high cap with blue ribbons, and zealously poured out wine for his neighbours, not overlooking himself. The countess, too, while mindful of her duties as hostess, cast significant glances from behind the pineapples at her husband, whose face and bald head struck her as looking particularly red against his grey hair. At the ladies' end there was a rhythmic murmur of talk, but at the other end of the table the men's voices grew louder and louder, especially the voice of the colonel of hussars, who, getting more and more flushed, ate and drank so much that the count held him up as a pattern to the rest. Berg with a tender smile was telling Vera that love was an emotion not of earth but of heaven. Boris was telling his new friend Pierre the names of the guests, while he exchanged glances with Natasha sitting opposite him. Pierre said little, looked about at the new faces, and ate a great deal. Of the two soups he chose *à la tortue*, and from that course to the fish-pasties and the grouse, he did not let a single dish pass, and took every sort of wine that the butler offered him, as he mysteriously poked a bottle wrapped in a napkin over his neighbour's shoulder, murmuring, 'Dry Madeira,' or 'Hungarian,' or 'Rhine wine.' Pierre took a wine-glass at random out of the four crystal glasses engraved with the count's crest that were set at each place, and drank with relish, staring at the guests with a countenance that became more and more amiable as the dinner went on. Natasha, who sat opposite him, gazed at Boris as girls of thirteen gaze at the boy whom they have just kissed for the first time, and with whom they are in love. This gaze sometimes strayed to Pierre, and at the look on the funny, excited little girl's face, he felt an impulse to laugh himself without knowing why.

Nikolay was sitting a long way from Sonya, beside Julie Karagin, and again smiling the same unconscious smile, he was talking to her. Sonya wore a company smile, but she was visibly in agonies of jealousy; at one moment she turned pale, then she crimsoned, and all her energies were concentrated on listening to what Nikolay and Julie were saying. The governess looked nervously about her, as though preparing to resent any slight that might be offered to the children. The German tutor was trying to learn by heart a list of all the kinds of dishes, desserts, and wines, in order to write a detailed description of them to the folks at home in Germany, and was greatly mortified that the butler with the bottle in the napkin had passed him over. The German knitted his brows, and tried to look as though he would not have cared to take that wine, but he was mortified because no one would understand that he had not wanted the wine to quench his thirst, or through greed, but from a conscientious desire for knowledge.

XVI

AT the men's end of the table the conversation was becoming more and more lively. The colonel was asserting that the proclamation of the declaration of war had already been issued in Petersburg, and that a copy, which he had seen himself, had that day been brought by a courier to the commander-in-chief.

'And what evil spirit must make us go to war with Bonaparte?' said Shinshin. 'He has already made Austria take a back seat. I am afraid it may be our turn this time.'

The colonel was a stout, tall, and plethoric German, evidently a zealous officer and good patriot. He resented Shinshin's words.

'The reason why, my good sir,' he said, speaking with a German accent, 'is just that the emperor knows that. In his proclamation he says that he cannot behold with equanimity the danger threatening Russia, and that the security of the empire, its dignity, and the sacredness of its *alliances*.' He laid a special emphasis on the word *alliances*, as though the gist of the matter lay in that word. And with the unfailing memory for official matters that was peculiar to him, he repeated the introductory words of the proclamation . . . 'and the desire, which constitutes the Sovereign's sole and immutable aim, to establish peace on a secure foundation, have determined him to despatch now a part of the troops abroad, and to make dispositions for carrying out this new project. That is the reason why, my dear sir,' he concluded, tossing off a glass of wine in edifying fashion, and looking towards the count for encouragement.

'Do you know the proverb, "Erema, Erema, you'd better stay at home and mind your spindle"?' said Shinshin, frowning and smiling. 'That suits us to a hair. Why, Suvorov even was defeated hollow, and where are our Suvorovs nowadays? I just ask you that?' he said, continually shifting from Russian to French and back again.

'We ought to fight to the last drop of our blood,' said the colonel, thumping the table, 'and to die for our emperor, and then all will be well. And to discuss it as little as possible,' he concluded, turning again to the count, and drawling out the word 'possible.' 'That's how we old hussars look at it; that's all we have to say. And how do you look at it, young man and young hussar?' he added, addressing Nikolay, who, catching that it was the war they were discussing, had dropped his conversation with Julie, and was all eyes and all ears, intent on the colonel.

'I perfectly agree with you,' answered Nikolay, growing hot all over, twisting his plate round, and changing the places of the glasses with a face as desperate and determined as though he were exposed to great danger at that actual moment. 'I am convinced that the Russians must die or conquer,' he said. He was himself, like the rest of the party, conscious after the words were uttered that he had spoken with an enthusiasm and fervour out of keeping with the occasion, and so he was embarrassed.

'That was very fine, what you just said,' Julie sitting beside him said breathlessly. Sonya trembled all over and crimsoned to her ears, and behind her ears, and down her neck and shoulders, while Nikolay was speaking. Pierre listened to the colonel's remarks, and nodded his head approvingly.

'That's capital,' said he.

'You're a true hussar, young man,' the colonel shouted, thumping on the table again.

'What are you making such a noise about over there?' Marya Dmitryevna's bass voice was suddenly heard asking across the table. 'What are you thumping the table for?' she addressed the colonel. 'Whom are you so hot against? You imagine, I suppose, that the French are before you?'

'I speak the truth,' said the hussar, smiling.

'It's all about the war,' the count shouted across the table. 'My son's going, you see, Marya Dmitryevna, my son's going.'

'And I've four sons in the army, but I don't grieve. All's in God's hands; one may die in one's bed, and in battle God may spare,' Marya Dmitryevna's deep voice boomed back, speaking without the slightest effort from the further end of the table.

'That's true.'

And the conversation concentrated into two groups again, one at the ladies' end, and one at the men's.

'You don't dare to ask!' said her little brother to Natasha, 'and you won't ask!'

'I will ask,' answered Natasha. Her face suddenly glowed, expressing a desperate and mirthful resolution. She rose in her seat, her eyes inviting Pierre to listen, and addressed her mother.

'Mamma!' her childish contralto rang out over the table.

'What is it?' the countess asked in dismay; but seeing from her daughter's face that it was mischief, she shook her hand at her sternly, with a threatening and forbidding movement of her head.

All conversation was hushed.

'Mamma! what pudding will there be?' Natasha's little voice rang out still more resolutely and deliberately.

The countess tried to frown, but could not. Marya Dmitryevna shook her fat finger.

'Cossack!' she said menacingly.

Most of the guests looked at the parents, not knowing how they were to take this sally.

'I'll give it to you,' said the countess.

'Mamma! what pudding will it be?' Natasha cried, with bold and saucy gaiety, feeling sure that her prank would be taken in the right spirit. Sonya and fat little Petya were hiding their giggles. 'You see I did ask,' Natasha whispered to her little brother and Pierre, at whom she glanced again.

'Ice-pudding, only you are not to have any,' said Marya Dmitryevna. Natasha saw there was nothing to be afraid of, and so she was not frightened at Marya Dmitryevna even.

'Marya Dmitryevna! what sort of ice-pudding? I don't like ice-cream.'

'Carrot-ices.'

'No, what sort, Marya Dmitryevna, what sort?' she almost shrieked. 'I want to know.' Marya Dmitryevna and the countess burst out laughing, and all the party followed their example. They all laughed, not at Marya Dmitryevna's answer, but at the irrepressible boldness and smartness of the little girl, who had the pluck and the wit to tackle Marya Dmitryevna in this fashion.

Natasha only desisted when she had been told it was to be pine-apple ice. Before the ices, champagne was passed round. Again the band struck up, the count kissed his countess, and the guests getting up from the table congratulated the countess, and clinked glasses across the table with the count, the children, and one another. Again the waiters darted about, chairs grated on the floor, and in the same order, but with flushed faces, the guests returned to the drawing-room and the count's study.

XVII

THE card-tables were opened, parties were made up for boston, and the count's guests settled themselves in the two drawing-rooms, the divan room, and the library.

The count holding his cards in a fan, with some difficulty kept himself from dropping into his customary after-dinner nap, and laughed at everything. The young people, at the countess's suggestion, gathered about the clavichord and the harp. Julie was first pressed by every one to perform, and played a piece with variations on the harp. Then she joined the other young ladies in begging Natasha and Nikolay, who were noted for their musical talents, to sing something. Natasha, who was treated by every one as though she were grown-up, was visibly very proud of it, and at the same time made shy by it.

'What are we to sing?' she asked.

'The "Spring,"' answered Nikolay.

'Well, then, let's make haste. Boris, come here,' said Natasha. 'But where's Sonya?' She looked round, and seeing that her friend was not in the room, she ran off to find her.

After running to Sonya's room, and not finding her there, Natasha ran to the nursery: Sonya was not there either. Natasha knew that she must be on the chest in the corridor. The chest in the corridor was the scene of the woes of the younger feminine generation of the house of Rostov. Yes, Sonya was on the chest, lying face downwards, crushing her gossamer pink frock on their old nurse's dirty striped feather-bed. Her face hidden in her fingers, she was sobbing, and her little bare shoulders were heaving. Natasha's birthday face that had been festive and excited all day, changed at once; her eyes wore a fixed look, then her broad neck quivered, and the corners of her lips drooped.

'Sonya! what is it? . . . what's the matter with you? Oo-oo-oo! . . .' and Natasha, letting her big mouth drop open and becoming quite ugly, wailed like a baby, not knowing why, simply because Sonya was crying. Sonya tried to lift up her head, tried to answer, but could not, and buried her face more than ever. Natasha cried, sitting on the edge of the blue feather-bed and hugging her friend. Making an effort, Sonya got up, began to dry her tears and to talk.

'Nikolinka's going away in a week, his . . . paper . . . has come . . . he told me himself. . . . But still I shouldn't cry . . .' (she showed a sheet of paper she was holding in her hand; on it were verses written by Nikolay). 'I shouldn't have cried; but you can't . . . no one can understand . . . what a soul he has.'

And again she fell to weeping at the thought of how noble his soul was.

'It's all right for you . . . I'm not envious . . . I love you and Boris too,' she said, controlling herself a little; 'he's so nice . . . there are no difficulties in your way. But Nikolay's my cousin . . . the metropolitan chief priest himself . . . has to . . . or else it's impossible. And so, if mamma's told' (Sonya looked on the countess and addressed her as a mother), 'she'll say that I'm spoiling Nikolay's career, that I have no heart, that I'm ungrateful, though really . . . in God's name' (she made the sign of the cross) 'I love her so, and all of you, only Vera . . . Why is it? What have I done to her? I am so grateful to you that I would be glad to sacrifice everything for you, but I have nothing. . . .'

Sonya could say no more, and again she buried her head in her hands and the feather-bed. Natasha tried to comfort her, but her face showed that she grasped all the gravity of her friend's trouble.

'Sonya!' she said all at once, as though she had guessed the real cause of her cousin's misery, 'of course Vera's been talking to you since dinner? Yes?'

'Yes, these verses Nikolay wrote himself, and I copied some others; and she found them on my table, and said she should show them to mamma, and she said too that I was ungrateful, and that mamma would never allow him to marry me, but that he would marry Julie. You see how he has been with her all day . . . Natasha! why is it?'

And again she sobbed more bitterly than ever. Natasha lifted her up, hugged her, and smiling through her tears, began comforting her.

'Sonya, don't you believe her, darling; don't believe her. Do you remember how we talked with Nikolay, all three of us together, in the divan room, do you remember, after supper? Why we settled how it should all be. I don't quite remember now, but do you remember, it was all right and all possible. Why, uncle Shinshin's brother is married to his first cousin, and we're only second cousins, you know. And Boris said that it's quite easily arranged. You know I told him all about it. He's so clever and so good,' said Natasha. . . . 'Don't cry, Sonya, darling, sweet one, precious, Sonya,' and she kissed her, laughing. 'Vera's spiteful; never mind her! and it will all come right, and she won't tell mamma. Nikolinka will tell her himself, and he's never thought of Julie.'

And she kissed her on the head. Sonya got up, and the kitten revived; its eyes sparkled, and it was ready, it seemed, to wag its tail, spring on its soft paws and begin to play with a ball, in its own natural, kittenish way.

'Do you think so? Really? Truly?' she said rapidly, smoothing her frock and her hair.

'Really, truly,' answered Natasha, putting back a stray coil of rough hair on her friend's head; and they both laughed. 'Well, come along and sing the "Spring."'

'Let's go, then.'

'And do you know that fat Pierre, who was sitting opposite me, he's so funny!' Natasha said suddenly, stopping. 'I am enjoying myself so,' and Natasha ran along the corridor.

Brushing off the feather fluff from her frock, and thrusting the verses into her bodice next to her little throat and prominent breast-bones, Sonya ran with flushed face and light, happy steps, following Natasha along the corridor to the divan room. At the request of their guests the young people sang the quartette the 'Spring,' with which every one was delighted; then Nikolay sang a song he had lately learnt.

> 'How sweet in the moon's kindly ray,
> In fancy to thyself to say,
> That earth holds still one dear to thee!
> Whose thoughts, whose dreams are all of thee!
> That her fair fingers as of old
> Stray still upon the harp of gold,
> Making sweet, passionate harmony,
> That to her side doth summon thee!
> Tomorrow and thy bliss is near!
> Alas! all's past! she is not here!'

And he had hardly sung the last words when the young people were getting ready to dance in the big hall, and the musicians began stamping with their feet and coughing in the orchestra.

Pierre was sitting in the drawing-room, where Shinshin had started a conversation with him on the political situation, as a subject likely to be of interest to any one who had just come home from abroad, though it did not in fact interest Pierre. Several other persons joined in the conversation. When the orchestra struck up, Natasha walked into the drawing-room, and going straight up to Pierre, laughing and blushing, she said, 'Mamma told me to ask you to dance.'

'I'm afraid of muddling the figures,' said Pierre, 'but if you will be my teacher . . .' and he gave his fat hand to the slim little girl, putting his arm low down to reach her level.

While the couples were placing themselves and the musicians were tuning up, Pierre sat down with his little partner. Natasha was perfectly happy; she was dancing with a grown-up person, with a man who had just come from abroad. She was sitting in view of every one and talking to him like a grown-up person. She had in her hand a fan, which some lady had given her to hold, and taking the most modish pose (God knows where and when she had learnt it) fanning herself and smiling all over her face, she talked to her partner.

'What a girl! Just look at her, look at her!' said the old countess, crossing the big hall and pointing to Natasha. Natasha coloured and laughed.

'Why, what do you mean, mamma? Why should you laugh? Is there anything strange about it?'

In the middle of the third écossaise there was a clatter of chairs in the drawing-room, where the count and Marya Dmitryevna were playing, and the greater number of the more honoured guests and elderly people stretching themselves after sitting so long, put their pocket-books and purses in their pockets and came out to the door of the big hall. In front of all came Marya Dmitryevna and the count, both with radiant faces. The count gave his arm, curved into a hoop, to Marya Dmitreyevna with playfully exaggerated ceremony, like a ballet-dancer. He drew himself up, and his face beamed with a peculiar, jauntily-knowing smile, and as soon as they had finished dancing the last figure of the écossaise, he clapped his hands to the orchestra, and shouted to the first violin: 'Semyon! do you know "Daniel Cooper?"'

That was the count's favourite dance that he had danced in his youth. (Daniel Cooper was the name of a figure of the anglaise.)

'Look at papa!' Natasha shouted to all the room (entirely forgetting that she was dancing with a grown-up partner), and ducking down till her curly head almost touched her knees, she went off into her ringing laugh that filled the hall. Every one in the hall was, in fact, looking with a smile of delight at the gleeful old gentleman. Standing beside his majestic partner, Marya Dmitryevna, who was taller than he was, he curved his arms, swaying them in time to the music, moved his shoulders, twirled with his legs, lightly tapping with his heels, and with a broadening grin on his round face, prepared the spectators for what was to come. As soon as the orchestra played the gay, irresistible air of Daniel Cooper, somewhat like a livelier Russian *trepak*, all the doorways of the big hall were suddenly filled with the smiling faces of the house-serfs—men on one side, and women on the other—come to look at their master making merry.

'Our little father! An eagle he is!' the old nurse said out loud at one door.

The count danced well and knew that he did, but his partner could not dance at all, and did not care about dancing well. Her portly figure stood erect, with her mighty arms hanging by her side (she had handed her reticule to the countess). It was only her stern, but comely face that danced. What was expressed by the whole round person of the count, was expressed by Marya Dmitryevna in her more and more beaming countenance and puckered nose. While the count, with greater and greater expenditure of energy, enchanted the spectators by the unexpectedness of the nimble pirouettes and capers of his supple legs, Marya Dmitryevna with the slightest effort in the movement of her shoulders or curving of her arms, when they turned or marked the time with their feet, produced no less impression from the contrast, which every one appreciated, with her portliness and her habitual severity of demeanour. The dance grew more and more animated. The *vis-à-vis* could not obtain one moment's attention, and did not attempt to do so. All attention was absorbed by the count and Marya Dmitryevna. Natasha pulled at the sleeve or gown of every one present, urging them to look at papa, though they never took their eyes off the dancers. In the pauses in the dance the count drew a deep breath, waved his hands and shouted to the musician to play faster. More and more quickly, more and more nimbly the count pirouetted, turning now on his toes and now on his heels, round Marya Dmitryevna. At last, twisting his lady round to her place, he executed the last steps, kicking his supple legs up behind him, and bowing his perspiring head and smiling face, with a round sweep of his right arm, amidst a thunder of applause and laughter, in which Natasha's laugh was loudest. Both partners stood still, breathing heavily, and mopping their faces with their batiste handkerchiefs.

'That's how they used to dance in our day, *ma chère*,' said the count.

'Bravo, Daniel Cooper!' said Marya Dmitryevna, tucking up her sleeves and drawing a deep, prolonged breath.

XVIII

WHILE in the Rostovs' hall they were dancing the sixth anglaise, while the weary orchestra played wrong notes, and the tired footmen and cooks were getting the supper, Count Bezuhov had just had his sixth stroke. The doctors declared that there was no hope of recovery; the sick man received absolution and the sacrament while unconscious.

Preparations were being made for administering extreme unction, and the house was full of the bustle and thrill of suspense usual at such moments. Outside the house undertakers were crowding beyond the gates, trying to escape the notice of the carriages that drove up, but eagerly anticipating a good order for the count's funeral. The governor of Moscow, who had been constantly sending his adjutants to inquire after the count's condition, came himself that evening to say good-bye to the renowned grandee of Catherine's court, Count Bezuhov.

The magnificent reception-room was full. Every one stood up respectfully when the governor, after being half an hour alone with the sick man, came out of the sick-room. Bestowing scanty recognition on the bows with which he was received, he tried to escape as quickly as possible from the gaze of the doctors, ecclesiastical personages, and relations. Prince Vassily, who had grown paler and thinner during the last few days, escorted the governor out, and softly repeated something to him several times over.

After seeing the governor, Prince Vassily sat down on a chair in the hall alone, crossing one leg high over the other, leaning his elbow on his knee, and covering his eyes with his hand. After sitting so for some time he got up, and with steps more hurried than his wont, he crossed the long corridor, looking round him with frightened eyes, and went to the back part of the house to the apartments of the eldest princess.

The persons he had left in the dimly lighted reception-room, next to the sick-room, talked in broken whispers among themselves, pausing, and looking round with eyes full of suspense and inquiry whenever the door that led into the dying man's room creaked as some one went in or came out.

'Man's limitation,' said a little man, an ecclesiastic of some sort, to a lady who was sitting near him listening naïvely to his words—'his limitation is fixed, there is no overstepping it.'

'I wonder if it won't be late for extreme unction?' inquired the lady, using his clerical title, and apparently having no opinion of her own on the matter.

'It is a great mystery, ma'am,' answered the cleric, passing his hands over his bald head, on which lay a few tresses of carefully combed, half grey hair.

'Who was that? was it the governor himself?' they were asking at the other end of the room. 'What a young-looking man!'

'And he's over sixty! . . . What, do they say, the count does not know any one? Do they mean to give extreme unction?'

'I knew a man who received extreme unction seven times.'

The second princess came out of the sick-room with tearful eyes, and sat down beside Doctor Lorrain, who was sitting in a graceful pose under the portrait of Catherine, with his elbow on the table.

'Very fine,' said the doctor in reply to a question about the weather; 'very fine, princess, and besides, at Moscow, one might suppose oneself in the country.'

'Might one not?' said the princess, sighing. 'So may he have something to drink?' Lorrain thought a moment.

'He has taken his medicine?'

'Yes.'

The doctor looked at his memoranda.

'Take a glass of boiled water and put in a pinch' (he showed with his delicate fingers what was meant by a pinch) 'of cream of tartar.'

'There has never been a case,' said the German doctor to the adjutant, speaking broken Russian, 'of recovery after having a third stroke.'

'And what a vigorous man he was!' said the adjutant. 'And to whom will this great wealth go?' he added in a whisper.

'Candidates will be found,' the German replied, smiling. Every one looked round again at the door; it creaked, and the second princess having made the drink according to Lorrain's direction, carried it into the sick-room. The German doctor went up to Lorrain.

'Can it drag on till tomorrow morning?' asked the German, with a vile French accent.

Lorrain, with compressed lips and a stern face, moved his finger before his nose to express a negative.

'Tonight, not later,' he said softly, and with a decorous smile of satisfaction at being able to understand and to express the exact position of the sick man, he walked away.

Meanwhile Prince Vassily had opened the door of the princess's room.

It was half dark in the room; there were only two lamps burning before the holy pictures, and there was a sweet perfume of incense and flowers. The whole room was furnished with miniature furniture, little sideboards, small bookcases, and small tables. Behind a screen could be seen the white coverings of a high feather-bed. A little dog barked.

'Ah, is that you, *mon cousin*?'

She got up and smoothed her hair, which was always, even now, so extraordinarily smooth that it seemed as though made out of one piece with her head and covered with varnish.

'Has anything happened?' she asked. 'I am in continual dread.'

'Nothing, everything is unchanged. I have only come to have a little talk with you, Katish, about business,' said the prince, sitting down wearily in the low chair from which she had just risen. 'How warm it is here, though,' he said. 'Come, sit here; let us talk.'

'I wondered whether anything had happened,' said the princess, and with her stonily severe expression unchanged, she sat down opposite the prince, preparing herself to listen. 'I have been trying to get some sleep, *mon cousin*, but I can't.'

'Well, my dear?' said Prince Vassily, taking the princess's hand, and bending it downwards as his habit was.

It was plain that this 'well?' referred to much that they both comprehended without mentioning it in words.

The princess, with her spare, upright figure, so disproportionately long in the body, looked straight at the prince with no sign of emotion in her prominent grey eyes. She shook her head, and sighing looked towards the holy pictures. Her gesture might have been interpreted as an expression of grief and devotion, or as an expression of weariness and the hope of a speedy release. Prince Vassily took it as an expression of weariness.

'And do you suppose it's any easier for me?' he said. 'I am as worn out as a post horse. I must have a little talk with you, Katish, and a very serious one.'

Prince Vassily paused, and his cheeks began twitching nervously, first on one side, then on the other, giving his face an unpleasant expression such as was never seen on his countenance when he was in drawing-rooms. His eyes, too, were different from usual: at one moment they stared with a sort of insolent jocoseness, at the next they looked round furtively.

The princess, pulling her dog on her lap with her thin, dry hands, gazed intently at the eyes of Prince Vassily, but it was evident that she would not break the silence, if she had to sit silent till morning.

'You see, my dear princess and cousin, Katerina Semyonovna,' pursued Prince Vassily, obviously with some inner conflict bracing himself to go on with what he wanted to say, 'at such moments as the present, one has to think of everything. One must think of the future, of you ... I care for all of you as if you were my own children; you know that.'

The princess looked at him with the same dull immovable gaze.

'Finally, we have to think of my family too,' continued Prince Vassily, angrily pushing away a little table and not looking at her: 'you know, Katish, that you three Mamontov sisters and my wife,—we are the only direct heirs of the count. I know, I know how painful it is for you to speak and think of such things. And it's as hard for me; but, my dear, I am a man over fifty, I must be ready for anything. Do you know that I have sent for Pierre, and that the count, pointing straight at his portrait, has asked for him?'

Prince Vassily looked inquiringly at the princess, but he could not make out whether she was considering what he had said, or was simply staring at him.

'I pray to God for one thing only continually, *mon cousin*,' she replied, 'that He may have mercy upon him, and allow his noble soul to leave this . . .'

'Yes, quite so,' Prince Vassily continued impatiently, rubbing his bald head and again wrathfully moving the table towards him that he had just moved away, 'but in fact . . . in fact the point is, as you are yourself aware, that last winter the count made a will by which, passing over his direct heirs and us, he bequeathed all his property to Pierre.'

'He may have made ever so many wills!' the princess said placidly; 'but he can't leave it to Pierre. Pierre is illegitimate.'

'*Ma chere*,' said Prince Vassily suddenly, pushing the table against him, growing more earnest and beginning to speak more rapidly: 'but what if a letter has been written to the Emperor, and the count has petitioned him to legitimise Pierre? You understand, that the count's services would make his petition carry weight . . .'

The princess smiled, as people smile who believe that they know much more about the subject than those with whom they are talking.

'I can say more,' Prince Vassily went on, clasping her hand; 'that letter has been written, though it has not been sent off, and the Emp҅ has heard about it. The question only is whether it has been destroy҅ or not. If not, as soon as all is over,' Prince Vassily sighed, giving her thereby to understand what he meant precisely by the words 'all is over,' 'and they open the count's papers, the will with the letter will be given to the Emperor, and his petition will certainly be granted. Pierre, as the legitimate son, will receive everything.'

'What about our share?' the princess inquired, smiling ironically as though anything but that might happen.

'Why, my poor Katish, it is as clear as daylight. He will then be the only legal heir of all, and you won't receive as much as this, see. You ought to know, my dear, whether the will and the petition were written, and whether they have been destroyed, and if they have somehow been overlooked, then you ought to know where they are and to find them, because . . .'

'That would be rather too much!' the princess interrupted him, smiling sardonically, with no change in the expression of her eyes. 'I am a woman, and you think we are all silly; but I do know so much, that an illegitimate son can't inherit . . . *Un bâtard*,' she added, supposing that by this translation of the word she was conclusively proving to the prince the groundlessness of his contention.

'How can you not understand, Katish, really! You are so intelligent; how is it you don't understand that if the count has written a letter to the Emperor, begging him to recognise his son as legitimate, then Pierre will not be Pierre but Count Bezuhov, and then he will inherit everything under the will? And if the will and the letter have not been destroyed, then except the consolation of having been dutiful and of all that results from having done your duty, nothing is left for you. That's the fact.'

'I know that the will was made, but I know, too, that it is invalid, and you seem to take me for a perfect fool, *mon cousin*,' said the princess, with the air with which women speak when they imagine they are saying something witty and biting.

'My dear princess, Katerina Semyonovna!' Prince Vassily began impatiently, 'I have come to you not to provoke you, but to talk to you as a kinswoman, a good, kind-hearted, true kinswoman, of your own interests. I tell you for the tenth time that if the letter to the Emperor and the will in Pierre's favour are among the count's papers, you, my dear girl, and your sisters are not heiresses. If you don't believe me, believe people who know; I have just been talking to Dmitry Onufritch' (this was the family solicitor); 'he said the same.'

There was obviously some sudden change in the princess's ideas; her thin lips turned white (her eyes did not change), and when she began to speak, her voice passed through transitions, which she clearly did not herself anticipate.

'That would be a pretty thing,' she said. 'I wanted nothing, and I want nothing.' She flung her dog off her lap and smoothed out the folds of her skirt.

'That's the gratitude, that's the recognition people get who have sacrificed everything for him,' she said. 'Very nice! Excellent! I don't want anything, prince.'

'Yes, but you are not alone, you have sisters,' answered Prince Vassily. But the princess did not heed him.

'Yes, I knew it long ago, but I'd forgotten that I could expect nothing in this house but baseness, deceit, envy, scheming, nothing but ingratitude, the blackest ingratitude . . .'

'Do you or do you not know where that will is?' asked Prince Vassily, the twitching of his cheeks more marked than ever.

'Yes, I have been foolish; I still kept faith in people, and cared for them and sacrificed myself. But no one succeeds except those who are base and vile. I know whose plotting this is.'

The princess would have risen, but the prince held her by the arm. The princess had the air of a person who has suddenly lost faith in the whole human race. She looked viciously at her companion.

'There is still time, my dear. Remember, Katish, that all this was done heedlessly, in a moment of anger, of illness, and then forgotten. Our duty, my dear girl, is to correct his mistake, to soften his last moments by not letting him commit this injustice, not letting him die with the thought that he has made miserable those . . .'

'Those who have sacrificed everything for him,' the princess caught him up; and she made an impulsive effort again to stand up, but the prince would not let her, 'a sacrifice he has never known how to appreciate. No, *mon cousin*,' she added, with a sigh, 'I will remember that one can expect no reward in this world, that in this world there is no honour, no justice. Cunning and wickedness is what one wants in this world.'

'Come, *voyons*, calm yourself; I know your noble heart.'

'No, I have a wicked heart.'

'I know your heart,' repeated the prince. 'I value your affection, and I could wish you had the same opinion of me. Calm yourself and let us talk sensibly while there is time—perhaps twenty-four hours, perhaps one. Tell me all you know about the will, and what's of most consequence, where it is; you must know. We will take it now at once and show it to the count. He has no doubt forgotten about it and would wish to destroy it. You understand that my one desire is to carry out his wishes religiously. That is what I came here for. I am only here to be of use to him and to you.'

'Now I see it all. I know whose plotting this is. I know,' the princess was saying.

'That's not the point, my dear.'

'It's all your precious Anna Mihalovna, your *protégée* whom I wouldn't take as a housemaid, the nasty creature.'

'Do not let us waste time.'

'Oh, don't talk to me! Last winter she forced her way in here and told such a pack of vile, mean tales to the count about all of us, especially Sophie—I can't repeat them—that it made the count ill, and he wouldn't see us for a fortnight. It was at that time, I know, he wrote that hateful, infamous document, but I thought it was of no consequence.'

'There we are. Why didn't you tell us about it before?'

'It's in the inlaid portfolio that he keeps under his pillow. Now I know,' said the princess, making no reply. 'Yes, if I have a sin to my account, a great sin, it's my hatred of that infamous woman,' almost shrieked the princess, utterly transformed. 'And why does she force herself in here? But I'll have it out with her. The time will come!'

XIX

AT the time that these conversations were taking place in the reception-room and the princess's room, a carriage with Pierre (who had been sent for) and Anna Mihalovna (who had thought fit to come with him) in it was driving into the court of Count Bezuhov's mansion. When the sound of the carriage wheels was muffled by the straw in the street, Anna Mihalovna turned with words of consolation to her companion, discovered that he was asleep in his corner of the carriage, and waked him up. Rousing himself, Pierre followed Anna Mihalovna out of the carriage, and only then began to think of the interview with his dying father that awaited him. He noticed that they had driven not up to the visitors' approach, but to the back entrance. As he got down from the carriage step, two men in the dress of tradesmen hastily scurried away from the entrance into the shadow of the wall. Pierre, as he stood waiting, noticed several other similar persons standing in the shadow of the house on both sides. But neither Anna Mihalovna nor the footman and coachman, who must have seen these people, took any notice of them. So it must be all right, Pierre decided, and he followed Anna Mihalovna. With hurrying footsteps Anna Mihalovna walked up the dimly lighted, narrow stone staircase, urging on Pierre, who lagged behind. Though Pierre had no notion why he had to go to the count at all, and still less why he had to go by the back stairs, yet, impressed by Anna Mihalovna's assurance and haste, he made up his mind that it was undoubtedly necessary for him to do so. Half-way up the stairs they were almost knocked over by some men with pails, who ran down towards them, tramping loudly with their big boots. These men huddled up against the wall to let Pierre and Anna Mihalovna pass, and showed not the slightest surprise at seeing them.

'Is this the princess's side of the house?' Anna Mihalovna asked of one of them . . .

'Yes, it is,' answered the footman in a bold, loud voice, as though anything were permissible at such a time; 'the door on the left, ma'am.'

'Perhaps the count has not asked for me,' said Pierre, as he reached the landing. 'I had better go to my own room.' Anna Mihalovna stopped for Pierre to catch her up.

'*Ah, mon ami,*' she said, touching his hand with just the same gesture as she had used in the morning with her son. 'Believe me, I am suffering as much as you; but be a man.'

'Really, had I not better go?' Pierre asked affectionately, looking at her over his spectacles.

'Ah, *mon ami*, forget the wrong that may have been done you, think that it is your father ... and perhaps in his death agony,' she sighed. 'I have loved you like a son from the first. Trust in me, Pierre. I shall not forget your interests.'

Pierre did not understand a word. Again he felt more strongly than before that all this had to be so, and he obediently followed Anna Mihalovna, who was already opening the door. The door led into the vestibule of the back stairs. In the corner sat the princess's old man-servant knitting stockings. Pierre had never been in this part of the house, and had not even suspected the existence of these apartments. A maid-servant carrying a tray with a decanter overtook them, and Anna Mihalovna (calling her 'my dear' and 'my good girl') asked her after the princesses' health, and drew Pierre further along the stone corridor. The first door to the left led out of the corridor into the princesses' living rooms, the maid with the decanter was in a hurry (everything seemed to be done in a hurry at that moment in the house), and she did not close the door after her. Pierre and Anna Mihalovna, as they passed by, glanced unconsciously into the room where the eldest princess and Prince Vassily were sitting close together talking. On catching sight of their passing figures, Prince Vassily made an impatient movement and drew back, the princess jumped up, and with a despairing gesture she closed the door, slamming it with all her might. This action was so unlike the princess's habitual composure, the dismay depicted on the countenance of Prince Vassily was so out of keeping with his dignity, that Pierre stopped short and looked inquiringly over his spectacles at his guide. Anna Mihalovna manifested no surprise; she simply smiled a little and sighed, as though to show that she had anticipated all that.

'Be a man, *mon ami*, I am looking after your interests,' she said in response to his look of inquiry, and she walked more quickly along the corridor.

Pierre had no notion what was going on, and no inkling of what was meant by watching over his interests. But he felt that all this had to be so. From the corridor they went into the half-lighted hall adjoining the count's reception-room. This was one of the cold, sumptuously furnished rooms which Pierre knew, leading from the visitors' staircase. But even in this apartment there was an empty bath standing in the middle of the floor, and water had been spilt on the carpet. They were met here by a servant and a church attendant with a censer, who walked on tiptoe and took no notice of them. They went into the reception-room opening into the winter garden, a room Pierre knew well, with its two Italian windows, its big bust and full-length portrait of Catherine. The same persons were all sitting almost in the same positions exchanging whispers in the reception-room. All ceased speaking and looked round at Anna Mihalovna, as she came in with her pale, tear-stained face, and at the big, stout figure of Pierre, as with downcast head he followed her submissively.

The countenance of Anna Mihalovna showed a consciousness that the crucial moment had arrived. With the air of a Petersburg lady of experience, she walked into the room even more boldly than in the morning, keeping Pierre at her side. She felt that as she was bringing the person the dying man wanted to see, she might feel secure as to her reception. With a rapid glance, scanning all the persons in the room, and observing the count's spiritual adviser, she did not precisely bow down, but seemed somehow suddenly to shrink in stature, and with a tripping amble swam up to the priest and reverentially received a blessing first from one and then from another ecclesiastic.

'Thank God that we are in time,' she said to the priest; 'all of us, his kinsfolk, have been in such alarm. This young man is the count's son,' she added more softly. 'It is a terrible moment.'

Having uttered these words she approached the doctor.

'Dear doctor,' she said to him, 'this young man is the count's son. Is there any hope?'

The doctor did not speak, but rapidly shrugged his shoulders and turned up his eyes. With precisely the same gesture Anna Mihalovna moved her shoulders and eyes, almost closing her eyelids, sighed and went away from the doctor to Pierre. She addressed Pierre with peculiar deference and tender melancholy.

'Have faith in His mercy,' she said to him, and indicating a sofa for him to sit down and wait for her, she went herself with inaudible steps towards the door, at which every one was looking, and after almost noiselessly opening it, she vanished behind it.

Pierre, having decided to obey his monitress in everything, moved towards the sofa she had pointed out to him. As soon as Anna Mihalovna had disappeared, he noticed that the eyes of all the persons in the room were fixed upon him with something more than curiosity and sympathy in their gaze. He noticed that they were all whispering together, looking towards him with something like awe and even obsequious deference. They showed him a respect such as had never been shown him before. A lady, a stranger to him, the one who had been talking to the priest, got up and offered him her place. An adjutant picked up the glove Pierre had dropped and handed it to him. The doctors respectfully paused in their talk when he passed by them and moved aside to make way for him. Pierre wanted at first to sit somewhere else, so as not to trouble the lady; he would have liked to pick up the glove himself and to walk round the doctors, who were really not at all in the way. But he felt all at once that to do so would be improper; he felt that he was that night a person who had to go through a terrible ceremony which every one expected of him, and that for that reason he was bound to accept service from every one. He took the glove from the adjutant in silence, sat down in the lady's place, laying his big hands on his knees, sitting in the naïvely symmetrical pose of an Egyptian statue, and decided mentally that it must all inevitably be like this, and that to avoid losing his head and doing something stupid, he must for that evening not act on his own ideas, but abandon himself wholly to the will of those who were guiding him.

Two minutes had not elapsed before Prince Vassily came majestically into the room, wearing his coat with three stars on it, and carrying his head high. He looked as though he had grown thinner since the morning. His eyes seemed larger than usual as he glanced round the room, and caught sight of Pierre. He went up to him, took his hand (a thing he had never done before), and drew it downwards, as though he wanted to try its strength.

'Courage, courage, *mon ami*. He has asked to see you, that is well . . .' and he would have gone on, but Pierre thought it fitting to ask: 'How is . . . ?' He hesitated, not knowing whether it was proper for him to call the dying man 'the count'; he felt ashamed to call him 'father.'

'He has had another stroke half-an-hour ago. Courage, *mon ami*.'

Pierre was in a condition of such mental confusion that the word stroke aroused in his mind the idea of a blow from some heavy body. He looked in perplexity at Prince Vassily, and only later grasped that an attack of illness was called a stroke. Prince Vassily said a few words to Lorrain as he passed and went to the door on tiptoe. He could not walk easily on tiptoe, and jerked his whole person up and down in an ungainly fashion. He was followed by the eldest princess, then by the clergy and church attendants; some servants too went in at the door. Through that door a stir could be heard, and at last Anna Mihalovna, with a face still pale but resolute in the performance of duty, ran out and, touching Pierre on the arm, said:

'The goodness of heaven is inexhaustible; it is the ceremony of extreme unction which they are beginning. Come.'

Pierre went in, stepping on to the soft carpet, and noticed that the adjutant and the unknown lady and some servants too, all followed him in, as though there were no need now to ask permission to enter that room.

XX

PIERRE knew well that great room, divided by columns and an arch, and carpeted with Persian rugs. The part of the room behind the columns, where on one side there stood a high mahogany bedstead with silken hangings, and on the other a huge case of holy pictures, was brightly and decoratively lighted up, as churches are lighted for evening service. Under the gleaming ornamentation of the case stood a long invalid chair, and in the chair, on snow-white, uncrumpled, freshly changed pillows, covered to the waist with a bright green quilt, Pierre recognised the majestic figure of his father, Count Bezuhov, with the grey shock of hair like a lion's mane over his broad forehead, and the characteristically aristocratic, deep lines on his handsome, reddish-yellow face. He was lying directly under the holy pictures: both his great stout arms were lying on the quilt. In his right hand, which lay with the palm downwards, a wax candle had been thrust between the thumb and forefinger, and an old servant bending over the chair held it in it. About the chair stood the clergy in their shining ceremonial vestments, with their long hair pulled out over them. They held lighted candles in their hands, and were performing the service with deliberate solemnity. A little behind them stood the two younger princesses holding handkerchiefs to their eyes, and in front of them the eldest, Katish, stood with a vindictive and determined air, never for an instant taking her eyes off the holy image, as though she were declaring to all that she would not answer for herself, if she were to look round. Anna Mihalovna with a countenance of meek sorrow and forgiveness stood at the door with the unknown lady. Prince Vassily was standing close to the invalid chair on the other side of the door. He had drawn a carved, velvet chair up to him, and was leaning on the back of it with his left hand, in which he held a candle, while with his right he crossed himself, turning his eyes upwards every time as he put his finger to his forehead. His face expressed quiet piety and submission to the will of God. 'If you don't understand such feelings, so much the worse for you,' his face seemed to say.

Behind him stood the adjutant, the doctors, and the men-servants; the men and the women had separated as though they were in church. All were silently crossing themselves, nothing was audible but the reading of the service, the subdued, deep bass singing, and in the intervals of silence sighs could be heard and the shuffling of feet. With a significant air, which showed she knew what she was about, Anna Mihalovna walked right across the room to Pierre and gave him a candle. He lighted it, and absorbed in watching the people around him, he absent-mindedly crossed himself with the hand in which he held the candle. The youngest princess, Sophie, the rosy, laughing one with the mole, was looking at him. She smiled, hid her face in her handkerchief, and for a long while did not uncover it. But looking at Pierre again, again she laughed. She was apparently unable to look at him without laughing, but could not resist looking at him, and to be out of temptation, she softly moved behind a column. In the middle of the service the voices of the priests suddenly ceased, and they whispered something to one another. The old servant, who was holding the count's hand, got up and turned to the ladies. Anna Mihalovna stepped forward and, stooping over the sick man, she beckoned behind her back to Lorrain. The French doctor had been leaning against the column without a candle, in the respectful attitude of the foreigner, who would show that in spite of the difference of religion he comprehends all the solemnity of the ceremony and even approves of it. With the noiseless steps of a man in the full vigour of his age, he went up to the sick man. His delicate, white fingers lifted his disengaged hand from the quilt, and turning away, the doctor began feeling the pulse in absorbed attention. They gave the sick man some drink; there was a slight bustle around him, then all went back to their places and the service was continued. During this break in the proceedings Pierre noticed that Prince Vassily moved away from his chair-back, and with that same air of being quite sure of what he was about, and of its being so much the worse for others, if they failed to understand it, he did not go up to the sick man, but passed by him and joined the eldest princess. Then together they went away to the further end of the room to the high bedstead under the silk canopy. When they moved away from the bed the prince and princess disappeared together by the further door, but before the end of the service they returned one after the other to their places. Pierre paid no more attention to this circumstance than to all the rest, having once for all made up his mind that all that he saw taking place that evening must inevitably be as it was.

The sounds of the church singing ceased and the voice of the chief ecclesiastic was heard, respectfully congratulating the sick man on his reception of the mystery. The dying man lay as lifeless and immovable as before. Every one was moving about him, there was the sound of footsteps and of whispers, Anna Mihalovna's whisper rising above the rest.

Pierre heard her say: 'Undoubtedly he must be moved on to the bed; it's impossible . . .'

The sick man was so surrounded by the doctors, the princesses and the servants, that Pierre could no longer see the reddish-yellow face with the grey mane, which he had never lost sight of for one instant during the ceremony, even though he had been watching other people too. Pierre guessed from the cautious movements of the people about the chair that they were lifting the dying man up and moving him.

'Hold on to my arm; you'll drop him so,' he heard the frightened whisper of one of the servants. 'Lower down . . . another one here,' said voices. And their heavy breathing and hurried tread seemed to show that the weight they carried was too heavy for them.

As they passed him—Anna Mihalovna among them—the young man caught a glimpse over people's backs and necks of the great muscular open chest, the grey, curly, leonine head, and the massive shoulders of the sick man, which were pushed up, as he was supported under the arm-pits. His head, with its extraordinarily broad brow and cheekbones, its beautiful sensual mouth, and haughty, cold eyes, was not disfigured by the proximity of death. It was just the same as Pierre had seen it three months before, when his father had been sending him off to Petersburg. But the head swayed helplessly with the jerky steps of the bearers, and the cold, apathetic eyes did not know on what to rest.

They were busy for several minutes round the high bed; then the people, who had moved the count, dispersed. Anna Mihalovna touched Pierre's arm and said, 'Come along.' With her Pierre approached the bed, on which the sick man had been laid in a ceremonial position in keeping with the sacred rite that had just been performed. He was lying with his head propped high on the pillows. His hands were laid symmetrically on the green silk quilt with the palms turned downwards. When Pierre came up, the count looked straight at him, but he looked at him with a gaze the intent and significance of which no man could fathom. Either these eyes said nothing, but simply looked because as eyes they must look at something, or they said too much. Pierre stopped, not knowing what he was to do, and looked inquiringly at his monitress. Anna Mihalovna gave him a hurried glance, with a gesture indicating the sick man's hand and with her lips wafting towards it a phantom kiss. Pierre did as he was bid, and carefully craning his neck to avoid entanglement with the quilt, kissed the broad-boned, muscular hand. There was not the faintest stir in the hand, nor in any muscle of the count's face. Pierre again looked inquiringly at Anna Mihalovna to learn what he was to do now. Anna Mihalovna glanced towards the arm-chair that stood beside the bed. Pierre proceeded obediently to sit down there, his eyes still inquiring whether he had done the right thing. Anna Mihalovna nodded approvingly. Again Pierre fell into the naïvely symmetrical pose of an Egyptian statue, obviously distressed that his ungainly person took up so much room, and doing his utmost to look as small as possible. He looked at the count. The count still gazed at the spot where Pierre's face had been, when he was standing up. Anna Mihalovna's attitude evinced her consciousness of the touching gravity of this last meeting between father and son. It lasted for two minutes, which seemed to Pierre an hour. Suddenly a shudder passed over the thick muscles and furrows of the count's face. The shudder grew more intense; the beautiful mouth was contorted (it was only then that Pierre grasped how near death his father was), and from the contorted mouth there came a husky, muffled sound. Anna Mihalovna looked intently at the sick man's mouth, and trying to guess what he wanted, pointed first to Pierre, then to some drink, then in an inquiring whisper she mentioned the name of Prince Vassily, then pointed to the quilt. The eyes and face of the sick man showed impatience. He made an effort to glance at the servant, who never moved away from the head of his bed.

'His excellency wants to be turned over on the other side,' whispered the servant, and he got up to turn the heavy body of the count facing the wall.

Pierre stood up to help the servant.

While the count was being turned over, one of his arms dragged helplessly behind, and he made a vain effort to pull it after him. Whether the count noticed the face of horror with which Pierre looked at that lifeless arm, or whether some other idea passed through his dying brain, he looked at the refractory arm, at the expression of horror on Pierre's face, again at his arm, and a smile came on to his face, strangely out of keeping with its features; a weak, suffering smile, which seemed mocking at his own helplessness. Suddenly, at the sight of that smile, Pierre felt a lump in his throat and a tickling in his nose, and tears dimmed his eyes. The sick man was turned towards the wall. He sighed.

'He has fallen into a doze,' said Anna Mihalovna, noticing the princess coming to take her turn by the bedside. 'Let us go.'

Pierre went out.

XXI

THERE was by now no one in the reception-room except Prince Vassily and the eldest princess, who were in eager conversation together, sitting under the portrait of Catherine. They were mute at once on seeing

Pierre and his companion, and the princess concealed something as Pierre fancied and murmured: 'I can't stand the sight of that woman.'

'Katish has had tea served in the little drawing-room,' Prince Vassily said to Anna Mihalovna. 'Go, my poor Anna Mihalovna, take something or you will not hold out.'

To Pierre he said nothing; he simply pressed his arm sympathetically. Pierre and Anna Mihalovna went on into the little drawing-room.

'There is nothing so reviving as a cup of this excellent Russian tea, after a sleepless night,' said Lorrain with an air of restrained briskness, sipping it out of a delicate china cup without a handle, as he stood in the little circular drawing-room close to a table laid with tea-things and cold supper-dishes. All who were in Count Bezuhov's house on that night had, with a view to fortifying themselves, gathered around the table. Pierre remembered well that little circular drawing-room with its mirrors and little tables. When there had been balls in the count's house, Pierre, who could not dance, had liked sitting in that little room full of mirrors, watching the ladies in ball-dresses with pearls and diamonds on their bare shoulders, as they crossed that room and looked at themselves in the brightly lighted mirrors that repeated their reflections several times. Now the same room was dimly lighted with two candles, and in the middle of the night the tea-set and supper-dishes stood in disorder on one of the little tables, and heterogeneous, plainly dressed persons were sitting at it, whispering together, and showing in every word that no one could forget what was passing at that moment and what was still to come in the bedroom. Pierre did not eat anything, though he felt very much inclined to. He looked round inquiringly towards his monitress, and perceived that she had gone out again on tiptoe into the reception-room where Prince Vassily had remained with the eldest princess. Pierre supposed that this too was an inevitable part of the proceedings, and, after a little delay, he followed her. Anna Mihalovna was standing beside the princess, and they were both talking at once in excited tones.

'Allow me, madam, to know what is and what is not to be done,' said the princess, who was apparently in the same exasperated temper as she had been when she slammed the door of her room.

'But, dear princess,' Anna Mihalovna was saying mildly and persuasively, blocking up the way towards the bedroom and not letting the princess pass. 'Would that not be too great a tax on poor uncle at such a moment, when he needs repose? At such moments to talk of worldly matters when his soul is already prepared...'

Prince Vassily was sitting in a low chair in his habitual attitude, with one leg crossed high above the other. His cheeks were twitching violently, and when they relaxed, they looked heavier below; but he wore the air of a man little interested in the two ladies' discussion.

'No, my dear Anna Mihalovna, let Katish act on her own discretion. You know how the count loves her.'

'I don't even know what is in this document,' said the princess, addressing Prince Vassily, and pointing to the inlaid portfolio which she held in her hand. 'All I know is that the real will is in the bureau, and this is a paper that has been forgotten....'

She tried to get round Anna Mihalovna, but the latter, with another little skip, barred her way again.

'I know, dear, sweet princess,' said Anna Mihalovna, taking hold of the portfolio, and so firmly that it was clear she would not readily let go of it again. 'Dear princess, I beg you, I beseech you, spare him. I entreat you.'

The princess did not speak. All that was heard was the sound of a scuffle over the portfolio. There could be no doubt that if she were to speak, she would say nothing complimentary to Anna Mihalovna. The latter kept a tight grip, but in spite of that her voice retained all its sweet gravity and softness.

'Pierre, come here, my dear boy. He will not be one too many, I should imagine, in a family council; eh, prince?'

'Why don't you speak, *mon cousin*?' the princess shrieked all of a sudden, so loudly that they heard her voice, and were alarmed by it in the drawing-room. 'Why don't you speak when here a meddling outsider takes upon herself to interfere, and make a scene on the very threshold of a dying man's room. Scheming creature,' she muttered viciously, and tugged at the portfolio with all her might, but Anna Mihalovna took a few steps forward so as not to lose her grasp of it and changed hands.

'Ah,' said Prince Vassily, in reproachful wonder. He got up. 'It is ridiculous. Come, let go. I tell you.' The princess let go.

'And you.'

Anna Mihalovna did not heed him.

'Let go, I tell you. I will take it all upon myself. I will go and ask him. I . . . you let it alone.'

'But, prince,' said Anna Mihalovna, 'after this solemn sacrament, let him have a moment's peace. Here, Pierre, tell me your opinion,' she turned to the young man, who going up to them was staring in surprise at the exasperated face of the princess, which had thrown off all appearance of decorum, and the twitching cheeks of Prince Vassily.

'Remember that you will have to answer for all the consequences,' said Prince Vassily sternly; 'you don't know what you are doing.'

'Infamous woman,' shrieked the princess, suddenly pouncing on Anna Mihalovna and tearing the portfolio from her. Prince Vassily bowed his head and flung up his hands.

At that instant the door, the dreadful door at which Pierre had gazed so long, and which had opened so softly, was flung rapidly, noisily open, banging against the wall, and the second princess ran out wringing her hands.

'What are you about?' she said, in despair. 'He is passing away, and you leave me alone.'

The eldest princess dropped the portfolio. Swiftly Anna Mihalovna stooped and, snatching up the object of dispute, ran into the bedroom. The eldest princess and Prince Vassily recovering themselves followed her. A few minutes later the eldest princess came out again with a pale, dry face, biting her underlip. At the sight of Pierre her face expressed irrepressible hatred.

'Yes, now you can give yourself airs,' she said, 'you have got what you wanted.' And breaking into sobs, she hid her face in her handkerchief and ran out of the room.

The next to emerge was Prince Vassily. He staggered to the sofa, on which Pierre was sitting, and sank on to it, covering his eyes with his hand. Pierre noticed that he was pale, and that his lower jaw was quivering and working as though in ague.

'Ah, my dear boy,' he said, taking Pierre by the elbow—and there was a sincerity and a weakness in his voice that Pierre had never observed in him before—'what sins, what frauds we commit, and all for what? I'm over fifty, my dear boy. . . . I too. . . . It all ends in death, all. Death is awful.' He burst into tears.

Anna Mihalovna was the last to come out. She approached Pierre with soft, deliberate steps. 'Pierre,' she said. Pierre looked inquiringly at her. She kissed the young man on the forehead, wetting him with her tears. She did not speak for a while.

'He is no more. . . .'

Pierre gazed at her over his spectacles.

'Come. I will take you back. Try to cry. Nothing relieves like tears.'

She led him back into the dark drawing-room, and Pierre was glad that no one could see his face. Anna Mihalovna left him, and when she came back he was fast asleep with his arm under his head.

The next morning Anna Mihalovna said to Pierre: 'Yes, my dear boy, it is a great loss for us all. I do not speak of you. But God will uphold you; you are young, and now you are at the head of an immense fortune, I hope. The will has not been opened yet. I know you well enough to know that this will not turn your head, but it will impose duties upon you and you must be a man.'

Pierre did not speak.

'Perhaps, later, I may tell you, my dear boy, that if I had not been there God knows what would have happened. You know, my uncle promised me, only the day before yesterday, not to forget Boris. But he had no time. I hope, dear friend, that you will fulfil your father's desire.'

Pierre did not understand a word, and colouring shyly, looked dumbly at Anna Mihalovna. After talking to him, Anna Mihalovna drove to the Rostovs, and went to bed. On waking in the morning, she told the Rostovs and all her acquaintances the details of Count Bezuhov's death. She said that the count had died, as she would wish to die herself, that his end had been not simply touching, but edifying; that the last interview of the father and son had been so touching that she could not recall it without tears; and that she did not know which had behaved more nobly in those terrible moments: the father, who had remembered everything and every one so well at the last, and had said such moving words to his son; or Pierre, whom it was heartbreaking to see, so utterly crushed was he, though he yet tried to conceal his grief, so as not to distress his dying father. 'It is painful, but it does one good; it uplifts the soul to see such men as the old count and his worthy son,' she said. She told them about the action of the princess and Prince Vassily too, but in great secrecy, in whispers, and with disapproval.

XXII

AT Bleak Hills, the estate of Prince Nikolay Andreivitch Bolkonsky, the arrival of young Prince Andrey and his wife was daily expected. But this expectation did not disturb the regular routine in which life moved in the old prince's household. Prince Nikolay Andreivitch, once a commander-in-chief, known in the fashionable world by the nickname of 'the Prussian king,' had been exiled to his estate in the reign of Paul, and had remained at Bleak Hills ever since with his daughter, Princess Marya, and her companion, Mademoiselle Bourienne. Even in the new reign, though he had received permission to return to the capital, he had never left his home in the country, saying that if any one wanted to see him, he could travel the hundred and fifty versts from Moscow to Bleak Hills, and, for his part, he wanted nobody and nothing. He used to maintain that human vices all sprang from only two sources—idleness and superstition, and that there were but two virtues—energy and intelligence. He had himself undertaken the education of his daughter; and to develop in her these important qualities, he continued giving her lessons in algebra and geometry up to her twentieth year, and mapped out her whole life in uninterrupted occupation. He was himself always occupied in writing his memoirs, working out problems in higher mathematics, turning snuff-boxes on his lathe, working in his garden, or looking after the erection of farm buildings which were always being built on his estate. Since the great thing for enabling one to get through work is regularity, he had carried regularity in his manner of life to the highest point of exactitude. His meals were served in a fixed and invariable manner, and not only at a certain hour, but at a certain minute. With those about him, from his daughter to his servants, the count was sharp and invariably exacting, and so, without being cruel, he inspired a degree of respect and awe that the most cruel man could not readily have commanded. In spite of the fact that he was now on the retired list, and had no influence whatever in political circles, every high official in the province in which was the prince's estate felt obliged to call upon him, and had, just like the architect, the gardener, or Princess Marya, to wait till the regular hour at which the prince always made his appearance in the lofty waiting-room. And every one in the waiting-room felt the same veneration, and even awe, when the immensely high door of the study opened and showed the small figure of the old man in a powdered wig, with his little withered hands and grey, overhanging eyebrows, that, at times when he scowled, hid the gleam in his shrewd, youthful-looking eyes.

On the day that the young people were expected to arrive, Princess Marya went as usual at the fixed hour in the morning into the waiting-room to say good-morning to her father, and with dread in her heart crossed herself and mentally repeated a prayer. Every day she went in to her father in the same way, and every day she prayed that her interview with her father might pass off well that day. The old man-servant, wearing powder, softly got up from his seat in the waiting-room and whispered: 'Walk in.'

Through the door came the regular sounds of the lathe. The princess kept timidly hold of the door, which opened smoothly and easily, and stood still in the doorway. The prince was working at his lathe, and glancing round, he went on with what he was doing.

The immense room was filled with things obviously in constant use. The large table, on which lay books and plans, the high bookcases with keys in the glass-covered doors, the high table for the prince to write at, standing up, with an open manuscript-book upon it, the carpenter's lathe, with tools ranged about it and shavings scattered around, all suggested continual, varied, and orderly activity. The movements of the prince's small foot in its Tatar, silver-embroidered boot, the firm pressure of his sinewy, lean hand, showed the strength of vigorous old age still strong-willed and wiry. After making a few more turns, he took his foot from the pedal of the lathe, wiped the plane, dropped it into a leather pouch attached to the lathe, and going up to the table called his daughter. He never gave the usual blessing to his children; he simply offered her his scrubby, not yet shaved cheek, and said sternly and yet at the same time with intense tenderness, as he looked her over: 'Quite well? All right, then, sit down!' He took a geometry exercise-book written by his own hand, and drew his chair up with his leg.

'For tomorrow,' he said quickly, turning to the page and marking it from one paragraph to the next with his rough nail. The princess bent over the exercise-book. 'Stop, there's a letter for you,' the old man said suddenly, pulling out of a pocket hanging over the table an envelope addressed in a feminine hand, and putting it on the table.

The princess's face coloured red in patches at the sight of the letter. She took it hurriedly and bent over it.

'From Heloise?' asked the prince, showing his still strong, yellow teeth in a cold smile.

'Yes, from Julie,' said the princess, glancing timidly at him, and timidly smiling.

'Two more letters I'll let pass, but the third I shall read,' said the prince severely; 'I'm afraid you write a lot of nonsense. The third I shall read.'

'Read this one, father,' answered the princess, colouring still more and handing him the letter.

'The third, I said the third,' the prince cried shortly; pushing away the letter and leaning his elbow on the table, he drew up to him the book with the figures of geometry in it.

'Now, madam,' began the old man, bending over the book close to his daughter, and laying one arm on the back of the chair she was sitting on, so that the princess felt herself surrounded on all sides by the peculiar acrid smell of old age and tobacco, which she had so long associated with her father. 'Come, madam, these triangles are equal: kindly look; the angle A B C. . . .'

The princess glanced in a scared way at her father's eyes gleaming close beside her. The red patches overspread her whole face, and it was evident that she did not understand a word, and was so frightened that terror prevented her from understanding all the subsequent explanations her father offered her, however clear they might be. Whether it was the teacher's fault or the pupil's, every day the same scene was repeated. The princess's eyes grew dim; she could see and hear nothing; she could feel nothing but the dry face of her stern father near her, his breath and the smell of him, and could think of nothing but how to escape as soon as possible from the study and to make out the problem in freedom in her room. The old man lost his temper; with a loud, grating noise he pushed back and drew up again the chair he was sitting on, made an effort to control himself, not to fly into a rage, and almost every time did fly into a rage, and scold, and sometimes flung the book away.

The princess answered a question wrong.

'Well, you are too stupid!' cried the prince, pushing away the book, and turning sharply away. But he got up immediately, walked up and down, laid his hand on the princess's hair, and sat down again. He drew himself up to the table and continued his explanations. 'This won't do; it won't do,' he said, when Princess Marya, taking the exercise back with the lesson set her, and shutting it, was about to leave the room: 'mathematics is a grand subject, madam. And to have you like the common run of our silly misses is what I don't want at all. Patience, and you'll get to like it.' He patted her on the cheek. 'It will drive all the nonsense out of your head.' She would have gone; he stopped her with a gesture, and took a new, uncut book from the high table.

'Here's a book, too, your Heloise sends you some sort of Key to the Mystery. Religious. But I don't interfere with any one's belief ... I have looked at it. Take it. Come, run along, run along.'

He patted her on the shoulder, and himself closed the door after her.

Princess Marya went back to her own room with that dejected, scared expression that rarely left her, and made her plain, sickly face even plainer. She sat down at her writing-table, which was dotted with miniature portraits, and strewn with books and manuscripts. The princess was as untidy as her father was tidy. She put down the geometry exercise-book and impatiently opened the letter. The letter was from the princess's dearest friend from childhood; this friend was none other than Julie Karagin, who had been at the Rostovs' name-day party.

Julie wrote in French:

'DEAR AND EXCELLENT FRIEND,—What a terrible and frightful thing is absence! I say to myself that half of my existence and of my happiness is in you, that notwithstanding the distance that separates us, our hearts are united by invisible bonds; yet mine rebels against destiny, and in spite of the pleasures and distractions around me, I cannot overcome a certain hidden sadness which I feel in the bottom of my heart since our separation. Why are we not together as we were this summer in your great study, on the blue sofa, the confidential sofa? Why can I not, as I did three months ago, draw new moral strength from that gentle, calm, penetrating look of yours, a look that I loved so well and that I seem to see before me as I write to you.'

When she reached this passage, Princess Marya sighed and looked round into the pier-glass that stood on her right. The glass reflected a feeble, ungraceful figure and a thin face. The eyes, always melancholy, were looking just now with a particularly hopeless expression at herself in the looking-glass. She flatters me, thought the princess, and she turned away and went on reading. But Julie did not flatter her friend: the princess's eyes—large, deep, and luminous (rays of warm light seemed at times to radiate in streams from them), were really so fine, that very often in spite of the plainness of the whole face her eyes were more attractive than beauty. But the princess had never seen the beautiful expression of her eyes; the expression that came into them when she was not thinking of herself. As is the case with every one, her face assumed an affected, unnatural, ugly expression as soon as she looked in the looking-glass.

She went on reading:

'All Moscow talks of nothing but war. One of my two brothers is already abroad, the other is with the Guards, who are starting on the march to the frontier. Our dear Emperor has left Petersburg, and, people declare, intends to expose his precious existence to the risks of war. God grant that the Corsican monster who is destroying the peace of Europe may be brought low by the angel whom the Almighty in His mercy has given us as sovereign. Without speaking of my brothers, this war has deprived me of one of my heart's dearest alliances. I mean the young Nicholas Rostov, whose enthusiasm could not endure inaction, and who has left the university to go and join the army. Well, dear Marie, I will own to you that, in spite of his extreme youth, his departure for the army has been a great grief to me. This young man, of whom I spoke to you in the summer, has so much nobility, so much real youthfulness, rarely to be met with in our age, among our old men of twenty. Above all, he has so much openness and so much heart. He is so pure and poetic that my acquaintance with him, though so transient, has been one of the dearest joys known by my poor heart, which has already had so much suffering. Some day I will tell you about our farewells and all that we said to each other as we parted. As yet, all that is too fresh. Ah, dear friend, you are fortunate in not knowing these joys and these pains which are so poignant. You are fortunate, because the latter are generally stronger! I know very well that Count Nicholas is too young ever to become more to me than a friend, but this sweet friendship, this poetic and pure intimacy have fulfilled a need of my heart. No more of this. The great news of the day, with which all Moscow is taken up, is the death of old Count Bezuhov, and his inheritance. Fancy, the three princesses have hardly got anything, Prince Vassily nothing, and everything has been left to M. Pierre, who has been acknowledged as a legitimate son into the bargain, so that he is Count Bezuhov and has the finest fortune in Russia. People say that Prince Vassily behaved very badly in all these matters and that he has gone back to Petersburg quite cast down.

'I own that I understand very little about all these details of legacies and wills; what I know is that since the young man whom we all used to know as plain M. Pierre has become Count Bezuhov and owner of one of the largest fortunes in Russia, I am much amused to observe the change in the tone and the manners of mammas burdened with marriageable daughters and of those young ladies themselves, towards that individual—who I may say in passing has always seemed to me a poor creature. As people have amused themselves for the last two years in giving me husbands whom I don't know, the matrimonial gossip of Moscow generally makes me Countess Bezuhov. But you, I am sure, feel that I have no desire to become so. About marriage, by the way, do you know that the *universal aunt*, Anna Mihalovna, has confided to me, under the seal of the deepest secrecy, a marriage scheme for you. It is no one more or less than Prince Vassily's son, Anatole, whom they want to settle by marrying him to some one rich and distinguished, and the choice of his relations has fallen on you. I don't know what view you will take of the matter, but I thought it my duty to let you know beforehand. He is said to be very handsome and very wild; that is all I have been able to find out about him.

'But enough of gossip. I am finishing my second sheet and mamma is sending for me to go and dine with the Apraxins. Read the mystical book which I send you, and which is the rage here. Though there are things in this book, difficult for our human conceptions to attain to, it is an admirable book, and reading it calms and elevates the soul. Farewell. My respects to your father and my compliments to Mlle. Bourienne. I embrace you as I love you.   JULIE.

'P.S.—Let me hear news of your brother and his charming little wife.'

Princess Marya thought a minute, smiling dreamily (her face, lighted up by her luminous eyes, was completely transformed). Suddenly getting up, she crossed over to the table, treading heavily. She got out a sheet of paper and her hand began rapidly moving over it. She wrote the following answer:

'DEAR AND EXCELLENT FRIEND,—Your letter of the 13th gave me great delight. So you still love me, my poetic Julie. So, absence, which you so bitterly denounce, has not had its usual effect upon you. You complain of absence—what might I say, if I ventured to complain, I, deprived of all who are dear to me? Ah, if we had not religion to console us, life would be very sad. Why do you suppose that I should look severe when you tell me of your affection for that young man? In such matters I am hard upon no one but myself. I understand such feelings in other people, and if, never having felt them, I cannot express approval, I do not condemn them. Only it seems to me that Christian love, the love of our neighbour, the love of our enemies, is more meritorious, sweeter and more beautiful than those feelings that may be inspired in a poetic and loving young girl like you, by the fine eyes of a young man.

'The news of Count Bezuhov's death reached us before your letter, and affected my father very much. He says that the count was the last representative but one of the great century and that it is his turn now; but that he will do his best to have his turn come as late as possible. May God save us from that terrible misfortune. I cannot agree with you about Pierre, whom I knew as a child. He always appeared to me to have an excellent heart, and that is the quality that I most esteem in people. As to his inheritance and Prince Vassily's behaviour about it, it is very sad for both. Ah, my dear friend, our divine Saviour's word, that it is easier for a camel to pass through the eye of a needle than for a rich man to enter into the kingdom of Heaven is a terribly true saying; I pity Prince Vassily, and I am yet more sorry for Pierre. So young and burdened with this wealth, to what temptations he will be exposed! If I were asked what I wished most in the world, it would be to be poorer than the poorest beggar. A thousand thanks, dear friend, for the work you send me, and which is all the rage where you are. As, however, you tell me that amid many good things there are others to which our weak human understanding cannot attain, it seems to me rather useless to busy oneself in reading an unintelligible book, since for that very reason it cannot yield any profit. I have never been able to comprehend the passion which some people have for confusing their minds by giving themselves to the study of mystical books which only awaken their doubts, inflaming their imagination, and giving them a disposition to exaggeration altogether contrary to Christian simplicity. Let us read the Apostles and the Gospel. Do not let us seek to penetrate what is mysterious in these, for how can we dare presume, miserable sinners as we are, to enter into the terrible and sacred secrets of Providence, while we wear this carnal husk that raises an impenetrable veil between us and the Eternal? Let us rather confine ourselves to studying those sublime principles which our divine Saviour has left us as guides for our conduct here below; let us seek to conform ourselves to those and follow them; let us persuade ourselves that the less range we give to our weak human understanding, the more agreeable it will be to God, who rejects all knowledge that does not come from Him; that the less we seek to dive into that which He has pleased to hide from our knowledge the sooner will He discover it to us by means of His divine Spirit.

'My father has not spoken to me of the suitor, but has only told me that he has received a letter, and was expecting a visit from Prince Vassily. In regard to a marriage-scheme concerning myself, I will tell you, my dear and excellent friend, that to my mind marriage is a divine institution to which we must conform. However painful it may be to me, if the Almighty should ever impose upon me the duties of a wife and mother, I shall try to fulfil them as faithfully as I can, without disquieting myself by examining my feelings in regard to him whom He may give me for a husband.

'I have received a letter from my brother, who announces his coming to Bleak Hills with his wife. It will be a pleasure of brief duration, since he is leaving us to take part in this unhappy war into which we have been drawn, God knows how and why. It is not only with you, in the centre of business and society, that people talk of nothing except war, for here also, amid those rustic labours and that calm of nature, which townspeople generally imagine in the country, rumours of war are heard and are felt painfully. My father talks of nothing but marches and counter-marches, things of which I understand nothing; and the day before yesterday, taking my usual walk in the village street, I witnessed a heartrending scene. . . . It was a convoy of recruits that had been enrolled in our district, and were being sent away to the army. You should have seen the state of the mothers, wives and children of the men who were going, and have heard the sobs on both sides. It seems as though humanity had forgotten the laws of its divine Saviour, Who preached love and the forgiveness of offences, and were making the greatest merit to consist in the art of killing one another.

'Adieu, dear and good friend: may our divine Saviour and His most Holy Mother keep you in their holy and powerful care.

MARIE'

'Ah, you are sending off your letters, Princess. I have already finished mine. I have written to my poor mother,' said Mademoiselle Bourienne quickly in her agreeable, juicy voice, with a roll of the *r*'s. She came in, all smiles, bringing into the intense, melancholy, gloomy atmosphere of the Princess Marya an alien world of gay frivolity and self-satisfaction. 'Princess, I must warn you,' she added, dropping her voice, 'the prince has had an altercation,' she said, with a peculiar roll of the *r*, seeming to listen to herself with pleasure. 'An altercation with Mihail Ivanov. He is in a very ill humour, very morose. Be prepared, you know.'

'Ah, *chère amie*,' answered Princess Marya, 'I have begged you never to tell me beforehand in what humour I shall find my father. I do not permit myself to judge him and I would not have others do so.'

The princess glanced at her watch, and seeing that it was already five minutes later than the hour fixed for her practice on the clavichord, she went with a face of alarm into the divan-room. In accordance with the rules by which the day was mapped out, the prince rested from twelve to two, while the young princess practised on the clavichord.

XXIII

THE grey-haired valet was sitting in the waiting-room dozing and listening to the prince's snoring in his immense study. From a far-off part of the house there came through closed doors the sound of difficult passages of a sonata of Dusseck's repeated twenty times over.

At that moment a carriage and a little cart drove up to the steps, and Prince Andrey got out of the carriage, helped his little wife out and let her pass into the house before him. Grey Tihon in his wig, popping out at the door of the waiting-room, informed him in a whisper that the prince was taking a nap and made haste to close the door. Tihon knew that no extraordinary event, not even the arrival of his son, would be permitted to break through the routine of the day. Prince Andrey was apparently as well aware of the fact as Tihon. He looked at his watch as though to ascertain whether his father's habits had changed during the time he had not seen him, and satisfying himself that they were unchanged, he turned to his wife.

'He will get up in twenty minutes. Let's go to Marie,' he said.

The little princess had grown stouter during this time, but her short upper lip, with the smile and the faint moustache on it, rose as gaily and charmingly as ever when she spoke.

'Why, it is a palace,' she said to her husband, looking round her with exactly the expression with which people pay compliments to the host at a ball. 'Come, quick, quick!' As she looked about her, she smiled at Tihon and at her husband, and at the footman who was showing them in.

'It is Marie practising? Let us go quietly, we must surprise her.' Prince Andrey followed her with a courteous and depressed expression.

'You're looking older, Tihon,' he said as he passed to the old man, who was kissing his hand.

Before they had reached the room, from which the sounds of the clavichord were coming, the pretty, fair-haired Frenchwoman emerged from a side-door. Mademoiselle Bourienne seemed overwhelmed with delight.

'Ah, what a pleasure for the princess!' she exclaimed. 'At last! I must tell her.'

'No, no, please not' . . . said the little princess, kissing her. 'You are Mademoiselle Bourienne; I know you already through my sister-in-law's friendship for you. She does not expect us!'

They went up to the door of the divan-room, from which came the sound of the same passage repeated over and over again. Prince Andrey stood still frowning as though in expectation of something unpleasant.

The little princess went in. The passage broke off in the middle; he heard an exclamation, the heavy tread of Princess Marya, and the sound of kissing. When Prince Andrey went in, the two ladies, who had only seen each other once for a short time at Prince Andrey's wedding, were clasped in each other's arms, warmly pressing their lips to the first place each had chanced upon. Mademoiselle Bourienne was standing near them, her hands pressed to her heart; she was smiling devoutly, apparently equally ready to weep and to laugh. Prince Andrey shrugged his shoulders, and scowled as lovers of music scowl when they hear a false note. The two ladies let each other go; then hastened again, as though each afraid of being remiss, to hug each other, began kissing each other's hands and pulling them away, and then fell to kissing each other on the face again. Then they quite astonished Prince Andrey by both suddenly bursting into tears and beginning the kissing over again. Mademoiselle Bourienne cried too. Prince Andrey was unmistakably ill at ease. But to the two women it seemed such a natural thing that they should weep; it seemed never to have occurred to them that their meeting could have taken place without tears.

'Ah, ma chère! . . . Ah, Marie!' . . . both the ladies began talking at once, and they laughed. 'I had a dream last night. Then you did not expect us? O Marie, you have got thinner.'

'And you are looking better . . .'

'I recognised the princess at once,' put in Mademoiselle Bourienne.

'And I had no idea!' ... cried Princess Marya. 'Ah, Andrey, I did not see you.'

Prince Andrey and his sister kissed each other's hands, and he told her she was just as great a cry-baby as she always had been. Princess Marya turned to her brother, and through her tears, her great, luminous eyes, that were beautiful at that instant, rested with a loving, warm and gentle gaze on Prince Andrey's face. The little princess talked incessantly. The short, downy upper lip was continually flying down to meet the rosy, lower lip when necessary, and parting again in a smile of gleaming teeth and eyes. The little princess described an incident that had occurred to them on Spasskoe hill, and might have been serious for her in her condition. And immediately after that she communicated the intelligence that she had left all her clothes in Petersburg, and God knew what she would have to go about in here, and that Andrey was quite changed, and that Kitty Odintsov had married an old man, and that a suitor had turned up for Princess Marya, 'who was a suitor worth having,' but that they would talk about that later. Princess Marya was still gazing mutely at her brother, and her beautiful eyes were full of love and melancholy. It was clear that her thoughts were following a train of their own, apart from the chatter of her sister-in-law. In the middle of the latter's description of the last fête-day at Petersburg, she addressed her brother.

'And is it quite settled that you are going to the war, Andrey?' she said, sighing. Liza sighed too.

'Yes, and tomorrow too,' answered her brother.

'He is deserting me here, and Heaven knows why, when he might have had promotion ...' Princess Marya did not listen to the end, but following her own train of thought, she turned to her sister-in-law, letting her affectionate eyes rest on her waist.

'Is it really true?' she said.

The face of her sister-in-law changed. She sighed.

'Yes, it's true,' she said. 'Oh! It's very dreadful ...'

Liza's lip drooped. She put her face close to her sister-in-law's face, and again she unexpectedly began to cry.

'She needs rest,' said Prince Andrey, frowning. 'Don't you, Liza? Take her to your room, while I go to father. How is he—just the same?'

'The same, just the same; I don't know what you will think,' Princess Marya answered joyfully.

'And the same hours, and the walks about the avenues, and the lathe?' asked Prince Andrey with a scarcely perceptible smile, showing that, in spite of all his love and respect for his father, he recognised his weaknesses.

'The same hours and the lathe, mathematics too, and my geometry lessons,' Princess Marya answered gaily, as though those lessons were one of the most delightful events of her life.

When the twenty minutes had elapsed, and the time for the old prince to get up had come, Tihon came to call the young man to his father. The old man made a departure from his ordinary routine in honour of his son's arrival. He directed that he should be admitted into his apartments during his time for dressing, before dinner. The old prince used to wear the old-fashioned dress, the kaftan and powder. And when Prince Andrey—not with the disdainful face and manners with which he walked into drawing-rooms, but with the eager face with which he had talked to Pierre—went in to his father's room, the old gentleman was in his dressing-room sitting in a roomy morocco chair in a *peignoir*, with his head in the hands of Tihon.

'Ah! the warrior! So you want to fight Bonaparte?' said the old man, shaking his powdered head as far as his plaited tail, which was in Tihon's hands, would permit him.

'Mind you look sharp after him, at any rate, or he'll soon be putting us on the list of his subjects. How are you?'

And he held out his cheek to him.

The old gentleman was in excellent humour after his nap before dinner. (He used to say that sleep after dinner was silver, but before dinner it was golden.) He took delighted, sidelong glances at his son from under his thick, overhanging brows. Prince Andrey went up and kissed his father on the spot indicated for him. He made no reply on his father's favourite topic—jesting banter at the military men of the period, and particularly at Bonaparte.

'Yes, I have come to you, father, bringing a wife with child,' said Prince Andrey, with eager and reverential eyes watching every movement of his father's face. 'How is your health?'

'None but fools, my lad, and profligates are unwell, and you know me; busy from morning till night and temperate, so of course I'm well.'

'Thank God,' said his son, smiling.

'God's not much to do with the matter. Come, tell me,' the old man went on, going back to his favourite hobby, 'how have the Germans trained you to fight with Bonaparte on their new scientific method—strategy as they call it?'

Prince Andrey smiled.

'Give me time to recover myself, father,' he said, with a smile that showed that his father's failings did not prevent his respecting and loving him. 'Why, I have only just got here.'

'Nonsense, nonsense,' cried the old man, shaking his tail to try whether it were tightly plaited, and taking his son by the hand. 'The house is ready for your wife. Marie will look after her and show her everything, and talk nineteen to the dozen with her too. That's their feminine way. I'm glad to have her. Sit down, talk to me. Mihelson's army, I understand, Tolstoy's too . . . a simultaneous expedition . . . but what's the army of the South going to do? Prussia, her neutrality . . . I know all that. What of Austria?' he said, getting up from his chair and walking about the room, with Tihon running after him, giving him various articles of his apparel. 'What about Sweden? How will they cross Pomerania?'

Prince Andrey, seeing the urgency of his father's questions, began explaining the plan of operations of the proposed campaign, speaking at first reluctantly, but becoming more interested as he went on, and unconsciously from habit passing from Russian into French. He told him how an army of ninety thousand troops was to threaten Prussia so as to drive her out of her neutrality and draw her into the war, how part of these troops were to join the Swedish troops at Strahlsund, how two hundred and twenty thousand Austrians were to combine with a hundred thousand Russians in Italy and on the Rhine, and how fifty thousand Russians and fifty thousand English troops were to meet at Naples, and how the army, forming a total of five hundred thousand, was to attack the French on different sides at once. The old prince did not manifest the slightest interest in what he told him. He went on dressing, as he walked about, apparently not listening, and three times he unexpectedly interrupted him. Once he stopped him and shouted: 'The white one! the white one!'

This meant that Tihon had not given him the waistcoat he wanted. Another time, he stood still, asked: 'And will she be confined soon?' and shook his head reproachfully: 'That's bad! Go on, go on.'

The third time was when Prince Andrey was just finishing his description. The old man hummed in French, in his falsetto old voice: 'Malbrook goes off to battle, God knows when he'll come back.'

His son only smiled.

'I don't say that this is a plan I approve of,' he said; 'I'm only telling you what it is. Napoleon has made a plan by now as good as this one.'

'Well, you have told me nothing new.' And thoughtfully the old man repeated, speaking quickly to himself: 'God knows when he'll come back. Go into the dining-room.'

XXIV

At the exact hour, the prince, powdered and shaven, walked into the dining-room, where there were waiting for him his daughter-in-law, Princess Marya, Mademoiselle Bourienne, and the prince's architect, who, by a strange whim of the old gentleman's, dined at his table, though being an insignificant person of no social standing, he would not naturally have expected to be treated with such honour. The prince, who was in practice a firm stickler for distinctions of rank, and rarely admitted to his table even important provincial functionaries, had suddenly pitched on the architect Mihail Ivanovitch, blowing his nose in a check pocket-handkerchief in the corner, to illustrate the theory that all men are equal, and had more than once impressed upon his daughter that Mihail Ivanovitch was every whit as good as himself and her. At table the prince addressed his conversation to the taciturn architect more often than to any one.

In the dining-room, which, like all the other rooms in the house, was immensely lofty, the prince's entrance was awaited by all the members of his household and the footmen, standing behind each chair. The butler with a table-napkin on his arm scanned the setting of the table, making signs to the footmen, and continually he glanced uneasily from the clock on the wall to the door, by which the prince was to enter. Prince Andrey stared at an immense golden frame on the wall that was new to him. It contained the genealogical tree of the Bolkonskys, and hanging opposite it was a frame, equally immense, with a badly painted representation (evidently the work of some household artist) of a reigning prince in a crown, intended for the descendant of Rurik and founder of the family of the Bolkonsky princes. Prince Andrey looked at this genealogical tree shaking his head, and he laughed as one laughs at a portrait ridiculously like.

'There you have him all over!' he said to Princess Marya as she came up to him.

Princess Marya looked at her brother in surprise. She did not know what he was smiling at. Everything her father did inspired in her a reverence that did not admit of criticism.

'Every one has his weak spot,' Prince Andrey went on; 'with *his* vast intellect to condescend to such triviality!'

Princess Marya could not understand the boldness of her brother's criticism and was making ready to protest, when the step they were all listening for was heard coming from the study. The prince walked in with a quick, lively step, as he always walked, as though intentionally contrasting the elasticity of his movements with the rigidity of the routine of the house. At that instant the big clock struck two, and another clock in the drawing-room echoed it in thinner tones. The prince stood still; his keen, stern eyes gleaming under his bushy, overhanging brows scanned all the company and rested on the little princess. The little princess experienced at that moment the sensation that courtiers know on the entrance of the Tsar, that feeling of awe and veneration that this old man inspired in every one about him. He stroked the little princess on the head, and then with an awkward movement patted her on her neck.

'I'm glad to see you,' he said, and looking intently into her eyes he walked away and sat down in his place. 'Sit down, sit down, Mihail Ivanovitch, sit down.'

He pointed his daughter-in-law to a seat beside him. The footman moved a chair back for her.

'Ho, ho!' said the old man, looking at her rounded figure. 'You've not lost time; that's bad!' He laughed a dry, cold, unpleasant laugh, laughing as he always did with his lips, but not with his eyes. 'You must have exercise, as much exercise as possible, as much as possible,' he said.

The little princess did not hear or did not care to hear his words. She sat dumb and seemed disconcerted. The prince asked after her father, and she began to talk and to smile. He asked her about common acquaintances; the princess became more and more animated, and began talking away, giving the prince greetings from various people and retailing the gossip of the town.

'Poor Countess Apraxin has lost her husband; she has quite cried her eyes out, poor dear,' she said, growing more and more lively.

As she became livelier, the prince looked more and more sternly at her, and all at once, as though he had studied her sufficiently and had formed a clear idea of her, he turned away and addressed Mihail Ivanovitch:

'Well, Mihail Ivanovitch, our friend Bonaparte is to have a bad time of it. Prince Andrey' (this was how he always spoke of his son) 'has been telling me what forces are being massed against him! While you and I have always looked upon him as a very insignificant person.'

Mihail Ivanovitch, utterly at a loss to conjecture when 'you and I' had said anything of the sort about Bonaparte, but grasping that he was wanted for the introduction of the prince's favourite subject, glanced in wonder at the young prince, not knowing what was to come next.

'He's a great tactician!' said the prince to his son, indicating the architect, and the conversation turned again on the war, on Bonaparte, and the generals and political personages of the day. The old prince was, it seemed, convinced that all the public men of the period were mere babes who had no idea of the A B C of military and political matters; while Bonaparte, according to him, was an insignificant Frenchman, who had met with success simply because there were no Potyomkins and Suvorovs to oppose him. He was even persuaded firmly that there were no political difficulties in Europe, that there was no war indeed, but only a sort of marionette show in which the men of the day took part, pretending to be doing the real thing. Prince Andrey received his father's jeers at modern people gaily, and with obvious pleasure drew his father out and listened to him.

'Does everything seem good that was done in the past?' he said; 'why, didn't Suvorov himself fall into the trap Moreau laid for him, and wasn't he unable to get out of it too?'

'Who told you that? Who said so?' cried the prince. 'Suvorov!' And he flung away his plate, which Tihon very neatly caught. 'Suvorov! . . . Think again, Prince Andrey. There were two men—Friedrich and Suvorov . . . Moreau! Moreau would have been a prisoner if Suvorov's hands had been free, but his hands were tied by the Hofskriegswurstschnappsrath; the devil himself would have been in a tight place. Ah, you'll find out what these Hofskriegswurstschnappsraths are like! Suvorov couldn't get the better of them, so how is Mihail Kutuzov going to do it? No, my dear,' he went on; 'so you and your generals aren't able to get round Bonaparte; you must needs call in Frenchmen—set a thief to catch a thief! The German, Pahlen, has been sent to New York in America to get the Frenchman Moreau,' he said, alluding to the invitation that had that year been made to Moreau to enter the Russian service. 'A queer business! . . . Why the Potyomkins, the Suvorovs, the Orloffs, were they Germans? No, my lad, either you have all lost your wits, or I have outlived mine. God help you, and we shall see. Bonaparte's become a great military leader among them! H'm! . . .'

'I don't say at all that all those plans are good,' said Prince Andrey; 'only I can't understand how you can have such an opinion of Bonaparte. Laugh, if you like, but Bonaparte is any way a great general!'

'Mihail Ivanovitch!' the old prince cried to the architect, who, absorbed in the roast meat, hoped they had forgotten him. 'Didn't I tell you Bonaparte was a great tactician? Here he says so too.'

'To be sure, your excellency,' replied the architect. The prince laughed again his frigid laugh.

'Bonaparte was born with a silver spoon in his mouth. He has splendid soldiers. And he attacked the Germans first too. And any fool can beat the Germans. From the very beginning of the world every one has beaten the Germans. And they've never beaten any one. They only conquer each other. He made his reputation fighting against them.'

And the prince began analysing all the blunders that in his opinion Bonaparte had committed in his wars and even in politics. His son did not protest, but it was evident that whatever arguments were advanced against him, he was as little disposed to give up his opinion as the old prince himself. Prince Andrey listened and refrained from replying. He could not help wondering how this old man, living so many years alone and never leaving the country, could know all the military and political events in Europe of the last few years in such detail and with such accuracy, and form his own judgment on them.

'You think I'm an old man and don't understand the actual position of affairs?' he wound up. 'But I'll tell you I'm taken up with it! I don't sleep at nights. Come, where has this great general of yours proved himself to be such?'

'That would be a long story,' answered his son.

'You go along to your Bonaparte. Mademoiselle Bourienne, here is another admirer of your blackguard of an emperor!' he cried in excellent French.

'You know that I am not a Bonapartist, Prince.'

'God knows when he'll come back . . .' the prince hummed in falsetto, laughed still more falsetto, and got up from the table.

The little princess had sat silent during the whole discussion and the rest of the dinner, looking in alarm first at Princess Marya and then at her father-in-law. When they left the dinner-table, she took her sister-in-law's arm and drew her into another room.

'What a clever man your father is,' she said; 'perhaps that is why I am afraid of him.'

'Oh, he is so kind!' said Princess Marya.

XXV

Prince Andrey was leaving the following evening. The old prince, not departing from his regular routine, went away to his own room after dinner. The little princess was with her sister-in-law. Prince Andrey, having changed his dress and put on a travelling-coat without epaulettes, had been packing with his valet in the rooms set apart for him. After himself inspecting the coach and the packing of his trunks on it, he gave orders for the horses to be put to. Nothing was left in the room but the things that Prince Andrey always carried with him: a travelling-case, a big silver wine-case, two Turkish pistols and a sabre, a present from his father, brought back from his campaign under Otchakov. All Prince Andrey's belongings for the journey were in good order; everything was new and clean, in cloth covers, carefully fastened with tape.

At moments of starting off and beginning a different life, persons given to deliberating on their actions are usually apt to be in a serious frame of mind. At such moments one reviews the past and forms plans for the future. The face of Prince Andrey was very dreamy and tender. Clasping his hands behind him, he walked rapidly up and down the room from corner to corner, looking straight before him and dreamily shaking his head. Whether he felt dread at going to the war, or grief at forsaking his wife—or possibly something of both—he evidently did not care to be seen in that mood, for, catching the sound of footsteps in the outer room, he hastily unclasped his hands, stood at the table, as though engaged in fastening the cover of the case, and assumed his habitual calm and impenetrable expression. It was the heavy step of Princess Marya.

'They told me you had ordered the horses to be put in,' she said, panting (she had evidently been running), 'and I did so want to have a little more talk with you alone. God knows how long we shall be parted again. You're not angry with me for coming? You're very much changed, Andryusha,' she added, as though to explain the question.

She smiled as she uttered the word 'Andryusha.' It was obviously strange to her to think that this stern, handsome man was the same as the thin, mischievous boy, the Andryusha who had been the companion of her childhood.

'And where's Liza?' he asked, only answering her question by a smile.

'She was so tired that she fell asleep on the sofa in my room. O Andrey, what a treasure of a wife you have,' she said, sitting down on the sofa, facing her brother. 'She is a perfect child; such a sweet, merry child. I like her so much.' Prince Andrey did not speak, but the princess noticed the ironical and contemptuous expression that came into his face.

'But one must be indulgent to little weaknesses. Who is free from them, Andrey? You mustn't forget that she has grown up and been educated in society. And then her position is not a very cheerful one. One must put oneself in every one's position. To understand everything is to forgive everything. Only think what it must be for her, poor girl, after the life she has been used to, to part from her husband and be left alone in the country, and in her condition too. It's very hard.'

Prince Andrey smiled, looking at his sister as we smile listening to people whom we fancy we see through.

'You live in the country and think the life so awful?' he said.

'I—that's a different matter. Why bring me in? I don't wish for any other life, and indeed I can't wish for anything different, for I know no other sort of life. But only think, Andrey, what it is for a young woman used to fashionable society to be buried for the best years of her life in the country, alone, because papa is always busy, and I . . . you know me . . . I am not a cheerful companion for women used to the best society. Mademoiselle Bourienne is the only person . . .'

'I don't like her at all, your Bourienne,' said Prince Andrey.

'Oh, no! she's a very good and sweet girl, and what's more, she's very much to be pitied. She has nobody, nobody. To tell the truth, she is of no use to me, but only in my way. I have always, you know, been a solitary creature, and now I'm getting more and more so. I like to be alone . . . *Mon père* likes her very much. She and Mihail Ivanovitch are the two people he is always friendly and good-tempered with, because he has been a benefactor to both of them; as Sterne says: "We don't love people so much for the good they have done us as for the good we have done them." *Mon père* picked her up an orphan in the streets, and she's very good-natured. And *mon père* likes her way of reading. She reads aloud to him in the evenings. She reads very well.'

'Come, tell me the truth, Marie, you suffer a good deal, I expect, sometimes from our father's character?' Prince Andrey asked suddenly. Princess Marya was at first amazed, then aghast at the question.

'Me? . . . me? . . . me suffer!' she said.

'He was always harsh, but he's growing very tedious, I should think,' said Prince Andrey, speaking so slightingly of his father with an unmistakable intention either of puzzling or of testing his sister.

'You are good in every way, Andrey, but you have a sort of pride of intellect,' said the princess, evidently following her own train of thought rather than the thread of the conversation, 'and that's a great sin. Do you think it right to judge our father? But if it were right, what feeling but *vénération* could be aroused by such a man as *mon père*? And I am so contented and happy with him. I could only wish you were all as happy as I am.'

Her brother shook his head incredulously.

'The only thing that troubles me,—I'll tell you the truth, Andrey,—is our father's way of thinking in religious matters. I can't understand how a man of such immense intellect can fail to see what is as clear as day, and can fall into such error. That is the one thing that makes me unhappy. But even in this I see a slight change for the better of late. Lately his jeers have not been so bitter, and there is a monk whom he received and talked to a long time.'

'Well, my dear, I'm afraid you and your monk are wasting your powder and shot,' Prince Andrey said ironically but affectionately.

'*Ah, mon ami!* I can only pray to God and trust that He will hear me. Andrey,' she said timidly after a minute's silence, 'I have a great favour to ask of you.'

'What is it, dear?'

'No; promise me you won't refuse. It will be no trouble to you, and there is nothing beneath you in it. Only it will be a comfort to me. Promise, Andryusha,' she said, putting her hand into her reticule and holding something in it, but not showing it yet, as though what she was holding was the object of her entreaty, and before she received a promise to grant it, she could not take that something out of her reticule. She looked timidly with imploring eyes at her brother.

'Even if it were a great trouble . . .' answered Prince Andrey, seeming to guess what the favour was.

'You may think what you please about it. I know you are like *mon père*. Think what you please, but do this for my sake. Do, please. The father of my father, our grandfather, always wore it in all his wars . . .' She still did not take out what she was holding in her reticule. 'You promise me, then?'

'Of course, what is it?'

'Andrey, I am blessing you with the holy image, and you must promise me you will never take it off. . . . You promise?'

'If it does not weigh a ton and won't drag my neck off . . . To please you,' said Prince Andrey. The same second he noticed the pained expression that came over his sister's face at this jest, and felt remorseful. 'I am very glad, really very glad, dear,' he added.

'Against your own will He will save and will have mercy on you and turn you to Himself, because in Him alone is truth and peace,' she said in a voice shaking with emotion, and with a solemn gesture holding in both hands before her brother an old-fashioned, little, oval holy image of the Saviour with a black face in a silver setting, on a little silver chain of delicate workmanship. She crossed herself, kissed the image, and gave it to Andrey.

'Please, Andrey, for my sake.'

Rays of kindly, timid light beamed from her great eyes. Those eyes lighted up all the thin, sickly face and made it beautiful. Her brother would have taken the image, but she stopped him. Andrey understood, crossed himself, and kissed the image. His face looked at once tender (he was touched) and ironical.

'*Merci, mon ami.*' She kissed him on the forehead and sat down again on the sofa. Both were silent.

'So as I was telling you, Andrey, you must be kind and generous as you always used to be. Don't judge Liza harshly,' she began; 'she is so sweet, so good-natured, and her position is a very hard one just now.'

'I fancy I have said nothing to you, Masha, of my blaming my wife for anything or being dissatisfied with her. What makes you say all this to me?'

Princess Marya coloured in patches, and was mute, as though she felt guilty.

'I have said nothing to you, but you have been *talked to*. And that makes me sad.'

The red patches grew deeper on the forehead and neck and cheeks of Princess Marya. She would have said something, but could not utter the words. Her brother had guessed right: his wife had shed tears after dinner, had said that she had a presentiment of a bad confinement, that she was afraid of it, and had complained of her hard lot, of her father-in-law and her husband. After crying she had fallen asleep. Prince Andrey felt sorry for his sister.

'Let me tell you one thing, Masha, I can't reproach *my wife* for anything, I never have and never shall, nor can I reproach myself for anything in regard to her, and that shall always be so in whatever circumstances I may be placed. But if you want to know the truth . . . if you want to know if I am happy. No. Is she happy? No. Why is it so? I don't know.'

As he said this, he went up to his sister, and stooping over her kissed her on the forehead. His fine eyes shone with an unaccustomed light of intelligence and goodness. But he was not looking at his sister, but towards the darkness of the open door, over her head.

'Let us go to her; I must say good-bye. Or you go alone and wake her up, and I'll come in a moment. Petrushka!' he called to his valet, 'come here and take away these things. This is to go in the seat and this on the right side.'

Princess Marya got up and moved toward the door. She stopped. 'Andrey, if you had faith, you would have appealed to God, to give you the love that you do not feel, and your prayer would have been granted.'

'Yes, perhaps so,' said Prince Andrey. 'Go, Masha, I'll come immediately.'

On the way to his sister's room, in the gallery that united one house to the other, Prince Andrey encountered Mademoiselle Bourienne smiling sweetly. It was the third time that day that with an innocent and enthusiastic smile she had thrown herself in his way in secluded passages.

'Ah, I thought you were in your own room,' she said, for some reason blushing and casting down her eyes. Prince Andrey looked sternly at her. A sudden look of wrathful exasperation came into his face. He said nothing to her, but stared at her forehead and her hair, without looking at her eyes, with such contempt that the Frenchwoman crimsoned and went away without a word. When he reached his sister's room, the little princess was awake and her gay little voice could be heard through the open door, hurrying one word after another. She talked as though, after being long restrained, she wanted to make up for lost time, and, as always, she spoke French.

'No, but imagine the old Countess Zubov, with false curls and her mouth full of false teeth as though she wanted to defy the years. *Ha, ha, ha, Marie!*'

Just the same phrase about Countess Zubov and just the same laugh Prince Andrey had heard five times already from his wife before outsiders. He walked softly into the room. The little princess, plump and rosy, was sitting in a low chair with her work in her hands, trotting out her Petersburg reminiscences and phrases. Prince Andrey went up, stroked her on the head, and asked if she had got over the fatigue of the journey. She answered him and went on talking.

The coach with six horses stood at the steps. It was a dark autumn night. The coachman could not see the shafts of the carriage. Servants with lanterns were running to and fro on the steps. The immense house glared with its great windows lighted up. The house-serfs were crowding in the outer hall, anxious to say good-bye to their young prince. In the great hall within stood all the members of the household: Mihail Ivanovitch, Mademoiselle Bourienne, Princess Marya, and the little princess. Prince Andrey had been summoned to the study of his father, who wanted to take leave of him alone. All were waiting for him to come out again. When Prince Andrey went into the study, the old prince was in his old-age spectacles and his white dressing-gown, in which he never saw any one but his son. He was sitting at the table writing. He looked round.

'Going?' And he went on writing again.

'I have come to say good-bye.'

'Kiss me here,' he touched his cheek; 'thanks, thanks!'

'What are you thanking me for?'

'For not lingering beyond your fixed time, for not hanging about a woman's petticoats. Duty before everything. Thanks, thanks!' And he went on writing, so that ink spurted from the scratching pen.

'If you want to say anything, say it. I can do these two things at once,' he added.

'About my wife . . . I'm ashamed as it is to leave her on your hands. . . .'

'Why talk nonsense? Say what you want.'

'When my wife's confinement is due, send to Moscow for an *accoucheur* . . . Let him be here.'

The old man stopped and stared with stern eyes at his son, as though not understanding.

'I know that no one can be of use, if nature does not assist,' said Prince Andrey, evidently confused. 'I admit that out of a million cases only one goes wrong, but it's her fancy and mine. They've been telling her things; she's had a dream and she's frightened.'

'H'm . . . h'm . . .' the old prince muttered to himself, going on with his writing. 'I will do so.' He scribbled his signature, and suddenly turned quickly to his son and laughed.

'It's a bad business, eh?'

'What's a bad business, father?'

'Wife!' the old prince said briefly and significantly.

'I don't understand,' said Prince Andrey.

'But there's no help for it, my dear boy,' said the old prince; 'they're all like that, and there's no getting unmarried again. Don't be afraid, I won't say a word to any one, but you know it yourself.'

He grasped his hand with his thin, little, bony fingers, shook it, looked straight into his son's face with his keen eyes, that seemed to see right through any one, and again he laughed his frigid laugh.

The son sighed, acknowledging in that sigh that his father understood him. The old man, still busy folding and sealing the letters with his habitual rapidity, snatched up and flung down again the wax, the seal, and the paper.

'It can't be helped. She's pretty. I'll do everything. Set your mind at rest,' he said jerkily, as he sealed the letter.

Andrey did not speak; it was both pleasant and painful to him that his father understood him. The old man got up and gave his son the letter.

'Listen,' said he. 'Don't worry about your wife; what can be done shall be done. Now, listen; give this letter to Mihail Ilarionovitch. I write that he is to make use of you on good work, and not to keep you long an adjutant; a vile duty! Tell him I remember him and like him. And write to me how he receives you. If he's all right, serve him. The son of Nikolay Andreitch Bolkonsky has no need to serve under any man as a favour. Now, come here.'

He spoke so rapidly that he did not finish half of his words, but his son was used to understanding him. He led his son to the bureau, opened it, drew out a drawer, and took out of it a manuscript book filled with his bold, big, compressed handwriting.

'I am sure to die before you. See, here are my notes, to be given to the Emperor after my death. Now here, see, is a bank note and a letter: this is a prize for any one who writes a history of Suvorov's wars. Send it to the academy. Here are my remarks, read them after I am gone for your own sake; you will find them profitable.'

Andrey did not tell his father that he probably had many years before him. He knew there was no need to say that.

'I will do all that, father,' he said.

'Well, now, good-bye!' He gave his son his hand to kiss and embraced him. 'Remember one thing, Prince Andrey, if you are killed, it will be a grief to me in my old age . . .' He paused abruptly, and all at once in a shrill voice went on: 'But if I learn that you have not behaved like the son of Nikolay Bolkonsky, I shall be . . . ashamed,' he shrilled.

'You needn't have said that to me, father,' said his son, smiling.

The old man did not speak.

'There's another thing I wanted to ask you,' went on Prince Andrey; 'if I'm killed, and if I have a son, don't let him slip out of your hands, as I said to you yesterday; let him grow up with you . . . please.'

'Not give him up to your wife?' said the old man, and he laughed.

They stood mutually facing each other. The old man's sharp eyes were fixed on his son's eyes. A quiver passed over the lower part of the old prince's face.

'We have said good-bye . . . go along!' he said suddenly. 'Go along!' he cried in a loud and wrathful voice, opening the study door.

'What is it, what's the matter?' asked the two princesses on seeing Prince Andrey, and catching a momentary glimpse of the old man in his white dressing-gown, wearing his spectacles and no wig, and shouting in a wrathful voice.

Prince Andrey sighed and made no reply.

'Now, then,' he said, turning to his wife, and that 'now then' sounded like a cold sneer, as though he had said, 'Now, go through your little performance.'

'Andrey? Already!' said the little princess, turning pale and looking with dismay at her husband. He embraced her. She shrieked and fell swooning on his shoulder.

He cautiously withdrew the shoulder, on which she was lying, glanced into her face and carefully laid her in a low chair.

'Good-bye, Masha,' he said gently to his sister, and they kissed one another's hands, then with rapid steps he walked out of the room.

The little princess lay in the arm-chair; Mademoiselle Bourienne rubbed her temples, Princess Marya, supporting her sister-in-law, still gazed with her fine eyes full of tears at the door by which Prince Andrey had gone, and she made the sign of the cross at it. From the study she heard like pistol shots the repeated and angry sounds of the old man blowing his nose. Just after Prince Andrey had gone, the door of the study was flung open, and the stern figure of the old man in his white dressing-gown peeped out.

'Gone? Well, and a good thing too!' he said, looking furiously at the fainting princess. He shook his head reproachfully and slammed the door.

PART II

I

IN THE OCTOBER of 1805 the Russian troops were occupying the towns and villages of the Austrian archduchy, and fresh regiments kept arriving from Russia and encamping about the fortress of Braunau, burdening the inhabitants on whom they were billeted. Braunau was the chief headquarters of the commander-in-chief, Kutuzov.

On the 11th of October 1805, one of the infantry regiments that had just reached Braunau had halted half a mile from the town, awaiting the inspection of the commander-in-chief. In spite of the un-Russian character of the country and the environment (the fruit gardens, the stone walls, the tiled roofs, the mountains in the distance, the foreign peasants, who looked with curiosity at the Russian soldiers), the regiment looked exactly as every Russian regiment always looks when it is getting ready for inspection anywhere in the heart of Russia. In the evening, on the last stage of the march, the order had been received that the commander-in-chief would inspect the regiment on the march. Though the wording of the order did not seem quite clear to the general in command of the regiment, and the question arose whether they were to take it to mean, in marching order or not, it was decided on a consultation between the majors to present the regiment in parade order on the ground, since, as the saying is, it is better to bow too low than not to bow low enough. And the soldiers after a twenty-five mile march had not closed their eyes, but had spent the night mending and cleaning, while the adjutants and officers had been reckoning up and calculating. And by the morning the regiment, instead of the straggling, disorderly crowd it had been on the last march, the previous evening, presented the spectacle of an organised mass of two thousand men, of whom every one knew his part and his duty, and had every button and every strap in its proper position, and shining with cleanliness. It was not only the outside that was in good order; if the commander-in-chief should think fit to peep below the uniform, he would see on every man alike a clean shirt, and in every knapsack he would find the regulation number of articles. There was only one circumstance which no one could feel comfortable about. That was their foot-gear. More than half the soldiers had holes in their boots. But this deficiency was not due to any shortcoming on the part of their commanding officer, since in spite of his repeated demands the boots had not yet been granted him by the Austrian authorities, and the regiment had marched nearly a thousand miles.

The commander of the regiment was a sanguine-looking general past middle age, with grey whiskers and eyebrows, broad and thick-set, and thicker through from the chest to the back than across the shoulders. He wore a brand-new uniform with the creases still in it where it had been folded, and rich gold epaulettes, which seemed to stand up instead of lying down on his thick shoulders. The general had the air of a man who has successfully performed one of the most solemn duties of his life. He walked about in front of the line, and quivered as he walked, with a slight jerk of his back at each step. The general was unmistakably admiring his regiment, and happy in it, and it was evident that his whole brain was engrossed by the regiment. But for all that, his quivering strut seemed to say that, apart from his military interests, he had plenty of warmth in his heart for the attractions of social life and the fair sex.

'Well, Mihail Mitritch, sir,' he said, addressing a major (the major came forward smiling; they were evidently in excellent spirits).

'We have had our hands full all night . . . But it'll do, I fancy; the regiment's not so bad as some . . . eh?'

The major understood this good-humoured irony and laughed.

'Even on the Tsaritsyn review ground they wouldn't be turned off.'

'Eh?' said the commander.

At that moment two figures on horseback came into sight on the road from the town, where sentinels had been posted to give the signal. They were an adjutant, and a Cossack riding behind him.

The adjutant had been sent by the commander-in-chief to confirm to the commander what had not been clearly stated in the previous order, namely, that the commander-in-chief wished to inspect the regiment exactly in the order in which it had arrived—wearing their overcoats, and carrying their baggage, and without any sort of preparation.

A member of the Hofkriegsrath from Vienna had been with Kutuzov the previous day, proposing and demanding that he should move on as quickly as possible to effect a junction with the army of Archduke Ferdinand and Mack; and Kutuzov, not considering this combination advisable, had intended, among other arguments in support of his view, to point out to the Austrian general the pitiable condition in which were the troops that had arrived from Russia. It was with this object, indeed, that he had meant to meet the regiment, so that the worse the condition of the regiment, the better pleased the commander-in-chief would be with it. Though the adjutant did not know these details, he gave the general in command of the regiment the message that the commander-in-chief absolutely insisted on the men being in their overcoats and marching order, and that, if the contrary were the case, the commander-in-chief would be displeased.

On hearing this the general's head sank; he shrugged his shoulders, and flung up his hands with a choleric gesture.

'Here's a mess we've made of it,' he said. 'Why, didn't I tell you, Mihail Mitritch, that on the march meant in their overcoats,' he said reproachfully to the major. 'Ah, my God!' he added, and stepped resolutely forward. 'Captains of the companies!' he shouted in a voice used to command. 'Sergeants! . . . Will his excellency be coming soon?' he said, turning to the adjutant with an expression of respectful deference, that related obviously only to the person he was speaking of.

'In an hour's time, I believe.'

'Have we time to change clothes?'

'I can't say, general. . . .'

The general, going himself among the ranks, gave orders for the men to change back to their overcoats. The captains ran about among the companies, the sergeants bustled to and fro (the overcoats were not quite up to the mark), and instantaneously the squadrons, that had been in regular order and silent, were heaving to and fro, straggling apart and humming with talk. The soldiers ran backwards and forwards in all directions, stooping with their shoulders thrown back, drawing their knapsacks off over their heads, taking out their overcoats and lifting their arms up to thrust them into the sleeves.

Half an hour later everything was in its former good order again, only the squadrons were now grey instead of black. The general walked in front of the regiment again with his quivering strut, and scanned it from some distance.

'What next? what's this!' he shouted, stopping short. 'Captain of the third company!'

'The captain of the third company to the general! The captain to the general of the third company to the captain!' . . . voices were heard along the ranks, and an adjutant ran to look for the tardy officer. When the sound of the officious voices, varying the command, and, by now, crying, 'the general to the third company,' reached their destination, the officer called for emerged from behind his company, and, though he was an elderly man and not accustomed to running, he moved at a quick trot towards the general, stumbling awkwardly over the toes of his boots. The captain's face showed the uneasiness of a schoolboy who is called up to repeat an unlearnt lesson. Patches came out on his red nose (unmistakably due to intemperance), and he did not know how to keep his mouth steady. The general looked the captain up and down as he ran panting up, slackening his pace as he drew nearer.

'You'll soon be dressing your men in petticoats! What's the meaning of it?' shouted the general, thrusting out his lower jaw and pointing in the ranks of the third division to a soldier in an overcoat of a colour different from the rest. 'Where have you been yourself? The commander-in-chief is expected, and you're not in your place? Eh? . . . I'll teach you to rig your men out in dressing-gowns for inspection! . . . Eh?'

The captain, never taking his eyes off his superior officer, pressed the peak of his cap more and more tightly with his two fingers, as though he saw in this compression his only hope of safety.

'Well, why don't you speak? Who's that dressed up like a Hungarian?' the general jested bitterly.

'Your excellency . . .'

'Well, what's your excellency? Your excellency! Your excellency! But what that means, your excellency, nobody knows.'

'Your excellency, that's Dolohov, the degraded officer,' the captain said softly.

'Well, is he degraded to be a field-marshal, or a common soldier? If he's a soldier, then he must be dressed like all the rest, according to regulation.'

'Your excellency, you gave him leave yourself on the march.'

'Gave him leave? There, you're always like that, you young men,' said the general, softening a little. 'Gave him leave? If one says a word to you, you go and . . .' The general paused. 'One says a word to you, and you go and . . . Eh?' he said with renewed irritation. 'Be so good as to clothe your men decently. . . .'

And the general, looking round at the adjutant, walked with his quivering strut towards the regiment. It was obvious that he was pleased with his own display of anger, and that, walking through the regiment, he was trying to find a pretext for wrath. Falling foul of one officer for an unpolished ensign, of another for the unevenness of the rank, he approached the third company.

'How are you standing? Where is your leg? Where is your leg?' the general shouted with a note of anguish in his voice, stopping five men off Dolohov, who was wearing his blue overcoat. Dolohov slowly straightened his bent leg, and looked with his clear, insolent eyes straight in the general's face.

'Why are you in a blue coat? Off with it! . . . Sergeant! change his coat . . . the dir . . .' Before he had time to finish the word—

'General, I am bound to obey orders, but I am not bound to put up with . . .' Dolohov hastened to say.

'No talking in the ranks! . . . No talking, no talking!'

'Not bound to put up with insults,' Dolohov went on, loudly and clearly. The eyes of the general and the soldier met. The general paused, angrily pulling down his stiff scarf.

'Change your coat, if you please,' he said as he walked away.

II

'COMING!' the sentinel shouted at that moment. The general, turning red, ran to his horse, with trembling hands caught at the stirrup, swung himself up, settled himself in the saddle, drew out his sword, and with a pleased and resolute face opened his mouth on one side, in readiness to shout. The regiment fluttered all over, like a bird preening its wings, and subsided into stillness.

'Silence!' roared the general, in a soul-quaking voice, expressing at once gladness on his own account, severity as regards the regiment, and welcome as regards the approaching commander-in-chief.

A high, blue Vienna coach with several horses was driving at a smart trot, rumbling on its springs, along the broad unpaved high-road, with trees planted on each side of it. The general's suite and an escort of Croats galloped after the coach. Beside Kutuzov sat an Austrian general in a white uniform, that looked strange among the black Russian ones. The coach drew up on reaching the regiment. Kutuzov and the Austrian general were talking of something in low voices, and Kutuzov smiled slightly as, treading heavily, he put his foot on the carriage step, exactly as though those two thousand men gazing breathlessly at him and at their general, did not exist at all.

The word of command rang out, again the regiment quivered with a clanking sound as it presented arms. In the deathly silence the weak voice of the commander-in-chief was audible. The regiment roared: 'Good health to your Ex . . lency . . lency . . lency!' And again all was still. At first Kutuzov stood in one spot, while the regiment moved; then Kutuzov began walking on foot among the ranks, the white general beside him, followed by his suite.

From the way that the general in command of the regiment saluted the commander-in-chief, fixing his eyes intently on him, rigidly respectful and obsequious, from the way in which, craning forward, he followed the generals through the ranks, with an effort restraining his quivering strut, and darted up at every word and every gesture of the commander-in-chief,—it was evident that he performed his duties as a subordinate with even greater zest than his duties as a commanding officer. Thanks to the strictness and assiduity of its commander, the regiment was in excellent form as compared with the others that had arrived at Braunau at the same time. The sick and the stragglers left behind only numbered two hundred and seventeen, and everything was in good order except the soldiers' boots.

Kutuzov walked through the ranks, stopping now and then, and saying a few friendly words to officers he had known in the Turkish war, and sometimes to the soldiers. Looking at their boots, he several times shook his head dejectedly, and pointed them out to the Austrian general, with an expression as much as to say that he blamed no one for it, but he could not help seeing what a bad state of things it was. The general in command of the regiment, on every occasion such as this, ran forward, afraid of missing a single word the commander-in-chief might utter regarding the regiment. Behind Kutuzov, at such a distance that every word, even feebly articulated, could be heard, followed his suite, consisting of some twenty persons. These gentlemen were talking among themselves, and sometimes laughed. Nearest of all to the commander-in-chief walked a handsome adjutant. It was Prince Bolkonsky. Beside him was his comrade Nesvitsky, a tall staff-officer, excessively stout, with a good-natured, smiling, handsome face, and moist eyes. Nesvitsky could hardly suppress his mirth, which was excited by a swarthy officer of hussars walking near him. This officer, without a smile or a change in the expression of his fixed eyes, was staring with a serious face at the commanding officer's back, and mimicking every movement he made. Every time the commanding officer quivered and darted forward, the officer of hussars quivered and darted forward in precisely the same way. Nesvitsky laughed, and poked the others to make them look at the mimic.

Kutuzov walked slowly and listlessly by the thousands of eyes which were almost rolling out of their sockets in the effort to watch him. On reaching the third company, he suddenly stopped. The suite, not foreseeing this halt, could not help pressing up closer to him.

'Ah, Timohin!' said the commander-in-chief, recognising the captain with the red nose who had got into trouble over the blue overcoat.

One would have thought it impossible to stand more rigidly erect than Timohin had done when the general in command of the regiment had made his remarks to him; but at the instant when the commander-in-chief addressed him, the captain stood with such erect rigidity that it seemed that, were the commander-in-chief to remain for some time looking at him, the captain could hardly sustain the ordeal, and for that reason Kutuzov, realising his position, and wishing him nothing but good, hurriedly turned away. A scarcely perceptible smile passed over Kutuzov's podgy face, disfigured by the scar of a wound.

'Another old comrade at Ismail!' he said. 'A gallant officer! Are you satisfied with him?' Kutuzov asked of the general in command.

And the general, all unconscious that he was being reflected as in a mirror in the officer of hussars behind him, quivered, pressed forward, and answered: 'Fully, your most high excellency.'

'We all have our weaknesses,' said Kutuzov, smiling and walking away from him. 'He had a predilection for Bacchus.'

The general in command was afraid that he might be to blame for this, and made no answer. The officer of hussars at that instant noticed the face of the captain with the red nose, and the rigidly drawn-in stomach, and mimicked his face and attitude in such a life-like manner that Nesvitsky could not restrain his laughter. Kutuzov turned round. The officer could apparently do anything he liked with his face; at the instant Kutuzov turned round, the officer had time to get in a grimace before assuming the most serious, respectful, and innocent expression.

The third company was the last, and Kutuzov seemed pondering, as though trying to recall something. Prince Andrey stepped forward and said softly in French: 'You told me to remind you of the degraded officer, Dolohov, serving in the ranks in this regiment.'

'Where is Dolohov?' asked Kutuzov.

Doholov, attired by now in the grey overcoat of a private soldier, did not wait to be called up. The slender figure of the fair-haired soldier, with his bright blue eyes, stepped out of the line. He went up to the commander-in-chief and presented arms.

'A complaint to make?' Kutuzov asked with a slight frown.

'This is Dolohov,' said Prince Andrey.

'Ah!' said Kutuzov. 'I hope this will be a lesson to you, do your duty thoroughly. The Emperor is gracious. And I shall not forget you, if you deserve it.'

The bright blue eyes looked at the commander-in-chief just as impudently as at the general of his regiment, as though by his expression tearing down the veil of convention that removed the commander-in-chief so far from the soldier.

'The only favour I beg of your most high excellency,' he said in his firm, ringing, deliberate voice, 'is to give me a chance to atone for my offence, and to prove my devotion to his majesty the Emperor, and to Russia.'

Kutuzov turned away. There was a gleam in his eyes of the same smile with which he had turned away from Captain Timohin. He turned away and frowned, as though to express that all Dolohov had said to him and all he could say, he had known long, long ago, that he was sick to death long ago of it, and that it was not at all what was wanted. He turned away and went towards the coach.

The regiment broke up into companies and went towards the quarters assigned them at no great distance from Braunau, where they hoped to find boots and clothes, and to rest after their hard marches.

'You won't bear me a grudge, Prohor Ignatitch?' said the commanding general, overtaking the third company and riding up to Captain Timohin, who was walking in front of it. The general's face beamed with a delight he could not suppress after the successful inspection. 'It's in the Tsar's service . . . can't be helped . . . sometimes one has to be a little sharp at inspection. I'm the first to apologise; you know me. . . .' He was very much pleased. And he held out his hand to the captain.

'Upon my word, general, as if I'd make so bold,' answered the Captain, his nose flushing redder. He smiled, and his smile revealed the loss of two front teeth, knocked out by the butt-end of a gun at Ismail.

'And tell Dolohov that I won't forget him; he can be easy about that. And tell me, please, what about him, how's he behaving himself. . . . I've been meaning to inquire . . .'

'He's very exact in the discharge of his duties, your excellency . . . but he's a character . . .' said Timohin.

'Why, what sort of a character?' asked the general.

'It's different on different days, your excellency,' said the captain; 'at one time he's sensible and well-educated and good-natured. And then he'll be like a wild beast. In Poland, he all but killed a Jew, if you please. . . .'

'Well, well,' said the general, 'still one must feel for a young man in trouble. He has great connections, you know. . . . So you . . .'

'Oh yes, your excellency,' said Timohin, with a smile that showed he understood his superior officer's wish in the matter.

'Very well, then, very well.'

The general sought out Dolohov in the ranks and pulled up his horse.

'In the first action you may win your epaulettes,' he said to him.

Dolohov looked round and said nothing. There was no change in the lines of his ironically-smiling mouth.

'Well, that's all right then,' the general went on. 'A glass of brandy to every man from me,' he added, so that the soldiers could hear. 'I thank you all. God be praised!' And riding round the company, he galloped off to another.

'Well, he's really a good fellow, one can get on very well under him,' said Timohin to the subaltern officer walking beside him.

'The king of hearts, that's the only word for him,' the subaltern said, laughing. (The general was nicknamed the king of hearts.)

The cheerful state of mind of the officers after the inspection was shared by the soldiers. The companies went along merrily. Soldiers' voices could be heard on all sides chatting away.

'Why, don't they say Kutuzov's blind of one eye?'

'To be sure he is. Quite blind of one eye.'

'Nay . . . lads, he's more sharp-eyed than you are. See how he looked at our boots and things.' . . .

'I say, mate, when he looked at my legs . . . well, thinks I . . .'

'And the other was an Austrian with him, that looked as if he'd been chalked all over. As white as flour. I bet they rub him up as we rub up our guns.'

'I say, Fedeshou . . . did he say anything as to when the battles are going to begin? You stood nearer. They did say Bonaparte himself was in Brunovo.'

'Bonaparte! What nonsense the fellow talks! What won't you know next! Now it's the Prussian that's revolting. The Austrian, do you see, is pacifying him. When he's quiet, then the war will begin with Bonaparte. And he talks of Bonaparte's being in Brunovo! It's plain the fellow's a fool. You'd better keep your ears open.'

'Those devils of quartermasters! . . . The fifth company's turned into the village by now, and they're cooking their porridge, and we're not there yet.'

'Give us a biscuit, old man.'

'And did you give me tobacco yesterday? All right, my lad. Well, well, God be with you.'

'They might have made a halt, or we'll have to do another four miles with nothing to eat.'

'I say, it was fine how those Germans gave us carriages. One drove along, something like.'

'But here, lads, the folks are regularly stripped bare. There it was all Poles of some sort, all under the Russian crown, but now we've come to the regular Germans, my boy.'

'Singers to the front,' the captain called. And from the different ranks about twenty men advanced to the front. The drummer, who was their leader, turned round facing the chorus and waving his arm, struck up a soldier's song, beginning: 'The sun was scarcely dawning,' and ending with the words: 'So, lads, we'll march to glory with Father Kamensky.' . . . This song had been composed in Turkey, and now was sung in Austria, the only change being the substitution of the words 'Father Kutuzov' for 'Father Kamensky.'

Jerking out the last words in soldierly fashion and waving his arms, as though he were flinging something on the ground, the drummer, a lean, handsome soldier of forty, looked sternly at the soldier-chorus and frowned. Then, having satisfied himself that all eyes were fixed upon him, he gesticulated, as though he were carefully lifting some unseen precious object over his head in both hands, holding it there some seconds, and all at once with a desperate movement flinging it away.

'Ah, the threshold of my cottage,
My new cottage.'

Here twenty voices caught up the refrain, and the castanet player, in spite of the weight of his weapon and knapsack, bounded nimbly forward, and walked backwards facing the company, shaking his shoulders, and seeming to menace some one with the castanets. The soldiers stepped out in time to the song, swinging their arms and unconsciously falling into step. Behind the company came the sound of wheels, the rumble of springs, and the tramp of horses. Kutuzov and his suite were going back to the town. The commander-in-chief made a sign for the soldiers to go on freely, and he and all his suite looked as though they took pleasure in the sound of the singing, and the spectacle of the dancing soldier and the gaily, smartly marching men. In the second row from the right flank, beside which the carriage passed, they could not help noticing the blue-eyed soldier, Dolohov, who marched with a special jauntiness and grace in time to the song, and looked at the faces of the persons driving by with an expression that seemed to pity every one who was not at that moment marching in the ranks. The cornet of hussars, the officer of Kutuzov's suite, who had mimicked the general, fell back from the carriage and rode up to Dolohov.

The cornet of hussars, Zherkov, had at one time belonged to the fast set in Petersburg, of which Dolohov had been the leader. Zherkov had met Dolohov abroad as a common soldier, and had not seen fit to recognise him. But now, after Kutuzov's conversation with the degraded officer, he addressed him with all the cordiality of an old friend.

'Friend of my heart, how are you?' he said, through the singing, making his horse keep pace with the marching soldiers.

'How am I?' Dolohov answered coldly. 'As you see.' The lively song gave a peculiar flavour to the tone of the free-and-easy gaiety, with which Zherkov spoke, and the studied coldness of Dolohov's replies.

'Well, how do you get on with your officers?' asked Zherkov.

'All right; they're good fellows. How did you manage to poke yourself on to the staff?'

'I was attached; I'm on duty.'

They were silent.

> 'My gay goshawk I took with me,
> From my right sleeve I set him free,'

said the song, arousing an involuntary sensation of courage and cheerfulness. Their conversation would most likely have been different, if they had not been talking while the song was singing.

'Is it true, the Austrians have been beaten?' asked Dolohov.

'Devil knows; they say so.'

'I'm glad,' Dolohov made a brief, sharp reply, as was required to fit in with the tune.

'I say, come round to us some evening; we'll have a game of faro,' said Zherkov.

'Is money so plentiful among you?'

'Do come.'

'I can't; I've sworn not to. I won't drink or play till I'm promoted.'

'Well, but in the first action . . .'

'Then we shall see.' Again they paused.

'You come, if you want anything; one can always be of use on the staff. . . .'

Dolohov grinned. 'Don't trouble yourself. What I want, I'm not going to ask for; I take it for myself.'

'Oh, well, I only . . .'

'Well, and I only.'

'Good-bye.'

'Good-bye.'

> 'And far and free
> To his own country.'

Zherkov put spurs to his horse, which three times picked up its legs excitedly, not knowing which to start from, then galloped off round the company, and overtook the carriage, keeping time too to the song.

III

ON returning from the review, Kutuzov, accompanied by the Austrian general, went to his private room, and calling his adjutant, told him to give him certain papers, relating to the condition of the newly arrived troops, and letters, received from Archduke Ferdinand, who was in command of the army at the front. Prince Andrey Bolkonsky came into the commander-in-chief's room with the papers he had asked for. Kutuzov and the Austrian member of the Hofkriegsrath were sitting over a plan that lay unfolded on the table.

'Ah!' . . . said Kutuzov, looking round at Bolkonsky; and inviting his adjutant, as it were, by this word to wait, he went on in French with the conversation.

'I have only one thing to say, general,' said Kutuzov, with an agreeable elegance of expression and intonation, that forced one to listen for each deliberately uttered word. It was evident that Kutuzov himself listened to his voice with pleasure. 'I can only say one thing, that if the matter depended on my personal wishes, the desire of his Majesty, the Emperor Francis, should long ago have been accomplished; I should long ago have joined the archduke. And, upon my honour, believe me that for me personally to hand over the chief command of the army to more experienced and skilful generals—such as Austria is so rich in—and to throw off all this weighty responsibility, for me personally would be a relief. But circumstances are too strong for us, general.' And Kutuzov smiled with an expression that seemed to say: 'You are perfectly at liberty not to believe me, and indeed it's a matter of perfect indifference to me whether you believe me or not, but you have no grounds for saying so. And that's the whole point.' The Austrian general looked dissatisfied, but he had no choice but to answer Kutuzov in the same tone.

'On the contrary,' he said in a querulous and irritated voice, that contrasted with the flattering intention of the words he uttered; 'on the contrary, the participation of your most high excellency in common action is highly appreciated by his majesty. But we imagine that the present delay robs the gallant Russian troops and their commander-in-chief of the laurels they are accustomed to winning in action,' he concluded a phrase he had evidently prepared beforehand.

Kutuzov bowed, still with the same smile.

'But I am convinced of this, and relying on the last letter with which his Highness the Archduke Ferdinand has honoured me, I imagine that the Austrian troops under the command of so talented a leader as General Mack, have by now gained a decisive victory and have no longer need of our aid,' said Kutuzov.

The general frowned. Though there was no positive news of the defeat of the Austrians, there were too many circumstances in confirmation of the unfavourable reports; and so Kutuzov's supposition in regard to an Austrian victory sounded very much like a sneer. But

Kutuzov smiled blandly, still with the same expression, which seemed to say that he had a right to suppose so. And in fact the last letter he had received from the army of General Mack had given him news of victory, and of the most favourable strategical position of the army.

'Give me that letter,' said Kutuzov, addressing Prince Andrey. 'Here, if you will kindly look'—and Kutuzov, with an ironical smile about the corners of his mouth, read in German the following passage from the letter of the Archduke Ferdinand:

'We have a force, perfectly kept together, of nearly 70,000 men, in order to attack and defeat the enemy if they should pass the Lech. As we are masters of Ulm, we cannot lose the advantage of remaining masters also of both sides of the Danube; and moreover able, should the enemy not cross the Lech, to pass over the Danube at any moment, throw ourselves upon their line of communication, recross the Danube lower down, and entirely resist the enemy's aim if they should attempt to turn their whole force upon our faithful ally. In this way we shall await courageously the moment when the Imperial Russian is ready, and shall then, in conjunction, easily find a possibility of preparing for the foe that fate which he so richly deserves.'

Kutuzov concluded this period with a heavy sigh and looked intently and genially at the member of the Hofkriegsrath.

'But you know, your excellency, the sage precept to prepare for the worst,' said the Austrian general, obviously wishing to have done with jests and to come to business. He could not help glancing round at the adjutant.

'Excuse me, general,' Kutuzov interrupted him, and he, too, turned to Prince Andrey. 'Here, my dear boy, get all the reports from our scouts from Kozlovsky. Here are two letters from Count Nostits, here is a letter from his Highness the Archduke Ferdinand, here is another,' he said, giving him several papers. 'And of all this make out clearly in French a memorandum showing all the information we have had of the movements of the Austrian army. Well, do so, and then show it to his excellency.'

Prince Andrey bowed in token of understanding from the first word not merely what had been said, but also what Kutusov would have liked to have said to him. He gathered up the papers, and making a comprehensive bow, stepped softly over the carpet and went out into the reception-room.

Although so short a time had passed since Prince Andrey had left Russia, he had changed greatly during that time. In the expression of his face, in his gestures, in his gait, there was scarcely a trace to be seen now of his former affectation, ennui, and indolence. He had the air of a man who has not time to think of the impression he is making on others, and is absorbed in work, both agreeable and interesting. His face showed more satisfaction with himself and those around him. His smile and his glance were more light-hearted and attractive.

Kutuzov, whom he had overtaken in Poland, had received him very cordially, had promised not to forget him, had marked him out among the other adjutants, had taken him with him to Vienna and given him the more serious commissions. From Vienna, Kutuzov had written to his old comrade, Prince Andrey's father.

'Your son,' he wrote, 'gives promise of becoming an officer, who will make his name by his industry, firmness, and conscientiousness. I consider myself lucky to have such an assistant at hand.'

On Kutuzov's staff, among his fellow-officers, and in the army generally, Prince Andrey had, as he had had in Petersburg society, two quite opposite reputations. Some, the minority, regarded Prince Andrey as a being different from themselves and from all other men, expected great things of him, listened to him, were enthusiastic in his praise, and imitated him, and with such people Prince Andrey was frank and agreeable. Others, the majority, did not like Prince Andrey, and regarded him as a sulky, cold, and disagreeable person. But with the latter class, too, Prince Andrey knew how to behave so that he was respected and even feared by them.

Coming out of Kutuzov's room into the reception-room, Prince Andrey went in with his papers to his comrade, the adjutant on duty, Kozlovsky, who was sitting in the window with a book.

'What is it, prince?' queried Kozlovsky.

'I am told to make a note of the reason why we are not moving forward.'

'And why aren't we?'

Prince Andrey shrugged his shoulders.

'No news from Mack?' asked Kozlovsky.

'No.'

'If it were true that he had been beaten, news would have come.'

'Most likely,' said Prince Andrey, and he moved towards the door to go out. But he was met on the way by a tall man who at that instant walked into the reception-room, slamming the door. The stranger, who had obviously just arrived, was an Austrian general in a long coat, with a black kerchief tied round his head, and the order of Maria Theresa on his neck. Prince Andrey stopped short.

'Commander-in-chief Kutuzov?' the general asked quickly, speaking with a harsh German accent. He looked about him on both sides, and without a pause walked to the door of the private room.

'The commander-in-chief is engaged,' said Kozlovsky, hurriedly going up to the unknown general and barring his way to the door. 'Whom am I to announce?'

The unknown general looked disdainfully down at the short figure of Kozlovsky, as though surprised that they could be ignorant of his identity.

'The commander-in-chief is engaged,' Kozlovsky repeated tranquilly.

The general's face contracted, his lips twitched and quivered. He took out a notebook, hurriedly scribbled something in pencil, tore out the leaf, handed it to Kozlovsky, and with rapid steps walked to the window, dropped on to a chair and looked round at the persons in the room, as though asking what they were looking at him for. Then the general lifted his head, craned his neck forward as though intending to say something, but immediately, as though carelessly beginning to hum to himself, uttered a strange sound which broke off at once. The door of the private room opened, and Kutuzov appeared in the doorway.

The general with the bandaged head, bent forward as though fleeing from danger, strode towards Kutuzov, his thin legs moving swiftly.

'You see the unfortunate Mack,' he articulated in French in a breaking voice.

The face of Kutuzov, as he stood in the doorway, remained for several instants perfectly unmoved. Then a frown seemed to run over his face, like a wave, leaving his forehead smooth again; he bowed his head respectfully, closed his eyes, ushered Mack in before him without a word, and closed the door behind him.

The report, which had been in circulation before this, of the defeat of the Austrians and the surrender of the whole army at Ulm, turned out to be the truth. Within half an hour adjutants had been despatched in various directions with orders. It was evident that the Russian troops which had hitherto been inactive, were destined soon to meet the enemy.

Prince Andrey was one of those rare staff-officers whose interests were concentrated on the general progress of the war. On seeing Mack and learning the details of his overthrow, he grasped the fact that half the campaign was lost; he perceived all the difficulty of the position of the Russian troops, and vividly pictured to himself what lay before the army, and the part he would have to play in the work in store for them. He could not help feeling a rush of joyful emotion at the thought of the humiliation of self-confident Austria, and the prospect within a week, perhaps, of seeing and taking part in the meeting of the Russians with the French, the first since Suvorov's day. But he was afraid of the genius of Bonaparte, which might turn out to be more powerful than all the bravery of the Russian troops; and at the same time he could not bear to entertain the idea of the disgrace of his favourite hero.

Excited and irritated by these ideas, Prince Andrey went towards his own room to write to his father, to whom he wrote every day. In the corridor he met Nesvitsky, the comrade with whom he shared a room, and the comic man, Zherkov. They were, as usual, laughing at some joke.

'What are you looking so dismal about?' asked Nesvitsky, noticing Prince Andrey's pale face and gleaming eyes.

'There's nothing to be gay about,' answered Bolkonsky.

Just as Prince Andrey met Nesvitsky and Zherkov, there came towards them from the other end of the corridor Strauch, an Austrian general, who was on Kutuzov's staff in charge of the provisioning of the Russian army, and the member of the Hofkriegsrath, who had arrived the previous evening. There was plenty of room in the wide corridor for the generals to pass the three officers easily. But Zherkov, pulling Nesvitsky back by the arm, cried in a breathless voice:

'They are coming! ... they are coming! ... move aside, make way! please, make way.'

The generals advanced with an air of wishing to avoid burdensome honours. The face of the comic man, Zherkov, suddenly wore a stupid smile of glee, which he seemed unable to suppress.

'Your Excellency,' he said in German, moving forward and addressing the Austrian general, 'I have the honour to congratulate you.' He bowed, and awkwardly, as children do at dancing-lessons, he began scraping first with one leg and then with the other. The member of the Hofkriegsrath looked severely at him, but seeing the seriousness of his stupid smile, he could not refuse him a moment's attention. He screwed up his eyes and showed that he was listening.

'I have the honour to congratulate you. General Mack has arrived, quite well, only slightly wounded here,' he added, pointing with a beaming smile to his head.

The general frowned, turned away and went on.

'*Gott, wie naïv!*' he said angrily, when he was a few steps away.

Nesvitsky with a chuckle threw his arms round Prince Andrey, but Bolkonsky, turning even paler, pushed him away with a furious expression, and turned to Zherkov. The nervous irritability, into which he had been thrown by the sight of Mack, the news of his defeat and the thought of what lay before the Russian army, found a vent in anger at the misplaced jest of Zherkov.

'If you, sir,' he began cuttingly, with a slight trembling in his lower jaw, 'like to be a *clown*, I can't prevent your being so, but if you *dare* to play the fool another time in my presence, I'll teach you how to behave.'

Nesvitsky and Zherkov were so astounded at this outburst that they gazed at Bolkonsky with open eyes.

'Why, I only congratulated them,' said Zherkov.

'I am not jesting with you; be silent, please!' shouted Bolkonsky, and taking Nesvitsky's arm, he walked away from Zherkov, who could not find any reply.

'Come, what is the matter, my dear boy?' said Nesvitsky, trying to soothe him.

'What's the matter?' said Prince Andrey, standing still from excitement. 'Why, you ought to understand that we're either officers, who serve their Tsar and their country and rejoice in the success, and grieve at the defeat of the common cause, or we're hirelings, who have no interest in our master's business. Forty thousand men massacred and the army of our allies destroyed, and you find something in that to laugh at,' he said, as though by this French phrase he were strengthening his view. 'It is all very well for a worthless fellow like that individual of whom you have made a friend, but not for you, not for you. None but *schoolboys* can find amusement in such jokes,' Prince Andrey added in Russian, uttering the word with a French accent. He noticed that Zherkov could still hear him, and waited to see whether the cornet would not reply. But the cornet turned and went out of the corridor.

IV

THE Pavlogradsky regiment of hussars was stationed two miles from Braunau. The squadron in which Nikolay Rostov was serving as ensign was billeted on a German village, Salzeneck. The officer in command of the squadron, Captain Denisov, known through the whole cavalry division under the name of Vaska Denisov, had been assigned the best quarters in the village. Ensign Rostov had been sharing his quarters, ever since he overtook the regiment in Poland.

On the 8th of October, the very day when at headquarters all was astir over the news of Mack's defeat, the routine of life was going on as before among the officers of this squadron.

Denisov, who had been losing all night at cards, had not yet returned home, when Rostov rode back early in the morning from a foraging expedition. Rostov, in his ensign's uniform, rode up to the steps, with a jerk to his horse, swung his leg over with a supple, youthful action, stood a moment in the stirrup as though loath to part from the horse, at last sprang down and called the orderly.

'Ah, Bondarenko, friend of my heart,' he said to the hussar who rushed headlong up to his horse. 'Walk him up and down, my dear fellow,' he said, with that gay and brotherly cordiality with which good-hearted young people behave to every one, when they are happy.

'Yes, your excellency,' answered the Little Russian, shaking his head good-humouredly.

'Mind now, walk him about well!'

Another hussar rushed up to the horse too, but Bondarenko had already hold of the reins.

It was evident that the ensign was liberal with his tips, and that his service was a profitable one. Rostov stroked the horse on the neck and then on the haunch, and lingered on the steps.

'Splendid! What a horse he will be!' he said to himself, and smiling and holding his sword, he ran up the steps, clanking his spurs. The German, on whom they were billeted, looked out of the cowshed, wearing a jerkin and a pointed cap, and holding a fork, with which he was clearing out the dung. The German's face brightened at once when he saw Rostov. He smiled good-humouredly and winked. 'Good-morning, good-morning!' he repeated, apparently taking pleasure in greeting the young man.

'At work already!' said Rostov, still with the same happy, fraternal smile that was constantly on his eager face. 'Long live the Austrians! Long live the Russians! Hurrah for the Emperor Alexander!' he said, repeating phrases that had often been uttered by the German. The German laughed, came right out of the cowshed, pulled off his cap, and waving it over his head, cried:

'And long live all the world!'

Rostov too, like the German, waved his cap over his head, and laughing cried: 'And hurrah for all the world!' Though there was no reason for any special rejoicing either for the German, clearing out his shed, or for Rostov, coming back from foraging for hay, both these persons gazed at one another in delighted ecstasy and brotherly love, wagged their heads at each other in token of their mutual affection, and parted with smiles, the German to his cowshed, and Rostov to the cottage he shared with Denisov.

'Where's your master?' he asked of Lavrushka, Denisov's valet, well known to all the regiment as a rogue.

'His honour's not been in since the evening. He's been losing, for sure,' answered Lavrushka. 'I know by now, if he wins, he'll come home early to boast of his luck; but if he's not back by morning, it means that he's lost,—he'll come back in a rage. Shall I bring coffee?'

'Yes, bring it.'

Ten minutes later, Lavrushka brought in the coffee.

'He's coming!' said he; 'now for trouble!'

Rostov glanced out of the window and saw Denisov returning home. Denisov was a little man with a red face, sparkling black eyes, towzled black whiskers and hair. He was wearing an unbuttoned tunic, wide breeches that fell in folds, and on the back of his head a crushed hussar's cap. Gloomily, with downcast head, he drew near the steps.

'Lavrushka,' he shouted, loudly and angrily, lisping the r, 'come, take it off, blockhead!'

'Well, I am taking it off,' answered Lavrushka's voice.

'Ah! you are up already,' said Denisov, coming into the room.

'Long ago,' said Rostov; 'I've been out already after hay, and I have seen Fraülein Mathilde.'

'Really? And I've been losing, my boy, all night, like the son of a dog,' cried Denisov, not pronouncing his r's. 'Such ill-luck! such ill-luck! ... As soon as you left, my luck was gone. Hey, tea?'

Denisov, puckering up his face as though he were smiling, and showing his short, strong teeth, began with his short-fingered hands ruffling up his thick, black hair, that was tangled like a forest.

'The devil was in me to go to that rat' (the nickname of an officer), he said, rubbing his brow and face with both hands. 'Only fancy, he didn't deal me one card, not one, not one card!' Denisov took the lighted pipe that was handed to him, gripped it in his fist, and scattering sparks, he tapped it on the floor, still shouting.

'He lets me have the simple, and beats the parole; lets me get the simple, and beats the parole.'

He scattered the sparks, broke the pipe, and threw it away. Then Denisov paused, and all at once he glanced brightly at Rostov with his gleaming black eyes.

'If there were only women. But here, except drinking, there's nothing to do. If only we could get to fighting soon. . . . Hey, who's there?' he called towards the door, catching the sounds of thick boots and clanking spurs that came to a stop, and of a respectful cough.

'The sergeant!' said Lavrushka. Denisov puckered up his face more than ever.

'That's a nuisance,' he said, flinging down a purse with several gold coins in it. 'Rostov, count, there's a dear boy, how much is left, and put the purse under the pillow,' he said, and he went out to the sergeant. Rostov took the money and mechanically sorting and arranging in heaps the old and new gold, he began counting it over.

'Ah, Telyanin! Good-morning! I was cleaned out last night,' he heard Denisov's voice saying from the other room.

'Where was that? At Bykov's? at the rat's? ... I knew it,' said a thin voice, and thereupon there walked into the room Lieutenant Telyanin, a little officer in the same squadron.

Rostov put the purse under the pillow, and shook the damp little hand that was offered him. Telyanin had for some reason been transferred from the guards just before the regiment set out. He had behaved very well in the regiment, but he was not liked, and Rostov, in particular, could not endure him, and could not conceal his groundless aversion for this officer.

'Well, young cavalryman, how is my Rook doing for you?' (Rook was a riding-horse Telyanin had sold to Rostov.) The lieutenant never looked the person he was speaking to in the face. His eyes were continually flitting from one object to another. 'I saw you riding today...'

'Oh, he's all right; a good horse,' answered Rostov, though the horse, for which he had paid seven hundred roubles, was not worth half that sum. 'He's begun to go a little lame in the left fore leg...' he added.

'The hoof cracked! That's no matter. I'll teach you, I'll show you the sort of thing to put on it.'

'Yes, please do,' said Rostov.

'I'll show you, I'll show you; it's not a secret. But you'll be grateful to me for that horse.'

'Then I'll have the horse brought round,' said Rostov, anxious to be rid of Telyanin. He went out to order the horse to be brought round.

In the outer room Denisov was squatting on the threshold with a pipe, facing the sergeant, who was giving him some report. On seeing Rostov, Denisov screwed up his eyes, and pointing over his shoulder with his thumb to the room where Telyanin was sitting, he frowned and shook his head with an air of loathing.

'Ugh! I don't like the fellow,' he said, regardless of the presence of the sergeant.

Rostov shrugged his shoulders as though to say, 'Nor do I, but what's one to do?' And having given his order, he went back to Telyanin.

The latter was still sitting in the same indolent pose in which Rostov had left him, rubbing his little white hands.

'What nasty faces there are in this world!' thought Rostov as he went into the room.

'Well, have you given orders for the horse to be fetched out?' said Telyanin, getting up and looking carelessly about him.

'Yes.'

'Well, you come along yourself. I only came round to ask Denisov about yesterday's order. Have you got it, Denisov?'

'Not yet. But where are you off to?'

'I'm going to show this young man here how to shoe a horse,' said Telyanin.

They went out down the steps and into the stable. The lieutenant showed how to put on the remedy, and went away to his own quarters.

When Rostov went back there was a bottle of vodka and some sausage on the table. Denisov was sitting at the table, and his pen was squeaking over the paper. He looked gloomily into Rostov's face.

'I am writing to her,' he said. He leaned his elbow on the table with the pen in his hand, and obviously rejoiced at the possibility of saying by word of mouth all he meant to write, he told the contents of his letter to Rostov. 'You see, my dear boy,' he said, 'we are plunged in slumber, we are the children of dust and ashes, until we love . . . but love, and you are a god, you are pure, as on the first day of creation. . . . Who's that now? Send him to the devil! I've no time!' he shouted to Lavrushka, who, not in the slightest daunted, went up to him.

'Why, who should it be? You told him to come yourself. The sergeant has come for the money.'

Denisov frowned, seemed about to shout some reply, but did not speak.

'It's a nuisance,' he said to himself. 'How much money was there left in the purse?' he asked Rostov.

'Seven new and three old gold pieces.'

'Oh, it's a nuisance! Well, why are you standing there, you mummy? Send the sergeant!' Denisov shouted to Lavrushka.

'Please, Denisov, take the money from me; I've plenty,' said Rostov, blushing.

'I don't like borrowing from my own friends; I dislike it,' grumbled Denisov.

'But if you won't take money from me like a comrade, you'll offend me. I've really got it,' repeated Rostov.

'Oh, no.' And Denisov went to the bed to take the purse from under the pillow.

'Where did you put it, Rostov?'

'Under the lower pillow.'

'But it's not there.' Denisov threw both the pillows on the floor. There was no purse. 'Well, that's a queer thing.'

'Wait a bit, haven't you dropped it?' said Rostov, picking the pillows up one at a time and shaking them. He took off the quilt and shook it. The purse was not there.

'Could I have forgotten? No, for I thought that you keep it like a secret treasure under your head,' said Rostov. 'I laid the purse here. Where is it?' He turned to Lavrushka.

'I never came into the room. Where you put it there it must be.'

'But it isn't.'

'You're always like that; you throw things down anywhere and forget them. Look in your pockets.'

'No, if I hadn't thought of its being a secret treasure,' said Rostov, 'but I remember where I put it.'

Lavrushka ransacked the whole bed, glanced under it and under the table, ransacked the whole room and stood still in the middle of the room. Denisov watched Lavrushka's movements in silence, and when Lavrushka flung up his hands in amazement to signify that it was nowhere, he looked round at Rostov.

'Rostov, none of your schoolboy jokes.'

Rostov, feeling Denisov's eyes upon him, lifted his eyes and instantly dropped them again. All his blood, which felt as though it had been locked up somewhere below his throat, rushed to his face and eyes. He could hardly draw his breath.

'And there's been no one in the room but the lieutenant and yourselves. It must be here somewhere,' said Lavrushka.

'Now then, you devil's puppet, bestir yourself and look for it!' Denisov shouted suddenly, turning purple and dashing at the valet with a threatening gesture. 'The purse is to be found, or I'll flog you! I'll flog you all!'

Rostov, his eyes avoiding Denisov, began buttoning up his jacket, fastening on his sword, and putting on his forage-cap.

'I tell you the purse is to be found,' roared Denisov, shaking the orderly by the shoulders and pushing him against the wall.

'Denisov, let him be; I know who has taken it,' said Rostov, going towards the door without raising his eyes.

Denisov stopped, thought a moment, and evidently understanding Rostov's hint, he clutched him by the arm.

'Nonsense!' he roared so that the veins stood out on his neck and forehead like cords. 'I tell you, you've gone out of your mind; I won't allow it. The purse is here: I'll flay the skin off this rascal, and it will be here.'

'I know who has taken it, repeated Rostov, in a shaking voice, and he went to the door.

'And I tell you, you're not to dare to do it,' shouted Denisov, making a dash at the ensign to detain him. But Rostov pulled his arm away, lifted his eyes, and looked directly and resolutely at Denisov with as much fury as if he had been his greatest enemy.

'Do you understand what you're saying?' he said in a trembling voice; 'except me, there has been no one else in the room. So that, if it's not so, why then . . .'

He could not utter the rest, and ran out of the room.

'Oh, damn you and all the rest,' were the last words Rostov heard.

Rostov went to Telyanin's quarters.

'The master's not at home, he's gone to the staff,' Telyanin's orderly told him. 'Has something happened?' the orderly added, wondering at the ensign's troubled face.

'No, nothing.'

'You've only just missed him,' said the orderly.

The staff quarters were two miles and a half from Salzeneck. Not having found him at home, Rostov took his horse and rode to the quarters of the staff. In the village, where the staff was quartered, there was a restaurant which the officers frequented. Rostov reached the restaurant and saw Telyanin's horse at the entry.

In the second room the lieutenant was sitting over a dish of sausages and a bottle of wine.

'Ah, you have come here too, young man,' he said, smiling and lifting his eyebrows.

'Yes,' said Rostov, speaking as though the utterance of the word cost him great effort; and he sat down at the nearest table.

Both were silent; there were two Germans and a Russian officer in the room. Every one was mute, and the only sounds audible were the clatter of knives on the plates and the munching of the lieutenant. When Telyanin had finished his lunch, he took out of his pocket a double purse; with his little white fingers, that were curved at the tips, he parted the rings, took out some gold, and raising his eyebrows, gave the money to the attendant.

'Make haste, please,' he said.

The gold was new. Rostov got up and went to Telyanin.

'Let me look at the purse,' he said in a low voice, scarcely audible.

With shifting eyes, but eyebrows still raised, Telyanin gave him the purse.

'Yes, it's a pretty purse . . . yes . . .' he said, and suddenly he turned white. 'You can look at it, young man,' he added.

Rostov took the purse in his hand and looked both at it and at the money in it, and also at Telyanin. The lieutenant looked about him, as his way was, and seemed suddenly to have grown very good-humoured.

'If we go to Vienna, I suspect I shall leave it all there, but now there's nowhere to spend our money in these wretched little places,' he said. 'Come, give it me, young man; I'm going.'

Rostov did not speak.

'What are you going to do? have lunch too? They give you decent food,' Telyanin went on. 'Give it me.' He put out his hand and took hold of the purse. Rostov let go of it. Telyanin took the purse and began carelessly dropping it into the pocket of his riding trousers, while his eyebrows were carelessly lifted and his mouth stood a little open, as though he would say: 'Yes, yes, I'm putting my purse in my pocket, and that's a very simple matter, and no one has anything to do with it.'

'Well, young man?' he said with a sigh, and from under his lifted eyebrows he glanced into Rostov's eyes. A kind of gleam passed with the swiftness of an electric flash from Telyanin's eyes to the eyes of Rostov, and back again and back again and again, all in one instant.

'Come here,' said Rostov, taking Telyanin by the arm. He almost dragged him to the window. 'That's Denisov's money; you took it . . .' he whispered in his ear.

'What? . . . what? . . . How dare you? What?' . . . said Telyanin. But the words sounded like a plaintive, despairing cry and prayer for forgiveness. As soon as Rostov heard the sound of his voice, a great weight of suspense, like a stone, rolled off his heart. He felt glad, and at the same instant he pitied the luckless creature standing before him, but he had to carry the thing through to the end.

'God knows what the people here may think,' muttered Telyanin, snatching up his forage-cap and turning towards a small empty toom. 'You must explain . . .'

'I know that, and I'll prove it,' said Rostov.

'I . . .'

The terrified, white face of Telyanin began twitching in every muscle; his eyes still moved uneasily, but on the ground, never rising to the level of Rostov's face, and tearful sobs could be heard.

'Count! . . . don't ruin a young man . . . here is the wretched money, take it.' . . . He threw it on the table. 'I've an old father and mother!' . . .

Rostov took the money, avoiding Telyanin's eyes, and without uttering a word, he went out of the room. But in the doorway he stopped and turned back.

'My God!' he said, with tears in his eyes, 'how could you do it?'

'Count,' said Telyanin, coming nearer to the ensign.

'Don't touch me,' said Rostov, drawing back. 'If you're in need, take the money.'

He thrust a purse on him and ran out of the restaurant.

V

In the evening of the same day a lively discussion was taking place in Denisov's quarters between some officers of the squadron.

'But I tell you, Rostov, that you must apologise to the colonel,' the tall staff-captain was saying, addressing Rostov, who was crimson with excitement. The staff-captain, Kirsten, a man with grizzled hair, immense whiskers, thick features and a wrinkled face, had been twice degraded to the ranks for affairs of honour, and had twice risen again to holding a commission.

'I permit no one to tell me I'm lying!' cried Rostov. 'He told me I was lying and I told him he was lying. And there it rests. He can put me on duty every day, he can place me under arrest, but no one can compel me to apologise, because if he, as the colonel, considers it beneath his dignity to give me satisfaction, then . . .'

'But you wait a bit, my good fellow; you listen to me,' interrupted the staff-captain in his bass voice, calmly stroking his long whiskers. 'You tell the colonel in the presence of other officers that an officer has stolen —

'I'm not to blame for the conversation being in the presence of other officers. Possibly I ought not to have spoken before them, but I'm not a diplomatist. That's just why I went into the hussars; I thought that here I should have no need of such finicky considerations, and he tells me I'm a liar . . . so let him give me satisfaction.'

'That's all very fine, no one imagines that you're a coward; but that's not the point. Ask Denisov if it's not utterly out of the question for an ensign to demand satisfaction of his colonel?'

Denisov was biting his moustache with a morose air, listening to the conversation, evidently with no desire to take part in it. To the captain's question, he replied by a negative shake of the head.

'You speak to the colonel in the presence of other officers of this dirty business,' pursued the staff-captain. 'Bogdanitch' (Bogdanitch was what they called the colonel) 'snubbed you . . .'

'No, he didn't. He said I was telling an untruth.'

'Quite so, and you talked nonsense to him, and you must apologise.'

'Not on any consideration!' shouted Rostov.

'I shouldn't have expected this of you,' said the staff-captain seriously and severely. 'You won't apologise, but, my good sir, it's not only him, but all the regiment, all of us, that you've acted wrongly by; you're to blame all round. Look here; if you'd only thought it over, and taken advice how to deal with the matter, but you must go and blurt it all straight out before the officers. What was the colonel to do then? Is he to bring the officer up for trial and disgrace the whole regiment? On account of one scoundrel is the whole regiment to be put to shame? Is that the thing for him to do, to your thinking? It is not to our thinking. And Bogdanitch did the right thing. He told you that you were telling an untruth. It's unpleasant, but what could he do? you brought it on yourself. And now when they try to smoothe the thing over, you're so high and mighty, you won't apologise, and want to have the whole story out. You're huffy at being put on duty, but what is it for you to apologise to an old and honourable officer! Whatever Bogdanitch may be, any way he's an honourable and gallant old colonel; you're offended at that, but disgracing the regiment's nothing to you.' The staff-captain's voice began to quaver. 'You, sir, have been next to no time in the regiment; you're here today, and tomorrow you'll be passed on somewhere as an adjutant; you don't care a straw for people saying: "There are thieves among the Pavlograd officers!" But we do care! Don't we, Denisov? Do we care?'

Denisov still did not speak or stir; his gleaming black eyes glanced now and then at Rostov.

'Your pride is dear to you, you don't want to apologise,' continued the staff-captain, 'but we old fellows, as we grew up in the regiment and, please God, we hope to die in it, it's the honour of the regiment is dear to us, and Bogdanitch knows that. Ah, isn't it dear to us! But this isn't right; it's not right! You may take offence or not; but I always speak the plain truth. It's not right!'

And the staff-captain got up and turned away from Rostov.

'That's the truth, damn it!' shouted Denisov, jumping up. 'Come, Rostov, come!'

Rostov, turning crimson and white again, looked first at one officer and then at the other.

'No, gentlemen, no . . . you mustn't think . . . I quite understand, you're wrong in thinking that of me . . . I . . . for me . . . for the honour of the regiment I'd . . . but why talk? I'll prove that in action and for me the honour of the flag . . . well, never mind, it's true, I'm to blame!' . . . There were tears in his eyes. 'I'm wrong, wrong all round! Well, what more do you want?' . . .

'Come, that's right, count,' cried the staff-captain, turning round and clapping him on the shoulder with his big hand.

'I tell you,' shouted Denisov, 'he's a capital fellow.'

'That's better, count,' repeated the captain, beginning to address him by his title as though in acknowledgment of his confession. 'Go and apologise, your excellency.'

'Gentlemen, I'll do anything, no one shall hear a word from me,' Rostov protested in an imploring voice, 'but I can't apologise, by God, I can't, say what you will! How can I apologise, like a little boy begging pardon!'

Denisov laughed.

'It'll be the worse for you, if you don't. Bogdanitch doesn't forget things; he'll make you pay for your obstinacy,' said Kirsten.

'By God, it's not obstinacy! I can't describe the feeling it gives me. I can't do it.'

'Well, as you like,' said the staff-captain. 'What has the scoundrel done with himself?' he asked Denisov.

'He has reported himself ill; tomorrow the order's given for him to be struck off,' said Denisov.

'It is an illness, there's no other way of explaining it,' said the staff-captain.

'Whether it's illness or whether it's not, he'd better not cross my path —I'd kill him,' Denisov shouted blood-thirstily.

Zherkov walked into the room.

'How do you come here?' the officers cried to the newcomer at once.

'To the front, gentlemen. Mack has surrendered with his whole army.'

'Nonsense!'

'I've seen him myself.'

'What? Seen Mack alive, with all his arms and legs?'

'To the front! to the front! Give him a bottle for such news. How did you come here?'

'I've been dismissed back to the regiment again on account of that devil, Mack. The Austrian general complained of me. I congratulated him on Mack's arrival. . . . What is it, Rostov, you look as if you'd just come out of a hot bath?'

'We've been in such a mess these last two days, old boy.'

The regimental adjutant came in and confirmed the news brought by Zherkov. They were under orders to advance next day.

'To the front, gentlemen!'

'Well, thank God! we've been sticking here too long.'

VI

KUTUZOV fell back to Vienna, destroying behind him the bridges over the river Inn (in Braunau) and the river Traun (in Linz). On the 23rd of October the Russian troops crossed the river Enns. The Russian baggage-waggons and artillery and the columns of troops were in the middle of that day stretching in a long string across the town of Enns on both sides of the bridge. The day was warm, autumnal, and rainy. The wide view that opened out from the heights where the Russian batteries stood guarding the bridge was at times narrowed by the slanting rain that shut it in like a muslin curtain, then again widened out, and in the bright sunlight objects could be distinctly seen in the distance, looking as if covered with a coat of varnish. The little town could be seen below with its white houses and its red roofs, its cathedral and its bridge, on both sides of which streamed masses of Russian troops, crowded together. At the bend of the Danube could be seen ships and the island and a castle with a park, surrounded by the waters formed by the Enns falling into the Danube, and the precipitous left bank of the Danube, covered with pine forest, with a mysterious distance of green tree-tops and bluish gorges. Beyond the pine forest, that looked wild and untouched by the hand of man, rose the turrets of a nunnery; and in the far distance in front, on the hill on the further side of the Enns, could be seen the scouts of the enemy.

Between the cannons on the height stood the general in command of the rear-guard and an officer of the suite scanning the country through a field-glass. A little behind them, there sat on the trunk of a cannon, Nesvitsky, who had been despatched by the commander-in-chief to the rear-guard. The Cossack who accompanied Nesvitsky had handed him over a knapsack and a flask, and Nesvitsky was regaling the officers with pies and real doppel-kümmel. The officers surrounded him in a delighted circle, some on their knees, some sitting cross-legged, like Turks, on the wet grass.

'Yes, there was some sense in that Austrian prince who built a castle here. It's a magnificent spot. Why aren't you eating, gentlemen?' said Nesvitsky.

'Thank you very much, prince,' answered one of the officers, enjoying the opportunity of talking to a staff-official of such importance. 'It's a lovely spot. We marched right by the park; we saw two deer and such a splendid house!'

'Look, prince,' said another, who would dearly have liked to take another pie, but was ashamed to, and therefore affected to be gazing at the countryside; 'look, our infantry have just got in there. Over there, near the meadow behind the village, three of them are dragging something. They will clean out that palace nicely,' he said, with evident approval.

'No doubt,' said Nesvitsky. 'No; but what I should like,' he added, munching a pie in his moist, handsome mouth, 'would be to slip in there.' He pointed to the turreted nunnery that could be seen on the mountainside. He smiled, his eyes narrowing and gleaming. 'Yes, that would be first-rate, gentlemen!' The officers laughed.

'One might at least scare the nuns a little. There are Italian girls, they say, among them. Upon my word, I'd give five years of my life for it!'

'They must be bored, too,' said an officer who was rather bolder, laughing.

Meanwhile the officer of the suite, who was standing in front, pointed something out to the general; the general looked through the field-glass.

'Yes, so it is, so it is,' said the general angrily, taking the field-glass away from his eye and shrugging his shoulders; 'they are going to fire at them at the crossing of the river. And why do they linger so?'

With the naked eye, looking in that direction, one could discern the enemy and their batteries, from which a milky-white smoke was rising. The smoke was followed by the sound of a shot in the distance, and our troops were unmistakably hurrying to the place of crossing.

Nesvitsky got up puffing and went up to the general, smiling.

'Wouldn't your excellency take some lunch,' he said.

'It's a bad business,' said the general, without answering him; 'our men have been too slow.'

'Shouldn't I ride over, your excellency,' said Nesvitsky.

'Yes, ride over, please,' said the general, repeating an order that had already once before been given in detail; 'and tell the hussars that they are to cross last and to burn the bridge, as I sent orders, and that they're to overhaul the burning materials on the bridge.'

'Very good,' answered Nesvitsky. He called the Cossack with his horse, told him to pick up the knapsack and flask, and lightly swung his heavy person into the saddle.

'Upon my word, I am going to pay a visit to the nuns,' he said to the officers who were watching him, smiling, and he rode along the winding path down the mountain.

'Now then, captain, try how far it'll carry,' said the general, turning to the artillery officer. 'Have a little fun to pass the time.'

'Men, to the guns!' commanded the officer, and in a moment the gunners ran gaily from the camp fires and loaded the big guns.

'One!' they heard the word of command. Number one bounded back nimbly. The cannon boomed with a deafening metallic sound, and whistling over the heads of our men under the mountainside, the grenade flew across, and falling a long way short of the enemy showed by the rising smoke where it had fallen and burst.

The faces of the soldiers and officers lightened up at the sound. Every one got up and busily watched the movements of our troops below, which could be seen as in the hollow of a hand, and the movements of the advancing enemy. At the same instant, the sun came out fully from behind the clouds, and the full note of the solitary shot and the brilliance of the bright sunshine melted into a single inspiring impression of light-hearted gaiety.

VII

OVER the bridge two of the enemy's shots had already flown and there was a crush on the bridge. In the middle of the bridge stood Nesvitsky. He had dismounted and stood with his stout person jammed against the railings. He looked laughingly back at his Cossack, who was standing several paces behind him holding the two horses by their bridles. Every time Nesvitsky tried to move on, the advancing soldiers and waggons bore down upon him and shoved him back against the railings. There was nothing for him to do but to smile.

'Hi! there, my lad,' said the Cossack to a soldier in charge of a waggon-load who was forcing his way through the foot-soldiers that pressed right up to his wheels and his horses; 'what are you about? No, you wait a bit; you see the general wants to pass.'

But the convoy soldier, taking no notice of the allusion to the general, bawled to the soldiers who blocked the way: 'Hi! fellows, keep to the left! wait a bit!' But the fellows, shoulder to shoulder, with their bayonets interlocked, moved over the bridge in one compact mass. Looking down over the rails, Prince Nesvitsky saw the noisy, rapid, but not high waves of the Enns, which, swirling in eddies round the piles of the bridge, chased one another down stream. Looking on the bridge he saw the living waves of the soldiers, all alike as they streamed by: shakoes with covers on them, knapsacks, bayonets, long rifles, and under the shakoes broad-jawed faces, sunken cheeks, and looks of listless weariness, and legs moving over the boards of the bridge, that were coated with sticky mud. Sometimes among the monotonous streams of soldiers, like a crest of white foam on the waves of the Enns, an officer forced his way through, in a cloak, with a face of a different type from the soldiers. Sometimes, like a chip whirling on the river, there passed over the bridge among the waves of infantry a dismounted hussar, an orderly, or an inhabitant of the town. Sometimes, like a log floating down the river, there moved over the bridge, hemmed in on all sides, a baggage-waggon, piled up high and covered with leather covers.

'Why, they're like a river bursting its banks,' said the Cossack, stopping hopelessly. 'Are there many more over there?'

'A million, all but one!' said a cheerful soldier in a torn coat, winking, as he passed out of sight; after him came another soldier, an older man.

'If *he*' (*he* meant the enemy) 'starts popping at the bridge just now,' said the old soldier dismally, addressing his companion, 'you'll forget to scratch yourself.' And he passed on. After him came another soldier riding on a waggon.

'Where the devil did you put the leg-wrappers?' said an orderly, running after the waggon and fumbling in the back part of it. And he too passed on with the waggon.

Then came some hilarious soldiers, who had unmistakably been drinking.

'And didn't he up with the butt end of his gun and give him one right in the teeth,' one soldier was saying gleefully with a wide sweep of his arm.

'It just was a delicious ham,' answered the other with a chuckle. And they passed on, so that Nesvitsky never knew who had received the blow in his teeth, and what the ham had to do with it.

'Yes, they're in a hurry now! When *he* let fly a bit of cold lead, one would have thought they were all being killed,' said an under officer, angrily and reproachfully.

'When it whizzed by me, uncle, the bullet,' said a young soldier with a huge mouth, scarcely able to keep from laughing, 'I turned fairly numb. Upon my soul, wasn't I in a fright, to be sure!' said the soldier, making a sort of boast of his terror.

He, too, passed on. After him came a waggon unlike all that had passed over before. It was a German *Vorspann* with two horses, loaded, it seemed, with the goods of a whole household. The horses were led by a German, and behind was fastened a handsome, brindled cow with an immense udder. On piled-up feather-beds sat a woman with a small baby, an old woman, and a good-looking, rosy-cheeked German girl. They were evidently country people, moving, who had been allowed through by special permit. The eyes of all the soldiers were turned upon the women, and while the waggon moved by, a step at a time, all the soldiers' remarks related to the two women. Every face wore almost the same smile, reflecting indecent ideas about the women.

'Hey, the sausage, he's moving away!'

'Sell us your missis,' said another soldier, addressing the German who strode along with downcast eyes, looking wrathful and alarmed.

'See how she's dressed herself up! Ah, you devils!'

'I say, wouldn't you like to be billeted on them, Fedotov!'

'I know a thing or two, mate!'

'Where are you going?' asked the infantry officer, who was eating an apple. He too was half smiling and staring at the handsome girl. The German, shutting his eyes, signified that he did not understand.

'Take it, if you like,' said the officer, giving the girl an apple. The girl smiled and took it. Nesvitsky, like all the men on the bridge, never took his eyes off the women till they had passed by. When they had passed by, again there moved by the same soldiers, with the same talk, and at last all came to a standstill. As often happens, the horses in a convoy-waggon became unmanageable at the end of the bridge, and the whole crowd had to wait.

'What are they standing still for? There's no order kept!' said the soldiers. 'Where are you shoving?' 'Damn it!' 'Can't you wait a little?' 'It'll be a bad look-out if *he* sets light to the bridge.'

'Look, there's an officer jammed in too,' the soldiers said in different parts of the stationary crowd, as they looked about them and kept pressing forward to the end of the bridge. Looking round at the waters of the Enns under the bridge, Nesvitsky suddenly heard a sound new to him, the sound of something rapidly coming nearer . . . something big, and then a splash in the water.

'Look where it reaches to!' a soldier standing near said sternly, looking round at the sound.

'He's encouraging us to get on quicker,' said another uneasily. The crowd moved again. Nesvitsky grasped that it was a cannon ball.

'Hey, Cossack, give me my horse!' he said. 'Now then, stand aside! stand aside! make way!'

With a mighty effort he succeeded in getting to his horse. Shouting continually, he moved forward. The soldiers pressed together to make way for him, but jammed upon him again, so that they squeezed his leg, and those nearest him were not to blame, for they were pressed forward even more violently from behind.

'Nesvitsky! Nesvitsky! You, old chap!' he heard a husky voice shouting from behind at that instant.

Nesvitsky looked round and saw, fifteen paces away, separated from him by a living mass of moving infantry, the red and black and towzled face of Vaska Denisov with a forage-cap on the back of his head, and a pelisse swung jauntily over his shoulder.

'Tell them to make way, the damned devils!' roared Denisov, who was evidently in a great state of excitement. He rolled his flashing, coal-black eyes, showing the bloodshot whites, and waved a sheathed sword, which he held in a bare hand as red as his face.

'Eh! Vaska!' Nesvitsky reponded joyfully. 'But what are you about?'

'The squadron can't advance!' roared Vaska Denisov, viciously showing his white teeth, and spurring his handsome, raven thoroughbred 'Bedouin,' which, twitching its ears at the bayonets against which it pricked itself, snorting and shooting froth from its bit, tramped with metallic clang on the boards of the bridge, and seemed ready to leap over the railings, if its rider would let it.

'What next! like sheep! for all the world like sheep! back ... make way! ... Stand there! go to the devil with the waggon! I'll cut you down with my sword!' he roared, actually drawing his sword out of the sheath and beginning to brandish it.

The soldiers, with terrified faces, squeezed together, and Denisov joined Nesvitsky.

'How is it you're not drunk today?' said Nesvitsky, when he came up.

'They don't even give us time to drink!' answered Vaska Denisov. 'They've been dragging the regiment to and fro the whole day. Fighting's all very well, but who the devil's to know what this is!'

'How smart you are today!' said Nesvitsky, looking at his new pelisse and fur saddle-cloth.

Denisov smiled, pulled out of his sabretache a handkerchief that diffused a smell of scent, and put it to Nesvitsky's nose.

'To be sure, I'm going into action! I've shaved, and cleaned my teeth and scented myself!'

Nesvitsky's imposing figure, accompanied by his Cossack, and the determination of Denisov, waving his sword and shouting desperately, produced so much effect that they stopped the infantry and got to the other end of the bridge. Nesvitsky found at the entry the colonel, to whom he had to deliver the command, and having executed his commission he rode back.

Having cleared the way for him, Denisov stopped at the entrance of the bridge. Carelessly holding in his horse, who neighed to get to his companions, and stamped with its foot, he looked at the squadron moving towards him. The clang of the hoofs on the boards of the bridge sounded as though several horses were galloping, and the squadron, with the officers in front, drew out four men abreast across the bridge and began emerging on the other side.

The infantry soldiers, who had been forced to stop, crowding in the trampled mud of the bridge, looked at the clean, smart hussars, passing them in good order, with that special feeling of aloofness and irony with which different branches of the service usually meet.

'They're a smart lot! They ought to be on the Podnovinsky!'

'They're a great deal of use! They're only for show!' said another.

'Infantry, don't you kick up a dust!' jested a hussar, whose horse, prancing, sent a spurt of mud on an infantry soldier.

'I should like to see you after two long marches with the knapsack on your shoulder. Your frogs would be a bit shabby,' said the foot-soldier, rubbing the mud off his face with his sleeve; 'perched up there you're more like a bird than a man!'

'Wouldn't you like to be popped on a horse, Zikin; you'd make an elegant rider,' jested a corporal at a thin soldier, bowed down by the weight of his knapsack.

'Put a stick between your legs and you'd have a horse to suit you,' responded the hussar.

VIII

THE rest of the infantry pressed together into a funnel shape at the entrance of the bridge, and hastily marched across it. At last all the baggage-waggons had passed over; the crush was less, and the last battalion were stepping on to the bridge. Only the hussars of Denisov's squadron were left on the further side of the river facing the enemy. The enemy, visible in the distance from the opposite mountain, could not yet be seen from the bridge below, as, from the valley, through which the river flowed, the horizon was bounded by rising ground not more than half a mile away. In front lay a waste plain dotted here and there with handfuls of our scouting Cossacks. Suddenly on the road, where it ran up the rising ground opposite, troops came into sight wearing blue tunics and accompanied by artillery. They were the French. A scouting party of Cossacks trotted away down the hillside. Though the officers and the men of Denisov's squadron tried to talk of other things, and to look in other directions, they all thought continually of nothing else but what was there on the hillside, and kept constantly glancing towards the dark patches they saw coming into sight on the sky-line, and recognised as the enemy's forces. The weather had cleared again after midday, and the sun shone brilliantly as it began to go down over the Danube and the dark mountains that encircle it. The air was still, and from the hillside there floated across from time to time the sound of bugles and of the shouts of the enemy. Between the squadron and the enemy there was no one now but a few scouting parties. An empty plain, about six hundred yards across, separated them from the hostile troops. The enemy had ceased firing, and that made even more keenly felt the stern menace of that inaccessible, unassailable borderland that was the dividing-line between the two hostile armies.

'One step across that line, that suggests the line dividing the living from the dead, and unknown sufferings and death. And what is there? and who is there? there, beyond that field and that tree and the roofs with the sunlight on them? No one knows, and one longs to know and dreads crossing that line, and longs to cross it, and one knows that sooner or later one will have to cross it and find out what there is on the other side of the line, just as one must inevitably find out what is on the other side of death. Yet one is strong and well and cheerful and nervously excited, and surrounded by men as strong in the same irritable excitement.' That is how every man, even if he does not think, feels in the sight of the enemy, and that feeling gives a peculiar brilliance and delightful keenness to one's impressions of all that takes place at such moments.

On the rising ground occupied by the enemy, there rose the smoke of a shot, and a cannon ball flew whizzing over the heads of the squadron of hussars. The officers, who had been standing together, scattered in different directions. The hussars began carefully getting their horses back into line. The whole squadron subsided into silence. All the men were looking at the enemy in front and at the commander of the squadron, expecting an order to be given. Another cannon ball flew by them, and a third. There was no doubt that they were firing at the hussars. But the cannon balls, whizzing regularly and rapidly, flew over the heads of the hussars and struck the ground beyond them. The hussars did not look round, but at each sound of a flying ball, as though at the word of command, the whole squadron, with their faces so alike, through all their dissimilarity, rose in the stirrups, holding their breath, as the ball whizzed by, then sank again. The soldiers did not turn their heads, but glanced out of the corners of their eyes at one another, curious to see the effect on their comrades. Every face from Denisov down to the bugler showed about the lips and chin the same lines of conflict and nervous irritability and excitement. The sergeant frowned, looking the soldiers up and down, as though threatening them with punishment. Ensign Mironov ducked at the passing of each cannon ball. On the left flank, Rostov on his Rook—a handsome beast, in spite of his unsound legs—had the happy air of a schoolboy called up before a large audience for an examination in which he is confident that he will distinguish himself. He looked serenely and brightly at every one, as though calling upon them all to notice how unconcerned he was under fire. But into his face too there crept, against his will, that line about the mouth that betrayed some new and strenuous feeling.

'Who's bobbing up and down there? Ensign Mironov! Not the thing! look at me!' roared Denisov, who could not keep still in one place, but galloped to and fro before the squadron.

The snub-nosed, black, hairy face of Vaska Denisov, and his little, battered figure, and the sinewy, short-fingered hand in which he held the hilt of his naked sword—his whole figure was just as it always was, especially in the evening after he had drunk a couple of bottles. He was only rather redder in the face than usual, and tossing back his shaggy head, as birds do when they drink, his little legs mercilessly driving the spurs into his good horse Bedouin, he galloped to the other flank of the squadron, looking as though he were falling backwards in the saddle, and shouted in a husky voice to the men to look to their pistols. He rode up to Kirsten. The staff-captain on his stout, steady charger rode at a walking pace to meet him. The staff-captain's face with its long whiskers was serious, as always, but his eyes looked brighter than usual.

'Well,' he said to Denisov, 'it won't come to a fight. You'll see, we shall retreat again.'

'Devil knows what they're about!' growled Denisov. 'Ah, Rostov!' he called to the ensign, noticing his beaming face. 'Well, you've not had long to wait.' And he smiled approvingly, unmistakably pleased at the sight of the ensign. Rostov felt perfectly blissful. At that moment the colonel appeared at the bridge. Denisov galloped up to him.

'Your excellency, let us attack! we'll settle them.'

'Attack, indeed!' said the colonel in a bored voice, puckering his face up as though at a teasing fly. 'And what are you stopping here for? You see the flanks are retreating. Lead the squadron back.'

The squadron crossed the bridge and passed out of range of the enemy's guns without losing a single man. It was followed by the second squadron, and the Cossacks last of all crossed, leaving the further side of the river clear.

The two squadrons of the Pavlograd regiment, after crossing the bridge, rode one after the other up the hill. Their colonel, Karl Bogdanitch Schubert, had joined Denisov's squadron, and was riding at a walking pace not far from Rostov, taking no notice of him, though this was the first time they had met since the incident in connection with Telyanin. Rostov, feeling himself at the front in the power of the man towards whom he now admitted that he had been to blame, never took his eyes off the athletic back, and flaxen head and red neck of the colonel. It seemed to Rostov at one time that Bogdanitch was only feigning inattention, and that his whole aim was now to test the ensign's pluck; and he drew himself up and looked about him gaily. Then he fancied that Bogdanitch was riding close by him on purpose to show off his own valour. Then the thought struck him that his enemy was now sending the squadron to a hopeless attack on purpose to punish him, Rostov. Then he dreamed of how after the attack he would go up to him as he lay wounded, and magnanimously hold out his hand in reconciliation. The high-shouldered figure of Zherkov, who was known to the Pavlograd hussars, as he had not long before left their regiment, rode up to the colonel. After Zherkov had been dismissed from the staff of the commander-in-chief, he had not remained in the regiment, saying that he was not such a fool as to go to hard labour at the front when he could get more pay for doing nothing on the staff, and he had succeeded in getting appointed an orderly on the staff of Prince Bagration. He rode up to his old colonel with an order from the commander of the rear guard.

'Colonel,' he said, with his gloomy seriousness, addressing Rostov's enemy, and looking round at his comrades, 'there's an order to go back and burn the bridge.'

'An order, *who to*?' asked the colonel grimly.

'Well, I don't know, colonel, *who to*?' answered the cornet, seriously, 'only the prince commanded me: "Ride and tell the colonel the hussars are to make haste back and burn the bridge."'

Zherkov was followed by an officer of the suite, who rode up to the colonel with the same command. After the officer of the suite the stout figure of Nesvitsky was seen riding up on a Cossack's horse, which had some trouble to gallop with him.

'Why, colonel,' he shouted, while still galloping towards him, 'I told you to burn the bridge, and now some one's got it wrong; they're all frantic over there, there's no making out anything.'

The colonel in a leisurely way stopped the regiment and turned to Nesvitsky.

'You told me about burning materials,' he said; 'but about burning it, you never said a word.'

'Why, my good man,' said Nesvitsky, as he halted, taking off his forage-cap and passing his plump hand over his hair, which was drenched with sweat, 'what need to say the bridge was to be burnt when you put burning materials to it?'

'I'm not your "good man," M. le staff-officer, and you never told me to set fire to the bridge! I know my duty, and it's my habit to carry out my orders strictly. You said the bridge will be burnt, but who was going to burn it I couldn't tell.'

'Well, that's always the way,' said Nesvitsky, with a wave of his arm. 'How do you come here?' he added, addressing Zherkov.

'Why, about the same order. You're sopping though, you want to be rubbed down.'

'You said, M. le staff-officer . . .' pursued the colonel in an aggrieved tone.

'Colonel,' interposed the officer of the suite, 'there is need of haste, or the enemy will have moved up their grape-shot guns.'

The colonel looked dumbly at the officer of the suite, at the stout staff-officer, at Zherkov, and scowled.

'I will burn the bridge,' he said in a solemn tone, as though he would express that in spite of everything they might do to annoy him, he would still do what he ought.

Beating his long muscular legs against his horse, as though he were to blame for it all, the colonel moved forward and commanded the second squadron, the one under Denisov's command, in which Rostov was serving, to turn back to the bridge.

'Yes, it really is so,' thought Rostov, 'he wants to test me!' His heart throbbed and the blood rushed to his face. 'Let him see whether I'm a coward!' he thought.

Again all the light-hearted faces of the men of the squadron wore that grave line, which had come upon them when they were under fire. Rostov looked steadily at his enemy, the colonel, trying to find confirmation of his suppositions on his face. But the colonel never once glanced at Rostov, and looked, as he always did at the front, stern and solemn. The word of command was given.

'Look sharp! look sharp!' several voices repeated around him.

Their swords catching in the reins and their spurs jingling, the hussars dismounted in haste, not knowing themselves what they were to do. The soldiers crossed themselves. Rostov did not look at the colonel now; he had no time. He dreaded, with a sinking heart he dreaded, being left behind by the hussars. His hand trembled as he gave his horse to an orderly, and he felt that the blood was rushing to his heart with a thud. Denisov, rolling backwards, and shouting something, rode by him. Rostov saw nothing but the hussars running around him, clinging spurs and jingling swords.

'Stretchers!' shouted a voice behind him. Rostov did not think of the meaning of the need of stretchers. He ran along, trying only to be ahead of all. But just at the bridge, not looking at his feet, he got into the slippery, trodden mud, and stumbling fell on his hands. The others outstripped him.

'On both sides, captain,' he heard shouted by the colonel, who, riding on ahead, had pulled his horse up near the bridge, with a triumphant and cheerful face.

Rostov, rubbing his muddy hands on his riding-breeches, looked round at his enemy, and would have run on further, imagining that the forwarder he went the better it would be. But though Bogdanitch was not looking, and did not recognise Rostov, he shouted to him.

'Who will go along the middle of the bridge? On the right side? Ensign, back!' he shouted angrily, and he turned to Denisov, who with swaggering bravado rode on horseback on to the planks of the bridge.

'Why run risks, captain? You should dismount,' said the colonel.

'Eh! it'll strike the guilty one,' said Vaska Denisov, turning in his saddle.

Meanwhile Nesvitsky, Zherkov, and the officer of the suite were standing together out of range of the enemy, watching the little group of men in yellow shakoes, dark-green jackets, embroidered with frogs, and blue riding-breeches, swarming about the bridge, and on the other side of the river the blue tunics and the groups with horses, that might so easily be taken for guns, approaching in the distance.

'Will they burn the bridge or not? Who'll get there first? Will they run there and burn it, or the French train their grape-shot on them and kill them?' These were the questions that, with a sinking of the heart, each man was asking himself in the great mass of troops overlooking the bridge. In the brilliant evening sunshine they gazed at the bridge and the hussars, and at the blue tunics, with bayonets and guns, moving up on the other side.

'Ugh! The hussars will be caught,' said Nesvitsky. 'They're not out of range of grape-shot now.'

'He did wrong to take so many men,' said the officer of the suite.

'Yes, indeed,' said Nesvitsky. 'If he'd sent two bold fellows it would have done as well.'

'Ah, your excellency,' put in Zherkov, his eyes fixed on the hussars, though he still spoke with his naïve manner, from which one could not guess whether he were speaking seriously or not. 'Ah, your excellency. How you look at things. Send two men, but who would give us the Vladimir and ribbon then? But as it is, even if they do pepper them, one can represent the squadron and receive the ribbon oneself. Our good friend Bogdanitch knows the way to do things.'

'I say,' said the officer of the suite, 'that's grape-shot.'

He pointed to the French guns, which had been taken out of the gun-carriages, and were hurriedly moving away.

On the French side, smoke rose among the groups that had cannons. One puff, a second and a third almost at the same instant; and at the very moment when they heard the sound of the first shot, there rose the smoke of a fourth; two booms came one after another, then a third.

'Oh, oh!' moaned Nesvitsky, clutching at the hand of the officer of the suite, as though in intense pain. 'Look, a man has fallen, fallen, fallen!'

'Two, I think.'

'If I were Tsar, I'd never go to war,' said Nesvitsky, turning away.

The French cannons were speedily loaded again. The infantry in their blue tunics were running towards the bridge. Again the puffs of smoke rose at different intervals, and the grape-shot rattled and cracked on the bridge. But this time Nesvitsky could not see what was happening at the bridge. A thick cloud of smoke had risen from it. The hussars had succeeded in setting fire to the bridge, and the French batteries were firing at them now, not to hinder them, but because their guns had been brought up and they had some one to fire at.

The French had time to fire three volleys of grape-shot before the hussars got back to their horses. Two were badly aimed, and the shot flew over them, but the last volley fell in the middle of the group of hussars and knocked down three men.

Rostov, absorbed by his relations with Bogdanitch, stepped on the bridge, not knowing what he had to do. There was no one to slash at with his sword (that was how he always pictured a battle to himself), and he could be of no use in burning the bridge, because he had not brought with him any wisps of straw, like the other soldiers. He stood and looked about him, when suddenly there was a rattle on the bridge, like a lot of nuts being scattered, and one of the hussars, the one standing nearest him, fell with a groan on the railing. Rostov ran up to him with the others. Again some one shouted. 'Stretchers!' Four men took hold of the hussar and began lifting him up. 'Oooo! . . . Let me be for Christ's sake!' shrieked the wounded man, but still they lifted him up and laid him on a stretcher. Nikolay Rostov turned away, and began staring into the distance, at the waters of the Danube, at the sky, at the sun, as though he were searching for something. How fair that sky seemed, how blue and calm and deep. How brilliant and triumphant seemed the setting sun. With what an enticing glimmer shone the water of the far-away Danube. And fairer still were the far-away mountains that showed blue beyond the Danube, the nunnery, the mysterious gorges, the pine forests, filled with mist to the tree-tops . . . there all was peace and happiness. . . . 'There is nothing, nothing I could wish for, if only I were there,' thought Rostov. 'In myself alone and in that sunshine there is so much happiness, while here . . . groans, agonies, and this uncertainty, this hurry. . . . Here they are shouting something again and again, all of them are running back somewhere, and I'm running with them, and here is *it, it*, death hanging over me, all round me. . . . One instant, and I shall never see that sunshine, that water, that mountain gorge again. . . .' At that moment the sun went behind the clouds; more stretchers came into view ahead of Rostov. And the terror of death and of the stretchers, and the loss of the sunshine and life, all blended into one sensation of sickening fear.

'Good God, Thou who art in that sky, save and forgive, and protect me,' Rostov whispered to himself.

The hussars ran back to their horses; their voices grew louder and more assured; the stretchers disappeared from sight.

'Well, lad, so you've had a sniff of powder!' Vaska Denisov shouted in his ear.

'It's all over, but I am a coward, yes, I am a coward,' thought Rostov, and with a heavy sigh he took his Rook, who had begun to go lame of one leg, from the man who held him and began mounting.

'What was that—grape-shot?' he asked of Denisov.

'Yes, and something like it too,' cried Denisov; 'they worked their guns in fine style. But it's a nasty business. A cavalry attack's a pleasant thing—slash away at the dogs; but this is for all the devil like aiming at a target.'

And Denisov rode away to a group standing not far from Rostov, consisting of the colonel, Nesvitsky, Zherkov, and the officer of the suite.

'It seems as if no one noticed it, though,' Rostov thought to himself. And indeed no one had noticed it at all, for every one was familiar with the feeling that the ensign, never before under fire, was experiencing for the first time.

'Now you'll have something to talk about,' said Zherkov; 'they'll be promoting me a sub-lieutenant before I know where I am, eh?'

'Inform the prince that I have burnt the bridge,' said the colonel, in a cheerful and triumphant tone.

'And if he inquires with what losses?'

'Not worth mentioning,' boomed the colonel; 'two hussars wounded, and one stark dead on the spot,' he said, with undisguised cheerfulness. The German was unable to repress a smile of satisfaction as he sonorously enunciated the idiomatic Russian colloquialism of the last phrase.

IX

PURSUED by the French army of a hundred thousand men under the command of Bonaparte, received with hostility by the inhabitants, losing confidence in their allies, suffering from shortness of supplies, and forced to act under circumstances unlike anything that had been foreseen, the Russian army of thirty-five thousand men, under the command of Kutuzov, beat a hasty retreat to the lower ground about the Danube. There they halted, and were overtaken by the enemy, and fought a few rear-guard skirmishes, avoiding an engagement, except in so far as it was necessary to secure a retreat without the loss of their baggage and guns. There were actions at Lambach, at Amsteten, and at Melk; but in spite of the courage and stubbornness—acknowledged even by the enemy—with which the Russians fought, the only consequence of these engagements was a still more rapid retreat. The Austrian troops that had escaped being taken at Ulm, and had joined Kutuzov's forces at Braunau, now parted from the Russian army, and Kutuzov was left unsupported with his weak and exhausted forces. The defence of Vienna could no longer be dreamed of. Instead of the elaborately planned campaign of attack, in accordance with the principles of the modern science of strategy, the plan of which had been communicated to Kutuzov during his sojourn in Vienna by the Austrian Hofkriegsrath, the sole aim—almost a hopeless one—that remained now for Kutuzov was to avoid losing his army, like Mack at Ulm, and to effect a junction with the fresh troops marching from Russia.

On the 28th of October, Kutuzov took his army across to the left bank of the Danube, and then for the first time halted, leaving the Danube between his army and the greater part of the enemy's forces. On the 30th he attacked Mortier's division, which was on the left bank of the Danube, and defeated it. In this action for the first time trophies were taken—a flag, cannons, and two of the enemy's generals. For the first time, after retreating for a fortnight, the Russian troops had halted, and after fighting had not merely kept the field of battle, but had driven the French off it. Although the troops were without clothing and exhausted, and had lost a third of their strength in wounded, killed, and missing; although they had left their sick and wounded behind on the other side of the Danube, with a letter from Kutuzov commending them to the humanity of the enemy; although the great hospitals and houses in Krems could not contain all the sick and wounded,—in spite of all that, the halt before Krems and the victory over Mortier had greatly raised the spirits of the troops. Throughout the whole army, and also at headquarters, there were the most cheerful but groundless rumours of the near approach of the columns from Russia, of some victory gained by the Austrians, and of the retreat of Bonaparte panic-stricken.

Prince Andrey had been during the engagement in attendance on the Austrian general Schmidt, who was killed in the battle. His horse had been wounded under him, and he had himself received a slight wound on his arm from a bullet. As a mark of special favour on the part of the commander-in-chief, he was sent with the news of this victory to the Austrian court, now at Brünn, as Vienna was threatened by the French. On the night of the battle, excited, but not weary (though Prince Andrey did not look robustly built, he could bear fatigue better than very strong men), he had ridden with a despatch from Dohturov to Krems to Kutuzov. The same night he had been sent on with a special despatch to Brünn. This commission, apart from its reward, meant an important step in promotion.

The night was dark and starlit; the road looked black in the white snow that had fallen on the day of the battle. With his mind filled with impressions of the battle, joyful anticipations of the effect that would be produced by the news of the victory, and recollections of the farewells of the commander-in-chief and his comrades, Prince Andrey trotted along in a light posting cart, with the sensations of a man who, after long waiting, has at last attained the first instalment of some coveted happiness. As soon as he closed his eyes, the firing of guns and cannons was echoing in his ears, and that sound blended with the rattle of the wheels and the sensation of victory. At one moment he would begin to dream that the Russians were flying, that he was himself slain; but he waked up in haste, and with fresh happiness realised anew that that was all unreal, and that it was the French, on the contrary, who were put to flight. He recalled again all the details of the victory, his own calm manliness during the battle, and, reassured, he began to doze. . . . The dark, starlit night was followed by a bright and sunny morning. The snow was thawing in the sun, the horses galloped quickly, and new and different-looking forests, fields, and trees flew by on both sides of the road alike.

At one of the stations he overtook a convoy of Russian wounded. The Russian officer in charge of the transport lay lolling back in the foremost cart, and was shouting coarse abuse at a soldier. In each of the long German *Vorspanns* six or more pale, bandaged, and dirty wounded men were being jolted over the stony roads. Some of them were talking (he caught the sound of Russian words), others were eating bread; the most severely wounded gazed dumbly at the posting cart trotting by, with the languid interest of sick children.

Prince Andrey told the driver to stop, and asked a soldier in what battle they had been wounded.

'The day before yesterday on the Danube,' answered the soldier. Prince Andrey took out his purse and gave the soldier three gold pieces.

'For all,' he added, addressing the officer as he came up. 'Get well, lads,' he said to the soldiers, 'there's a lot to do yet.'

'What news?' asked the officer, evidently anxious to get into conversation.

'Good news! Forward!' he called to the driver, and galloped on.

It was quite dark when Prince Andrey rode into Brünn, and saw himself surrounded by high houses, lighted shops, the lighted windows of houses, and street lamps, handsome carriages noisily rolling over the pavement, and all that atmosphere of a great town full of life, which is so attractive to a soldier after camp. In spite of the rapid drive and sleepless night, Prince Andrey felt even more alert, as he drove up to the palace, than he had on the previous evening. Only his eyes glittered with a feverish brilliance, and his ideas followed one another with extreme rapidity and clearness. He vividly pictured again all the details of the battle, not in confusion, but definitely, in condensed shape, as he meant to present them to the Emperor Francis. He vividly imagined the casual questions that might be put to him, and the answers he would make to them. He imagined that he would be at once presented to the Emperor. But at the chief entrance of the palace an official ran out to meet him, and learning that he was a special messenger, led him to another entrance.

'Turning to the right out of the corridor, *Euer Hochgeboren*, you will find the adjutant on duty,' the official said to him. 'He will conduct you to the minister of war.'

The adjutant on duty, meeting Prince Andrey, asked him to wait, and went in to the war minister. Five minutes later the adjutant returned, and with marked courtesy, bowing and ushering Prince Andrey before him, he led him across the corridor to the private room of the war minister. The adjutant, by his elaborately formal courtesy, seemed to wish to guard himself from any attempt at familiarity on the part of the Russian adjutant. The joyous feeling of Prince Andrey was considerably damped as he approached the door of the minister's room. He felt slighted, and the feeling of being slighted passed instantaneously—without his being aware of it himself—into a feeling of disdain, which was quite uncalled for. His subtle brain at the same instant supplied him with the point of view from which he had the right to feel disdain both of the adjutant and the minister of war. 'No doubt it seems to them a very simple matter to win victories, never having smelt powder!' he thought. His eyelids drooped disdainfully; he walked with peculiar deliberateness into the war minister's room. This feeling was intensified when he saw the minister of war sitting at a big table, and for the first two minutes taking no notice of his entrance. The minister of war had his bald head, with grey curls on the temples, held low between two wax candles; he was reading some papers, and marking them with a pencil. He went on reading to the end, without raising his eyes at the opening of the door and the sound of footsteps.

'Take this and give it him,' said the minister of war to his adjutant, handing him the papers, and taking no notice of the Russian attaché.

Prince Andrey felt that either the minister of war took less interest in the doings of Kutuzov's army than in any other subject demanding his attention, or that he wanted to make the Russian attaché feel this. 'But that's a matter of complete indifference to me,' thought he. The minister of war put the other remaining papers together, making their edges level, and lifted his head. He had an intellectual and characteristic head. But the instant he turned to Prince Andrey, the shrewd and determined expression of the war minister's face changed in a manner evidently conscious and habitual. On his face was left the stupid smile —hypocritical, and not disguising its hypocrisy—of a man who receives many petitioners, one after another.

'From General—Field Marshal Kutuzov?' he queried. 'Good news, I hope? Has there been an engagement with Mortier? A victory? It was high time!'

He took the despatch, which was addressed to him, and began to read it with a mournful expression.

'Ah! My God! my God! Schmidt!' he said in German. 'What a calamity! what a calamity!' Skimming through the despatch, he laid it on the table and glanced at Prince Andrey, visibly meditating on something.

'Ah, what a calamity! So the action, you say, was a decisive one?' ('Mortier was not taken, however,' he reflected.) 'Very glad you have brought good news, though the death of Schmidt is a costly price for the victory. His majesty will certainly wish to see you, but not today. I thank you; you must need repose. Tomorrow, be at the levée after the review. But I will let you know.'

The stupid smile, which had disappeared while he was talking, reappeared on the war minister's face.

'*Au revoir*, I thank you indeed. His majesty the Emperor will most likely wish to see you,' he repeated, and he bowed his head.

As Prince Andrey left the palace, he felt that all the interest and happiness that had been given him by his victory had been left behind by him now in the indifferent hands of the minister and the formal adjutant. The whole tenor of his thoughts had instantaneously changed. The battle figured in his mind as a remote, far-away memory.

X

PRINCE ANDREY stayed at Brünn with a Russian of his acquaintance in the diplomatic service, Bilibin.

'Ah, my dear prince, there's no one I could have been more pleased to see,' said Bilibin, coming to meet Prince Andrey. 'Franz, take the prince's things to my bedroom,' he said to the servant, who was ushering Bolkonsky in. 'What, a messenger of victory? That's capital. I'm kept indoors ill, as you see.'

After washing and dressing, Prince Andrey came into the diplomat's luxurious study and sat down to the dinner prepared for him. Bilibin was sitting quietly at the fireplace.

Not his journey only, but all the time he had spent with the army on the march, deprived of all the conveniences of cleanliness and the elegancies of life, made Prince Andrey feel now an agreeable sense of repose among the luxurious surroundings to which he had been accustomed from childhood. Moreover, after his Austrian reception, he was glad to speak—if not in Russian, for they talked French—at least to a Russian, who would, he imagined, share the general Russian dislike (which he felt particularly keenly just then) for the Austrians.

Bilibin was a man of five-and-thirty, a bachelor, of the same circle as Prince Andrey. They had been acquainted in Petersburg, but had become more intimate during Prince Andrey's last stay at Vienna with Kutuzov. Just as Prince Andrey was a young man, who promised to rise high in a military career, Bilibin promised to do even better in diplomacy. He was still a young man, but not a young diplomat, as he had been in the service since he was sixteen. He had been in Paris and in Copenhagen; and now in Vienna he filled a post of considerable importance. Both the foreign minister and our ambassador at Vienna knew him and valued him. He was not one of that great multitude of diplomats whose qualification is limited to the possession of negative qualities, who need simply avoid doing certain things and speak French in order to be very good diplomats. He was one of those diplomats who like work and understand it, and in spite of his natural indolence, he often spent nights at his writing-table. He worked equally well whatever the object of his work might be. He was interested not in the question 'Why?' but in the question 'How?' What constituted his diplomatic work, he did not mind, but to draw up a circular, a memorandum, or a report subtly, pointedly, and elegantly, was a task which gave him great pleasure. Apart from such labours, Bilibin's merits were esteemed the more from his ease in moving and talking in the higher spheres.

Bilibin enjoyed conversation just as he enjoyed work, only when the conversation could be elegantly witty. In society he was continually watching for an opportunity of saying something striking, and did not enter into conversation except under such circumstances. Bilibin's conversation was continually sprinkled with original, epigrammatic, polished phrases of general interest. These phrases were fashioned in the inner laboratory of Bilibin's mind, as though intentionally, of portable form, so that insignificant persons could easily remember them and carry them from drawing-room to drawing-room. And Bilibin's good things were hawked about in Viennese drawing-rooms and afterwards had an influence on so-called great events.

His thin, lean, yellow face was all covered with deep creases, which always looked as clean and carefully washed as the tips of one's fingers after a bath. The movement of these wrinkles made up the chief play of expression of his countenance. At one moment his forehead wrinkled up in broad furrows, and his eyebrows were lifted, at another moment his eyebrows drooped again and deep lines creased his cheeks. His deep-set, small eyes looked out frankly and good-humouredly.

'Come, now, tell us about your victories,' he said. Bolkonsky in the most modest fashion, without once mentioning himself in connection with it, described the engagement, and afterwards his reception by the war minister.

'They received me and my news like a dog in a game of skittles,' he concluded.

Bilibin grinned, and the creases in his face disappeared.

'All the same, my dear fellow,' he said, gazing from a distance at his finger-nails, and wrinkling up the skin over his left eye, 'notwithstanding my high esteem for the holy Russian armament, I own that your victory is not so remarkably victorious.'

He went on talking in French, only uttering in Russian those words to which he wished to give a contemptuous intonation.

'Why? with the whole mass of your army you fell upon the unlucky Mortier with one division, and Mortier slipped through your fingers? Where's the victory?'

'Seriously speaking, though,' answered Prince Andrey, 'we can at least say without boasting that it's rather better than Ulm . . .'

'Why didn't you capture us one, at least, one marshal?'

'Because everything isn't done as one expects it will be, and things are not as regular as on parade. We had expected, as I told you, to attack the enemy in the rear at seven o'clock in the morning, but we did not arrive at it until five o'clock in the evening.'

'But why didn't you do it at seven in the morning? You ought to have done it at seven in the morning,' said Bilibin, smiling; 'you ought to have done it at seven in the morning.'

'Why didn't you succeed in impressing on Bonaparte by diplomatic methods that he had better leave Genoa alone?' said Prince Andrey in the same tone.

'I know,' broke in Bilibin, 'you are thinking that it's very easy to capture marshals, sitting on the sofa by one's fireside. That's true, but still why didn't you capture him? And you needn't feel surprised if the most august Emperor and King Francis, like the war minister, is not very jubilant over your victory. Why, even I, a poor secretary of the Russian Embassy, feel no necessity to testify my rejoicing by giving my Franz a thaler and sending him out for a holiday to disport himself with his Liebchen on the Prater . . . though it's true there is no Prater here . . .' He looked straight at Prince Andrey and suddenly let the creases drop out of his puckered forehead.

'Now it's my turn to ask you "why," my dear boy,' said Bolkonsky. 'I must own that I don't understand it; perhaps there are diplomatic subtleties in it that are beyond my feeble intellect; but I can't make it out. Mack loses a whole army, Archduke Ferdinand and Archduke Karl give no sign of life and make one blunder after another; Kutuzov alone gains at last a decisive victory, breaks the prestige of invincibility of the French, and the minister of war does not even care to learn the details!'

'For that very reason, my dear boy, don't you see! Hurrah for the Tsar, for Russia, for the faith! That's all very nice; but what have we, I mean the Austrian court, to do with your victories? You bring us good news of a victory of Archduke Karl or Ferdinand—one archduke's as good as the other, as you know—if it's only a victory over a fire brigade of Bonaparte, and it will be another matter, it will set the cannons booming. But this can only tantalize us, as if it were done on purpose. Archduke Karl does nothing, Archduke Ferdinand covers himself with disgrace, you abandon Vienna, give up its defence, as though you would say to us, God is with us, and the devil take you and your capital. One general, whom we all loved, Schmidt, you put in the way of a bullet, and then congratulate us on your victory! . . . You must admit that anything more exasperating than the news you have brought could not be conceived. It's as though it were done on purpose, done on purpose. But apart from that, if you were to gain a really brilliant victory, if Archduke Karl even were to win a victory, what effect could it have on the general course of events? It's too late now, when Vienna is occupied by the French forces.'

'Occupied? Vienna occupied?'

'Not only is Vienna occupied, but Bonaparte is at Schönbrunn, and the count—our dear Count Urbna—is setting off to receive his orders.'

After the fatigues and impressions of his journey and his reception, and even more after the dinner he had just eaten, Bolkonsky felt that he could not take in all the significance of the words he had just heard.

'Count Lichtenfels was here this morning,' pursued Bilibin, 'and he showed me a letter containing a full description of the parade of the French at Vienna. Prince Murat and all the rest of it . . . You see that your victory is not a great matter for rejoicing, and that you can't be received as our deliverer . . .'

'Really, I don't care about that, I don't care in the slightest!' said Prince Andrey, beginning to understand that his news of the battle before Krems was really of little importance in view of such an event as the taking of the capital of Austria. 'How was Vienna taken? And its bridge and its famous fortifications, and Prince Auersperg? We heard rumours that Prince Auersperg was defending Vienna,' said he.

'Prince Auersperg is stationed on this side—our side—and is defending us; defending us very ineffectually, I imagine, but any way he is defending us. But Vienna's on the other side of the river. No, the bridge has not been taken, and I hope it won't be taken, because it is mined and orders have been given to blow it up. If it were not so, we should have long ago been in the mountains of Bohemia, and you and your army would have spent a bad quarter of an hour between two fires.'

'But still that doesn't mean that the campaign is over,' said Prince Andrey.

'But I believe that it is over. And so do all the big-wigs here, though they don't dare to say so. It will be as I said at the beginning of the campaign, that the matter will not be settled by your firing before Dürenstein, not by gunpowder, but by those who invented it,' said Bilibin, repeating one of his *mots*, letting the creases run out of his forehead and pausing. 'The only question is what the meeting of the Emperor Alexander and the Prussian king may bring forth. If Prussia enters the alliance, they will force Austria's hand and there will be war. If not, the only point will be to arrange where to draw up the articles of the new Campo Formio.'

'But what an extraordinary genius!' cried Prince Andrey suddenly, clenching his small hand and bringing it down on the table. 'And what luck the man has!'

'Buonaparte?' said Bilibin interrogatively, puckering up his forehead and so intimating that a *mot* was coming. 'Buonaparte?' he said, with special stress on the *u*. 'I think, though, that now when he is dictating laws to Austria from Schönbrunn, we must let him off the *u*. I shall certainly adopt the innovation, and call him simply Bonaparte.'

'No, joking apart,' said Prince Andrey, 'do you really believe the campaign is over?'

'I'll tell you what I think. Austria has been made a fool of, and she is not used to that. And she'll avenge it. And she has been made a fool of, because in the first place her provinces have been pillaged (they say the Holy Russian armament is plundering them cruelly), her army has been destroyed, her capital has been taken, and all this for the sweet sake of his Sardinian Majesty. And so between ourselves, my dear boy, my instinct tells me we are being deceived; my instinct tells me of negotiations with France and projects of peace, a secret peace, concluded separately.'

'Impossible!' said Prince Andrey. 'That would be too base.'

'Time will show,' said Bilibin, letting the creases run off his forehead again in token of being done with the subject.

When Prince Andrey went to the room that had been prepared for him, and lay down in the clean linen on the feather bed and warmed and fragrant pillows, he felt as though the battle of which he brought tidings was far, far away from him. The Prussian alliance, the treachery of Austria, the new triumph of Bonaparte, the levée and parade and the audience of Emperor Francis next day, engrossed his attention. He closed his eyes and instantly his ears were ringing with the cannonade, the firing of muskets, and the creaking of wheels, and again he saw the long line of musketeers running down-hill and the French firing, and he felt his heart beating and saw himself galloping in front of the lines with Schmidt, and the bullets whizzing merrily around him, and he knew that sense of intensified joy in living that he had not experienced since childhood. He waked up.

'Yes, that all happened!' . . . he said, with a happy, childlike smile to himself. And he fell into the deep sleep of youth.

XI

NEXT day he waked up late. Going over the impressions of the past, what he recalled most vividly was that he was to be presented to the Emperor Francis; he remembered the minister of war, the ceremonious adjutant, Bilibin, and the conversation of the previous evening. He dressed for his attendance at court in full court-dress, which he had not worn for a long time, and fresh, eager, and handsome, he walked into Bilibin's room with his arm in a sling. Four gentlemen of the diplomatic corps were already there. With Prince Ippolit Kuragin, who was a secretary to the embassy, Bolkonsky was already acquainted; Bilibin introduced him to the others.

The gentlemen calling on Bilibin were a set of fashionable, wealthy, and lively young men, who here, as at Vienna, made up a circle apart, a circle which Bilibin, its leader, spoke of as *les nôtres*. This circle, consisting almost exclusively of diplomatists, evidently had its own interests—quite apart from the war and politics—interests, that revolved round the fashionable world, relations with certain women and the formal side of the service. They gave Prince Andrey an unmistakably cordial reception, as one of themselves (a distinction they allowed to few). From civility and to break the ice they asked him a few questions about the army and the battle, and the conversation slipped back again to disconnected, good-humoured jests and gossip.

'But what was so particularly nice,' said one, relating a disaster that had befallen a colleague, 'was that the minister told him in so many words that his appointment to London was a promotion and that that was how he ought to regard it. Can you fancy his figure at the moment?' . . .

'But the worst of all is to come, gentlemen. I'm going to betray Kuragin—here is this Don Juan going to profit by his misfortune; he's a shocking fellow!'

Prince Ippolit lounged in a reclining chair, with his legs over the arm. He laughed.

'Tell me about that,' said he.

'O Don Juan! O serpent!' cried the voices.

'You're not aware, I dare say, Bolkonsky,' said Bilibin, turning to Prince Andrey, 'that all the atrocities of the French army (I was almost saying of the Russian) are nothing in comparison with the exploits of this fellow among the ladies.'

'Woman . . . is the companion of man,' Prince Ippolit enunciated, and he stared through his eyeglass at his elevated legs.

Bilibin and *les nôtres* roared, looking Ippolit straight in the face. Prince Andrey saw that this Ippolit, of whom—he could not disguise it from himself—he had been almost jealous on his wife's account, was the butt of this set.

'No, I must entertain you with a specimen of Kuragin,' said Bilibin aside to Bolkonsky. 'He's exquisite, when he airs his views upon politics; you must see his gravity.'

He sat down by Ippolit, and, wrinkling up his forehead, began talking to him about politics. Prince Andrey and the others stood round the two.

'The Berlin cabinet cannot express a feeling of alliance,' Ippolit began, looking consequentially round at all of them, 'without expressing . . . as in its last note . . . you understand . . . you understand . . . and besides, if his Majesty the Emperor does not give up the principle of our alliance.'

'Wait, I have not finished,' he said to Prince Andrey, taking him by the arm. 'I suppose that intervention will be stronger than non-intervention. And . . .' He paused. 'Our dispatch of the 28th of November cannot be reckoned as an exception. That is how it will all end.' And he dropped Bolkonsky's arm as a sign that he had now quite concluded.

'Demosthenes, I recognise you by the pebble that you hide in your golden mouth,' said Bilibin, whose thick thatch of hair moved forward on his head from the puckering of his brows with delight.

Every one laughed. Ippolit laughed louder than any. He was visibly distressed; he breathed painfully, but he could not help breaking into a savage laugh, that convulsed his usually impassive face.

'Well now, gentlemen,' said Bilibin, 'Bolkonsky is my guest here in Brünn and I want to show him, as far as I can, all the attractions of our life here. If we were in Vienna, it would be easy enough; but here, in this vile Moravian hole it is more difficult, and I beg you all for assistance. We must do him the honour of Brünn. You undertake the theatre and I will undertake society; you, Ippolit, of course, the ladies.'

'We ought to let him see Amélie; she's exquisite!' said one of *les nôtres*, kissing his finger-tips.

'Altogether,' said Bilibin, 'we must turn this bloodthirsty man to more humane interests.'

'I fear I can hardly take advantage of your hospitality, gentlemen; it's time I was off even now,' said Bolkonsky, glancing at his watch.

'Where to?'

'To the Emperor!'

'Oh! oh! oh!'

'Well, *au revoir*, Bolkonsky! *Au revoir*, prince! Come early to dinner,' said voices. 'We reckon upon you.'

'Try to make the most of the good discipline of the troops, in the provisioning of supplies and on the lines of march, when you talk to the Emperor,' said Bilibin, accompanying Bolkonsky to the hall.

'I should like to speak well of it, but as far as my observation goes, I can't,' answered Bolkonsky, smiling.

'Well, talk as much as you can, any way. Audiences are his passion, but he doesn't like talking himself, and can't talk either, as you will see.'

XII

AT the levée the Emperor Francis only looked intently into Prince Andrey's face, and nodded his long head to him as he stood in the place assigned him among the Austrian officers. But after the levée the adjutant of the previous evening ceremoniously communicated to Bolkonsky the Emperor's desire to give him an audience. The Emperor Francis received him, standing in the middle of the room. Prince Andrey was struck by the fact that before beginning the conversation, the Emperor seemed embarrassed, didn't know what to say, and reddened.

'Tell me when the battle began,' he asked hurriedly. Prince Andrey answered. The question was followed by others, as simple: 'Was Kutuzov well?' 'How long was it since he left Krems?' and so on. The Emperor spoke as though his sole aim was to put a certain number of questions. The answers to these questions, as was only too evident, could have no interest for him.

'At what o'clock did the battle begin?' asked the Emperor.

'I cannot inform your majesty at what o'clock the battle began in the front lines, but at Dürenstein, where I was, the troops began the attack about six in the evening,' said Bolkonsky, growing more eager, and conceiving that now there was a chance for him to give an accurate description, just as he had it ready in his head, of all he knew and had seen. But the Emperor smiled and interrupted him:

'How many miles?'

'From where to where, your majesty?'

'From Dürenstein to Krems?'

'Three and a half miles, your majesty.'

'The French abandoned the left bank?'

'As our scouts reported, the last crossed the river on rafts in the night.'

'Have you enough provisions at Krems?'

'Provisions have not been furnished to the amount . . .'

The Emperor interrupted him:

'At what o'clock was General Schmidt killed?'

'At seven o'clock, I think.'

'At seven o'clock? Very sad! very sad!'

The Emperor said that he thanked him, and bowed. Prince Andrey withdrew, and was at once surrounded by courtiers on all sides. Everywhere he saw friendly eyes gazing at him, and heard friendly voices addressing him. The adjutant of the preceding evening reproached him for not having stopped at the palace, and offered him his own house. The minister of war came up and congratulated him on the Order of Maria Theresa of the third grade, with which the Emperor was presenting him. The Empress's chamberlain invited him to her majesty. The archduchess, too, wished to see him. He did not know whom to answer, and for a few seconds he was trying to collect his ideas. The Russian ambassador took him by the shoulder, led him away to a window, and began to talk to him.

Contrary to Bilibin's prognostications, the news he brought was received with rejoicing. A thanksgiving service was arranged. Kutuzov was decorated with the great cross of Maria Theresa, and rewards were bestowed on the whole army. Bolkonsky received invitations on all hands, and had to spend the whole morning paying visits to the principal personages in the Austrian Government. After paying his visits, Prince Andrey, at five o'clock in the evening, was returning homewards to Bilibin's, mentally composing a letter to his father about the battle and his reception at Brünn. At the steps of Bilibin's house stood a cart packed half full of things, and Franz, Bilibin's servant, came out of the doorway, with difficulty dragging a travelling-trunk.

Before going back to Bilibin's, Prince Andrey had driven to a bookseller's to lay in a stock of books for the campaign, and had spent some time in the shop.

'What is it?' asked Bolkonsky.

'Ah, your excellency!' said Franz, with some exertion rolling the trunk on the cart. 'We are to move on still farther. The scoundrel is already at our heels again!'

'Eh? what?' queried Prince Andrey.

Bilibin came out to meet Bolkonsky. His ordinarily composed face looked excited.

'No, no, confess that this is charming,' he said, 'this story of the bridge of Tabor. They have crossed it without striking a blow.'

Prince Andrey could not understand.

'Why, where do you come from not to know what every coachman in the town knows by now?'

'I come from the archduchess. I heard nothing there.'

'And didn't you see that people are packing up everywhere?'

'I have seen nothing . . . But what's the matter?' Prince Andrey asked impatiently.

'What's the matter? The matter is that the French have crossed the bridge that Auersperg was defending, and they haven't blown up the bridge, so that Murat is at this moment running along the road to Brunn, and today or tomorrow they'll be here.'

'Here? But how is it the bridge wasn't blown up, since it was mined?'

'Why, that's what I ask you. No one—not Bonaparte himself—can tell why.' Bolkonsky shrugged his shoulders.

'But if they have crossed the bridge, then it will be all over with the army; it will be cut off,' he said.

'That's the whole point,' answered Bilibin. 'Listen. The French enter Vienna, as I told you. Everything is satisfactory. Next day, that is yesterday, *Messieurs les Maréchaux*, Murat, Lannes, and Beliard get on their horses and ride off to the bridge. (Remark that all three are Gascons.) "Gentlemen," says one, "you know that the Tabor bridge has been mined and countermined, and is protected by a formidable fortification and fifteen thousand troops, who have orders to blow up the bridge and not to let us pass. But our gracious Emperor Napoleon will be pleased if we take the bridge. Let us go us three and take it." "Yes, let us go," say the others; and they start off and take the bridge, cross it, and now with their whole army on this side of the Danube, they are coming straight upon us, and upon you and your communications.'

'Leave off jesting,' said Prince Andrey, with mournful seriousness. The news grieved Prince Andrey, and yet it gave him pleasure. As soon as he heard that the Russian army was in such a hopeless position, the idea struck him that he was the very man destined to extricate the Russian army from that position, and that it had come—the Toulon—that would lift him for ever from out of the ranks of unknown officers, and open the first path to glory for him! As he listened to Bilibin, he was already considering how, on reaching the army, he would, at a council of war, give the opinion that alone could save the army, and how he would be entrusted alone to execute the plan.

'Leave off joking,' he said.

'I'm not joking,' Bilibin went on. 'Nothing could be more truthful or more melancholy. These three gentlemen advance to the bridge alone and wave white handkerchiefs; they declare that it's a truce, and that they, the marshals, are come for a parley with Prince Auersperg. The officer on duty lets them into the *tête du pont*. They tell him a thousand Gascon absurdities; say that the war is over, that Emperor Francis has arranged a meeting with Bonaparte, that they desire to see Prince Auersperg, and so on. The officer sends for Auersperg. These Gascon gentlemen embrace the officers, make jokes, and sit about on the cannons, while a French battalion meantime advances unnoticed on the bridge, flings the sacks of inflammable material into the river, and marches up to the *tête du pont*. Finally the lieutenant-general himself appears, our dear Prince Auersperg von Mautern. "My dear enemy! Flower of Austrian chivalry! hero of the Turkish war! Hostility is at end, we can take each other's hands . . . the Emperor Napoleon burns with impatience to make the acquaintance of Prince Auersperg." In a word, these gentlemen—not Gascons for nothings—so bewilder Auersperg with fair words—he is so flattered at this speedy intimacy with French marshals, so dazzled by the spectacle of their cloaks, and of the ostrich feathers of Murat—that their fire gets into his eyes and makes him forget that he ought to be firing on the enemy' (in spite of the interest of his story, Bilibin did not omit to pause after this *mot*, to give time for its appreciation). 'A French battalion runs into the *tête du pont*, spikes the cannons, and the bridge is taken. No, but really the best part of the whole episode,' he went on, his excitement subsiding under the interest of his own story, 'is that the sergeant in charge of the cannon which was to give the signal for firing the mines and blowing up the bridge, this sergeant seeing the French troops running on to the bridge wanted to fire, but Lannes pulled his arm away. The sergeant, who seems to have been sharper than his general, goes up to Auersperg and says: "Prince, they're deceiving you, here are the French!" Murat sees the game is up if he lets the sergeant have his say. With an affectation of surprise (a true Gascon!) he addresses Auersperg: "Is this the Austrian discipline so highly extolled all over the world," says he, "do you let a man of low rank speak to you like this?" It was a stroke of genius. The Prince of Auersperg is touched in his honour and has the sergeant put under arrest. No, but confess that all this story of the bridge of Tabor is charming. It is neither stupidity, nor cowardice . . .'

'It is treason, perhaps,' said Prince Andrey, vividly picturing to himself grey overcoats, wounds, the smoke and sound of firing, and the glory awaiting him.

'Not that either. This puts the court into a pretty pickle,' pursued Bilibin. 'It is not treason, nor cowardice, nor stupidity; it is just as it was at Ulm . . .' He seemed to ponder, seeking the phrase, 'it is . . . *c'est du Mack. Nous sommes mackés*,' he said, feeling he was uttering *un mot*, and a fresh one, one that would be repeated. His creased-up brows let the puckers smoothe out quickly in sign of satisfaction, and with a faint smile he fell to scrutinizing his finger-nails.

'Where are you off to?' he said, suddenly turning to Prince Andrey, who had got up and was going to his room.

'I must start.'

'Where to?'

'To the army.'

'But you meant to stay another two days?'

'But now I am going at once'; and Prince Andrey, after a few words arranging about his journey, went to his room.

'Do you know, my dear boy,' said Bilibin, coming into his room, 'I have been thinking about you. What are you going for?' And in support of the irrefutability of his arguments on the subject, all the creases ran off his face.

Prince Andrey looked inquiringly at him and made no reply.

'Why are you going? I know you consider that it's your duty to gallop off to the army now that the army is in danger. I understand that, my boy, it's heroism.'

'Nothing of the kind,' said Prince Andrey.

'But you are *un philosophe*, be one fully, look at things from the other side, and you will see that it is your duty, on the contrary, to take care of yourself. Leave that to others who are no good for anything else ... You have received no orders to go back, and you are not dismissed from here, so that you can remain and go with us, where our ill luck takes us. They say they are going to Olmütz. And Olmutz is a very charming town. And we can travel there comfortably together in my carriage.'

'That's enough joking, Bilibin,' said Bolkonsky.

'I am speaking to you sincerely as a friend. Consider where are you going and with what object now, when you can stay here. You have two alternatives before you' (he puckered up the skin of his left temple) 'either you won't reach the army before peace will be concluded, or you will share the defeat and disgrace with Kutuzov's whole army.' And Bilibin let his brow go smooth again, feeling that his dilemma was beyond attack.

'That I can't enter into,' said Prince Andrey coldly, but he thought: 'I am going to save the army.'

'My dear fellow, you are a hero,' said Bilibin.

XIII

THE same night, after taking leave of the minister of war, Bolkonsky set off to join the army, not knowing where he should find it, at the risk of being caught by the French on the way to Krems.

At Brünn all the court and every one connected with it was packing up, and the heavy baggage was already being despatched to Olmütz. Near Esselsdorf, Prince Andrey came out on the road along which the Russian army was moving in the utmost haste and in the greatest disorder. The road was so obstructed with baggage-waggons that it was impossible to get by in a carriage. Prince Andrey procured a horse and a Cossack from the officer in command of the Cossacks, and hungry and weary he threaded his way in and out between the waggons and rode in search of the commander-in-chief and his own luggage. The most sinister rumours as to the position of the army reached him on the road, and the appearance of the army fleeing in disorder confirmed these rumours.

'As for that Russian army which English gold has brought from the ends of the universe, we are going to inflict upon it the same fate (the fate of the army of Ulm)'; he remembered the words of Bonaparte's address to his army at the beginning of the campaign, and these words aroused in him simultaneously admiration for the genius of his hero, a feeling of mortified pride, and the hope of glory. 'And if there's nothing left but to die?' he thought. 'Well if it must be! I will do it no worse than others.'

Prince Andrey looked disdainfully at the endless, confused mass of companies, of baggage-waggons, parks of artillery, and again store-waggons, carts, and waggons of every possible form, pursuing one another and obstructing the muddy road three and four abreast. On every side, behind and before, as far as the ear could reach in every direction there was the rumble of wheels, the rattle of carts, of waggons, and of gun-carriages, the tramp of horses, the crack of whips, the shouts of drivers, the swearing of soldiers, of orderlies, and officers. At the sides of the roads he saw fallen horses, and sometimes their skinned carcases, broken-down waggons, with solitary soldiers sitting on them, waiting for something, detached groups of soldiers strayed from their companies, starting off to neighbouring villages, or dragging back from them fowls, sheep, hay, or sacks of stores of some sort. Where the road went uphill or downhill the crush became greater, and there was an uninterrupted roar of shouts. The soldiers floundering knee-deep in the mud clutched the guns and clung to the waggons in the midst of cracking whips, slipping hoofs, breaking traces and throat-splitting yells. The officers superintending their movements rode to and fro in front and behind the convoys. Their voices were faintly audible in the midst of the general uproar, their faces betrayed that they despaired of the possibility of checking the disorder.

'*Voilà le cher* holy armament,' thought Bolkonsky, recalling Bilibin's words.

He rode up to a convoy, intending to ask of some one of these men where he could find the commander-in-chief. Directly opposite to him came a strange vehicle, with one horse, obviously rigged up by soldiers with the resources at their disposal, and looking like something between a cart, a cabriolet, and a coach. A soldier was driving it, and under the leathern tilt behind a cover sat a woman, muffled up in shawls. Prince Andrey rode up and was just addressing a question to the soldier, when his attention was taken off by the despairing shrieks of the woman in this conveyance. The officer, directing the traffic, aimed a blow at the soldier who sat in the coachman's seat, for trying to push in ahead of others, and the lash fell on the cover of the equipage. The woman shrieked shrilly. On catching sight of Prince Andrey, she looked out from under the cover and putting her thin arms out from the shawls and waving them, she screamed:

'Adjutant! sir! . . . For God's sake! . . . protect me. . . . What will happen to us? . . . I am the wife of the doctor of the Seventh Chasseurs . . . they won't let us pass, we have dropped behind, lost our own people. . . .'

'I'll thrash you into mincemeat! turn back!' shouted the exasperated officer to the soldier: 'turn back with your hussy!'

'Sir, protect us. What does it mean?' screamed the doctor's wife.

'Kindly let this cart get through. Don't you see that it is a woman?' said Prince Andrey, riding up to the officer.

The officer glanced at him, and without making any reply turned again to the soldier. 'I'll teach you how to push in. . . . Back! . . .'

'Let it pass, I tell you,' repeated Prince Andrey, setting his lips tightly.

'And who are you?' cried the officer, turning upon him suddenly with drunken fury. 'Who are you? Are *you*' (he put a peculiarly offensive intonation into the word) 'in command, pray? I'm commanding officer here, not you. Back you go,' he repeated, 'or I'll lash you into mincemeat.' The expression evidently pleased the officer.

'A nice snub he gave the little adjutant,' said a voice in the background.

Prince Andrey saw that the officer was in that stage of drunken unreasoning fury, when men do not remember what they say. He saw that his championship of the doctor's wife in the queer conveyance was exposing him to what he dreaded more than anything else in the world, what is called in French *ridicule*, but his instinct said something else. The officer had hardly uttered the last words when Prince Andrey rode up to him with a face distorted by frenzied anger, and raised his riding-whip: 'Let—them—pass!'

The officer flourished his arm and hurriedly rode away.

'It's all their doing, these staff-officers, all the disorder,' he grumbled. 'Do as you like.'

Prince Andrey, without lifting his eyes, made haste to escape from the doctor's wife, who called him her deliverer. And dwelling on the minutest detail of this humiliating scene with loathing, he galloped on towards the village, where he was told that the commander-in-chief was.

On reaching the village, he got off his horse, and went into the first house with the intention of resting for a moment at least, eating something, and getting all the mortifying impressions that were torturing him into some clear shape. 'This is a mob of scoundrels, not an army,' he thought, going up to the window of the first house, when a familiar voice called him by his name.

He looked round. Out of a little window was thrust the handsome face of Nesvitsky. Nesvitsky, munching something in his moist mouth and beckoning to him, called him in.

'Bolkonsky! Bolkonsky! Don't you hear, eh? Make haste,' he shouted.

Going into the house, Prince Andrey found Nesvitsky and another adjutant having a meal. They hastily turned to Bolkonsky with the enquiry, had he any news? On their familiar faces Prince Andrey read alarm and uneasiness. That expression was particularly noticeable in Nesvitsky's face, usually so full of laughter.

'Where is the commander-in-chief?' asked Bolkonsky.

'Here in this house,' answered the adjutant.

'Well, is it true, about the peace and capitulation?' asked Nesvitsky.

'I ask you. I know nothing except that I have had great difficulty in getting through to you.'

'And the things that have been going on, my boy! Awful! I was wrong to laugh at Mack; there's worse in store for us,' said Nesvitsky. 'But sit down, have something to eat.'

'You won't find your baggage or anything now, prince, and God knows what's become of your Pyotr,' said the other adjutant.

'Where are the headquarters?'

'We shall spend the night in Znaim.'

'Well, I got everything I wanted packed up on two horses,' said Nesvitsky; 'and capital packs they made for me, fit to scamper as far as the Bohemian mountains at least. Things are in a bad way, my boy. But, I say, you must be ill, shivering like that?' Nesvitsky queried, noticing how Prince Andrey shuddered, as though in contact with a galvanic battery.

'No; I'm all right,' answered Prince Andrey. He had recalled at that instant the incident with the doctor's wife and the transport officer.

'What is the commander-in-chief doing here?' he asked.

'I can't make out anything,' said Nesvitsky.

'I know one thing, that it's all loathsome, loathsome,' said Prince Andrey, and he went into the house where the commander-in-chief was stopping.

Passing by Kutuzov's carriage, the exhausted saddle-horses of his suite, and the Cossacks talking loudly together, Prince Andrey went into the outer room. Kutuzov himself was, as Prince Andrey had been told, in the inner room of the hut with Prince Bagration and Weierother. The latter was the Austrian general, who had taken

Schmidt's place. In the outer room little Kozlovsky was squatting on his heels in front of a copying-clerk. The latter was sitting on a tub turned upside down, he was writing rapidly with the cuffs of his uniform tucked up. Kozlovsky's face was careworn; he too looked as if he had not slept all night. He glanced at Prince Andrey, and did not even nod to him.

'The second line. . . . Ready?' he went on, dictating to the clerk: 'the Kiev Grenadiers, the Podolsky . . .'

'Don't be in such a hurry, your honour,' the clerk answered rudely and angrily, looking at Kozlovsky. Through the door he heard at that moment Kutuzov's voice, eager and disatisfied, and other unfamiliar voices interrupting him. The sound of those voices, the inattention with which Kozlovsky glanced at him, the churlishness of the harassed clerk, the fact that the clerk and Kozlovsky were sitting round a tub on the floor at so little distance from the commander-in-chief, and that the Cossacks holding the horses laughed so loudly at the window—all made Prince Andrey feel that some grave calamity was hanging over them.

Prince Andrey turned to Kozlovsky with urgent questions.

'In a minute, prince,' said Kozlovsky. 'The disposition of Bagration's troops . . .'

'What about capitulation?'

'Nothing of the sort; arrangements have been made for a battle!'

Prince Andrey went towards the door from which the sound of voices came. But at the moment when he was going to open the door, the voices in the room paused, the door opened of itself, and Kutuzov with his eagle nose and podgy face appeared in the doorway. Prince Andrey was standing exactly opposite Kutuzov; but from the expression of the commander-in-chief's one seeing eye it was evident that thought and anxiety so engrossed him as to veil, as it were, his vision. He looked straight into his adjutant's face and did not recognise him.

'Well, have you finished?' he addressed Kozlovsky.

'In a second, your Excellency.'

Bagration, a short lean man, not yet elderly, with a resolute and impassive face of oriental type, came out after the commander-in-chief.

'I have the honour to report myself,' Prince Andrey said for the second time, rather loudly, as he handed Kutuzov an envelope.

'Ah, from Vienna? Very good! Later, later!' Kutuzov went out to the steps with Bagration.

'Well, prince, good-bye,' he said to Bagration. 'Christ be with you! May my blessing bring you a great victory!' Kutuzov's face suddenly softened, and there were tears in his eyes. With his left arm he drew Bagration to him, while with his right hand, on which he wore a ring, he crossed him with a gesture evidently habitual. He offered him his podgy cheek, but Bagration kissed him on the neck. 'Christ be with you!' repeated Kutuzov, and he went towards his carriage. 'Get in with me,' he said to Bolkonsky.

'Your Most High Excellency, I should have liked to be of use here. Allow me to remain in Prince Bagration's detachment.'

'Get in,' said Kutuzov, and noticing that Bolkonsky still delayed: 'I have need of good officers myself, myself.'

They took their seats in the carriage and drove for some minutes in silence.

'There is a great deal, a great deal of everything still before us,' he said, with an expression of old-age clairvoyance, as though he saw all that was passing in Bolkonsky's heart. 'If one-tenth part of his detachment comes in, I shall thank God,' added Kutuzov, as though talking to himself.

Prince Andrey glanced at Kutuzov, and unconsciously his eyes were caught by the carefully washed seams of the scar on his temple, where the bullet had gone through his head at Ismail, and the empty eye-socket, not a yard from him. 'Yes, he has the right to speak so calmly of the destruction of these men,' thought Bolkonsky.

'That's why I ask you to send me to that detachment,' he said.

Kutuzov made no reply. He seemed to have forgotten what was said to him, and sat plunged in thought. Five minutes later, swaying easily in the soft carriage springs, Kutuzov addressed Prince Andrey. There was no trace of emotion on his face now. With delicate irony he questioned Prince Andrey about the details of his interview with the emperor, about the comments he had heard at Court on the Krems engagement, and about ladies of their common acquaintance.

XIV

KUTUZOV had, on the 1st of November, received from one of his spies information that showed the army he commanded to be in an almost hopeless position. The spy reported that the French, after crossing the bridge at Vienna, were moving in immense force on Kutuzov's line of communications with the reinforcements marching from Russia. If Kutuzov were to determine to remain at Krems, Napoleon's army of a hundred and fifty thousand men would cut him off from all communications, and would surround his exhausted army of forty thousand, and he would find himself in the position of Mack before Ulm. If Kutuzov decided to leave the road leading to a junction with the Russian reinforcements, he would have to make his way with no road through unknown country to the mountains of Bohemia, pursued by the cream of the enemy's forces, and to give up all hope of effecting a junction with Buxhevden. If Kutuzov decided to march by the road from Krems to Olmütz to join the forces from Russia he ran the risk of finding the French, who had crossed the Vienna bridge, in advance of him on this road, and so being forced to give battle on the march, encumbered with all his stores and transport, with an enemy three times as numerous and hemming him in on both sides. Kutuzov chose the last course.

The French, after crossing the river, had, as the spy reported, set off at a quick march towards Znaim, which lay on Kutuzov's line of route, more than a hundred versts in front of him. To reach Znaim before the French offered the best hopes of saving the army. To allow the French to get to Znaim before him would mean exposing the whole army to a disgrace like that of the Austrians at Ulm, or to complete destruction. But to arrive there before the French with the whole army was impossible. The road of the French army from Vienna to Znaim was shorter and better than the Russian's road from Krems to Znaim.

On the night of receiving the news Kutuzov sent Bagration's advance guard of four thousand soldiers to the right over the mountains from the Krems-Znaim road to the Vienna and Znaim road. Bagration was to make a forced march, to halt facing towards Vienna and with his back to Znaim, and if he succeeded in getting on the road in advance of the French, he was to delay them as long as he could. Kutuzov himself with all the transport was making straight for Znaim.

Bagration marched forty-five versts, by night in stormy weather, through the mountains, with no road, and with hungry, barefoot soldiers. Leaving a third of his men straggling behind him, Bagration reached Hollabrunn, on the Vienna and Znaim road, a few hours before the French, who marched upon Hollabrunn from Vienna. Kutuzov needed fully another twenty-four hours to get to Znaim with all the transport, and so to save the army Bagration would have had, with his four thousand hungry and exhausted soldiers, to have kept at bay the whole army of the enemy confronting him at Hollabrunn for four-and-twenty hours, and this was obviously impossible. But a freak of fate made the impossible possible. The success of the trick that had given the Vienna bridge into the hands of the French encouraged Murat to try and take in Kutuzov too. Murat, on meeting Bagration's weak detachment on the Znaim road, supposed it to be the whole army of Kutuzov. To give this army a final and crushing defeat he waited for the troops still on the road from Vienna, and to that end he proposed a truce for three days, on the condition that neither armies should change their positions nor stir from where they were. Murat averred that negotiations for peace were now proceeding, and that he proposed a truce therefore to avoid useless bloodshed. The Austrian general, Nostits, who was in charge of the advance posts, believed the statements of Murat's messengers and retired, leaving Bagration's detachment unprotected. The other messengers rode off to the Russian line to make the same announcement about peace negotiations, and to propose a truce of three days to the Russian troops. Bagration replied that he was not authorised to accept or to decline a truce, and sent his adjutant to Kutuzov with a report of the proposition made to him.

A truce gave Kutuzov the only possibility of gaining time, of letting Bagration's exhausted forces rest, and of getting the transport and heavy convoys (the movement of which was concealed from the French) a further stage on their journey. The offer of a truce gave the one—and totally unexpected—chance of saving the army. On receiving information of it, Kutuzov promptly despatched the general-adjutant, Winzengerode, who was with him, to the enemy's camp. Winzengerode was instructed not only to accept the truce, but to propose terms of capitulation, while Kutuzov meanwhile sent his adjutants back to hasten to the utmost the transport of the luggage of the whole army along the Krems and Znaim road. Bagration's hungry and exhausted detachment alone was to cover the movements of the transport and of the whole army, by remaining stationary in face of an enemy eight times stronger numerically.

Kutuzov's anticipations were correct both as to the proposals of capitulation, which bound him to nothing, giving time for part of the transport to reach Znaim, and as to Murat's blunder being very quickly discovered. As soon as Bonaparte, who was at Schobrunn, only twenty-five versts from Hollabrunn, received Murat's despatch and projects of truce and capitulation, he detected the deception and despatched the following letter to Murat:

To Prince Murat.

Schönbrunn, 25 Brumaire, year 1805
at 8 o'clock in the morning.

'It is impossible to find terms in which to express to you my displeasure. You only command my advance guard and you have no right to make any truce without my order. You are causing me to lose the results of a campaign. Break the truce immediately and march upon the enemy. You must make a declaration to them that the general who signed this capitulation had no right to do so, and that only the Emperor of Russia has that right.

'Whenever the Emperor of Russia ratifies the aforesaid convention, however, I will ratify it; but it is only a stratagem. March on, destroy the Russian army . . . you are in a position to take its baggage and artillery.

'The Emperor of Russia's aide-de-camp is a . . . Officers are nothing when they have not powers; this one had none. . . . The Austrians let themselves be tricked about the crossing of the bridge of Vienna, you are letting yourself be tricked by one of the Emperor's aides-de-camp.
NAPOLEON.'

Bonaparte's adjutant dashed off at full gallop with this menacing letter to Murat. Not trusting his generals, Bonaparte himself advanced to the field of battle with his whole guard, fearful of letting the snared victim slip through his fingers. Meanwhile the four thousand men of Bagration's detachment, merrily lighting camp-fires, dried and warmed themselves, and cooked their porridge for the first time for three days, and not one among them knew or dreamed of what was in store for them.

XV

BEFORE four o'clock in the afternoon Prince Andrey, who had persisted in his petition to Kutuzov, reached Grunte, and joined Bagration. Bonaparte's adjutant had not yet reached Murat's division, and the battle had not yet begun. In Bagration's detachment, they knew nothing of the progress of events. They talked about peace, but did not believe in its possibility. They talked of a battle, but did not believe in a battle's being close at hand either.

Knowing Bolkonsky to be a favourite and trusted adjutant, Bagration received him with a commanding officer's special graciousness and condescension. He informed him that there would probably be an engagement that day or the next day, and gave him full liberty to remain in attendance on him during the battle, or to retire to the rear-guard to watch over the order of the retreat, also a matter of great importance.

'Today, though, there will most likely be no action,' said Bagration, as though to reassure Prince Andrey.

'If this is one of the common run of little staff dandies, sent here to win a cross, he can do that in the rear-guard, but if he wants to be with me, let him . . . he'll be of use, if he's a brave officer,' thought Bagration. Prince Andrey, without replying, asked the prince's permission to ride round the position and find out the disposition of the forces, so that, in case of a message, he might know where to take it. An officer on duty, a handsome and elegantly dressed man, with a diamond ring on his forefinger, who spoke French badly, but with assurance, was summoned to conduct Prince Andrey.

On all sides they saw officers drenched through, with dejected faces, apparently looking for something, and soldiers dragging doors, benches, and fences from the village.

'Here we can't put a stop to these people,' said the staff-officer, pointing to them. 'Their commanders let their companies get out of hand. And look here,' he pointed to a canteen-keeper's booth, 'they gather here, and here they sit. I drove them all out this morning, and look, it's full again. I must go and scare them, prince. One moment.'

'Let us go together, and I'll get some bread and cheese there,' said Prince Andrey, who had not yet had time for a meal.

'Why didn't you mention it, prince? I would have offered you something.'

They got off their horses and went into the canteen-keeper's booth. Several officers, with flushed and exhausted faces, were sitting at the tables, eating and drinking.

'Now what does this mean, gentlemen?' said the staff-officer, in the reproachful tone of a man who has repeated the same thing several times. 'You mustn't absent yourselves like this. The prince gave orders that no one was to leave his post. Come, really, captain,' he remonstrated with a muddy, thin little artillery officer, who in his stockings (he had given his boots to the canteen-keeper to dry) stood up at their entrance, smiling not quite naturally.

'Now aren't you ashamed, Captain Tushin?' pursued the staff-officer. 'I should have thought you as an artillery officer ought to set an example, and you have no boots on. They'll sound the alarm, and you'll be in a pretty position without your boots on.' (The staff-officer smiled.) 'Kindly return to your posts, gentlemen, all, all,' he added in a tone of authority.

Prince Andrey could not help smiling as he glanced at Captain Tushin. Smiling, without a word, Tushin shifted from one bare foot to the other, looking inquiringly, with his big, shrewd, and good-natured eyes, from Prince Andrey to the staff-officer.

'The soldiers say it's easier barefoot,' said Captain Tushin, smiling shyly, evidently anxious to carry off his awkward position in a jesting tone. But before he had uttered the words, he felt that his joke would not do and had not come off. He was in confusion.

'Kindly go to your places,' said the staff-officer, trying to preserve his gravity.

Prince Andrey glanced once more at the little figure of the artillery officer. There was something peculiar about it, utterly unsoldierly, rather comic, but very attractive.

The staff-officer and Prince Andrey got on their horses and rode on.

Riding out beyond the village, continually meeting or overtaking soldiers and officers of various ranks, they saw on the left earthworks being thrown up, still red with the freshly dug clay. Several battalions of soldiers, in their shirt-sleeves, in spite of the cold wind were toiling like white ants at these entrenchments; from the trench they saw spadefuls of red clay continually being thrown out by unseen hands. They rode up to the entrenchment, examined it, and were riding on further. Close behind the entrenchment they came upon dozens of soldiers continually running to and from the earthworks, and they had to hold their noses and put their horses to a gallop to get by the pestilential atmosphere of this improvised sewer.

'*Voilà l'agrément des camps, monsieur le prince*,' said the staff-officer. They rode up the opposite hill. From that hill they had a view of the French. Prince Andrey stopped and began looking closer at what lay before them.

'You see here is where our battery stands,' said the staff-officer, pointing to the highest point, 'commanded by that queer fellow sitting without his boots; from there you can see everything; let us go there, prince.'

'I am very grateful to you, I'll go on alone now,' said Prince Andrey, anxious to be rid of the staff-officer; 'don't trouble yourself further, please.'

The staff-officer left him, and Prince Andrey rode on alone.

The further forward and the nearer to the enemy he went, the more orderly and cheerful he found the troops. The greatest disorder and depression had prevailed in the transport forces before Znaim, which Prince Andrey had passed that morning, ten versts from the French. At Grunte too a certain alarm and vague dread could be felt. But the nearer Prince Andrey got to the French line, the more self-confident was the appearance of our troops. The soldiers, in their greatcoats, stood ranged in lines with their sergeant, and the captain was calling over the men, poking the last soldier in the line in the ribs, and telling him to hold up his hand. Soldiers were dotted all over the plain, dragging logs and brushwood, and constructing shanties, chatting together, and laughing good-humouredly. They were sitting round the fires, dressed and stripped, drying shirts and foot-gear. Or they thronged round the porridge-pots and cauldrons, brushing their boots and their coats. In one company dinner was ready, and the soldiers, with greedy faces, watched the steaming pots, and waited for the sample, which was being taken in a wooden bowl to the commissariat officer, sitting on a piece of wood facing his shanty.

In another company—a lucky one, for not all had vodka—the soldiers stood in a group round a broad-shouldered, pock-marked sergeant, who was tilting a keg of vodka, and pouring it into the covers of the canteens held out to him in turn. The soldiers, with reverential faces, lifted the covers to their mouths, drained them, and licking their lips and rubbing them with the sleeves of their coats, they walked away looking more good-humoured than before. Every face was as serene as though it were all happening not in sight of the enemy, just before an action in which at least half the detachment must certainly be left on the field, but somewhere at home in Russia, with every prospect of a quiet halting-place. Prince Andrey rode by the Chasseur regiment, and as he advanced into the ranks of the Kiev Grenadiers, stalwart fellows all engaged in the same peaceful pursuits, not far from the colonel's shanty, standing higher than the rest, he came upon a platoon of grenadiers, before whom lay a man stripped naked. Two soldiers were holding him, while two others were brandishing supple twigs and bringing them down at regular intervals on the man's bare back. The man shrieked unnaturally. A stout major was walking up and down in front of the platoon, and regardless of the screams, he kept saying: 'It's a disgrace for a soldier to steal; a soldier must be honest, honourable, and brave, and to steal from a comrade, he must be without honour indeed, a monster. Again, again!'

And still he heard the dull thuds and the desperate but affected scream.

'Again, again,' the major was saying.

A young officer, with an expression of bewilderment and distress in his face, walked away from the flogging, looking inquiringly at the adjutant.

Prince Andrey, coming out to the foremost line, rode along in front of it. Our line and the enemy's were far from one another at the left and also at the right flank; but in the centre, at the spot where in the morning the messengers had met, the lines came so close that the soldiers of the two armies could see each other's faces and talk together. Besides these soldiers, whose place was in that part of the line, many others had gathered there from both sides, and they were laughing, as they scrutinised the strange and novel dress and aspect of their foes.

Since early morning, though it was forbidden to go up to the line, the commanding officers could not keep the inquisitive soldiers back. The soldiers, whose post was in that part of the line, like showmen exhibiting some curiosity, no longer looked at the French, but made observations on the men who came up to look, and waited with a bored face to be relieved. Prince Andrey stopped to look carefully at the French.

'Look'ee, look'ee,' one soldier was saying to a comrade, pointing to a Russian musketeer, who had gone up to the lines with an officer and was talking warmly and rapidly with a French grenadier. 'I say, doesn't he jabber away fine! I bet the Frenchy can't keep pace with him. Now, then, Sidorov?'

'Wait a bit; listen. Aye, it's fine!' replied Sidorov, reputed a regular scholar at talking French.

The soldier, at whom they had pointed laughing, was Dolohov. Prince Andrey recognised him and listened to what he was saying. Dolohov, together with his captain, had come from the left flank, where his regiment was posted.

'Come, again, again!' the captain urged, craning forward and trying not to lose a syllable of the conversation, though it was unintelligible to him. 'Please, go on. What's he saying?'

Dolohov did not answer the captain; he had been drawn into a hot dispute with the French grenadier. They were talking, as was to be expected, of the campaign. The Frenchman, mixing up the Austrians and the Russians, was maintaining that the Russians had been defeated and had been fleeing all the way from Ulm. Dolohov declared that the Russians had never been defeated, but had beaten the French.

'We have orders to drive you away from here, and we shall too,' said Dolohov.

'You had better take care you are not all captured with all your Cossacks,' said the French grenadier.

Spectators and listeners on the French side laughed.

'We shall make you dance, as you danced in Suvorov's day' (*on vous fera danser*), said Dolohov.

'What is he prating about?' said a Frenchman.

'Ancient history,' said another, guessing that the allusion was to former wars. 'The emperor will show your Suvorov, like the others . . .'

'Bonaparte . . .' Dolohov was beginning, but the Frenchman interrupted him.

'Not Bonaparte. He is the Emperor! *Sacré nom* . . .' he said angrily.

'Damnation to him, your Emperor!'

And Dolohov swore a coarse soldier's oath in Russian, and, shouldering his gun, walked away.

'Come along, Ivan Lukitch,' he said to his captain.

'So that's how they talk French,' said the soldiers in the line. 'Now then, you, Sidorov.' Sidorov winked, and, turning to the French, he fell to gabbling disconnected syllables very rapidly.

'Kari-ma-la-ta-fa-sa-fi-mu-ter-kess-ka,' he jabbered, trying to give the most expressive intonation to his voice.

'Ho, ho, ho! ha ha! ha ha! Oh! oo!' the soldiers burst into a roar of such hearty, good-humoured laughter, in which the French line too could not keep from joining, that after it it seemed as though they must unload their guns, blow up their ammunition, and all hurry away back to their homes. But the guns remained loaded, the port-holes in the houses and earthworks looked out as menacingly as ever, and the cannons, taken off their platforms, confronted one another as before.

XVI

AFTER making a circuit round the whole line of the army, from the right flank to the left, Prince Andrey rode up to that battery from which the staff-officer told him that the whole field could be seen. Here he dismounted and stood by the end one of the four cannons, which had been taken off their platforms. An artilleryman on sentinel duty in front of the cannons was just confronting the officer, but at a sign being made to him, he renewed his regular, monotonous pacing. Behind the cannons stood their platforms, and still further behind, the picket-ropes and camp-fires of the artillerymen. To the left, not far from the end cannon, was a little newly rigged-up shanty, from which came the sounds of officers' voices in eager conversation. From the battery there was in fact a view of almost the whole disposition of the Russian forces, and the greater part of the enemy's. Directly facing the battery on the skyline of the opposite hill could be seen the village of Schöngraben; to the left and to the right could be discerned in three places through the smoke of the camp-fires masses of the French troops, of which the greater number were undoubtedly in the village itself and behind the hill. To the left of the village there was something in the smoke that looked like a battery, but it could not be made out clearly by the naked eye. Our right flank was stationed on a rather steep eminence, which dominated the French position. About it were disposed our infantry regiments, and on the very ridge could be seen dragoons. In the centre, where was placed Tushin's battery, from which Prince Andrey was surveying the position, there was the most sloping and direct descent to the stream that separated us from Schöngraben. On the left our troops were close to a copse, where there was the smoke of the camp-fires of our infantry, chopping wood in it. The French line was wider than ours, and it was obviously easy for the French to outflank us on both sides. Behind our position was a precipitous and deep ravine, down which it would be difficult to retreat with artillery and cavalry. Prince Andrey leaned his elbow on the cannon, and taking out a notebook, sketched for himself a plan of the disposition of the troops. In two places he made notes with a pencil, intending to speak on the points to Bagration. He meant to suggest first concentrating all the artillery in the centre, and secondly drawing the cavalry back to the further side of the ravine. Prince Andrey, who was constantly in attendance on the commander-in-chief, watching the movements of masses of men and manoeuvring of troops, and also continually studying the historical accounts of battles, could not help viewing the course of the military operations that were to come only in their general features. His imagination dwelt on the broad possibilities, such as the following: 'If the enemy makes the right flank the point of attack,' he said to himself, 'the Kiev grenadiers and Podolsky Chasseurs will have to defend their position, till the reserves from the centre come to their support. In that case the dragoons can get them in the flank and drive them back. In case of an attack on the centre, we station on this height the central battery, and under its cover we draw off the left flank and retreat to the ravine by platoons,' he reasoned. . . . All the while he was on the cannon, he heard, as one often does, the sounds of the voices of the officers talking in the shanty, but he did not take in a single word of what they were saying. Suddenly a voice from the shanty impressed him by a tone of such earnestness that he could not help listening.

'No, my dear fellow,' said a pleasant voice that seemed somehow familiar to Prince Andrey. 'I say that if one could know what will happen after death, then not one of us would be afraid of death. That's so, my dear fellow.'

Another younger voice interrupted him: 'But afraid or not afraid, there's no escaping it.'

'Why, you're always in fear! Fie on you learned fellows,' said a third, a manly voice, interrupting both. 'To be sure, you artillerymen are clever fellows, because you can carry everything with you to eat and to drink.'

And the owner of the manly voice, apparently an infantry officer, laughed.

'Still one is in fear,' pursued the first voice, the one Prince Andrey knew. 'One's afraid of the unknown, that's what it is. It's all very well to say the soul goes to heaven . . . but this we do know, that there is no heaven, but only atmosphere.'

Again the manly voice interrupted.

'Come, give us a drop of your herb-brandy, Tushin,' it said.

'Oh, it's the captain, who had his boots off in the booth,' thought Prince Andrey, recognising with pleasure the agreeable philosophising voice.

'Herb-brandy by all means,' said Tushin; 'but still to conceive of a future life...' He did not finish his sentence.

At that moment there was a whiz heard in the air: nearer, nearer, faster and more distinctly, and faster it came; and the cannon-ball, as though not uttering all it had to say, thudded into the earth not far from the shanty, tearing up the soil with superhuman force. The earth seemed to moan at the terrible blow. At the same instant there dashed out of the shanty, before any of the rest, little Tushin with his short pipe in his mouth; his shrewd, good-humoured face was rather pale. After him emerged the owner of the manly voice, a stalwart infantry officer, who ran off to his company, buttoning his coat as he ran.

XVII

PRINCE ANDREY mounted his horse but lingered at the battery, looking at the smoke of the cannon from which the ball had flown. His eyes moved rapidly over the wide plain. He only saw that the previously immobile masses of the French were heaving to and fro, and that it really was a battery on the left. The smoke still clung about it. Two Frenchmen on horseback, doubtless adjutants, were galloping on the hill. A small column of the enemy, distinctly visible, were moving downhill, probably to strengthen the line. The smoke of the first shot had not cleared away, when there was a fresh puff of smoke and another shot. The battle was beginning. Prince Andrey turned his horse and galloped back to Grunte to look for Prince Bagration. Behind him he heard the cannonade becoming louder and more frequent. Our men were evidently beginning to reply. Musket shots could be heard below at the spot where the lines were closest. Lemarrois had only just galloped to Murat with Napoleon's menacing letter, and Murat, abashed and anxious to efface his error, at once moved his forces to the centre and towards both flanks, hoping before evening and the arrival of the Emperor to destroy the insignificant detachment before him.

'It has begun! Here it comes!' thought Prince Andrey, feeling the blood rush to his heart. 'But where? What form is my Toulon to take?' he wondered.

Passing between the companies that had been eating porridge and drinking vodka a quarter of an hour before, he saw everywhere nothing but the same rapid movements of soldiers forming in ranks and getting their guns, and on every face he saw the same eagerness that he felt in his heart. 'It has begun! Here it comes! Terrible and delightful!' said the face of every private and officer. Before he reached the earth-works that were being thrown up, he saw in the evening light of the dull autumn day men on horseback crossing towards him. The foremost, wearing a cloak and an astrachan cap, was riding on a white horse. It was Prince Bagration. Prince Andrey stopped and waited for him to come up. Prince Bagration stopped his horse, and recognising Prince Andrey nodded to him. He still gazed on ahead while Prince Andrey told him what he had been seeing.

The expression: 'It has begun! it is coming!' was discernible even on Prince Bagration's strong, brown face, with his half-closed, lustreless, sleepy-looking eyes. Prince Andrey glanced with uneasy curiosity at that impassive face, and he longed to know: Was that man thinking and feeling, and what was he thinking and feeling at that moment? 'Is there anything at all there behind that impassive face?' Prince Andrey wondered, looking at him. Prince Bagration nodded in token of his assent to Prince Andrey's words, and said: 'Very good,' with an expression that seemed to signify that all that happened, and all that was told him, was exactly what he had foreseen. Prince Andrey, panting from his rapid ride, spoke quickly. Prince Bagration uttered his words in his Oriental accent with peculiar deliberation, as though impressing upon him that there was no need of hurry. He did, however, spur his horse into a gallop in the direction of Tushin's battery. Prince Andrey rode after him with his suite. The party consisted of an officer of the suite, Bagration's private adjutant, Zherkov, an orderly officer, the staff-officer on duty, riding a beautiful horse of English breed, and a civilian official, the auditor, who had asked to be present from curiosity to see the battle. The auditor, a plump man with a plump face, looked about him with a naïve smile of amusement, swaying about on his horse, and cutting a queer figure in his cloak on his saddle among the hussars, Cossacks, and adjutants.

'This gentleman wants to see a battle,' said Zherkov to Bolkonsky, indicating the auditor, 'but has begun to feel queer already.'

'Come, leave off,' said the auditor, with a beaming smile at once naïve and cunning, as though he were flattered at being the object of Zherkov's jests, and was purposely trying to seem stupider than he was in reality.

'It's very curious, *mon Monsieur Prince*,' said the staff-officer on duty. (He vaguely remembered that the title *prince* was translated in some peculiar way in French, but could not get it quite right.) By this time they were all riding up to Tushin's battery, and a ball struck the ground before them.

'What was that falling?' asked the auditor, smiling naïvely.

'A French pancake,' said Zherkov.

'That's what they hit you with, then?' asked the auditor. 'How awful!' And he seemed to expand all over with enjoyment. He had hardly uttered the words when again there was a sudden terrible whiz, which ended abruptly in a thud into something soft, and flop—a Cossack, riding a little behind and to the right of the auditor, dropped from his horse to the ground. Zherkov and the staff-officer bent forward over their saddles and turned their horses away. The auditor stopped facing the Cossack, and looking with curiosity at him. The Cossack was dead, the horse was still struggling.

Prince Bagration dropped his eyelids, looked round, and seeing the cause of the delay, turned away indifferently, seeming to ask, 'Why notice these trivial details?' With the ease of a first-rate horseman he stopped his horse, bent over a little and disengaged his sabre, which had caught under his cloak. The sabre was an old-fashioned one, unlike what are worn now. Prince Andrey remembered the story that Suvorov had given his sabre to Bagration in Italy, and the recollection was particularly pleasant to him at that moment. They had ridden up to the very battery from which Prince Andrey had surveyed the field of battle.

'Whose company?' Prince Bagration asked of the artilleryman standing at the ammunition boxes.

He asked in words: 'Whose company?' but what he was really asking was, 'You're not in a panic here?' And the artilleryman understood that.

'Captain Tushin's, your excellency,' the red-haired, freckled artilleryman sang out in a cheerful voice, as he ducked forward.

'To be sure, to be sure,' said Bagration, pondering something, and he rode by the platforms up to the end cannon. Just as he reached it, a shot boomed from the cannon, deafening him and his suite, and in the smoke that suddenly enveloped the cannon the artilleryman could be seen hauling at the cannon, dragging and rolling it back to its former position. A broad-shouldered, gigantic soldier, gunner number one, with a mop, darted up to the wheel and planted himself, his legs wide apart; while number two, with a shaking hand, put the charge into the cannon's mouth; a small man with stooping shoulders, the officer Tushin, stumbling against the cannon, dashed forward, not noticing the general, and looked out, shading his eyes with his little hand.

'Another two points higher, and it will be just right,' he shouted in a shrill voice, to which he tried to give a swaggering note utterly out of keeping with his figure. 'Two!' he piped. 'Smash away, Medvyedev!'

Bagration called to the officer, and Tushin went up to the general, putting three fingers to the peak of his cap with a timid and awkward gesture, more like a priest blessing some one than a soldier saluting. Though Tushin's guns had been intended to cannonade the valley, he was throwing shells over the village of Schöngraben, in part of which immense masses of French soldiers were moving out.

No one had given Tushin instructions at what or with what to fire, and after consulting his sergeant, Zaharchenko, for whom he had a great respect, he had decided that it would be a good thing to set fire to the village. 'Very good!' Bagration said, on the officer's submitting that he had done so, and he began scrutinizing the whole field of battle that lay unfolded before him. He seemed to be considering something. The French had advanced nearest on the right side. In the hollow where the stream flowed, below the eminence on which the Kiev regiment was stationed, could be heard a continual roll and crash of guns, the din of which was overwhelming. And much further to the right, behind the dragoons, the officer of the suite pointed out to Bagration a column of French outflanking our flank. On the left the horizon was bounded by the copse close by. Prince Bagration gave orders for two battalions from the centre to go to the right to reinforce the flank. The officer of the suite ventured to observe to the prince that the removal of these battalions would leave the cannon unprotected. Prince Bagration turned to the officer of the suite and stared at him with his lustreless eyes in silence. Prince Andrey thought that the officer's observation was a very just one, and that really there was nothing to be said in reply. But at that instant an adjutant galloped up with a message from the colonel of the regiment in the hollow that immense masses of the French were coming down upon them, that his men were in disorder and retreating upon the Kiev grenadiers. Prince Bagration nodded to signify his assent and approval. He rode at a walking pace to the right, and sent an adjutant to the dragoons with orders to attack the French. But the adjutant returned half an hour later with the news that the colonel of the dragoons had already retired beyond the ravine, as a destructive fire had been opened upon him, and he was losing his men for nothing, and so he had concentrated his men in the wood.

'Very good!' said Bagration.

Just as he was leaving the battery, shots had been heard in the wood on the left too; and as it was too far to the left flank for him to go himself, Prince Bagration despatched Zherkov to tell the senior general—

the general whose regiment had been inspected by Kutuzov at Braunau —to retreat as rapidly as possible beyond the ravine, as the right flank would probably not long be able to detain the enemy. Tushin, and the battalion that was to have defended his battery, was forgotten. Prince Andrey listened carefully to Prince Bagration's colloquies with the commanding officers, and to the orders he gave them, and noticed, to his astonishment, that no orders were really given by him at all, but that Prince Bagration confined himself to trying to appear as though everything that was being done of necessity, by chance, or at the will of individual officers, was all done, if not by his orders, at least in accordance with his intentions. Prince Andrey observed, however, that, thanks to the tact shown by Prince Bagration, notwithstanding that what was done was due to chance, and not dependent on the commander's will, his presence was of the greatest value. Commanding officers, who rode up to Bagration looking distraught, regained their composure; soldiers and officers greeted him cheerfully, recovered their spirits in his presence, and were unmistakably anxious to display their pluck before him.

XVIII

AFTER riding up to the highest point of our right flank, Prince Bagration began to go downhill, where a continuous roll of musketry was heard and nothing could be seen for the smoke. The nearer they got to the hollow the less they could see, and the more distinctly could be felt the nearness of the actual battlefield. They began to meet wounded men. Two soldiers were dragging one along, supporting him on each side. His head was covered with blood; he had no cap, and was coughing and spitting. The bullet had apparently entered his mouth or throat. Another one came towards them, walking pluckily alone without his gun, groaning aloud and wringing his hands from the pain of a wound from which the blood was flowing, as though from a bottle, over his greatcoat. His face looked more frightened than in pain. He had been wounded only a moment before. Crossing the road, they began going down a deep descent, and on the slope they saw several men lying on the ground. They were met by a crowd of soldiers, among them some who were not wounded. The soldiers were hurrying up the hill, gasping for breath, and in spite of the general's presence, they were talking loudly together and gesticulating with their arms. In the smoke ahead of them they could see now rows of grey coats, and the commanding officer, seeing Bagration, ran after the group of retreating soldiers, calling upon them to come back. Bagration rode up to the ranks, along which there was here and there a rapid snapping of shots drowning the talk of the soldiers and the shouts of the officers. The whole air was reeking with smoke. The soldiers' faces were all full of excitement and smudged with powder. Some were plugging with their ramrods, others were putting powder on the touch-pans, and getting charges out of their pouches, others were firing their guns. But it was impossible to see at whom they were firing from the smoke, which the wind did not lift. The pleasant hum and whiz of the bullets was repeated pretty rapidly. 'What is it?' wondered Prince Andrey, as he rode up to the crowd of soldiers. 'It can't be the line, for they are all crowded together; it can't be an attacking party, for they are not moving; it can't be a square, they are not standing like one.'

A thin, weak-looking colonel, apparently an old man, with an amiable smile, and eyelids that half-covered his old-looking eyes and gave him a mild air, rode up to Prince Bagration and received him as though he were welcoming an honoured guest into his house. He announced to Prince Bagration that his regiment had had to face a cavalry attack of the French, that though the attack had been repulsed, the regiment had lost more than half of its men. The colonel said that the attack had been repulsed, supposing that to be the proper military term for what had happened; but he did not really know himself what had been taking place during that half hour in the troops under his command, and could not have said with any certainty whether the attack had been repelled or his regiment had been beaten by the attack. All he knew was that at the beginning of the action balls and grenades had begun flying all about his regiment, and killing men, that then some one had shouted 'cavalry,' and our men had begun firing. And they were firing still, though not now at the cavalry, who had disappeared, but at the French infantry, who had made their appearance in the hollow and were firing at our men. Prince Bagration nodded his head to betoken that all this was exactly what he had desired and expected. Turning to an adjutant, he commanded him to bring down from the hill the two battalions of the Sixth Chasseurs, by whom they had just come. Prince Andrey was struck at that instant by the change that had come over Prince Bagration's face. His face wore the look of concentrated and happy determination, which may be seen in a man who in a hot day takes the final run before a header into the water. The lustreless, sleepy look in the eyes, the affectation of profound thought had gone. The round, hard, eagle eyes looked ecstatically and rather disdainfully before him, obviously not resting on anything, though there was still the same deliberation in his measured movements.

The colonel addressed a protest to Prince Bagration, urging him to go back, as there it was too dangerous for him. 'I beg of you, your excellency, for God's sake!' he kept on saying, looking for support to the officer of the suite, who only turned away from him.

'Only look, your excellency!' He called his attention to the bullets which were continually whizzing, singing, and hissing about them. He spoke in the tone of protest and entreaty with which a carpenter speaks to a gentleman who has picked up a hatchet. 'We are used to it, but you may blister your fingers.' He talked as though these bullets could not kill him, and his half-closed eyes gave a still more persuasive effect to his words. The staff-officer added his protests to the colonel's, but Bagration made them no answer. He merely gave the order to cease firing, and to form so as to make room for the two battalions of reinforcements. Just as he was speaking the cloud of smoke covering the hollow was lifted as by an unseen hand and blown by the rising wind from right to left, and the opposite hill came into sight with the French moving across it. All eyes instinctively fastened on that French column moving down upon them and winding in and out over the ups and downs of the ground. Already they could see the fur caps of the soldiers, could distinguish officers from privates, could see their flag flapping against its staff.

'How well they're marching,' said some one in Bagration's suite.

The front part of the column was already dipping down into the hollow. The engagement would take place then on the nearer side of the slope . . .

The remnants of the regiment that had already been in action, forming hurriedly, drew off to the right; the two battalions of the Sixth Chasseurs marched up in good order, driving the last stragglers before them. They had not yet reached Bagration, but the heavy, weighty tread could be heard of the whole mass keeping step. On the left flank, nearest of all to Bagration, marched the captain, a round-faced imposing-looking man, with a foolish and happy expression of face. It was the same infantry officer who had run out of the shanty after Tushin. He was obviously thinking of nothing at that moment, but that he was marching before his commander in fine style. With the complacency of a man on parade, he stepped springing on his muscular legs, drawing himself up without the slightest effort, as though he were swinging, and this easy elasticity was a striking contrast to the heavy tread of the soldiers keeping step with him. He wore hanging by his leg an unsheathed, slender, narrow sword (a small bent sabre, more like a toy than a weapon), and looking about him, now at the commander, now behind, he turned his whole powerful frame round without getting out of step. It looked as though all the force of his soul was directed to marching by his commander in the best style possible. And conscious that he was accomplishing this, he was happy. 'Left . . . left . . . left . . .' he seemed to be inwardly repeating at each alternate step. And the wall of soldierly figures, weighed down by their knapsacks and guns, with their faces all grave in different ways, moved by in the same rhythm, as though each of the hundreds of soldiers were repeating mentally at each alternate step, 'Left . . . left . . . left . . .' A stout major skirted a bush on the road, puffing and shifting his step. A soldier, who had dropped behind, trotted after the company, looking panic-stricken at his own defection. A cannon ball, whizzing through the air flew over the heads of Prince Bagration and his suite, and in time to the same rhythm, 'Left . . . left . . .' it fell into the column.

'Close the ranks!' rang out the jaunty voice of the captain. The soldiers marched in a half circle round something in the place where the ball had fallen, and an old cavalryman, an under officer, lingered near the dead, and overtaking his line, changed feet with a hop, got into step, and looked angrily about him. 'Left . . . left . . . left . . .' seemed to echo out of the menacing silence and the monotonous sound of the simultaneous tread of the feet on the ground.

'Well done, lads!' said Prince Bagration.

'For your ex . . . slen, slen, slency!' rang out along the ranks. A surly-looking soldier, marching on the left, turned his eyes on Bagration as he shouted, with an expression that seemed to say, 'We know that without telling.' Another, opening his mouth wide, shouted without glancing round, and marched on, as though afraid of letting his attention stray. The order was given to halt and take off their knapsacks.

Bagration rode round the ranks of men who had marched by him, and then dismounted from his horse. He gave the reins to a Cossack, took off his cloak and handed it to him, stretched his legs and set his cap straight on his head. The French column with the officers in front came into sight under the hill.

'With God's help!' cried Bagration in a resolute, sonorous voice. He turned for one instant to the front line, and swinging his arms a little, with the awkward, lumbering gait of a man always on horseback, he walked forward over the uneven ground. Prince Andrey felt that some unseen force was drawing him forward, and he had a sensation of great happiness.[1]

The French were near. Already Prince Andrey, walking beside

[1] This was the attack of which Thiers says: 'The Russians behaved valiantly and, which is rare in warfare, two bodies of infantry marched resolutely upon each other, neither giving way before the other came up.' And Napoleon on St. Helena said: 'Some Russian battalions showed intrepidity.'

Bagration, could distinguish clearly the sashes, the red epaulettes, even the faces of the French. (He saw distinctly one bandy-legged old French officer, wearing Hessian boots, who was getting up the hill with difficulty, taking hold of the bushes.) Prince Bagration gave no new command, and still marched in front of the ranks in the same silence. Suddenly there was the snap of a shot among the French, another and a third . . . and smoke rose and firing rang out in all the broken-up ranks of the enemy. Several of our men fell, among them the round-faced officer, who had been marching so carefully and complacently. But at the very instant of the first shot, Bagration looked round and shouted, 'Hurrah!' 'Hura . . . a . . . a . . . ah!' rang out along our lines in a prolonged roar, and out-stripping Prince Bagration and one another, in no order, but in an eager and joyous crowd, our men ran downhill after the routed French.

XIX

THE attack of the Sixth Chasseurs covered the retreat of the right flank. In the centre Tushin's forgotten battery had succeeded in setting fire to Schongraben and delaying the advance of the French. The French stayed to put out the fire, which was fanned by the wind, and this gave time for the Russians to retreat. The retreat of the centre beyond the ravine was hurried and noisy; but the different companies kept apart. But the left flank, which consisted of the Azovsky and Podolsky infantry and the Pavlograd hussars, was simultaneously attacked in front and surrounded by the cream of the French army under Lannes, and was thrown into disorder. Bagration had sent Zherkov to the general in command of the left flank with orders to retreat immediately.

Zherkov, keeping his hand still at his cap, had briskly started his horse and galloped off. But no sooner had he ridden out of Bagration's sight than his courage failed him. He was overtaken by a panic he could not contend against, and he could not bring himself to go where there was danger.

After galloping some distance towards the troops of the left flank, he rode not forward where he heard firing, but off to look for the general and the officers in a direction where they could not by any possibility be; and so it was that he did not deliver the message.

The command of the left flank belonged by right of seniority to the general of the regiment in which Dolohov was serving—the regiment which Kutuzov had inspected before Braunau. But the command of the extreme left flank had been entrusted to the colonel of the Pavlograd hussars, in which Rostov was serving. Hence arose a misunderstanding. Both commanding officers were intensely exasperated with one another, and at a time when fighting had been going on a long while on the right flank, and the French had already begun their advance on the left, these two officers were engaged in negotiations, the sole aim of which was the mortification of one another. The regiments —cavalry and infantry alike—were by no means in readiness for the engagement. No one from the common soldier to the general expected a battle; and they were all calmly engaged in peaceful occupations— feeding their horses in the cavalry, gathering wood in the infantry.

'He is my senior in rank, however,' said the German colonel of the hussars, growing very red and addressing an adjutant, who had ridden up. 'So let him do as he likes. I can't sacrifice my hussars. Bugler! Sound the retreat!'

But things were becoming urgent. The fire of cannon and musketry thundered in unison on the right and in the centre, and the French tunics of Lannes's sharpshooters had already passed over the milldam, and were forming on this side of it hardly out of musket-shot range.

The infantry general walked up to his horse with his quivering strut, and mounting it and drawing himself up very erect and tall, he rode up to the Pavlograd colonel. The two officers met with affable bows and concealed fury in their hearts.

'Again, colonel,' the general said, 'I cannot leave half my men in the wood. I *beg* you, I *beg* you,' he repeated, 'to occupy the *position*, and prepare for an attack.'

'And I beg you not to meddle in what's not your business,' answered the colonel, getting hot. 'If you were a cavalry officer . . .'

'I am not a cavalry officer, colonel, but I am a Russian general, and if you are unaware of the fact . . .'

'I am fully aware of it, your excellency,' the colonel screamed suddenly, setting his horse in motion and becoming purple in the face. 'If you care to come to the front, you will see that this position cannot be held. I don't want to massacre my regiment for your satisfaction.'

'You forget yourself, colonel. I am not considering my own satisfaction, and I do not allow such a thing to be said.'

Taking the colonel's proposition as a challenge to his courage, the general squared his chest and rode scowling beside him to the front line, as though their whole difference would inevitably be settled there under the enemy's fire. They reached the line, several bullets flew by them, and they stood still without a word. To look at the front line was a useless proceeding, since from the spot where they had been standing before, it was clear that the cavalry could not act, owing to the bushes and the steep and broken character of the ground, and that the French were outflanking the left wing. The general and the colonel glared sternly and significantly at one another, like two cocks preparing for a fight, seeking in vain for a symptom of cowardice. Both stood the test without flinching. Since there was nothing to be said, and neither was willing to give the other grounds for asserting that he was the first to withdraw from under fire, they might have remained a long while standing there, mutually testing each other's pluck, if there had not at that moment been heard in the copse, almost behind them, the snap of musketry and a confused shout of voices. The French were attacking the soldiers gathering wood in the copse. The hussars could not now retreat, nor could the infantry. They were cut off from falling back on the left by the French line. Now, unfavourable as the ground was, they must attack to fight a way through for themselves.

The hussars of the squadron in which Rostov was an ensign had hardly time to mount their horses when they were confronted by the enemy. Again, as on the Enns bridge, there was no one between the squadron and the enemy, and between them lay that terrible border-line of uncertainty and dread, like the line dividing the living from the dead. All the soldiers were conscious of that line, and the question whether they would cross it or not, and how they would cross it, filled them with excitement.

The colonel rode up to the front, made some angry reply to the questions of the officers, and, like a man desperately insisting on his rights, gave some command. No one said anything distinctly, but through the whole squadron there ran a vague rumour of attack. The command to form in order rang out, then there was the clank of sabres being drawn out of their sheaths. But still no one moved. The troops of the left flank, both the infantry and the hussars, felt that their commanders themselves did not know what to do, and the uncertainty of the commanders infected the soldiers.

'Make haste, if only they'd make haste,' thought Rostov, feeling that at last the moment had come to taste the joys of the attack, of which he had heard so much from his comrades.

'With God's help, lads,' rang out Denisov's voice, 'forward, quick, gallop!'

The horses' haunches began moving in the front line. Rook pulled at the reins and set off of himself.

On the right Rostov saw the foremost lines of his own hussars, and still further ahead he could see a dark streak, which he could not distinguish clearly, but assumed to be the enemy. Shots could be heard, but at a distance.

'Quicker!' rang out the word of command, and Rostov felt the drooping of Rook's hindquarters as he broke into a gallop. He felt the joy of the gallop coming, and was more and more lighthearted. He noticed a solitary tree ahead of him. The tree was at first in front of him, in the middle of that borderland that had seemed so terrible. But now they had crossed it and nothing terrible had happened, but he felt more lively and excited every moment. 'Ah, won't I slash at him!' thought Rostov, grasping the hilt of his sabre tightly. 'Hur . . . r . . . a . . . a!' roared voices.

'Now, let him come on, whoever it may be,' thought Rostov, driving the spurs into Rook, and outstripping the rest, he let him go at full gallop. Already the enemy could be seen in front. Suddenly something swept over the squadron like a broad broom. Rostov lifted his sabre, making ready to deal a blow, but at that instant the soldier Nikitenko galloped ahead and left his side, and Rostov felt as though he were in a dream being carried forward with supernatural swiftness and yet remaining at the same spot. An hussar, Bandartchuk, galloped up from behind close upon him and looked angrily at him. Bandartchuk's horse started aside, and he galloped by.

'What's the matter? I'm not moving? I've fallen, I'm killed . . .' Rostov asked and answered himself all in one instant. He was alone in the middle of the field. Instead of the moving horses and the hussars' backs, he saw around him the motionless earth and stubblefield. There was warm blood under him.

'No, I'm wounded, and my horse is killed.' Rook tried to get up on his forelegs, but he sank again, crushing his rider's leg under his leg. Blood was flowing from the horse's head. The horse struggled, but could not get up. Rostov tried to get up, and fell down too. His sabretache had caught in the saddle. Where our men were, where were the French, he did not know. All around him there was no one.

Getting his leg free, he stood up. 'Which side, where now was that line that had so sharply divided the two armies?' he asked himself, and could not answer. 'Hasn't something gone wrong with me? Do such things happen, and what ought one to do in such cases?' he wondered as he was getting up. But at that instant he felt as though something superfluous was hanging on his benumbed left arm. The wrist seemed not to belong to it. He looked at his hand, carefully searching for blood on it. 'Come, here are some men,' he thought joyfully, seeing some men running towards him. 'They will help me!' In front of these men ran a single figure in a strange shako and a blue coat, with a swarthy sunburnt face and a hooked nose. Then came two men, and many more were running up behind. One of them said some strange words, not

Russian. Between some similar figures in similar shakos behind stood a Russian hussar. He was being held by the arms; behind him they were holding his horse too.

'It must be one of ours taken prisoner.... Yes. Surely they couldn't take me too? What sort of men are they?' Rostov was still wondering, unable to believe his own eyes. 'Can they be the French?' He gazed at the approaching French, and although only a few seconds before he had been longing to get at these Frenchmen and to cut them down, their being so near seemed to him now so awful that he could not believe his eyes. 'Who are they? What are they running for? Can it be to me? Can they be running to me? And what for? To kill me? *Me*, whom every one's so fond of?' He recalled his mother's love, the love of his family and his friends, and the enemy's intention of killing him seemed impossible. 'But they may even kill me.' For more than ten seconds he stood, not moving from the spot, nor grasping his position. The foremost Frenchman with the hook nose was getting so near that he could see the expression of his face. And the excited, alien countenance of the man, who was running so lightly and breathlessly towards him, with his bayonet lowered, terrified Rostov. He snatched up his pistol, and instead of firing with it, flung it at the Frenchman and ran to the bushes with all his might. Not with the feeling of doubt and conflict with which he had moved at the Enns bridge, did he now run, but with the feeling of a hare fleeing from the dogs. One unmixed feeling of fear for his young, happy life took possession of his whole being. Leaping rapidly over the hedges with the same impetuosity with which he used to run when he played games, he flew over the field, now and then turning his pale, good-natured, youthful face, and a chill of horror ran down his spine. 'No, better not to look,' he thought, but as he got near to the bushes he looked round once more. The French had given it up, and just at the moment when he looked round the foremost man was just dropping from a run into a walk, and turning round to shout something loudly to a comrade behind. Rostov stopped. 'There's some mistake,' he thought; 'it can't be that they meant to kill me.' And meanwhile his left arm was as heavy as if a hundred pound weight were hanging on it. He could run no further. The Frenchman stopped too and took aim. Rostov frowned and ducked. One bullet and then another flew hissing by him; he took his left hand in his right, and with a last effort ran as far as the bushes. In the bushes there were Russian sharpshooters.

XX

THE infantry, who had been caught unawares in the copse, had run away, and the different companies all confused together had retreated in disorderly crowds. One soldier in a panic had uttered those words—terrible in war and meaningless: 'Cut off!' and those words had infected the whole mass with panic.

'Outflanked! Cut off! Lost!' they shouted as they ran.

When their general heard the firing and the shouts in the rear he had grasped at the instant that something awful was happening to his regiment; and the thought that he, an exemplary officer, who had served so many years without ever having been guilty of the slightest shortcoming, might be held responsible by his superiors for negligence or lack of discipline, so affected him that, instantly oblivious of the insubordinate cavalry colonel and his dignity as a general, utterly oblivious even of danger and of the instinct of self-preservation, he clutched at the crupper of his saddle, and spurring his horse, galloped off to the regiment under a perfect hail of bullets that luckily missed him. He was possessed by the one desire to find out what was wrong, and to help and correct the mistake whatever it might be, if it were a mistake on his part, so that after twenty-two years of exemplary service, without incurring a reprimand for anything, he might avoid being responsible for this blunder.

Galloping successfully between the French forces, he reached the field behind the copse across which our men were running downhill, not heeding the word of command. That moment had come of moral vacillation which decides the fate of battles. Would these disorderly crowds of soldiers hear the voice of their commander, or, looking back at him, run on further? In spite of the despairing yell of the commander, who had once been so awe-inspiring to his solders, in spite of his infuriated, purple face, distorted out of all likeness to itself, in spite of his brandished sword, the soldiers still ran and talked together, shooting into the air and not listening to the word of command. The moral balance which decides the fate of battle was unmistakably falling on the side of panic.

The general was choked with screaming and gunpowder-smoke, and he stood still in despair. All seemed lost; but at that moment the French, who had been advancing against our men, suddenly, for no apparent reason, ran back, vanished from the edge of the copse, and Russian sharpshooters appeared in the copse. This was Timohin's division, the only one that had retained its good order in the copse, and hiding in ambush in the ditch behind the copse, had suddenly attacked the French. Timohin had rushed with such a desperate yell upon the French, and with such desperate and drunken energy he had dashed at the enemy with only a sword in his hand, that the French flung down their weapons and fled without pausing to recover themselves. Dolohov, running beside Timohin, killed one French soldier at close quarters, and was the first to seize by the collar an officer who surrendered. The fleeing Russians came back; the battalions were brought together; and the French, who had been on the point of splitting the forces of the left flank into two parts, were for the moment held in check. The reserves had time to join the main forces, and the runaways were stopped. The general stood with Major Ekonomov at the bridge, watching the retreating companies go by, when a soldier ran up to him, caught hold of his stirrup and almost clung on to it. The soldier was wearing a coat of blue fine cloth, he had no knapsack nor shako, his head was bound up, and across his shoulders was slung a French cartridge case. In his hand he held an officer's sword. The soldier was pale, his blue eyes looked impudently into the general's face, but his mouth was smiling. Although the general was engaged in giving instructions to Major Ekonomov, he could not help noticing this soldier.

'Your excellency, here are two trophies,' said Dolohov, pointing to the French sword and cartridge case. 'An officer was taken prisoner by me. I stopped the company.' Dolohov breathed hard from weariness; he spoke in jerks. 'The whole company can bear me witness. I beg you to remember me, your excellency!'

'Very good, very good,' said the general, and he turned to Major Ekonomov. But Dolohov did not leave him; he undid the bandage, and showed the blood congealed on his head.

'A bayonet wound; I kept my place in the front. Remember me, your excellency.'

Tushin's battery had been forgotten, and it was only at the very end of the action that Prince Bagration, still hearing the cannonade in the centre, sent the staff-officer on duty and then Prince Andrey to command the battery to retire as quickly as possible. The force which had been stationed near Tushin's cannons to protect them had by somebody's orders retreated in the middle of the battle. But the battery still kept up its fire, and was not taken by the French simply because the enemy could not conceive of the reckless daring of firing from four cannons that were quite unprotected. The French supposed, on the contrary, judging from the energetic action of the battery, that the chief forces of the Russians were concentrated here in the centre, and twice attempted to attack that point, and both times were driven back by the grapeshot fired on them from the four cannons which stood in solitude on the heights. Shortly after Prince Bagration's departure, Tushin had succeeded in setting fire to Schöngraben.

'Look, what a fuss they're in! It's flaming! What a smoke! Smartly done! First-rate! The smoke! the smoke!' cried the gunners, their spirits reviving.

All the guns were aimed without instructions in the direction of the conflagration. The soldiers, as though they were urging each other on, shouted at every volley: 'Bravo! That's something like now! Go it! ... First-rate!' The fire, fanned by the wind, soon spread. The French columns, who had marched out beyond the village, went back, but as though in revenge for this mischance, the enemy stationed ten cannons a little to the right of the village, and began firing from them on Tushin.

In their childlike glee at the conflagration of the village, and the excitement of their successful firing on the French, our artillerymen only noticed this battery when two cannonballs and after them four more fell among their cannons, and one knocked over two horses and another tore off the foot of a gunner. Their spirits, however, once raised, did not flag; their excitement simply found another direction. The horses were replaced by others from the ammunition carriage; the wounded were removed, and the four cannons were turned facing the ten of the enemy's battery. The other officer, Tushin's comrade, was killed at the beginning of the action, and after an hour's time, of the forty gunners of the battery, seventeen were disabled, but they were still as merry and as eager as ever. Twice they noticed the French appearing below close to them, and they sent volleys of grapeshot at them.

The little man with his weak, clumsy movements, was continually asking his orderly *for just one more pipe for that stroke*, as he said, and scattering sparks from it, he kept running out in front and looking from under his little hand at the French.

'Smash away, lads!' he was continually saying, and he clutched at the cannon wheels himself and unscrewed the screws. In the smoke, deafened by the incessant booming of the cannons that made him shudder every time one was fired, Tushin ran from one cannon to the other, his short pipe never out of his mouth. At one moment he was taking aim, then reckoning the charges, then arranging for the changing and unharnessing of the killed and wounded horses, and all the time shouting in his weak, shrill, hesitating voice. His face grew more and more eager. Only when men were killed and wounded he knitted his brows, and turning away from the dead man, shouted angrily to the men, slow, as they always are, to pick up a wounded man or a dead body. The soldiers, for the most part fine, handsome fellows (a couple of heads taller than their officer and twice as broad in the chest, as they mostly are in the artillery), all looked to their commanding officer like children in a difficult position, and the expression they found on his face was invariably reflected at once on their own.

Owing to the fearful uproar and noise and the necessity of attention and activity, Tushin experienced not the slightest unpleasant sensation of fear; and the idea that he might be killed or badly wounded never entered his head. On the contrary, he felt more and more lively. It seemed to him that the moment in which he had first seen the enemy and had fired the first shot was long, long ago, yesterday perhaps, and that the spot of earth on which he stood was a place long-familiar to him, in which he was quite at home. Although he thought of everything, considered everything, did everything the very best officer could have done in his position, he was in a state of mind akin to the delirium of fever or the intoxication of a drunken man.

The deafening sound of his own guns on all sides, the hiss and thud of the enemy's shells, the sight of the perspiring, flushed gunners hurrying about the cannons, the sight of the blood of men and horses, and of the puffs of smoke from the enemy on the opposite side (always followed by a cannon-ball that flew across and hit the earth, a man, a horse, or a cannon)—all these images made up for him a fantastic world of his own, in which he found enjoyment at the moment. The enemy's cannons in his fancy were not cannons, but pipes from which an invisible smoker blew puffs of smoke at intervals.

'There he's puffing away again,' Tushin murmured to himself as a cloud of smoke rolled downhill, and was borne off by the wind in a wreath to the left. 'Now, your ball—throw it back.'

'What is it, your honour?' asked a gunner who stood near him, and heard him muttering something.

'Nothing, a grenade . . .' he answered. 'Now for it, our Matvyevna,' he said to himself. Matvyevna was the name his fancy gave to the big cannon, cast in an old-fashioned mould, that stood at the end. The French seemed to be ants swarming about their cannons. The handsome, drunken soldier, number one gunner of the second cannon, was in his dream-world 'uncle'; Tushin looked at him more often than at any of the rest, and took delight in every gesture of the man. The sound—dying away, then quickening again—of the musketry fire below the hill seemed to him like the heaving of some creature's breathing. He listened to the ebb and flow of these sounds.

'Ah, she's taking another breath again,' he was saying to himself. He himself figured in his imagination as a mighty man of immense stature, who was flinging cannon-balls at the French with both hands.

'Come, Matvyevna, old lady, stick by us!' he was saying, moving back from the cannon, when a strange, unfamiliar voice called over his head. 'Captain Tushin! Captain!'

Tushin looked round in dismay. It was the same staff-officer who had turned him out of the booth at Grunte. He was shouting to him in a breathless voice:

'I say, are you mad? You've been commanded twice to retreat, and you . . .'

'Now, what are they pitching into me for?' . . . Tushin wondered, looking in alarm at the superior officer.

'I . . . don't . . .' he began, putting two fingers to the peak of his cap. 'I . . .'

But the staff-officer did not say all he had meant to. A cannon-ball flying near him made him duck down on his horse. He paused, and was just going to say something more, when another ball stopped him. He turned his horse's head and galloped away.

'Retreat! All to retreat!' he shouted from a distance.

The soldiers laughed. A minute later an adjutant arrived with the same message. This was Prince Andrey. The first thing he saw, on reaching the place where Tushin's cannons were stationed, was an unharnessed horse with a broken leg, which was neighing beside the harnessed horses. The blood was flowing in a perfect stream from its leg. Among the platforms lay several dead men. One cannon-ball after another flew over him as he rode up, and he felt a nervous shudder running down his spine. But the very idea that he was afraid was enough to rouse him again. 'I can't be frightened,' he thought, and he deliberately dismounted from his horse between the cannons. He gave his message, but he did not leave the battery. He decided to stay and assist in removing the cannons from the position and getting them away. Stepping over the corpses, under the fearful fire from the French, he helped Tushin in getting the cannons ready.

'The officer that came just now ran off quicker than he came,' said a gunner to Prince Andrey, 'not like your honour.'

Prince Andrey had no conversation with Tushin. They were both so busy that they hardly seemed to see each other. When they had got the two out of the four cannons that were uninjured on to the platforms and were moving downhill (one cannon that had been smashed and a howitzer were left behind), Prince Andrey went up to Tushin.

'Well, good-bye till we meet again,' said Prince Andrey, holding out his hand to Tushin.

'Good-bye, my dear fellow,' said Tushin, 'dear soul! good-bye, my dear fellow,' he said with tears, which for some unknown reason started suddenly into his eyes.

XXI

THE wind had sunk, black storm-clouds hung low over the battlefield, melting on the horizon into the clouds of smoke from the powder. Darkness had come, and the glow of conflagrations showed all the more distinctly in two places. The cannonade had grown feebler, but the snapping of musketry-fire in the rear and on the right was heard nearer and more often. As soon as Tushin with his cannons, continually driving round the wounded and coming upon them, had got out of fire and were descending the ravine, he was met by the staff, among whom was the staff-officer and Zherkov, who had twice been sent to Tushin's battery, but had not once reached it. They all vied with one another in giving him orders, telling him how and where to go, finding fault and making criticisms. Tushin gave no orders, and in silence, afraid to speak because at every word he felt, he could not have said why, ready to burst into tears, he rode behind on his artillery nag. Though orders were given to abandon the wounded, many of them dragged themselves after the troops and begged for a seat on the cannons. The jaunty infantry-officer—the one who had run out of Tushin's shanty just before the battle—was laid on Matvyevna's carriage with a bullet in his stomach. At the bottom of the hill a pale ensign of hussars, holding one arm in the other hand, came up to Tushin and begged for a seat.

'Captain, for God's sake. I've hurt my arm,' he said timidly. 'For God's sake. I can't walk. For God's sake!' It was evident that this was not the first time the ensign had asked for a lift, and that he had been everywhere refused. He asked in a hesitating and piteous voice, 'Tell them to let me get on, for God's sake!'

'Let him get on, let him get on,' said Tushin. 'Put a coat under him, you, uncle.' He turned to his favourite soldier. 'But where's the wounded officer?'

'We took him off; he was dead,' answered some one.

'Help him on. Sit down, my dear fellow, sit down. Lay the coat there, Antonov.'

The ensign was Rostov. He was holding one hand in the other. He was pale, and his lower jaw was trembling as though in a fever. They put him on Matvyevna, the cannon from which they had just removed the dead officer. There was blood on the coat that was laid under him, and Rostov's riding-breeches and arm were smeared with it.

'What, are you wounded, my dear?' said Tushin, going up to the cannon on which Rostov was sitting.

'No; it's a sprain.'

'How is it there's blood on the frame?' asked Tushin.

'That was the officer, your honour, stained it,' answered an artilleryman, wiping the blood off with the sleeve of his coat, and as it were apologising for the dirty state of the cannon.

With difficulty, aided by the infantry, they dragged the cannon uphill, and halted on reaching the village of Guntersdorf. It was by now so dark that one could not distinguish the soldiers' uniforms ten paces away, and the firing had begun to subside. All of a sudden there came the sound of firing and shouts again close by on the right side. The flash of the shots could be seen in the darkness. This was the last attack of the French. It was met by the soldiers in ambush in the houses of the village. All rushed out of the village again, but Tushin's cannons could not move, and the artillerymen, Tushin, and the ensign looked at one another in anticipation of their fate. The firing on both sides began to subside, and some soldiers in lively conversation streamed out of a side street.

'Not hurt, Petrov?' inquired one.

'We gave it them hot, lads. They won't meddle with us now,' another was saying.

'One couldn't see a thing. Didn't they give it to their own men! No seeing for the darkness, mates. Isn't there something to drink?'

The French had been repulsed for the last time. And again, in the complete darkness, Tushin's cannons moved forward, surrounded by the infantry, who kept up a hum of talk.

In the darkness they flowed on like an unseen, gloomy river always in the same direction, with a buzz of whisper and talk and the thud of hoofs and rumble of wheels. Above all other sounds, in the confused uproar, rose the moans and cries of the wounded, more distinct than anything in the darkness of the night. Their moans seemed to fill all the darkness surrounding the troops. Their moans and the darkness seemed to melt into one. A little later a thrill of emotion passed over the moving crowd. Some one followed by a suite had ridden by on a white horse, and had said something as he passed.

'What did he say? Where we are going now? To halt, eh? Thanked us, what?' eager questions were heard on all sides, and the whole moving mass began to press back on itself (the foremost, it seemed, had halted), and a rumour passed through that the order had been given to halt. All halted in the muddy road, just where they were.

Fires were lighted and the talk became more audible. Captain Tushin, after giving instructions to his battery, sent some of his soldiers to look for an ambulance or a doctor for the ensign, and sat down by the fire his soldiers had lighted by the roadside. Rostov too dragged himself to the fire. His whole body was trembling with fever from the pain, the cold, and the damp. He was dreadfully sleepy, but he could not go to sleep for the agonising pain in his arm, which ached and would not be easy in any position. He closed his eyes, then opened them to stare at the fire, which seemed to him dazzlingly red, and then at the stooping, feeble figure of Tushin, squatting in Turkish fashion near him. The big, kindly, and shrewd eyes of Tushin were fixed upon him with sympathy and commiseration. He saw that Tushin wished with all his soul to help him, but could do nothing for him.

On all sides they heard the footsteps and the chatter of the infantry going and coming and settling themselves round them. The sounds of voices, of steps, and of horses' hoofs tramping in the mud, the crackling firewood far and near, all melted into one fluctuating roar of sound.

It was not now as before an unseen river flowing in the darkness, but a gloomy sea subsiding and still agitated after a storm. Rostov gazed vacantly and listened to what was passing before him and around him. An infantry soldier came up to the fire, squatted on his heels, held his hands to the fire, and turned his face.

'You don't mind, your honour?' he said, looking inquiringly at Tushin. 'Here I've got lost from my company, your honour; I don't know myself where I am. It's dreadful!'

With the soldier an infantry officer approached the fire with a bandaged face. He asked Tushin to have the cannon moved a very little, so as to let a store waggon pass by. After the officer two soldiers ran up to the fire. They were swearing desperately and fighting, trying to pull a boot from one another.

'No fear! you picked it up! that's smart!' one shouted in a husky voice.

Then a thin, pale soldier approached, his neck bandaged with a blood-stained rag. With a voice of exasperation he asked the artillerymen for water.

'Why, is one to die like a dog?' he said.

Tushin told them to give him water. Next a good-humoured soldier ran up, to beg for some red-hot embers for the infantry.

'Some of your fire for the infantry! Glad to halt, lads. Thanks for the loan of the firing; we'll pay it back with interest,' he said, carrying some glowing firebrands away into the darkness.

Next four soldiers passed by, carrying something heavy in an overcoat. One of them stumbled.

'Ay, the devils, they've left firewood in the road,' grumbled one.

'He's dead; why carry him?' said one of them.

'Come on, you!' And they vanished into the darkness with their burden.

'Does it ache, eh?' Tushin asked Rostov in a whisper.

'Yes, it does ache.'

'Your honour's sent for to the general. Here in a cottage he is,' said a gunner, coming up to Tushin.

'In a minute, my dear.' Tushin got up and walked away from the fire, buttoning up his coat and setting himself straight.

In a cottage that had been prepared for him not far from the artillerymen's fire, Prince Bagration was sitting at dinner, talking with several commanding officers, who had gathered about him. The little old colonel with the half-shut eyes was there, greedily gnawing at a mutton-bone, and the general of twenty-two years irreproachable service, flushed with a glass of vodka and his dinner, and the staff-officer with the signet ring, and Zherkov, stealing uneasy glances at every one, and Prince Andrey, pale with set lips and feverishly glittering eyes.

In the corner of the cottage room stood a French flag, that had been captured, and the auditor with the naïve countenance was feeling the stuff of which the flag was made, and shaking his head with a puzzled air, possibly because looking at the flag really interested him, or possibly because he did not enjoy the sight of the dinner, as he was hungry and no place had been laid for him. In the next cottage there was the French colonel, who had been taken prisoner by the dragoons. Our officers were flocking in to look at him. Prince Bagration thanked the several commanding officers, and inquired into details of the battle and of the losses. The general, whose regiment had been inspected at Braunau, submitted to the prince that as soon as the engagement began, he had fallen back from the copse, mustered the men who were cutting wood, and letting them pass by him, had made a bayonet charge with two battalions and repulsed the French.

'As soon as I saw, your excellency, that the first battalion was thrown into confusion, I stood in the road and thought, "I'll let them get through and then open fire on them"; and that's what I did.'

The general had so longed to do this, he had so regretted not having succeeded in doing it, that it seemed to him now that this was just what had happened. Indeed might it not actually have been so? Who could make out in such confusion what did and what did not happen?

'And by the way I ought to note, your excellency,' he continued, recalling Dolohov's conversation with Kutuzov and his own late interview with the degraded officer, 'that the private Dolohov, degraded to the ranks, took a French officer prisoner before my eyes and particularly distinguished himself.'

'I saw here, your excellency, the attack of the Pavlograd hussars,' Zherkov put in, looking uneasily about him. He had not seen the hussars at all that day, but had only heard about them from an infantry officer. 'They broke up two squares, your excellency.'

When Zherkov began to speak, several officers smiled, as they always did, expecting a joke from him. But as they perceived that what he was saying all redounded to the glory of our arms and of the day, they assumed a serious expression, although many were very well aware that what Zherkov was saying was a lie utterly without foundation. Prince Bagration turned to the old colonel.

'I thank you all, gentlemen; all branches of the service behaved heroically—infantry, cavalry, and artillery. How did two cannons come to be abandoned in the centre?' he inquired, looking about for some one. (Prince Bagration did not ask about the cannons of the left flank; he knew that all of them had been abandoned at the very beginning of the action.) 'I think it was you I sent,' he added, addressing the staff-officer.

'One had been disabled,' answered the staff-officer, 'but the other, I can't explain; I was there all the while myself, giving instructions, and I had scarcely left there. . . . It was pretty hot, it's true,' he added modestly.

Some one said that Captain Tushin was close by here in the village, and that he had already been sent for.

'Oh, but you went there,' said Prince Bagration, addressing Prince Andrey.

'To be sure, we rode there almost together,' said the staff-officer, smiling affably to Bolkonsky.

'I had not the pleasure of seeing you,' said Prince Andrey, coldly and abruptly. Every one was silent.

Tushin appeared in the doorway, timidly edging in behind the generals' backs. Making his way round the generals in the crowded hut, embarrassed as he always was before his superior officers, Tushin did not see the flag-staff and tumbled over it. Several of the officers laughed.

'How was it a cannon was abandoned?' asked Bagration, frowning, not so much at the captain as at the laughing officers, among whom Zherkov's laugh was the loudest. Only now in the presence of the angry-looking commander, Tushin conceived in all its awfulness the crime and disgrace of his being still alive when he had lost two cannons. He had been so excited that till that instant he had not had time to think of that. The officers' laughter had bewildered him still more. He stood before Bagration, his lower jaw quivering, and could scarcely articulate:

'I don't know . . . your excellency . . . I hadn't the men, your excellency.'

'You could have got them from the battalions that were covering your position!' That there were no battalions there was what Tushin did not say, though it was the fact. He was afraid of getting another officer into trouble by saying that, and without uttering a word he gazed straight into Bagration's face, as a confused schoolboy gazes at the face of an examiner.

The silence was rather a lengthy one. Prince Bagration, though he had no wish to be severe, apparently found nothing to say; the others did not venture to intervene. Prince Andrey was looking from under his brows at Tushin and his fingers moved nervously.

'Your excellency,' Prince Andrey broke the silence with his abrupt voice, 'you sent me to Captain Tushin's battery. I went there and found two-thirds of the men and horses killed, two cannons disabled and no forces near to defend them.'

Prince Bagration and Tushin looked now with equal intensity at Bolkonsky, as he went on speaking with suppressed emotion.

'And if your excellency will permit me to express my opinion,' he went on, 'we owe the success of the day more to the action of that battery and the heroic steadiness of Captain Tushin and his men than to anything else,' said Prince Andrey, and he got up at once and walked away from the table, without waiting for a reply.

Prince Bagration looked at Tushin and, apparently loath to express his disbelief in Bolkonsky's off-handed judgment, yet unable to put complete faith in it, he bent his head and said to Tushin that he could go. Prince Andrey walked out after him.

'Thanks, my dear fellow, you got me out of a scrape,' Tushin said to him.

Prince Andrey looked at Tushin, and walked away without uttering a word. Prince Andrey felt bitter and melancholy. It was all so strange, so unlike what he had been hoping for.

'Who are they? Why are they here? What do they want? And when will it all end?' thought Rostov, looking at the shadowy figures that kept flitting before his eyes. The pain in his arm became even more agonising. He was heavy with sleep, crimson circles danced before his eyes, and the impression of these voices and these faces and the sense of his loneliness all blended with the misery of the pain. It was they, these soldiers, wounded and unhurt alike, it was they crushing and weighing upon him, and twisting his veins and burning the flesh in his sprained arm and shoulder. To get rid of them he closed his eyes.

He dozed off for a minute, but in that brief interval he dreamed of innumerable things. He saw his mother and her large, white hand; he saw Sonya's thin shoulders, Natasha's eyes and her laugh, and Denisov with his voice and his whiskers, and Telyanin, and all the affair with Telyanin and Bogdanitch. All that affair was inextricably mixed up with this soldier with the harsh voice, and that affair and this soldier here were so agonisingly, so ruthlessly pulling, crushing, and twisting his arm always in the same direction. He was trying to get away from them, but they would not let go of his shoulder for a second. It would not ache, it would be all right if they wouldn't drag at it; but there was no getting rid of them.

He opened his eyes and looked upwards. The black pall of darkness hung only a few feet above the light of the fire. In the light fluttered tiny flakes of falling snow. Tushin had not returned, the doctor had not come. He was alone, only a soldier was sitting now naked on the other side of the fire, warming his thin, yellow body.

'Nobody cares for me!' thought Rostov. 'No one to help me, no one to feel sorry for me. And I too was once at home, and strong, and happy and loved,' he sighed, and with the sigh unconsciously he moaned.

'In pain, eh?' asked the soldier, shaking his shirt out before the fire, and without waiting for an answer, he added huskily: 'Ah, what a lot of fellows done for today—awful!'

Rostov did not hear the soldier. He gazed at the snowflakes whirling over the fire and thought of the Russian winter with his warm, brightly lighted home, his cosy fur cloak, his swift sledge, his good health, and all the love and tenderness of his family. 'And what did I come here for!' he wondered.

On the next day, the French did not renew the attack and the remnant of Bagration's detachment joined Kutuzov's army.

PART III

I

PRINCE VASSILY used not to think over his plans. Still less did he think of doing harm to others for the sake of his own interest. He was simply a man of the world, who had been successful in the world, and had formed a habit of being so. Various plans and calculations were continually forming in his mind, arising from circumstances and the persons he met, but he never deliberately considered them, though they constituted the whole interest of his life. Of such plans and calculations he had not one or two, but dozens in train at once, some of them only beginning to occur to him, others attaining their aim, others again coming to nothing. He never said to himself, for instance: 'That man is now in power, I must secure his friendship and confidence, and through him obtain a grant from the Single-Assistance Fund'; nor, 'Now Pierre is a wealthy man, I must entice him to marry my daughter and borrow the forty thousand I need.' But the man in power met him, and at the instant his instinct told him that that man might be of use, and Prince Vassily made friends with him, and at the first opportunity by instinct, without previous consideration, flattered him, became intimate with him, and told him of what he wanted.

Pierre was ready at hand in Moscow, and Prince Vassily secured an appointment as gentleman of the bedchamber for him, a position at that time reckoned equal in status to that of a councillor of state, and insisted on the young man's travelling with him to Petersburg, and staying at his house. Without apparent design, but yet with unhesitating conviction that it was the right thing, Prince Vassily did everything to ensure Pierre's marrying his daughter. If Prince Vassily had definitely reflected upon his plans beforehand, he could not have been so natural in his behaviour and so straightforward and familiar in his relations with every one, of higher and of lower rank than himself. Something drew him infallibly towards men richer or more powerful than himself, and he was endowed with a rare instinct for hitting on precisely the moment when he should and could make use of such persons.

Pierre, on unexpectedly becoming rich and Count Bezuhov, after his lonely and careless manner of life, felt so surrounded, so occupied, that he never succeeded in being by himself except in his bed. He had to sign papers, to present himself at legal institutions, of the significance of which he had no definite idea, to make some inquiry of his chief steward, to visit his estate near Moscow, and to receive a great number of persons, who previously had not cared to be aware of his existence, but now would have been hurt and offended if he had not chosen to see them. All these various people, business men, relations, acquaintances, were all equally friendly and well disposed towards the young heir. They were all obviously and unhesitatingly convinced of Pierre's noble qualities. He was continually hearing phrases, such as, 'With your exceptionally kindly disposition'; or, 'Considering your excellent heart'; or, 'You are so pure-minded yourself, count . . .' or, 'If he were as clever as you,' and so on, so that he was beginning genuinely to believe in his own exceptional goodness and his own exceptional intelligence, the more so, as at the bottom of his heart it had always seemed to him that he really was very good-natured and very intelligent. Even people, who had before been spiteful and openly hostile to him, became tender and affectionate. The hitherto ill-tempered, eldest princess, with the long waist and the hair plastered down like a doll, had gone into Pierre's room after the funeral. Dropping her eyes and repeatedly turning crimson, she said that she very much regretted the misunderstanding that had arisen between them, and that now she felt she had no right to ask him for anything except permission, after the blow that had befallen her, to remain for a few weeks longer in the house which she was so fond of, and in which she had made such sacrifices. She could not control herself, and wept at these words. Touched at seeing the statue-like princess so changed, Pierre took her by the hand and begged her pardon, though he could not have said what for. From that day the princess began knitting a striped scarf for Pierre, and was completely changed towards him.

'Do this for my sake, my dear boy; she had to put up with a great deal from the deceased, any way,' Prince Vassily said to him, giving him some deed to sign for the princess's benefit. Prince Vassily reflected that this note of hand for thirty thousand was a sop worth throwing to the poor princess, that it might not occur to her to gossip about Prince Vassily's part in the action taken with the inlaid portfolio. Pierre signed the note, and from that time the princess became even more amiable. The younger sisters became as affectionate too, especially the youngest one, the pretty one with the mole, who often disconcerted Pierre with her smiles and her confusion at the sight of him.

To Pierre it seemed so natural that every one should be fond of him, it would have seemed to him so unnatural if any one had not liked him, that he could not help believing in the sincerity of the people surrounding him. Besides, he had no time to doubt their sincerity or insincerity. He never had a moment of leisure, and felt in a continual state of mild and agreeable intoxication. He felt as though he were the centre of some important public function, felt that something was continually being expected of him; that if he did not do this or that, he would wound many people and disappoint them, but that if he did this and that, all would be well, and he did what was expected of him, but still that happy result loomed in the future.

In these early days Prince Vassily, more than all the rest, took control of Pierre's affairs, and of Pierre himself. On the death of Count Bezuhov he did not let Pierre slip out of his hands. Prince Vassily had the air of a man weighed down by affairs, weary, worried, but from sympathetic feeling, unable in the last resort to abandon this helpless lad, the son, after all, of his friend, and the heir to such an immense fortune, to leave him to his fate to become a prey to plotting knaves. During the few days he had stayed on in Moscow after Count Bezuhov's death, he had invited Pierre to him, or had himself gone to see Pierre, and had dictated to him what he was to do in a tone of weariness and certainty which seemed to be always saying: 'You know that I am overwhelmed with business and that it is out of pure charity that I concern myself with you, and moreover you know very well that what I propose to you is the only feasible thing.'

'Well, my dear boy, tomorrow we are off at last,' he said one day, closing his eyes, drumming his fingers on his elbow, and speaking as though the matter had long ago been settled between them, and could not be settled in any other way.

'Tomorrow we set off; I'll give you a place in my coach. I'm very glad. Here all our important business is settled. And I ought to have been back long ago. Here, I have received this from the chancellor. I petitioned him in your favour, and you are put on the diplomatic corps, and created a gentleman of the bedchamber. Now a diplomatic career lies open to you.'

Notwithstanding the effect produced on him by the tone of weariness and certainty with which these words were uttered, Pierre, who had so long been pondering over his future career, tried to protest. But Prince Vassily broke in on his protest in droning, bass tones, that precluded all possibility of interrupting the flow of his words; it was the resource he fell back upon when extreme measures of persuasion were needed.

'But, my dear boy, I have done it for my own sake, for my conscience' sake, and there is no need to thank me. No one has ever complained yet of being too much loved; and then you are free, you can give it all up tomorrow. You'll see for yourself in Petersburg. And it is high time you were getting away from these terrible associations.' Prince Vassily sighed. 'So that's all settled, my dear fellow. And let my valet go in your coach. Ah, yes, I was almost forgetting,' Prince Vassily added. 'You know, my dear boy, I had a little account to settle with your father, so as I have received something from the Ryazan estate, I'll keep that; you don't want it. We'll go into accounts later.'

What Prince Vassily called 'something from the Ryazan estate' was several thousands of roubles paid in lieu of service by the peasants, and this sum he kept for himself.

In Petersburg, Pierre was surrounded by the same atmosphere of affection and tenderness as in Moscow. He could not decline the post, or rather the title (for he did nothing) that Prince Vassily had obtained for him, and acquaintances, invitations, and social duties were so numerous that Pierre was even more than in Moscow conscious of the feeling of stupefaction, hurry and continual expectation of some future good which was always coming and was never realised.

Of his old circle of bachelor acquaintances there were not many left in Petersburg. The Guards were on active service, Dolohov had been degraded to the ranks; Anatole had gone into the army and was somewhere in the provinces; Prince Andrey was abroad; and so Pierre had not the opportunity of spending his nights in the way he had so loved spending them before, nor could he open his heart in intimate talk with the friend who was older than himself and a man he respected. All his time was spent at dinners and balls, or at Prince Vassily's in the society of the fat princess, his wife, and the beauty, his daughter Ellen.

Like every one else, Anna Pavlovna Scherer showed Pierre the change that had taken place in the attitude of society towards him.

In former days, Pierre had always felt in Anna Pavlovna's presence that what he was saying was unsuitable, tactless, not the right thing; that the phrases, which seemed to him clever as he formed them in his mind, became somehow stupid as soon as he uttered them aloud, and that, on the contrary, Ippolit's most pointless remarks had the effect of being clever and charming. Now everything he said was always 'delightful'. Even if Anna Pavlovna did not say so, he saw she was longing to say so, and only refraining from doing so from regard for his modesty.

At the beginning of the winter, in the year 1805, Pierre received one of Anna Pavlovna's customary pink notes of invitation, in which the words occurred: 'You will find the fair Helene at my house, whom one never gets tired of seeing.'

On reading that passage, Pierre felt for the first time that there was being formed between himself and Ellen some sort of tie, recognised by other people, and this idea at once alarmed him, as though an obligation were being laid upon him which he could not fulfil, and pleased him as an amusing supposition.

Anna Pavlovna's evening party was like her first one, only the novel attraction which she had provided for her guests was not on this occasion Mortemart, but a diplomat, who had just arrived from Berlin, bringing the latest details of the Emperor Alexander's stay at Potsdam, and of the inviolable alliance the two exalted friends had sworn together, to maintain the true cause against the enemy of the human race. Pierre was welcomed by Anna Pavlovna with a shade of melancholy, bearing unmistakable reference to the recent loss sustained by the young man in the death of Count Bezuhov (every one felt bound to be continually assuring Pierre that he was greatly afflicted at the death of his father, whom he had hardly known). Her melancholy was of precisely the same kind as that more exalted melancholy she always displayed at any allusion to Her Most August Majesty the Empress Mariya Fyodorovna. Pierre felt flattered by it. Anna Pavlovna had arranged the groups in her drawing-room with her usual skill. The larger group, in which were Prince Vassily and some generals, had the benefit of the diplomat. Another group gathered about the tea-table. Pierre would have liked to join the first group, but Anna Pavlovna, who was in the nervous excitement of a general on the battlefield, that mental condition in which numbers of brilliant new ideas occur to one that one has hardly time to put into execution—Anna Pavlovna, on seeing Pierre, detained him with a finger on his coat sleeve: 'Wait, I have designs on you for this evening.'

She looked round at Ellen and smiled at her.

'My dear Hélène, you must show charity to my poor aunt, who has an adoration for you. Go and keep her company for ten minutes. And that you may not find it too tiresome, here's our dear count, who certainly won't refuse to follow you.'

The beauty moved away towards the old aunt; but Anna Pavlovna still detained Pierre at her side, with the air of having still some last and essential arrangement to make with him.

'She is exquisite, isn't she?' she said to Pierre, indicating the majestic beauty swimming away from them. 'And how she carries herself! For such a young girl, what tact, what a finished perfection of manner. It comes from the heart. Happy will be the man who wins her. The most unworldly of men would take a brilliant place in society as her husband. That's true, isn't it? I only wanted to know your opinion,' and Anna Pavlovna let Pierre go.

Pierre was perfectly sincere in giving an affirmative answer to her question about Ellen's perfection of manner. If ever he thought of Ellen, it was either of her beauty that he thought, or of her extraordinary capacity for serene, dignified silence in society.

The old aunt received the two young people in her corner, but appeared anxious to conceal her adoration of Ellen, and rather to show her fear of Anna Pavlovna. She glanced at her niece, as though to inquire what she was to do with them. Anna Pavlovna again laid a finger on Pierre's sleeve and said: 'I hope you will never say in future that people are bored at my house,' and glanced at Ellen. Ellen smiled with an air, which seemed to say that she did not admit the possibility of any one's seeing her without being enchanted. The old aunt coughed, swallowed the phlegm, and said in French that she was very glad to see Ellen; then she addressed Pierre with the same greeting and the same grimace. In the middle of a halting and tedious conversation, Ellen looked round at Pierre and smiled at him with the bright, beautiful smile with which she smiled at every one. Pierre was so used to this smile, it meant so little to him, that he did not even notice it. The aunt was speaking at that moment of a collection of snuff-boxes belonging to Pierre's father, Count Bezuhov, and she showed them her snuff-box. Prince Ellen asked to look at the portrait of the aunt's husband, which was on the snuff-box.

'It's probably the work of Vines,' said Pierre, mentioning a celebrated miniature painter. He bent over the table to take the snuff-box, listening all the while to the conversation going on in the larger group. He got up to move towards it, but the aunt handed him the snuff-box, passing it across Ellen, behind her back. Ellen bent forward to make room, and looked round smiling. She was, as always in the evening, wearing a dress cut in the fashion of the day, very low in the neck both in front and behind. Her bust, which had always to Pierre looked like marble, was so close to his short-sighted eyes that he could discern all the living charm of her neck and shoulders, and so near his lips that he need scarcely have stooped to kiss it. He felt the warmth of her body, the fragrance of scent, and heard the creaking of her corset as she moved. He saw not her marble beauty making up one whole with her gown: he saw and felt all the charm of her body, which was only veiled by her clothes. And having once seen this, he could not see it otherwise, just as we cannot return to an illusion that has been explained.

'So you have never noticed till now that I am lovely?' Ellen seemed to be saying. 'You haven't noticed that I am a woman? Yes, I am a woman, who might belong to any one—to you, too,' her eyes said. And at that moment Pierre felt that Ellen not only could, but would become his wife, that it must be so.

He knew it at that moment as surely as he would have known it, standing under the wedding crown beside her. How would it be? and when? He knew not, knew not even if it would be a good thing (he had a feeling, indeed, that for some reason it would not), but he knew it would be so.

Pierre dropped his eyes, raised them again, and tried once more to see her as a distant beauty, far removed from him, as he had seen her every day before. But he could not do this. He could not, just as a man who has been staring in a fog at a blade of tall steppe grass and taking it for a tree cannot see a tree in it again, after he has once recognised it as a blade of grass. She was terribly close to him. Already she had power over him. And between him and her there existed no barriers of any kind, but the barrier of his own will.

'Very good, I will leave you in your little corner. I see you are very comfortable there,' said Anna Pavlovna's voice. And Pierre, trying panic-stricken to think whether he had done anything reprehensible, looked about him, crimsoning. It seemed to him as though every one knew, as well as he did, what was passing in him. A little later, when he went up to the bigger group, Anna Pavlovna said to him:

'I am told you are making improvements in your Petersburg house.' (This was the fact: the architect had told him it was necessary, and Pierre, without knowing with what object, was having his immense house in Petersburg redecorated.) 'That is all very well, but do not move from Prince Vassily's. It is a good thing to have such a friend as the prince,' she said, smiling to Prince Vassily. 'I know something about that. Don't I? And you are so young. You need advice. You mustn't be angry with me for making use of an old woman's privileges.' She paused, as women always do pause, in anticipation of something, after speaking of their age. 'If you marry, it's a different matter.' And she united them in one glance. Pierre did not look at Ellen, nor she at him. But she was still terribly close to him.

He muttered something and blushed.

After Pierre had gone home, it was a long while before he could get to sleep; he kept pondering on what was happening to him. What was happening? Nothing. Simply he had grasped the fact that a woman, whom he had known as a child, of whom he had said, without giving her a thought, 'Yes, she's nice-looking,' when he had been told she was a beauty, he had grasped the fact that that woman might belong to him.

'But she's stupid, I used to say myself that she was stupid,' he thought. 'There is something nasty in the feeling she excites in me, something not legitimate. I have been told that her brother, Anatole, was in love with her, and she in love with him, that there was a regular scandal, and that's why Anatole was sent away. Her brother is Ippolit. . . . Her father is Prince Vassily. . . . That's bad,' he mused; and at the very moment that he was reflecting thus (the reflections were not followed out to the end) he caught himself smiling, and became conscious that another series of reflections had risen to the surface across the first, that he was at the same time meditating on her worthlessness, and dreaming of how she would be his wife, how she might love him, how she might become quite different, and how all he had thought and heard about her might be untrue. And again he saw her, not as the daughter of Prince Vassily, but saw her whole body, only veiled by her grey gown. 'But, no, why didn't that idea ever occur to me before?' And again he told himself that it was impossible, that there would be something nasty, unnatural, as it seemed to him, and dishonourable in this marriage. He recalled her past words and looks, and the words and looks of people, who had seen them together. He remembered the words and looks of Anna Pavlovna, when she had spoken about his house, he recollected thousands of such hints from Prince Vassily and other people, and he was overwhelmed with terror that he might have bound himself in some way to do a thing obviously wrong, and not what he ought to do. But at the very time that he was expressing this to himself, in another part of his mind her image floated to the surface in all its womanly beauty.

II

IN the November of 1805 Prince Vassily was obliged to go on a tour of inspection through four provinces. He had secured this appointment for himself, in order to be able at the same time to visit his estates, which were in a neglected state. He intended to pick up his son, Anatole, on the way (where his regiment was stationed), and to pay a visit to Prince Nikolay Andreivitch Bolkonsky, with a view to marrying his son to the rich old man's daughter. But before going away and entering on these new affairs, Prince Vassily wanted to settle matters with Pierre, who had, it was true, of late spent whole days at home, that is, at Prince Vassily's, where he was staying, and was as absurd, as agitated, and as stupid in Ellen's present, as a young man in love should be, but still made no offer.

'This is all very fine, but the thing must come to a conclusion,' Prince Vassily said to himself one morning, with a melancholy sigh, recognising that Pierre, who was so greatly indebted to him (But there! God bless the fellow!), was not behaving quite nicely to him in the matter. 'Youth . . . frivolity . . . well, God be with him,' thought Prince Vassily, enjoying the sense of his own goodness of heart, 'but the thing must come to a conclusion. The day after tomorrow is Ellen's name-day, I'll invite some people, and if he doesn't understand what he's to do, then it will be my affair to see to it. Yes, my affair. I'm her father.'

Six weeks after Anna Pavlovna's party, and the sleepless and agitated night after it, in which Pierre had made up his mind that a marriage with Ellen would be a calamity, and that he must avoid her and go away; six weeks after that decision Pierre had still not left Prince Vassily's, and felt with horror that every day he was more and more connected with her in people's minds, that he could not go back to his former view of her, that he could not tear himself away from her even, that it would be an awful thing, but that he would have to unite his life to hers. Perhaps he might have mastered himself, but not a day passed without a party at Prince Vassily's (where receptions had not been frequent), and Pierre was bound to be present if he did not want to disturb the general satisfaction and disappoint every one. At the rare moments when Prince Vassily was at home, he took Pierre's hand if he passed him, carelessly offered him his shaven, wrinkled cheek for a kiss, and said, 'till tomorrow,' or 'be in to dinner, or I shan't see you,' or 'I shall stay at home on your account,' or some such remark. But although, when Prince Vassily did stay at home for Pierre (as he said), he never spoke two words to him, Pierre did not feel equal to disappointing him. Every day he said the same thing over and over to himself. 'I must, really, understand her and make up my mind, what she is. Was I mistaken before, or am I mistaken now? No, she's not stupid; no, she's a good girl,' he said to himself sometimes. 'She never makes a mistake, nor has said anything stupid. She says very little, but what she does say is always simple and clear. So she's not stupid. She has never been abashed, and she is not abashed now. So she isn't a bad woman.' It often happened that he began to make reflections, to think aloud in her company, and every time she had replied either by a brief, but appropriate remark, that showed she was not interested in the matter, or by a mute smile and glance, which more palpably than anything proved to Pierre her superiority. She was right in regarding all reflections as nonsense in comparison with that smile.

She always addressed him now with a glad, confiding smile—a smile having reference to him alone, and full of something more significant than the society smile that always adorned her face. Pierre knew that every one was only waiting for him to say one word, to cross a certain line, and he knew that sooner or later he would cross it. But a kind of uncomprehended horror seized upon him at the mere thought of this fearful step. A thousand times in the course of those six weeks, during which he felt himself being drawn on further and further toward the abyss that horrified him, Pierre had said to himself: 'But what does it mean? I must act with decision! Can it be that I haven't any?' He tried to come to a decision, but felt with dismay that he had not in this case the strength of will which he had known in himself and really did possess. Pierre belonged to that class of persons who are only strong when they feel themselves perfectly pure. And ever since the day when he had been overcome by the sensation of desire, that he had felt stooping over the snuff-box at Anna Pavlovna's, an unconscious sense of the sinfulness of that impulse paralysed his will.

On Ellen's name-day, Prince Vassily was giving a little supper party of just their own people, as his wife said, that is, of friends and relations. All these friends and relations were made to feel that the day was to be a momentous one in the young lady's life. The guests were seated at supper. Princess Kuragin, a massive woman of imposing presence, who had once been beautiful, sat in the hostess' place, with the most honoured guests on each side of her—an old general and his wife, and Anna Pavlovna Scherer. Towards the bottom of the table sat the less elderly and less honoured guests, and there too sat as members of the family Pierre and Ellen, side by side. Prince Vassily did not take supper. He moved to and fro about the table, in excellent spirits, sitting down beside one guest after another. To every one he dropped a few careless and agreeable words, except to Pierre and Ellen, whose presence he seemed not to notice. Prince Vassily enlivened the whole company. The wax candles burned brightly, there was a glitter of silver and crystal on the table, of ladies' ornaments and the gold and silver of epaulettes. The servants threaded their way in and out round the table in their red coats. There was a clatter of knives, glasses, and plates, and the sound of eager talk from several separate conversations round the table. The old kammerherr at one end could be heard asseverating to an elderly baroness his ardent love for her, while she laughed. At the other end an anecdote was being told of the ill-success of some Marya Viktorovna. In the centre Prince Vassily concentrated the attention on himself. With a playful smile on his lips, he was telling the ladies about the last Wednesday's session of the privy council, at which Sergey Kuzmitch Vyazmitinov, the new military governor-general of Petersburg, had received and read a rescript—

much talked of at the time—from the Emperor Alexander Pavlovitch. The Emperor, writing from the army to Sergey Kuzmitch, had said that on all sides he was receiving proofs of the devotion of his people, and that the testimony from Petersburg was particularly gratifying to him, that he was proud of the honour of being at the head of such a people, and would do his best to be worthy of it. This rescript began with the words: 'Sergey Kuzmitch. From all sides reports reach me,' etc.

'So that he never got further with it than "Sergey Kuzmitch,"' one lady asked.

'No, no, not a syllable,' Prince Vassily answered laughing. "Sergey Kuzmitch . . . from all sides." "From all sides . . . Sergey Kuzmitch. . . ." Poor Vyazmitinov could not get any further. Several times he started upon the letter again, but no sooner did he utter "Sergey," . . . than a sniff . . . "Kus . . . mi . . . itch"—tears . . . and "from all sides" is smothered in sobs, and he can get no further. And again the handkerchief and again "Sergey Kuzmitch from all sides" and tears, . . . so that we begged some one else to read it. . . .'

'"Kuzmitch . . . from all sides" . . . and tears. . . .' some one repeated, laughing.

'Don't be naughty,' said Anna Pavlovna, from the other end of the table, shaking her finger at him. 'He is such a worthy, excellent man, our good Vyazmitinov.'

Every one laughed heartily. At the upper end of the table, the place of honour, every one seemed in good spirits, under the influence of various enlivening tendencies. Only Pierre and Ellen sat mutely side by side almost at the bottom of the table. The faces of both wore a restrained but beaming smile that had no connection with Sergey Kuzmitch—the smile of bashfulness at their own feelings. Gaily as the others laughed and talked and jested, appetising as were the Rhine wine, the *sauté*, and the ices they were discussing, carefully as they avoided glancing at the young couple, heedless and unobservant as they seemed of them, yet it was somehow perceptible from the glances stolen at times at them, that the anecdote about Sergey Kuzmitch, and the laughter and the dishes, were all affectation, and that the whole attention of all the party was really concentrated simply on that pair—Pierre and Ellen. Prince Vassily mimicked the sniffs of Sergey Kuzmitch, and at the same time avoided glancing at his daughter, and at the very time that he was laughing, his expression seemed to say: 'Yes, yes, it's all going well, it will all be settled today.' Anna Pavlovna shook her finger at him for laughing at 'our good Vyazmitinov,' but in her eyes, which at that second flashed a glance in Pierre's direction, Prince

Vassily read congratulation on his future son-in-law and his daughter's felicity. Old Princess Kuragin, offering wine to the lady next her with a pensive sigh, looking angrily at her daughter, seemed in that sigh to be saying: 'Yes, there's nothing left for you and me now, my dear, but to drink sweet wine, now that the time has come for the young people to be so indecently, provokingly happy!' 'And what stupid stuff it all is that I'm talking about, as though it interested me,' thought the diplomat, glancing at the happy faces of the lovers. 'That's happiness!'

Into the midst of the petty trivialities, the conventional interests, which made the common tie uniting that company, had fallen the simple feeling of the attraction of two beautiful and healthy young creatures to one another. And this human feeling dominated everything and triumphed over all their conventional chatter. The jests fell flat, the news was not interesting, the liveliness was unmistakably forced. Not the guests only, but the footmen waiting at table seemed to feel the same and forget their duties, glancing at the lovely Ellen with her radiant face and the broad, red, happy and uneasy face of Pierre. The very light of the candles seemed concentrated on those two happy faces.

Pierre felt that he was the centre of it all, and this position both pleased him and embarrassed him. He was like a man absorbed in some engrossing occupation. He had no clear sight, nor hearing; no understanding of anything. Only from time to time disconnected ideas and impressions of the reality flashed unexpectedly into his mind.

'So it is all over!' he thought. 'And how has it all been done? So quickly! Now I know that not for her sake, nor for my sake alone, but for every one *it* must inevitably come to pass. They all expect it so, they are all so convinced that it will be, that I cannot, I cannot, disappoint them. But how will it be? I don't know, but it will be infallibly, it will be!' mused Pierre, glancing at the dazzling shoulders that were so close to his eyes.

Then he suddenly felt a vague shame. He felt awkward at being the sole object of the general attention, at being a happy man in the eyes of others, with his ugly face being a sort of Paris in possession of a Helen. 'But, no doubt, it's always like this, and must be so,' he consoled himself. 'And yet what have I done to bring it about? When did it begin? I came here from Moscow with Prince Vassily, then there was nothing. Afterwards what reason was there for not staying with him? Then I played cards with her and picked up her reticule, and went skating with her. When did it begin, when did it all come about?' And here he was sitting beside her as her betrothed, hearing, seeing, feeling her closeness, her breathing, her movements, her beauty.. Then it suddenly seemed to him that it was not she, but he who was himself extraordinarily beautiful, that that was why they were looking at him so, and he, happy in the general admiration, was drawing himself up, lifting his head and rejoicing in his happiness. All at once he heard a voice, a familiar voice, addressing him for the second time.

But Pierre was so absorbed that he did not understand what was said to him.

'I'm asking you, when you heard last from Bolkonsky,' Prince Vassily repeated a third time. 'How absent-minded you are, my dear boy.' Prince Vassily smiled, and Pierre saw that every one, every one was smiling at him and at Ellen.

'Well, what of it, since you all know,' Pierre was saying to himself. 'What of it? it's the truth,' and he smiled himself his gentle, childlike smile, and Ellen smiled.

'When did you get a letter? From Olmütz?' repeated Prince Vassily, who wanted to know in order to settle some disputed question.

'How can people talk and think of such trifles?' thought Pierre.

'Yes, from Olmütz,' he answered with a sigh.

Pierre took his lady in behind the rest from supper to the drawing-room. The guests began to take leave, and several went away without saying good-bye to Ellen. As though unwilling to take her away from a serious occupation, several went up to her for an instant and made haste to retire again, refusing to let her accompany them out. The diplomat went out of the drawing-room in dumb dejection. He felt vividly all the vanity of his diplomatic career by comparison with Pierre's happiness. The old general growled angrily at his wife when she inquired how his leg was. 'The old fool,' he thought. 'Look at Elena Vassilyevna; she'll be beautiful at fifty.'

'I believe I may congratulate you,' Anna Pavlovna whispered to Princess Kuragin, as she kissed her warmly. 'If I hadn't a headache, I would stay on.' The princess made no answer; she was tormented by envy of her daughter's happiness.

While the guests were taking leave, Pierre was left a long while alone with Ellen in the little drawing-room, where they were sitting. Often before, during the last six weeks he had been left alone with Ellen, but he had never spoken of love to her. Now he felt that this was inevitable, but he could not make up his mind to this final step. He felt ashamed; it seemed to him that here at Ellen's side he was filling some other man's place. 'This happiness is not for you,' some inner voice said to him. 'This happiness is for those who have not in them what you have within you.' But he had to say something, and he began to speak. He asked her whether she had enjoyed the evening. With her habitual directness in replying, she answered that this name-day had been one of the pleasantest she had ever had.

A few of the nearest relations were still lingering on. They were sitting in the big drawing-room. Prince Vassily walked with languid steps towards Pierre. Pierre rose and observed that it was getting late. Prince Vassily levelled a look of stern inquiry upon him, as though what he had said was so strange that one could not believe one's ears. But the expression of severity immediately passed away, and Prince Vassily taking Pierre's hand drew him down into a seat and smiled affectionately.

'Well, Ellen?' he said at once, addressing his daughter in that careless tone of habitual tenderness which comes natural to parents who have petted their children from infancy, but in Prince Vassily's case was only arrived at by imitation of other parents. And he turned to Pierre again: '"Sergey Kuzmitch on all sides,"' he repeated, unbuttoning the top button of his waistcoat.

Pierre smiled, but his smile betrayed that he understood that it was not the anecdote of Sergey Kuzmitch that interested Prince Vassily at that moment, and Prince Vassily knew that Pierre knew it. Prince Vassily all at once muttered something and went away. It seemed to Pierre that Prince Vassily was positively disconcerted. The sight of the discomfiture of this elderly man of the world touched Pierre; he looked round at Ellen—and she, he fancied, was disconcerted too, and her glance seemed to say: 'Well, it's your own fault.'

'I must inevitably cross the barrier, but I can't, I can't,' thought Pierre, and he began again speaking of extraneous subjects, of Sergey Kuzmitch, inquiring what was the point of the anecdote, as he had not caught it all. Ellen, with a smile, replied that she did not know it either.

When Prince Vassily went into the drawing-room, the princess was talking in subdued tones with an elderly lady about Pierre.

'Of course it is a very brilliant match, but happiness, my dear . . .'

'Marriages are made in heaven,' responded the elderly lady.

Prince Vassily walked to the furthest corner and sat down on a sofa, as though he had not heard the ladies. He closed his eyes and seemed to doze. His head began to droop, and he roused himself.

'Aline,' he said to his wife, 'go and see what they are doing.'

The princess went up to the door, walked by it with a countenance full of meaning and affected nonchalance, and glanced into the little drawing-room. Pierre and Ellen were sitting and talking as before.

'Just the same,' she said in answer to her husband. Prince Vassily frowned, twisting his mouth on one side, his cheeks twitched with the unpleasant, brutal expression peculiar to him at such moments. He shook himself, got up, flung his head back, and with resolute steps passed the ladies and crossed over to the little drawing-room. He walked quickly, joyfully up to Pierre. The prince's face was so extraordinarily solemn that Pierre got up in alarm on seeing him.

'Thank God!' he said. 'My wife has told me all about it.' He put one arm round Pierre, the other round his daughter. 'My dear boy! Ellen! I am very, very glad.' His voice quavered. 'I loved your father ... and she will make you a good wife ... God's blessing on you! ...' He embraced his daughter, then Pierre again, and kissed him with his elderly lips. Tears were actually moist on his cheeks. 'Aline, come here,' he called.

The princess went in and wept too. The elderly lady also put her handkerchief to her eye. They kissed Pierre, and he several times kissed the hand of the lovely Ellen. A little later they were again left alone.

'All this had to be so and could not have been otherwise,' thought Pierre, 'so that it's no use to inquire whether it was a good thing or not. It's a good thing because it's definite, and there's none of the agonising suspense there was before.' Pierre held his betrothed's hand in silence, and gazed at the heaving and falling of her lovely bosom.

'Ellen!' he said aloud, and stopped. 'There's something special is said on these occasions,' he thought; but he could not recollect precisely what it was that was said on these occasions. He glanced into her face. She bent forward closer to him. Her face flushed rosy red.

'Ah, take off those ... those ...' she pointed to his spectacles.

Pierre took off his spectacles, and there was in his eyes besides the strange look people's eyes always have when they remove spectacles, a look of dismay and inquiry. He would have bent over her hand and have kissed it. But with an almost brutal movement of her head, she caught at his lips and pressed them to her own. Pierre was struck by the transformed, the unpleasantly confused expression of her face.

'Now it's too late, it's all over, and besides I love her,' thought Pierre.

'I love you!' he said, remembering what had to be said on these occasions. But the words sounded so poor that he felt ashamed of himself.

Six weeks later he was married, and the lucky possessor of a lovely wife and millions of money, as people said; he took up his abode in the great, newly decorated Petersburg mansion of the Counts Bezuhov.

III

In the December of 1805, the old Prince Nikolay Andreitch Bolkonsky received a letter from Prince Vassily, announcing that he intended to visit him with his son. ('I am going on an inspection tour, and of course a hundred versts is only a step out of the way for me to visit you, my deeply-honoured benefactor,' he wrote. 'My Anatole is accompanying me on his way to the army, and I hope you will permit him to express to you in person the profound veneration that, following his father's example, he entertains for you.')

'Well, there's no need to bring Marie out, it seems; suitors come to us of themselves,' the little princess said heedlessly on hearing of this. Prince Nikolay Andreitch scowled and said nothing.

A fortnight after receiving the letter, Prince Vassily's servants arrived one evening in advance of him, and the following day he came himself with his son.

Old Bolkonsky had always had a poor opinion of Prince Vassily's character, and this opinion had grown stronger of late since Prince Vassily had, under the new reigns of Paul and Alexander, advanced to high rank and honours. Now from the letter and the little princess's hints, he saw what the object of the visit was, and his poor opinion of Prince Vassily passed into a feeling of ill-will and contempt in the old prince's heart. He snorted indignantly whenever he spoke of him. On the day of Prince Vassily's arrival, the old prince was particularly discontented and out of humour. Whether he was out of humour because Prince Vassily was coming, or whether he was particularly displeased at Prince Vassily's coming because he was out of humour, no one can say. But he was out of humour, and early in the morning Tihon had dissuaded the architect from going to the prince with his report.

'Listen how he's walking,' said Tihon, calling the attention of the architect to the sound of the prince's footsteps. 'Stepping flat on his heels ... then we know ...'

At nine o'clock, however, the old prince went out for a walk, as usual, wearing his short, velvet, fur-lined cloak with a sable collar and a sable cap. There had been a fall of snow on the previous evening. The path along which Prince Nikolay Andreitch walked to the conservatory had been cleared; there were marks of a broom in the swept snow, and a spade had been left sticking in the crisp bank of snow that bordered the path on both sides. The prince walked through the conservatories, the servants' quarters, and the out-buildings, frowning and silent.

'Could a sledge drive up?' he asked the respectful steward, who was escorting him to the house, with a countenance and manners like his own.

'The snow is deep, your excellency. I gave orders for the avenue to be swept too.'

The prince nodded, and was approaching the steps. 'Glory to Thee, O Lord!' thought the steward, 'the storm has passed over!'

'It would have been hard to drive up, your excellency,' added the steward. 'So I hear, your excellency, there's a minister coming to visit your excellency?' The prince turned to the steward and stared with scowling eyes at him.

'Eh? A minister? What minister? Who gave you orders?' he began in his shrill, cruel voice. 'For the princess my daughter, you do not clear the way, but for the minister you do! For me there are no ministers!'

'Your excellency, I supposed . . .'

'You supposed,' shouted the prince, articulating with greater and greater haste and incoherence. 'You supposed . . . Brigands! blackguards! . . . I'll teach you to suppose,' and raising his stick he waved it at Alpatitch, and would have hit him, had not the steward instinctively shrunk back and escaped the blow. 'You supposed . . . Blackguards! . . .' he still cried hurriedly. But although Alpatitch, shocked at his own insolence in dodging the blow, went closer to the prince, with his bald head bent humbly before him, or perhaps just because of this, the prince did not lift the stick again, and still shouting, 'Blackguards! . . . fill up the road . . .' he ran to his room.

Princess Marya and Mademoiselle Bourienne stood, waiting for the old prince before dinner, well aware that he was out of temper. Mademoiselle Bourienne's beaming countenance seemed to say, 'I know nothing about it, I am just the same as usual,' while Princess Marya stood pale and terrified with downcast eyes. What made it harder for Princess Marya was that she knew that she ought to act like Mademoiselle Bourienne at such times, but she could not do it. She felt, 'If I behave as if I did not notice it, he'll think I have no sympathy with him. If I behave as if I were depressed and out of humour myself, he'll say (as indeed often happened) that I'm sulky . . .' and so on.

The prince glanced at his daughter's scared face and snorted.

'Stuff!' or perhaps 'stupid!' he muttered. 'And the other is not here! they've been telling tales to her already,' he thought, noticing that the little princess was not in the dining-room.

'Where's Princess Liza?' he asked. 'In hiding?'

'She's not quite well,' said Mademoiselle Bourienne with a bright smile; 'she is not coming down. In her condition it is only to be expected.'

'H'm! h'm! kh! kh!' growled the prince, and he sat down to the table. He thought his plate was not clean: he pointed to a mark on it and threw it away. Tihon caught it and handed it to a footman. The little princess was quite well, but she was in such overwhelming terror of the prince, that on hearing he was in a bad temper, she had decided not to come in.

'I am afraid for my baby,' she said to Mademoiselle Bourienne; 'God knows what might not be the result of a fright.'

The little princess, in fact, lived at Bleak Hills in a state of continual terror of the old prince, and had an aversion for him, of which she was herself unconscious, so completely did terror overbear every other feeling. There was the same aversion on the prince's side, too; but in his case it was swallowed up in contempt. As she went on staying at Bleak Hills, the little princess became particularly fond of Mademoiselle Bourienne; she spent her days with her, begged her to sleep in her room, and often talked of her father-in-law, and criticised him to her.

'We have company coming, prince,' said Mademoiselle Bourienne, her rosy fingers unfolding her dinner-napkin. 'His excellency Prince Kuragin with his son, as I have heard say?' she said in a tone of inquiry.

'H'm! . . . his *excellence* is an upstart. I got him his place in the college,' the old prince said huffily. 'And what his son's coming for, I can't make out. Princess Lizaveta Karlovna and Princess Marya can tell us, maybe; I don't know what he's bringing this son here for. I don't want him.' And he looked at his daughter, who turned crimson.

'Unwell, eh? Scared of the minister, as that blockhead Alpatitch called him today?'

'*Non, mon pere*.'

Unsuccessful as Mademoiselle Bourienne had been in the subject she had started, she did not desist, but went on prattling away about the conservatories, the beauty of a flower that had just opened, and after the soup the prince subsided.

After dinner he went to see his daughter-in-law. The little princess was sitting at a little table gossiping with Masha, her maid. She turned pale on seeing her father-in-law.

The little princess was greatly changed. She looked ugly rather than pretty now. Her cheeks were sunken, her lip was drawn up, and her eyes were hollow.

'Yes, a sort of heaviness,' she said in answer to the prince's inquiry how she felt.

'Isn't there anything you need?'

'Non, merci, mon père.'

'Oh, very well then, very well.'

He went out and into the waiting-room. Alpatitch was standing there with downcast head.

'Filled up the road again?'

'Yes, your excellency; for God's sake, forgive me, it was simply a blunder.'

The prince cut him short with his unnatural laugh.

'Oh, very well, very well.' He held out his hand, which Alpatitch kissed, and then he went to his study.

In the evening Prince Vassily arrived. He was met on the way by the coachmen and footmen of the Bolkonskys, who with shouts dragged his carriages and sledge to the lodge, over the road, which had been purposely obstructed with snow again.

Prince Vassily and Anatole were conducted to separate apartments.

Taking off his tunic, Anatole sat with his elbows on the table, on a corner of which he fixed his handsome, large eyes with a smiling, unconcerned stare. All his life he had looked upon as an uninterrupted entertainment, which some one or other was, he felt, somehow bound to provide for him. In just the same spirit he had looked at his visit to the cross old gentleman and his rich and hideous daughter. It might all, according to his anticipations, turn out very jolly and amusing. 'And why not get married, if she has such a lot of money? That never comes amiss,' thought Anatole.

He shaved and scented himself with the care and elegance that had become habitual with him, and with his characteristic expression of all-conquering good-humour, he walked into his father's room, holding his head high. Two valets were busily engaged in dressing Prince Vassily; he was looking about him eagerly, and nodded gaily to his son, as he entered with an air that said, 'Yes, that's just how I wanted to see you looking.'

'Come, joking apart, father, is she so hideous? Eh?' he asked in French, as though reverting to a subject more than once discussed on the journey.

'Nonsense! The great thing for you is to try and be respectful and sensible with the old prince.'

'If he gets nasty, I'm off,' said Anatole. 'I can't stand those old gentlemen. Eh?'

'Remember that for you everything depends on it.'

Meanwhile, in the feminine part of the household not only the arrival of the minister and his son was already known, but the appearance of both had been minutely described. Princess Marya was sitting alone in her room doing her utmost to control her inner emotion.

'Why did they write, why did Liza tell me about it? Why, it cannot be!' she thought, looking at herself in the glass. 'How am I to go into the drawing-room? Even if I like him, I could never be myself with him now.' The mere thought of her father's eyes reduced her to terror. The little princess and Mademoiselle Bourienne had already obtained all necessary information from the maid, Masha; they had learned what a handsome fellow the minister's son was, with rosy cheeks and black eyebrows; how his papa had dragged his legs upstairs with difficulty, while he, like a young eagle, had flown up after him three steps at a time. On receiving these items of information, the little princess and Mademoiselle Bourienne, whose eager voices were audible in the corridor, went into Princess Marya's room.

'They are come, Marie, do you know?' said the little princess, waddling in and sinking heavily into an armchair. She was not wearing the gown in which she had been sitting in the morning, but had put on one of her best dresses. Her hair had been carefully arranged, and her face was full of an eager excitement, which did not, however, conceal its wasted and pallid look. In the smart clothes which she had been used to wear in Petersburg in society, the loss of her good looks was even more noticeable. Mademoiselle Bourienne, too, had put some hardly perceptible finishing touches to her costume, which made her fresh, pretty face even more attractive.

'What, and you are staying just as you are, dear princess. They will come in a minute to tell us the gentlemen are in the drawing-room,' she began. 'We shall have to go down, and you are doing nothing at all to your dress.'

The little princess got up from her chair, rang for the maid, and hurriedly and eagerly began to arrange what Princess Marya was to wear, and to put her ideas into practice. Princess Marya's sense of personal dignity was wounded by her own agitation at the arrival of her suitor, and still more was she mortified that her two companions should not even conceive that she ought not to be so agitated. To have told them how ashamed she was of herself and of them would have been to betray her own excitement. Besides, to refuse to be dressed up, as they suggested, would have been exposing herself to reiterated raillery and insistence. She flushed; her beautiful eyes grew dim; her face was suffused with patches of crimson; and with the unbeautiful, victimised expression which was the one most often seen on her face, she abandoned herself to Mademoiselle Bourienne and Liza. Both women exerted themselves with *perfect sincerity* to make her look well. She was so plain that the idea of rivalry with her could never have entered their heads. Consequently it was with perfect sincerity, in the naïve and unhesitating conviction women have that dress can make a face handsome, that they set to work to attire her.

'No, really, *ma bonne amie*, that dress isn't pretty,' said Liza, looking sideways at Princess Marya from a distance; 'tell her to put you on your maroon velvet there. Yes, really! Why, you know, it may be the turning-point in your whole life. That one's too light, it's not right, no, it's not!'

It was not the dress that was wrong, but the face and the whole figure of the princess, but that was not felt by Mademoiselle Bourienne and the little princess. They still fancied that if they were to put a blue ribbon in her hair, and do it up high, and to put the blue sash lower on the maroon dress and so on, then all would be well. They forgot that the frightened face and figure of Princess Marya could not be changed, and therefore, however presentable they might make the setting and decoration of the face, the face itself would still look piteous and ugly. After two or three changes, to which Princess Marya submitted passively, when her hair had been done on the top of her head (which completely changed and utterly disfigured her), and the blue sash and best maroon velvet dress had been put on, the little princess walked twice round, and with her little hand stroked out a fold here and pulled down the sash there, and gazed at her with her head first on one side and then on the other.

'No, it won't do,' she said resolutely, throwing up her hands. 'No, Marie, decidedly that does not suit you. I like you better in your little grey everyday frock. No, please do that for me. Katya,' she said to the maid, 'bring the princess her grey dress, and look, Mademoiselle Bourienne, how I'll arrange it,' she said, smiling with a foretaste of artistic pleasure. But when Katya brought the dress, Princess Marya was still sitting motionless before the looking-glass, looking at her own face, and in the looking-glass she saw that there were tears in her eyes and her mouth was quivering, on the point of breaking into sobs.

'Come, dear princess,' said Mademoiselle Bourienne, 'one more little effort.'

The little princess, taking the dress from the hands of the maid, went up to Princess Marya.

'Now, we'll try something simple and charming,' she said. Her voice and Mademoiselle Bourienne's and the giggle of Katya blended into a sort of gay babble like the twitter of birds.

'No, leave me alone,' said the princess; and there was such seriousness and such suffering in her voice that the twitter of the birds ceased at once. They looked at the great, beautiful eyes, full of tears and of thought, looking at them imploringly and they saw that to insist was useless and even cruel.

'At least alter you hair,' said the little princess. 'I told you,' she said reproachfully to Mademoiselle Bourienne, 'there were faces which that way of doing the hair does not suit a bit. Not a bit, not a bit, please alter it.'

'Leave me alone, leave me alone, all that is nothing to me,' answered a voice scarcely able to struggle with tears.

Mademoiselle Bourienne and the little princess could not but admit to themselves that Princess Marya was very plain in this guise, far worse than usual, but it was too late. She looked at them with an expression they knew well, an expression of deep thought and sadness. That expression did not inspire fear. (That was a feeling she could never have inspired in any one.) But they knew that when that expression came into her face, she was mute and inflexible in her resolutions.

'You will alter it, won't you?' said Liza, and when Princess Marya made no reply, Liza went out of the room.

Princess Marya was left alone. She did not act upon Liza's wishes, she did not re-arrange her hair, she did not even glance into the looking-glass. Letting her eyes and her hands drop helplessly, she sat mentally dreaming. She pictured her husband, a man, a strong, masterful, and inconceivably attractive creature, who would bear her away all at once into an utterly different, happy world of his own. A child, *her own*, like the baby she had seen at her old nurse's daughter's, she fancied at her own breast. The husband standing, gazing tenderly at her and the child. 'But no, it can never be, I am too ugly,' she thought.

'Kindly come to tea. The prince will be going in immediately,' said the maid's voice at the door. She started and was horrified at what she had been thinking. And before going downstairs she went into the oratory, and fixing her eyes on the black outline of the great image of the Saviour, she stood for several minutes before it with clasped hands. Princess Marya's soul was full of an agonising doubt. Could the joy of love, of earthly love for a man, be for her? In her reveries of marriage, Princess Marya dreamed of happiness in a home and children of her own, but her chief, her strongest and most secret dream was of earthly love. The feeling became the stronger the more she tried to conceal it from others, and even from herself. 'My God,' she said, 'how am I to subdue in my heart these temptings of the devil? How am I to renounce for ever all evil thoughts, so as in peace to fulfil Thy will?' And scarcely had she put this question than God's answer came to her in her own heart. 'Desire nothing for thyself, be not covetous, anxious, envious. The future of men and thy destiny too must be unknown for thee; but live that thou mayest be ready for all. If it shall be God's will to prove thee in the duties of marriage, be ready to obey His will.' With this soothing thought (though still she hoped for the fulfilment of that forbidden earthly dream) Princess Marya crossed herself, sighing, and went downstairs, without thinking of her dress nor how her hair was done, of how she would go in nor what she would say. What could all that signify beside the guidance of Him, without Whose will not one hair falls from the head of man.

IV

WHEN Princess Marya went into the room, Prince Vassily and his son were already in the drawing-room, talking to the little princess and Mademoiselle Bourienne. When she walked in with her heavy step, treading on her heels, the gentlemen and Mademoiselle Bourienne rose, and the little princess, with a gesture indicating her to the gentlemen, said: 'Here is Marie!' Princess Marya saw them all and saw them in detail. She saw the face of Prince Vassily, growing serious for an instant at the sight of her, and then hastily smiling, and the face of the little princess, scanning the faces of the guests with curiosity to detect the impression Marie was making on them. She saw Mademoiselle Bourienne, too, with her ribbon and her pretty face, turned towards *him* with a look of more eagerness than she had ever seen on it. But *him* she could not see, she could only see something large, bright-coloured, and handsome moving towards her, as she entered the room. Prince Vassily approached her first; and she kissed his bald head, as he bent over to kiss her hand, and in reply to his words said, that on the contrary, she remembered him very well. Then Anatole went up to her. She still could not see him. She only felt a soft hand taking her hand firmly, and she touched with her lips a white forehead, over which there was beautiful fair hair, smelling of pomade. When she glanced at him, she was impressed by his beauty. Anatole was standing with the thumb of his right hand at a button of his uniform, his chest squared and his spine arched; swinging one foot, with his head a little on one side, he was gazing in silence with a beaming face on the princess, obviously not thinking of her at all. Anatole was not quick-witted, he was not ready, not eloquent in conversation, but he had that faculty, so invaluable for social purposes, of composure and imperturbable assurance. If a man of no self-confidence is dumb at first making acquaintance, and betrays a consciousness of the impropriety of this dumbness and an anxiety to find something to say, the effect will be bad. But Anatole was dumb and swung his leg, as he watched the princess's hair with a radiant face. It was clear that he could be silent with the same serenity for a very long while. 'If anybody feels silence awkward, let him talk, but I don't care about it,' his demeanour seemed to say. Moreover, in his manner to women, Anatole had that air, which does more than anything else to excite curiosity, awe, and even love in women, the air of supercilious consciousness of his own superiority. His manner seemed to say to them: 'I know you, I know, but why trouble my head about you? You'd be pleased enough, of course!' Possibly he did not think this on meeting women (it is probable, indeed, that he did not, for he thought very little at any time), but that was the effect of his air and his manner. Princess Marya felt it, and as though to show him she did not even venture to think of inviting his attention, she turned to his father. The conversation was general and animated, thanks to the voice and the little downy lip, that flew up and down over the white teeth of the little princess. She met Prince Vassily in that playful tone so often adopted by chatty and lively persons, the point of which consists in the assumption that there exists a sort of long-established series of jokes and amusing, partly private, humorous reminiscences between the persons so addressed and oneself, even when no such reminiscences are really shared, as indeed was the case with Prince Vassily and the little princess. Prince Vassily readily fell in with this tone; the little princess embellished their supposed common reminiscences with all sorts of droll incidents that had never occurred, and drew Anatole too into them, though she had scarcely known him. Mademoiselle Bourienne too succeeded in taking a part in them, and even Princess Marya felt with pleasure that she was being made to share in their gaiety.

'Well, anyway, we shall take advantage of you to the utmost now we have got you, dear prince,' said the little princess, in French, of course, to Prince Vassily. 'Here it is not as it used to be at our evenings at Annette's, where you always ran away. Do you remember our dear Annette?'

'Ah yes, but then you mustn't talk to me about politics, like Annette!'

'And our little tea-table?'

'Oh yes!'

'Why is it you never used to be at Annette's?' the little princess asked of Anatole. 'Ah, I know, I know,' she said, winking; 'your brother, Ippolit, has told me tales of your doings. Oh!' She shook her finger at him. 'I know about your exploits in Paris too!'

'But he, Ippolit, didn't tell you, did he? said Prince Vassily (addressing his son and taking the little princess by the arm, as though she would have run away and he were just in time to catch her); 'he didn't tell you how he, Ippolit himself, was breaking his heart over our sweet princess, and how she turned him out of doors.'

'Oh! she is the pearl of women, princess,' he said, addressing Princess Marya. Mademoiselle Bourienne on her side, at the mention of Paris, did not let her chance slip for taking a share in the common stock of recollections.

She ventured to inquire if it were long since Anatole was in Paris, and how he had liked that city. Anatole very readily answered the Frenchwoman, and smiling and staring at her, he talked to her about her native country. At first sight of the pretty Mademoiselle, Anatole had decided that even here at Bleak Hills he should not be dull. 'Not half bad-looking,' he thought, scrutinising her, 'she's not half bad-looking, that companion! I hope she'll bring her along when we're married,' he mused; 'she is a nice little thing.'

The old prince was dressing deliberately in his room, scowling and ruminating on what he was to do. The arrival of these visitors angered him. 'What's Prince Vassily to me, he and his son? Prince Vassily is a braggart, an empty-headed fool, and a nice fellow the son is, I expect,' he growled to himself. What angered him was that this visit revived in his mind the unsettled question, continually thrust aside, the question in regard to which the old prince always deceived himself. That question was whether he would ever bring himself to part with his daughter and give her to a husband. The prince could never bring himself to put this question directly to himself, knowing beforehand that if he did he would have to answer it justly, but against justice in this case was ranged more than feeling, the very possibility of life. Life without Princess Marya was unthinkable to the old prince, little as in appearance he prized her. 'And what is she to be married for?' he thought; 'to be unhappy, beyond a doubt. Look at Liza with Andrey (and a better husband, I should fancy, it would be difficult to find nowadays), but she's not satisfied with her lot. And who would marry her for love? She's plain and ungraceful. She'd be married for her connections, her wealth. And don't old maids get on well enough? They are happier really!' So Prince Nikolay Andreivitch mused, as he dressed, yet the question constantly deferred demanded an immediate decision. Prince Vassily had brought his son obviously with the intention of making an offer, and probably that day or the next he would ask for a direct answer. The name, the position in the world, was suitable. 'Well, I'm not against it,' the prince kept saying to himself, 'only let him be worthy of her. That's what we shall see. That's what we shall see,' he said aloud, 'that's what we shall see,' and with his usual alert step he walked into the drawing-room, taking in the whole company in a rapid glance. He noticed the change in the dress of the little princess and Mademoiselle Bourienne's ribbon, and the hideous way in which Princess Marya's hair was done, and the smiles of the Frenchwoman and Anatole, and the isolation of his daughter in the general talk. 'She's decked herself out like a fool!' he thought, glancing vindictively at his daughter. 'No shame in her; while he doesn't care to speak to her!'

He went up to Prince Vassily.

'Well, how d'ye do, how d' ye do, glad to see you.'

'For a friend that one loves seven versts is close by,' said Prince Vassily, quoting the Russian proverb, and speaking in his usual rapid, self-confident, and familiar tone. 'This is my second, I beg you to love him and welcome him, as they say.'

Prince Nikolay Andreivitch scrutinised Anatole.

'A fine fellow, a fine fellow!' he said. 'Well, come and give me a kiss,' and he offered him his cheek. Anatole kissed the old man, and looked at him with curiosity and perfect composure, waiting for some instance of the eccentricity his father had told him to expect.

The old prince sat down in his customary place in the corner of the sofa, moved up an armchair for Prince Vassily, pointed to it, and began questioning him about political affairs and news. He seemed to be listening with attention to what Prince Vassily was saying, but glanced continually at Princess Marya.

'So they're writing from Potsdam already?' He repeated Prince Vassily's last words, and suddenly getting up, he went up to his daughter.

'So it was for visitors you dressed yourself up like this, eh?' he said. 'Nice of you, very nice. You do your hair up in some new fashion before visitors, and before visitors, I tell you, never dare in future to change your dress without my leave.'

'It was my fault . . .' stammered the little princess, flushing.

'You are quite at liberty,' said the old prince, with a scrape before his daughter-in-law, 'but she has no need to disfigure herself—she's ugly enough without that.' And he sat down again in his place, taking no further notice of his daughter, whom he had reduced to tears.

'On the contrary, that coiffure is extremely becoming to the princess,' said Prince Vassily.

'Well, my young prince, what's your name?' said the old prince, turning to Anatole. 'Come here, let us talk to you a little and make your acquaintance.'

'Now the fun's beginning,' thought Anatole, and with a smile he sat down by the old prince.

'That's it; they tell me, my dear boy, you have been educated abroad. Not taught to read and write by the deacon, like your father and me. Tell me, are you serving now in the Horse Guards?' asked the old man, looking closely and intently at Anatole.

'No, I have transferred into the line,' answered Anatole, with difficulty restraining his laughter.

'Ah! a good thing. So you want to serve your Tsar and your country, do you? These are times of war. Such a fine young fellow ought to be on service, he ought to be on service. Ordered to the front, eh?'

'No, prince, our regiment has gone to the front. But I'm attached. What is it I'm attached to, papa?' Anatole turned to his father with a laugh.

'He is a credit to the service, a credit. What is it I'm attached to! Ha-ha-ha!' laughed the old prince, and Anatole laughed still louder. Suddenly the old prince frowned. 'Well, you can go,' he said to Anatole. With a smile Anatole returned to the ladies.

'So you had them educated abroad, Prince Vassily? Eh?' said the old prince to Prince Vassily.

'I did what I could, and I assure you the education there is far better than ours.'

'Yes, nowadays everything's different, everything's new-fashioned. A fine fellow! a fine fellow! Well, come to my room.' He took Prince Vassily's arm and led him away to his study.

Left alone with the old prince, Prince Vassily promptly made known to him his wishes and his hopes.

'Why, do you imagine,' said the old prince wrathfully, 'that I keep her, that I can't part with her? What an idea!' he protested angrily. 'I am ready for it tomorrow! Only, I tell you, I want to know my future son-in-law better. You know my principles: everything open! Tomorrow I will ask her in your presence; if she wishes it, let him stay on. Let him stay on, and I'll see.' The prince snorted. 'Let her marry, it's nothing to me,' he screamed in the piercing voice in which he had screamed at saying good-bye to his son.

'I will be frank with you,' said Prince Vassily in the tone of a crafty man, who is convinced of the uselessness of being crafty with so penetrating a companion. 'You see right through people, I know. Anatole is not a genius, but a straightforward, good-hearted lad, good as a son or a kinsman.'

'Well, well, very good, we shall see.'

As is always the case with women who have for a long while been living a secluded life apart from masculine society, on the appearance of Anatole on the scene, all the three women in Prince Nikolay Andreivitch's house felt alike that their life had not been real life till then. Their powers of thought, of feeling, of observation, were instantly redoubled. It seemed as though their life had till then been passed in darkness, and was all at once lighted up by a new brightness that was full of significance.

Princess Marya did not remember her face and her coiffure. The handsome, open face of the man who might, perhaps, become her husband, absorbed her whole attention. She thought him kind, brave, resolute, manly, and magnanimous. She was convinced of all that. Thousands of dreams of her future married life were continually floating into her imagination. She drove them away and tried to disguise them.

'But am I not too cold with him?' thought Princess Marya. 'I try to check myself, because at the bottom of my heart I feel myself too close to him. But of course he doesn't know all I think of him, and may imagine I don't like him.'

And she tried and knew not how to be cordial to him.

'The poor girl is devilish ugly,' Anatole was thinking about her.

Mademoiselle Bourienne, who had also been thrown by Anatole's arrival into a high state of excitement, was absorbed in reflections of a different order. Naturally, a beautiful young girl with no defined position in society, without friends or relations, without even a country of her own, did not look forward to devoting her life to waiting on Prince Nikolay Andreivitch, to reading him books and being a friend to Princess Marya. Mademoiselle Bourienne had long been looking forward to the Russian prince, who would have the discrimination to discern her superiority to the ugly, badly dressed, ungainly Russian princesses—who would fall in love with her and bear her away. And now this Russian prince at last had come. Mademoiselle Bourienne knew a story she had heard from her aunt, and had finished to her own taste, which she loved to go over in her own imagination. It was the story of how a girl had been seduced, and her poor mother (*sa pauvre mère*) had appeared to her and reproached her for yielding to a man's allurements without marriage. Mademoiselle was often touched to tears, as in imagination she told '*him*,' her seducer, this tale. Now this '*he*,' a real Russian prince, had appeared. He would elope with her, then 'my poor mother' would come on the scene, and he would marry her. This was how all her future history shaped itself in Mademoiselle Bourienne's brain at the very moment when she was talking to him of Paris. Mademoiselle Bourienne was not guided by calculations (she did not even consider for one instant what she would do), but it had all been ready within her long before, and now it all centred about Anatole as soon as he appeared, and she wished and tried to attract him as much as possible.

The little princess, like an old warhorse hearing the blast of the trumpet, was prepared to gallop off into a flirtation as her habit was, unconsciously forgetting her position, with no ulterior motive, no struggle, nothing but simple-hearted, frivolous gaiety in her heart.

Although in feminine society Anatole habitually took up the attitude of a man weary of the attentions of women, his vanity was agreeably flattered by the spectacle of the effect he produced on these three women. Moreover, he was beginning to feel towards the pretty and provocative Mademoiselle Bourienne that violent, animal feeling, which was apt to come upon him with extreme rapidity, and to impel him to the coarsest and most reckless actions.

After tea the party moved into the divan-room, and Princess Marya was asked to play on the clavichord. Anatole leaned on his elbow facing her, and near Mademoiselle Bourienne, and his eyes were fixed on Princess Marya, full of laughter and glee. Princess Marya felt his eyes upon her with troubled and joyful agitation. Her favourite sonata bore her away to a world of soul-felt poetry, and the feeling of his eyes upon her added still more poetry to that world. The look in Anatole's eyes, though they were indeed fixed upon her, had reference not to her, but to the movements of Mademoiselle's little foot, which he was at that very time touching with his own under the piano. Mademoiselle Bourienne too was gazing at Princess Marya, and in her fine eyes, too, there was an expression of frightened joy and hope that was new to the princess.

'How she loves me!' thought Princess Marya. 'How happy I am now and how happy I may be with such a friend and such a husband! Can he possibly be my husband?' she thought, not daring to glance at his face, but still feeling his eyes fastened upon her.

When the party broke up after supper, Anatole kissed Princess Marya's hand. She was herself at a loss to know how she had the hardihood, but she looked straight with her short-sighted eyes at the handsome face as it came close to her. After the princess, he bent over the hand of Mademoiselle Bourienne (it was a breach of etiquette, but he did everything with the same ease and simplicity), and Mademoiselle Bourienne crimsoned and glanced in dismay at the princess.

'*Quelle délicatesse!*' thought Princess Marya. 'Can Amélie' (Mademoiselle's name) 'suppose I could be jealous of her, and fail to appreciate her tenderness and devotion to me?' She went up to Mademoiselle Bourienne and kissed her warmly. Anatole went to the little princess.

'No, no, no! When your father writes me word that you are behaving well, I will give you my hand to kiss.' And shaking her little finger at him, she went smiling out of the room.

V

THEY all went to their rooms, and except Anatole, who fell asleep the instant he got into bed, no one could get to sleep for a long while that night. 'Can he possibly be—my husband, that stranger, that handsome, kind man; yes, he is certainly kind,' thought Princess Marya, and a feeling of terror, such as she scarcely ever felt, came upon her. She was afraid to look round; it seemed to her that there was some one there—the devil, and he was that man with his white forehead, black eye-brows, and red lips.

She rang for her maid and asked her to sleep in her room.

Mademoiselle Bourienne walked up and down the winter garden for a long while that evening, in vain expectation of some one; at one moment she was smiling at that some one, the next, moved to tears by an imaginary reference to *ma pauvre mere* reproaching her for her fall.

The little princess kept grumbling to her maid that her bed had not been properly made. She could not lie on her side nor on her face. She felt uncomfortable and ill at ease in every position. Her burden oppressed her, oppressed her more than ever that night, because Anatole's presence had carried her vividly back to another time when it was not so, and she had been light and gay. She sat in a low chair in her nightcap and dressing-jacket. Katya, sleepy and dishevelled, for the third time beat and turned the heavy feather bed, murmuring something.

'I told you it was all in lumps and hollows,' the little princess repeated; 'I should be glad enough to go to sleep, so it's not my fault.' And her voice quivered like a child's when it is going to cry.

The old prince too could not sleep. Tihon, half asleep, heard him pacing angrily up and down and blowing his nose. The old prince felt as though he had been insulted through his daughter. The insult was the more bitter because it concerned not himself, but another, his daughter, whom he loved more than himself. He said to himself that he would think the whole matter over thoroughly and decide what was right and what must be done, but instead of doing so, he only worked up his irritation more and more.

'The first stray comer that appears! and father and all forgotten, and she runs upstairs, and does up her hair, and rigs herself out, and doesn't know what she's doing! She's glad to abandon her father! And she knew I should notice it. Fr . . . fr . . . fr . . . And don't I see the fool has no eyes but for Bourienne (must get rid of her). And how can she have so little pride, as not to see it? If not for her own sake, if she has no pride, at least for mine. I must show her that the blockhead doesn't give her a thought, and only looks at Bourienne. She has no pride, but I'll make her see it . . .'

By telling his daughter that she was making a mistake, that Anatole was getting up a flirtation with Mademoiselle Bourienne, the old prince knew that he would wound her self-respect, and so his object (not to be parted from his daughter) would be gained, and so at this reflection he grew calmer. He called Tihon and began undressing.

'The devil brought them here!' he thought, as Tihon slipped his nightshirt over his dried-up old body and his chest covered with grey hair.

'I didn't invite them. They come and upset my life. And there's not much of it left. Damn them!' he muttered, while his head was hidden in the nightshirt. Tihon was used to the prince's habit of expressing his thoughts aloud, and so it was with an unmoved countenance that he met the wrathful and inquiring face that emerged from the nightshirt.

'Gone to bed?' inquired the prince.

Tihon, like all good valets, indeed, knew by instinct the direction of his master's thoughts. He guessed that it was Prince Vassily and his son who were meant.

'Their honours have gone to bed and put out their lights, your excellency.'

'They had no reason, no reason . . .' the prince articulated rapidly, and slipping his feet into his slippers and his arms into his dressing-gown, he went to the couch on which he always slept.

Although nothing had been said between Anatole and Mademoiselle Bourienne, they understood each other perfectly so far as the first part of the romance was concerned, the part previous to the *pauvre mere* episode. They felt that they had a great deal to say to each other in private, and so from early morning they sought an opportunity of meeting alone. While the princess was away, spending her hour as usual with her father, Mademoiselle Bourienne was meeting Anatole in the winter garden.

That day it was with even more than her usual trepidation that Princess Marya went to the door of the study. It seemed to her not only that every one was aware that her fate would be that day decided, but that all were aware of what she was feeling about it. She read it in Tihon's face and in the face of Prince Vassily's valet, who met her in the corridor with hot water, and made her a low bow.

The old prince's manner to his daughter that morning was extremely affectionate, though strained. That strained expression Princess Marya knew well. It was the expression she saw in his face at the moments when his withered hands were clenched with vexation at Princess Marya's not understanding some arithmetical problem, and he would get up and walk away from her, repeating the same words over several times in a low voice.

He came to the point at once and began talking. 'A proposal has been made to me on your behalf,' he said, with an unnatural smile. 'I dare say, you have guessed,' he went on, 'that Prince Vassily has not come here and brought his protégé' (for some unknown reason the old prince elected to refer to Anatole in this way) 'for the sake of my charms. Yesterday, they made me a proposal on your behalf. And as you know my principles, I refer the matter to you.'

'How am I to understand you, *mon père?*' said the princess, turning pale and red.

'How understand me!' cried her father angrily. 'Prince Vassily finds you to his taste as a daughter-in-law, and makes you a proposal for his protégé. That's how to understand it. How understand it! ... Why, I ask you.'

'I don't know how you, *mon pere* . . .' the princess articulated in a whisper.

'I? I? what have I to do with it? leave me out of the question. I am not going to be married. What do you say? that's what it's desirable to learn.'

The princess saw that her father looked with ill-will on the project, but at that instant the thought had occurred to her that now or never the fate of her life would be decided. She dropped her eyes so as to avoid the gaze under which she felt incapable of thought, and capable of nothing but her habitual obedience: 'My only desire is to carry out your wishes,' she said; 'if I had to express my own desire . . .'

She had not time to finish. The prince cut her short. 'Very good, then!' he shouted. 'He shall take you with your dowry, and hook on Mademoiselle Bourienne into the bargain. She'll be his wife, while you . . .' The prince stopped. He noticed the effect of these words on his daughter. She had bowed her head and was beginning to cry.

'Come, come, I was joking, I was joking,' he said. 'Remember one thing, princess; I stick to my principles, that a girl has a full right to choose. And I give you complete freedom. Remember one thing; the happiness of your life depends on your decision. No need to talk about me.'

'But I don't know . . . father.'

'No need for talking! He's told to, and he's ready to marry any one, but you are free to choose . . . Go to your own room, think it over, and come to me in an hour's time and tell me in his presence: yes or no. I know you will pray over it. Well, pray if you like. Only you'd do better to think. You can go.'

'Yes or no, yes or no, yes or no!' he shouted again as the princess went out of the room, reeling in a sort of fog. Her fate was decided, and decided for happiness. But what her father had said about Mademoiselle Bourienne, that hint was horrible. It was not true, of course, but still it was horrible; she could not help thinking of it. She walked straight forward through the winter garden, seeing and hearing nothing, when all of a sudden she was roused by the familiar voice of Mademoiselle Bourienne. She lifted her eyes, and only two paces before her she saw Anatole with his arms round the Frenchwoman, whispering something to her. With a terrible expression on his handsome face, Anatole looked round at Princess Marya, and did not for the first second let go the waist of Mademoiselle Bourienne, who had not seen her.

'Who's there? What do you want? Wait a little!' was what Anatole's face expressed. Princess Marya gazed blankly at them. She could not believe her eyes. At last Mademoiselle Bourienne shrieked and ran away. With a gay smile Anatole bowed to Princess Marya, as though inviting her to share his amusement at this strange incident, and with a shrug of his shoulders he went to the door that led to his apartment.

An hour later Tihon came to summon Princess Marya to the old prince, and added that Prince Vassily was with him. When Tihon came to her, Princess Marya was sitting on the sofa in her own room holding in her arms the weeping Mademoiselle Bourienne. Princess Marya was softly stroking her head. Her beautiful eyes had regained all their luminous peace, and were gazing with tender love and commiseration at the pretty little face of Mademoiselle Bourienne.

'Oh, princess, I am ruined for ever in your heart,' Mademoiselle Bourienne was saying.

'Why? I love you more than ever,' said Princess Marya, 'and I will try to do everything in my power for your happiness.'

'But you despise me, you who are so pure, you will never understand this frenzy of passion. Ah, it is only my poor mother . . .'

'I understand everything,' said Princess Marya, smiling mournfully. 'Calm yourself, my dear. I am going to my father,' she said, and she went out.

When the princess went in, Prince Vassily was sitting with one leg crossed high over the other, and a snuff-box in his hand. There was a smile of emotion on his face, and he looked as though moved to such an extreme point that he could but regret and smile at his own sensibility. He took a hasty pinch of snuff.

'Ah, my dear, my dear!' he said, getting up and taking her by both hands. He heaved a sigh, and went on: 'My son's fate is in your hands. Decide, my good dear, sweet Marie, whom I have always loved like a daughter.' He drew back. There was a real tear in his eye.

'Fr .. ffr . . .' snorted the old prince. 'The prince in his protégé's ... his son's name makes you a proposal. Are you willing or not to be the wife of Prince Anatole Kuragin? You say: yes or no,' he shouted, 'and then I reserve for myself the right to express my opinion. Yes, my opinion, and nothing but my opinion,' added the old prince, to Prince Vassily in response to his supplicating expression, 'Yes or no!'

'My wish, *mon père*, is never to leave you; never to divide my life from yours. I do not wish to marry,' she said resolutely, glancing with her beautiful eyes at Prince Vassily and at her father.

'Nonsense, fiddlesticks! Nonsense, nonsense!' shouted the old prince, frowning. He took his daughter's hand, drew her towards him and did not kiss her, but bending over, touched her forehead with his, and wrung the hand he held so violently that she winced and uttered a cry. Prince Vassily got up.

'My dear, let me tell you that this is a moment I shall never forget, never; but, dear, will you not give us a little hope of touching so kind and generous a heart. Say that perhaps. . . . The future is so wide. . . . Say: perhaps.'

'Prince, what I have said is all that is in my heart. I thank you for the honour you do me, but I shall never be your son's wife.'

'Well, then it's all over, my dear fellow. Very glad to have seen you, very glad to have seen you. Go to your room, princess; go along now,' said the old prince. 'Very, very glad to have seen you,' he repeated, embracing Prince Vassily.

'My vocation is a different one,' Princess Marya was thinking to herself; 'my vocation is to be happy in the happiness of others, in the happiness of love and self-sacrifice. And at any cost I will make poor Amelie happy. She loves him so passionately. She is so passionately penitent. I will do everything to bring about their marriage. If he is not rich I will give her means, I will beg my father, I will beg Andrey. I shall be so happy when she is his wife. She is so unhappy, a stranger, solitary and helpless! And, my God, how passionately she must love him to be able to forget herself so. Perhaps I might have done the same! . . .' thought Princess Marya.

VI

IT was a long while since the Rostovs had had news of their Nikolushka. But in the middle of the winter a letter was handed to Count Rostov, on the envelope of which he recognised his son's handwriting. On receiving the letter the count, in alarm and in haste, ran on tiptoe to his room, trying to escape notice, shut himself in and read the letter. Anna Mihalovna had learned (as she always did learn all that passed in the house) that he had received a letter, and treading softly, she went in to the count and found him with the letter in his hand, sobbing and laughing at once. Anna Mihalovna, though her fortunes had been looking up, was still an inmate of the Rostov household.

'My dear friend?' Anna Mihalovna brought out in a voice of melancholy inquiry, equally ready for sympathy in any direction. The count sobbed more violently.

'Nikolushka . . . letter . . . wounded . . . he would . . . my dear . . . wounded . . . my darling boy . . . the little countess . . . promoted . . . thank God . . . how are we to tell the little countess?'

Anna Mihalovna sat down by his side, with her own handkerchief wiped the tears from his eyes and from the letter, then dried her own tears, read the letter, soothed the count, and decided that before dinner and before tea she would prepare the countess; and after tea, with God's help, tell her all. During dinner Anna Mihalovna talked of the rumours from the war, of dear Nikolay, inquired twice when his last letter had been received, though she knew perfectly well, and observed that they might well be getting a letter from him today. Every time that the countess began to be uneasy under these hints and looked in trepidation from the count to Anna Mihalovna, the latter turned the conversation in the most unnoticeable way to insignificant subjects. Natasha, who was of all the family the one most gifted with the faculty of catching the shades of intonations, of glances, and expressions, had been on the alert from the beginning of dinner, and was certain that there was some secret between her father and Anna Mihalovna, and that it had something to do with her brother, and that Anna Mihalovna was paving the way for it. Natasha knew how easily upset her mother was by any references to news from Nikolushka, and in spite of all her recklessness she did not venture at dinner to ask a question. But she was too much excited to eat any dinner and kept wriggling about on her chair, regardless of the protests of her governess. After dinner she rushed headlong to overtake Anna Mihalovna, and in the divan-room dashed at her and flung herself on her neck: 'Auntie, darling, do tell me what it is?'

'Nothing, my dear.'

'No, darling, sweet, precious peach, I won't leave off; I know you know something.'

Anna Mihalovna shook her head. 'You are sharp, my child!' she said.

'A letter from Nikolinka? I'm sure of it!' cried Natasha, reading an affirmative answer on the face of Anna Mihalovna.

'But, for God's sake, be more careful; you know what a shock it may be to your mamma.'

'I will be, I will, but tell me about it. You won't? Well, then, I'll run and tell her this minute.'

Anna Mihalovna gave Natasha a brief account of what was in the letter, on condition that she would not tell a soul.

'On my word of honour,' said Natasha, crossing herself, 'I won't tell any one,' and she ran at once to Sonya. 'Nikolinka . . . wounded . . . a letter . . .' she proclaimed in gleeful triumph.

'Nikolinka!' was all Sonya could articulate, instantly turning white. Natasha seeing the effect of the news of her brother's wound on Sonya, for the first time felt the painful aspect of the news.

She rushed at Sonya, hugged her, and began to cry. 'A little wounded, but promoted to be an officer; he's all right now, he writes himself,' she said through her tears.

'One can see all you women are regular cry-babies,' said Petya, striding with resolute steps up and down the room: 'I'm very glad, really very glad, that my brother has distinguished himself so. You all start blubbering! you don't understand anything about it.' Natasha smiled through her tears.

'You haven't read the letter?' asked Sonya.

'No; but she told me it was all over, and that he's an officer now . . .'

'Thank God,' said Sonya, crossing herself. 'But perhaps she was deceiving you. Let us go to mamma.'

Petya had been strutting up and down in silence.

'If I were in Nikolinka's place, I'd have killed a lot more of those Frenchmen,' he said, 'they're such beasts! I'd have killed them till there was a regular heap of them,' Petya went on.

'Hold your tongue, Petya, what a silly you are! . . .'

'I'm not a silly; people are silly who cry for trifles,' said Petya.

'Do you remember him?' Natasha asked suddenly, after a moment's silence. Sonya smiled.

'Do I remember Nikolinka?'

'No, Sonya, but do you remember him so as to remember him thoroughly, to remember him quite,' said Natasha with a strenuous gesture, as though she were trying to put into her words the most earnest meaning. 'And I do remember Nikolinka, I remember him,' she said. 'But I don't remember Boris. I don't remember him a bit . . .'

'What? You don't remember Boris?' Sonya queried with surprise.

'I don't mean I don't remember him. I know what he's like, but not as I remember Nikolinka. I shut my eyes and I can see him, but not Boris' (she shut her eyes), 'no, nothing!'

'Ah, Natasha!' said Sonya, looking solemnly and earnestly at her friend, as though she considered her unworthy to hear what she meant to say, and was saying it to some one else with whom joking was out of the question. 'I have come to love your brother once for all, and whatever were to happen to him and to me, I could never cease to love him all my life.'

With inquisitive, wondering eyes, Natasha gazed at Sonya, and she did not speak. She felt that what Sonya was saying was the truth, that there was love such as Sonya was speaking of. But Natasha had never known anything like it. She believed that it might be so, but she did not understand it.

'Shall you write to him?' she asked. Sonya sank into thought. How she should write to Nikolay, and whether she ought to write to him, was a question that worried her. Now that he was an officer, and a wounded hero, would it be nice on her part to remind him of herself, and as it were of the obligations he had taken on himself in regard to her. 'I don't know. I suppose if he writes to me I shall write,' she said, blushing.

'And you won't be ashamed to write to him?'

Sonya smiled.

'No.'

'And I should be ashamed to write to Boris, and I'm not going to write.'

'But why should you be ashamed?'

'Oh, I don't know. I feel awkward, ashamed.'

'I know why she'd be ashamed,' said Petya, offended at Natasha's previous remark, 'because she fell in love with that fat fellow in spectacles' (this was how Petya used to describe his namesake, the new Count Bezuhov); 'and now she's in love with that singing fellow' (Petya meant Natasha's Italian singing-master), 'that's why she's ashamed.'

'Petya, you're stupid,' said Natasha.

'No stupider than you, ma'am,' said nine-year-old Petya, exactly as though he had been an elderly brigadier.

The countess had been prepared by Anna Mihalovna's hints during dinner. On returning to her room she had sat down in a low chair with her eyes fixed on the miniature of her son, painted on the lid of her snuff-box, and the tears started into her eyes. Anna Mihalovna, with the letter, approached the countess's room on tiptoe, and stood still at the door.

'Don't come in,' she said to the old count, who was following her; 'later,' and she closed the door after her. The count put his ear to the keyhole, and listened.

At first he heard the sound of indifferent talk, then Anna Mihalovna's voice alone, uttering a long speech, then a shriek, then silence, then both voices talking at once with joyful intonations, then there were steps, and Anna Mihalovna opened the door. Her face wore the look of pride of an operator who has performed a difficult amputation, and invites the public in to appreciate his skill.

'It is done,' she said to the count triumphantly, motioning him to the countess, who was holding in one hand the snuff-box with the portrait, in the other the letter and pressing her lips first to one and then to the other. On seeing the count, she held out her arms to him, embraced his bald head, and looked again over the bald head at the letter and the portrait, and in order again to press them to her lips, slightly repelled the bald head from her. Vera, Natasha, Sonya, and Petya came into the room, and the reading of the letter began. The letter briefly described the march and the two battles in which Nikolushka had taken part, and the receiving of his commission, and said that he kissed the hands of his mamma and papa, begging their blessing, and sent kisses to Vera, Natasha, and Petya. He sent greetings, too, to Monsieur Schelling and Madame Schoss, and his old nurse, and begged them to kiss for him his darling Sonya, whom he still loved and thought of the same as ever. On hearing this, Sonya blushed till the tears came into her eyes. And unable to stand the eyes fixed upon her, she ran into the big hall, ran about with a flushed and smiling face, whirled round and round and ducked down, making her skirts into a balloon. The countess was crying.

'What are you crying about, mamma?' said Vera. 'From all he writes, we ought to rejoice instead of crying.'

This was perfectly true, but the count and the countess and Natasha all looked at her reproachfully. 'And who is it that she takes after!' thought the countess.

Nikolushka's letter was read over hundreds of times, and those who were considered worthy of hearing it had to come in to the countess, who did not let it go out of her hands. The tutors went in, the nurses,

Mitenka, and several acquaintances, and the countess read the letter every time with fresh enjoyment, and every time she discovered from it new virtues in her Nikolushka. How strange, extraordinary, and joyful it was to her to think that her son—the little son, whose tiny limbs had faintly stirred within her twenty years ago, for whose sake she had so often quarrelled with the count, who would spoil him, the little son, who had first learnt to say *grusha*, and then had learnt to say *baba* —that that son was now in a foreign land, in strange surroundings, a manly warrior, alone without help or guidance, doing there his proper manly work. All the world-wide experience of ages, proving that children do imperceptibly from the cradle grow into men, did not exist for the countess. The growth of her son had been for her at every stage of his growth just as extraordinary as though millions of millions of men had not grown up in the same way. Just as, twenty years before, she could not believe that the little creature that was lying somewhere under her heart, would one day cry and suck her breast and learn to talk, now she could not believe that the same little creature could be that strong, brave man, that paragon of sons and of men that, judging by this letter, he was now.

'What *style*, how charmingly he describes everything!' she said, reading over the descriptions in the letter. 'And what soul! Of himself not a word . . . not a word! A great deal about a man called Denisov, though he was himself, I dare say, braver than any one. He doesn't write a word about his sufferings. What a heart! How like him it is! How he thinks of every one! No one forgotten. I always, always said, when he was no more than that high, I always used to say . . .'

For over a week they were hard at work preparing a letter to Nikolushka from all the household, writing out rough copies, copying out fair copies. With the watchful care of the countess, and the fussy solicitude of the count, all sorts of necessary things were got together, and money, too, for the equipment and the uniform of the young officer. Anna Mihalovna, practical woman, had succeeded in obtaining special patronage for herself and her son in the army, that even extended to their correspondence. She had opportunities of sending her letters to the Grand Duke Konstantin Pavlovitch, who was in command of the guards. The Rostovs assumed that 'The Russian Guards Abroad,' was quite a sufficiently definite address, and that if a letter reached the grand duke in command of the guards, there was no reason why it should not reach the Pavlograd regiment, who were presumably somewhere in the same vicinity. And so it was decided to send off their letters and money by the special messenger of the grand duke to Boris, and Boris would have to forward them to Nikolushka. There were letters from the count, the countess, Petya, Vera, Natasha, and Sonya, a sum of six thousand roubles for his equipment, and various other things which the count was sending to his son.

VII

On the 12th of November, Kutuzov's army, encamped near Olmütz, was preparing to be reviewed on the following day by the two Emperors—the Russian and the Austrian. The guards, who had only just arrived from Russia, spent a night fifteen versts from Olmütz, and at ten o'clock the next morning went straight to be reviewed in the Olmütz plain.

That day Nikolay Rostov had received a note from Boris informing him that the Ismailovsky regiment was quartered for the night fifteen versts from Olmütz, and that he wanted to see him to give him a letter and some money. The money Rostov particularly needed just now, when the troops after active service were stationed near Olmütz, and the camp swarmed with well-equipped canteen keepers and Austrian Jews, offering all kinds of attractions. The Pavlograd hussars had been keeping up a round of gaiety, fêtes in honour of the promotions received in the field, and excursions to Olmütz to a certain Caroline la Hongroise, who had recently opened a restaurant there with girls as waiters. Rostov had just been celebrating his commission as a cornet; he had bought Denisov's horse Bedouin, too, and was in debt all round to his comrades and the canteen keepers. On getting the note from Boris, Rostov rode into Olmütz with a comrade, dined there, drank a bottle of wine, and rode on alone to the guards' camp to find the companion of his childhood. Rostov had not yet got his uniform. He was wearing a shabby ensign's jacket with a private soldier's cross, equally shabby riding-trousers lined with worn leather, and an officer's sabre with a sword-knot. The horse he was riding was of the Don breed, bought of a Cossack on the march. A crushed hussars' cap was stuck jauntily back on one side of his head. As he rode up to the camp of the Ismailovsky regiment, he was thinking of how he would impress Boris and all his comrades in the guards by looking so thoroughly a hussar who has been under fire and roughed it at the front.

The guards had made their march as though it were a pleasure excursion, priding themselves on their smartness and discipline. They moved by short stages, their knapsacks were carried in the transport waggons, and at every halt the Austrian government provided the officers with excellent dinners. The regiments made their entry into towns and their exit from them with bands playing, and, according to the grand duke's order, the whole march had (a point on which the guards prided themselves) been performed by the soldiers in step, the officers too walking in their proper places. Boris had throughout the march walked and stayed with Berg, who was by this time a captain. Berg, who had received his company on the march, had succeeded in gaining the confidence of his superior officers by his conscientiousness and accuracy, and had established his financial position on a very satisfactory basis. Boris had during the same period made the acquaintance of many persons likely to be of use to him, and by means of a letter of recommendation brought from Pierre, had made the acquaintance of Prince Andrey Bolkonsky, through whom he had hopes of obtaining a post on the staff of the commander-in-chief. Berg and Boris, who had rested well after the previous day's march, were sitting smartly and neatly dressed, in the clean quarters assigned them, playing draughts at a round table. Berg was holding between his knees a smoking pipe. Boris, with his characteristic nicety, was building the draughts into a pyramid with his delicate, white fingers, while he waited for Berg to play. He was watching his partner's face, obviously thinking of the game, his attention concentrated, as it always was, on what he was engaged in.

'Well, how are you going to get out of that?' he said.

'I am going to try,' answered Berg, touching the pieces, and taking his hand away again.

At that instant the door opened.

'Here he is at last!' shouted Rostov. 'And Berg too. *Ah, petisanfan, alley cooshey dormir*!' he cried, repeating the saying of their old nurse's that had once been a joke with him and Boris.

'Goodness, how changed you are!' Boris got up to greet Rostov, but as he rose, he did not forget to hold the board, and to put back the falling pieces. He was about to embrace his friend, but Nikolay drew back from him. With that peculiarly youthful feeling of fearing beaten tracks, of wanting to avoid imitation, to express one's feelings in some new way of one's own, so as to escape the forms often conventionally used by one's elders, Nikolay wanted to do something striking on meeting his friend. He wanted somehow to give him a pinch, to give Berg a shove, anything rather than to kiss, as people always did on such occasions. Boris, on the contrary, embraced Rostov in a composed and friendly manner, and gave him three kisses.

It was almost six months since they had seen each other. And being at the stage when young men take their first steps along the path of life, each found immense changes in the other, quite new reflections of the different society in which they had taken those first steps. Both had changed greatly since they were last together, and both wanted to show as soon as possible what a change had taken place.

'Ah, you damned floor polishers! Smart and clean, as if you'd been enjoying yourselves; not like us poor devils at the front,' said Rostov, with martial swagger, and with baritone notes in his voice that were new to Boris. He pointed to his mud-stained riding-breeches. The German woman of the house popped her head out of a door at Rostov's loud voice.

'A pretty woman, eh?' said he, winking.

'Why do you shout so? You are frightening them,' said Boris. 'I didn't expect you today,' he added. 'I only sent the note off to you yesterday—through an adjutant of Kutuzov's, who's a friend of mine —Bolkonsky. I didn't expect he would send it to you so quickly. Well, how are you? Been under fire already?' asked Boris.

Without answering, Rostov, in soldierly fashion, shook the cross of St. George that hung on the cording of his uniform, and pointing to his arm in a sling, he glanced smiling at Berg.

'As you see,' he said.

'To be sure, yes, yes,' said Boris, smiling; 'and we have had a capital march here too. You know his Highness kept all the while with our regiment, so that we had every convenience and advantage. In Poland, the receptions, the dinners, the balls!—I can't tell you. And the Tsarevitch was very gracious to all our officers.' And both the friends began describing one, the gay revels of the hussars and life at the front; the other, the amenities and advantages of service under the command of royalty.

'Oh, you guards,' said Rostov. 'But, I say, send for some wine.'

Boris frowned.

'If you really want some,' he said. And he went to the bedstead, took a purse from under the clean pillows, and ordered some wine. 'Oh, and I have a letter and money to give you,' he added.

Rostov took the letter, and flinging the money on the sofa, put both his elbows on the table and began reading it. He read a few lines, and looked wrathfully at Berg. Meeting his eyes, Rostov hid his face with the letter.

'They sent you a decent lot of money, though,' said Berg, looking at the heavy bag, that sank into the sofa. 'But we manage to scrape along on our pay, count, I can tell you in my own case....'

'I say, Berg, my dear fellow,' said Rostov; 'when you get a letter from home and meet one of your own people, who you want to talk everything over with, and I'm on the scene, I'll clear out at once, so as not to be in your way. Do you hear, be off, please, anywhere, anywhere ... to the devil!' he cried, and immediately seizing him by the shoulder, and looking affectionately into his face, evidently to soften the rudeness of his words, he added: 'you know, you're not angry, my dear fellow, I speak straight from the heart to an old friend like you.'

'Why, of course, count, I quite understand,' said Berg, getting up and speaking in his deep voice.

'You might go and see the people of the house; they did invite you,' added Boris.

Berg put on a spotless clean coat, brushed his lovelocks upwards before the looking-glass, in the fashion worn by the Tsar Alexander Pavlovitch, and having assured himself from Rostov's expression that his coat had been observed, he went out of the room with a bland smile.

'Ah, what a beast I am, though,' said Rostov, as he read the letter.

'Oh, why?'

'Ah, what a pig I've been, never once to have written and to have given them such a fright. Ah, what a pig I am!' he repeated, flushing all at once. 'Well, did you send Gavrila for some wine? That's right, let's have some!' said he.

With the letters from his family there had been inserted a letter of recommendation to Prince Bagration, by Anna Mihalovna's advice, which Countess Rostov had obtained through acquaintances, and had sent to her son, begging him to take it to its address, and to make use of it.

'What nonsense! Much use to me,' said Rostov, throwing the letter under the table.

'What did you throw that away for?' asked Boris.

'It's a letter of recommendation of some sort; what the devil do I want with a letter like that!'

'What the devil do you want with it?' said Boris, picking it up and reading the address; 'that letter would be of great use to you.'

'I'm not in want of anything, and I'm not going to be an adjutant to anybody.'

'Why not?' asked Boris.

'A lackey's duty.'

'You are just as much of an idealist as ever, I see,' said Boris, shaking his head.

'And you're just as much of a diplomat. But that's not the point. . . . Come, how are you?' asked Rostov.

'Why, as you see. So far everything's gone well; but I'll own I should be very glad to get a post as adjutant, and not to stay in the line.'

'What for?'

'Why, because if once one goes in for a military career, one ought to try to make it as successful a career as one can.'

'Oh, that's it,' said Rostov, unmistakably thinking of something else. He looked intently and inquiringly into his friend's eyes, apparently seeking earnestly the solution of some question.

Old Gavrila brought in the wine.

'Shouldn't we send for Alphonse Karlitch now?' said Boris. 'He'll drink with you, but I can't.'

'Send for him, send for him. Well, how do you get on with the Teuton?' said Rostov, with a contemptuous smile.

'He's a very, very nice, honest, and pleasant fellow,' said Boris.

Rostov looked intently into Boris's face once more and he sighed. Berg came back, and over the bottle the conversation between the three officers became livelier. The guardsmen told Rostov about their march and how they had been fêted in Russia, in Poland, and abroad. They talked of the sayings and doings of their commander, the Grand-Duke, and told anecdotes of his kind-heartedness and his irascibility. Berg was silent, as he always was, when the subject did not concern him personally, but *à propos of* the irascibility of the Grand-Duke he related with gusto how he had had some words with the Grand-Duke in Galicia, when his Highness had inspected the regiments and had flown into a rage over some irregularity in their movements. With a bland smile on his face he described how the Grand-Duke had ridden up to him in a violent rage, shouting 'Arnauts,' ('Arnauts' was the Tsarevitch's favourite term of abuse when he was in a passion), and how he had asked for the captain. 'Would you believe me, count, I wasn't in the least alarmed, because I knew I was right. Without boasting, you know, count, I may say I know all the regimental drill-book by heart, and the standing orders, too, I know as I know "Our Father that art in Heaven." And so that's how it is, count, there's never the slightest detail neglected in my company. So my conscience was at ease. I came forward.' (Berg stood up and mimicked how he had come forward with his hand to the beak of his cap. It would certainly have been difficult to imagine more respectfulness and more self-complacency in a face.) 'Well, he scolded, and scolded, and rated at me, and shouted his "Arnauts," and damns, and "to Siberia,"' said Berg, with a subtle smile. 'I knew I was right, and so I didn't speak; how could I, count? "Why are you dumb?" he shouted. Still I held my tongue, and what do you think, count? Next day there was nothing about it in the orders of the day; that's what comes of keeping one's head. Yes, indeed, count,' said Berg, pulling at his pipe and letting off rings of smoke.

'Yes, that's capital,' said Rostov, smiling; but Boris, seeing that Rostov was disposed to make fun of Berg, skilfully turned the conversation. He begged Rostov to tell them how and where he had been wounded. That pleased Rostov, and he began telling them, getting more and more eager as he talked. He described to them his battle at Schöngraben exactly as men who have taken part in battles always do describe them, that is, as they would have liked them to be, as they have heard them described by others, and as sounds well, but not in the least as it really had been. Rostov was a truthful young man, he would not have intentionally told a lie. He began with the intention of telling everything precisely as it had happened, but imperceptibly, unconsciously, and inevitably he passed into falsehood. If he had told the truth to his listeners, who, like himself, had heard numerous descriptions of cavalry charges, and had formed a definite idea of what a charge was like and were expecting a similar description, either they would not have believed him, or worse still, would have assumed that Rostov was himself to blame for not having performed the exploits usually performed by those who describe cavalry charges. He could not tell them simply that they had all been charging full gallop, that he had fallen off his horse, sprained his arm, and run with all his might away from the French into the copse. And besides, to tell everything exactly as it happened, he would have had to exercise considerable self-control in order to tell nothing beyond what happened. To tell the truth is a very difficult thing; and young people are rarely capable of it. His listeners expected to hear how he had been all on fire with excitement, had forgotten himself, had flown like a tempest on the enemy's square, had cut his way into it, hewing men down right and left, how a sabre had been thrust into his flesh, how he had fallen unconscious, and so on. And he described all that. In the middle of his tale, just as he was saying: 'You can't fancy what a strange frenzy takes possession of one at the moment of the charge,' there walked into the room Prince Andrey Bolkonsky, whom Boris was expecting. Prince Andrey liked to encourage and assist younger men, he was flattered at being applied to for his influence, and well disposed to Boris, who had succeeded in making a favourable impression on him the previous day; he was eager to do for the young man what he desired. Having been sent with papers from Kutuzov to the Tsarevitch, he called upon Boris, hoping to find him alone. When he came into the room and saw the hussar with his soldierly swagger describing his warlike exploits (Prince Andrey could not endure the kind of men who are fond of doing so), he smiled cordially to Boris, but frowned and dropped his eyelids as he turned to Rostov with a slight bow. Wearily and languidly he sat down on the sofa, regretting that he had dropped into such undesirable society. Rostov, perceiving it, grew hot, but he did not care; this man was nothing to him. Glancing at Boris, he saw, however, that he too seemed ashamed of the valiant hussar. In spite of Prince Andrey's unpleasant, ironical manner, in spite of the disdain with which Rostov, from his point of view of a fighting man in the regular army, regarded the whole race of staff-adjutants in general—the class to which the newcomer unmistakably belonged—he yet felt abashed, reddened, and subsided into silence. Boris inquired what news there was on the staff and whether he could not without indiscretion tell them something about our plans.

'Most likely they will advance,' answered Bolkonsky, obviously unwilling to say more before outsiders. Berg seized the opportunity to inquire with peculiar deference whether the report was true, as he had heard, that the allowance of forage to captains of companies was to be doubled. To this Prince Andrey replied with a smile that he could not presume to offer an opinion on state questions of such gravity, and Berg laughed with delight.

'As to your business,' Prince Andrey turned again to Boris, 'we will talk of it later,' and he glanced at Rostov. 'You come to me after the review, and we'll do what we can.' And looking round the room he addressed Rostov, whose childish, uncontrollable embarrassment, passing now into anger, he did not think fit to notice: 'You were talking, I think, about the Schöngraben action? Were you there?'

'I was there,' Rostov said in a tone of exasperation, which he seemed to intend as an insult to the adjutant. Bolkonsky noticed the hussar's state of mind, and it seemed to amuse him. He smiled rather disdainfully.

'Ah! there are a great many stories now about that engagement.'

'Yes, stories!' said Rostov loudly, looking from Boris to Bolkonsky with eyes full of sudden fury, 'a great many stories, I dare say, but our stories are the stories of men who have been under the enemy's fire, our stories have some weight, they're not the tales of little staff upstarts, who draw pay for doing nothing.'

'The class to which you assume me to belong,' said Prince Andrey, with a calm and particularly amiable smile.

A strange feeling of exasperation was mingled in Rostov's heart with respect for the self-possession of this person.

'I'm not talking about you,' he said; 'I don't know you, and, I'll own, I don't want to. I'm speaking of staff-officers in general.'

'Let me tell you this,' Prince Andrey cut him short in a tone of quiet authority, 'you are trying to insult me, and I'm ready to agree with you that it is very easy to do so, if you haven't sufficient respect for yourself. But you will agree that the time and place is ill-chosen for this squabble. In a day or two we have to take part in a great and more serious duel, and besides, Drubetskoy, who tells me he is an old friend of yours, is in no way to blame because my physiognomy is so unfortunate as to displease you. However,' he said, getting up, 'you know my name, and know where to find me; but don't forget,' he added, 'that I don't consider either myself or you insulted, and my advice, as a man older than you, is to let the matter drop. So on Friday, after the review, I shall expect you, Drubetskoy; good-bye till then,' cried Prince Andrey, and he went out, bowing to both.

Rostov only bethought him of what he ought to have answered when he had gone. And he was more furious still that he had not thought of saying it. He ordered his horse to be brought round at once, and taking leave of Boris coldly, he rode back. Whether to ride tomorrow to headquarters and challenge that conceited adjutant, or whether really to let the matter drop, was the question that worried him all the way. At one moment he thought vindictively how he would enjoy seeing the fright that feeble, little, conceited fellow would be in, facing his pistol, at the next he was feeling with surprise that, of all the men he knew, there was no one he would be more glad to have for his friend than that detested little adjutant.

VIII

THE day after Rostov's visit to Boris, the review took place of the Austrian and Russian troops, both the reinforcements freshly arrived from Russia and the troops that had been campaigning with Kutuzov. Both Emperors, the Russian Emperor with the Tsarevitch, and the Austrian with the arch-duke, were to assist at this review of the allied forces, making up together an army of eighty thousand men. From early morning the troops, all smart and clean, had been moving about the plain before the fortress. Thousands of legs and bayonets moved with flags waving, and halted at the word of command, turned and formed at regular intervals, moving round other similar masses of infantry in different uniforms. With the rhythmic tramp of hoofs, the smartly dressed cavalry in blue, and red, and green laced uniforms rode jingling by on black and chestnut and grey horses, the bandsmen in front covered with embroidery. Between the infantry and the cavalry the artillery, in a long line of polished, shining cannons quivering on their carriages, crawled slowly by with their heavy, brazen sound, and their peculiar smell from the linstocks, and ranged themselves in their places. Not only the generals in their full parade uniform, wearing scarves and all their decorations, with waists, portly and slim alike, pinched in to the uttermost, and red necks squeezed into stiff collars, not only the pomaded, dandified officers, but every soldier, with his clean, washed, and shaven face, and weapons polished to the utmost possibility of glitter, every horse rubbed down till its coat shone like satin, and every hair in its moistened mane lay in place—all alike felt it no joking matter, felt that something grave and solemn was going forward. Every general and every soldier was conscious of his own insignificance, feeling himself but a grain of sand in that ocean of humanity, and at the same time was conscious of his might, feeling himself a part of that vast whole. There had been strenuous exertion and bustle since early morning, and by ten o'clock everything was in the required order. The rows of soldiers were standing on the immense plain. The whole army was drawn out in three lines. In front was the cavalry; behind, the artillery; still further back, the infantry.

Between each two ranks of soldiery there was as it were a street. The army was sharply divided into three parts: Kutuzov's army (on the right flank of which stood the Pavlograd hussars in the front line), the regiments of the line and the guards that had arrived from Russia, and the Austrian troops. But all stood in one line, under one command, and in similar order.

Like a wind passing over the leaves, the excited whisper fluttered over the plain: 'They are coming! they are coming!' There was a sound of frightened voices, and the hurried men's fuss over the last finishing touches ran like a wave over the troops.

A group came into sight moving towards them from Olmütz in front of them. And at the same moment, though there had been no wind, a faint breeze fluttered over the army, and stirred the streamers on the lances, and sent the unfurled flags flapping against their flag-staffs. It looked as though in this slight movement the army itself were expressing its joy at the approach of the Emperors. One voice was heard saying; 'Steady!' Then like cocks at sunrise, voices caught up and repeated the sound in different parts of the plain. And all sank into silence.

In the deathlike stillness, the only sound was the tramp of hoofs. It was the Emperors' suite. The Emperors rode towards the flank, and the trumpets of the first cavalry regiment began playing a march. It seemed as though the sound did not come from the trumpeters, but that the army itself was naturally giving forth this music in its delight at the Emperors' approach. Through the music could be distinctly heard one voice, the genial, youthful voice of the Emperor Alexander. He uttered some words of greeting, and the first regiment boomed out: 'Hurrah!'.

with a shout so deafening, so prolonged, so joyful, that the men themselves felt awestruck at the multitude and force of the mass they made up.

Rostov, standing in the foremost ranks of Kutuzov's army, which the Tsar approached first of all, was possessed by the feeling, common to every man in that army—a feeling of self-oblivion, of proud consciousness of their might and passionate devotion to the man who was the centre of that solemn ceremony.

He felt that at one word from that man all that vast mass (and he, an insignificant atom bound up with it), would rush through fire and water, to crime, to death, or to the grandest heroism, and so he could not but thrill and tremble at the sight of the man who was the embodiment of that word.

'Hurrah! hurrah! hurrah!' thundered on all sides, and one regiment after another greeted the Tsar with the strains of the march, then hurrah! . . . then the march, and again hurrah! and hurrah! which growing stronger and fuller, blended into a deafening roar.

Before the Tsar had reached it, each regiment in its speechless immobility seemed like a lifeless body. But as soon as the Tsar was on a level with it, each regiment broke into life and noise, which joined with the roar of all the line, by which the Tsar had passed already. In the terrific, deafening uproar of those voices, between the square masses of troops, immobile as though turned to stone, moved carelessly, but symmetrically and freely, some hundreds of men on horseback, the suite, and in front of them two figures—the Emperors. Upon these was entirely concentrated the repressed, passionate attention of all that mass of men.

The handsome, youthful Emperor Alexander, in the uniform of the Horse Guards, in a triangular hat with the base in front, attracted the greater share of attention with his pleasant face and sonorous, low voice.

Rostov was standing near the trumpeters, and with his keen eyes he recognised the Tsar from a distance and watched him approaching. When the Tsar was only twenty paces away, and Nikolay saw clearly in every detail the handsome, young, and happy face of the Emperor, he experienced a feeling of tenderness and ecstasy such as he had never known before. Everything in the Tsar—every feature, every movement —seemed to him full of charm.

Halting before the Pavlograd regiment, the Tsar said something in French to the Austrian Emperor and smiled.

Seeing that smile, Rostov unconsciously began to smile himself and felt an even stronger rush of love for his Emperor. He longed to express his love for the Tsar in some way. He knew it was impossible, and he wanted to cry. The Tsar called up the colonel of the regiment and said a few words to him.

'By God! what would happen to me if the Emperor were to address me!' thought Rostov; 'I should die of happiness.'

The Tsar addressed the officers, too.

'All of you, gentlemen' (every word sounded to Rostov like heavenly music), 'I thank you with all my heart.'

How happy Rostov would have been if he could have died on the spot for his Emperor.

'You have won the flags of St. George and will be worthy of them.'

'Only to die, to die for him!' thought Rostov.

The Tsar said something more which Rostov did not catch, and the soldiers, straining their lungs, roared 'hurrah!'

Rostov, too, bending over in his saddle, shouted with all his might, feeling he would like to do himself some injury by this shout, if only he could give full expression to his enthusiasm for the Tsar.

The Tsar stood for several seconds facing the hussars, as though he were hesitating.

'How could the Emperor hesitate?' Rostov wondered; but then, even that hesitation seemed to him majestic and enchanting, like all the Tsar did.

The Tsar's hesitation lasted only an instant. The Tsar's foot in the narrow-pointed boot of the day, touched the belly of the bay English thoroughbred he was riding. The Tsar's hand in its white glove gathered up the reins and he moved off, accompanied by the irregularly heaving sea of adjutants. Further and further he rode away, stopping at the other regiments, and at last the white plume of his hat was all that Rostov could see above the suite that encircled the Emperors.

Among the gentlemen of the suite, Rostov noticed Bolkonsky, sitting his horse in a slack, indolent pose. Rostov remembered his quarrel with him on the previous day and his doubt whether he ought or ought not to challenge him. 'Of course, I ought not,' Rostov reflected now.... 'And is it worth thinking and speaking of it at such a moment as the present? At the moment of such a feeling of love, enthusiasm, and self-sacrifice, what are all our slights and squabbles? I love every one, I forgive every one at this moment,' thought Rostov.

When the Tsar had made the round of almost all the regiments, the troops began to file by him in a parade march, and Rostov on Bedouin, which he had lately bought from Denisov, was the officer at the rear, that is, had to pass last, alone, and directly in view of the Tsar.

Before he reached the Tsar, Rostov, who was a capital horseman, set spurs twice to his Bedouin, and succeeded in forcing him into that frantic form of gallop into which Bedouin always dropped when he was excited. Bending his foaming nose to his chest, arching his tail, and seeming to skim through the air without touching the earth, Bedouin, as though he, too, were conscious of the Tsar's eye upon him, flew by in superb style, with a graceful high action of his legs.

Rostov himself drew back his legs and drew in his stomach, and feeling himself all of a piece with his horse, rode by the Tsar with a frowning but blissful face, looking a regular devil, as Denisov used to say.

'Bravo, Pavlograds!' said the Tsar.

'My God! shouldn't I be happy if he bade me fling myself into fire this instant,' thought Rostov.

When the review was over, the officers, both of the reinforcements and of Kutuzov's army, began to gather together in groups. Conversations sprang up about the honours that had been conferred, about the Austrians and their uniforms, and their front line, about Bonaparte and the bad time in store for him now, especially when Essen's corps, too, should arrive, and Prussia should take our side. But the chief subject of conversation in every circle was the Emperor Alexander, every word he had uttered, every gesture was described and expatiated upon with enthusiasm.

There was but one desire in all; under the Emperor's leadership to face the enemy as soon as possible. Under the command of the Emperor himself they would not fail to conquer any one whatever: so thought Rostov and most of the officers after the review.

After the review they all felt more certain of victory than they could have been after two decisive victories.

IX

THE day after the review Boris Drubetskoy put on his best uniform, and accompanied by his comrade Berg's good wishes for his success, rode to Olmütz to see Bolkonsky, in the hope of profiting by his friendliness to obtain a better position, especially the position of an adjutant in attendance on some personage of importance, a post which seemed to him particularly alluring.

'It's all very well for Rostov, whose father sends him ten thousand at a time, to talk about not caring to cringe to any one, and not being a lackey to any man. But I, with nothing of my own but my brains, have my career to make, and mustn't let opportunities slip, but must make the most of them.'

He did not find Prince Andrey at Olmütz that day. But the sight of

Olmütz—where were the headquarters and the diplomatic corps, and where both Emperors with their suites, their households, and their court, were staying—only strengthened his desire to belong to this upper world.

He knew no one; and in spite of his smart guardsman's uniform, all these exalted persons, racing to and fro about the streets in their elegant carriages, plumes, ribbons, and orders, courtiers and military alike, all seemed to be so immeasurably above him, a little officer in the Guards, as to be not simply unwilling, but positively unable to recognise his existence. At the quarters of the commander-in-chief, Kutuzov, where he asked for Bolkonsky, all the adjutants and even the orderlies looked at him as though they wished to impress on him that a great many officers of his sort came hanging about here, and that they were all heartily sick of seeing them. In spite of this, or rather in consequence of it, he went again the following day, the 15th, after dinner, to Olmütz, and going into the house occupied by Kutuzov, asked for Bolkonsky. Prince Andrey was at home, and Boris was ushered into a large room, probably at some time used for dancing. Now there were five bedsteads in it and furniture of various kinds: a table, chairs, a clavichord. One adjutant was sitting in a Persian dressing-gown writing at a table near the door. Another, the stout, red-faced Nesvitsky, was lying on a bed, his arms under his head, laughing with an officer sitting by the bedside. A third was playing a Vienna waltz on the clavichord, while a fourth lay on the clavichord, humming to the tune. Bolkonsky was not in the room. Not one of these gentlemen changed his position on observing Boris. The one who was writing, on being applied to by Boris, turned round with an air of annoyance, and told him that Bolkonsky was the adjutant on duty, and that he should go to the door to the left, into the reception-room, if he wanted to see him. Boris thanked him, and went to the reception-room. There he found some ten officers and generals.

At the moment when Boris entered, Prince Andrey dropping his eyelids disdainfully (with that peculiar air of courteous weariness which so distinctly says, 'If it were not my duty, I would not stay talking to you for a minute'), was listening to an old Russian general with many decorations, who, rigidly erect, almost on tiptoe, was laying some matter before Prince Andrey with the obsequious expression of a common soldier on his purple face.

'Very good, be so kind as to wait a moment,' he said to the general in Russian, with that French accent with which he always spoke when he meant to speak disdainfully, and noticing Boris, Prince Andrey took no further notice of the general (who ran after him with entreaties, begging him to hear something more), but nodded to Boris with a bright smile, as he turned towards him. At that moment Boris saw distinctly what he had had an inkling of before, that is, that quite apart from that subordination and discipline, which is written down in the drill-book, and recognised in the regiment and known to him, there was in the army another and more actual subordination, that which made this rigid, purple-faced general wait respectfully while Prince Andrey —of captain's rank—found it more in accordance with his pleasure to talk to Lieutenant Drubetskoy. Boris felt more than ever determined to follow in future the guidance not of the written code laid down in the regulations, but of this unwritten code. He felt now that simply because he had been recommended to Prince Andrey, he had become at one step superior to the general, who in other circumstances, at the front, could annihilate a mere lieutenant in the guards like him. Prince Andrey went up to him and shook hands.

'Very sorry you didn't find me in yesterday. I was busy the whole day with the Germans. We went with Weierother to survey the disposition. When Germans start being accurate, there's no end to it!'

Boris smiled, as though he understood, as a matter of common knowledge, what Prince Andrey was referring to. But it was the first time he had heard the name of Weierother, or even the word 'disposition' used in that sense.

'Well, my dear boy, you still want an adjutant's post? I have been thinking about you since I saw you.'

'Yes,' said Boris, involuntarily flushing for some reason, 'I was thinking of asking the commander-in-chief; he has had a letter about me from Prince Kuragin; and I wanted to ask him simply because,' he added, as though excusing himself, 'I am afraid the guards won't be in action.'

'Very good, very good! we will talk it over later,' said Prince Andrey, 'only let me report on this gentleman's business and I am at your disposal.' While Prince Andrey was away reporting to the commander-in-chief on the business of the purple-faced general, that general, who apparently did not share Boris's views as to the superior advantages of the unwritten code, glared at the insolent lieutenant, who had hindered his having his say out, so that Boris began to be uncomfortable. He turned away and waited with impatience for Prince Andrey to come out of the commander-in-chief's room.

'Well, my dear fellow, I have been thinking about you,' said Prince Andrey, when they had gone into the big room with the clavichord in it. 'It's no use your going to the commander-in-chief; he will say a lot of polite things to you, will ask you to dine with him' ('that wouldn't come amiss in the service of that unwritten code,' thought Boris), 'but nothing more would come of it; we shall soon have a complete battalion of adjutants and orderly officers. But I tell you what we will do; I have a friend, a general adjutant and an excellent fellow, Prince Dolgorukov. And though you may not be aware of it, the fact is that Kutuzov and his staff and all of us are just now of no account at all. Everything now is concentrated about the Emperor, so we'll go together to Dolgorukov. I have to go to see him, and I have already spoken of you to him. So we can see whether he may not think it possible to find a post for you on his staff, or somewhere there nearer to the sun.'

Prince Andrey was always particularly keen over guiding a young man and helping him to attain worldly success. Under cover of this help for another, which he would never have accepted for himself, he was brought into the circle which bestowed success, and which attracted him. He very readily took up Boris's cause, and went with him to Prince Dolgorukov.

It was late in the evening as they entered the palace at Olmütz, occupied by the Emperors and their retinues.

There had been on that same day a council of war, at which all the members of the Hofkriegsrath and the two Emperors had been present. At the council it had been decided, contrary to the advice of the elder generals, Kutuzov and Prince Schwarzenberg, to advance at once and to fight a general engagement with Bonaparte. The council of war was only just over when Prince Andrey, accompanied by Boris, went into the palace in search of Prince Dolgorukov. Every one at headquarters was still under the spell of the victory gained that day by the younger party at the council of war. The voices of those who urged delay, and counselled waiting for something and not advancing, had been so unanimously drowned and their arguments had been confuted by such indubitable proofs of the advantages of advancing, that what had been discussed at the council, the future battle and the victory certain to follow it, seemed no longer future but past. All the advantages were on our side. Our immense forces, undoubtedly superior to those of Napoleon, were concentrated in one place; the troops were encouraged by the presence of the two Emperors, and were eager for battle. The strategic position on which they were to act was to the minutest detail known to the Austrian general Weierother, who was at the head of the troops (as a lucky chance would have it, the Austrian troops had chosen for their manœuvres the very fields in which they had now to fight the French). Every detail of the surrounding neighbourhood was known and put down on maps, while Bonaparte, apparently growing feebler, was taking no measures.

Dolgorukov, who had been one of the warmest advocates of attack, had just come back from the council, weary, exhausted, but eager and proud of the victory he had gained. Prince Andrey presented the officer for whom he was asking his influence, but Prince Dolgorukov, though he shook hands politely and warmly, said nothing to Boris. Obviously unable to restrain himself from uttering the thoughts which were engrossing him at that moment, he addressed Prince Andrey in French.

'Well, my dear fellow, what a battle we have won! God only grant that the one which will be the result of it may be as victorious. I must own, though, my dear fellow,' he said jerkily and eagerly, 'my shortcomings compared with the Austrians and especially Weierother. What accuracy, what minuteness, what knowledge of the locality, what foresight of every possibility, every condition, of every minutest detail! No, my dear boy, anything more propitious than the circumstances we are placed in could not have been found, if one had arranged it purposely. The union of Austrian exactitude with Russian valour—what could you wish for more?'

'So an attack has been finally decided upon?' said Bolkonsky.

'And do you know, I fancy, Bonaparte really has lost his head. You know that a letter came from him today to the Emperor.' Dolgorukov smiled significantly.

'You don't say so! What does he write?' asked Balkonsky.

'What can he write? Tradi-ri-di-ra—all simply to gain time. I tell you he's in our hands; that's the fact! But the most amusing part of it all,' he said, breaking all at once into a good-natured laugh, 'is that they couldn't think how to address an answer to him. If not "consul," and of course not "emperor," it should be "general" Bonaparte, it seemed to me.'

'But between not recognising him as emperor and calling him General Bonaparte, there's a difference,' said Bolkonsky.

'That's just the point,' Dolgorukov interrupted quickly, laughing. 'You know Bilibin, he's a very clever fellow; he suggested addressing it, "To the Usurper and Enemy of the Human Race,"' Dolgorukov chuckled merrily.

'And nothing more?' observed Bolkonsky.

'But still it was Bilibin who found the suitable form of address in earnest. He's both shrewd and witty . . .'

'How was it?'

'To the Chief of the French Government: *au chef du gouvernement français*,' Dolgorukov said seriously and with satisfaction. 'That was the right thing, wasn't it?'

'It was all right, but he will dislike it extremely,' observed Bolkonsky.

'Oh, extremely! My brother knows him; he's dined more than once with him—nowadays the emperor—in Paris, and used to tell me that he'd never seen a subtler and more crafty diplomat; you know, a combination of French adroitness and the Italian actor-faculty! You know the anecdote about Bonaparte and Count Markov? Count Markov was the only person who knew how to treat him. You know the story of the handkerchief? It's a gem!' And the talkative Dolgorukov turning from Boris to Prince Andrey told the story of how Bonaparte, to test Markov, our ambassador, had purposely dropped his handkerchief before him, and had stood looking at him, probably expecting Markov to pick it up for him, and how Markov promptly dropped his own beside it, and had picked up his own without touching Bonaparte's.

'Capital,' said Bolkonsky. 'But, prince, I have come to you as a petitioner in behalf of this young friend. You see . . .' But before Prince Andrey could finish, an adjutant came into the room to summon Prince Dolgorukov to the Emperor.

'Ah, how annoying!' said Dolgorukov, getting up hurriedly and shaking hands with Prince Andrey and Boris. 'You know I shall be very glad to do all that depends on me both for you and for this charming young man.' Once more he shook hands with Boris with an expression of good-natured, genuine, heedless gaiety. 'But you see . . . another time!'

Boris was excited by the thought of being so close to the higher powers, as he felt himself to be at that instant. He was conscious here of being in contact with the springs that controlled all those vast movements of the masses, of which in his regiment he felt himself a tiny, humble, and insignificant part. They followed Prince Dolgorukov out into the corridor and met (coming out of the door of the Tsar's room at which Dolgórukov went in) a short man in civilian dress with a shrewd face and a sharply projecting lower jaw, which, without spoiling his face, gave him a peculiar alertness and shiftiness of expression. This short man nodded to Dolgorukov, as if he were an intimate friend, and stared with an intently cold gaze at Prince Andrey, walking straight towards him and apparently expecting him to bow or move out of his way. Prince Andrey did neither; there was a vindictive look on his face, and the short young man turned away and walked at the side of the corridor.

'Who's that?' asked Boris.

'That's one of the most remarkable men—and the most unpleasant to me. The minister of foreign affairs, Prince Adam Tchartorizhsky.'

'Those are the men,' added Bolkonsky with a sigh which he could not suppress, as they went out of the palace, 'those are the men who decide the fates of nations.'

Next day the troops set off on the march, and up to the time of the battle of Austerlitz, Boris did not succeed in seeing Bolkonsky or Dolgorukov again, and remained for a while in the Ismailov regiment.

X

AT dawn on the 16th, Denisov's squadron, in which Nikolay Rostov was serving, and which formed part of Prince Bagration's detachment, moved on from its halting place for the night—to advance into action, as was said. After about a mile's march, in the rear of other columns, it was brought to a standstill on the high-road. Rostov saw the Cossacks, the first and second squadrons of hussars, and the infantry battalions with the artillery pass him and march on ahead; he also saw the Generals Bagration and Dolgorukov ride by with their adjutants. All the panic he had felt, as before, at the prospect of battle, all the inner conflict by means of which he had overcome that panic, all his dreams of distinguishing himself in true hussar style in this battle—all were for nothing. His squadron was held back in reserve, and Nikolay Rostov spent a tedious and wretched day. About nine o'clock in the morning he heard firing ahead of him, and shouts of hurrah, saw the wounded being brought back (there were not many of them), and finally saw a whole detachment of French cavalry being brought away in the midst of a company of Cossacks. Obviously the action was over, and the action had, obviously, been a small one, but successful. The soldiers and officers as they came back were talking of a brilliant victory, of the taking of the town of Vishau, and a whole French squadron taken prisoners. The day was bright and sunny after a sharp frost at night, and the cheerful brightness of the autumn day was in keeping with the news of victory, which was told not only by the accounts of those who had taken part in it, but by the joyful expression of soldiers, officers, generals, and adjutants, who rode to and fro by Rostov. All the greater was the pang in Nikolay's heart that he should have suffered the dread that goes before the battle for nothing, and have spent that happy day in inactivity.

'Rostov, come here, let's drink "begone, dull care!"' shouted Denisov, sitting at the roadside before a bottle and some edibles. The officers gathered in a ring, eating and talking, round Denisov's wine-case.

'Here they're bringing another!' said one of the officers, pointing to a French prisoner, a dragoon, who was being led on foot by two Cossacks.

One of them was leading by the bridle the prisoner's horse, a tall and beautiful French beast.

'Sell the horse?' Denisov called to the Cossacks.

'If you will, your honour.'

The officers got up and stood round the Cossacks and the prisoner. The French dragoon was a young fellow, an Alsatian who spoke French with a German accent. He was breathless with excitement, his face was red, and hearing French spoken he began quickly speaking to the officers, turning from one to another. He said that they wouldn't have taken him, that it wasn't his fault he was taken, but the fault of the corporal, who had sent him to get the horse-cloths, that he had told him the Russians were there. And at every word he added: 'But don't let anybody hurt my little horse,' and stroked his horse. It was evident that he did not quite grasp where he was. At one moment he was excusing himself for having been taken prisoner, at the next, imagining himself before his superior officers, he was trying to prove his soldierly discipline and zeal for the service. He brought with him in all its freshness into our rearguard the atmosphere of the French army, so alien to us.

The Cossacks sold the horse for two gold pieces, and Rostov, being the richest of the officers since he had received money from home, bought it.

'Be good to the little horse!' the Alsatian said with simple-hearted good-nature to Rostov, when the horse was handed to the hussar.

Rostov smiling, soothed the dragoon, and gave him money.

'Alley! Alley!' said the Cossack, touching the prisoner's arm to make him go on.

'The Emperor! the Emperor!' was suddenly heard among the hussars. Everything was bustle and hurry, and Rostov saw behind them on the road several horsemen riding up with white plumes in their hats. In a single moment all were in their places and eagerly expectant.

Rostov had no memory and no consciousness of how he ran to his post and got on his horse. Instantly his regret at not taking part in the battle, his humdrum mood among the men he saw every day—all was gone; instantly all thought of self had vanished. He was entirely absorbed in the feeling of happiness at the Tsar's being near. His nearness alone made up to him by itself, he felt, for the loss of the whole day. He was happy, as a lover is happy when the moment of the longed-for meeting has come. Not daring to look round from the front line, by an ecstatic instinct without looking round, he felt his approach. And he felt it not only from the sound of the tramping hoofs of the approaching cavalcade, he felt it because as the Tsar came nearer everything grew brighter, more joyful and significant, and more festive. Nearer and nearer moved this sun, as he seemed to Rostov, shedding around him rays of mild and majestic light, and now he felt himself enfolded in that radiance, he heard his voice—that voice caressing, calm, majestic, and yet so simple. A deathlike silence had come—as seemed to Rostov fitting—and in that silence he heard the sound of the Tsar's voice.

'The Pavlograd hussars?' he was saying interrogatively.

'The reserve, sire,' replied a voice—such a human voice, after the superhuman voice that had said: *'Les hussards de Pavlograd?'*

The Tsar was on a level with Rostov, and he stood still there. Alexander's face was even handsomer than it had been at the review three days before. It beamed with such gaiety and youth, such innocent youthfulness, that suggested the playfulness of a boy of fourteen, and yet it was still the face of the majestic emperor. Glancing casually along the squadron, the Tsar's eyes met the eyes of Rostov, and for not more than two seconds rested on them. Whether it was that the Tsar saw what was passing in Rostov's soul (it seemed to Rostov that he saw everything), any way he looked for two seconds with his blue eyes into Rostov's face. (A soft, mild radiance beamed from them.) Then all at once he raised his eyebrows, struck his left foot sharply against his horse, and galloped on.

The young emperor could not restrain his desire to be present at the battle, and in spite of the expostulations of his courtiers, at twelve o'clock, escaping from the third column which he had been following, he galloped to the vanguard. Before he reached the hussars, several adjutants met him with news of the successful issue of the engagement. The action, which had simply consisted in the capture of a squadron of the French, was magnified into a brilliant victory over the enemy, and so the Tsar and the whole army believed, especially while the smoke still hung over the field of battle, that the French had been defeated, and had been forced to retreat against their will. A few minutes after the Tsar had galloped on, the division of the Pavlograd hussars received orders to move forward. In Vishau itself, a little German town, Rostov saw the Tsar once more. In the market-place of the town where there had been rather a heavy firing before the Tsar's arrival, lay several dead and wounded soldiers, whom there had not been time to pick up. The Tsar, surrounded by his suite of officers and courtiers, was mounted on a different horse from the one he had ridden at the review, a chestnut English thoroughbred. Bending on one side with a graceful gesture, holding a gold field-glass to his eyes, he was looking at a soldier lying on his face with a blood-stained and uncovered head. The wounded soldier was an object so impure, so grim, and so revolting, that Rostov was shocked at his being near the Emperor. Rostov saw how the Tsar's stooping shoulders shuddered, as though a cold shiver had passed over them, how his left foot convulsively pressed the spur into the horse's side, and how the trained horse looked round indifferently and did not stir. An adjutant dismounting lifted the soldier up under his arms, and began laying him on a stretcher that came up. The soldier groaned.

'Gently, gently, can't you do it more gently?' said the Tsar, apparently suffering more than the dying soldier, and he rode away.

Rostov saw the tears in the Tsar's eyes, and heard him say in French to Tchartorizhsky, as he rode off: 'What an awful thing war is, what an awful thing!'

The forces of the vanguard were posted before Vishau in sight of the enemy's line, which had been all day retreating before us at the slightest exchange of shots. The Tsar's thanks were conveyed to the vanguard, rewards were promised, and a double allowance of vodka was served out to the men. Even more gaily than on the previous night the bivouac fires crackled, and the soldiers sang their songs. Denisov on that night celebrated his promotion to major, and, towards the end of the carousal, after a good deal of drinking, Rostov proposed a toast to the health of the Emperor, but 'not our Sovereign and Emperor, as they say at official dinners,' said he, 'but to the health of the Emperor, the good, enchanting, great man, let us drink to his health, and to a decisive victory over the French!'

'If we fought before,' said he, 'and would not yield an inch before the French, as at Schöngraben, what will it be now when he is at our head? We will all die, we will gladly die for him. Eh, gentlemen? Perhaps I'm not saying it right. I've drunk a good deal, but that's how I feel, and you do too. To the health of Alexander the First! Hurrah!'

'Hurrah!' rang out the cheery voices of the officers. And the old captain Kirsten shouted no less heartily and sincerely than Rostov, the boy of twenty.

When the officers had drunk the toast and smashed their glasses, Kirsten filled some fresh ones, and in his shirt-sleeves and riding-breeches went out to the soldiers' campfires, glass in hand, and waving his hand in the air stood in a majestic pose, with his long grey whiskers and his white chest visible through the open shirt in the light of the camp-fire.

'Lads, to the health of our Sovereign the Emperor, to victory over our enemies, hurrah!' he roared in his stalwart old soldier's baritone.

The hussars thronged about him and responded by a loud shout in unison.

Late at night, when they had all separated, Denisov clapped his short hand on the shoulder of his favourite Rostov. 'To be sure he'd no one to fall in love with in the field, so he's fallen in love with the Tsar,' he said.

'Denisov, don't joke about that,' cried Rostov, 'it's such a lofty, such a sublime feeling, so . . .'

'I believe you, I believe you, my dear, and I share the feeling and approve . . .'

'No, you don't understand!' And Rostov got up and went out to wander about among the camp-fires, dreaming of what happiness it would be to die—not saving the Emperor's life—(of that he did not even dare to dream), but simply to die before the Emperor's eyes. He really was in love with the Tsar and the glory of the Russian arms and the hope of coming victory. And he was not the only man who felt thus in those memorable days that preceded the battle of Austerlitz: nine-tenths of the men in the Russian army were at that moment in love, though less ecstatically, with their Tsar and the glory of the Russian arms.

XI

THE following day the Tsar stayed in Vishau. His medical attendant, Villier, was several times summoned to him. At headquarters and among the troops that were nearer, the news circulated that the Tsar was unwell. He was eating nothing and had slept badly that night, so those about him reported. The cause of this indisposition was the too violent shock given to the sensitive soul of the Tsar by the sight of the killed and wounded.

At dawn on the 17th, a French officer was conducted from our outposts into Vishau. He came under a flag of truce to ask for an interview with the Russian Emperor. This officer was Savary. The Tsar had only just fallen asleep, and so Savary had to wait. At midday he was admitted to the emperor, and an hour later he rode away accompanied by Prince Dolgorukov to the outposts of the French army. Savary's mission was, so it was rumoured, to propose a meeting between Alexander and Napoleon. A personal interview was, to the pride and rejoicing of the whole army, refused, and instead of the Tsar, Prince Dolgorukov, the general victorious in the action at Vishau, was despatched with Savary to undertake negotiations with Napoleon, if these negotiations—contrary to expectation—were founded on a real desire for peace. In the evening Dolgorukov came back, went straight to the Tsar and remained a long while alone with him.

On the 18th and 19th the troops moved forward two days' march, and the enemy's outposts, after a brief interchange of shots, retired. In the higher departments of the army an intense, bustling excitement and activity prevailed from midday of the 19th till the morning of the following day, the 20th of November, on which was fought the memorable battle of Austerlitz. Up to midday of the 19th the activity, the eager talk, the bustle, and the despatching of adjutants was confined to the headquarters of the Emperors; after midday the activity had reached the headquarters of Kutuzov and the staff of the commanding officers of the columns. By evening this activity had been carried by the adjutants in all directions into every part of the army, and in the night of the 19th the multitude of the eighty thousands of the allied army rose from its halting-place, and with a hum of talk moved on, a vast heaving mass nine versts long.

The intense activity that had begun in the morning in the headquarters of the Emperors, and had given the impetus to all the activity in remoter parts, was like the first action in the centre wheel of a great tower clock. Slowly one wheel began moving, another began turning, and a third, and more and more rapidly, levers, wheels, and blocks began to revolve, chimes began playing, figures began to pop out, and the hands began moving rhythmically, as a result of that activity.

Just as in the mechanism of the clock, in the mechanism of the military machine too, once the impetus given, it was carried on to the last results, and just as unsympathetically stationary were the parts of the machinery which the impulse had not yet reached. Wheels creak on their axles, and teeth bite into cogs, and blocks whir in rapid motion, while the next wheel stands as apathetic and motionless as though it were ready to stand so for a hundred years. But the momentum reaches it—the lever catches, and the wheel, obeying the impulse, creaks and takes its share in the common movement, the result and aim of which are beyond its ken.

Just as in the clock, the result of the complex action of countless different wheels and blocks is only the slow, regular movement of the hand marking the time, so the result of all the complex human movement of those 160,000 Russians and Frenchmen—of all the passions, hopes, regrets, humiliations, sufferings, impulses of pride, of fear, and of enthusiasm of those men—was only the loss of the battle of Austerlitz, the so-called battle of the three Emperors, that is, the slow shifting of the registering hand on the dial of the history of mankind.

Prince Andrey was on duty that day, and in close attendance on the commander-in-chief. At six o'clock in the evening Kutuzov visited the headquarters of the Emperors, and after a brief interview with the Tsar, went in to see the Ober-Hofmarschal Count Tolstoy.

Bolkonsky took advantage of this interval to go in to Dolgorukov to try and learn details about the coming action. Prince Andrey felt that Kutuzov was disturbed and displeased about something, and that they were displeased with him at headquarters, and that all the persons at the Emperor's headquarters took the tone with him of people who knew something other people are not aware of; and for that reason he wanted to have some talk with Dolgorukov.

'Oh, good evening, my dear boy,' said Dolgorukov, who was sitting at tea with Bilibin. 'The fête's for tomorrow. How's your old fellow? out of humour?'

'I won't say he's out of humour, but I fancy he would like to get a hearing.'

'But he did get a hearing at the council of war, and he will get a hearing when he begins to talk sense. But to delay and wait about now when Bonaparte fears a general engagement more than anything—is out of the question.'

'Oh yes, you have seen him,' said Prince Andrey. 'Well, what did you think of Bonaparte? What impression did he make on you?'

'Yes, I saw him, and I'm persuaded he fears a general engagement more than anything in the world,' repeated Dolgorukov, who evidently attached great value to this general deduction he had made from his interview with Napoleon. 'If he weren't afraid of an engagement what reason has he to ask for this interview, to open negotiations, and, above all, to retreat, when retreat is contrary to his whole method of conducting warfare? Believe me, he's afraid, afraid of a general engagement; his hour has come, mark my words.'

'But tell me what was he like, how did he behave?' Prince Andrey still insisted.

'He's a man in a grey overcoat, very anxious to be called "your majesty," but disappointed at not getting a title of any kind out of me. That's the sort of man he is, that's all,' answered Dolgorukov, looking round with a smile at Bilibin.

'In spite of my profound respect for old Kutuzov,' he pursued, 'a pretty set of fools we should be to wait about and let him have a chance to get away or cheat us, when as it is he's in our hands for certain. No, we mustn't forget Suvorov and his rule—never to put oneself in a position to be attacked, but to make the attack oneself. Believe me, the energy of young men is often a safer guide in warfare than all the experience of the old cunctators.'

'But in what position are you going to attack him? I have been at the outposts today, and there was no making out where his chief forces are concentrated,' said Prince Andrey. He was longing to explain to Dolgorukov his own idea, the plan of attack he had formed.

'Ah, that's a matter of no consequence whatever,' Dolgorukov said quickly, getting up and unfolding a map on the table. 'Every contingency has been provided for; if he is concentrated at Brünn. . . .' And Prince Dolgorukov gave a rapid and vague account of Weierother's plan of a flank movement.

Prince Andrey began to make objections and to explain his own plan, which may have been as good as Weierother's, but had the fatal disadvantage that Weierother's plan had already been accepted. As soon as Prince Andrey began to enlarge on the drawbacks of the latter and the advantages of his own scheme, Prince Dolgorukov ceased to attend, and looked without interest not at the map, but at Prince Andrey's face.

'There is to be a council of war at Kutuzov's tonight, though; you can explain all that then,' said Dolgorukov.

'That's what I am going to do,' said Prince Andrey, moving away from the map.

'And what are you worrying yourselves about, gentlemen?' said Bilibin, who had till then been listening to their talk with a beaming smile, but now unmistakably intended to make a joke. 'Whether there is victory or defeat tomorrow, the glory of the Russian arms is secure. Except your Kutuzov, there's not a single Russian in command of a column. The commanders are: Herr General Wimpfen, le comte de Langeron, le prince de Lichtenstein, le prince de Hohenlohe and Prishprshiprsh, or some such Polish name.'

'Hold your tongue, backbiter,' said Dolgorukov. 'It's not true, there are two Russians: Miloradovitch and Dohturov, and there would have been a third, Count Araktcheev, but for his weak nerves.'

'Mihail Ilarionovitch has come out, I think,' said Prince Andrey. 'Good luck and success to you, gentlemen,' he added, and went out, after shaking hands with Dolgorukov and Bilibin.

On returning home Prince Andrey could not refrain from asking Kutuzov, who sat near him in silence, what he thought about the coming battle. Kutuzov looked sternly at his adjutant, and after a pause, answered: 'I think the battle will be lost, and I said so to Count Tolstoy and asked him to give that message to the Tsar. And what do you suppose was the answer he gave me? *"Eh, mon cher général, je me mêle de riz et de côtelettes, mêlez-vous des affaires de la guerre."* Yes. . . . That's the answer I got!'

XII

At ten o'clock in the evening, Weierother with his plans rode over to Kutuzov's quarters, where the council of war was to take place. All the commanders of columns were summoned to the commander-in-chief's, and with the exception of Prince Bagration, who declined to come, all of them arrived at the hour fixed.

Weierother, who was entirely responsible for all the arrangements for the proposed battle, in his eagerness and hurry, was a striking contrast to the ill-humoured and sleepy Kutuzov, who reluctantly played the part of president and chairman of the council of war. Weierother obviously felt himself at the head of the movement that had been set going and could not be stopped. He was like a horse in harness running downhill with a heavy load behind him. Whether he were pulling it or it were pushing him, he could not have said, but he was flying along at full speed with no time to consider where this swift motion would land him. Weierother had been twice that evening to make a personal inspection up to the enemy's line, and twice he had been with the Emperors, Russian and Austrian, to report and explain, and to his office, where he had dictated the disposition of the German troops. He came now, exhausted, to Kutuzov's.

He was evidently so much engrossed that he even forgot to be respectful to the commander-in-chief. He interrupted him, talked rapidly and indistinctly, without looking at the person he was addressing, failed to answer questions that were put to him, was spattered with mud, and had an air pitiful, exhausted, distracted, and at the same time self-confident and haughty.

Kutuzov was staying in a small nobleman's castle near Austerlitz. In the drawing-room, which had been made the commander-in-chief's study, were gathered together: Kutuzov himself, Weierother, and the members of the council of war. They were drinking tea. They were only waiting for Prince Bagration to open the council. Presently Bagration's orderly officer came with a message that the prince could not be present. Prince Andrey came in to inform the commander-in-chief of this; and, profiting by the permission previously given him by Kutuzov to be present at the council, he remained in the room.

'Well, since Prince Bagration isn't coming, we can begin,' said Weierother, hastily getting up from his place and approaching the table, on which an immense map of the environs of Brünn lay unfolded.

Kutuzov, his uniform unbuttoned, and his fat neck as though set free from bondage, bulging over the collar, was sitting in a low chair with his podgy old hands laid symmetrically on the arms; he was almost asleep.

At the sound of Weierother's voice, he made an effort and opened his solitary eye.

'Yes, yes, please, it's late as it is,' he assented, and nodding his head, he let it droop and closed his eyes again.

If the members of the council had at first believed Kutuzov to be shamming sleep, the nasal sounds to which he gave vent during the reading that followed, proved that the commander-in-chief was concerned with something of far greater consequence than the desire to show his contempt for their disposition of the troops or anything else whatever; he was concerned with the satisfaction of an irresistible human necessity—sleep. He was really asleep. Weierother, with the gesture of a man too busy to lose even a minute of his time, glanced at Kutuzov, and satisfying himself that he was asleep, he took up a paper and in a loud, monotonous tone began reading the disposition of the troops in the approaching battle under a heading, which he also read.

'Disposition for the attack of the enemy's position behind Kobelnitz and Sokolnitz, November 20, 1805.'

The disposition was very complicated and intricate.

'As the enemy's left wing lies against the wooded hills and their right wing is advancing by way of Kobelnitz and Sokolnitz behind the swamps that lie there, while on the other hand our left wing stretches far beyond their right, it will be advantageous to attack this last-named wing, especially if we have possession of the villages of Sokolnitz and Kobelnitz, by which means we can at once fall on them in the rear, and pursue them in the open between Schlapanitz and the Thuerassa-Wald, thereby avoiding the defiles of Schlapanitz and Bellowitz, which are covered by the enemy's front. With this ultimate aim it will be necessary.... The first column marches.... The second column marches. ... The third column marches'... read Weierother.

The generals seemed to listen reluctantly to the intricate account of the disposition of the troops. The tall, fair-haired general, Buxhevden, stood leaning his back against the wall, and fixing his eyes on a burning candle, he seemed not to be listening, not even to wish to be thought to be listening. Exactly opposite to Weierother, with his bright, wide-open eyes fixed upon him was Miloradovitch, a ruddy man, with whiskers and shoulders turned upwards, sitting in a military pose with his hands on his knees and his elbows bent outwards. He sat in obstinate silence, staring into Weierother's face, and only taking his eyes off him when the Austrian staff-commander ceased speaking. Then

Miloradovitch looked round significantly at the other generals. But from that significant glance it was impossible to tell whether he agreed or disagreed, was pleased or displeased, at the arrangements. Next to Weierother sat Count Langeron, with a subtle smile that never left his Southern French face during the reading; he gazed at his delicate fingers as he twisted round a golden snuff-box with a portrait on it. In the middle of one of the lengthy paragraphs he stopped the rotatory motion of the snuff-box, lifted his head, and with hostile courtesy lurking in the corners of his thin lips, interrupted Weierother and would have said something. But the Austrian general, continuing to read, frowned angrily with a motion of the elbows that seemed to say: 'Later, later, you shall give your opinion, now be so good as to look at the map and listen.' Langeron turned up his eyes with a look of bewilderment, looked round at Miloradovitch, as though seeking enlightenment, but meeting the significant gaze of Miloradovitch, that signified nothing, he dropped his eyes dejectedly, and fell to twisting his snuff-box again.

'A geography lesson,' he murmured as though to himself, but loud enough to be heard.

Przhebyshevsky, with respectful but dignified courtesy, put his hand up to his ear on the side nearest Weierother, with the air of a man absorbed in attention. Dohturov, a little man, sat opposite Weierother with a studious and modest look on his face. Bending over the map, he was conscientiously studying the arrangement of the troops and the unfamiliar locality. Several times he asked Weierother to repeat words and difficult names of villages that he had not caught. Weierother did so, and Dohturov made a note of them.

When the reading, which lasted more than an hour, was over, Langeron, stopping his twisting snuff-box, began to speak without looking at Weierother or any one in particular. He pointed out how difficult it was to carry out such a disposition, in which the enemy's position was assumed to be known, when it might well be uncertain seeeing that the enemy was in movement. Langeron's objections were well founded, yet it was evident that their principal object was to make Weierother, who had read his plans so conceitedly, as though to a lot of schoolboys, feel that he had to deal not with fools, but with men who could teach him something in military matters.

When the monotonous sound of Weierother's voice ceased, Kutuzov opened his eyes, as the miller wakes up at any interruption in the droning of the mill-wheels, listened to what Langeron was saying, and as though saying to himself: 'Oh, you're still at the same nonsense!' made haste to close his eyes again, and let his head sink still lower.

Langeron, trying to deal the most malignant thrusts possible at

Weierother's military vanity as author of the plan, showed that Bonaparte might easily become the attacking party instead of waiting to be attacked, and so render all this plan of the disposition of the troops utterly futile. Weierother met all objections with a confident and contemptuous smile, obviously prepared beforehand for every objection, regardless of what they might say to him.

'If he could have attacked us, he would have done so today,' he said.

'You suppose him, then, to be powerless?' said Langeron.

'I doubt if he has as much as forty thousand troops,' answered Weierother with the smile of a doctor to whom the sick-nurse is trying to expound her own method of treatment.

'In that case, he is going to meet his ruin in awaiting our attack,' said Langeron with a subtle, ironical smile, looking round again for support to Miloradovitch near him. But Miloradovitch was obviously thinking at that instant of anything in the world rather than the matter in dispute between the generals.

'*Ma foi*,' he said, 'tomorrow we shall see all that on the field of battle.'

Weierother smiled again, a smile that said that it was comic and queer for *him* to meet with objections from Russian generals and to have to give proofs to confirm what he was not simply himself convinced of, but had thoroughly convinced their majesties the Emperors of too.

'The enemy have extinguished their fires and a continual noise has been heard in their camp,' he said. 'What does that mean? Either they are retreating—the only thing we have to fear, or changing their position' (he smiled ironically). 'But even if they were to take up their position at Turas, it would only be saving us a great deal of trouble, and all our arrangements will remain unchanged in the smallest detail.'

'How can that be? . . .' said Prince Andrey, who had a long while been looking out for an opportunity of expressing his doubts. Kutuzov waked up, cleared his throat huskily, and looked round at the generals.

'Gentlemen, the disposition for tomorrow, for today indeed (for it's going on for one o'clock), can't be altered now,' he said. 'You have heard it, and we will all do our duty. And before a battle nothing is of so much importance . . .' (he paused) 'as a good night's rest.'

He made a show of rising from his chair. The generals bowed themselves out. It was past midnight. Prince Andrey went out.

The council of war at which Prince Andrey had not succeeded in expressing his opinion, as he had hoped to do, had left on him an impression of uncertainty and uneasiness. Which was right—Dolgorukov and Weierother, or Kutuzov and Langeron and the others, who did not approve of the plan of attack—he did not know. But had it really been impossible for Kutuzov to tell the Tsar his views directly? Could it not have been managed differently? On account of personal and court considerations were tens of thousands of lives to be risked—'and my life, *mine*?' he thought.

'Yes, it may well be that I shall be killed tomorrow,' he thought.

And all at once, at that thought of death, a whole chain of memories, the most remote and closest to his heart, rose up in his imagination. He recalled his last farewell to his father and his wife; he recalled the early days of his love for her, thought of her approaching motherhood; and he felt sorry for her and for himself, and in a nervously overwrought and softened mood he went out of the cottage at which he and Nesvitsky were putting up, and began to walk to and fro before it. The night was foggy, and the moonlight glimmered mysteriously through the mist. 'Yes, tomorrow, tomorrow!' he thought. 'Tomorrow, may be, all will be over for me, all these memories will be no more, all these memories will have no more meaning for me. Tomorrow, perhaps—for certain, indeed—tomorrow, I have a presentiment, I shall have for the first time to show all I can do.' And he pictured the engagement, the loss of it, the concentration of the fighting at one point, and the hesitation of all the commanding officers. And then the happy moment —that Toulon he had been waiting for so long—at last comes to him. Resolutely and clearly he speaks his opinion to Kutuzov and Weierother and the Emperors. All are struck by the justness of his view, but no one undertakes to carry it into execution, and behold, he leads the regiment, only making it a condition that no one is to interfere with his plans, and he leads his division to the critical point and wins the victory alone. 'And death and agony!' said another voice. But Prince Andrey did not answer that voice, and went on with his triumphs. The disposition of the battle that ensues is all his work alone. Nominally, he is an adjutant on the staff of Kutuzov, but he does everything alone. The battle is gained by him alone. Kutuzov is replaced, he is appointed. . . . 'Well, and then?' said the other voice again, 'what then, if you do a dozen times over escape being wounded, killed, or deceived before that; well, what then?' 'Why, then . . .' Prince Andrey answered himself, 'I don't know what will come then, I can't know, and don't want to; but if I want that, if I want glory, want to be known to men, want to be loved by them, it's not my fault that I want it, that it's the only thing I care for, the only thing I live for. Yes, the only thing! I shall never say so to any one, but, my God! what am I to do, if I care for nothing but glory, but men's love? Death, wounds, the loss of my family—nothing has terrors for me. And dear and precious as many people are to me: father, sister, wife—the people dearest to me; yet dreadful and unnatural as it seems, I would give them all up for a moment of glory, of triumph over men, of love from men whom I don't know, and shall never know, for the love of those people there,' he thought, listening to the talk in the courtyard of Kutuzov's house. He could hear the voices of the officers' servants packing up; one of them, probably a coachman, was teasing Kutuzov's old cook, a man called Tit, whom Prince Andrey knew. He kept calling him and making a joke on his name.

'Tit, hey, Tit?' he said.

'Well?' answered the old man.

'*Tit, stupay molotit*' ('Tit, go a thrashing'), said the jester.

'Pooh, go to the devil, do,' he heard the cook's voice, smothered in the laughter of the servants.

'And yet, the only thing I love and prize is triumph over all of them, that mysterious power and glory which seems hovering over me in this mist!'

XIII

ROSTOV had been sent that night with a platoon on picket duty to the line of outposts in the foremost part of Bagration's detachment. His hussars were scattered in couples about the outposts; he himself rode about the line of the outposts trying to struggle against the sleepiness which kept overcoming him. Behind him could be seen the immense expanse of the dimly burning fires of our army; before him was the misty darkness. However intently Rostov gazed into this misty distance, he could see nothing; at one moment there seemed something greyish, at the next something blackish, then something like the glimmer of a fire over there where the enemy must be, then he fancied the glimmer had been only in his own eyes. His eyes kept closing, and there floated before his mind the image of the Emperor, then of Denisov, and Moscow memories, and again he opened his eyes and saw close before him the head and ears of the horse he was riding, and sometimes black figures of hussars, when he rode within six paces of them, but in the distance still the same misty darkness. 'Why? it may well happen,' mused Rostov, 'that the Emperor will meet me and give me some commission, as he might to any officer; he'll say, "Go and find out what's there." There are a lot of stories of how quite by chance he has made the acquaintance of officers and given them some place close to him too. Oh, if he were to give me a place in attendance on him! Oh, what care I would take of him, how I would tell him the whole truth, how I would unmask all who deceive him!' And to picture his love and devotion to the Tsar more vividly, Rostov imagined some enemy or treacherous German, whom he would with great zest not simply kill, but slap in the face before the Tsar's eyes. All at once a shout in the distance roused Rostov. He started and opened his eyes. 'Where am I? Yes, in the picket line; the pass and watchword—shaft, Olmütz. How annoying that our squadron will be in reserve . . .' he thought. 'I'll ask to go to the front. It may be my only chance of seeing the Emperor. And now it's not long before I'm off duty. I'll ride round once more, and as I come back, I'll go to the general and ask him.' He sat up straight in the saddle and set off to ride once more round his hussars. It seemed to him that it was lighter. On the left side he could see a sloping descent that looked lighted up and a black knoll facing it that seemed steep as a wall. On this knoll was a white patch which Rostov could not understand; was it a clearing in the wood, lighted up by the moon, or the remains of snow, or white horses? It seemed to him indeed that something was moving over the white spot. 'It must be snow—that spot: a spot—*une tache*,' Rostov mused dreamily. 'But that's not a *tache* . . . Na . . . tasha, my sister, her black eyes. Na . . . tasha (won't she be surprised when I tell her how I've seen the Emperor!) Natasha . . . tasha . . . sabretache. . . .' 'Keep to the right, your honour, there are bushes here,' said the voice of an hussar, by whom Rostov was riding as he fell asleep. Rostov lifted his head, which had dropped on to his horse's mane, and pulled up beside the hussar. He could not shake off the youthful, childish drowsiness that overcame him. 'But, I say, what was I thinking? I mustn't forget. How I am going to speak to the Emperor? No, not that —that's tomorrow. Yes, yes! Natasha, attacks, tacks us,—whom? The hussars. Ah, the hussars with their moustaches . . . Along the Tversky boulevard rode that hussar with the moustaches, I was thinking of him too, just opposite Guryev's house. . . . Old Guryev. . . Ah, a fine fellow Denisov! But that's all nonsense. The great thing is that the Emperor's here now. How he looked at me and longed to say something, but he did not dare. . . No, it was I did not dare. But that's nonsense, and the great thing is not to forget something important I was thinking of, yes. Natasha, attacks us, yes, yes, yes. That's right.' And again he dropped with his head on his horse's neck. All at once it seemed to him that he was being fired at. 'What? what? . . . Cut them down! What?' Rostov was saying, as he wakened up. At the instant that he opened his eyes, Rostov heard in front, over where the enemy were, the prolonged shouting of thousands of voices. His horse and the horse of the hussar near him pricked up their ears at these shouts. Over where the shouts came from, a light was lighted and put out, then another, and all along the line of the French troops on the hillside fires were lighted and the shouts grew louder and louder. Rostov heard the sound of French words though he could not distinguish them. He could only hear: aaaa! and rrrr!

'What is it? What do you think?' Rostov said to the hussar near him. 'That's in the enemy's camp surely?'

The hussar made no reply.

'Why, don't you hear it?' Rostov asked again, after waiting some time for a reply.

'Who can tell, your honour,' the hussar answered reluctantly.

'From the direction it must be the enemy,' Rostov said again.

'May be 'tis, and may be not,' said the hussar; 'it's dark. Now! steady,' he shouted to his horse, who fidgeted. Rostov's horse too was restless, and pawed the frozen ground as it listened to the shouts and looked at the lights. The shouting grew louder and passed into a mingled roar that could only be produced by an army of several thousands. The lights stretched further and further probably along the line of the French camp. Rostov was not sleepy now. The gay, triumphant shouts in the enemy's army had a rousing effect on him. *'Vive l'Empereur! l'Empereur!'* Rostov could hear distinctly now.

'Not far off, beyond the stream it must be,' he said to the hussar near him.

The hussar merely sighed without replying, and cleared his throat angrily. They heard the thud of a horse trotting along the line of hussars, and there suddenly sprang up out of the night mist, looking huge as an elephant, the figure of a sergeant of hussars.

'Your honour, the generals!' said the sergeant, riding up to Rostov. Rostov, still looking away towards the lights and shouts, rode with the sergeant to meet several men galloping along the line. One was on a white horse. Prince Bagration with Prince Dolgorukov and his adjutant had ridden out to look at the strange demonstration of lights and shouts in the enemy's army. Rostov going up to Bagration, reported what he had heard and seen to him, and joined the adjutants, listening to what the generals were saying.

'Take my word for it,' Prince Dolgorukov was saying to Bagration, 'it's nothing but a trick; they have retreated and ordered the rearguard to light fires and make a noise to deceive us.'

'I doubt it,' said Bagration; 'since evening I have seen them on that knoll; if they had retreated, they would have withdrawn from there too. Monsieur l'officier,' Prince Bagration turned to Rostov, 'are the enemy's pickets still there?'

'They were there this evening, but now I can't be sure, your excellency. Shall I go with some hussars and see?' said Rostov.

Bagration stood still, and before answering, tried to make out Rostov's face in the mist.

'Well, go and see,' he said after a brief pause.

'Yes, sir.'

Rostov put spurs to his horse, called up the sergeant Fedtchenko, and two other hussars, told them to ride after him, and trotted off downhill in the direction of the shouting, which still continued. Rostov felt both dread and joy in riding alone with three hussars into that mysterious and dangerous, misty distance, where no one had been before him. Bagration shouted to him from the hill not to go beyond the stream, but Rostov made as though he had not heard his words, and rode on without stopping, further and further, continually mistaking bushes for trees and ravines for men, and continually discovering his mistakes. As he galloped downhill he lost sight both of our men and the enemy, but more loudly and distinctly he heard the shouts of the French. In the valley he saw ahead of him something that looked like a river, but when he had ridden up to it, he found out it was a road. As he got out on the road he pulled up his horse, hesitating whether to go along it or to cut across it, and ride over the black field up the hillside. To follow the road, which showed lighter in the mist, was more dangerous, because figures could be more easily descried upon it. 'Follow me,' he said; 'cut across the road,' and began galloping up the hill towards the point where the French picket had been in the evening.

'Your honour, here he is!' said one of the hussars behind; and before Rostov had time to make out something that rose up suddenly black in the mist, there was a flash of light, the crack of a shot and a bullet, that seemed whining a complaint, whizzed high in the air and flew away out of hearing. Another shot missed fire, but there was a flash in the pan. Rostov turned his horse's head and galloped back. He heard four more shots at varying intervals, and four more bullets whistled in varying tones somewhere in the mist. Rostov held in his horse, who seemed inspirited, as he was himself by the shots, and rode back at a walking-pace. 'Now, then, some more; now then, more!' a sort of light-hearted voice murmured in his soul. But there were no more shots. Only as he approached Bagration, Rostov put his horse into a gallop again, and with his hand to his cap, rode up to him.

Dolgorukov was still insisting on his opinion that the French were retreating, and had only lighted fires to mislead them. 'What does it prove?' he was saying, as Rostov rode up to them. 'They might have retreated and left pickets.'

'It's clear they have not all retired, prince,' said Bagration. 'We must wait till morning; tomorrow we shall know all about it.'

'The picket's on the hill, your excellency, still where it was in the evening,' Rostov announced, his hand to his cap, unable to restrain the smile of delight that had been called up by his expedition and the whiz of the bullets.

'Very good, very good,' said Bagration, 'I thank you, monsieur l'officier.'

'Your excellency,' said Rostov, 'may I ask a favour?'

'What is it?'

'Tomorrow our squadron is ordered to the rear; may I beg you to attach me to the first squadron?'

'What's your name?'

'Count Rostov.'

'Ah, very good! You may stay in attendance on me.'

'Ilya Andreitch's son?' said Dolgorukov. But Rostov made him no reply.

'So I may reckon on it, your excellency.'

'I will give the order.'

'Tomorrow, very likely, they will send me with some message to the Emperor,' he thought. 'Thank God!'

The shouts and lights in the enemy's army had been due to the fact that while Napoleon's proclamation had been read to the troops, the Emperor had himself ridden among the bivouacs. The soldiers on seeing the Emperor had lighted wisps of straw and run after him, shouting, '*Vive l'empereur!*' Napoleon's proclamation was as follows:—

'Soldiers! The Russian army is coming to meet you, to avenge the Austrian army, the army of Ulm. They are the forces you have defeated at Hollabrunn, and have been pursuing ever since up to this place. The position we occupy is a powerful one, and while they will march to outflank me on the right, they will expose their flank to me! Soldiers! I will myself lead your battalions. I will keep out of fire, if you, with your habitual bravery, carry defeat and disorder into the ranks of the enemy. But if victory is for one moment doubtful, you will see your Emperor exposed to the enemy's hottest attack, for there can be no uncertainty of victory, especially on this day, when it is a question of the honour of the French infantry, on which rests the honour of our nation. Do not, on the pretext of removing the wounded, break the order of the ranks! Let every man be fully penetrated by the idea that we must subdue these minions of England, who are inspired by such hatred of our country. This victory will conclude our campaign, and we can return to winter quarters, where we shall be reinforced by fresh forces now being formed in France; and then the peace I shall conclude will be one worthy of my people, of you and me.   NAPOLEON.'

XIV

AT five o'clock in the morning it was still quite dark. The troops of the centre, of the reserves, and of Bagration's right flank, were still at rest. But on the left flank the columns of the infantry, cavalry, and artillery, destined to be the first to descend from the heights, so as to attack the French right flank, and, according to Weierother's plan, to drive it back to the Bohemian mountains, were already up and astir. The smoke from the camp-fires, into which they were throwing everything superfluous, made the eyes smart. It was cold and dark. The officers were hurriedly drinking tea and eating breakfast; the soldiers were munching biscuits, stamping their feet rhythmically, while they gathered about the fires warming themselves, and throwing into the blaze remains of shanties, chairs, tables, wheels, tubs, everything superfluous that they could not take away with them. Austrian officers were moving in and out among the Russian troops, coming everywhere as heralds of their advance. As soon as an Austrian officer appeared near a commanding officer's quarters, the regiment began to bestir themselves; the soldiers ran from the fires, thrust pipes into boot-legs, bags into waggons, saw to their muskets, and formed into ranks. The officers buttoned themselves up, put on their sabres and pouches, and moved up and down the ranks shouting. The commissariat men and officers' servants harnessed the horses, packed and tied up the waggons. The adjutants and the officers in command of regiments and battalions got on their horses, crossed themselves, gave final orders, exhortations and commissions to the men who remained behind with the baggage, and the monotonous thud of thousands of feet began. The columns moved, not knowing where they were going, and unable from the crowds round them, the smoke, and the thickening fog, to see either the place which they were leaving, or that into which they were advancing.

The soldier in movement is as much shut in, surrounded, drawn along by his regiment, as the sailor is by his ship. However great a distance he traverses, however strange, unknown, and dangerous the regions to which he penetrates, all about him, as the sailor has the deck and masts and rigging of his ship, he has always everywhere the same comrades, the same ranks, the same sergeant Ivan Mitritch, the same regimental dog Zhutchka, the same officers. The soldier rarely cares to know into what region his ship has sailed; but on the day of battle—

God knows how or whence it comes—there may be heard in the moral world of the troops a sterner note that sounds at the approach of something grave and solemn, and rouses them to a curiosity unusual in them. On days of battle, soldiers make strenuous efforts to escape from the routine of their regiment's interests, they listen, watch intently, and greedily inquire what is being done around them.

The fog had become so thick that though it was growing light, they could not see ten steps in front of them. Bushes looked like huge trees, level places looked like ravines and slopes. Anywhere, on any side, they might stumble upon unseen enemies ten paces from them. But for a long while the columns marched on in the same fog, going downhill and uphill, passing gardens and fences, in new and unknown country, without coming upon the enemy anywhere. On the contrary, the soldiers became aware that in front, behind, on all sides, were the Russian columns moving in the same direction. Every soldier felt cheered at heart by knowing that where he was going, to that unknown spot were going also many, many more of our men.

'I say, the Kurskies have gone on,' they were saying in the ranks.

'Stupendous, my lad, the forces of our men that are met together! Last night I looked at the fires burning, no end of them. A regular Moscow!'

Though not one of the officers in command of the columns rode up to the ranks nor talked to the soldiers (the commanding officers, as we have seen at the council of war, were out of humour, and displeased with the plans that had been adopted, and so they simply carried out their orders without exerting themselves to encourage the soldiers), yet the soldiers marched on in good spirits, as they always do when advancing into action, especially when on the offensive.

But after they had been marching on for about an hour in the thick fog, a great part of the troops had to halt, and an unpleasant impression of mismanagement and misunderstanding spread through the ranks. In what way that impression reached them it is very difficult to define. But there is no doubt that it did reach them, and with extraordinary correctness and rapidity, and spread imperceptibly and irresistibly, like water flowing over a valley. Had the Russian army been acting alone, without allies, possibly it would have taken a long time for this impression of mismanagement to become a general conviction. But as it was, it was so particularly pleasant and natural to ascribe the mismanagement to the senseless Germans, and all believed that there was some dangerous muddle due to a blunder on the part of the sausage-makers.

'What are they stopping for? Blocked up the way, eh? Or hit upon the French at last?'

'No, not heard so. There'd have been firing. After hurrying us to march off, and we've marched off—to stand in the middle of a field for no sense—all the damned Germans making a muddle of it. The senseless devils! I'd have sent them on in front. But no fear, they crowd to the rear. And now one's to stand with nothing to eat.'

'I say, will they be quick there?'

'The cavalry is blocking up the road, they say,' said an officer.

'Ah, these damned Germans, they don't know their own country,' said another.

'Which division are you?' shouted an adjutant, riding up.

'Eighteenth.'

'Then why are you here? You ought to have been in front long ago; you won't get there now before evening.'

'The silly fools' arrangements, they don't know themselves what they're about,' said the officer, and he galloped away. Then a general trotted up, and shouted something angrily in a foreign tongue.

'*Ta-fa-la-fa*, and no making out what he's jabbering,' said a soldier, mimicking the retreating general. 'I'd like to shoot the lot of them, the blackguards!'

'Our orders were to be on the spot before ten o'clock, and we're not halfway there. That's a nice way of managing things!' was repeated on different sides, and the feeling of energy with which the troops had started began to turn to vexation and anger against the muddled arrangements and the Germans.

The muddle originated in the fact that while the Austrian cavalry were in movement, going to the left flank, the chief authorities had come to the conclusion that our centre was too far from the right flank, and all the cavalry had received orders to cross over to the right. Several thousands of mounted troops had to cross in front of the infantry, and the infantry had to wait till they had gone by.

Ahead of the troops a dispute had arisen between the Austrian officer and the Russian general. The Russian general shouted a request that the cavalry should stop. The Austrian tried to explain that he was not responsible, but the higher authorities. The troops meanwhile stood, growing listless and dispirited. After an hour's delay the troops moved on at last, and began going downhill. The fog, that overspread the hill, lay even more densely on the low ground to which the troops were descending. Ahead in the fog they heard one shot, and another, at first at random, at irregular intervals; tratta-tat, then growing more regular and frequent, and the skirmish of the little stream, the Holdbach, began.

Not having reckoned on meeting the enemy at the stream, and coming upon them unexpectedly in the fog, not hearing a word of encouragement from their commanding officers, with a general sense of being too late, and seeing nothing before or about them in the fog, the Russians fired slowly and languidly at the enemy, never receiving a command in time from the officers and adjutants, who wandered about in the fog in an unknown country, unable to find their own divisions. This was how the battle began for the first, the second, and the third columns, who had gone down into the low-lying ground. The fourth column, with which Kutuzov was, was still on the plateau of Pratzen.

The thick fog still hung over the low ground where the action was beginning; higher up it was beginning to clear, but still nothing could be seen of what was going on in front. Whether all the enemy's forces were, as we had assumed, ten versts away from us, or whether they were close by in that stretch of fog, no one knew till nine o'clock.

Nine o'clock came. The fog lay stretched in an unbroken sea over the plain, but at the village of Schlapanitz, on the high ground where Napoleon was, surrounded by his marshals, it was now perfectly clear. There was bright blue sky over his head, and the vast orb of the sun, like a huge, hollow, purple float, quivered on the surface of the milky sea of fog. Not the French troops only, but Napoleon himself with his staff were not on the further side of the streams, and the villages of Sokolnitz and Schlapanitz, beyond which we had intended to take up our position and begin the attack, but were on the nearer side, so close indeed to our forces that Napoleon could distinguish a cavalry man from a foot soldier in our army with the naked eye. Napoleon was standing a little in front of his marshals, on a little grey Arab horse, wearing the same blue overcoat he had worn through the Italian campaign. He was looking intently and silently at the hills, which stood up out of the sea of mist, and the Russian troops moving across them in the distance, and he listened to the sounds of firing in the valley. His face —still thin in those days—did not stir a single muscle; his gleaming eyes were fixed intently on one spot. His forecasts were turning out correct. Part of the Russian forces were going down into the valley towards the ponds and lakes, while part were evacuating the heights of Pratzen, which he regarded as the key of the position, and had intended to take. He saw through the fog, in the dip between two hills near the village of Pratzen, Russian columns with glittering bayonets moving always in one direction towards the valleys, and vanishing one after another into the mist. From information he had received over night, from the sounds of wheels and footsteps he had heard in the night at the outposts, from the loose order of the march of the Russian columns, from all the evidence, he saw clearly that the allies believed him to be a long way in front of them, that the columns moving close to Pratzen constituted the centre of the Russian army, and that the centre was by this time too much weakened to be able to attack him successfully. But still he delayed beginning the battle.

That day was for him a day of triumph—the anniversary of his coronation. He had slept for a few hours in the early morning, and feeling fresh, and in good health and spirits, in that happy frame of mind in which everything seems possible and everything succeeds, he got on his horse and rode out. He stood without stirring, looking at the heights that rose out of the fog, and his cold face wore that peculiar shade of confident, self-complacent happiness, seen on the face of a happy boy in love. The marshals stood behind him, and did not venture to distract his attention. He looked at the heights of Pratzen, then at the sun floating up out of the mist.

When the sun had completely emerged from the fog, and was glittering with dazzling brilliance over the fields and the mist (as though he had been waiting for that to begin the battle), he took his glove off his handsome white hand, made a signal with it to his marshals, and gave orders for the battle to begin. The marshals, accompanied by adjutants, galloped in various directions, and in a few minutes the chief forces of the French army were moving towards those heights of Pratzen, which were left more and more exposed by the Russian troops as the latter kept moving to the left towards the valley.

XV

AT eight o'clock Kutuzov rode out to Pratzen at the head of Miloradovitch's fourth column, the one which was to occupy the place left vacant by the columns of Przhebyshevsky and Langeron, who had by this time gone down to the plain. He greeted the men of the foremost regiment, and gave them the command to march, showing thereby that he meant to lead that column himself. On reaching the village of Pratzen he halted. Prince Andrey was behind among the immense number of persons who made up the commander-in-chief's suite. Prince Andrey was in a state of excitement, of irritation, and at the same time of repressed calm, as a man often is on attaining a long-desired moment. He was firmly convinced that today would be the day of his Toulon or his bridge of Arcola. How it would come to pass he knew not, but he was firmly convinced that it would be so. The locality and the position of our troops he had mastered to the minutest detail, so far as they could be known to any one in our army. His own strategic plan, which obviously could not conceivably be carried out now, was forgotten by him. Throwing himself into Weierother's plan, Prince Andrey was now deliberating over the contingencies that might arise, and inventing new combinations, in which his rapidity of resource and decision might be called for.

On the left, below in the fog, could be heard firing between unseen forces. There, it seemed to Prince Andrey, the battle would be concentrated, there 'the difficulty would arise, and there I shall be sent,' he thought, 'with a brigade or a division, and there, flag in hand, I shall march forward and shatter all before me.'

Prince Andrey could not look unmoved upon the flags of the passing battalions. Looking at the flag, he kept thinking; perhaps it is that very flag with which I shall have to lead the men. Towards morning nothing was left of the fog on the heights but a hoar frost passing into dew, but in the valleys the fog still lay in a milky-white sea. Nothing could be seen in the valley to the left into which our troops had vanished, and from which sounds of firing were coming. Above the heights stood a clear, dark blue sky, and on the right the vast orb of the sun. In the distance in front, on the coast of that sea of mist, rose up the wooded hills, on which the enemy's army should have been, and something could be descried there. On the right there was the tramp of hoofs and rumble of wheels, with now and then the gleam of bayonets, as the guards plunged into the region of mist; on the left, behind the village, similar masses of cavalry were moving and disappearing into the sea of fog. In front and behind were the marching infantry. The commander-in-chief was standing at the end of the village, letting the troops pass before him. Kutuzov seemed exhausted and irritable that morning. The infantry marching by him halted without any command being given, apparently because something in front blocked up the way.

'Do tell the men to form in battalion columns and go round the village,' said Kutuzov angrily to a general who rode up. 'How is it you don't understand, my dear sir, that it's out of the question to let them file through the defile of the village street, when we are advancing to meet the enemy.'

'I had proposed forming beyond the village, your most high excellency,' replied the general.

Kutuzov laughed bitterly.

'A nice position you'll be in, deploying your front in sight of the enemy—very nice.'

'The enemy is a long way off yet, your most high excellency. According to the disposition. . . .'

'The disposition!' Kutuzov cried with bitter spleen; 'but who told you so.... Kindly do as you are commanded.'

'Yes, sir.'

'My dear boy,' Nesvitsky whispered to Prince Andrey, 'the old fellow is in a vile temper.'

An Austrian officer wearing a white uniform and green plumes in his hat, galloped up to Kutuzov and asked him in the Emperor's name: Had the fourth column started?

Kutuzov turned away without answering, and his eye fell casually on Prince Andrey, who was standing near him. Seeing Bolkonsky, Kutuzov let his vindictive and bitter expression soften, as though recognising that his adjutant was not to blame for what was being done. And still not answering the Austrian adjutant, he addressed Bolkonsky.

'Go and see, my dear fellow, whether the third division has passed the village. Tell them to stop and wait for my orders.'

Prince Andrey had scarcely started when he stopped him.

'And ask whether the sharpshooters are posted,' he added. 'What they are doing, what they are doing!' he murmured to himself, still making no reply to the Austrian.

Prince Andrey galloped off to do his bidding. Overtaking all the advancing battalions, he stopped the third division and ascertained that there actually was no line of sharpshooters in advance of our columns. The officer in command of the foremost regiment was greatly astounded on the order being brought him from the commander-in-chief to send a flying line of sharpshooters in advance. The officer had been resting in the full conviction that there were other troops in front of him, and that the enemy could not be less than ten versts away. In reality there was nothing in front of him but an empty stretch of ground, sloping downhill and covered with fog. Giving him the commander-in-chief's order to rectify the omission, Prince Andrey galloped back. Kutuzov was still at the same spot; his bulky frame drooped in the saddle with the lassitude of old age, and he was yawning wearily with closed eyes. The troops had not yet moved on, but were standing at attention.

'Good, good,' he said to Prince Andrey, and he turned to the general who, watch in hand, was saying that it was time they started, as all the columns of the left flank had gone down already.

'We have plenty of time yet, your excellency,' Kutuzov interpolated between his yawns. 'Plenty of time!' he repeated.

At that moment in the distance behind Kutuzov there were sounds of regiments saluting; the shouts came rapidly nearer along the whole drawn-out line of the advancing Russian columns. Clearly he who was the object of these greetings was riding quickly. When the soldiers of the regiment, in front of which Kutuzov was standing, began to shout he rode off a little on one side, and wrinkling up his face, looked round. Along the road from Pratzen, galloped what looked like a whole squadron of horsemen of different colours. Two of them galloped side by side ahead of the rest. One was in a black uniform with a white plume, on a chestnut English thoroughbred, the other in a white uniform on a black horse. These were the two Emperors and their suites. With a sort of affectation of the manner of an old soldier at the head of his regiment, Kutuzov gave the command, 'Steady,' to the standing troops and rode up to the Emperors, saluting. His whole figure and manner were suddenly transformed. He assumed the air of a subordinate, a man who accepts without criticism. With an affectation of respectfulness which unmistakably made an unpleasant impression on Alexander, he rode up and saluted him.

The unpleasant impression, like the traces of fog in a clear sky, merely flitted across the young and happy face of the Emperor and vanished. He looked that day rather thinner after his illness than he had been at the review at Olmütz, where Bolkonsky had seen him for the first time abroad. But there was the same bewitching combination of majesty and mildness in his fine, grey eyes, and on his delicate lips the same possibility of varying expressions and the predominant expression of noble-hearted, guileless youth.

At the Olmutz review he had been more majestic, here he was livelier and more energetic. He was flushed a little from the rapid three-verst gallop, and as he pulled up his horse, he breathed a sigh of relief, and looked round at those among the faces of his suite that were as young and eager as his own. Behind the Tsar were Tchartorizhsky, and Novosiltsov, and Prince Volkonsky, and Stroganov, and the rest, all richly dressed, gay young men on splendid, well-groomed, fresh horses, slightly heated from the gallop. The Emperor Francis, a rosy, long-faced young man, sat excessively erect on his handsome sable horse, casting deliberate and anxious looks around him. He beckoned one of his white adjutants and asked him a question. 'Most likely at what o'clock they started,' thought Prince Andrey, watching his old acquaintance with a smile, which he could not repress, as he remembered his audience with him. With the Emperors' suite were a certain number of fashionable young aristocrats—Russians and Austrians—selected from the regiments of the guards and the line. Among them were postillions leading extra horses, beautiful beasts from the Tsar's stables, covered with embroidered horsecloths.

Like a breath of fresh country air rushing into a stuffy room through an open window was the youth, energy, and confidence of success that the cavalcade of brilliant young people brought with them into Kutuzov's cheerless staff.

'Why aren't you beginning, Mihail Larionovitch?' the Emperor Alexander said hurriedly, addressing Kutuzov, while he glanced courteously towards the Emperor Francis.

'I am waiting to see, your majesty,' Kutuzov answered, bowing reverentially.

The Emperor turned his ear towards him, with a slight frown and an air of not having caught his words.

'I'm waiting to see, your majesty,' repeated Kutuzov (Prince Andrey noticed that Kutuzov's upper lip quivered unnaturally as he uttered that: 'I'm waiting'). 'Not all the columns are massed yet, your majesty.'

The Tsar heard him, but the answer apparently did not please him; he shrugged his sloping shoulders, and glanced at Novosiltsov, who stood near, with a look that seemed to complain of Kutuzov.

'We are not on the Tsaritsin field, you know, Mihail Larionovitch, where the parade is not begun till all the regiments are ready,' said the Tsar, glancing again at the Emperor Francis as though inviting him, if not to take part, at least to listen to what he was saying. But the Emperor Francis still gazed away and did not listen.

'That's just why I'm not beginning, sire,' said Kutuzov in a resounding voice, as though foreseeing a possibility his words might be ignored, and once more there was a quiver in his face. 'That's why I am not beginning, sire; because we are not on parade and not on the Tsaritsin field,' he articulated clearly and distinctly.

All in the Tsar's suite exchanged instantaneous glances with one another, and every face wore an expression of regret and reproach. 'However old he may be, he ought not, he ought never to speak like that,' the faces expressed.

The Tsar looked steadily and attentively into Kutuzov's face, waiting to see if he were not going to say more. But Kutuzov too on his side, bending his head respectfully, seemed to be waiting. The silence lasted about a minute.

'However, if it's your majesty's command,' said Kutuzov, lifting his head and relapsing into his former affectation of the tone of a stupid, uncritical general, who obeys orders. He moved away, and beckoning the commanding officer of the column, Miloradovitch, gave him the command to advance.

The troops began to move again, and two battalions of the Novgorod regiment and a battalion of the Apsheron regiment passed before the Tsar.

While the Apsheron battalion was marching by, Miloradovitch, a red-faced man, wearing a uniform and orders, with no overcoat, and a turned-up hat with huge plumes stuck on one side, galloped ahead of them, and saluting in gallant style, reined up his horse before the Tsar.

'With God's aid, general,' said the Tsar.

'*Ma foi*, sire, we will do whatever is in our power to do,' he answered gaily, arousing none the less an ironical smile among the gentlemen of the Tsar's suite by his bad French accent. Miloradovitch wheeled his horse round sharply, and halted a few steps behind the Tsar. The Apsheron men, roused by the presence of the Tsar, stepped out gallantly as they marched by the Emperors and their suites.

'Lads!' shouted Miloradovitch in his loud, self-confident, and cheery voice. He was apparently so excited by the sounds of the firing, the anticipation of battle, and the sight of the gallant Apsheron men, his old comrades with Suvorov, that he forgot the Tsar's presence. 'Lads! it's not the first village you've had to take!' he shouted.

'Glad to do our best,' roared the soldiers. The Tsar's horse reared at the unexpected sound. This horse, who had carried the Tsar at reviews in Russia, bore his rider here on the field of Austerlitz, patiently enduring the heedless blows of his left foot, and pricked up his ears at the sound of shots as he had done on the review ground with no comprehension of the significance of these sounds, nor of the nearness of the raven horse of Emperor Francis, nor of all that was said and thought and felt that day by the man who rode upon his back.

The Tsar turned with a smile to one of his courtiers, pointing to the gallant-looking Apsheron regiment, and said something to him.

XVI

KUTUZOV, accompanied by his adjutants, followed the carabineers at a walking pace.

After going on for half a mile at the tail of the column, he stopped at a solitary, deserted house (probably once an inn), near the branching of two roads. Both roads led downhill, and troops were marching along both.

The fog was beginning to part, and a mile and a half away the enemy's troops could be indistinctly seen on the opposite heights. On the left below, the firing became more distinct. Kutuzov stood still in conversation with an Austrian general. Prince Andrey standing a little behind watched them intently, and turned to an adjutant, meaning to ask him for a field-glass.

'Look, look!' this adjutant said, looking not at the troops in the distance, but down the hill before him. 'It's the French!'

The two generals and the adjutant began snatching at the field-glass, pulling it from one another. All their faces suddenly changed, and horror was apparent in them all. They had supposed the French to be over a mile and a half away, and here they were all of a sudden confronting us.

'Is it the enemy? ... No. ... But, look, it is ... for certain. ... What does it mean?' voices were heard saying.

With the naked eye Prince Andrey saw to the right, below them, a dense column of French soldiers coming up towards the Apsheron regiment, not over five hundred paces from where Kutuzov was standing.

'Here it is, it is coming, the decisive moment! My moment has come,' thought Prince Andrey, and slashing his horse, he rode up to Kutuzov.

'We must stop the Apsheron regiment,' he shouted, 'your most high excellency.'

But at that instant everything was lost in a cloud of smoke, there was a sound of firing close by, and a voice in naïve terror cried not two paces from Prince Andrey: 'Hey, mates, it's all up!' And this voice was like a command. At that voice there was a general rush, crowds, growing larger every moment, ran back in confusion to the spot where five minutes before they had marched by the Emperors. It was not simply difficult to check this rushing crowd, it was impossible not to be carried back with the stream oneself. Bolkonsky tried only not to be left behind by it, and looked about him in bewilderment, unable to grasp what was taking place. Nesvitsky, with an exasperated, crimson face, utterly unlike himself, was shouting to Kutuzov that if he didn't get away at once he'd be taken prisoner to a certainty. Kutuzov was standing in the same place: he was taking out his handkerchief, and did not answer. The blood was flowing from his cheek. Prince Andrey forced his way up to him.

'You are wounded?' he asked, hardly able to control the quivering of his lower jaw.

'The wound's not here, but there, see!' said Kutuzov, pressing the handkerchief to his wounded cheek, and pointing to the running soldiers.

'Stop them!' he shouted, and at the same time convinced that it was impossible to stop them, he lashed his horse and rode to the right. A fresh rush of flying crowds caught him up with it and carried him back.

The troops were running in such a dense multitude, that once getting into the midst of the crowd, it was a hard matter to get out of it. One was shouting: 'Get on! what are you lagging for?' Another was turning round to fire in the air; another striking the very horse on which Kutuzov was mounted. Getting out with an immense effort from the stream on the left, Kutuzov, with his suite diminished to a half, rode towards the sounds of cannon close by. Prince Andrey, trying not to be left behind by Kutuzov, saw, as he got out of the racing multitude, a Russian battery still firing in the smoke on the hillside and the French running towards it. A little higher up stood Russian infantry, neither moving forward to the support of the battery, nor back in the same direction as the runaways. A general on horseback detached himself from the infantry and rode towards Kutuzov. Of Kutuzov's suite only four men were left. They were all pale and looking at one another dumbly.

'Stop those wretches!' Kutuzov gasped to the officer in command of the regiment, pointing to the flying soldiers. But at the same instant, as though in revenge for the words, the bullets came whizzing over the regiment and Kutuzov's suite like a flock of birds. The French were attacking the battery, and catching sight of Kutuzov, they were shooting at him. With this volley the general clutched at his leg; several soldiers fell, and the second lieutenant standing with the flag let it drop out of his hands. The flag tottered and was caught on the guns of the nearest soldiers. The soldiers had begun firing without orders.

'Oogh!' Kutuzov growled with an expression of despair, and he looked round him. 'Bolkonsky,' he whispered in a voice shaking with the consciousness of his old age and helplessness. 'Bolkonsky,' he whispered, pointing to the routed battalion and the enemy, 'what's this?'

But before he had uttered the words, Prince Andrey, feeling the tears of shame and mortification rising in his throat, was jumping off his horse and running to the flag.

'Lads, forward!' he shrieked in a voice of childish shrillness. 'Here, it is come!' Prince Andrey thought, seizing the staff of the flag, and hearing with relief the whiz of bullets, unmistakably aimed at him. Several soldiers dropped.

'Hurrah!' shouted Prince Andrey, and hardly able to hold up the heavy flag in both his hands, he ran forward in the unhesitating conviction that the whole battalion would run after him. And in fact it was only for a few steps that he ran alone. One soldier started, then another, and then the whole battalion with a shout of 'hurrah!' was running forward and overtaking him. An under-officer of the battalion ran up and took the flag which tottered from its weight in Prince Andrey's hands, but he was at once killed. Prince Andrey snatched up the flag again, and waving it by the staff, ran on with the battalion. In front of him he saw our artillery men, of whom some were fighting, while others had abandoned their cannons and were running towards him. He saw French infantry soldiers, too, seizing the artillery horses and turning the cannons round. Prince Andrey and the battalion were within twenty paces of the cannons. He heard the bullets whizzing over him incessantly, and continually the soldiers moaned and fell to the right and left of him. But he did not look at them; his eyes were fixed on what was going on in front of him—at the battery. He could now see distinctly the figure of the red-haired artilleryman, with a shako crushed on one side, pulling a mop one way, while a French soldier was tugging it the other way. Prince Andrey could see distinctly now the distraught, and at the same time exasperated expression of the faces of the two men, who were obviously quite unconscious of what they were doing.

'What are they about?' wondered Prince Andrey, watching them; 'why doesn't the red-haired artilleryman run, since he has no weapon? Why doesn't the Frenchman stab him? He won't have time to run away before the Frenchman will think of his gun, and knock him on the head.' Another Frenchman did, indeed, run up to the combatants with his gun almost overblancing him, and the fate of the red-haired artilleryman, who still had no conception of what was awaiting him, and was pulling the mop away in triumph, was probably sealed. But Prince Andrey did not see how it ended. It seemed to him as though a hard stick were swung full at him by some soldier near, dealing him a violent blow on the head. It hurt a little, but the worst of it was that the pain distracted his attention, and prevented him from seeing what he was looking at.

'What's this? am I falling? my legs are giving way under me,' he thought, and fell on his back. He opened his eyes, hoping to see how the struggle of the French soldiers with the artilleryman was ending, and eager to know whether the red-haired artilleryman was killed or not, whether the cannons had been taken or saved. But he saw nothing of all that. Above him there was nothing but the sky—the lofty sky, not clear, but still immeasurably lofty, with grey clouds creeping quietly over it. 'How quietly, peacefully, and triumphantly, and not like us running, shouting, and fighting, not like the Frenchmen and artillerymen dragging the mop from one another with frightened and frantic faces, how differently are those clouds creeping over that lofty, limitless sky. How was it I did not see that lofty sky before? And how happy I am to have found it at last. Yes! all is vanity, all is a cheat, except that infinite sky. There is nothing, nothing but that. But even that is not, there is nothing but peace and stillness. And thank God! ...'

XVII

ON the right flank in Bagration's detachment, at nine o'clock the battle had not yet begun. Not caring to assent to Dolgorukov's request that he should advance into action, and anxious to be rid of all responsibility, Prince Bagration proposed to Dolgorukov to send to inquire of the commander-in-chief. Bagration was aware that as the distance between one flank and the other was almost eight miles, if the messenger sent were not killed (which was highly probable), and if he were to succeed in finding the commander-in-chief (which would be very difficult), he would hardly succeed in making his way back before the evening.

Bagration looked up and down his suite with his large, expressionless, sleepy eyes, and the childish face of Rostov, unconsciously all a-quiver with excitement and hope, was the first that caught his eye. And he sent him.

'And if I meet his majesty before the commander-in-chief, your excellency?' said Rostov, with his hand to the peak of his cap.

'You can give the message to his majesty,' said Dolgorukov, hurriedly interposing before Bagration.

On being relieved from picket duty, Rostov had managed to get a few hours' sleep before morning, and felt cheerful, bold, and resolute, with a peculiar springiness in his movements, and confidence in his luck, and in that frame of mind in which everything seems easy and possible.

All his hopes had been fulfilled that morning: there was to be a general engagement, he was taking part in it; more than that, he was in attendance on the bravest general; more than that, he was being sent on a commission to Kutuzov, perhaps even to the Tsar himself. It was a fine morning, he had a good horse under him, his heart was full of joy and happiness. On receiving his orders, he spurred his horse and galloped along the line. At first he rode along the line of Bagration's troops which had not yet advanced into action, and were standing motionless, then he rode into the region occupied by Uvarov's cavalry, and here he began to observe activity and signs of preparation for battle. After he had passed Uvarov's cavalry, he could distinctly hear the sound of musket-fire and the booming of cannons ahead of him. The firing grew louder and more intense.

The sound that reached him in the fresh morning air was not now, as before, the report of two or three shots at irregular intervals, and then one or two cannons booming. Down the slopes of the hillsides before Pratzen, he could hear volleys of musketry, interspersed with such frequent shots of cannon that sometimes several booming shots could not be distinguished from one another, but melted into one mingled roar of sound.

He could see the puffs of musket smoke flying down the hillsides, as though racing one another, while the cannon smoke hung in clouds, that floated along and melted into one another. He could see, from the gleam of bayonets in the smoke, that masses of infantry were moving down, and narrow lines of artillery with green caissons.

On a hillock Rostov stopped his horse to try and make out what was going on. But however much he strained his attention, he could not make out and understand what he saw; there were men of some sort moving about there in the smoke, lines of troops were moving both backwards and forwards; but what for? Who? where were they going? it was impossible to make out. This sight, and these sounds, so far from exciting any feeling of depression or timidity in him, only increased his energy and determination.

'Come, fire away, at them again!' was his mental response to the sounds he heard. Again he galloped along the line, penetrating further and further into the part where the troops were already in action.

'How it will be there, I don't know, but it will all be all right!' thought Rostov.

After passing Austrian troops of some sort, Rostov noticed that the next part of the forces (they were the guards) had already advanced into action.

'So much the better! I shall see it close,' he thought.

He was riding almost along the front line. A body of horsemen came galloping towards him. They were a troop of our Uhlans returning in disorder from the attack. Rostov, as he passed them, could not help noticing one of them covered with blood, but he galloped on.

'That's no affair of mine!' he thought.

He had not ridden on many hundred paces further when there came into sight, on his left, across the whole extent of the field, an immense mass of cavalry on black horses, in dazzling white uniforms, trotting straight towards him, cutting off his advance. Rostov put his horse to his utmost speed to get out of the way of these cavalrymen, and he would have cleared them had they been advancing at the same rate, but they kept increasing their pace, so that several horses broke into a gallop. More and more loudly Rostov could hear the thud of their horses' hoofs, and the jingle of their weapons, and more and more distinctly he could see their horses, their figures, and even their faces. These were our horse-guards, charging to attack the French cavalry, who were advancing to meet them.

The cavalry guards were galloping, though still holding in their horses. Rostov could see their faces now, and hear the word of command, 'Charge!' uttered by an officer, as he let his thoroughbred go at full speed. Rostov, in danger of being trampled underfoot or carried away to attack the French, galloped along before their lines as fast as his horse could go, and still he was not in time to escape them.

The last of the line of cavalry, a pock-marked man of immense stature, scowled viciously on seeing Rostov just in front of him, where he must inevitably come into collision with him. This horse-guard would infallibly have overturned Rostov and his Bedouin (Rostov felt himself so little and feeble beside these gigantic men and horses) if he had not bethought himself of striking the horse-guard's horse in the face with his riding-whip. The heavy, black, high horse twitched its ears and reared, but its pock-marked rider brought it down with a violent thrust of the spurs into its huge sides, and the horse, lashing its tail and dragging its neck, flew on faster than ever. The horse-guard had hardly passed Rostov when he heard their shout 'Hurrah!' and looking round saw their foremost ranks mixed up with some strange cavalry, in red epaulettes, probably French. He could see nothing more, for immediately after cannons were fired from somewhere, and everything was lost in the smoke.

At the moment when the horse-guards passing him vanished into the smoke, Rostov hesitated whether to gallop after them or to go on where he had to go. This was the brilliant charge of the horse-guards of which the French themselves expressed their admiration. Rostov was appalled to hear afterwards that of all that mass of huge, fine men, of all those brilliant, rich young officers and ensigns who had galloped by him on horses worth thousands of roubles, only eighteen were left after the charge.

'I have no need to envy them, my share won't be taken from me, and may be I shall see the Emperor in a minute!' thought Rostov, and he galloped on.

When he reached the infantry of the guards, he noticed that cannon-balls were flying over and about them, not so much from the sound of the cannon-balls as from the uneasiness he saw in the faces of the soldiers and the unnatural, martial solemnity on the faces of the officers.

As he rode behind one of the lines of the regiments of foot-guards, he heard a voice calling him by name: 'Rostov!'

'Eh?' he called back, not recognising Boris.

'I say, we've been in the front line! Our regiment marched to the attack!' said Boris, smiling that happy smile that is seen in young men who have been for the first time under fire. Rostov stopped.

'Really!' he said. 'Well, how was it?'

'We beat them!' said Boris, growing talkative in his eagerness. 'You can fancy . . .' And Boris began describing how the guards having taken up their position, and seeing troops in front of them had taken them for Austrians, and all at once had found out from the cannon-balls aimed at them from those troops that they were in the front line, and had quite unexpectedly to advance to battle. Rostov set his horse moving without waiting to hear Boris to the end.

'Where are you off to?' asked Boris.

'To his majesty with a commission.'

'Here he is!' said Boris, who had not caught what Rostov said, and thinking it was the grand duke he wanted, he pointed him out, standing a hundred paces from them, wearing a helmet and a horse-guard's white elk tunic, with his high shoulders and scowling brows, shouting something to a pale, white-uniformed Austrian officer.

'Why, that's the grand duke, and I must see the commander-in-chief or the Emperor,' said Rostov, and he was about to start again.

'Count, count!' shouted Berg, running up on the other side, as eager as Boris. 'I was wounded in my right hand' (he pointed to his blood-stained hand, bound up with a pocket-handkerchief), 'and I kept my place in the front. Count, I held my sabre in my left hand. All my family, count, the Von Bergs, have been knights.' Berg would have said more, but Rostov rode on without listening.

After riding by the guards, and on through an empty space, Rostov rode along the line of the reserves for fear of getting in the way of the front line, as he had done in the charge of the horse guards, and made a wide circuit round the place where he heard the hottest musket-fire and cannonade. All of a sudden, in front of him and behind our troops, in a place where he could never have expected the enemy to be, he heard the sound of musket-fire quite close.

'What can it be?' thought Rostov. 'The enemy in the rear of our troops? It can't be,' thought Rostov, but a panic of fear for himself and for the issue of the whole battle came over him all at once. 'Whatever happens, though,' he reflected, 'it's useless to try and escape now. It's my duty to seek the commander-in-chief here, and if everything's lost, it's my duty to perish with all the rest.'

The foreboding of evil that had suddenly come upon Rostov grew stronger and stronger the further he advanced into the region behind the village of Pratzen, which was full of crowds of troops of all sorts.

'What does it mean? What is it? Whom are they firing at? Who is firing?' Rostov kept asking, as he met Austrian and Russian soldiers running in confused crowds across his path.

'Devil knows! Killed them all! Damn it all,' he was answered in Russian, in German, and in Tchekh, by the hurrying rabble, who knew no more than he what was being done.

'Kill the Germans!' shouted one.

'To hell with them—the traitors.'

'*Zum Henker diese Russen*,' muttered a German.

Several wounded were among the crowds on the road. Shouts, oaths, moans were mingled in the general hubbub. The firing began to subside, and, as Rostov found out later, the Russian and Austrian soldiers had been firing at one another.

'My God! how can this be?' thought Rostov. 'And here, where any minute the Emperor may see them.... No, these can only be a few wretches. It will soon be over, it's not the real thing, it can't be,' he thought. 'Only to make haste, make haste, and get by them.'

The idea of defeat and flight could not force its way into Rostov's head. Though he saw the French cannons and troops precisely on Pratzen hill, the very spot where he had been told to look for the commander-in-chief, he could not and would not believe in it.

XVIII

NEAR the village of Pratzen Rostov had been told to look for Kutuzov and the Emperor. But there they were not, nor was there a single officer to be found in command, nothing but disorderly crowds of troops of different sorts. He urged on his weary horse to hasten through this rabble, but the further he went the more disorderly the crowds became. The high road, along which he rode, was thronged with carriages, with vehicles of all sorts, and Austrian and Russian soldiers of every kind, wounded and unwounded. It was all uproar and confused bustle under the sinister whiz of the flying cannon-balls from the French batteries stationed on the heights of Pratzen.

'Where's the Emperor? Where's Kutuzov?' Rostov kept asking of every one he could stop, and from no one could he get an answer.

At last clutching a soldier by the collar, he forced him to answer him.

'Aye! brother! they've all bolted long ago!' the soldier said to Rostov, laughing for some reason as he pulled himself away. Letting go that soldier, who must, he thought, be drunk, Rostov stopped the horse of a groom or postillion of some personage of consequence, and began to cross-question him. The groom informed Rostov that an hour before the Tsar had been driven at full speed in a carriage along this very road, and that the Tsar was dangerously wounded.

'It can't be,' said Rostov; 'probably some one else.'

'I saw him myself,' said the groom with a self-satisfied smirk; 'it's high time I should know the Emperor, I should think, after the many times I've seen him in Petersburg; I saw him as it might be here. Pale, deadly pale, sitting in the carriage. The way they drove the four raven horses! my goodness, didn't they dash by us! It would be strange, I should think, if I didn't know the Tsar's horses and Ilya Ivanitch; why, Ilya never drives any one else but the Tsar.'

Rostov let go of the horse and would have gone on. A wounded officer passing by addressed him, 'Why, who is it you want?' asked the officer, 'the commander-in-chief? Oh, he was killed by a cannon-ball, struck in the breast before our regiment.'

'Not killed—wounded,' another officer corrected him.

'Who? Kutuzov?' asked Rostov.

'Not Kutuzov, but what's his name—well, it's all the same, there are not many left alive. Go that way, over there to that village, all the commanding officers are there,' said the officer, pointing to the village of Gostieradeck, and he walked on.

Rostov rode on at a walking pace, not knowing to whom and with what object he was going now. The Tsar was wounded, the battle was lost. There was no refusing to believe in it now. Rostov rode in the direction which had been pointed out to him, and saw in the distance turrets and a church. What had he to hasten for now? What was he to say now to the Tsar or to Kutuzov, even if they were alive and not wounded?

'Go along this road, your honour, that way you will be killed in a trice!' a soldier shouted to him. 'You'll be killed that way!'

'Oh! what nonsense!' said another. 'Where is he to go? That way's nearest.' Rostov pondered, and rode off precisely in the direction in which he had been told he would be killed.

'Now, nothing matters; if the Emperor is wounded, can I try and save myself?' he thought. He rode into the region where more men had been killed than anywhere, in fleeing from Pratzen. The French had not yet taken that region, though the Russians—those who were slightly wounded or unhurt—had long abandoned it. All over the field, like ridges of dung on well-kept plough-land, lay the heaps of dead and wounded, a dozen or fifteen bodies to every three acres. The wounded were crawling two or three together, and their shrieks and groans had a painful and sometimes affected sound, it seemed to Rostov. Rostov put his horse to a trot to avoid the sight of all those suffering people, and he felt afraid. He was afraid of losing not his life, but his pluck, which he needed so much, which he knew would not stand the sight of those luckless wretches. The French had ceased firing at this field that was dotted over with dead and wounded, because there seemed no one living upon it, but seeing an adjutant trotting across it, they turned a cannon upon him and shot off several cannon-balls. The sense of these whizzing, fearful sounds, and of the dead bodies all round him melted into a single impression of horror and pity for himself in Rostov's heart. He thought of his mother's last letter. 'What would she be feeling now?' he thought, 'if she could see me here now on this field with cannons aimed at me?'

In the village of Gostieradeck there were Russian troops, in some confusion indeed, but in far better discipline, who had come from the field of battle. Here they were out of range of the French cannons, and the sounds of firing seemed far away. Here every one saw clearly that the battle was lost, and all were talking of it. No one to whom Rostov applied could tell him where was the Tsar, or where was Kutuzov. Some said that the rumour of the Tsar's wound was correct, others said not, and explained this widely spread false report by the fact that the Ober-Hofmarschal Tolstoy, who had come out with others of the Emperor's suite to the field of battle, had been seen pale and terrified driving back at full gallop in the Tsar's carriage. One officer told Rostov that, behind the village to the left, he had seen some one from headquarters, and Rostov rode off in that direction, with no hope now of finding any one, but simply to satisfy his conscience. After going about two miles and passing the last of the Russian troops, Rostov saw, near a kitchen-garden enclosed by a ditch, two horsemen standing facing the ditch. One with a white plume in his hat seemed somehow a familiar figure to Rostov, the other, a stranger on a splendid chestnut horse (the horse Rostov fancied he had seen before) rode up to the ditch, put spurs to his horse, and lightly leaped over the ditch into the garden. A little earth from the bank crumbled off under his horse's hind hoofs. Turning the horse sharply, he leaped the ditch again and deferentially addressed the horseman in the white plume, apparently urging him to do the same. The rider, whose figure seemed famili r to Rostov and somehow riveted his attention, made a gesture of refusal with his head and his hand, and in that gesture Rostov instantly recognised his lamented, his idolised sovereign.

'But it can't be he, alone, in the middle of this empty field,' thought Rostov. At that moment Alexander turned his head and Rostov saw the beloved features so vividly imprinted on his memory. The Tsar was pale, his cheeks looked sunken, and his eyes hollow, but the charm, the mildness of his face was only the more striking. Rostov felt happy in the certainty that the report of the Emperor's wound was false. He was happy that he was seeing him. He knew that he might, that he ought, indeed, to go straight to him and to give him the message he had been commanded to give by Dolgorukov.

But, as a youth in love trembles and turns faint and dares not utter what he has spent nights in dreaming of, and looks about in terror, seeking aid or a chance of delay or flight, when the moment he has longed for comes and he stands alone at her side, so Rostov, now when he was attaining what he had longed for beyond everything in the world, did not know how to approach the Emperor, and thousands of reasons why it was unsuitable, unseemly, and impossible came into his mind.

'What! it's as though I were glad to take advantage of his being alone and despondent. It may be disagreeable and painful to him, perhaps, to see an unknown face at such a moment of sadness; besides, what can I say to him now, when at the mere sight of him my heart is throbbing and leaping into my mouth?' Not one of the innumerable speeches he had addressed to the Tsar in his imagination recurred to his mind now. These speeches for the most part were appropriate to quite other circumstances; they had been uttered for the most part at moments of victory and triumph, and principally on his deathbed when, as he lay dying of his wounds, the Emperor thanked him for his heroic exploits, and he gave expression as he died to the love he had proved in deeds. 'And then, how am I to ask the Emperor for his instructions to the right flank when it's four o'clock in the afternoon and the battle is lost? No, certainly I ought not to ride up to him, I ought not to break in on his sorrow. Better die a thousand deaths than that he should give me a glance, a thought of disapproval,' Rostov decided, and with grief and despair in his heart he rode away, continually looking back at the Tsar, who still stood in the attitude of indecision.

While Rostov was making these reflections and riding mournfully away from the Tsar, Captain Von Toll happened to ride up to the same spot, and seeing the Emperor, went straight up to him, offered him his services, and assisted him to cross the ditch on foot. The Tsar, feeling unwell and in need of rest, sat down under an apple-tree, and Von Toll remained standing by his side. Rostov from a distance saw with envy and remorse how Von Toll talked a long while warmly to the Emperor, how the Emperor, apparently weeping, hid his face in his hand, and pressed Von Toll's hand.

'And it might have been I in his place!' Rostov thought, and hardly restraining his tears of sympathy for the Tsar, he rode away in utter despair, not knowing where and with what object he was going now.

His despair was all the greater from feeling that it was his own weakness that was the cause of his regret.

He might . . . not only might, but ought to have gone up to the Emperor. And it was a unique chance of showing his devotion to the Emperor. And he had not made use of it. . . . 'What have I done?' he thought. And he turned his horse and galloped back to the spot where he had seen the Emperor; but there was no one now beyond the ditch. There were only transport waggons and carriages going by. From one carrier Rostov learned that Kutuzov's staff were not far off in the village towards which the transport waggons were going. Rostov followed them.

In front of him was Kutuzov's postillion leading horses in horse-cloths. A baggage-waggon followed the postillion, and behind the waggon walked an old bandy-legged servant in a cap and a cape.

'Tit, hey. Tit!' said the postillion.

'Eh,' responded the old man absent-mindedly.

'*Tit! Stupay molotit!*' ('Tit, go a thrashing!')

'Ugh, the fool, pugh!' said the old man, spitting angrily. A short interval of silence followed, and then the same joke was repeated.

By five o'clock in the evening the battle had been lost at every point. More than a hundred cannons were in the possession of the French. Przhebyshevsky and his corps had surrendered. The other columns had retreated, with the loss of half their men, in confused, disorderly masses. All that were left of Langeron's and Dohturov's forces were crowded together in hopeless confusion on the dikes and banks of the ponds near the village of Augest.

At six o'clock the only firing still to be heard was a heavy cannonade on the French side from numerous batteries ranged on the slope of the table-land of Pratzen, and directed at our retreating troops.

In the rearguard Dohturov and the rest, rallying their battalions, had been firing at the French cavalry who were pursuing them. It was beginning to get dark. On the narrow dam of Augest, where the old miller in his peaked cap had sat for so many years with his fishing tackle, while his grandson, with tucked-up shirt sleeves, turned over the silvery, floundering fish in the net; on that dam where the Moravians, in their shaggy caps and blue jackets, had for so many years peacefully driven their horses and waggons, loaded with wheat, to the mill and driven back over the same dam, dusty with flour that whitened their waggons —on that narrow dam men, made hideous by the terror of death, now crowded together, amid army waggons and cannons, under horses' feet and between carriage-wheels, crushing each other, dying, stepping over the dying, and killing each other, only to be killed in the same way a few steps further on.

Every ten seconds a cannon-ball flew lashing the air and thumped down, or a grenade burst in the midst of that dense crowd, slaying men and splashing blood on those who stood near. Dolohov, wounded in the hand, with some dozen soldiers of his company on foot (he was already an officer) and his general on horseback, were the sole representatives of a whole regiment. Carried along by the crowd, they were squeezed in the approach to the dam and stood still, jammed in on all sides because a horse with a cannon had fallen, and the crowd were dragging it away. A cannon-ball killed some one behind them, another fell in front of them and spurted the blood upon Dolohov. The crowd moved forward desperately, was jammed, moved a few steps and was stopped again. 'Only to get over these hundred steps and certain safety: stay here two minutes and death to a certainty,' each man was thinking.

Dolohov standing in the centre of the crowd, forced his way to the edge of the dam, knocking down two soldiers, and ran on to the slippery ice that covered the millpond.

'Turn this way!' he shouted, bounding over the ice, which cracked under him. 'Turn this way!' he kept shouting to the cannon. 'It bears! ...' The ice bore him, but swayed and cracked, and it was evident that, not to speak of a cannon or a crowd of people, it would give way in a moment under him alone. Men gazed at him and pressed to the bank, unable to bring themselves to step on to the ice. The general of his regiment on horseback at the end of the dam lifted his hand and opened his mouth to speak to Dolohov. Suddenly one of the cannon-balls flew so low over the heads of the crowd that all ducked. There was a wet splash, as the general fell from his horse into a pool of blood. No one glanced at the general, no one thought of picking him up.

'On to the ice! Get on the ice! Get on! turn! don't you hear! Get on!' innumerable voices fell to shouting immediately after the ball had struck the general, not knowing themselves what and why they were shouting.

One of the hindmost cannons that had been got on to the dam was turned off upon the ice. Crowds of soldiers began running from the dam on to the frozen pond. The ice cracked under one of the foremost soldiers, and one leg slipped into the water. He tried to right himself and floundered up to his waist. The soldiers nearest tried to draw back, the driver of the cannon pulled up his horse, but still the shouts were heard from behind: 'Get on to the ice, why are you stopping? go on! go on!' And screams of terror were heard in the crowd. The soldiers near the cannon waved at the horses, and lashed them to make them turn and go on. The horses moved from the dam's edge. The ice that had held under the foot-soldiers broke in a huge piece, and some forty men who were on it dashed, some forwards, some backwards, drowning one another.

Still the cannon-balls whizzed as regularly and thumped on to the ice, into the water, and most often into the crowd that covered the dam, the pond, and the bank.

XIX

PRINCE ANDREY BOLKONSKY was lying on the hill of Pratzen, on the spot where he had fallen with the flag-staff in his hands. He was losing blood, and kept moaning a soft, plaintive, childish moan, of which he himself knew nothing. Towards evening he ceased moaning and became perfectly still. He did not know how long his unconsciousness lasted. Suddenly he felt again that he was alive and suffering from a burning, lacerating pain in his head.

'Where is it, that lofty sky that I knew not till now and saw today?' was his first thought. 'And this agony I did not know either,' he thought. 'Yes, I knew nothing, nothing till now. But where am I?'

He fell to listening, and caught the sound of approaching hoofs and voices speaking French. He opened his eyes. Above him was again the same lofty sky, with clouds higher than ever floating over it, and between them stretches of blue infinity. He did not turn his head and did not see the men who, judging from the voices and the thud of hoofs, had ridden up to him and stopped.

They were Napoleon and two adjutants escorting him. Bonaparte, making a tour of the field of battle, had been giving his last instructions for the strengthening of the battery firing at the Augest dam, and was inspecting the dead and wounded on the field of battle.

'Fine men!' said Napoleon, looking at a dead Russian grenadier, who with his face thrust into the earth and blackened neck lay on his stomach, one stiff arm flung wide.

'The field-guns have exhausted their ammunition,' said an adjutant, arriving that moment from the battery that was firing at Augest.

'Bring up more from the reserve,' said Napoleon, and riding a few steps away stood still, looking at Prince Andrey, who lay on his back with the abandoned flag-staff beside him (the flag had been taken by the French as a trophy).

'That's a fine death!' said Napoleon, looking at Bolkonsky. Prince Andrey knew that it was said of him, and that it was Napoleon saying it. He heard the speaker of those words addressed as 'your majesty.' But he heard the words as he heard the buzzing of flies. It was not merely that he took no interest in them, but he did not attend to them and at once forgot them. There was a burning pain in his head; he felt he was losing blood, and he saw above him the high, far-away, everlasting sky. He knew it was Napoleon—his hero—but at that moment Napoleon seemed to him such a small, insignificant creature in comparison with what was passing now between his soul and that lofty, limitless sky with the clouds flying over it. It meant nothing to him at that moment who was standing over him, what was being said of him. He was only glad that people were standing over him, and his only desire was that these people should help him and bring him back to life, which seemed to him so good, because he saw it all quite differently now. He made a supreme effort to stir and utter some sound. He moved his leg faintly, and uttered a weak, sickly moan that touched himself. 'Ah, he's alive,' said Napoleon. 'Pick up this young man and carry him to an ambulance!' Saying this, Napoleon rode on to meet Marshal Lannes, who rode up to meet the conqueror, smiling, taking off his hat and congratulating him on his victory.

Prince Andrey remembered nothing more; he lost consciousness from the excruciating pain caused by being laid on the stretcher, the jolting while he was being moved, and the sounding of his wound at the ambulance. He only regained consciousness towards the end of the day when with other Russian officers, wounded and prisoners, he was being taken to the hospital. On this journey he felt a little stronger, and could look about him and even speak.

The first words he heard on coming to himself were from a French convoy officer who was saying hurriedly: 'They must stop here; the Emperor will be here directly; it will be a pleasure for him to see these prisoners.'

'There are such a lot of prisoners today, almost the whole of the Russian army, that he is probably weary of seeing them,' said another officer.

'Well, but this one, they say, is the commander of all the Emperor Alexander's guards,' said the first speaker, pointing to a wounded Russian officer in the white uniform of the horse-guards. Bolkonsky recognised Prince Repnin, whom he had met in Petersburg society. Beside him stood another officer of the horse-guards, a lad of nineteen, also wounded.

Bonaparte rode up at a gallop and pulled up, 'Who is the senior officer?' he said, on seeing the prisoners.

They named the colonel, Prince Repnin.

'Are you the commander of the regiment of Emperor Alexander's horse-guards?' asked Napoleon.

'I was in command of a squadron,' replied Repnin.

'Your regiment did its duty honourably,' said Napoleon.

'The praise of a great general is a soldier's best reward,' said Repnin.

'I bestow it upon you with pleasure,' said Napoleon. 'Who is this young man beside you?' Prince Repnin gave his name, Lieutenant Suhtelen.

Looking at him, Napoleon said with a smile: 'He has come very young to meddle with us.'

'Youth is no hindrance to valour,' said Suhtelen in a breaking voice.

'A fine answer,' said Napoleon; 'young man, you will go far.'

Prince Andrey, who had been thrust forward under the Emperor's eyes to complete the show of prisoners, could not fail to attract his notice. Napoleon apparently remembered seeing him on the field, and addressing him he used the same epithet, 'young man,' with which his first sight of Bolkonsky was associated in his memory.

'And you, young man,' he said to him, 'how are you feeling, *mon brave?*'

Although five minutes previously Prince Andrey had been able to say a few words to the soldiers who were carrying him, he was silent now, with his eyes fastened directly upon Napoleon. So trivial seemed to him at that moment all the interests that were engrossing Napoleon, so petty seemed to him his hero, with his paltry vanity and glee of victory, in comparison with that lofty, righteous, and kindly sky which he had seen and comprehended, that he could not answer him. And all indeed seemed to him so trifling and unprofitable beside the stern and solemn train of thought aroused in him by weakness from loss of blood, by suffering and the nearness of death. Gazing into Napoleon's eyes, Prince Andrey mused on the nothingness of greatness, on the nothingness of life, of which no one could comprehend the significance, and on the nothingness—still more—of death, the meaning of which could be understood and explained by none of the living.

The Emperor, after vainly pausing for a reply, turned away and said to one of the officers in command—

'See that they look after these gentlemen and take them to my bivouac; let my doctor Larrey attend to their wounds. *Au revoir*, Prince Repnin,' and he galloped away.

His face was radiant with happiness and self-satisfaction.

The soldiers, who had been carrying Prince Andrey, had come across the golden relic Princess Marya had hung upon her brother's neck, and taken it off him, but seeing the graciousness the Emperor had shown to the prisoners, they made haste to restore the holy image.

Prince Andrey did not see who put it on him again, nor how it was replaced, but all at once he found the locket on its delicate gold chain on his chest outside his uniform.

'How good it would be,' thought Prince Andrey, as he glanced at the image which his sister had hung round his neck with such emotion and reverence, 'how good it would be if all were as clear and simple as it seems to Marie. How good to know where to seek aid in this life and what to expect after it, there, beyond the grave!'

'How happy and at peace I should be, if I could say now: "Lord have mercy on me! ..." But to whom am I to say that? Either a Power infinite, inconceivable, to which I cannot appeal, which I cannot even put into words, the great whole, or nothing,' he said to himself, 'or that God, who has been sewn up here in this locket by Marie? There is nothing, nothing certain but the nothingness of all that is comprehensible to us, and the grandeur of something incomprehensible, but more important!'

The stretchers began to be moved. At every jolt he felt intolerable pain again. The fever became higher, and he fell into delirium. Visions of his father, his wife, his sister, and his future son, and the tenderness he had felt for them on the night before the battle, the figure of that little, petty Napoleon, and over all these the lofty sky, formed the chief substance of his delirious dreams. The quiet home life and peaceful happiness of Bleak Hills passed before his imagination. He was enjoying that happiness when suddenly there appeared that little Napoleon with his callous, narrow look of happiness in the misery of others, and there came doubts and torments, and only the sky promised peace. Towards morning all his dreams mingled and melted away in the chaos and darkness of unconsciousness and oblivion, far more likely, in the opinion of Napoleon's doctor, Larrey, to be ended by death than by recovery.

'He is a nervous, bilious subject,' said Larrey; 'he won't recover.'

Prince Andrey, with the rest of the hopeless cases, was handed over to the care of the inhabitants of the district.

PART IV

I

AT THE BEGINNING of the year 1806, Nikolay Rostov was coming home on leave. Denisov, too, was going home to Voronezh, and Rostov persuaded him to go with him to Moscow and to pay him a visit there. Denisov met his comrade at the last posting station but one, drank three bottles of wine with him, and, in spite of the jolting of the road on the journey to Moscow, slept soundly lying at the bottom of the posting sledge beside Rostov, who grew more and more impatient, as they got nearer to Moscow.

'Will it come soon? Soon? Oh, these insufferable streets, bunshops, street lamps, and sledge drivers!' thought Rostov, when they had presented their papers at the town gates and were driving into Moscow.

'Denisov, we're here! Asleep!' he kept saying, flinging his whole person forward as though by that position he hoped to hasten the progress of the sledge. Denisov made no response.

'Here's the corner of the cross-roads, where Zahar the sledge-driver used to stand; and here is Zahar, too, and still the same horse. And here's the little shop where we used to buy cakes. Make haste! Now!'

'Which house is it?' asked the driver.

'Over there, at the end, the big one; how is it you don't see it? That's our house,' Rostov kept saying; 'that's our house, of course.'

'Denisov! Denisov! we shall be there in a minute.'

Denisov raised his head, cleared his throat, and said nothing.

'Dmitry,' said Rostov to his valet on the box, 'surely that light is home?'

'To be sure it is; it's the light in your papa's study, too.'

'They've not gone to bed yet? Eh? What do you think?'

'Mind now, don't forget to get me out my new tunic,' added Rostov, fingering his new moustaches.

'Come, get on,' he shouted to the driver. 'And do wake up, Vasya,' he said to Denisov, who had begun nodding again.

'Come, get on, three silver roubles for vodka—get on!' shouted Rostov, when they were only three houses from the entrance. It seemed to him that the horses were not moving. At last the sledge turned to the right into the approach, Rostov saw the familiar cornice with the broken plaster overhead, the steps, the lamp-post. He jumped out of the sledge while it was moving and ran into the porch. The house stood so inhospitably, as though it were no concern of its who had come into it. There was no one in the porch. 'My God! is everything all right?' wondered Rostov, stopping for a moment with a sinking heart, and then running on again along the porch and up the familiar, crooked steps. Still the same door handle, the dirtiness of which so often angered the countess, turned in the same halting fashion. In the hall there was a single tallow candle burning.

Old Mihailo was asleep on his perch.

Prokofy, the footman, a man so strong that he had lifted up a carriage, was sitting there in his list shoes. He glanced towards the opening door and his expression of sleepy indifference was suddenly transformed into one of frightened ecstasy.

'Merciful Heavens! The young count!' he cried, recognising his young master. 'Can it be? my darling?' And Prokofy, shaking with emotion, made a dash towards the drawing-room door, probably with the view of announcing him; but apparently he changed his mind, for he came back and fell on his young master's shoulder.

'All well?' asked Rostov, pulling his hand away from him.

'Thank God, yes! All, thank God! Only just finished supper! Let me have a look at you, your excellency!'

'Everything perfectly all right?'

'Thank God, yes, thank God!'

Rostov, completely forgetting Denisov, flung off his fur coat and, anxious that no one should prepare the way for him, he ran on tip-toe into the big, dark reception-hall. Everything was the same, the same card-tables, the same candelabra with a cover over it, but some one had already seen the young master, and he had not reached the drawing-room when from a side door something swooped headlong, like a storm upon him, and began hugging and kissing him. A second and a third figure dashed in at a second door and at a third; more huggings, more kisses, more outcries and tears of delight. He could not distinguish where and which was papa, which was Natasha, and which was Petya. All were screaming and talking and kissing him at the same moment. Only his mother was not among them, that he remembered.

'And I never knew... Nikolenka... my darling!'

'Here he is... our boy... my darling Kolya... Isn't he changed! Where are the candles? Tea!'

'Kiss me too!'

'Dearest... and me too.'

Sonya, Natasha, Petya, Anna Mihalovna, Vera, and the old count were all hugging him; and the servants and the maids flocked into the room with talk and outcries.

Petya hung on his legs.

'Me too!' he kept shouting.

Natasha, after pulling him down to her and kissing his face all over, skipped back from him and, keeping her hold of his jacket, pranced like a goat up and down in the same place, uttering shrill shrieks of delight.

All round him were loving eyes shining with tears of joy, all round were lips seeking kisses.

Sonya too, as red as crimson baize, clung to his arm and beamed all over, gazing blissfully at his eyes for which she had so long been waiting. Sonya was just sixteen and she was very pretty, especially at this moment of happy, eager excitement. She gazed at him, unable to take her eyes off him, smiling and holding her breath. He glanced gratefully at her; but still he was expectant and looking for some one, and the old countess had not come in yet. And now steps were heard at the door. The steps were so rapid that they could hardly be his mother's footsteps.

But she it was in a new dress that he did not know, made during his absence. All of them let him go, and he ran to her. When they came together, she sank on his bosom, sobbing. She could not lift up her face, and only pressed it to the cold braiding of his hussar's jacket. Denisov, who had come into the room unnoticed by any one, stood still looking at them and rubbing his eyes.

'Vassily Denisov, your son's friend,' he said, introducing himself to the count, who looked inquiringly at him.

'Very welcome. I know you, I know you,' said the count, kissing and embracing Denisov. 'Nikolenka wrote to us... Natasha, Vera, here he is, Denisov.'

The same happy, ecstatic faces turned to the touzled figure of Denisov and surrounded him.

'Darling Denisov,' squealed Natasha, and, beside herself with delight, she darted up to him, hugging and kissing him. Every one was disconcerted by Natasha's behaviour. Denisov too reddened, but he smiled, took Natasha's hand and kissed it.

Denisov was conducted to the room assigned him, while the Rostovs all gathered about Nikolenka in the divan-room.

The old countess sat beside him, keeping tight hold of his hand, which she was every minute kissing. The others thronged round them, gloating over every movement, every glance, every word he uttered, and never taking their enthusiastic and loving eyes off him. His brother and sisters quarrelled and snatched from one another the place nearest him and disputed over which was to bring him tea, a handkerchief, a pipe.

Rostov was very happy in the love they showed him. But the first minute of meeting them had been so blissful that his happiness now seemed a little thing, and he kept expecting something more and more and more.

Next morning after his journey he slept on till ten o'clock.

The adjoining room was littered with swords, bags, sabretaches, open trunks, and dirty boots. Two pairs of cleaned boots with spurs had just been stood against the wall. The servants brought in wash-hand basins, hot water for shaving, and their clothes well brushed. The room was full of a masculine odour and reeked of tobacco.

'Hi, Grishka, a pipe!' shouted the husky voice of Vaska Denisov. 'Rostov, get up!'

Rostov, rubbing his eyelids that seemed glued together, lifted his touzled head from the warm pillow.

'Why, is it late?'

'It is late, nearly ten,' answered Natasha's voice, and in the next room they heard the rustle of starched skirts and girlish laughter. The door was opened a crack, and there was a glimpse of something blue, of ribbons, black hair and merry faces. Natasha with Sonya and Petya had come to see if he were not getting up.

'Nikolenka, get up!' Natasha's voice was heard again at the door.

'At once!' Meanwhile in the outer room Petya had caught sight of the swords and seized upon them with the rapture small boys feel at the sight of a soldier brother, and regardless of its not being the proper thing for his sisters to see the young men undressed, he opened the bedroom door.

'Is this your sword?' he shouted.

The girls skipped away. Denisov hid his hairy legs under the bedclothes, looking with a scared face to his comrade for assistance. The door admitted Petya and closed after him. A giggle was heard from outside.

'Nikolenka, come out in your dressing-gown,' cried Natasha's voice.

'Is this your sword?' asked Petya, 'or is it yours?' he turned with deferential respect to the swarthy, whiskered Denisov.

Rostov made haste to get on his shoes and stockings, put on his dressing-gown and went out. Natasha had put on one spurred boot and was just getting into the other. Sonya was 'making cheeses,' and had just whirled her skirt into a balloon and was ducking down, when he came in. They were dressed alike in new blue frocks, both fresh, rosy, and good-humoured. Sonya ran away, but Natasha, taking her brother's arm, led him into the divan-room, and a conversation began between them. They had not time to ask and answer all the questions about the thousand trifling matters which could only be of interest to them. Natasha laughed at every word he said and at every word she said, not because what they said was amusing, but because she was in high spirits and unable to contain her joy, which brimmed over in laughter.

'Ah, isn't it nice, isn't it splendid!' she kept saying every moment. Under the influence of the warm sunshine of love, Rostov felt that for the first time for a year and a half his soul and his face were expanding in that childish smile, he had not once smiled since he left home.

'No, I say,' she said, 'you're quite a man now, eh? I'm awfully glad you're my brother.' She touched his moustache. 'I do want to know what sort of creatures you men are. Just like us? No.'

'Why did Sonya run away?' asked Rostov.

'Oh, there's a lot to say about that! How are you going to speak to Sonya? Shall you call her "thou" or "you?"'

'As it happens,' said Rostov.

'Call her "you," please; I'll tell you why afterwards.'

'But why?'

'Well, I'll tell you now. You know that Sonya's my friend, such a friend that I burnt my arm for her sake. Here, look.' She pulled up her muslin sleeve and showed him on her long, thin, soft arm above the elbow near the shoulder (on the part which is covered even in a ball-dress) a red mark.

'I burnt that to show her my love. I simply heated a ruler in the fire and pressed it on it.'

Sitting in his old schoolroom on the sofa with little cushions on the arms, and looking into Natasha's wildly eager eyes, Rostov was carried back into that world of home and childhood which had no meaning for any one else but gave him some of the greatest pleasures in his life. And burning one's arm with a ruler as a proof of love did not strike him as pointless; he understood it, and was not surprised at it.

'Well, is that all?' he asked.

'Well, we are such friends, such great friends! That's nonsense—the ruler; but we are friends for ever. If she once loves any one, it's for ever; I don't understand that, I forget so quickly.'

'Well, what then?'

'Yes, so she loves me and you.' Natasha suddenly flushed. 'Well, you remember before you went away . . . She says you are to forget it all . . . She said, I shall always love him, but let him be free. That really is splendid, noble! Yes, yes; very noble? Yes?' Natasha asked with such seriousness and emotion that it was clear that what she was saying now she had talked of before with tears. Rostov thought a little.

'I never take back my word,' he said. 'And besides, Sonya's so charming that who would be such a fool as to renounce his own happiness?'

'No, no,' cried Natasha. 'She and I have talked about that already. We knew that you'd say that. But that won't do, because, don't you see, if you say that—if you consider yourself bound by your words, then it makes it as though she had said that on purpose. It makes it as though you were, after all, obliged to marry her, and it makes it all wrong.'

Rostov saw that it had all been well thought over by them. On the previous day, Sonya had struck him by her beauty; in the glimpse he had caught of her today, she seemed even prettier. She was a charming girl of sixteen, obviously passionately in love with him (of that he could not doubt for an instant). 'Why should he not love her now, even if he did not marry her,' mused Rostov, 'but . . . just now he had so many other joys and interests!'

'Yes, that's a very good conclusion on their part,' he thought; 'I must remain free.'

'Well, that's all right, then,' he said; 'we'll talk about it later on. Ah, how glad I am to be back with you!' he added. 'Come, tell me, you've not been false to Boris?'

'That's nonsense!' cried Natasha, laughing. 'I never think of him nor of any one else, and don't want to.'

'Oh, you don't, don't you! Then what do you want?'

'I?' Natasha queried, and her face beamed with a happy smile. 'Have you seen Duport?'

'No.'

'Not seen Duport, the celebrated dancer? Oh, well then, you won't understand. I—that's what I am.' Curving her arms, Natasha held out her skirt, as dancers do, ran back a few steps, whirled round, executed a pirouette, bringing her little feet together and standing on the very tips of her toes, moved a few steps forward.

'You see how I stand? there, like this,' she kept saying; but she could not keep on her toes. 'So that's what I'm going to be! I'm never going to be married to any one; I'm going to be a dancer. Only, don't tell anybody.'

Rostov laughed so loudly and merrily that Denisov in his room felt envious, and Natasha could not help laughing with him.

'No, isn't it all right?' she kept saying.

'Oh, quite. So you don't want to marry Boris now?'

Natasha got hot.

'I don't want to marry any one. I'll tell him so myself when I see him.'

'Oh, will you?' said Rostov.

'But that's all nonsense,' Natasha prattled on. 'And, I say, is Denisov nice?' she asked.

'Yes, he's nice.'

'Well, good-bye, go and dress. Is he a dreadful person Denisov?'

'How, dreadful?' asked Nikolay. 'No, Vaska's jolly.'

'You call him Vaska? . . . that's funny. Well, is he very nice?'

'Very nice.'

'Make haste and come to tea, then. We are all going to have it together.'

And Natasha rose on to her toes and stepped out of the room, as dancers do, but smiling as only happy girls of fifteen can smile. Rostov reddened on meeting Sonya in the drawing-room. He did not know how to behave with her. Yesterday they had kissed in the first moment of joy at meeting, but today they felt that out of the question. He felt that every one, his mother and his sisters, were looking inquiringly at him, and wondering how he would behave with her. He kissed her hand, and called her *you* and *Sonya*. But their eyes when they met spoke more fondly and kissed tenderly. Her eyes asked his forgiveness for having dared, by Natasha's mediation, to remind him of his promise, and thanked him for his love. His eyes thanked her for offering him his freedom, and told her that whether so, or otherwise, he should never cease to love her, because it was impossible not to love her.

'How queer it is, though,' said Vera, selecting a moment of general silence, 'that Sonya and Nikolenka meet now and speak like strangers.'

Vera's observation was true, as were all her observations; but like most of her observations it made every one uncomfortable—not Sonya Nikolay, and Natasha only crimsoned; the countess, too, who was afraid of her son's love for Sonya as a possible obstacle to his making a brilliant marriage, blushed like a girl.

To Rostov's surprise, Denisov in his new uniform, pomaded and perfumed, was quite as dashing a figure in a drawing-room as on the field of battle, and was polite to the ladies and gentlemen as Rostov had never expected to see him.

II

O N his return to Moscow from the army, Nikolay Rostov was received by his family as a hero, as the best of sons, their idolised Nikolenka;

by his relations, as a charming, agreeable, and polite young man; by his acquaintances as a handsome lieutenant of hussars, a good dancer, and one of the best matches in Moscow.

All Moscow was acquainted with the Rostovs; the old count had plenty of money that year, because all his estates had been mortgaged, and so Nikolenka, who kept his own racehorse, and wore the most fashionable riding-breeches of a special cut, unlike any yet seen in Moscow, and the most fashionable boots, with extremely pointed toes, and little silver spurs, was able to pass his time very agreeably. After the first brief interval of adapting himself to the old conditions of life, Rostov felt very happy at being home again. He felt that he had grown up and become a man. His despair at failing in a Scripture examination, his borrowing money from Gavrilo for his sledge-drivers, his stolen kisses with Sonya—all that he looked back upon as childishness from which he was now immeasurably remote. Now he was a lieutenant of hussars with a silver-braided jacket, and a soldier's cross of St. George, he had a horse in training for a race, and kept company with well-known racing men, elderly and respected persons. He had struck up an acquaintance, too, with a lady living in a boulevard, whom he used to visit in the evening. He led the mazurka at the Arharovs' balls, talked to Field-Marshal Kamensky about the war, and used familiar forms of address to a colonel of forty, to whom he had been introduced by Denisov.

His passion for the Tsar flagged a little in Moscow, as he did not see him, and had no chance of seeing him all that time. But still he often used to talk about the Emperor and his love for him, always with a suggestion in his tone that he was not saying all that there was in his feeling for the Emperor, something that every one could not understand; and with his whole heart he shared the general feeling in Moscow of adoration for the Emperor Alexander Pavlovitch, who was spoken of at that time in Moscow by the designation of the 'angel incarnate.'

During this brief stay in Moscow, before his return to the army, Rostov did not come nearer to Sonya, but on the contrary drifted further away from her. She was very pretty and charming, and it was obvious that she was passionately in love with him. But he was at that stage of youth when there seems so much to do, that one has not time to pay attention to love, and a young man dreads being bound, and prizes his liberty, which he wants for so much else. When he thought about Sonya during this stay at Moscow, he said to himself: 'Ah! there are many, many more like her to come, and there are many of them somewhere now, though I don't know them yet. There's plenty of time before me to think about love when I want to, but I have not the time now.' Moreover, it seemed to him that feminine society was somehow beneath his manly dignity. He went to balls, and into ladies' society with an affectation of doing so against his will. Races, the English club, carousals with Denisov, and the nocturnal visits that followed—all that was different, all that was the correct thing for a dashing young hussar.

At the beginning of March the old count, Ilya Andreivitch Rostov, was very busily engaged in arranging a dinner at the English Club, to be given in honour of Prince Bagration.

The count, in his dressing-gown, was continually walking up and down in the big hall, seeing the club manager, the celebrated Feoktista, and the head cook, and giving them instructions relative to asparagus, fresh cucumbers, strawberries, veal, and fish, for Prince Bagration's dinner. From the day of its foundation, the count had been a member of the club, and was its steward. He had been entrusted with the organisation of the banquet to Bagration by the club, because it would have been hard to find any one so well able to organise a banquet on a large and hospitable scale, and still more hard to find any one so able and willing to advance his own money, if funds were needed, for the organisation of the fête. The cook and the club manager listened to the count's orders with good-humoured faces, because they knew that with no one better than with him could one make a handsome profit out of a dinner costing several thousands.

'Well, then, mind there are scallops, scallops in pie-crust, you know.'

'Cold *entrées*, I suppose—three? . . .' questioned the cook.

The count pondered.

'Couldn't do with less, three . . . *mayonnaise*, one,' he said, crooking his finger.

'Then it's your excellency's order to take the big sturgeons?' asked the manager.

'Yes; it can't be helped, we must take them, if they won't knock the price down. Ah, mercy on us, I was forgetting. Of course we must have another *entrée* on the table. Ah, good heavens!' He clutched at his head. 'And who's going to get me the flowers? Mitenka! Hey, Mitenka! You gallop, Mitenka,' he said to the steward who came in at his call, 'you gallop off to the Podmoskovny estate' (the count's property in the environs of Moscow), 'and tell Maksimka the gardener to set the serfs to work to get decorations from the greenhouses. Tell him everything from his conservatories is to be brought here, and is to be packed in felt. And that I'm to have two hundred pots here by Friday.'

After giving further and yet further directions of all sorts, he was just going off to the countess to rest from his labours, but he recollected something else, turned back himself, brought the cook and manager back, and began giving orders again. They heard in the doorway a light, manly tread and a jingling of spurs, and the young count came in, handsome and rosy, with his darkening moustache, visibly sleeker and in better trim for his easy life in Moscow.

'Ah, my boy! my head's in a whirl,' said the old gentleman, with a somewhat shamefaced smile at his son. 'You might come to my aid! We have still the singers to get, you see. The music is all settled, but shouldn't we order some gypsy singers? You military gentlemen are fond of that sort of thing.'

'Upon my word, papa, I do believe that Prince Bagration made less fuss over getting ready for the battle of Schöngraben than you are making now,' said his son, smiling.

The old count pretended to be angry.

'Well, you talk, you try!' And the count turned to the cook, who with a shrewd and respectful face looked observantly and sympathetically from father to son.

'What are the young people coming to, eh, Feoktista?' said he; 'they laugh at us old fellows!'

'To be sure, your excellency, all they have to do is to eat a good dinner, but to arrange it all and serve it up, that's no affair of theirs!'

'True, true!' cried the count; and gaily seizing his son by both hands, he cried: 'Do you know now I've got hold of you! Take a sledge and pair this minute and drive off to Bezuhov, and say that Count Ilya Andreivitch has sent, say, to ask him for strawberries and fresh pineapples. There's no getting them from any one else. If he's not at home himself, you go in and give the message to the princesses; and, I say, from there you drive off to the Gaiety—Ipatka the coachman knows the place—and look up Ilyushka there, the gypsy who danced at Count Orlov's, do you remember, in a white Cossack dress, and bring him here to me.'

'And bring his gypsy girls here with him?' asked Nikolay, laughing.

'Come, come! ...'

At this moment Anna Mihalovna stepped noiselessly into the room with that air of Christian meekness, mingled with practical and anxious preoccupation that never left her face. Although Anna Mihalovna came upon the count in his dressing-gown every day, he was invariably disconcerted at her doing so, and apologised for his costume.

'Don't mention it, my dear count,' she said, closing her eyes meekly. 'I am just going to see Bezuhov,' she said. 'Young Bezuhov has arrived, and now we shall get all we want, count, from his greenhouses. I was wanting to see him on my own account, too. He has forwarded me a letter from Boris. Thank God, Boris is now on the staff.'

The count was overjoyed at Anna Mihalovna's undertaking one part of his commissions, and gave orders for the carriage to be brought round for her.

'Tell Bezuhov to come. I'll put his name down. Brought his wife with him?' he asked.

Anna Mihalovna turned up her eyes, and an expression of profound sadness came into her face.

'Ah, my dear, he's very unhappy,' she said. 'If it's true what we have been hearing, it's awful. How little did we think of this when we were rejoicing in his happiness! and such a lofty, angelic nature, that young Bezuhov! Yes, I pity him from my soul, and will do my utmost to give him any consolation in my power.'

'Why, what is the matter?' inquired both the Rostovs, young and old together.

Anna Mihalovna heaved a deep sigh.

'Dolohov, Marya Ivanovna's son,' she said in a mysterious whisper, 'has, they say, utterly compromised her. He brought him forward, invited him to his house in Petersburg, and now this! . . . She has come here, and that scapegrace has come after her,' said Anna Mihalovna. She wished to express nothing but sympathy with Pierre, but in her involuntary intonations and half smile, she betrayed her sympathy with the scapegrace, as she called Dolohov. 'Pierre himself, they say, is utterly crushed by his trouble.'

'Well, any way, tell him to come to the club—it will divert his mind. It will be a banquet on a grand scale.'

On the next day, the 3rd of March, at about two in the afternoon, the two hundred and fifty members of the English Club and fifty of their guests were awaiting the arrival of their honoured guest, the hero of the Austrian campaign, Prince Bagration.

On receiving the news of the defeat of Austerlitz, all Moscow had at first been thrown into bewilderment. At that period the Russians were so used to victories, that on receiving news of a defeat, some people were simply incredulous, while others sought an explanation of so strange an event in exceptional circumstances of some kind. At the English Club, where every one of note, every one who had authentic information and weight gathered together, during December, when the news began to arrive, not a word was said about the war and about the last defeat; it was as though all were in a conspiracy of silence. The men who took the lead in conversation at the club, such as Count Rostoptchin, Prince Yury Vladimirovitch Dolgoruky, Valuev, Count Markov, and Prince Vyazemsky, did not put in an appearance at the club, but met together in their intimate circles at each other's houses.

That section of Moscow society which took its opinions from others (to which, indeed, Count Ilya Andreivitch Rostov belonged) remained for a short time without leaders and without definite views upon the progress of the war. People felt in Moscow that something was wrong, and that it was difficult to know what to think of the bad news, and so better to be silent. But a little later, like jurymen coming out of their consultation room, the leaders reappeared to give their opinion in the club, and a clear and definite formula was found. Causes had been discovered to account for the fact—so incredible, unheard-of, and impossible—that the Russians had been beaten, and all became clear, and the same version was repeated from one end of Moscow to the other. These causes were: the treachery of the Austrians; the defective commissariat; the treachery of the Pole Przhebyshevsky and the Frenchman Langeron; the incapacity of Kutuzov; and (this was murmured in subdued tones) the youth and inexperience of the Emperor, who had put faith in men of no character and ability. But the army, the Russian army, said every one, had been extraordinary, and had performed miracles of valour. The soldiers, the officers, the generals—all were heroes. But the hero among heroes was Prince Bagration, who had distinguished himself in his Schöngraben engagement and in the retreat from Austerlitz, where he alone had withdrawn his column in good order, and had succeeded in repelling during the whole day an enemy twice as numerous. What contributed to Bagration's being chosen for the popular hero at Moscow was the fact that he was an outsider, that he had no connections in Moscow. In his person they could do honour to the simple fighting Russian soldier, unsupported by connections and intrigues, and still associated by memories of the Italian campaign with the name of Suvorov. And besides, bestowing upon him such honours was the best possible way of showing their dislike and disapproval of Kutuzov.

'If there had been no Bagration, somebody would have to invent him,' said the wit, Shinshin, parodying the words of Voltaire.

Of Kutuzov people did not speak at all, or whispered abuse of him, calling him the court weathercock and the old satyr.

All Moscow was repeating the words of Prince Dolgorukov: 'Chop down trees enough and you're bound to cut your finger,' which in our defeat suggested a consolatory reminder of former victories, and the saying of Rostopchin, that French soldiers have to be excited to battle by high-sounding phrases; that Germans must have it logically proved to them that it is more dangerous to run away than to go forward; but that all Russian soldiers need is to be held back and urged not to be too reckless! New anecdotes were continually to be heard on every side of individual feats of gallantry performed by our officers and men at Austerlitz. Here a man had saved a flag, another had killed five Frenchmen, another had kept five cannons loaded single-handed. The story was told of Berg, by those who did not know him, that wounded in his right hand, he had taken his sword in his left and charged on the enemy. Nothing was said about Bolkonsky, and only those who had known him intimately regretted that he had died so young, leaving a wife with child, and his queer old father.

III

ON the 3rd of March all the rooms of the English Club were full of the hum of voices, and the members and guests of the club, in uniforms and frock-coats, some even in powder and Russian kaftans, were standing, meeting, parting, and running to and fro like bees swarming in spring. Powdered footmen in livery, wearing slippers and stockings, stood at every door, anxiously trying to follow every movement of the guests and club members, so as to proffer their services. The majority of those present were elderly and respected persons, with broad, self-confident faces, fat fingers, and resolute gestures and voices. Guests and members of this class sat in certain habitual places, and met together in certain habitual circles. A small proportion of those present were casual guests—chiefly young men, among them Denisov, Rostov, and Dolohov, who was now an officer in the Semyonovsky regiment again. The faces of the younger men, especially the officers, wore that expression of condescending deference to their elders which seems to say to the older generation, 'Respect and deference we are prepared to give you, but remember all the same the future is for us.' Nesvitsky, an old member of the club, was there too. Pierre, who at his wife's command had let his hair grow and left off spectacles, was walking about the rooms dressed in the height of the fashion, but looking melancholy and depressed. Here, as everywhere, he was surrounded by the atmosphere of people paying homage to his wealth, and he behaved to them with the careless, contemptuous air of sovereignty that had become habitual with him.

In years, he belonged to the younger generation, but by his wealth and connections he was a member of the older circles, and so he passed from one set to the other. The most distinguished of the elder members formed the centres of circles, which even strangers respectfully approached to listen to the words of well-known men. The larger groups were formed round Count Rostoptchin, Valuev, and Naryshkin. Rostoptchin was describing how the Russians had been trampled underfoot by the fleeing Austrians, and had had to force a way with the bayonet through the fugitives. Valuev was confidentially informing his circle that Uvarov had been sent from Petersburg to ascertain the state of opinion in Moscow in regard to Austerlitz.

In the third group Naryshkin was repeating the tale of the meeting of the Austrian council of war, at which, in reply to the stupidity of the Austrian general, Suvorov crowed like a cock. Shinshin, who stood near, tried to make a joke, saying that Kutuzov, it seemed, had not even been able to learn from Suvorov that not very difficult art—of crowing like a cock—but the elder club members looked sternly at the wit, giving him thereby to understand that even such a reference to Kutuzov was out of place on that day.

Count Ilya Andreitch Rostov kept anxiously hurrying in his soft boots to and fro from the dining-room to the drawing-room, giving hasty greetings to important and unimportant persons, all of whom he knew, and all of whom he treated alike, on an equal footing. Now and then his eyes sought out the graceful, dashing figure of his young son, rested gleefully on him, and winked to him. Young Rostov was standing at the window with Dolohov, whose acquaintance he had lately made, and greatly prized. The old count went up to them, and shook hands with Dolohov.

'I beg you will come and see us; so you're a friend of my youngster's ... been together, playing the hero out there. . . . Ah! Vassily Ignatitch . . . a good day to you, old man,' he turned to an old gentleman who had just come in, but before he had time to finish his greetings to him there was a general stir, and a footman running in with an alarmed countenance, announced: 'He has arrived!'

Bells rang: the stewards rushed forward; the guests, scattered about the different rooms, gathered together in one mass, like rye shaken together in a shovel, and waited at the door of the great drawing-room.

At the door of the ante-room appeared the figure of Bagration, without his hat or sword, which, in accordance with the club custom, he had left with the hall porter. He was not wearing an astrachan cap, and had not a riding-whip over his shoulder, as Rostov had seen him on the night before the battle of Austerlitz, but wore a tight new uniform with Russian and foreign orders and the star of St. George on the left side of his chest. He had, obviously with a view to the banquet, just had his hair cut and his whiskers clipped, which changed his appearance for the worse. He had a sort of naïvely festive air, which, in conjunction with his determined, manly features, gave an expression positively rather comic to his face. Bekleshov and Fyodor Petrovitch Uvarov, who had come with him, stood still in the doorway trying to make him, as the guest of most importance, precede them. Bagration was embarrassed, and unwilling to avail himself of their courtesy; there was a hitch in the proceedings at the door, but finally Bagration did, after all, enter first. He walked shyly and awkwardly over the parquet of the reception-room, not knowing what to do with his hands. He would have been more at home and at his ease walking over a ploughed field under fire, as he had walked at the head of the Kursk regiment at Schöngraben. The stewards met him at the first door, and saying a few words of their pleasure at seeing such an honoured guest, they surrounded him without waiting for an answer, and, as it were, taking possession of him, led him off to the drawing-room. There was no possibility of getting in at the drawing-room door from the crowds of members and guests, who were crushing one another in their efforts to get a look over each other's shoulders at Bagration, as if he were some rare sort of beast. Count Ilya Andreitch laughed more vigorously than any one, and continually repeating, "Make way for him, my dear boy, make way, make way," shoved the crowd aside, led the guests into the drawing-room, and seated them on the sofa in the middle of it. The great men, and the more honoured members of the club, surrounded the newly arrived guests. Count Ilya Andreitch, shoving his way again through the crowd, went out of the drawing-room, and reappeared a minute later with another steward carrying a great silver dish, which he held out to Prince Bagration. On the dish lay a poem, composed and printed in the hero's honour. Bagration, on seeing the dish, looked about him in dismay, as though seeking assistance. But in all eyes he saw the expectation that he would submit. Feeling himself in their power. Bagration resolutely took the dish in both hands, and looked angrily and reproachfully at the count, who had brought it. Some one officiously took the dish from Bagration (or he would, it seemed, have held it so till nightfall, and have carried it with him to the table), and drew his attention to the poem. 'Well, I'll read it then,' Bagration seemed to say, and fixing his weary eyes on the paper, he began reading it with a serious and concentrated expression. The author of the verses took them, and began to read them aloud himself. Prince Bagration bowed his head and listened.

> 'Be thou the pride of Alexander's reign!
> And save for us our Titus on the throne!
> Be thou our champion and our country's stay!

> A noble heart, a Caesar in the fray!
> Napoleon in the zenith of his fame
> Learns to his cost to fear Bagration's name,
> Nor dares provoke a Russian foe again,' etc. etc.

But he had not finished the poem, when the butler boomed out sonorously: 'Dinner is ready!' The door opened, from the dining-room thundered the strains of the Polonaise: 'Raise the shout of victory, valiant Russians, festive sing,' and Count Ilya Andreitch, looking angrily at the author, who still went on reading his verses, bowed to Bagration as a signal to go in. All the company rose, feeling the dinner of more importance than the poem, and Bagration, again preceding all the rest, went in to dinner. In the place of honour between two Alexanders—Bekleshov and Naryshkin—(this, too, was intentional, in allusion to the name of the Tsar) they put Bagration: three hundred persons were ranged about the tables according to their rank and importance, those of greater consequence, nearer to the distinguished guest—as naturally as water flows to find its own level.

Just before dinner, Count Ilya Andreitch presented his son to the prince. Bagration recognised him, and uttered a few words, awkward and incoherent, as were indeed all he spoke that day. Count Ilya Andreitch looked about at every one in gleeful pride while Bagration was speaking to his son.

Nikolay Rostov, with Denisov and his new acquaintance Dolohov, sat together almost in the middle of the table. Facing them sat Pierre with Prince Nesvitsky. Count Ilya Andreitch was sitting with the other stewards facing Bagration, and, the very impersonation of Moscow hospitality, did his utmost to regale the prince.

His labours had not been in vain. All the banquet—the meat dishes and the Lenten fare alike—was sumptuous, but still he could not be perfectly at ease till the end of dinner. He made signs to the carver, gave whispered directions to the footmen, and not without emotion awaited the arrival of each anticipated dish. Everything was capital. At the second course, with the gigantic sturgeon (at the sight of which Ilya Andreitch flushed with shamefaced delight), the footman began popping corks and pouring out champagne. After the fish, which made a certain sensation, Count Ilya Andreitch exchanged glances with the other stewards. 'There will be a great many toasts, it's time to begin!' he whispered, and, glass in hand, he got up. All were silent, waiting for what he would say.

'To the health of our sovereign, the Emperor!' he shouted, and at the moment his kindly eyes grew moist with tears of pleasure and enthusiasm. At that instant they began playing: 'Raise the shout of victory!' All rose from their seats and shouted 'Hurrah!' And Bagration shouted 'Hurrah!' in the same voice in which he had shouted it in the field at Schöngraben. The enthusiastic voice of young Rostov could be heard above the three hundred other voices. He was on the very point of tears. 'The health of our sovereign, the Emperor,' he roared, 'hurrah!' Emptying his glass at one gulp, he flung it on the floor. Many followed his example. And the loud shouts lasted for a long while. When the uproar subsided, the footmen cleared away the broken glass, and all began settling themselves again; and smiling at the noise they had made, began talking. Count Ilya Andreitch rose once more, glanced at a note that lay beside his plate, and proposed a toast to the health of the hero of our last campaign, Prince Pyotr Ivanovitch Bagration, and again the count's blue eyes were dimmed with tears. 'Hurrah!' was shouted again by the three hundred voices of the guests, and instead of music this time a chorus of singers began to sing a cantata composed by Pavel Ivanovitch Kutuzov:

> 'No hindrance bars a Russian's way,
> Valour's the pledge of victory,
> We have our Bagrations,
> Our foes will all be at our feet,' etc. etc.

As soon as the singers had finished, more and more toasts followed, at which Count Ilya Andreitch became more and more moved, and more glass was broken and even more uproar was made. They drank to the health of Bekleshov, of Naryshkin, of Uvarov, of Dolgorukov, of Apraxin, of Valuev, to the health of the stewards, to the health of the committee, to the health of all the club members, to the health of all the guests of the club, and finally and separately to the health of the organiser of the banquet, Count Ilya Andreitch. At that toast the count took out his handkerchief and, hiding his face in it, fairly broke down.

IV

PIERRE was sitting opposite Dolohov and Nikolay Rostov. He ate greedily and drank heavily, as he always did. But those who knew him slightly could see that some great change was taking place in him that day. He was silent all through dinner, and blinking and screwing up his eyes, looked about him, or letting his eyes rest on something with an air of complete absent-mindedness, rubbed the bridge of his nose with his finger. His face was depressed and gloomy. He seemed not to be seeing or hearing what was passing about him and to be thinking of some one thing, something painful and unsettled.

This unsettled question that worried him was due to the hints dropped by the princess, his cousin, at Moscow in regard to Dolohov's close intimacy with his wife, and to an anonymous letter he had received that morning, which, with the vile jocoseness peculiar to all anonymous letters, had said that he didn't seem to see clearly through his spectacles, and that his wife's connection with Dolohov was a secret from no one but himself. Pierre did not absolutely believe either the princess's hints, or the anonymous letter, but he was afraid now to look at Dolohov, who sat opposite him. Every time his glance casually met Dolohov's handsome, insolent eyes, Pierre felt as though something awful, hideous was rising up in his soul, and he made haste to turn away. Involuntarily recalling all his wife's past and her attitude to Dolohov, Pierre saw clearly that what was said in the letter might well be true, might at least appear to be the truth, if only it had not related to *his wife*. Pierre could not help recalling how Dolohov, who had been completely reinstated, had returned to Petersburg and come to see him. Dolohov had taken advantage of his friendly relations with Pierre in their old rowdy days, had come straight to his house, and Pierre had established him in it and lent him money. Pierre recalled how Ellen, smiling, had expressed her dissatisfaction at Dolohov's staying in their house, and how cynically Dolohov had praised his wife's beauty to him, and how he had never since left them up to the time of their coming to Moscow.

'Yes, he is very handsome,' thought Pierre, 'and I know him. There would be a particular charm for him in disgracing my name and turning me into ridicule, just because I have exerted myself in his behalf, have befriended him and helped him. I know, I understand what zest that would be sure to give to his betrayal of me, if it were true. Yes, if it were true, but I don't believe it. I have no right to and I can't believe it.' He recalled the expression on Dolohov's face in his moments of cruelty, such as when he was tying the police officer on to the bear and dropping him into the water, or when he had utterly without provocation challenged a man to a duel or killed a sledge-driver's horse with a shot from his pistol. That expression often came into Dolohov's face when he was looking at him. 'Yes, he's a duelling bully,' thought Pierre; 'to him it means nothing to kill a man, it must seem to him that every one's afraid of him. He must like it. He must think I am afraid of him. And, in fact, I really am afraid of him,' Pierre mused; and again at these thoughts he felt as though something terrible and hideous were rising up in his soul. Dolohov, Denisov, and Rostov were sitting facing Pierre and seemed to be greatly enjoying themselves. Rostov talked away merrily to his two friends, of whom one was a dashing hussar, the other a notorious duellist and scapegrace, and now and then cast ironical glances at Pierre, whose appearance at the dinner was a striking one, with his preoccupied, absent-minded, massive figure. Rostov looked with disfavour upon Pierre. In the first place, because Pierre, in the eyes of the smart hussar, was a rich civilian, and husband of a beauty, was altogether, in fact, an old woman. And secondly, because Pierre in his preoccupation and absent-mindedness had not recognised Rostov and had failed to respond to his bow. When they got up to drink the health of the Tsar, Pierre, plunged in thought, did not rise nor take up his glass.

'What are you about?' Rostov shouted to him, looking at him with enthusiastic and exasperated eyes. 'Don't you hear: the health of our sovereign the Emperor!'

Pierre with a sigh obeyed, got up, emptied his glass, and waiting till all were seated again, he turned with his kindly smile to Rostov. 'Why, I didn't recognise you,' he said. But Rostov had no thoughts for him, he was shouting 'Hurrah!'

'Why don't you renew the acquaintance?' said Dolohov to Rostov.

'Oh, bother him, he's a fool,' said Rostov.

'One has to be sweet to the husbands of pretty women,' said Denisov. Pierre did not hear what they were saying, but he knew they were talking of him. He flushed and turned away. 'Well, now to the health of pretty women,' said Dolohov, and with a serious expression, though a smile lurked in the corners of his mouth, he turned to Pierre.

'To the health of pretty women, Petrusha, and their lovers too,' he said.

Pierre, with downcast eyes, sipped his glass, without looking at Dolohov or answering him. The footman, distributing copies of Kutuzov's cantata, laid a copy by Pierre, as one of the more honoured guests. He would have taken it, but Dolohov bent forward, snatched the paper out of his hands and began reading it. Pierre glanced at Dolohov, and his eyes dropped; something terrible and hideous, that had been torturing him all through the dinner, rose up and took possession of him. He bent the whole of his ungainly person across the table. 'Don't you dare to take it!' he shouted.

Hearing that shout and seeing to whom it was addressed, Nesvitsky and his neighbour on the right side turned in haste and alarm to Bezuhov.

'Hush, hush, what are you about?' whispered panic-stricken voices. Dolohov looked at Pierre with his clear, mirthful, cruel eyes, still with the same smile, as though he were saying, 'Come now, this is what I like.'

'I won't give it up,' he said distinctly.

Pale and with quivering lips, Pierre snatched the copy.

'You . . . you . . . blackguard! . . . I challenge you,' he said, and moving back his chair, he got up from the table. At the second Pierre did this and uttered these words he felt that the question of his wife's guilt, that had been torturing him for the last four and twenty hours, was finally and incontestably answered in the affirmative. He hated her and was severed from her for ever. In spite of Denisov's entreaties that Rostov would have nothing to do with the affair, Rostov agreed to be Dolohov's second, and after dinner he discussed with Nesvitsky, Bezuhov's second, the arrangements for the duel. Pierre had gone home, but Rostov with Dolohov and Denisov stayed on at the club listening to the gypsies and the singers till late in the evening.

'So good-bye till tomorrow, at Sokolniky,' said Dolohov, as he parted from Rostov at the club steps.

'And do you feel quite calm?' asked Rostov.

Dolohov stopped.

'Well, do you see, in a couple of words I'll let you into the whole secret of duelling. If, when you go to a duel, you make your will and write long letters to your parents, if you think that you may be killed, you're a fool and certain to be done for. But go with the firm intention of killing your man, as quickly and as surely as may be, then everything will be all right. As our bear-killer from Kostroma used to say to me: "A bear," he'd say, "why, who's not afraid of one? but come to see one and your fear's all gone, all you hope is he won't get away!" Well, that's just how I feel. *A demain, mon cher.*'

Next day at eight o'clock in the morning, Pierre and Nesvitsky reached the Sokolniky copse, and found Dolohov, Denisov, and Rostov already there. Pierre had the air of a man absorbed in reflections in no way connected with the matter in hand. His face looked hollow and yellow. He had not slept all night. He looked about him absent-mindedly, and screwed up his eyes, as though in glaring sunshine. He was exclusively absorbed by two considerations: the guilt of his wife, of which after a sleepless night he had not a vestige of doubt, and the guiltlessness of Dolohov, who was in no way bound to guard the honour of a man, who was nothing to him. 'Maybe I should have done the same in his place,' thought Pierre. 'For certain, indeed, I should have done the same; then why this duel, this murder? Either I shall kill him, or he will shoot me in the head, in the elbow, or the knee. To get away from here, to run, to bury myself somewhere,' was the longing that came into his mind. But precisely at the moments when such ideas were in his mind, he would turn with a peculiarly calm and unconcerned face, which inspired respect in the seconds looking at him, and asked: 'Will it be soon?' or 'Aren't we ready?'

When everything was ready, the swords stuck in the snow to mark the barrier, and the pistols loaded, Nesvitsky went up to Pierre.

'I should not be doing my duty, count,' he said in a timid voice, 'nor justifying the confidence and the honour you have done me in choosing me for your second, if at this grave moment, this very grave moment, I did not speak the whole truth to you. I consider that the quarrel has not sufficient grounds and is not worth shedding blood over. . . . You were not right, not quite in the right; you lost your temper. . . .'

'Oh, yes, it was awfully stupid,' said Pierre.

'Then allow me to express your regret, and I am convinced that our opponents will agree to accept your apology,' said Nesvitsky (who, like the others assisting in the affair, and every one at such affairs, was unable to believe that the quarrel would come to an actual duel). 'You know, count, it is far nobler to acknowledge one's mistake than to push things to the irrevocable. There was no great offence on either side. Permit me to convey . . .'

'No, what are you talking about?' said Pierre; 'it doesn't matter. . . . Ready then?' he added. 'Only tell me how and where I am to go, and what to shoot at?' he said with a smile unnaturally gentle. He took up a pistol, and began inquiring how to let it off, as he had never had a pistol in his hand before, a fact he did not care to confess. 'Oh, yes, of course, I know, I had only forgotten,' he said.

'No apologies, absolutely nothing,' Dolohov was saying to Denisov, who for his part was also making an attempt at reconciliation, and he too went up to the appointed spot.

The place chosen for the duel was some eighty paces from the road, on which their sledges had been left, in a small clearing in the pine wood, covered with snow that had thawed in the warmer weather of the last few days. The antagonists stood forty paces from each other at the further edge of the clearing. The seconds, in measuring the paces, left tracks in the deep, wet snow from the spot where they had been standing to the swords of Nesvitsky and Denisov, which had been thrust in the ground ten paces from one another to mark the barrier. The thaw and mist persisted; forty paces away nothing could be seen. In three minutes everything was ready, but still they delayed beginning. Every one was silent.

V

'WELL, let us begin,' said Dolohov.

'To be sure,' said Pierre, still with the same smile.

A feeling of dread was in the air. It was obvious that the affair that had begun so lightly could not now be in any way turned back, that it was going forward of itself, independently of men's will, and must run its course. Denisov was the first to come forward to the barrier and pronounce the words:

'Since the antagonists refuse all reconciliation, would it not be as well to begin. Take your pistols, and at the word "three" begin to advance together. O . . . one! Two! Three! . . .' Denisov shouted angrily, and he walked away from the barrier. Both walked along the trodden tracks closer and closer together, beginning to recognise one another in the mist. The combatants had the right to fire when they chose as they approached the barrier. Dolohov walked slowly, not lifting his pistol, and looking intently with his clear, shining blue eyes into the face of his antagonist. His mouth wore, as always, the semblance of a smile.

'So when I like, I can fire,' said Pierre, and at the word *three*, he walked with rapid steps forward, straying off the beaten track and stepping over the untrodden snow. Pierre held his pistol at full length in his right hand, obviously afraid of killing himself with that pistol. His left arm he studiously held behind him, because he felt inclined to use it to support his right arm, and he knew that was not allowed. After advancing six paces, and getting off the track into the snow, Pierre looked about under his feet, glanced rapidly again at Dolohov, and stretching out his finger, as he had been shown, fired. Not at all expecting so loud a report, Pierre started at his own shot, then smiled at his own sensation and stood still. The smoke, which was made thicker by the fog, hindered him from seeing for the first moment; but the other shot that he was expecting did not follow. All that could be heard were Dolohov's rapid footsteps, and his figure came into view through the smoke. With one hand he was clutching at his left side, the other was clenched on the lowered pistol. His face was pale. Rostov was running up and saying something to him.

'N . . . no,' Dolohov muttered through his teeth, 'no, it's not over': and struggling on a few sinking, staggering steps up to the sword, he sank on to the snow beside it. His left hand was covered with blood, he rubbed it on his coat and leaned upon it. His face was pale, frowning and trembling.

'Co . . .' Dolohov began, but he could not at once articulate the words: 'come up,' he said, with an effort. Pierre, hardly able to restrain his sobs, ran towards Dolohov, and would have crossed the space that separated the barriers, when Dolohov cried: 'To the barrier!' and Pierre, grasping what was wanted, stood still just at the sword. Only ten paces divided them. Dolohov putting his head down, greedily bit at the snow, lifted his head again, sat up, tried to get on his legs and sat down, trying to find a secure centre of gravity. He took a mouthful of the cold snow, and sucked it; his lips quivered, but still he smiled; his eyes glittered with the strain and the exasperation of the struggle with his failing forces. He raised the pistol and began taking aim.

'Sideways, don't expose yourself to the pistol,' said Nesvitsky.

'Don't face it!' Denisov could not help shouting, though it was to an antagonist.

With his gentle smile of sympathy and remorse, Pierre stood with his legs and arms straddling helplessly, and his broad chest directly facing Dolohov, and looked at him mournfully. Denisov, Rostov, and Nesvitsky screwed up their eyes. At the same instant they heard a shot and Dolohov's wrathful cry.

'Missed!' shouted Dolohov, and he dropped helplessly, face downwards, in the snow. Pierre clutched at his head, and turning back, walked into the wood, off the path in the snow, muttering aloud incoherent words.

'Stupid . . . stupid! Death . . . lies . . .' he kept repeating, scowling. Nesvitsky stopped him and took him home.

Rostov and Denisov got the wounded Dolohov away.

Dolohov lay in the sledge with closed eyes, in silence, and uttered not a word in reply to questions addressed to him. But as they were driving into Moscow, he suddenly came to himself, and lifting his head with an effort, he took the hand of Rostov, who was sitting near him. Rostov was struck by the utterly transformed and unexpectedly passionately tender expression on Dolohov's face.

'Well? How do you feel?' asked Rostov.

'Bad! but that's not the point. My friend,' said Dolohov, in a breaking voice, 'where are we? We are in Moscow, I know. I don't matter, but I have killed her, killed her. . . . She won't get over this. She can't bear . . .'

'Who?' asked Rostov.

'My mother. My mother, my angel, my adored angel, my mother,' and squeezing Rostov's hand, Dolohov burst into tears. When he was a little calmer, he explained to Rostov that he was living with his mother, that if his mother were to see him dying, she would not get over the shock. He besought Rostov to go to her and prepare her.

Rostov drove on ahead to carry out his wish, and to his immense astonishment he had learned that Dolohov, this bully, this noted duellist Doholov, lived at Moscow with his old mother and a hunchback sister, and was the tenderest son and brother.

VI

PIERRE had of late rarely seen his wife alone. Both at Petersburg and at Moscow their house had been constantly full of guests. On the night following the duel he did not go to his bedroom, but spent the night, as he often did, in his huge study, formerly his father's room, the very room indeed in which Count Bezuhov had died.

He lay down on the couch and tried to go to sleep, so as to forget all that had happened to him, but he could not do so. Such a tempest of feelings, thoughts, and reminiscences suddenly arose in his soul, that, far from going to sleep, he could not even sit still in one place, and was forced to leap up from the couch and pace with rapid steps about the room. At one moment he had a vision of his wife, as she was in the first days of their marriage, with her bare shoulders, and languid, passionate eyes; and then immediately by her side he saw the handsome, impudent, hard, and ironical face of Dolohov, as he had seen it at the banquet, and again the same face of Dolohov, pale, quivering, in agony, as it had been when he turned and sank in the snow.

'What has happened?' he asked himself; 'I have killed *her lover*; yes, killed the lover of my wife. Yes, that has happened. Why was it? How have I come to this?' 'Because you married her,' answered an inner voice.

'But how am I to blame?' he asked. 'For marrying without loving her, for deceiving yourself and her.' And vividly he recalled that minute after supper at Prince Vassily's when he had said those words he found so difficult to utter: 'I love you.' 'It has all come from that. Even then I felt it,' he thought; 'I felt at the time that it wasn't the right thing, that I had no right to do it. And so it has turned out.' He recalled the honeymoon, and blushed at the recollection of it. Particularly vivid, humiliating, and shameful was the memory of how one day soon after his marriage he had come in his silk dressing-gown out of his bedroom into his study at twelve o'clock in the day, and in his study had found his head steward, who had bowed deferentially, and looking at Pierre's face and his dressing-gown, had faintly smiled, as though to express by that smile his respectful sympathy with his patron's happiness. 'And how often I have been proud of her, proud of her majestic beauty, her social tact,' he thought; 'proud of my house, in which she received all Petersburg, proud of her unapproachability and beauty. So this was what I prided myself on. I used to think then that I did not understand her. How often, reflecting on her character, I have told myself that I was to blame, that I did not understand her, did not understand that everlasting composure and complacency, and the absence of all preferences and desires, and the solution of the whole riddle lay in that fearful word, that she is a dissolute woman; I have found that fearful word, and all has become clear.

'Anatole used to come to borrow money of her, and used to kiss her on her bare shoulders. She didn't give him money; but she let herself be kissed. Her father used to try in joke to rouse her jealousy; with a serene smile she used to say she was not fool enough to be jealous. Let him do as he likes, she used to say about me. I asked her once if she felt no symptoms of pregnancy. She laughed contemptuously, and said she was not such a fool as to want children, and that she would never have a child by me.'

Then he thought of the coarseness, the bluntness of her ideas, and the vulgarity of the expressions that were characteristic of her, although she had been brought up in the highest aristocratic circles. 'Not quite such a fool . . . you just try it on . . . you clear out of this,' she would say. Often, watching the favourable impression she made on young and old, on men and women, Pierre could not understand why it was he did not love her. 'Yes; I never loved her,' Pierre said to himself; 'I knew she was a dissolute woman,' he repeated to himself; 'but I did not dare own it to myself.'

'And now Dolohov: there he sits in the snow and forces himself to smile; and dies with maybe some swaggering affectation on his lips in answer to my remorse.'

Pierre was one of those people who in spite of external weakness of character—so-called—do not seek a confidant for their sorrows. He worked through his trouble alone.

'She, she alone is to blame for everything,' he said to himself: 'but what of that? Why did I bind myself to her; why did I say to her that "I love you," which was a lie, and worse than a lie,' he said to himself; 'I am to blame, and ought to bear . . . What? The disgrace to my name, the misery of my life? Oh, that's all rubbish,' he thought, 'disgrace to one's name and honour, all that's relative, all that's apart from myself.

'Louis XVI. was executed because *they* said he was dishonourable and a criminal' (the idea crossed Pierre's mind), 'and they were right from their point of view just as those were right too who died a martyr's death for his sake, and canonised him as a saint. Then Robespierre was executed for being a tyrant. Who is right, who is wrong? No one. But live while you live, tomorrow you die, as I might have died an hour ago.

And is it worth worrying oneself, when life is only one second in comparison with eternity?' But at the moment when he believed himself soothed by reflections of that sort, he suddenly had a vision of *her*, and of her at those moments when he had most violently expressed his most insincere love to her, and he felt a rush of blood to his heart, and had to jump up again, and move about and break and tear to pieces anything that his hands came across. 'Why did I say to her "I love you"?' he kept repeating to himself. And as he repeated the question for the tenth time the saying of Molière came into his head: 'But what the devil was he doing in that galley?' and he laughed at himself.

In the night he called for his valet and bade him pack to go to Petersburg. He could not conceive how he was going to speak to her now. He resolved that next day he would go away, leaving her a letter, in which he would announce his intention of parting from her for ever.

In the morning when the valet came into the study with his coffee, Pierre was lying on an ottoman asleep with an open book in his hand.

He woke up and looked about him for a long while in alarm, unable to grasp where he was.

'The countess sent to inquire if your excellency were at home,' said the valet.

But before Pierre had time to make up his mind what answer he would send, the countess herself walked calmly and majestically into the room. She was wearing a white satin dressing-gown embroidered with silver, and had her hair in two immense coils wound like a coronet round her exquisite head. In spite of her calm, there was a wrathful line on her rather prominent, marble brow. With her accustomed self-control and composure she did not begin to speak till the valet had left the room. She knew of the duel and had come to talk of it. She waited till the valet had set the coffee and gone out. Pierre looked timidly at her over his spectacles, and as the hare, hemmed in by dogs, goes on lying with its ears back in sight of its foes, so he tried to go on reading. But he felt that this was senseless and impossible, and again he glanced timidly at her. She did not sit down, but stood looking at him with a disdainful smile, waiting for the valet to be gone.

'What's this about now? What have you been up to? I'm asking you,' she said sternly.

'I? I? what?' said Pierre.

'You going in for deeds of valour! Now, answer me, what does this duel mean? What did you want to prove by it? Eh! I ask you the question.' Pierre turned heavily on the sofa, opened his mouth but could not answer.

'If you won't answer, I'll tell you . . .' Ellen went on. 'You believe everything you're told. You were told . . .' Ellen laughed, 'that Dolohov was my lover,' she said in French, with her coarse plainness of speech, uttering the word '*amant*' like any other word, 'and you believed it! But what have you proved by this? What have you proved by this duel? That you're a fool; but every one knew that as it was. What does it lead to? Why, that I'm made a laughing-stock to all Moscow; that every one's saying that when you were drunk and didn't know what you were doing, you challenged a man of whom you were jealous without grounds,' Ellen raised her voice and grew more and more passionate; 'who's a better man than you in every respect . . . .'

'Hem . . . hem . . .' Pierre growled, wrinkling up his face, and neither looking at her nor stirring a muscle.

'And how came you to believe that he's my lover? . . . Eh? Because I like his society? If you were cleverer and more agreeable, I should prefer yours.'

'Don't speak to me . . . I beseech you,' Pierre muttered huskily.

'Why shouldn't I speak? I can speak as I like, and I tell you boldly that it's not many a wife who with a husband like you wouldn't have taken a lover, but I haven't done it,' she said. Pierre tried to say something, glanced at her with strange eyes, whose meaning she did not comprehend, and lay down again. He was in physical agony at that moment; he felt a weight on his chest so that he could not breathe. He knew that he must do something to put an end to this agony but what he wanted to do was too horrible.

'We had better part,' he articulated huskily.

'Part, by all means, only if you give me a fortune,' said Ellen. . . . 'Part—that's a threat to frighten me!'

Pierre leaped up from the couch and rushed staggering towards her.

'I'll kill you!' he shouted, and snatching up a marble slab from a table with a strength he had not known in himself till then, he made a step towards her and waved it at her.

Ellen's face was terrible to see; she shrieked and darted away from him. His father's nature showed itself in him. Pierre felt the abandonment and the fascination of frenzy. He flung down the slab, shivering it into fragments, and with open arms swooping down upon Ellen, screamed 'Go!' in a voice so terrible that they heard it all over the house with horror. God knows what Pierre would have done at that moment if Ellen had not run out of the room.

A week later Pierre had made over to his wife the revenue from all his estates in Great Russia, which made up the larger half of his property, and had gone away alone to Petersburg.

VII

Two months had passed since the news of the defeat of Austerlitz and the loss of Prince Andrey had reached Bleak Hills. In spite of all researches and letters through the Russian embassy, his body had not been found, nor was he among the prisoners. What made it worst of all for his father and sister was the fact that there was still hope that he might have been picked up on the battlefield by the people of the country, and might perhaps be lying, recovering, or dying somewhere alone, among strangers, incapable of giving any account of himself. The newspapers, from which the old prince had first heard of the defeat at Austerlitz, had, as always, given very brief and vague accounts of how the Russians had been obliged after brilliant victories to retreat and had made their withdrawal in perfect order. The old prince saw from this official account that our army had been defeated. A week after the newspaper that had brought news of the defeat of Austerlitz, came a letter from Kutuzov, who described to the old prince the part taken in it by his son.

'Before my eyes,' wrote Kutuzov, 'your son with the flag in his hands, at the head of a regiment, fell like a hero, worthy of his father and his fatherland. To my regret and the general regret of the whole army it has not been ascertained up to now whether he is alive or dead. I comfort myself and you with the hope that your son is living, as, otherwise, he would have been mentioned among the officers found on the field of battle, a list of whom has been given me under flag of truce.'

After receiving this letter, late in the evening when he was alone in his study, the old prince went for his morning walk as usual next day. But he was silent with the bailiff, the gardener, and the architect, and though he looked wrathful, said nothing to them. When Princess Marya went in to him at the usual hour, he was standing at the lathe and went on turning as usual, without looking round at her. 'Ah? Princess Marya!' he said suddenly in an unnatural voice, and he let the lathe go. (The wheel swung round from the impetus. Long after, Princess Marya remembered the dying creak of the wheel, which was associated for her with what followed.)

Princess Marya went up to him; she caught sight of his face, and something seemed suddenly to give way within her. Her eyes could not see clearly. From her father's face—not sad nor crushed, but vindictive and full of unnatural conflict—she saw that there was hanging over her, coming to crush her, a terrible calamity, the worst in life, a calamity she had not known till then, a calamity irrevocable, irremediable, the death of one beloved.

'Father! Andrey?...' said the ungainly, awkward princess with such unutterable beauty of sorrow and self-forgetfulness that her father could not bear to meet her eyes and turned away sobbing.

'I have had news. Not among the prisoners, not among the killed, Kutuzov writes,' he screamed shrilly, as though he would drive his daughter away with that shriek. 'Killed!'

The princess did not swoon, she did not fall into a faint. She was pale, but when she heard those words her face was transformed, and there was a radiance of something in her beautiful, luminous eyes. Something like joy, an exalted joy, apart from the sorrows and joys of this world, flooded the bitter grief she felt within her. She forgot all her terror of her father, went up to him, took him by the hand, drew him to her, and put her arm about his withered, sinewy neck.

'Father,' she said, 'do not turn away from me, let us weep for him together.'

'Blackguards, scoundrels!' screamed the old man, turning his face away from her. 'Destroying the army, destroying men! What for? Go, go and tell Liza.'

Princess Marya sank helplessly into an armchair beside her father and burst into tears. She could see her brother now at the moment when he parted from her and from Liza with his tender and at the same time haughty expression. She saw him at the moment when tenderly and ironically he had put the image on. 'Did he believe now? Had he repented of his unbelief? Was he there now? There in the realm of eternal peace and blessedness?' she wondered. 'Father, tell me how it was,' she asked through her tears.

'Go away, go—killed in a defeat in which they led the best men of Russia and the glory of Russia to ruin. Go away, Princess Marya. Go and tell Liza. I will come.' When Princess Marya went back from her father, the little princess was sitting at her work, and she looked up with that special inward look of happy calm that is peculiar to women with child. It was clear that her eyes were not seeing Princess Marya, but looking deep within herself, at some happy mystery that was being accomplished within her.

'Marie,' she said, moving away from the embroidery frame and leaning back, 'give me your hand.' She took her sister-in-law's hand and laid it below her waist. Her eyes smiled, expectant, her little dewy lip was lifted and stayed so in childlike rapture. Princess Marya knelt down before her, and hid her face in the folds of her sister-in-law's dress. 'There—there—do you feel it? I feel so strange. And do you know, Marie, I am going to love him very much,' said Liza, looking at her sister-in-law with shining, happy eyes. Princess Marya could not lift her head; she was crying.

'What's the matter with you, Marie?'

'Nothing . . . only I felt sad . . . sad about Andrey,' she said, brushing away the tears on the folds of her sister-in-law's dress. Several times in the course of the morning Princess Marya began trying to prepare her sister-in-law's mind, and every time she began to weep. These tears, which the little princess could not account for, agitated her, little as she was observant in general. She said nothing, but looked about her uneasily, as though seeking for something. Before dinner the old prince, of whom she was always afraid, came into her room, with a particularly restless and malignant expression, and went out without uttering a word. She looked at Princess Marya with that expression of attention concentrated within herself that is only seen in women with child, and suddenly she burst into tears.

'Have you heard news from Andrey?' she said.

'No; you know news could not come yet; but father is uneasy, and I feel frightened.'

'Then you have heard nothing?'

'Nothing,' said Princess Marya, looking resolutely at her with her luminous eyes. She had made up her mind not to tell her, and had persuaded her father to conceal the dreadful news from her till her confinement, which was expected before many days. Princess Marya and the old prince, in their different ways, bore and hid their grief. The old Prince refused to hope; he made up his mind that Prince Andrey had been killed, and though he sent a clerk to Austria to seek for traces of his son, he ordered a monument for him in Moscow and intended to put it up in his garden, and he told every one that his son was dead. He tried to keep up his old manner of life unchanged, but his strength was failing him: he walked less, ate less, slept less, and every day he grew weaker. Princess Marya went on hoping. She prayed for her brother, as living, and every moment she expected news of his return.

VIII

'*Ma bonne amie*,' said the little princess, after breakfast, on the morning of the 19th of March, and her little downy lip was lifted as of old; but as in that house since the terrible news had come, smiles, tones of voice, movements even bore the stamp of mourning, so now the smile of the little princess, who was influenced by the general temper without knowing its cause, was such that more than all else it was eloquent of the common burden of sorrow.

'My dear, I am afraid that this morning's *fruschtique* (as Foka calls it) has disagreed with me.'

'What is the matter with you, my darling? You look pale. Oh, you are very pale,' said Princess Marya in alarm, running with her soft, ponderous tread up to her sister-in-law.

'Shouldn't we send for Marya Bogdanovna, your excellency?' said one of the maids who was present. Marya Bogdanovna was a midwife from a district town, who had been for the last fortnight at Bleak Hills.

'Yes, truly,' assented Princess Marya, 'perhaps it is really that. I'll go and get her. Courage, my angel.' She kissed Liza and was going out of the room.

'Oh, no, no!' And besides her pallor, the face of the little princess expressed a childish terror at the inevitable physical suffering before her.

'No, it is indigestion, say it is indigestion, say so, Marie, say so!' And the little princess began to cry, wringing her little hands with childish misery and capriciousness and affected exaggeration too. Princess Marya ran out of the room to fetch Marya Bogdanovna.

'*Mon Dieu! mon Dieu!* Oh!' she heard behind her. The midwife was already on her way to meet her, rubbing her plump, small, white hands, with a face of significant composure.

'Marya Bogdanovna! I think it has begun,' said Princess Marya, looking with wide-open, frightened eyes at the midwife.

'Well, I thank God for it,' said Marya Bogdanovna, not hastening her step. 'You young ladies have no need to know anything about it.'

'But how is it the doctor has not come from Moscow yet?' said the princess. (In accordance with the wishes of Liza and Prince Andrey, they had sent to Moscow for a doctor, and were expecting him every minute.)

'It's no matter, princess, don't be uneasy,' said Marya Bogdanovna; 'we shall do very well without the doctor.'

Five minutes later the princess from her room heard something heavy being carried by. She peeped out; the footmen were for some reason moving into the bedroom the leather sofa which stood in Prince Andrey's study. There was a solemn and subdued look on the men's faces.

Princess Marya sat alone in her room, listening to the sounds of the house, now and then opening the door when any one passed by and looking at what was taking place in the corridor. Several women passed to and fro treading softly; they glanced at the princess and turned away from her. She did not venture to ask questions, and going back to her room closed the door and sat still in an armchair, or took up her prayer-book, or knelt down before the shrine. To her distress and astonishment she felt that prayer did not soothe her emotion. All at once the door of her room was softly opened, and she saw on the threshold her old nurse, Praskovya Savvishna, with a kerchief over her head. The old woman hardly ever, owing to the old prince's prohibition, came into her room.

'I've come to sit a bit with thee, Mashenka,' said the nurse; 'and here I've brought the prince's wedding candles to light before his saint, my angel,' she said, sighing.

'Ah, how glad I am, nurse!'

'God is merciful, my darling.' The nurse lighted the gilt candles before the shrine, and sat down with her stocking near the door. Princess Marya took a book and began reading. Only when they heard steps or voices, the princess and the nurse looked at one another, one with alarmed inquiry, the other with soothing reassurance in her face. The feeling that Princess Marya was experiencing as she sat in her room had overpowered the whole house and taken possession of every one. Owing to the belief that the fewer people know of the sufferings of a woman in labour, the less she suffers, every one tried to affect to know nothing of it; no one talked about it, but over and above the habitual staidness and respectfulness of good manners that always reigned in the prince's household, there was apparent in all a sort of anxiety, a softening of the heart, and a consciousness of some great, unfathomable mystery being accomplished at that moment. There was no sound of laughter in the big room where the maids sat. In the waiting-room the men all sat in silence, as it were on the alert. Torches and candles were burning in the serfs' quarters, and no one slept. The old prince walked about his study, treading on his heels, and sent Tihon to Marya Bogdanovna to ask what news.

'Only say: the prince has sent to ask, what news, and come and tell me what she says.'

'Inform the prince that the labour has commenced,' said Marya Bogdanovna, looking significantly at the messenger. Tihon went and gave the prince that information.

'Very good,' said the prince, closing the door behind him, and Tihon heard not the slightest sound in the study after that. After a short interval Tihon went into the study, as though to attend to the candles. Seeing the prince lying on the couch, Tihon looked at him, looked at his perturbed face, shook his head, went up to him dumbly and kissed him on the shoulder, then went out without touching the candles or saying why he had come. The most solemn mystery in the world was being accomplished. Evening passed, night came on. And the feeling of suspense and softening of the heart before the unfathomable did not wane, but grew more intense. No one slept.

It was one of those March nights when winter seems to regain its sway, and flings its last snows and storms with malignant desperation. A relay of horses had been sent to the high-road for the German doctor who was expected every minute, and men were despatched on horseback with lanterns to the turning at the cross-roads to guide him over the holes and treacherous places in the ice.

Princess Marya had long abandoned her book; she sat in silence, her luminous eyes fixed on the wrinkled face of her old nurse (so familiar to her in the minutest detail), on the lock of grey hair that had escaped from the kerchief, on the baggy looseness of the skin under her chin.

The old nurse, with her stocking in her hand, talked away in a soft voice, not hearing it herself nor following the meaning of her own words; telling, as she had told hundreds of times before, how the late princess had been brought to bed of Princess Marya at Kishinyov, and had only a Moldavian peasant woman instead of a midwife.

'God is merciful, doctors are never wanted,' she said.

Suddenly a gust of wind blew on one of the window-frames (by the prince's decree the double frames were always taken out of every window when the larks returned), and flinging open a badly fastened window bolt, set the stuff curtain fluttering; and the chill, snowy draught blew out the candle. Princess Marya shuddered; the nurse putting down her stocking went to the window, and putting her head out tried to catch the open frame. The cold wind flapped the ends of her kerchief and the grey locks of her hair.

'Princess, my dearie, there's some one driving up the avenue!' she said, holding the window-frame and not closing it. 'With lanterns; it must be the doctor. . . .'

'Ah, my God! Thank God!' said Princess Marya. 'I must go and meet him; he does not know Russian.'

Princess Marya flung on a shawl and ran to meet the stranger. As she passed through the ante-room, she saw through the window a carriage and lanterns standing at the entrance. She went out on to the stairs. At the post of the balustrade stood a tallow-candle guttering in the draught. The footman Filipp, looking scared, stood below on the first landing of the staircase, with another candle in his hand. Still lower down, at the turn of the winding stairs, steps in thick overshoes could be heard coming up. And a voice—familiar it seemed to Princess Marya—was saying something.

'Thank God!' said the voice. 'And father?'

'He has gone to bed,' answered the voice of the butler, Demyan, who was below.

Then the voice said something more, Demyan answered something, and the steps in thick overshoes began approaching more rapidly up the unseen part of the staircase.

'It is Andrey!' thought Princess Marya. 'No, it cannot be, it would be too extraordinary,' she thought; and at the very instant she was thinking so, on the landing where the footman stood with a candle, there came into sight the face and figure of Prince Andrey, in a fur coat, with a deep collar covered with snow. Yes, it was he, but pale and thin, and with a transformed, strangely softened, agitated expression on his face. He went up the stairs and embraced his sister.

'You did not get my letter, then?' he asked; and not waiting for an answer, which he would not have received, for the princess could not speak, he turned back, and with the doctor who was behind him (they had met at the last station), he ran again rapidly upstairs and again embraced his sister.

'What a strange fate!' he said, 'Masha, darling!' And flinging off his fur coat and overboots, he went towards the little princess's room.

IX

THE little princess was lying on the pillows in her white nightcap (the agony had only a moment left her). Her black hair lay in curls about her swollen and perspiring cheeks; her rosy, charming little mouth, with the downy lip, was open, and she was smiling joyfully. Prince Andrey went into the room, and stood facing her at the foot of the bed on which she lay. The glittering eyes, staring in childish terror and excitement, rested on him with no change in their expression. 'I love you all, I have done no one any harm; why am I suffering? help me,' her face seemed to say. She saw her husband, but she did not take in the meaning of his appearance now before her. Prince Andrey went round the bed and kissed her on the forehead.

'My precious,' he said, a word he had never used speaking to her before. 'God is merciful. . . .' She stared at him with a face of inquiry, of childish reproach.

'I hoped for help from you, and nothing, nothing, you too!' her eyes said. She was not surprised at his having come; she did not understand that he had come. His coming had nothing to do with her agony and its alleviation. The pains began again, and Marya Bogdanovna advised Prince Andrey to go out of the room.

The doctor went into the room. Prince Andrey came out, and, meeting Princess Marya, went to her again. They talked in whispers, but every moment their talk was hushed. They were waiting and listening.

'Go, *mon ami*,' said Princess Marya. Prince Andrey went again to his wife and sat down in the adjoining room, waiting. A woman ran out of the bedroom with a frightened face, and was disconcerted on seeing Prince Andrey. He hid his face in his hands and sat so for some minutes. Piteous, helpless, animal groans came from the next room. Prince Andrey got up, went to the door, and would have opened it. Some one was holding the door.

'Can't come in, can't!' a frightened voice said from within. He began walking about the room. The screams ceased; several seconds passed. Suddenly a fearful scream—not her scream, could she scream like that?—came from the room. Prince Andrey ran to the door; the scream ceased; he heard the cry of a baby.

'What have they taken a baby in there for?' Prince Andrey wondered for the first second. 'A baby? What baby? ... Why a baby there? Or is the baby born?'

When he suddenly realised all the joyful significance of that cry, tears choked him, and leaning both elbows on the window-sill he cried, sobbing as children cry. The door opened. The doctor with his shirt sleeves tucked up, and no coat on, came out of the room, pale, and his lower jaw twitching. Prince Andrey addressed him, but the doctor, looking at him in a distracted way, passed by without uttering a word. A woman ran out, and, seeing Prince Andrey, stopped hesitating in the door. He went into his wife's room. She was lying dead in the same position in which he had seen her five minutes before, and in spite of the fixed gaze and white cheeks, there was the same expression still on the charming childish face with the little lip covered with fine dark hair. 'I love you all, and have done no harm to any one, and what have you done to me?' said her charming, piteous, dead face. In a corner of the room was something red and tiny, squealing and grunting in the trembling white hands of Marya Bogdanovna.

Two hours later Prince Andrey went with soft steps into his father's room. The old man knew everything already. He was standing near the door, and, as soon as it opened, his rough old arms closed like a vice round his son's neck, and without a word he burst into sobs like a child.

Three days afterwards the little princess was buried, and Prince Andrey went to the steps of the tomb to take his last farewell of her. Even in the coffin the face was the same, though the eyes were closed. 'Ah, what have you done to me?' it still seemed to say; and Prince Andrey felt that something was being torn out of his soul, that he was guilty of a crime that he could never set right nor forget. He could not weep. The old man, too, went in and kissed the little waxen hand that lay so peacefully crossed over the other, and to him, her face said: 'Ah, what have you done to me, and why?' And the old man turned angrily away, when he caught sight of the face.

In another five days there followed the christening of the young prince, Nikolay Andreitch. The nurse held the swaddling clothes up to her chin, while the priest with a goose feather anointed the baby's red, wrinkled hands and feet.

His grandfather, who was his godfather, trembling and afraid of dropping the baby, carried him round the battered tin font, and handed him over to the godmother, Princess Marya. Faint with terror that they would let the baby drown in the font, Prince Andrey sat in an adjoining room, waiting for the conclusion of the ceremony. He looked joyfully at the baby when the nurse brought him out, and nodded approvingly when the nurse told him that a bit of wax with the baby's hairs in it, thrown into the font, had not sunk in the water but floated on the surface.

X

ROSTOV'S share in the duel between Dolohov and Bezuhov had been hushed up by the efforts of the old count, and instead of being degraded to the ranks, as Nikolay had expected, he had been appointed an adjutant to the governor of Moscow. In consequence of this, he could not go to the country with the rest of the family, but was kept by his new duties all the summer in Moscow. Dolohov recovered, and Rostov became particularly friendly with him during his convalescence. Dolohov lay ill in the house of his mother, who was tenderly and passionately devoted to him. Marya Ivanovna, who had taken a fancy to Rostov, seeing his attachment to her Fedya, often talked to him about her son.

'Yes, count, he is too noble, too pure-hearted,' she would say, 'for the corrupt society of our day. Virtue is in favour with no one; it is apt to be a reproach to everybody. Come, tell me, count, was it right, was it honourable on Bezuhov's part? Fedya in his noble-hearted way loved him, and even now he never says a word against him. In Petersburg those pranks with the police constables, those practical jokes they played there, didn't they do everything together? And Bezuhov got nothing for it, while Fedya took all the blame on his shoulders. What he has had to go through! He has been reinstated, I know, but how could they help reinstating him? I don't suppose there were many such gallant, true sons of their fatherland out there! And now, what—this duel! Is there any feeling, any honour left in men? Knowing he was the only son, to call him out and aim so straight at him! We may be thankful God has been merciful to us. And what was it all for? Why, who hasn't intrigues nowadays? Why, if he were so jealous—I can understand it—he ought to have let it be seen long before, you know, and it had been going on for a year. And then to call him out, reckoning on Fedya's not fighting him because he was indebted to him. What baseness! What vileness! I know you understand Fedya, my dear count, and that's why I love you, believe me, from my heart. Few do understand him. His is such a lofty, heavenly nature!'

Dolohov himself, during his convalescence, often said to Rostov things which could never have been expected from him.

'People think me a wicked man, I know,' he would say; 'and they're welcome to think so. I don't care to know any one except those whom I love. But those I do love, I love in such a way that I would give my life for them, and all the rest I will crush if they get in my way. I have a precious and adored mother, and two or three friends, you among them; and as to the rest, I only pay attention to them in so far as they are useful or mischievous. And almost all are mischievous, especially the women. Yes, my dear,' he went on, 'men I have met who were loving, noble, and lofty-minded. But women that were not cattle for sale—countesses and cooks, they're all alike—I have not come across yet. I have not yet met the angelic purity and devotion which I look for in woman. If I could find such a woman, I would give my life for her! But these creatures! . . .' He made a gesture of contempt. 'But believe me, if I still care for life, I care for it because I still hope to meet such a heavenly creature, who would regenerate and purify and elevate me. But you don't understand that.'

'Yes, I quite understand,' answered Rostov, who was very much under the influence of his new friend.

In the autumn the Rostov family returned to Moscow. At the beginning of the winter Denisov too came back and stayed again with the Rostovs. The early part of the winter of 1806, spent by Nikolay Rostov in Moscow, was one of the happiest and liveliest periods for him and all the family. Nikolay brought a lot of young men about him into his parents' house. Vera was a handsome girl of twenty; Sonya, a girl of sixteen, with all the charm of an opening flower; Natasha, half grown up, half a child, at one time childishly absurd, and at another fascinating with the charm of a young girl.

The Rostovs' house was at that time full of a sort of peculiar atmosphere of love-making, as commonly happens in a household where there are very young and very charming girls. Among those young girls' faces, impressionable and always smiling (probably at their own happiness), in that whirl of eager bustle, amid that young feminine chatter, so inconsequent, but so friendly to every one, so ready for anything, so full of hope, and the inconsequent sound of singing and of music, any young man who came into the house felt the same sensation of readiness to fall in love and longing for happiness, that the younger members of the Rostov household were feeling themselves.

Among the young men Rostov brought to the house, one of the foremost was Dolohov, who was liked by every one in the house except Natasha. She almost had a quarrel with her brother over Dolohov. She persisted that he was a spiteful man; that in the duel with Bezuhov, Pierre had been in the right and Dolohov in the wrong, and that he was horrid and not natural.

'I know nothing about it, indeed,' Natasha would cry with self-willed obstinacy; 'he's spiteful and heartless. Your Denisov now, you see, I like; he's a rake, and all that, but still I like him, so I do understand. I don't know how to tell you; with him everything is done on a plan, and I don't like that. Denisov, now . . .'

'Oh, Denisov's another matter,' answered Nikolay, in a tone that implied that in comparison with Dolohov even Denisov was not of much account. 'One must understand what soul there is in that Dolohov; one must see him with his mother; such a noble heart!'

'I know nothing about that, but I don't feel at home with him. And do you know he's falling in love with Sonya?'

'What nonsense!'

'I am sure, you will see he is.'

Natasha's prediction was fulfilled. Dolohov, who did not as a rule care for ladies, began to come often to the house; and the question, for whose sake he came, was soon (though no one spoke of it) decided—it was on Sonya's account. And though Sonya would never have ventured to say so, she knew it, and blushed scarlet every time Dolohov made his appearance.

Dolohov often dined at the Rostovs', never missed a performance at which they were to be present, and attended Iogel's balls for the boys and girls,' at which the Rostovs were always to be found. He showed marked attention to Sonya, and looked at her with such an expression in his eyes that Sonya could not bear his eyes on her without turning crimson, and even the old countess and Natasha blushed when they saw that look.

It was evident that this strong, strange man could not shake off the impression made on him by the dark, graceful young girl, who was in love with another man.

Rostov noticed something new between Dolohov and Sonya, but he did not define to himself precisely what that new attitude was. 'They are all in love with some one,' he thought of Sonya and Natasha. But he did not feel quite at his ease as before with Sonya and Dolohov, and he began to be less often at home.

In the autumn of 1806 every one was beginning to talk again of war with Napoleon, and with even greater fervour than in the previous year. A levy was decreed, not only of ten recruits for active service, but of nine militiamen for the reserve as well, from every thousand of the population. Everywhere Bonaparte was anathematised, and the only thing talked of in Moscow was the impending war. To the Rostov family the interest of these preparations for war was entirely centred in the fact that Nikolushka refused to remain longer in Moscow, and was only waiting for the end of Denisov's leave to rejoin his regiment with him after the holidays. His approaching departure, far from hindering him from enjoying himself, gave an added zest to his pleasures. The greater part of his time he spent away from home, at dinners, parties, and balls.

XI

ON the third day after Christmas Nikolay dined at home, which he had rarely done of late. This was a farewell dinner in Nikolay's honour, as he was to set off with Denisov after the baptism festival to rejoin his regiment. Twenty persons were dining, among them Dolohov and Denisov.

Never had the love in the air of the Rostovs' house, never had the atmosphere of being in love, made itself so strongly felt as during those Christmas holidays. 'Seize the moment of happiness, love and be loved! That is the only thing real in the world; the rest is all nonsense. And that is the one thing we are interested in here,' was the sentiment that atmosphere was eloquent of.

After exhausting two pairs of horses, as he did every day without having been everywhere he ought to have been, and everywhere he had been invited, Nikolay reached home just at dinner-time. As soon as he went in he felt that intense atmosphere of love in the house, but in addition to that he became conscious of a strange embarrassment that seemed to prevail between certain persons in the company. Sonya seemed particularly disturbed, so did Dolohov and the old countess, and in a lesser degree Natasha. Nikolay saw that something must have passed before dinner between Sonya and Dolohov, and with the delicate instinct characteristic of him, he was very sympathetic and wary with both of them during dinner. On that evening there was to be one of the dances given by Iogel, the dancing-master, during the holidays to his pupils.

'Nikolenka, are you going to Iogel's? Please, do go,' said Natasha; 'he particularly begged you to, and Vassily Dmitritch' (this was Denisov) 'is going.'

'Where would I not go at the countess's commands!' said Denisov, who had jestingly taken up the *rôle* of Natasha's knight in the Rostov household. 'I am ready to dance the *pas de châle*.'

'If I have time! I promised the Arharovs; they have a party,' said Nikolay.

'And you? . . .' he turned to Dolohov. And as soon as he had asked the question, he saw that he should not have asked it.

'Yes, possibly . . .' Dolohov answered coldly and angrily, glancing at Sonya; and he glanced again, scowling at Nikolay with exactly the same look with which he had looked at Pierre at the club dinner.

'There's something wrong,' thought Nikolay; and he was still more confirmed in that surmise, when immediately after dinner Dolohov went away. He beckoned Natasha, and asked her what had happened.

'I was looking for you,' said Natasha, running out to him. 'I told you so, and still you wouldn't believe me,' she said triumphantly; 'he has made Sonya an offer.'

Little as Nikolay had been thinking of Sonya of late, he felt as if something were being torn from him when he heard this. Dolohov was a good, and in some respects a brilliant, match for the portionless orphan Sonya. From the point of view of the countess and of society it was out of the question for her to refuse him. And so Nikolay's first feeling when he heard of it was one of exasperation against Sonya. He braced himself up to say, 'And a capital thing, too; of course she must forget her childish promises and accept the offer'; but he had not succeeded in saying this when Natasha said:

'Only fancy! she has refused him, absolutely refused him! She says she loves some one else,' she added after a brief pause.

'Yes, my Sonya could not do otherwise!' thought Nikolay.

'Mamma begged her ever so many times not to, but she refused; and I know she won't change, if she has said a thing....'

'And mamma begged her not to!' Nikolay said reproachfully.

'Yes,' said Natasha. 'Do you know, Nikolenka—don't be angry—but I know you won't marry her. I know—I don't know why—but I know for certain that you won't marry her.'

'Well, you can't know that,' said Nikolay; 'but I want to talk to her. How charming Sonya is!' he added, smiling.

'Yes, she is so charming! I'll send her in to you.' And Natasha kissed her brother and ran way.

A minute later Sonya came in, looking frightened, distraught, and guilty. Nikolay went up to her and kissed her hand. It was the first time since his return that they had talked alone and of their love.

'Sophie,' he said to her, at first timidly, but more and more boldly as he went on, 'if you were simply refusing a brilliant, an advantageous match—but he's a splendid, noble fellow...he's my friend...'

Sonya interrupted him.

'I have refused him,' she said hastily.

'If you are refusing him for my sake, I am afraid that I...'

Sonya again cut him short. With frightened, imploring eyes she looked at him.

'Nikolenka, don't say that to me,' she said.

'No, I must. Perhaps it's *suffisance* on my part, but still it's better to say it. If you are refusing him on my account, I ought to tell you the whole truth. I love you, I believe, more than any one...'

'That's enough for me,' said Sonya, flushing crimson.

'No; but I have been in love a thousand times, and I shall fall in love again, though such a feeling of affection, confidence, and love I have for no one as for you. Then I am young. Mamma does not wish it. Well—in fact—I can make no promise. And I beg you to consider the offer of Dolohov,' he said, with an effort articulating the name of his friend.

'Don't speak to me of it. I want nothing. I love you as a brother, and shall always love you, and I want nothing more.'

'You are an angel; I'm not worthy of you, but I am only afraid of deceiving you.'

Nikolay kissed her hand once more.

XII

IOGEL'S were the most enjoyable balls in Moscow. So the mammas said as they looked at their boys and girls executing the steps they had only lately learnt. So too said the boys and girls themselves, who danced till they were ready to drop; so too said the grown-up girls and young men, who came to those dances in a spirit of condescension, and found in them the greatest enjoyment. That year two matches had been made at those dances. The two pretty young princesses Gortchakov had found suitors there, and had been married, and this had given the dances even greater vogue than before. What distinguished these dances from others was the absence of host and hostess, and the presence of the good-humoured Iogel, who had sold tickets for lessons to all his guests, and fluttered about like a feather, bowing and scraping in accordance with the rules of his art. Another point of difference, too, was that none came to these dances but those who really wanted to dance and enjoy themselves, in the way that girls of thirteen and fourteen do, putting on long dresses for the first time. All with rare exceptions were or looked pretty, so ecstatically they smiled and so rapturously their eyes sparkled. The *pas de châle* even was sometimes danced by the best pupils, among whom Natasha was the best of all, and conspicuous for her gracefulness. But at this last ball they only danced ecossaises, anglaises, and a mazurka that was just coming into fashion. A great hall had been taken by Iogel in the house of Bezuhov, and the ball, as every one said, was a great success. There were many pretty girls, and the Rostov girls were among the prettiest. They were both particularly happy and gay. That evening Sonya, elated by Dolohov's offer, her refusal, and her interview with Nikolay, had kept whirling round at home, not letting her maid have a chance of doing her hair, and now at the dance she was transparently radiant with impulsive happiness.

Natasha, no less elated at being for the first time at a real ball in a long skirt, was even happier. Both the girls wore white muslin dresses with pink ribbons.

Natasha fell in love the moment she walked into the ballroom. She was not in love with any one in particular, but in love with every one. Whomever she looked at, for the moment that she was looking at him, she was in love with.

'Oh, how nice it is!' she kept saying, running up to Sonya.

Nikolay and Denisov walked about the room, and looked with friendly patronage at the dancers.

'How sweet she is; she will be a beauty,' said Denisov.

'Who?'

'Countess Natasha,' answered Denisov.

'And how she dances; what grace!' he said again, after a short pause.

'Of whom are you speaking?'

'Why, of your sister,' cried Denisov angrily.

Rostov laughed.

'My dear count, you are one of my best pupils, you must dance,' said little Iogel, coming up to Nikolay. 'Look at all these pretty young ladies!' He turned with the same request to Denisov, who had also at one time been his pupil.

'No, my dear fellow, I will be a wallflower,' said Denisov. 'Don't you remember how little credit I did to your teaching?'

'Oh no!' said Iogel, hastening to reassure him. 'You were only inattentive, but you had talent, you had talent.'

They began to play the new mazurka. Nikolay could not refuse Iogel, and asked Sonya to dance. Denisov sat down by the elderly ladies, and leaning his elbow on his sword, and beating time with his foot, he began telling something amusing and making the old ladies laugh, while he watched the young ones dancing. Iogel was dancing in the first couple with Natasha, his best pupil and his pride. With soft and delicate movements of his little slippered feet, Iogel first flew across the room with Natasha—shy, but conscientiously executing her steps. Denisov did not take his eyes off her, and beat time with his sword with an air that betrayed, that if he were not dancing it was because he would not, and not because he could not, dance. In the middle of a figure he beckoned Rostov to him.

'That's not the right thing a bit,' he said. 'Is that the Polish Mazurka? But she does dance splendidly.'

Knowing that Denisov had been renowned even in Poland for his fine dancing of the Polish mazurka, Nikolay ran up to Natasha.

'Go and choose Denisov. He does dance. It's a marvel!' he said.

When it was Natasha's turn again, she got up, and tripping rapidly in her ribbon-trimmed dancing-shoes, she timidly ran alone across the room to the corner where Denisov was sitting. She saw that every one was looking at her, waiting to see what she would do. Nikolay saw that Denisov and Natasha were carrying on a smiling dispute, and that Denisov was refusing, though his face wore a delighted smile. He ran up.

'Please do, Vassily Dmitritch,' Natasha was saying; 'come, please.'

'Oh, have mercy on me, countess,' Denisov was saying jocosely.

'Come now, nonsense, Vasya,' said Nikolay.

'They coax me like the pussy-cat Vaska,' said Denisov good-humouredly.

'I'll sing to you a whole evening,' said Natasha.

'The little witch, she can do anything with me!' said Denisov; and he unhooked his sword. He came out from behind the chairs, clasped his partner firmly by the hand, raised his head and stood with one foot behind the other, waiting for the time. It was only on horseback and in the mazurka that Denisov's low stature was not noticeable, and that he looked the dashing hero he felt himself to be. At the right bar in the time he glanced sideways with a triumphant and amused air at his partner, and making an unexpected tap with one foot he bounded springily like a ball from the floor and flew round, whirling his partner round with him. He flew inaudibly across the hall with one leg forward, and seemed not to see the chairs standing before him, darting straight at them; but all at once with a clink of his spurs and a flourish of his foot he stopped short on his heels, stood so a second, with a clanking of spurs stamped with both feet, whirled rapidly round, and clapping the left foot against the right, again he flew round. Natasha's instinct told her what he was going to do, and without herself knowing how she did it, she followed his lead, abandoning herself to him. At one moment he spun her round, first on his right arm, then on his left arm, then falling on one knee, twirled her round him and again galloped, dashing forward with such vehemence that he seemed to intend to race through the whole suite of rooms without taking breath. Then he stopped suddenly again and executed new and unexpected steps in the dance. When after spinning his partner round before her seat he drew up smartly with a clink of his spurs, bowing to her, Natasha did not even make him a curtsey. She looked at him smiling with a puzzled face, as though she did not recognise him.

'What does it mean?' she said.

Although Iogel would not acknowledge this mazurka as the real one, every one was enchanged with Denisov's dancing of it, and he was continually being chosen as partner; while the old gentlemen, smiling, talked about Poland and the good old days. Denisov, flushed with his exertions and mopping his face with his handkerchief, sat by Natasha and would not leave her side all the rest of the ball.

XIII

For two days after the dance, Rostov had not seen Dolohov at his people's house nor found him at home; on the third day he received a note from him.

'As I do not intend to be at your house again owing to causes of which you are aware, and am going to rejoin the regiment, I am giving a farewell supper to my friends—come to the English Hotel.' On the day fixed Rostov went at about ten o'clock, from the theatre where he had been with his family and Denisov, to the English Hotel. He was at once conducted to the best room in the hotel, which Dolohov had taken for the occasion.

Some twenty men were gathered about a table before which Dolohov was sitting between two candles. On the table lay money and notes, and Dolohov was keeping the bank. Nikolay had not seen him again since his offer and Sonya's refusal, and he felt uneasy at the thought of meeting him.

Dolohov's clear, cold glance met Rostov in the doorway as though he had been expecting him a long while.

'It's a long while since we've met,' said he; 'thanks for coming. I'll just finish dealing here, and Ilyushka will make his appearance with his chorus.'

'I did go to see you,' said Rostov, flushing.

Dolohov made him no reply.

'You might put down a stake,' he said.

Rostov recalled at that instant a strange conversation he once had with Dolohov. 'None but fools trust to luck in play,' Dolohov had said then. 'Or are you afraid to play with me?' Dolohov said now, as though divining Rostov's thought; and he smiled. Behind his smile Rostov saw in him that mood which he had seen in him at the club dinner and at other times, when Dolohov seemed, as it were, weary of the monotony of daily life, and felt a craving to escape from it by some strange, for the most part cruel, act.

Rostov felt ill at ease; he racked his brain and could not find in it a joke in which to reply to Dolohov's words. But before he had time to do so, Dolohov, looking straight into Rostov's face, said to him slowly and deliberately so that all could hear: 'Do you remember, I was talking to you about play . . . he's a fool who trusts to luck in play; one must play a sure game, and I want to try.'

'Try his luck, or try to play a sure game?' wondered Rostov.

'Indeed, and you'd better not play,' he added; and throwing down a pack he had just torn open, he said: 'Bank, gentlemen!'

Moving the money forward, Dolohov began dealing.

Rostov sat near him, and at first he did not play. Dolohov glanced at him.

'Why don't you play?' said Dolohov. And, strange to say, Nikolay felt that he could not help taking up a card, staking a trifling sum on it, and beginning to play.

'I have no money with me,' said Rostov.

'I'll trust you!'

Rostov staked five roubles on a card and lost it, staked again and again lost. Dolohov 'killed,' that is, beat ten cards in succession from Rostov.

'Gentlemen,' he said, after dealing again for a little while, 'I beg you to put the money on the cards or else I shall get muddled over the reckoning.'

One of the players said that he hoped he could trust him.

'I can trust you, but I'm afraid of making mistakes; I beg you to lay the money on the cards,' answered Dolohov. 'You needn't worry, we'll settle our accounts,' he added to Rostov.

The play went on; a footman never ceased carrying round champagne.

All Rostov's cards were beaten, and the sum of eight hundred roubles was scored against him. He wrote on a card eight hundred roubles, but while champagne was being poured out for him, he changed his mind and again wrote down the usual stake, twenty roubles.

'Leave it,' said Dolohov, though he did not seem to be looking at Rostov; 'you'll win it back all the sooner. I lose to the rest, while I win from you. Or perhaps you are afraid of me,' he repeated.

Rostov excused himself, left the stake of eight hundred and laid down the seven of hearts, a card with a corner torn, which he had picked up from the ground. Well he remembered that card afterwards. He laid down the seven of hearts, wrote on it with a broken piece of chalk 800 in bold round figures; he drank the glass of warmed champagne that had been given him, smiled at Dolohov's words, and with a sinking at his heart, waiting for the seven of hearts, he watched Dolohov's hands that held the pack. The loss or gain of that card meant a great deal for Rostov. On the previous Sunday Count Ilya Andreitch had given his son two thousand roubles, and though he never liked speaking of money difficulties, he told him that this money was the last they would get till May, and so he begged him to be a little more careful. Nikolay said that that was too much really for him, and that he would give him his word of honour not to come for more before May. Now there was only twelve hundred out of that two thousand left. So that on the seven of hearts there hung not merely the loss of sixteen hundred roubles, but the consequent inevitable betrayal of his word. With a sinking heart he watched Dolohov's hands, and thought: 'Well, make haste and deal me that card, and I'll take my cap and drive home to supper with Denisov, Natasha, and Sonya, and I'm sure I'll never take a card in my hand again.' At that moment his home life, his jokes with Petya, his talks with Sonya, his duets with Natasha, his game of picquet with his father, even his comfortable bed in the house in Povarsky, rose before his imagination with such vividness, such brightness, and such charm, that it seemed as though it were all some long past, lost, and hitherto unappreciated happiness. He could not conceive that a stupid chance, leading the seven to the right rather than to the left, could deprive him of all that happiness felt now with new comprehension and seen in a new radiance, could hurl him into the abyss of unknown and undefined misery. It could not be; but yet it was with a thrill of dread that he waited for the movement of Dolohov's hands. Those broad-boned, reddish hands, with hairs visible under the shirt-cuffs, laid down the pack of cards and took up the glass and pipe that had been handed him.

'So you're not afraid to play with me?' repeated Dolohov; and as though he were about to tell a good story, he laid down the cards, leaned back in his chair, and began deliberately with a smile:

'Yes, gentlemen, I have been told there's a story going about Moscow that I'm too sharp with cards, so I advise you to be a little on your guard with me.'

'Come, deal away!' said Rostov.

'Ugh, these Moscow gossips!' said Dolohov, and he took up the cards with a smile.

'Aaah!' Rostov almost screamed, putting both his hands up to his hair. The seven he needed was lying uppermost, the first card in the pack. He had lost more than he could pay.

'Don't swim beyond your depth, though,' said Dolohov, with a passing glance at Rostov, and he went on.

XIV

WITHIN an hour and a half the greater number of the players were no longer seriously interested in their own play.

The whole interest of the game was concentrated on Rostov. Instead of a mere loss of sixteen hundred roubles he had by now scored against him a long column of figures, which he had added up to the tenth thousand, though he vaguely supposed that by now it had risen to fifteen thousand. In reality the score already exceeded twenty thousand roubles. Dolohov was not now listening to stories, or telling them, he followed every movement of Rostov's hands, and from time to time took a cursory survey of his score with him. He had resolved to keep the play up till that score had reached forty-three thousand. He had fixed on that number because it represented the sum of his and Sonya's ages. Rostov sat with his head propped in both hands, before the wine-stained table scrawled over with scorings and littered with cards. One torturing sensation never left him; those broad-boned, reddish hands, with the hairs visible under the shirt-cuffs, those hands which he loved and hated, held him in their power.

'Six hundred roubles, ace, corner, nine; winning it back's out of the question! . . . And how happy I should be at home. . . . The knave, double or quits, it can't be! . . . And why is he doing this to me? . . .' Rostov pondered and thought. Sometimes he put a higher stake on a card; but Dolohov refused it and fixed the stake himself. Nikolay submitted to him, and at one moment he was praying to God, as he had prayed under fire on the bridge of Amschteten; at the next he tried his fortune on the chance that the card that he would first pick up among the heap of crumpled ones under the table would save him; then he reckoned up the rows of braidings on his coat, and tried staking the whole amount of his losses on a card of that number, then he looked round for help to the others playing, or stared into Dolohov's face, which looked quite cold now, and tried to penetrate into what was passing within him.

'He knows, of course, what this loss means to me. Surely he can't want me to be ruined? Why, he was my friend. I loved him. . . . But, indeed, it's not his fault; what's he to do, if he has all the luck? And it's not my fault,' he kept saying to himself. 'I have done nothing wrong. I haven't murdered or hurt any one, or wished any one harm, have I? What is this awful calamity for? And when did it begin? Such a little while ago I came to this table with the idea of winning a hundred roubles, and buying mamma that little casket for her name-day, and going home. I was so happy, so free, so light-hearted. And I didn't even know then how happy I was. When did all that end, and when did this new awful state of things begin? What was the outward token of that change? I still went on sitting in the same place at this table, and in the same way picking out cards and putting them forward, and watching those deft, broad-boned hands. When did it come to pass, and what has come to pass? I am strong and well, and still the same, and still in the same place. No; it cannot be. It will all be sure to end in nothing.'

He was all red and in a sweat, though the room was not hot. And his face was painful and piteous to see, particularly from its helpless efforts to seem calm.

The score reached the fateful number of forty-three thousand roubles. Rostov already had the card ready which he meant to stake for double or quits on the three thousand, that had just been put down to his score, when Dolohov slapped the pack of cards down on the table, pushed it away, and taking the chalk began rapidly in his clear, strong hand, writing down the total of Rostov's losses, breaking the chalk as he did so.

'Supper, supper-time. And here are the gypsies.' And some swarthy men and women did in fact come in from the cold outside, saying something with their gypsy accent. Nikolay grasped that it was all over; but he said in an indifferent voice:

'What, won't you go on? And I have such a nice little card all ready.' As though what chiefly interested him was the game itself.

'It's all over, I'm done for,' he thought. 'Now a bullet through the head's the only thing left for me,' and at the same time he was saying in a cheerful voice:

'Come, just one more card.'

'Very good,' answered Dolohov, finishing his addition. 'Very good. Twenty-one roubles . . . done,' he said, pointing to the figure 21, over and above the round sum of forty-three thousands, and taking a pack, he made ready to deal, Rostov submissively turned down the corner, and instead of the 8000 he had meant to write, noted down 21.

'It's all the same to me,' he said; 'only it's interesting to me to know whether you will win on that ten or let me have it.'

Dolohov began seriously dealing. Oh, how Rostov hated at that moment those reddish hands, with their short fingers and the hairs visible under the shirt sleeves, those hands that held him in their clutches. . . . The ten was not beaten. Forty-three thousand to your score, count,' said Dolohov, and he got up from the table stretching. 'One does get tired sitting so long,' he said.

'Yes, I'm tired too,' said Rostov.

Dolohov cut him short, as though to warn him it was not for him to take a light tone.

'When am I to receive the money, count?'

Rostov flushing hotly drew Dolohov away into the other room.

'I can't pay it all at once, you must take an I.O.U.,' said he.

'Listen, Rostov,' said Dolohov, smiling brightly, and looking straight into Nikolay's eyes, 'you know the saying: "Lucky in love, unlucky at cards." Your cousin is in love with you. I know it.'

'Oh! this is awful to feel oneself in this man's power like this,' thought Rostov. He knew the shock the news of this loss would be to his father and mother; he knew what happiness it would be to be free of it all, and felt that Dolohov knew that he could set him free from this shame and grief, and wanted now to play cat and mouse with him.

'Your cousin . . .' Dolohov would have said, but Nikolay cut him short.

'My cousin has nothing to do with the matter, and there is no need to mention her!' he cried, with fury.

'Then, when am I to receive it?' asked Dolohov.

'Tomorrow,' said Rostov, and went out of the room.

XV

To say 'tomorrow,' and maintain the right tone was not difficult; but to arrive home alone, to see his sisters and brother, his mother and father, to confess and beg for money to which he had no right after giving his word of honour, was terrible.

At home they had not yet gone to bed. The younger members of the family after coming home from the theatre had had supper, and were now in a group about the clavichord. As soon as Nikolay entered the hall, he felt himself enfolded in the poetic atmosphere of love which dominated their household that winter; and now, since Dolohov's proposal and Iogel's ball seemed to have grown thicker about Sonya and Natasha, like the air before a storm. Sonya and Natasha, wearing the light blue dresses they had put on for the theatre, stood at the clavichord, pretty, and conscious of being so, happy and smiling. Vera was playing draughts with Shinshin in the drawing-room. The old countess, waiting for her son and her husband to come in, was playing patience with an old gentlewoman, who was one of their household. Denisov, with shining eyes and ruffled hair, was sitting with one leg behind him at the clavichord. He was striking chords with his short fingers, and rolling his eyes, as he sang in his small, husky, but true voice a poem of his own composition, 'The Enchantress,' to which he was trying to fit music.

> 'Enchantress, say what hidden fire
> Draws me to my forsaken lyre?
> What rapture thrills my fingers slow,
> What passion sets my heart aglow?'

he sang in his passionate voice, his black, agate eyes gleaming at the frightened and delighted Natasha.

'Splendid, capital!' Natasha cried. 'Another couplet,' she said, not noticing Nikolay.

'Everything's just the same with them,' thought Nikolay, peeping into the drawing-room, where he saw Vera and his mother and the old lady playing patience with her.

'Ah, and here's Nikolenka.' Natasha ran up to him. 'Is papa at home?' he asked.

'How glad I am that you have come,' said Natasha, not answering his question, 'we are having such fun. Vassily Dmitritch is staying a day longer for me, do you know?'

'No, papa has not come in yet,' answered Sonya.

'Kolya, you there? Come to me, darling,' said the voice of the countess from the drawing-room. Nikolay went up to his mother, kissed her hand, and sitting down by her table, began silently watching her hands as they dealt the cards. From the hall he kept hearing the sound of laughter and merry voices, persuading Natasha to do something.

'Oh, very well, very well!' Denisov cried; 'now it's no use crying off, it's your turn to sing the barcarolle, I entreat you.'

The countess looked round at her silent son.

'What's the matter?' his mother asked Nikolay.

'Oh, nothing,' he said, as though sick of being continually asked the same question: 'Will papa soon be in?'

'I expect so.'

'Everything's the same with them. They know nothing about it. What am I to do with myself?' thought Nikolay, and he went back to the hall, where the clavichord was.

Sonya was sitting at the clavichord, playing the prelude of the barcarolle that Denisov particularly liked. Natasha was preparing to sing. Denisov was watching her with impassioned eyes.

Nikolay began walking to and fro in the room.

'What can induce her to want to sing. What can she sing? And there's nothing to be so happy about in it,' thought Nikolay.

Sonya struck the first chord of the prelude. 'My God, I'm ruined, I'm a dishonoured man. Bullet through my head, that's the only thing left for me, and not singing,' he thought. 'Go away? But where? It makes no difference, let them sing.'

Still walking about the room, Nikolay glanced gloomily at Denisov and the girls, avoiding their eyes.

'Nikolenka, what's the matter?' Sonya's eyes asked, looking intently at him. She saw at once that something had happened to him.

Nikolay turned away from her. Natasha, too, with her quick instinct instantly detected her brother's state of mind. She noticed him, but she was herself in such high spirits at that moment, she was so far from sorrow, from sadness, from reproaches, that purposely she deceived herself (as young people so often do). 'No, I'm too happy just now to spoil my enjoyment by sympathy with any one's sorrow,' she felt, and she said to herself: 'No, I'm most likely mistaken, he must be happy, just as I am.'

'Come, Sonya,' she said, walking into the very middle of the room, where to her mind the resonance was best of all. Holding her head up, letting her arms hang lifelessly as dancers do, Natasha, with a vigorous turn from her heel on to her toe, walked over to the middle of the room and stood still.

'Behold me, here I am!' she seemed to say, in response to the enthusiastic gaze with which Denisov followed her. 'And what can she find to be so pleased at!' Nikolay wondered, looking at his sister. 'How is it she isn't feeling dull and ashamed!' Natasha took the first note, her throat swelled, her bosom heaved, a serious expression came into her face. She was thinking of no one and of nothing at that moment, and from her smiling mouth poured forth notes, those notes that any one can produce at the same intervals, and hold for the same length of time, yet a thousand times they leave us cold, and the thousand and first time they set us thrilling and weeping.

Natasha had for the first time begun that winter to take singing seriously, especially since Denisov had been so enthusiastic over her singing. She did not now sing like a child; there was not now in her singing that comical childish effort which used to be perceptible in it. But she did not yet sing well, said the musical connoisseurs who heard her. 'Not trained; a fine voice, it must be trained,' every one said. But this was usually said a good while after her voice was hushed. While that untrained voice, with its irregular breathing and its strained transitions sounded, even connoisseurs said nothing, and simply enjoyed that untrained voice, and simply longed to hear it again. Her voice had a virginal purity, an ignorance of its capacities, and an unlaboured velvety softness, so closely connected with its lack of art in singing, that it seemed as though nothing could be changed in that voice without spoiling it.

'How is it?' thought Nikolay, hearing her voice and opening his eyes wide; 'what has happened to her? How she is singing today!' he thought. And all at once the whole world was for him concentrated into anticipations of the next note, the next bar, and everything in the world seemed divided up into three motives: '*Oh, mio crudele affetto* ... One, two, three . . . one . . . *Oh, mio crudele affetto* . . . One, two, three . . . one. Ugh, this senseless life of ours!' thought Nikolay. 'All that, this calamity, and money, and Dolohov, and anger, and honour—it's all nonsense . . . and this is what's the real thing . . . Now, Natasha! now, darling! now, my girl! . . how will she take that *si*? taken it! thank God!' and without being conscious that he was singing, he himself sung a second to support her high note. 'My God! how fine! Can I have taken that note? how glorious!' he thought.

Oh, how that note had thrilled, and how something better that was in Rostov's soul began thrilling too. And that something was apart from everything in the world, and above everything in the world. What were losses, and Dolohovs, and honour beside it! . . . All nonsense! One might murder, and steal, and yet be happy. . . .

XVI

I T was long since Rostov had derived such enjoyment from music as on that day. But as soon as Natasha had finished her barcarolle, the reality forced itself upon his mind again. Saying nothing, he went out, and went down stairs to his own room. A quarter of an hour later, the old prince came in, good-humoured and satisfied from his club. Nikolay heard him come in, and went in to him.

'Well, had a good time?' said Ilya Andreivitch, smiling proudly and joyfully to his son. Nikolay tried to say 'Yes,' but could not; he was on the point of sobbing. The count was lighting his pipe, and did not notice his son's condition.

'Ugh, it's inevitable!' thought Nikolay, for the first and last time. And all at once, as though he were asking for the carriage to drive into town, he said to his father in the most casual tone, that made him feel vile to himself:

'Papa, I have come to you on a matter of business I was almost forgetting. I want some money.'

'You don't say so?' said his father, who happened to be in particularly good spirits. 'I told you that we shouldn't be having any. Do you want a large sum?'

'Very large,' said Nikolay, flushing and smiling a stupid, careless smile, for which long after he could not forgive himself. 'I have lost a little at cards, that is, a good deal, really, a great deal, forty-three thousand.'

'What! To whom? . . . You're joking!' cried the count, flushing, as old people flush, an apoplectic red over his neck and the back of his head.

'I have promised to pay it tomorrow,' said Nikolay.

'Oh!' . . . said the count, flinging up his arms; and he dropped helplessly on the sofa.

'It can't be helped! It happens to every one,' said his son in a free and easy tone, while in his heart he was feeling himself a low scoundrel, whose whole life could not atone for his crime. He would have liked to kiss his father's hands, to beg his forgiveness on his knees, while carelessly, rudely even, he was telling him that it happened to every one.

Count Ilya Andreivitch dropped his eyes when he heard those words from his son, and began moving hurriedly, as though looking for something.

'Yes, yes,' he brought out, 'it will be difficult, I fear, difficult to raise . . . happens to every one! yes, it happens to every one . . .' And the count cast a fleeting glance at his son's face and walked out of the room. . . . Nikolay had been prepared to face resistance, but he had not expected this.

'Papa! pa . . . pa!' he cried after him, sobbing; 'forgive me!' And clutching at his father's hand, he pressed it to his lips and burst into tears.

While the father and son were having this interview, another, hardly less important, was taking place between the mother and daughter. Natasha, in great excitement, had run in to her mother.

'Mamma! . . . Mamma! . . . he has made me . . .'

'Made you what?'

'He's made, made an offer. Mamma! Mamma!' she kept crying.

The countess could not believe her ears. Denisov had made an offer . . . to whom? . . . To this chit of a girl Natasha, who had only just given up playing with dolls, and was still having lessons.

'Natasha, enough of this silliness!' she said, hoping it was a joke.

'Silliness indeed! I am telling you the fact,' said Natasha angrily. 'I have come to ask you what to do, and you talk to me of "silliness" . . .'

The countess shrugged her shoulders.

'If it is true that Monsieur Denisov has made you an offer, then tell him he is a fool, that's all.'

'No, he's not a fool,' said Natasha, resentfully and seriously.

'Well, what would you have then? You are all in love, it seems, nowadays. Oh, well if you're in love with him, better marry him,' said the countess, laughing angrily, 'and God bless you.'

'No, mamma, I'm not in love with him. I suppose I'm not in love with him.'

'Well, then, tell him so.'

'Mamma, are you cross? Don't be cross, darling; it's not my fault, is it?'

'No, but upon my word, my dear, if you like, I will go and tell him so,' said the countess, smiling.

'No, I'll do it myself; only tell me how to say it. Everything comes easy to you,' she added, responding to her smile. 'And if you could have seen how he said it to me! I know he did not mean to say it, but said it by accident.'

'Well, any way you must refuse him.'

'No, I mustn't. I feel so sorry for him! He's so nice.'

'Oh, well, accept his proposal, then. High time you were married, I suppose,' said her mother angrily and ironically.

'No, mamma, but I'm so sorry for him. I don't know how to say it.'

'Well, there's no need for you to say anything. I'll speak to him myself,' said the countess, indignant that any one should have dared to treat this little Natasha as grown up.

'No, not on any account; I'll go myself, and you listen at the door,'— and Natasha ran across the drawing-room to the hall, where Denisov, his face in his hands, was still sitting in the same chair at the clavichord. He jumped up at the sound of her light footsteps.

'Natalie,' he said, moving with rapid steps towards her, 'decide my fate. It is in your hands!'

'Vassily Dmitritch, I'm so sorry for you! . . . No, but you are so nice . . . but it won't do . . . that . . . but I shall always love you as I do now.'

Denisov bent over her, and she heard strange sounds that she did not understand. She kissed his tangled curly black head. At that moment they heard the hurried rustle of the countess's skirts. She came up to them.

'Vassily Dmitritch, I thank you for the honour you do us,' said the countess, in an embarrassed voice, which sounded severe to Denisov, 'but my daughter is so young, and I should have thought that as my son's friend you would have come first to me. In that case you would not have forced me to make this refusal.'

'Countess! . . .' said Denisov, with downcast eyes and a guilty face; he tried to say more, and stammered.

Natasha could not see him in such a piteous plight without emotion. She began to whimper loudly.

'Countess, I have acted wrongly,' Denisov went on in a breaking voice, 'but believe me, I so adore your daughter and all your family that I'd give my life twice over . . .' He looked at the countess and noticed her stern face. . . . 'Well, good-bye, countess,' he said, kissing her hand, and without glancing at Natasha he walked with rapid and resolute steps out of the room.

Next day Rostov saw Denisov off, as he was unwilling to remain another day in Moscow. All his Moscow friends gave him a farewell entertainment at the Gypsies', and he had no recollection of how they got him into his sledge, or of the first three stations he passed.

After Denisov's departure Rostov spent another fortnight in Moscow, waiting for the money to pay his debt, which the count was unable to raise all at once. He hardly left the house, and spent most of his time in the young girls' room.

Sonya was more affectionate and devoted to him than ever. She seemed to want to show him that his loss at cards was an exploit for which she loved him more than ever. But now Nikolay regarded himself as unworthy of her.

He copied music for the girls, and wrote verses in their albums, and after at last sending off all the forty-three thousand roubles, and receiving Dolohov's receipt for it, he left Moscow towards the end of November without taking leave of any of his acquaintances, and overtook his regiment, which was already in Poland.

PART V

I

AFTER HIS interview with his wife, Pierre had set off for Petersburg. At the station of Torzhok there were no horses, or the overseer was unwilling to let him have them. Pierre had to wait. Without removing his outdoor things, he lay down on a leather sofa, in front of a round table, put up his big feet in their thick overboots on this table and sank into thought.

'Shall I bring in the trunks? Make up a bed? Will you take tea?' the valet kept asking.

Pierre made no reply, for he heard nothing and said nothing. He had been deep in thought since he left the last station, and still went on thinking of the same thing—of something so important that he did not notice what was passing around him. Far from being concerned whether he reached Petersburg sooner or later, or whether there would or would not be a place for him to rest in at this station, in comparison with the thoughts that engrossed him now, it was a matter of utter indifference to him whether he spent a few hours or the rest of his life at that station.

The overseer and his wife, his valet, and a peasant woman with Torzhok embroidery for sale, came into the room, offering their services. Without changing the position of his raised feet, Pierre gazed at them over his spectacles, and did not understand what they could want and how they all managed to live, without having solved the questions that absorbed him. These same questions had possessed his mind ever since that day when he had come back after the duel from Sokolniky and had spent that first agonising, sleepless night. But now in the solitude of his journey they seized upon him with special force. Of whatever he began thinking he came back to the same questions, which he could not answer, and from which he could not escape. It was as though the chief screw in his brain upon which his whole life rested were loose. The screw moved no forwarder, no backwarder, but still it turned, catching on nothing, always in the same groove, and there was no making it cease turning.

The overseer came in and began humbly begging his excellency to wait only a couple of hours, after which he would (come what might of it) let his excellency have the special mail service horses. The overseer was unmistakably lying, with the sole aim of getting an extra tip from the traveller. 'Was that good or bad?' Pierre wondered. 'For me good, for the next traveller bad, and for himself inevitable because he has nothing to eat; he said that an officer had thrashed him for it. And the officer thrashed him because he had to travel in haste. And I shot Dolohov because I considered myself injured. Louis XVI. was executed because they considered him to be a criminal, and a year later his judges were killed too for something. What is wrong? What is right? What must one love, what must one hate? What is life for, and what am I? What is life? What is death? What force controls it all?' he asked himself. And there was no answer to one of these questions, except one illogical reply that was in no way an answer to any of them. That reply was: 'One dies and it's all over. One dies and finds it all out or ceases asking.' But dying too was terrible.

The Torzhok pedlar woman in a whining voice proffered her wares, especially some goatskin slippers. 'I have hundreds of roubles I don't know what to do with, and she's standing in her torn cloak looking timidly at me,' thought Pierre. 'And what does she want the money for? As though that money could give her one hairsbreadth of happiness, of peace of soul. Is there anything in the world that can make her and me less enslaved to evil and to death? Death, which ends all, and must come today or tomorrow—which beside eternity is the same as in an instant's time.' And again he turned the screw that did not bite in anything, and the screw still went on turning in the same place.

His servant handed him a half-cut volume of a novel in the form of letters by Madame Suza. He began reading of the sufferings and the virtuous struggles of a certain 'Amélie de Mansfeld.' 'And what did she struggle against her seducer for?' he thought, when she loved him. God could not have put in her heart an impulse that was against His will. My wife—as she was once—didn't struggle, and perhaps she was right. Nothing has been discovered,' Pierre said to himself again, 'nothing has been invented. We can only know that we know nothing. And that's the highest degree of human wisdom.'

Everything within himself and around him struck him as confused, meaningless, and loathsome. But in this very loathing of everything surrounding him Pierre found a sort of tantalising satisfaction.

'I make bold to beg your excellency to make room the least bit for this gentleman here,' said the overseer, coming into the room and ushering in after him another traveller, brought to a standstill from lack of horses. The traveller was a thickset, square-shouldered, yellow, wrinkled old man, with grey eyelashes overhanging gleaming eyes of an indefinite grey colour.

Pierre took his feet off the table, stood up and went to lie down on the bed that had been made ready for him, glancing now and then at the newcomer, who, without looking at Pierre, with an air of surly fatigue was wearily taking off his outer wraps with the aid of his servant. The traveller, now clothed in a shabby nankin-covered sheepskin coat with felt highboots on his thin bony legs, sat down on the sofa, and leaning on its back with his close-cropped head, which was very large and broad across the temples, he glanced at Bezuhov. The stern, shrewd, and penetrating expression in that glance impressed Pierre. He felt disposed to speak to the traveller, but by the time he had ready a question about the road with which to address him, the traveller had closed his eyes, and folded his wrinkled old hands, on one finger of which there was a large iron ring with a seal representing the head of Adam. He sat without stirring, either resting or sunk, as it seemed to Pierre, in profound and calm meditation. The newcomer's servant was also a yellow old man, covered with wrinkles. He had neither moustache nor beard, not because he was shaved, but obviously had never had any. The old servant was active in unpacking a travelling-case, in setting the tea-table, and in bringing in a boiling samovar. When everything was ready, the traveller opened his eyes, moved to the table, and pouring out a glass of tea for himself, poured out another for the beardless old man and gave it him. Pierre began to feel an uneasiness and a sense of necessity, of the inevitability of entering into conversation with the traveller.

The servant brought back his empty glass turned upside down with an unfinished piece of nibbled sugar beside it, and asked if anything were wanted.

'Nothing. Give me my book,' said the traveller. The servant gave him a book, which seemed to Pierre to be of a devotional character, and the traveller became absorbed in its perusal. Pierre looked at him. All at once the stranger laid down the book, and putting a mark in it, shut it up. Then closing his eyes and leaning his arms on the back of the sofa, he fell back into his former attitude. Pierre stared at him, and had not time to look away when the old man opened his eyes and bent his resolute and stern glance upon Pierre. Pierre felt confused and tried to turn away from that glance, but the gleaming old eyes drew him irresistibly to them.

II

'I HAVE the pleasure of speaking to Count Bezuhov, if I am not mistaken,' said the stranger, in a loud deliberate voice. Pierre looked in silence and inquiringly over his spectacles at the speaker. 'I have heard of you,' continued the stranger, 'and I have heard, sir, of what has happened to you, of your misfortune.' He underlined, as it were, the last word, as though to say: 'Yes, misfortune, whatever you call it, I know that what happened to you in Moscow was a misfortune.'

'I am very sorry for it, sir.' Pierre reddened, and hurriedly dropping his legs over the edge of the bed, he bent forward towards the old man, smiling timidly and unnaturally.

'I have not mentioned this to you, sir, from curiosity, but from graver reasons.' He paused, not letting Pierre escape from his gaze, and moved aside on the sofa, inviting him by this movement to sit beside him. Pierre disliked entering into conversation with this old man, but involuntarily submitting to him, he came up and sat down beside him.

'You are unhappy, sir,' he went on, 'you are young, and I am old. I should like, as far as it is in my power, to help you.'

'Oh, yes,' said Pierre, with an unnatural smile. 'Very much obliged to you . . . where have you been travelling from?' The stranger's face was not cordial, it was even cold and severe, but in spite of that, both the speech and the face of his new acquaintance were irresistibly attractive to Pierre.

'But if for any reason you dislike conversing with me,' said the old man, 'then you say so, sir.' And suddenly he smiled a quite unexpected smile of fatherly kindliness.

'Oh, no, not at all; on the contrary, I am very glad to make your acquaintance,' said Pierre, and glancing once more at the stranger's hands, he examined the ring more closely. He saw the head of Adam, the token of masonry.

'Allow me to inquire,' he said, 'are you a mason?'

'Yes, I belong to the brotherhood of the freemasons,' said the stranger, looking now more searchingly into Pierre's eyes. 'And from myself and in their name I hold out to you a brotherly hand.'

'I am afraid,' said Pierre, smiling and hesitating between the confidence inspired in him by the personality of the freemason and the habit of ridiculing the articles of the masons' creed; 'I am afraid that I am very far from a comprehension—how shall I say—I am afraid that my way of thinking in regard to the whole theory of the universe is so opposed to yours that we shall not understand one another.'

'I am aware of your way of thinking,' said the freemason, 'and that way of thinking of which you speak, which seems to you the result of your own thought, is the way of thinking of the majority of men, and is the invariable fruit of pride, indolence, and ignorance. Excuse my saying, sir, that if I had not been aware of it, I should not have addressed you. Your way of thinking is a melancholy error.'

'Just as I may take for granted that you are in error,' said Pierre, faintly smiling.

'I would never be so bold as to say I know the truth,' said the mason, the definiteness and decision of whose manner of speaking impressed Pierre more and more. 'No one alone can attain truth; only stone upon stone, with the co-operation of all, by the millions of generations from our first father Adam down to our day is that temple being reared that should be a fitting dwelling-place of the Great God,' said the freemason, and he shut his eyes.

'I ought to tell you that I don't believe, don't . . . believe in God,' said Pierre regretfully and with effort, feeling it essential to speak the whole truth.

The freemason looked intently at Pierre and smiled as a rich man, holding millions in his hands, might smile to a poor wretch, who should say to him that he, the poor man, has not five roubles that would secure him happiness.

'Yes, you do not know Him, sir,' said the freemason. 'You cannot know Him. You know not Him, that is why you are unhappy.'

'Yes, yes, I am unhappy,' Pierre assented; 'but what am I to do?'

'You know not Him, sir, and that's why you are very unhappy. You know not Him, but He is here, He is within me, He is in my words, He is in thee, and even in these scoffing words that thou hast just uttered,' said the mason in a stern, vibrating voice.

He paused and sighed, evidently trying to be calm.

'If He were not,' he said softly, 'we should not be speaking of Him, sir. Of what, of whom were we speaking? Whom dost thou deny?' he said all at once, with enthusiastic austerity and authority in his voice. 'Who invented Him, if He be not? How came there within thee the conception that there is such an incomprehensible Being? How comes it that thou and all the world have assumed the existence of such an inconceivable Being, a Being all powerful, eternal and infinite in all His qualities? . . .' He stopped and made a long pause.

Pierre could not and would not interrupt this silence.

'He exists, but to comprehend Him is hard,' the mason began again, not looking into Pierre's face, but straight before him, while his old hands, which could not keep still for inward emotion, turned the leaves of the book. 'If it had been a man of whose existence thou hadst doubts, I could have brought thee the man, taken him by the hand, and shown him thee. But how am I, an insignificant mortal, to show all the power, all the eternity, all the blessedness of Him to one who is blind, or to one who shuts his eyes that he may not see, may not understand Him, and may not see, and not understand all his own vileness and viciousness.'

He paused. 'Who art thou? What art thou? Thou dreamest that thou art wise because thou couldst utter those scoffing words,' he said, with a gloomy and scornful irony, 'while thou art more foolish and artless than a little babe, who, playing with the parts of a cunningly fashioned watch, should rashly say that because he understands not the use of that watch, he does not believe in the maker who fashioned it. To know Him is a hard matter. For ages, from our first father Adam to our day, have we been striving for this knowledge, and are infinitely far from the attainment of our aim; but in our lack of understanding we see only our own weakness and His greatness . . .'

Pierre gazed with shining eyes into the freemason's face, listening with a thrill at his heart to his words; he did not interrupt him, nor ask questions, but with all his soul he believed what this strange man was telling him. Whether he believed on the rational grounds put before him by the freemason, or believed, as children do, through the intonations, the conviction, and the earnestness, of the mason's words, the quiver in his voice that sometimes almost broke his utterance, or the gleaming old eyes that had grown old in that conviction, or the calm, the resolution, and the certainty of his destination, which were conspicuous in the whole personality of the old man, and struck Pierre with particular force, beside his own abjectness and hopelessness,—any way, with his whole soul he longed to believe, and believed and felt a joyful sense of soothing, of renewal, and of return to life.

'It is not attained by the reason, but by life,' said the mason.

'I don't understand,' said Pierre, feeling with dismay that doubt was stirring within him. He dreaded obscurity and feebleness in the freemason's arguments, he dreaded being unable to believe in him. 'I don't understand,' he said, 'in what way human reason cannot attain that knowledge of which you speak.'

The freemason smiled his mild, fatherly smile.

'The highest wisdom and truth is like the purest dew, which we try to hold within us,' said he. 'Can I hold in an impure vessel that pure dew and judge of its purity? Only by the inner purification of myself can I bring that dew contained within me to some degree of purity.'

'Yes, yes; that's so,' Pierre said joyfully.

'The highest wisdom is founded not on reason only, not on those worldly sciences, of physics, history, chemistry, etc., into which knowledge of the intellect is divided. The highest wisdom is one. The highest wisdom knows but one science—the science of the whole, the science that explains the whole creation and the place of man in it. To instil this science into one's soul, it is needful to purify and renew one's inner man, and so, before one can know, one must believe and be made perfect. And for the attainment of these aims there has been put into our souls the light of God, called the conscience.'

'Yes, yes,' Pierre assented.

'Look with the spiritual eye into thy inner man, and ask of thyself whether thou art content with thyself. What hast thou attained with the guidance of the intellect alone? What art thou? You are young, you are wealthy, you are cultured, sir. What have you made of all the blessings voushsafed you? Are you satisfied with yourself and your life?'

'No, I hate my life,' said Pierre, frowning.

'Thou hatest it; then change it, purify thyself, and as thou art purified, thou wilt come to know wisdom. Look at your life, sir. How have you been spending it? In riotous orgies and debauchery, taking everything from society and giving nothing in return. You have received wealth. How have you used it? What have you done for your neighbour? Have you given a thought to the tens of thousands of your slaves, have you succoured them physically and morally? No. You have profited by their toil to lead a dissipated life. That's what you have done. Have you chosen a post in the service where you might be of use to your neighbour? No. You have spent your life in idleness. Then you married, sir, took upon yourself the responsibility of guiding a young woman in life, and what have you done? You have not helped her, sir, to find the path of truth, but have cast her into an abyss of deception and misery. A man injured you, and you have killed him, and you say you do not know God, and that you hate your life. There is no wisdom in all that, sir.'

After these words the freemason leaned his elbow again on the back of the sofa and closed his eyes, as though weary of prolonged talking. Pierre gazed at that stern, immovable, old, almost death-like face, and moved his lips without uttering a sound. He wanted to say, 'Yes, a vile, idle, vicious life,' and he dared not break the silence. The freemason cleared his throat huskily, as old men do, and called his servant.

'How about horses?' he asked, without looking at Pierre.

'They have brought round some that were given up,' answered the old man. 'You won't rest?'

'No, tell them to harness them.'

'Can he really be going away and leaving me all alone, without telling me everything and promising me help?' thought Pierre, getting up with downcast head, beginning to walk up and down the room, casting a glance from time to time at the freemason. 'Yes, I had not thought of it, but I have led a contemptible, dissolute life, but I did not like it, and I didn't want to,' thought Pierre, 'and this man knows the truth, and if he liked he could reveal it to me.' Pierre wanted to say this to the freemason and dared not. After packing his things with his practised old hands, the traveller buttoned up his sheepskin. On finishing these preparations, he turned to Bezuhov, and in a polite, indifferent tone, said to him:

'Where are you going now, sir?'

'I? . . . I'm going to Petersburg,' answered Pierre in a tone of childish indecision. 'I thank you. I agree with you in everything. But do not suppose that I have been so bad. With all my soul I have desired to be what you would wish me to be; but I have never met with help from any one. . . . Though I was myself most to blame for everything. Help me, instruct me, and perhaps I shall be able . . .'

Pierre could not say more; his voice broke and he turned away.

The freemason was silent, obviously pondering something.

'Help comes only from God,' he said, 'but such measure of aid as it is in the power of our order to give you, it will give you, sir. You go to Petersburg, and give this to Count Villarsky' (he took out his notebook and wrote a few words on a large sheet of paper folded into four). 'One piece of advice let me give you. When you reach the capital, devote your time at first there to solitude and to self-examination, and do not return to your old manner of life. Therewith I wish you a good journey, sir,' he added, noticing that his servant had entered the room, 'and all success . . .'

The stranger was Osip Alexyevitch Bazdyev, as Pierre found out from the overseer's book. Bazdyev had been one of the most well-known freemasons and Martinists even in Novikov's day. For a long while after he had gone, Pierre walked about the station room, neither lying down to sleep nor asking for horses. He reviewed his vicious past, and with an ecstatic sense of beginning anew, pictured to himself a blissful, irreproachably virtuous future, which seemed to him easy of attainment. It seemed to him that he had been vicious, simply because he had accidentally forgotten how good it was to be virtuous. There was left in his soul not a trace of his former doubts. He firmly believed in the possibility of the brotherhood of man, united in the aim of supporting one another in the path of virtue. And freemasonry he pictured to himself as such a brotherhood.

III

ON reaching Petersburg, Pierre let no one know of his arrival, went out to see nobody, spent whole days in reading Thomas à Kempis, a book which had been sent him, he did not know from whom. One thing, and one thing only, Pierre thoroughly understood in reading that book;

he understood what he had hitherto known nothing of, all the bliss of believing in the possibility of attaining perfection, and in the possibility of brotherly and active love between men, revealed to him by Osip Alexyevitch. A week after his arrival, the young Polish count, Villarsky, whom Pierre knew very slightly in Petersburg society, came one evening into his room with the same official and ceremonious air with which Dolohov's second had called on him. Closing the door behind him, and assuring himself that there was nobody in the room but Pierre, he addressed him:

'I have come to you with a message and a suggestion, count,' he said to him, not sitting down. 'A personage of very high standing in our brotherhood has been interceding for you to be admitted into our brotherhood before the usual term, and has asked me to be your sponsor. I regard it as a sacred duty to carry out that person's wishes. Do you wish under my sponsorship to enter the brotherhood of freemasons?'

Pierre was impressed by the cold and austere tone of this man, whom he had almost always seen before at balls wearing an agreeable smile, in the society of the most brilliant women.

'Yes, I do wish it,' said Pierre.

Villarsky bent his head.

'One more question, count,' he said, 'to which I beg you, not as a future mason, but as an honest man (*galant homme*) to answer me in all sincerity: have you renounced your former convictions? do you believe in God?'

Pierre thought a moment.

'Yes... yes, I do believe in God,' he said.

'In that case...' Villarsky was beginning, but Pierre interrupted him.

'Yes, I believe in God,' he said once more.

'In that case, we can go,' said Villarsky. 'My carriage is at your disposal.'

Throughout the drive Villarsky was silent. In answer to Pierre's inquiries, what he would have to do, and how he would have to answer, Villarsky simply said that brothers, more worthy than he, would prove him, and that Pierre need do nothing but tell the truth.

They drove in at the gates of a large house, where the lodge had its quarters, and, passing up a dark staircase, entered a small, lighted anteroom, where they took off their overcoats without the assistance of servants. From the ante-room they walked into another room. A man in strange attire appeared at the door. Villarsky, going in to meet him, said something to him in French in a low voice, and went up to a small cupboard, where Pierre noticed garments unlike any he had seen before. Taking a handkerchief from the cupboard, Villarsky put it over Pierre's eyes and tied it in a knot behind, catching his hair painfully in the knot. Then he drew him towards himself, kissed him, and taking him by the hand led him away somewhere. Pierre had been hurt by his hair being pulled in the knot: he puckered up his face from the pain, and smiled with vague shame. His huge figure with his arms hanging at his sides, and his face puckered up and smiling, moved after Villarsky with timid and uncertain steps.

After leading him for about ten steps, Villarsky stopped.

'Whatever happens to you,' said he, 'you must endure all with good courage if you are firmly resolved to enter our brotherhood.' (Pierre answered affirmatively by an inclination of his head.) 'When you hear a knock at the door, you may uncover your eyes,' added Villarsky; 'I wish you good courage and success,' and, pressing Pierre's hand, Villarsky went away.

When he was left alone, Pierre still went on smiling in the same way. Twice he shrugged his shoulders and raised his hand to the handkerchief, as though he would have liked to take it off, but he let it drop again. The five minutes he had spent with his eyes bandaged seemed to him an hour. His arms felt numb, his legs tottered, he felt as though he were tired out. He was aware of the most complex and conflicting feelings. He was afraid of what would be done to him, and still more afraid of showing fear. He felt inquisitive to know what was coming, what could be revealed to him; but above everything, he felt joy that the moment had come when he would at last enter upon that path of regeneration and of an actively virtuous life, of which he had been dreaming ever since his meeting with Osip Alexyevitch.

There came loud knocks at the door. Pierre took off the bandage and looked about him. It was black darkness in the room; only in one spot there was a little lamp burning before something white. Pierre went nearer and saw that the little lamp stood on a black table, on which there lay an open book. The book was the gospel: the white thing in which the lamp was burning was a human skull with its eye-holes and teeth. After reading the first words of the Gospel, 'In the beginning was the Word and the Word was with God,' Pierre went round the table and caught sight of a large open box filled with something. It was a coffin full of bones. He was not in the least surprised by what he saw. Hoping to enter upon a completely new life, utterly unlike the old life, he was ready for anything extraordinary, more extraordinary indeed than what he was seeing. The skull, the coffin, the gospel—it seemed to him that he had been expecting all that; had been expecting more, indeed. He tried to stir up a devotional feeling in himself; he looked about him. 'God, death, love, the brotherhood of man,' he kept saying to himself, associating with those words vague but joyful conceptions of some sort. The door opened and some one came in. In the faint light, in which Pierre could, however, see a little by this time, a short man approached. Apparently dazed by coming out of the light into the darkness, the man stopped, then with cautious steps moved again towards the table, and laid on it both his small hands covered with leather gloves.

This short man was wearing a white leather apron, that covered his chest and part of his legs; upon his neck could be seen something like a necklace, and a high white ruffle stood up from under the necklace, framing his long face, on which the light fell from below.

'For what are you come hither?' asked the newcomer, turning towards Pierre at a faint rustle made by the latter. 'For what are you, an unbeliever in the truth of the light, who have not seen the light, for what are you come here? What do you seek from us? Wisdom, virtue, enlightenment?'

At the moment when the door opened and the unknown person came in, Pierre had a sensation of awe and reverence, such as he had felt in childhood at confession; he felt himself alone with a man who was in the circumstances of life a complete stranger, and yet through the brotherhood of men so near. With a beating heart that made him gasp for breath, Pierre turned to the *rhetor*, as in the phraseology of freemasonry the man is called who prepares the *seeker* for entering the brotherhood. Going closer, Pierre recognised in the rhetor a man he knew, Smolyaninov, but it was mortifying to him to think that the newcomer was a familiar figure; he was to him only a brother and a guide in the path of virtue. For a long while Pierre could not utter a word, so that the rhetor was obliged to repeat his question.

'Yes; I . . . I . . . wish to begin anew,' Pierre articulated with difficulty.

'Very good,' said Smolyaninov, and went on at once.

'Have you any idea of the means by which our holy order will assist you in attaining your aim? . . .' said the rhetor calmly and rapidly.

'I . . . hope for . . . guidance . . . for help . . . in renewing . . .' said Pierre, with a tremble in his voice and a difficulty in utterance due both to emotion and to being unaccustomed to speak of abstract subjects in Russian.

'What idea have you of freemasonry?'

'I assume that freemasonry is the *fraternité* and equality of men with virtuous aims,' said Pierre, feeling ashamed as he spoke of the incongruity of his words with the solemnity of the moment. 'I assume . . .'

'Very good,' said the rhetor hastily, apparently quite satisfied with the reply. 'Have you sought the means of attaining your aim in religion?'

'No; I regarded it as untrue and have not followed it,' said Pierre, so softly that the rhetor did not catch it, and asked him what he was saying. 'I was an atheist,' answered Pierre.

'You seek the truth in order to follow its laws in life; consequently, you seek wisdom and virtue, do you not?' said the rhetor, after a moment's pause.

'Yes, yes,' assented Pierre.

The rhetor cleared his throat, folded his gloved hands across his chest, and began speaking.

'Now I must reveal to you the chief aim of our order,' he said, 'and if that aim coincides with yours, you may with profit enter our brotherhood. The first and greatest aim and united basis of our order, on which it is established and which no human force can destroy, is the preservation and handing down to posterity of a certain important mystery . . . that has come down to us from the most ancient times, even from the first man—a mystery upon which, perhaps, the fate of the human race depends. But since this mystery is of such a kind that no one can know it and profit by it if he has not been prepared by a prolonged and diligent self-purification, not everyone can hope to attain to it quickly. Hence we have a second aim, which consists in preparing our members, as far as possible reforming their hearts, purifying and enlightening their intelligence by those means which have been revealed to us by tradition from men who have striven to attain this mystery, and thereby to render them fit for the reception of it. Purifying and regenerating our members, we endeavour, thirdly, to improve the whole human race, offering it in our members an example of piety and virtue, and thereby we strive with all our strength to combat the evil that is paramount in the world. Ponder on these things, and I will come again to you,' he said, and went out of the room.

'To combat the evil that is paramount in the world . . .' Pierre repeated, and a mental image of his future activity in that direction rose before him. He seemed to see men such as he had been himself a fortnight ago, and he was mentally addressing an edifying exhortation to them. He pictured to himself persons vicious and unhappy, whom he would help in word and in deed; he pictured oppressors whose victims he would rescue. Of the three aims enumerated by the rhetor the last— the reformation of the human race—appealed particularly to Pierre. The great mystery of which the rhetor had made mention, though it excited his curiosity, did not strike his imagination as a reality; while the second aim, the purification and regeneration of himself, had little interest for him, because at that moment he was full of a blissful sense of being completely cured of all his former vices, and being ready for nothing but goodness.

Half an hour later the rhetor returned to enumerate to the seeker the seven virtues corresponding to the seven steps of the temple of Solomon, in which every freemason must train himself. Those virtues were: (1) discretion, the keeping of the secrets of the order; (2) obedience to the higher authorities of the order; (3) morality; (4) love for mankind; (5) courage; (6) liberality; and (7) love of death.

'Seventhly, strive,' said the rhetor, 'by frequent meditation upon death to bring yourself to feel it not an enemy to be dreaded, but a friend ... which delivers the soul grown weary in the labours of virtue from this distressful life and leads it to its place of recompense and peace.'

'Yes, that's as it should be,' thought Pierre, when the rhetor after these words left him again to solitary reflection; 'that's as it ought to be, but I'm still so weak as to love this life, the meaning of which is only now by degrees being revealed to me.' But the other five virtues which Pierre recalled, reckoning them on his fingers, he felt already in his soul: courage and liberality, morality and love for mankind, and above all, obedience, which seemed to him not to be a virtue, indeed, but a happiness. (It was such a joy to him now to be escaping from the guidance of his own caprice, and to be submitting his will to those who knew the absolute truth.) The seventh virtue Pierre had forgotten, and he could not recall it.

The third time the rhetor came back sooner, and asked Pierre whether he were still resolute in his intention, and whether he were prepared to submit to everything that would be demanded of him.

'I am ready for anything, said Pierre.

'I must inform you further,' said the rhetor, 'that our order promulgates its doctrine not by word only, but by certain means which have perhaps on the true seeker after wisdom and virtue a more potent effect than merely verbal explanations. This temple, with what you see therein, should shed more light on your heart, if it is sincere, than any words can do. You will see, maybe, a like method of enlightenment in the further rites of your admittance. Our order follows the usage of ancient societies which revealed their doctrine in hieroglyphs. A hieroglyph,' said the rhetor, 'is the name given to a symbol of some object, imperceptible to the senses and possessing qualities similar to those of the symbol.

Pierre knew very well what a hieroglyph was, but he did not venture to say so. He listened to the rhetor in silence, feeling from everything he said that his ordeal was soon to begin.

'If you are resolved, I must proceed to your initiation,' said the rhetor, coming closer to Pierre. 'In token of liberality I beg you to give me everything precious you have.'

'But I have nothing with me,' said Pierre, supposing he was being asked to give up all his possessions.

'What you have with you: watch, money, rings...'

Pierre made haste to get out his purse and his watch, and was a long time trying to get his betrothal ring off his fat finger. When this had been done, the freemason said:

'In token of obedience I beg you to undress.' Pierre took off his coat and waistcoat and left boot at the rhetor's instructions. The mason opened his shirt over the left side of his chest and pulled up his breeches on the left leg above the knee. Pierre would hurriedly have taken off the right boot and tucked up the trouser-leg, to save this stranger the trouble of doing so, but the mason told him this was not necessary and gave him a slipper to put on his left foot. With a childish smile of embarrassment, of doubt, and of self-mockery, which would come into his face in spite of himself, Pierre stood with his legs wide apart and his hands hanging at his side, facing the rhetor and awaiting his next commands.

'And finally, in token of candour, I beg you to disclose to me your chief temptation,' he said.

'My temptation! I *had* so many,' said Pierre.

'The temptation which does more than all the rest to make you stumble on the path of virtue,' said the freemason.

Pierre paused, seeking a reply.

'Wine? gluttony? frivolity? laziness? hasty temper? anger? women?' he went through his vices, mentally balancing them, and not knowing to which to give the pre-eminence.

'Women,' said Pierre in a low, hardly audible voice. The freemason did not speak nor stir for a long while after that reply. At last he moved up to Pierre, took the handkerchief that lay on the table, and again tied it over his eyes.

'For the last time I say to you: turn all your attention upon yourself, put a bridle on your feelings, and seek blessedness not in your passions, but in your own heart. The secret of blessing is not without but within us....'

Pierre had for a long while been conscious of this refreshing fount of blessing within him, that now flooded his heart with joy and emotion.

IV

SHORTLY after this, there walked into the dark temple to fetch Pierre, not the rhetor, but his sponsor Villarsky, whom he recognised by his voice. In reply to fresh inquiries as to the firmness of his resolve, Pierre answered:

'Yes, yes, I agree,' and with a beaming, childlike smile he walked forward, stepping timidly and unevenly with one booted and one slippered foot, while Villarsky held a sword pointed at his fat, uncovered chest. He was led out of the room along corridors, turning backwards and forwards, till at last he was brought to the doors of the lodge. Villarsky coughed; he was answered by masonic taps with hammers; the door opened before them. A bass voice (Pierre's eyes were again bandaged) put questions to him, who he was, where and when he was born, and so on. Then he was again led away somewhere with his eyes still bandaged, and as he walked they spoke to him in allegories of the toils of his pilgrimage, and of holy love, of the Eternal Creator of the world, of the courage with which he was to endure toils and dangers. During this time Pierre noticed that he was called sometimes the *seeker*, sometimes the *sufferer*, and sometimes the *postulant*, and that they made various tapping sounds with hammers and with swords. While he was being led up to some object, he noticed that there was hesitation and uncertainty among his conductors. He heard a whispered dispute among the people round him, and one of them insisting that he should be made to cross a certain carpet. After this they took his right hand, laid it on something, while they bade him with the left hold a compass to his left breast, while they made him repeat after some one who read the words aloud, the oath of fidelity to the laws of the order. Then the candles were extinguished and the spirit was lighted, as Pierre knew from the smell of it, and he was told that he would see the lesser light. The bandage was taken off his eyes, and in the faint light of the burning spirit Pierre saw, as though it were in a dream, several persons who stood facing him in aprons like the rhetor's, and held swords pointed at his breast. Among them stood a man in a white shirt stained with blood. On seeing this, Pierre moved with his chest forward towards the swords, meaning them to stab him. But the swords were drawn back, and the bandage was at once replaced on his eyes.

'Now you have seen the lesser light,' said a voice. Then again they lighted the candles, told him that he had now to see the full light, and again removed the bandage, and more than ten voices said all at once: '*Sic transit gloria mundi.*'

Pierre gradually began to regain his self-possession, and to look about at the room and the people in it. Round a long table covered with black were sitting some dozen men, all in the same strange garment that he had seen before. Several of them Pierre knew in Petersburg society. In the president's chair sat a young man, with a peculiar cross on his neck, whom he did not know. On his right hand sat the Italian abbé whom Pierre had seen two years before at Anna Pavlovna's. There were among them a dignitary of very high standing and a Swiss tutor, who had once been in the Kuragin family. All preserved a solemn silence, listening to the president, who held a hammer in his hand. In the wall was carved a blazing star; on one side of the table was a small rug with various figures worked upon it; on the other was something like an altar with the gospel and a skull on it. Round the table stood seven big ecclesiastical-looking candlesticks. Two of the brothers led Pierre up to the altar, set his feet at right angles and bade him lie down, saying that he would be casting himself down at the gates of the temple.

'He ought first to receive the spade,' said one of the brothers in a whisper.

'Oh! hush, please,' said another.

Pierre did not obey, but with uneasy short-sighted eyes looked about him, and suddenly doubt came over him. 'Where am I? What am I doing? Aren't they laughing at me? Shan't I be ashamed to remember this?' But this doubt only lasted a moment. Pierre looked round at the serious faces of the people round him, thought of all he had just been through, and felt that there was no stopping halfway. He was terrified at his own hesitation, and trying to arouse in himself his former devotional feeling, he cast himself down at the gates of the temple. And the devotional feeling did in fact come more strongly than ever upon him. When he had lain there some time, he was told to get up, and a white leather apron such as the others wore was put round him, and a spade and three pairs of gloves were put in his hands; then the grand master addressed him. He told him that he must try never to stain the whiteness of that apron, which symbolised strength and purity. Then of the unexplained spade he told him to toil with it at clearing his heart from vice, and with forbearing patience smoothing the way in the heart of his neighbour. Then of the first pair of gloves he said that he could not know yet their significance, but must treasure them; of the second pair he said that he must put them on at meetings; and finally of the third pair—they were women's gloves—he said:

'Dear brother, and these woman's gloves are destined for you too. Give them to the woman whom you shall honour beyond all others. That gift will be a pledge of your purity of heart to her whom you select as a worthy helpmeet in masonry.' After a brief pause, he added: 'But beware, dear brother, that these gloves never deck hands that are impure.'

While the grand master uttered the last words it seemed to Pierre that he was embarrassed. Pierre was even more embarrassed; he blushed to the point of tears, as children blush, looking about him uneasily, and an awkward silence followed.

This silence was broken by one of the brothers who, leading Pierre to the rug, began reading out of a manuscript book the interpretation of all the figures delineated upon it: the sun, the moon, the hammer, the balance, the spade, the rough stone and the shaped stone, the post, the three windows, etc. Then Pierre was shown his appointed place, he was shown the signs of the lodge, told the password, and at last permitted to sit down. The grand master began reading the exhortation. The exhortation was very long, and Pierre in his joy, his emotion, and his embarrassment was hardly in a condition to understand what was read. He only grasped the last words of the exhortation, which stuck in his memory.

'In our temples we know of no distinction,' read the grand master, 'but those between virtue and vice. Beware of making any difference that may transgress against equality. Fly to the succour of a brother whoever he may be, exhort him that goeth astray, lift up him that falleth, and cherish not malice nor hatred against a brother. Be thou friendly and courteous. Kindle in all hearts the fire of virtue. Share thy happiness with thy neighbour, and never will envy trouble that pure bliss. Forgive thy enemy, revenge not thyself on him but by doing him good. Fulfilling in this wise the highest law, thou wilt regain traces of the ancient grandeur thou hadst lost,' he concluded, and getting up he embraced Pierre and kissed him.

Pierre looked round with tears of joy in his eyes, not knowing how to answer the congratulations and greetings from acquaintances with which he was surrounded. He did not recognise any acquaintances; in all these men he saw only brothers, and he burned with impatience to get to work with them. The grand master tapped with his hammer, all sat down in their places, and one began reading a sermon on the necessity of meekness.

The grand master proposed that the last duty be performed, and the great dignitary whose duty it was to collect the alms began making the round of all the brothers. Pierre would have liked to give to the list of alms all the money he had in the world, but he feared thereby to sin by pride, and only wrote down the same sum as the others.

The sitting was over, and it seemed to Pierre on returning home that he had come back from a long journey on which he had spent dozens of years, and had become utterly changed, and had renounced his old habits and manner of life.

V

THE day after his initiation at the Lodge, Pierre was sitting at home reading a book, and trying to penetrate to the significance of the square, which symbolised by one of its sides, God, by another the moral, by the third the physical, by the fourth the nature of both mingled. Now and then he broke off from the book and the symbolic square, and in his imagination shaped his new plan of life. On the previous day he had been told at the lodge that the rumour of the duel had reached the Emperor's ears, and that it would be more judicious for him to withdraw for a while from Petersburg. Pierre proposed going to his estates in the south, and there occupying himself with the care of his peasants. He was joyfully dreaming of this new life when Prince Vassily suddenly walked into his room.

'My dear fellow, what have you been about in Moscow? What have you been quarrelling over with Ellen, my dear boy? You have been making a mistake,' said Prince Vassily, as he came into the room. 'I have heard all about it; I can tell you for a fact that Ellen is as innocent in her conduct towards you as Christ was to the Jews.'

Pierre would have answered, but he interrupted him.

'And why didn't you come simply and frankly to me as to a friend? I know all about it; I understand it all,' said he. 'You have behaved as was proper for a man who valued his honour, too hastily, perhaps, but we won't go into that. One thing you must think of, the position you are placing her and me in, in the eyes of society and even of the court,' he added, dropping his voice. 'She is in Moscow, while you are here. Think of it, my dear boy.' He drew him down by the arm. 'It's simply a misunderstanding; I expect you feel it so yourself. Write a letter with me now at once, and she'll come here, and everything will be explained, or else, I tell you plainly, my dear boy, you may very easily have to suffer for it.'

Prince Vassily looked significantly at Pierre.

'I have learned from excellent sources that the Dowager Empress is taking a keen interest in the whole affair. You know she is very graciously disposed to Ellen.'

Several times Pierre had prepared himself to speak, but on one hand Prince Vassily would not let him, and on the other hand Pierre himself was loth to begin to speak in the tone of resolute refusal and denial, in which he was firmly resolved to answer his father-in-law. Moreover the words of the masonic precept: 'Be thou friendly and courteous,' recurred to his mind. He blinked and blushed, got up and sank back again, trying to force himself to do what was for him the hardest thing in life—to say an unpleasant thing to a man's face, to say what was not expected by that man, whoever he might be. He was so much in the habit of submitting to that tone of careless authority in which Prince Vassily spoke, that even now he felt incapable of resisting it. But he felt, too, that on what he said now all his future fate would depend; that it would decide whether he continued along the old way of his past life, or advanced along the new path that had been so attractively pointed out to him by the masons, and that he firmly believed would lead him to regeneration in a new life.

'Come, my dear boy,' said Prince Vassily playfully, 'simply say "yes," and I'll write on my own account to her, and we'll kill the fatted calf.' But before Prince Vassily had finished uttering his playful words, Pierre not looking at him, but with a fury in his face that made him like his father, whispered, 'Prince, I did not invite you here: go, please, go!' He leaped up and opened the door to him. 'Go!' he repeated, amazed at himself and enjoying the expression of confusion and terror in the countenance of Prince Vassily.

'What's the matter with you? are you ill?'

'Go!' the quivering voice repeated once more. And Prince Vassily had to go, without receiving a word of explanation.

A week later Pierre went away to his estates, after taking leave of his new friends, the freemasons, and leaving large sums in their hands for alms. His new brethren gave him letters for Kiev and Odessa, to masons living there, and promised to write to him and guide him in his new activity.

VI

PIERRE'S duel with Dolohov was smoothed over, and in spite of the Tsar's severity in regard to duels at that time, neither the principals nor the seconds suffered for it. But the scandal of the duel, confirmed by Pierre's rupture with his wife, made a great noise in society. Pierre had been looked upon with patronising condescension when he was an illegitimate son; he had been made much of and extolled for his virtues while he was the wealthiest match in the Russian empire; but after his marriage, when young ladies and their mothers had nothing to hope from him, he had fallen greatly in the opinion of society, especially as he had neither the wit nor the wish to ingratiate himself in public favour. Now the blame of the whole affair was thrown on him; it was said that he was insanely jealous, and subject to the same fits of bloodthirsty fury as his father had been. And when, after Pierre's departure, Ellen returned to Petersburg, she was received by all her acquaintances not only cordially, but with a shade of deference that was a tribute to her distress. When the conversation touched upon her husband, Ellen assumed an expression of dignity, which her characteristic tact prompted her to adopt, though she had no conception of its significance. That expression suggested that she had resolved to bear her affliction without complaint, and that her husband was a cross God had laid upon her. Prince Vassily expressed his opinion more openly. He shrugged his shoulders when the conversation turned upon Pierre, and pointing to his forehead, said:

'Crackbrained, I always said so.'

'I used to say so even before,' Anna Pavlovna would say of Pierre, 'at the time I said at once and before every one' (she insisted on her priority) 'that he was an insane young man, corrupted by the dissolute ideas of the age. I used to say so at the time when every one was in such ecstasies over him; and he had only just come home from abroad, and do you remember at one of my *soirées* he thought fit to pose as a sort of Marat? And how has it ended? Even then I was against this marriage, and foretold all that has come to pass.'

Anna Pavlovna used still to give *soirées* on her free days as before, *soirées* such as only she had the gift of arranging, *soirées* at which were gathered together 'the cream of really good society, the flower of the intellectual essence of Petersburg society,' as Anna Pavlovna herself used to say. Besides this fine sifting of the society, Anna Pavlovna's *soirées* were further distinguished by some new interesting person, secured by the hostess on every occasion for the entertainment of the company. Moreover, the point on the political thermometer, at which the temperature of loyal court society stood in Petersburg, was nowhere so clearly and unmistakably marked as at these *soirées*.

Towards the end of the year 1806, when all the melancholy details of Napoleon's destruction of the Prussian army at Jena and Auerstadt, and the surrender of the greater number of the Prussian forts, had arrived, when our troops were already entering Prussia, and our second war with Napoleon was beginning, Anna Pavlovna was giving one of her *soirées*. 'The cream of really good society' consisted of the fascinating and unhappy Ellen, abandoned by her husband, of Mortemart, of the fascinating Prince Ippolit, who had just come home from Vienna, of two diplomats, of the old aunt; of a young man, always referred to in that society by the designation, 'a man of a great deal of merit . . .'; of a newly appointed maid of honour and her mother, and several other less noteworthy persons.

The novelty Anna Pavlovna was offering her guests for their entertainment that evening was Boris Drubetskoy, who had just arrived as a special messenger from the Prussian army, and was in the suite of a personage of very high rank.

What the political thermometer indicated at that *soirée* was something as follows: All the European rulers and generals may do their utmost to flatter Bonaparte with the object of causing *me* and *us* generally these annoyances and mortifications, but our opinion in regard to Bonaparte can undergo no change. We do not cease giving undisguised expression to our way of thinking on the subject, and can only say to the Prussian king and others: 'So much the worse for you.' '*Tu l'as voulou, George Dandin,*' that's all we can say. This was what the political thermometer indicated at Anna Pavlovna's *soirée*. When Boris, who was to be offered up to the guests, came into the drawing-room, almost all the company had assembled, and the conversation, guided by Anna Pavlovna, was of our diplomatic relations with Austria, and the hope of an alliance with her.

Boris, fresh, rosy, and manlier looking, walked easily into the drawing-room, wearing the elegant uniform of an adjutant. He was duly conducted to pay his respects to the aunt, and then joined the general circle.

Anna Pavlovna gave him her shrivelled hand to kiss, introduced him to several persons whom he did not know, and gave him a whispered description of each of them. 'Prince Ippolit Kuragin, M. Krug, *chargé d'affaires* from Copenhagen, a profound intellect and simply, M. Shitov, a man of a great deal of merit . . .' this of the young man always so spoken of.

Thanks to the efforts of Anna Mihalovna, his own tastes and the peculiarities of his reserved character, Boris had succeeded by that time in getting into a very advantageous position in the service. He was an adjutant in the suite of a personage of very high rank, he had received a very important commission in Prussia, and had only just returned thence as a special messenger. He had completely assimilated that unwritten code which had so pleased him at Olmütz, that code in virtue of which a lieutenant may stand infinitely higher than a general, and all that is needed for success in the service is not effort, not work, not gallantry, not perseverance, but simply the art of getting on with those who have the bestowal of promotion, and he often himself marvelled at the rapidity of his own progress, and that others failed to grasp the secret of it. His whole manner of life, all his relations with his old friends, all his plans for the future were completely transformed in consequence of this discovery. He was not well off, but he spent his last copeck to be better dressed than others. He would have deprived himself of many pleasures rather than have allowed himself to drive in an inferior carriage, or to be seen in the streets of Petersburg in an old uniform. He sought the acquaintance and cultivated the friendship only of persons who were in a higher position, and could consequently be of use to him. He loved Petersburg and despised Moscow. His memories of the Rostov household and his childish passion for Natasha were distasteful to him, and he had not once been at the Rostov's since he had entered the army. In Anna Pavlovna's drawing-room, his entry into which he looked upon as an important step upward in the service, he at once took his cue, and let Anna Pavlovna make the most of what interest he had to offer, while himself attentively watching every face and appraising the advantages and possibilities of intimacy with every one of the persons present. He sat on the seat indicated to him beside the fair Ellen and listened to the general conversation.

'Vienna considers the bases of the proposed treaty so unattainable that not even a continuance of the most brilliant successes would put them within reach, and doubts whether any means could gain them for us. These are the actual words of the ministry in Vienna,' said the Danish *chargé d'affaires*.

'It is polite of them to doubt,' said the man of profound intellect with a subtle smile.

'We must distinguish between the ministry in Vienna and the Emperor of Austria,' said Mortemart. 'The Emperor of Austria can never have thought of such a thing; it is only the ministers who say it.'

'Ah, my dear vicomte,' put in Anna Pavlovna; 'Europe will never be our sincere ally.'

Then Anna Pavlovna turned the conversation upon the courage and firmness of the Prussian king, with the object of bringing Boris into action.

Boris listened attentively to the person who was speaking, and waited for his turn, but meanwhile he had leisure to look round several times at the fair Ellen, who several times met the handsome young adjutant's eyes with a smile.

Very naturally, speaking of the position of Prussia, Anna Pavlovna asked Boris to describe his journey to Glogau, and the position in which he had found the Prussian army. Boris in his pure, correct French, told them very deliberately a great many interesting details about the armies, and the court, studiously abstaining from any expression of his own opinion in regard to the facts he was narrating. For some time Boris engrossed the whole attention of the company, and Anna Pavlovna felt that the novelty she was serving her guests was being accepted by them all with pleasure. Of all the party, the person who showed most interest in Boris's description was Ellen. She asked him several questions about his expedition, and seemed to be extremely interested in the position of the Prussian army. As soon as he had finished, she turned to him with her habitual smile.

'You absolutely must come and see me,' she said in a tone that suggested that for certain considerations, of which he could have no knowledge, it was absolutely essential. 'On Tuesday between eight and nine. It will give me great pleasure.'

Boris promised to do so, and was about to enter into conversation with her, when Anna Pavlovna drew him aside on the pretext that her aunt wished to hear his story.

'You know her husband, of course?' said Anna Pavlovna, dropping her eyelids, and with a melancholy gesture indicating Ellen. 'Ah, such an unhappy and exquisite woman! Don't speak of him before her; pray, don't speak of him. It's too much for her!'

VII

WHEN Boris and Anna Pavlovna returned to the rest, Prince Ippolit was in possession of the ear of the company. Bending forward in his low chair, he was saying:

'The King of Prussia!' and as he said it, he laughed. Every one turned towards him. 'The King of Prussia,' Ippolit said interrogatively, and again he laughed and again settled himself placidly and seriously in the depths of his big, low chair. Anna Pavlovna paused a little for him, but as Ippolit seemed quite certainly not intending to say more, she began to speak of how the godless Bonaparte had at Potsdam carried off the sword of Frederick the Great.

'It is the sword of Frederick the Great, which I . . .' she was beginning, but Ippolit interrupted her with the words:

'The King of Prussia . . .' and again as soon as all turned to listen to him, he excused himself and said no more. Anna Pavlovna frowned. Mortemart, Ippolit's friend, addressed him with decision:

'Come, what are you after with your King of Prussia?'

Ippolit laughed as though he were ashamed of his own laughter.

'No, it's nothing. I only meant . . .' (He had intended to repeat a joke that he had heard in Vienna and had been trying all the evening to get in.) 'I only meant that we are wrong to make war for the King of Prussia.'[1]

Boris smiled circumspectly, a smile that might do duty either for a sneer or a tribute to the jest, according to the way it was received. Every one laughed.

'It is too bad, your joke, very witty but unjust,' said Anna Pavlovna, shaking her little wrinkled finger at him. 'We are not making war for the sake of the King of Prussia, but for the sake of right principles. Ah, *le méchant, ce Prince Hippolyte*!' she said.

The conversation did not flag all the evening, and turned principally upon the political news. Towards the end of the evening it became particularly eager, when the rewards bestowed by the Tsar were the subjects of discussion.

'Why, last year N. N. received the snuff-box with the portrait,' said the man of profound intellect. 'Why shouldn't S. S. receive the same reward?'

'I beg your pardon, a snuff-box with the Emperor's portrait is a reward, but not a distinction,' said a diplomatist. 'A present, rather.'

'There are precedents. I would instance Schwartzenberg.'

'It is impossible,' retorted another.

'A bet on it. The ribbon of the order is different.'

When every one got up to take leave, Ellen, who had said very little all the evening, turned to Boris again with a request, and a caressing, impressive command that he would come to her on Tuesday.

'It is of great importance to me,' she said with a smile, looking round at Anna Pavlovna, and Anna Pavlovna, with the same mournful smile with which she accompanied any reference to her royal patroness, gave her support to Ellen's wishes. It appeared that from some words Boris had uttered that evening about the Prussian army, Ellen had suddenly discovered the absolute necessity of seeing him. She seemed to promise him that when he came on Tuesday she would disclose to him that necessity. When Boris entered Ellen's magnificent reception-room on Tuesday evening he received no clear explanation of the urgent reasons for his visit. Other guests were present, the countess talked little to him, and only as he kissed her hand at taking leave, with a strangely unsmiling face, she whispered to him unexpectedly:

'Come to dinner tomorrow . . . in the evening . . . you must come . . . come.'

During that stay in Petersburg Boris was constantly at the house of the Countess Bezuhov on a footing of the closest intimacy.

---

[1] '*Faire quelque chose pour le roi de Prusse*', is a French idiom meaning to do anything for insufficient reason or in vain.

VIII

WAR had broken out and the theatre of it was closer to the borders of Russia. On all sides could be heard curses upon the enemy of the human race, Bonaparte; in the villages there were levies of recruits and reserve men, and from the theatre of war came news of the most conflicting kind, false as usual, and hence variously interpreted.

The life of the old Prince Bolkonsky, of Prince Andrey, and of Princess Marya was greatly changed since the year 1805.

In 1806 the old prince had been appointed one of the eight commanders-in-chief, created at that time for the equipment of the militia throughout all Russia. In spite of his weakness and age, which had been particularly noticeable during the time when he believed his son to have been killed, the old prince did not think it right to refuse a duty to which he had been appointed by the Emperor himself, and this new field for his activity gave him fresh energy and strength. He was continually away on tours about the three provinces that were put under his command; he was punctilious to pedantry in the performance of his duties, severe to cruelty with his subordinates, and entered into the minutest details of the work himself. Princess Marya no longer took lessons on mathematics from her father, and only went into her father's room on the mornings when he was at home, accompanied by the wet nurse and little Prince Nikolay (as his grandfather called him). The baby, Prince Nikolay, with his wet nurse and the old nurse Savishna, occupied the rooms that had been his mother's, and Princess Marya spent most of her time in the nursery taking a mother's place to her little nephew, to the best of her powers. Mademoiselle Bourienne, too, appeared to be passionately fond of the child, and Princess Marya often sacrificed herself by giving up to her friend the pleasure of dandling and playing with the little *angel* (as she called the baby).

Near the altar of the church at Bleak Hills was a little chapel over the tomb of the little princess, and in the chapel had been placed a marble monument brought from Italy, representing an angel with its wings parted about to take flight for heaven. The angel had the upper lip lifted as though about to smile, and one day Prince Andrey and Princess Marya, as they came out of the chapel, confessed to one another that, strange to say, the face of the angel reminded them of the face of the little princess. But what was stranger, though this Prince Andrey did not confess to his sister, was that in the expression the sculptor had chanced to put into the angel's face, Prince Andrey read the same words of reproach which he had read then on the face of his dead wife: 'Ah, why have you done this to me? . . .'

Soon after Prince Andrey's return, the old prince made over a part of the property to him, giving him Bogutcharovo, a large estate about thirty miles from Bleak Hills. Partly to escape the painful memories associated with Bleak Hills, partly because Prince Andrey did not always feel equal to bearing with his father's peculiarities, and partly from a craving for solitude, Prince Andrey made use of Bogutcharovo, established himself there and spent the greater part of his time there.

After the Austerlitz campaign, Prince Andrey had firmly resolved never to serve again in the army. And when war broke out and all were bound to serve, he took service under his father in the levying of the militia, so as to escape active service. Since the campaign of 1805 the old prince and his son had as it were exchanged parts. The old prince, stimulated by activity, expected the best results from the present campaign. Prince Andrey, on the contrary, taking no part in the war, and secretly regretting his inaction, saw in it nothing but what was bad.

On the 26th of February 1807 the old prince set off on a tour of inspection. Prince Andrey was staying at Bleak Hills, as he usually did in his father's absence. Little Nikolushka had been ill for the last three days. The coachman, who had driven the old prince away, returned bringing papers and letters from the town for Prince Andrey. The valet with the letters not finding the young prince in his study, went to Princess Marya's apartments, but he was not there either. The valet was told that the prince had gone to the nursery. 'If you please, your excellency, Petrusha has come with some papers,' said one of the nursery maids, addressing Prince Andrey, who was sitting on a child's little chair. Screwing up his eyes, he was with trembling hands pouring drops from a medicine bottle into a glass half full of water.

'What is it?' he said angrily, and his hand shaking, he accidentally poured too many drops from the bottle into the glass. He tipped the medicine out of the glass on to the floor and asked for some more water. The maid gave it him.

In the room were a couple of armchairs, a child's crib, a table and a child's table and a little chair, on which Prince Andrey was sitting. The windows were curtained, and on the table a single candle was burning, screened by a note book, so that the light did not fall on the crib.

'My dear,' said Princess Marya, turning to her brother from beside the crib where she was standing, 'it would be better to wait a little . . . later.'

'Oh, please, do as I say, what nonsense you keep talking; you have kept putting things off, and see what's come of it!' said Prince Andrey in an exasperated whisper, evidently meaning to wound his sister.

'My dear, it's really better not to wake him, he has fallen asleep,' said the princess in a voice of entreaty.

Prince Andrey got up and went on tiptoe to the crib with the glass in his hand.

'Should we really not wake him?' he said, hesitating.

'As you think—really . . . I believe so . . . but as you think,' said Princess Marya, obviously intimidated and ashamed that her opinion should triumph. She drew her brother's attention to the maid, who was summoning him in a whisper.

It was the second night that they had been without sleep looking after the baby who was feverish. Mistrusting their own household doctor and expecting the doctor they had sent from the town, they had spent all that time trying first one remedy and then another. Agitated and worn out by sleeplessness, they vented their anxiety on each other, found fault with each other, and quarrelled.

'Petrusha with papers from your papa,' whispered the maid. Prince Andrey went out.

'Damn them all!' he commented angrily, and after listening to the verbal instructions sent him from his father, and taking the correspondence and his father's letter, he went back to the nursery. 'Well?' queried Prince Andrey.

'No change, wait a little, for God's sake. Karl Ivanitch always says sleep is better than anything,' Princess Marya whispered with a sigh. Prince Andrey went up to the baby and felt him. He was burning hot. 'Bother you and your Karl Ivanitch!' He took the glass with the drops of medicine in it and again went up to the crib.

'Andryusha, you shouldn't!' said Princess Marya. But he scowled at her with an expression of anger and at the same time of anguish, and bent over the child with the glass.

'But I wish it,' he said. 'Come, I beg you, give it him . . .'

Princess Marya shrugged her shoulders, but obediently she took the glass, and calling the nurse, began giving the child the medicine. The baby screamed and wheezed. Prince Andrey, scowling and clutching at his head, went out of the room and sat down on the sofa in the adjoining one.

The letters were still in his hand. Mechanically he opened them and began to read. The old prince in his big, sprawling hand, making use of occasional abbreviations, wrote on blue paper as follows:

'I have this moment received, through a special messenger, very joyful news, if it's not a falsehood. Bennigsen has gained it seems a complete victory over Bonaparte near Eylau. In Petersburg every one's jubilant and rewards have been sent to the army without stint. Though he's a German—I congratulate him. Commander in Kortchevo, a certain Handrikov, I can't make out what he's about; full contingent of men and regulation provision not yet arrived. Gallop over at once and say I'll have his head off if it's not all here within the week. I have a letter too about the Prussian battle at Preussisch-Eylau from Petenka, he took part in it,—it's all true. If people don't meddle who've no business to meddle, even a German beats Bonaparte. They say he's running away in great disorder. Mind you gallop over to Kortchevo and do the business without delay!'

Prince Andrey sighed and broke open the other letter. It was a letter from Bilibin, two sheets covered with fine hand-writing. He folded it up without reading it, and read through once more his father's letter, ending with the words: 'Mind you gallop over to Kortchevo and do the business without delay!'

'No, excuse me, I'm not going now till the child is better,' he thought, and going to the door he glanced into the nursery. Princess Marya was still standing at the crib, softly rocking the baby. 'Oh, and what was the other unpleasant thing he writes about?' Prince Andrey thought of the contents of his father's letter. 'Yes. Our troops have gained a victory over Bonaparte precisely when I'm not in the army. Yes, yes, everything mocks at me . . . well and welcome too . . .' and he began reading the letter in French from Bilibin. He read, not understanding half of it, read simply to escape for one moment from thinking of what he had too long, too exclusively and too anxiously been dwelling upon.

IX

BILIBIN was now in a diplomatic capacity at the headquarters of the army, and though he wrote in French, with French jests, and French turns of speech, he described the whole campaign with an impartial self-criticism and self-mockery exclusively Russian. Bilibin wrote that the obligation of diplomatic discretion was a torture to him, and that he was happy to have in Prince Andrey a trustworthy correspondent to whom he could pour out all the spleen that had been accumulating in him at the sight of what was going on in the army. The letter was dated some time back, before the battle of Eylau.

'Since our great success at Austerlitz, you know, my dear prince,' wrote Bilibin, 'that I have not left headquarters. Decidedly I have acquired a taste for warfare, and it is just as well for me. What I have seen in these three months is incredible.

'I will begin *ab ovo*. "The enemy of the human race," as you know, is attacking the Prussians. The Prussians are our faithful allies, who have only deceived us three times in three years. We stand up for them. But it occurs that the enemy of the human race pays no attention to our fine speeches, and in his uncivil and savage way flings himself upon the Prussians without giving them time to finish the parade that they had begun, and by a couple of conjuring tricks thrashes them completely, and goes to take up his quarters in the palace of Potsdam.

'"I most earnestly desire," writes the King of Prussia to Bonaparte, "that your majesty may be received and treated in my palace in a manner agreeable to you, and I have hastened to take all the measures to that end which circumstances allowed. May I have succeeded!" The Prussian generals pride themselves on their politeness towards the French, and lay down their arms at the first summons.

'The head of the garrison at Glogau, who has ten thousand men, asks the King of Prussia what he is to do if he is summoned to surrender.... All these are actual facts.

'In short, hoping only to produce an effect by our military attitude, we find ourselves at war in good earnest, and, what is more, at war on our own frontiers *with and for the King of Prussia*. Everything is fully ready, we only want one little thing, that is the commander-in-chief. As it is thought that the successes at Austerlitz might have been more decisive if the commander-in-chief had not been so young, the men of eighty have been passed in review, and of Prosoróvsky and Kamensky the latter is preferred. The general comes to us in a *kibik* after the fashion of Suvorov, and is greeted with acclamations of joy and triumph.

'On the 4th comes the first post from Petersburg. The mails are taken to the marshal's room, for he likes to do everything himself. I am called to sort the letters and take those meant for us. The marshal looks on while we do it, and waits for the packets addressed to him. We seek—there are none. The marshal gets impatient, sets to work himself, and finds letters from the Emperor for Count T., Prince V., and others. Then he throws himself into one of his furies. He rages against everybody, snatches hold of the letters, opens them, and reads those from the Emperor to other people.

'"Ah, so that's how I'm being treated! No confidence in me! Oh, ordered to keep an eye on me, very well; get along with you!"

'And then he writes the famous order of the day to General Bennigsen:

'"I am wounded, I cannot ride on horseback, consequently cannot command the army. You have led your corps d'armée defeated to Pultusk! Here it remains exposed and destitute of wood and of forage, and in need of assistance, and so, as you reported yourself to Count Buxhevden yesterday, you must think of retreat to our frontier, and so do today."

'"All my expeditions on horseback," he writes to the Emperor, "have given me a saddle sore, which, after my former journeys, quite prevents my sitting a horse, and commanding an army so widely scattered; and therefore I have handed over the said command to the general next in seniority to me, Count Buxhevden, having despatched to him all my suite and appurtenances of the same, advising him, if bread should run short, to retreat further into the interior of Prussia, seeing that bread for one day's rations only is left, and some regiments have none, as the commanders Osterman and Sedmoretsky have reported, and the peasantry of the country have had everything eaten up. I shall myself remain in the hospital at Ostrolenka till I am cured. In regard to which I must humbly submit the report that if the army remains another fortnight in its present bivouac, by spring not a man will be left in health.

'"Graciously discharge from his duty an old man who is sufficiently disgraced by his inability to perform the great and glorious task for which he was chosen. I shall await here in the hospital your most gracious acceptance of my retirement, that I may not have to act the part of a secretary rather than a commander. My removal is not producing the slightest sensation—a blind man is leaving the army, that is all. More like me can be found in Russia by thousands!"

'The marshal is angry with the Emperor and punishes all of us; isn't it logical!

'That is the first act. In the next the interest and the absurdity rise, as they ought. After the marshal has departed it appears that we are within sight of the enemy and shall have to give battle. Buxhevden is commanding officer by right of seniority, but General Bennigsen is not of that opinion, the rather that it is he and his corps who face the enemy, and he wants to seize the opportunity to fight a battle "on his own hand," as the Germans say. He fights it. It is the battle of Pultusk, which is counted a great victory, but which in my opinion is nothing of the kind. We civilians, you know, have a very ugly way of deciding whether battles are lost or won. The side that retreats after the battle has lost, that is what we say, and according to that we have lost the battle of Pultusk. In short, we retreat after the battle, but we send a message to Petersburg with news of a victory, and the general does not give up the command to Buxhevden, hoping to receive from Petersburg the title of commander-in-chief in return for his victory. During this interregnum we begin an excessively interesting and original scheme of manoeuvres. The aim does not, as it should, consist in avoiding or attacking the enemy, but solely in avoiding General Buxhevden, who by right of seniority should be our commanding officer. We pursue this object with so much energy that even when we cross a river which is not fordable we burn the bridges in order to separate ourselves from our enemy, who, at the moment, is not Bonaparte but Buxhevden. General Buxhevden was nearly attacked and taken by a superior force of the enemy, in consequence of one of our fine manoeuvres which saved us from him. Buxhevden pursues us; we scuttle. No sooner does he cross to our side of the river than we cross back to the other. At last our enemy Buxhevden catches us and attacks us. The two generals quarrel. There is even a challenge on Buxhevden's part and an epileptic fit on Bennigsen's. But at the critical moment the messenger who carried the news of our Pultusk victory brings us from Petersburg our appointment as commander-in-chief, and the first enemy, Buxhevden, being overthrown, we are able to think of the second, Bonaparte. But what should happen at that very moment but the rising against us of a third enemy, which is the "holy armament" fiercely crying out for bread, meat, biscuits, hay, and I don't know what else! The storehouses are empty, the roads impassable. The "holy armament" sets itself to pillage, and that in a way of which the last campaign can give you no notion. Half the regiments have turned themselves into free companies, and are overrunning the country with fire and sword. The inhabitants are totally ruined, the hospitals are overflowing with sick, and famine is everywhere. Twice over the headquarters have been attacked by bands of marauders, and the commander-in-chief himself has had to ask for a battalion to drive them off. In one of these attacks my empty trunk and my dressing-gown were carried off. The Emperor proposes to give authority to all the commanders of divisions to shoot marauders, but I greatly fear this will oblige one half of the army to shoot the other.'

Prince Andrey at first read only with his eyes, but unconsciously what he read (though he knew how much faith to put in Bilibin) began to interest him more and more. When he reached this passage, he crumpled up the letter and threw it away. It was not what he read that angered him; he was angry that the far-away life out there—in which he had no part—could trouble him. He closed his eyes, rubbed his forehead with his hand, as though to drive out all interest in what he had been reading, and listened to what was passing in the nursery. Suddenly he fancied a strange sound through the door. A panic seized him; he was afraid something might have happened to the baby while he was reading the letter. He went on tiptoe to the door of the nursery and opened it.

At the instant that he went in, he saw that the nurse was hiding something from him with a scared face, and Princess Marya was no longer beside the crib.

'My dear,' he heard behind him Princess Marya whisper—in a tone of despair it seemed to him. As so often happens after prolonged sleeplessness and anxiety, he was seized by a groundless panic; the idea came into his mind that the baby was dead. All he saw and heard seemed a confirmation of his terror.

'All is over,' he thought, and a cold sweat came out on his forehead. He went to the crib, beside himself, believing that he would find it empty, that the nurse had been hiding the dead baby. He opened the curtains, and for a long while his hurrying, frightened eyes could not find the baby. At last he saw him. The red-cheeked child lay stretched across the crib, with its head lower than the pillow; and it was making a smacking sound with its lips in its sleep and breathing evenly.

Prince Andrey rejoiced at seeing the child, as though he had already lost him. He bent down and tried with his lips whether the baby was feverish, as his sister had shown him. The soft forehead was moist; he touched the head with his hand—even the hair was wet: the child was in such a thorough perspiration. He was not dead; on the contrary, it was evident that the crisis was over and he was better. Prince Andrey longed to snatch up, to squeeze, to press to his heart that little helpless creature; he did not dare to do so. He stood over him, gazing at his head and his little arms and legs that showed beneath the quilt. He heard a rustle beside him, and a shadow seemed to come under the canopy of the crib. He did not look round, and still gazing at the baby's face, listened to his regular breathing. The dark shadow was Princess Marya, who with noiseless steps had approached the crib, lifted the canopy, and let it fall again behind her. Prince Andrey knew it was she without looking round, and held out his hand to her. She squeezed his hand.

'He is in a perspiration,' said Prince Andrey.

'I was coming to tell you so.'

The baby faintly stirred in its sleep, smiled and rubbed its forehead against the pillow.

Prince Andrey looked at his sister. In the even half light under the hanging of the crib, Princess Marya's luminous eyes shone more than usual with the happy tears that stood in them. She bent forward to her brother and kissed him, her head catching in the canopy of the crib. They shook their fingers at one another, and still stood in the twilight of the canopy, as though unwilling to leave that seclusion where they three were alone, shut off from all the world. Prince Andrey, ruffling his hair against the muslin hangings, was the first to move away. 'Yes, that is the one thing left me now,' he said with a sigh.

X

SHORTLY after his reception into the brotherhood of the freemasons, Pierre set off to the Kiev province, where were the greater number of his peasants, with full instructions written for his guidance in doing his duty on his estates.

On reaching Kiev, Pierre sent for all his stewards to his head counting-house, and explained to them his intentions and his desires. He told them that steps would very shortly be taken for the complete liberation of his peasants from serfdom, that till that time his peasants were not to be overburdened with labour, that the women with children were not to be sent out to work, that assistance was to be given to the peasants, that wrong-doing was to be met with admonishment, and not with corporal punishment; and that on every estate there must be founded hospitals, almshouses, and schools. Several of the stewards (among them were some bailiffs barely able to read and write) listened in dismay, supposing the upshot of the young count's remarks to be that he was dissatisfied with their management and embezzlement of his money. Others, after the first shock of alarm, derived amusement from Pierre's lisp and the new words he used that they had not heard before. Others again found a simple satisfaction in hearing the sound of their master's voice. But some, among them the head steward, divined from this speech how to deal with their master for the attainment of their own ends.

The head steward expressed great sympathy with Pierre's projects; but observed that, apart from these innovations, matters were in a bad way and needed thoroughly going into.

In spite of Count Bezuhov's enormous wealth, Pierre ever since he had inherited it, and had been, as people said, in receipt of an annual income of five hundred thousand, had felt much less rich than when he had been receiving an allowance of ten thousand from his father. In general outlines he was vaguely aware of the following budget. About eighty thousand was being paid into the Land Bank as interest on mortgages on his estates. About thirty thousand went to the maintenance of his estate in the suburbs of Moscow, his Moscow house, and his cousins, the princesses. About fifteen thousand were given in pensions, and as much more to benevolent institutions. One hundred and fifty thousand were sent to his countess for her maintenance. Some seventy thousand were paid away as interest on debts. The building of a new church had for the last two years been costing about ten thousand. The remainder—some one hundred thousand—was spent—he hardly knew how—and almost every year he was forced to borrow. Moreover every year the head steward wrote to him of conflagrations, or failures of crops, or of the necessity of rebuilding factories or workshops. And so the first duty with which Pierre was confronted was the one for which he had the least capacity and inclination—attention to practical business.

Every day Pierre *went into* things with the head steward. But he felt that what he was doing did not advance matters one inch. He felt that all he did was quite apart from the reality, that his efforts had no grip on the business, and would not set it in progress. One one side the head steward put matters in their worst light, proving to Pierre the necessity of paying his debts, and entering upon new undertakings with the labour of his serf peasants, to which Pierre would not agree. On the other side, Pierre urged their entering upon the work of liberation, to which the head steward objected the necessity of first paying off the loans from the Land Bank, and the consequent impossibility of haste in the matter. The head steward did not say that this was utterly impossible; he proposed as the means for attaining this object, the sale of the forests in the Kostroma province, the sale of the lands on the lower Volga, and of the Crimean estate. But all these operations were connected in the head steward's talk with such a complexity of processes, the removal of certain prohibitory clauses, the obtaining of certain permissions, and so on, that Pierre lost the thread, and could only say: 'Yes, yes, do so then.'

Pierre had none of that practical tenacity, which would have made it possible for him to undertake the business himself, and so he did not like it, and only tried to keep up a pretence of going into business before the head steward. The steward too kept up a pretence before the count of regarding his participation in it as of great use to his master, and a great inconvenience to himself.

In Kiev he had acquaintances: persons not acquaintances made haste to become so, and gave a warm welcome to the young man of fortune, the largest landowner of the province, who had come into their midst. The temptations on the side of Pierre's besetting weakness, the one to which he had given the first place at his initiation into the lodge, were so strong that he could not resist them. Again whole days, weeks, and months of his life were busily filled up with parties, dinners, breakfasts, and balls, giving him as little time to think as at Petersburg. Instead of the new life Pierre had hoped to lead, he was living just the same old life only in different surroundings.

Of the three precepts of freemasonry, Pierre had to admit that he had not fulfilled that one which prescribes for every mason the duty of being a model of moral life; and of the seven virtues he was entirely without two—morality and love of death. He comforted himself by reflecting that, on the other hand, he was fulfilling the other precept—the improvement of the human race; and had other virtues, love for his neighbour and liberality.

In the spring of 1807, Pierre made up his mind to go back again to Petersburg. On the way back he intended to make the tour of all his estates, and to ascertain personally what had been done of what had been prescribed by him, and in what position the people now were who had been entrusted to him by God, and whom he had been striving to benefit.

The head steward, who regarded all the young count's freaks as almost insanity—disastrous to him, to himself, and to his peasants—made concessions to his weaknesses. While continuing to represent the liberation of his serfs as impracticable, he made arrangements on all his estates for the building of schools, hospitals, and asylums on a large scale to be begun ready for the master's visit, prepared everywhere for him to be met, not with ceremonious processions, which he knew would not be to Pierre's taste, but with just the devotionally grateful welcomes, with holy images and bread and salt, such as would, according to his understanding of the count, impress him and delude him.

The southern spring, the easy, rapid journey in his Vienna carriage, and the solitude of the road, had a gladdening influence on Pierre. The estates, which he had not before visited, were one more picturesque than the other; the peasantry seemed everywhere thriving, and touchingly grateful for the benefits conferred on them. Everywhere he was met by welcomes, which though they embarrassed Pierre, yet at the bottom of his heart rejoiced him. At one place the peasants had brought him bread and salt and the images of Peter and Paul, and begged permission in honour of his patron saints, Peter and Paul, and in token of love and gratitude for the benefits conferred on them, to erect at their own expense a new chapel in the church. At another place he was welcomed by women with babies in their arms, who came to thank him for being released from the obligation of heavy labour. In a third place he was met by a priest with a cross, surrounded by children, whom by the favour of the count he was instructing in reading and writing and religion. On all his estates Pierre saw with his own eyes stone buildings erected, or in course of erection, all on one plan, hospitals, schools, and almshouses, which were in a short time to be opened. Everywhere Pierre saw the steward's reckoning of service due to him diminished in comparison with the past, and heard touching thanks for what was remitted from deputations of peasants in blue, full-skirted coats.

But Pierre did not know that where they brought him bread and salt and were building a chapel of Peter and Paul there was a trading village, and a fair on St. Peter's day, that the chapel had been built long ago by wealthy peasants of the village, and that nine-tenths of the peasants of that village were in the utmost destitution. He did not know that since by his orders nursing mothers were not sent to work on their master's land, those same mothers did even harder work on their own bit of land. He did not know that the priest who met him with the cross oppressed the peasants with his exactions, and that the pupils gathered around him were yielded up to him with tears and redeemed for large sums by their parents. He did not know that the stone buildings were being raised by his labourers, and increased the forced labour of his peasants, which was only less upon paper. He did not know that where the steward pointed out to him in the account book the reduction of rent to one-third in accordance with his will, the labour exacted had been raised by one half. And so Pierre was enchanted by his journey over his estates, and came back completely to the philanthropic frame of mind in which he had left Petersburg, and wrote enthusiastic letters to his preceptor and brother, as he called the grand master.

'How easy it is, how little effort is needed to do so much good,' thought Pierre, 'and how little we trouble ourselves to do it!'

He was happy at the gratitude shown him, but abashed at receiving it. That gratitude reminded him how much more he could do for those simple, good-hearted people.

The head steward, a very stupid and crafty man, who thoroughly understood the clever and naïve count, and played with him like a toy, seeing the effect produced on Pierre by these carefully arranged receptions, was bolder in advancing arguments to prove the impossibility, and even more, the uselessness of liberating the peasants, who were so perfectly happy without that.

In the recesses of his own heart, Pierre agreed with the steward that it was difficult to imagine people happier, and that there was no knowing what their future would be in freedom. But though reluctantly, he stuck to what he thought the right thing. The steward promised to use every effort to carry out the count's wishes, perceiving clearly that the count would never be in a position to verify whether every measure had been taken for the sale of the forests and estates for the repayment of the loans from the bank, would never probably even inquire, and would certainly never find out that the buildings, when finished, stood empty, and that the peasants were giving in labour and money just what they gave with other masters, that is, all that could be got out of them.

XI

RETURNING from his southern tour in the happiest frame of mind, Pierre carried out an intention he had long had, of visiting his friend Bolkonsky, whom he had not seen for two years.

Bogutcharovo lay in a flat, ugly part of the country, covered with fields and copses of fir and birch-trees, in parts cut down. The manor house was at the end of the straight village that ran along each side of the high road, behind an overflowing pond newly dug, and still bare of grass on its banks in the midst of a young copse, with several large pines standing among the smaller trees.

The homestead consisted of a threshing floor, serfs' quarters, stables, bath-houses, lodges, and a large stone house with a semi-circular façade, still in course of erection. Round the house a garden had been newly laid out. The fences and gates were solid and new; under a shed stood two fire-engines and a tub painted green. The paths were straight, the bridges were strong and furnished with stone parapets. Everything had an air of being cared for and looked after. The house serfs on the way, in reply to inquiries where the prince was living, pointed to a small new lodge at the very edge of the pond. Prince Andrey's old body-servant, Anton, after assisting Pierre out of his carriage, said that the prince was at home, and conducted him into a clean little lobby.

Pierre was struck by the modesty of this little, clean house, after the splendid surroundings in which he had last seen his friend in Petersburg.

He went hurriedly into the little parlour, still unplastered and smelling of pine wood, and would have gone further, but Anton ran ahead on tiptoe and knocked at the door.

'What is it?' he heard a harsh, unpleasant voice.

'A visitor,' answered Anton.

'Ask him to wait'; and there was the sound of a chair being pushed back.

Pierre went with rapid steps to the door, and came face to face with

Prince Andrey, who came out frowning and looking older. Pierre embraced him, and taking off his spectacles, kissed him and looked close at him.

'Well, I didn't expect you; I am glad,' said Prince Andrey.

Pierre said nothing; he was looking in wonder at his friend, and could not take his eyes off him. He was struck by the change in Prince Andrey. His words were warm, there was a smile on the lips and the face, but there was a lustreless, dead look in his eyes, into which, in spite of his evident desire to seem glad, Prince Andrey could not throw a gleam of happiness. It was not only that his friend was thinner, paler, more manly looking, but the look in his eyes and the line on his brow, that expressed prolonged concentration on some one subject, struck Pierre and repelled him till he got used to it.

On meeting after a long separation, the conversation, as is always the case, did not for a long while rest on one subject. They asked questions and gave brief replies about things of which they knew themselves they must talk at length. At last the conversation began gradually to revolve more slowly about questions previously touched only in passing, their life in the past, their plans for the future, Pierre's journeys, and what he had been doing, the war, and so on. The concentrated and crushed look which Pierre had noticed in Prince Andrey's eyes was still more striking now in the smile with which he listened to him, especially when he was telling him with earnestness and delight of his past or his future. It was as though Prince Andrey would have liked to take interest in what he was telling him, but could not. Pierre began to feel that to express enthusiasm, ideals, and hopes of happiness and goodness was unseemly before Prince Andrey. He felt ashamed of giving expression to all the new ideas he had gained from the masons, which had been revived and strengthened in him by his last tour. He restrained himself, afraid of seeming naïve. At the same time he felt an irresistible desire to show his friend at once that he was now a quite different Pierre, better than the one he had known in Petersburg.

'I can't tell you how much I have passed through during this time. I shouldn't know my old self.'

'Yes, you are very, very much changed since those days,' said Prince Andrey.

'Well, and what of you?' asked Pierre. 'What are your plans?'

'Plans?' repeated Prince Andrey ironically. 'My plans?' he repeated, as though wondering what was the meaning of such a word. 'Why, you see, I am building; I want next year to settle in here altogether...'

Pierre looked silently and intently into the face of Prince Andrey, which had grown so much older.

'No, I'm asking about . . .' Pierre began, but Prince Andrey interrupted him.

'But why talk about me . . . talk to me, and tell me about your journey, about everything you have been doing on your estates.'

Pierre began describing what he had been doing on his estates, trying as far as he could to disguise his share in the improvements made on them. Prince Andrey several times put in a few words before Pierre could utter them, as though all Pierre's doings were an old, familiar story, and he were hearing it not only without interest, but even as it were a little ashamed of what was told him.

Pierre began to feel awkward and positively wretched in his friend's company. He relapsed into silence.

'I tell you what, my dear fellow,' said Prince Andrey, who was unmistakably dreary and ill at ease with his visitor, 'I'm simply bivouacking here; I only came over to have a look at things. I'm going back again to my sister today. I will introduce you to her. But I think you know her, though,' he added, obviously trying to provide entertainment for his guest, with whom he now found nothing in common. 'We will set off after dinner. And now would you care to see my place?' They went out and walked about till dinner time, talking of political news and common acquaintances, like people not very intimate. The only thing of which Prince Andrey now spoke with some eagerness and interest was the new buildings and homestead he was building; but even in the middle of a conversation on this subject, on the scaffolding, when Prince Andrey was describing to Pierre the plan of the house, he suddenly stopped. 'There's nothing interesting in that, though, let us go in to dinner and set off.'

At dinner the conversation fell on Pierre's marriage.

'I was very much surprised when I heard of it,' said Prince Andrey.

Pierre blushed as he always did at any reference to his marriage, and said hurriedly: 'I'll tell you one day how it all happened. But you know that it's all over and for ever.'

'For ever?' said Prince Andrey; 'nothing's for ever.'

'But do you know how it all ended? Did you hear of the duel?'

'Yes, you had to go through that too!'

'The one thing for which I thank God is that I didn't kill that man,' said Pierre.

'Why so?' said Prince Andrey. 'To kill a vicious dog is a very good thing to do, really.'

'No, to kill a man is bad, wrong . . .'

'Why is it wrong?' repeated Prince Andrey; 'what's right and wrong is a question it has not been given to men to decide. Men are for ever in error, and always will be in error, and in nothing more than in what they regard as right and wrong.'

'What does harm to another man is wrong,' said Pierre, feeling with pleasure that for the first time since his arrival Prince Andrey was roused and was beginning to speak and eager to give expression to what had made him what he now was.

'And who has told you what is harm to another man?' he asked.

'Harm? harm?' said Pierre; 'we all know what harms ourselves.'

'Yes, we know that, but it's not the same harm we know about for ourselves that we do to another man,' said Prince Andrey, growing more and more eager, and evidently anxious to express to Pierre his new view of things. He spoke in French. 'I only know two very real ills in life, remorse and sickness. There is no good except the absence of those ills. To live for myself so as to avoid these two evils: that's the sum of my wisdom now.'

'And love for your neighbour, and self-sacrifice?' began Pierre. 'No, I can't agree with you! To live with the sole object of avoiding doing evil, so as not to be remorseful, that's very little. I used to live so, I used to live for myself, and I spoilt my life. And only now, when I'm living, at least trying to live' (modesty impelled Pierre to correct himself) 'for others, only now I have learnt to know all the happiness of life. No, I don't agree with you, and indeed, you don't believe what you're saying yourself.'

Prince Andrey looked at Pierre without speaking, and smiled ironically. 'Well, you'll see my sister Marie. You will get on with her,' said he. 'Perhaps you are right for yourself,' he added, after a brief pause, 'but every one lives in his own way; you used to live for yourself, and you say that by doing so you almost spoiled your life, and have only known happiness since you began to live for others. And my experience has been the reverse. I used to live for glory. (And what is glory? The same love for others, the desire to do something for them, the desire of their praise.) In that way I lived for others, and not almost, but quite spoilt my life. And I have become more peaceful since I live only for myself.'

'But how are you living only for yourself?' Pierre asked, getting hot. 'What of your son, your sister, your father?'

'Yes, but that's all the same as myself, they are not others,' said Prince Andrey; 'but others, one's neighbours, as you and Marie call them, they are the great source of error and evil. One's neighbours are those—your Kiev peasants—whom one wants to do good to.'

And he looked at Pierre with a glance of ironical challenge. He unmistakably meant to draw him on.

'You are joking,' said Pierre, getting more and more earnest. 'What error and evil can there be in my wishing (I have done very little and done it very badly), but still wishing to do good, and doing indeed something any way? Where can be the harm if unhappy people, our peasants, people just like ourselves, growing up and dying with no other idea of God and the truth, but a senseless prayer and ceremony, if they are instructed in the consoling doctrines of a future life, of retribution, and recompense and consolation? What harm and error can there be in my giving them doctors, and a hospital, and a refuge for the aged, when men are dying of disease without help, and it is so easy to give them material aid? And isn't there palpable, incontestable good, when the peasants and the women with young children have no rest day or night, and I give them leisure and rest? . . .' said Pierre, talking hurriedly and lisping. 'And I have done that; badly it's true, and too little of it, but I have done something towards it, and you'll not only fail to shake my conviction that I have done well, you'll not even shake my conviction that you don't believe that yourself. And the great thing,' Pierre continued, 'is that I know this—and know it for a certainty—that the enjoyment of doing this good is the only real happiness in life.'

'Oh, if you put the question like that, it's a different matter,' said Prince Andrey. 'I'm building a house and laying out a garden, while you are building hospitals. Either occupation may serve to pass the time. But as to what's right and what's good—leave that to one who knows all to judge; it's not for us to decide. Well, you want an argument,' he added; 'all right, let us have one.' They got up from the table and sat out on the steps in default of a balcony. 'Come, let us argue the matter,' said Prince Andrey. 'You talk of schools,' he went on, crooking one finger, 'instruction, and so forth, that is, you want to draw him' (he pointed to a peasant who passed by them taking off his cap), 'out of his animal condition and to give him spiritual needs, but it seems to me that the only possible happiness is animal happiness, and you want to deprive him of it. I envy him, while you are trying to make him into me, without giving him my circumstances. Another thing you speak of is lightening his toil. But to my notions, physical labour is as much a necessity for him, as much a condition of his existence, as intellectual work is for me and for you. You can't help thinking. I go to bed at three o'clock, thoughts come into my mind, and I can't go to sleep; I turn over, and can't sleep till morning, because I'm thinking, and I can't help thinking, just as he can't help ploughing and mowing. If he didn't, he would go to the tavern, or become ill. Just as I could not stand his terrible physical labour, but should die of it in a week, so he could not stand my physical inactivity, he would grow fat and die. The third thing—what was it you talked about?'

Prince Andrey crooked his third finger.

'Oh, yes, hospitals, medicine. He has a fit and dies, but you have him bled and cure him. He will drag about an invalid for ten years, a burden to every one. It would be ever so much simpler and more comfortable for him to die. Others are born, and there are always plenty. If you grudge losing a labourer—that's how I look at him—but you want to cure him from love for him. But he has no need of that. And besides, what a notion that medicine has ever cured any one! Killed them—yes!' he said, scowling and turning away from Pierre.

Prince Andrey gave such clear and precise utterance to his ideas that it was evident he had thought more than once of this already, and he talked rapidly and eagerly, as a man does who has long been silent. His eyes grew keener, the more pessimistic were the views he expressed.

'Oh, this is awful, awful!' said Pierre. 'I don't understand how one can live with such ideas. I have had moments of thinking like that; it was not long ago at Moscow and on a journey, but then I become so abject that I don't live at all, everything's hateful to me ... myself, most of all. Then I don't eat, I don't wash ... how can you go on? ...'

'Why not wash, that's not clean,' said Prince Andrey; 'on the contrary, one has to try and make one's life more agreeable as far as one can. I'm alive, and it's not my fault that I am, and so I have to try without hurting others to get on as well as I can till death.'

'But what impulse have you to live with such ideas? You would sit still without stirring, taking no part in anything....'

'Life won't leave you in peace even so. I should be glad to do nothing, but here you see on one side, the local nobility have done me the honour of electing me a marshal; it was all I could do to get out of it. They could not understand that I haven't what's needed, haven't that good-natured, fussy vulgarity we all know so well, that's needed for it. Then there's this house here, which had to be built that I might have a nook of my own where I could be quiet. Now there's the militia.'

'Why aren't you serving in the army?'

'After Austerlitz!' said Prince Andrey gloomily. 'No, thank you; I swore to myself that I would never serve in the Russian army again. And I will not, if Bonaparte were stationed here at Smolensk, threatening Bleak Hills! even then I wouldn't serve in the Russian army. Well, so I was saying,' Prince Andrey went on, regaining his composure. 'Now, there's the militia; my father's commander-in-chief of the third circuit, and the only means for me to escape from active service is to serve under him.'

'So you are in the service, then?'

'Yes.' He was silent for a while.

'Then why do you serve?'

'I'll tell you why. My father is one of the most remarkable men of his time. But he's grown old, and he's not cruel exactly, but he's of too energetic a character. He's terrible from his habit of unlimited power, and now with this authority given him by the Emperor as a commander-in-chief in the militia. If I had been two hours later a fortnight ago, he would have hanged the register-clerk at Yuhnovo,' said Prince Andrey with a smile. 'So I serve under him now because no one except me has any influence over my father, and I sometimes save him from an act which would be a source of misery to him afterwards.'

'Ah, there you see!'

'Yes, it is not as you think,' Prince Andrey continued. 'I didn't, and I don't wish well in the slightest to that scoundrelly register-clerk who had stolen boots or something from the militiamen; indeed, I would have been very glad to see him hanged, but I feel for my father, that is again myself.'

Prince Andrey grew more and more eager. His eyes glittered feverishly, as he tried to prove to Pierre that there was never the slightest desire to do good to his neighbour in his actions.

'Well, you want to liberate your serfs, too,' he pursued; 'that's a very good thing, but not for you—I expect you have never flogged a man nor sent one to Siberia—and still less for your peasants. If a peasant is beaten, flogged, sent to Siberia, I dare say he's not a bit the worse for it. In Siberia he can lead the same brute existence; the stripes on the body heal, and he's as happy as before. But it's needed for the people who are ruined morally, who are devoured by remorse, who stifle that remorse and grow callous from being able to inflict punishment all round them. Perhaps you have not seen it, but I have seen good men, brought up in the traditions of unlimited power with years, as they grew more irritable, become cruel and brutal, conscious of it, and unable to control themselves, and growing more and more miserable.'

Prince Andrey spoke with such earnestness that Pierre could not help thinking those ideas were suggested to him by his father. He made him no reply.

'So that's what I grieve for—for human dignity, for peace of conscience, for purity, and not for their backs or their heads, which always remain just the same backs and heads, however you thrash or shave them.'

'No, no, a thousand times no! I shall never agree with you,' said Pierre.

XII

IN the evening Prince Andrey and Pierre got into the coach and drove to Bleak Hills. Prince Andrey watched Pierre and broke the silence from time to time with speeches that showed he was in a good humour.

Pointing to the fields, he told him of the improvements he was making in the management of his land.

Pierre preserved a gloomy silence, replying only by monosyllables, and apparently plunged in his own thoughts.

Pierre was reflecting that Prince Andrey was unhappy, that he was in error, that he did not know the true light, and that he ought to come to his aid, enlighten him and lift him up. But as soon as he began to deliberate on what he would say, he foresaw that Prince Andrey with one word, one argument, would annihilate everything in his doctrine; and he was afraid to begin, afraid of exposing his most cherished and holiest to possible ridicule.

'No, what makes you think so?' Pierre began all at once, lowering his head and looking like a butting bull; 'what makes you think so? You ought not to think so.'

'Think so, about what?' asked Prince Andrey in surprise.

'About life. About the destination of man. It can't be so. I used to think like that, and I have been saved, do you know, by what?—freemasonry. No, you must not smile. Freemasonry is not a religious sect, nor mere ceremonial rites, as I used to suppose; freemasonry is the best, the only expression of the highest, eternal aspects of humanity.' And he began expounding to Prince Andrey freemasonry, as he understood it.

He said that freemasonry is the teaching of Christianity, freed from its political and religious fetters; the teaching of equality, fraternity, and love.

'Our holy brotherhood is the only thing that has real meaning in life; all the rest is a dream,' said Pierre. 'You understand, my dear fellow, that outside this brotherhood all is filled with lying and falsehood, and I agree with you that there's nothing left for an intelligent and good-hearted man but, like you, to get through his life, only trying not to hurt others. But make our fundamental convictions your own, enter into our brotherhood, give yourself up to us, let us guide you, and you will at once feel yourself, as I felt, a part of a vast, unseen chain, the origin of which is lost in the skies,' said Pierre, looking straight before him.

Prince Andrey listened to Pierre's words in silence. Several times he did not catch words from the noise of the wheels, and he asked Pierre to repeat what he had missed. From the peculiar light that glowed in Prince Andrey's eyes, and from his silence, Pierre saw that his words were not in vain, that Prince Andrey would not interrupt him nor laugh at what he said.

They reached a river that had overflowed its banks, and had to cross it by a ferry. While the coach and horses waited they crossed on the ferry. Prince Andrey with his elbow on the rail gazed mutely over the stretch of water shining in the setting sun.

'Well, what do you think about it?' asked Pierre. 'Why are you silent?'

'What do I think? I have heard what you say. That's all right,' said Prince Andrey. 'But you say, enter into our brotherhood, and we will show you the object of life and the destination of man, and the laws that govern the universe. But who are we?—men? How do you know it all? Why is it I alone don't see what you see? You see on earth the dominion of good and truth, but I don't see it.'

Pierre interrupted him. 'Do you believe in a future life?' he asked.

'In a future life?' repeated Prince Andrey.

But Pierre did not give him time to answer, and took this repetition as a negative reply, the more readily as he knew Prince Andrey's atheistic views in the past. 'You say that you can't see the dominion of good and truth on the earth. I have not seen it either, and it cannot be seen if one looks upon our life as the end of everything. On earth, this earth here' (Pierre pointed to the open country), 'there is no truth —all is deception and wickedness. But in the world, the whole world, there is a dominion of truth, and we are now the children of earth, but eternally the children of the whole universe. Don't I feel in my soul that I am a part of that vast, harmonious whole? Don't I feel that in that vast, innumerable multitude of beings, in which is made manifest the Godhead, the higher power—what you choose to call it—I constitute one grain, one step upward from lower beings to higher ones? If I see, see clearly that ladder that rises up from the vegetable to man, why should I suppose that ladder breaks off with me and does not go on further and further? I feel that I cannot disappear as nothing does disappear in the universe, that indeed I always shall be and always have been. I feel that beside me, above me, there are spirits, and that in their world there is truth.'

'Yes, that's Herder's theory,' said Prince Andrey. 'But it's not that, my dear boy, convinces me; but life and death are what have convinced me. What convinces me is seeing a creature dear to me, and bound up with me, to whom one has done wrong, and hoped to make it right'

(Prince Andrey's voice shook and he turned away), 'and all at once that creature suffers, is in agony, and ceases to be. . . . What for? It cannot be that there is no answer! And I believe there is. . . . That's what convinces, that's what has convinced me,' said Prince Andrey.

'Just so, just so,' said Pierre; 'isn't that the very thing I'm saying?'

'No. I only say that one is convinced of the necessity of a future life, not by argument, but when one goes hand-in-hand with some one, and all at once that some one slips away *yonder into nowhere*, and you are left facing that abyss and looking down into it. And I have looked into it . . .'

'Well, that's it then! You know there is a *yonder* and there is *some one*. *Yonder* is the future life; *Some One* is God.'

Prince Andrey did not answer. The coach and horses had long been taken across to the other bank, and had been put back into the shafts, and the sun had half sunk below the horizon, and the frost of evening was starring the pools at the fording-place; but Pierre and Andrey, to the astonishment of the footmen, coachmen, and ferrymen, still stood in the ferry and were still talking.

'If there is God and there is a future life, then there is truth and there is goodness; and the highest happiness of man consists in striving for their attainment. We must live, we must love, we must believe,' said Pierre, 'that we are not only living today on this clod of earth, but have lived and will live for ever there in everything' (he pointed to the sky). Prince Andrey stood with his elbow on the rail of the ferry, and as he listened to Pierre he kept his eyes fixed on the red reflection of the sun on the bluish stretch of water. Pierre ceased speaking. There was perfect stillness. The ferry had long since come to a standstill, and only the eddies of the current flapped with a faint sound on the bottom of the ferry boat. It seemed to Prince Andrey that the lapping of the water kept up a refrain to Pierre's words: 'It's the truth, believe it.'

Prince Andrey sighed, and with a radiant, child-like, tender look in his eyes glanced at the face of Pierre—flushed and triumphant, though still timidly conscious of his friend's superiority.

'Yes, if only it were so!' he said. 'Let us go and get in, though,' added Prince Andrey, and as he got out of the ferry he looked up at the sky, to which Pierre had pointed him, and for the first time since Austerlitz he saw the lofty, eternal sky, as he had seen it lying on the field of Austerlitz, and something that had long been slumbering, something better that had been in him, suddenly awoke with a joyful, youthful feeling in his soul. That feeling vanished as soon as Prince Andrey returned again to the habitual conditions of life, but he knew that that feeling—though he knew not how to develop it—was still within him.

Pierre's visit was for Prince Andrey an epoch, from which there began, though outwardly unchanged, a new life in his inner world.

XIII

IT was dark by the time Prince Andrey and Pierre drove up to the principal entrance of the house at Bleak Hills. While they were driving in, Prince Andrey with a smile drew Pierre's attention to a commotion that was taking place at the back entrance. A bent little old woman with a wallet on her back, and a short man with long hair, in a black garment, ran back to the gate on seeing the carriage driving up. Two women ran out after them, and all the four, looking round at the carriage with scared faces, ran in at the back entrance.

'Those are Masha's God's folk,' said Prince Andrey. 'They took us for my father. It's the one matter in which she does not obey him. He orders them to drive away these pilgrims, but she receives them.'

'But what are God's folk?' asked Pierre.

Prince Andrey had not time to answer him. The servants came out to meet them, and he inquired where the old prince was and whether they expected him home soon. The old prince was still in the town, and they were expecting him every minute.

Prince Andrey led Pierre away to his own suite of rooms, which were always in perfect readiness for him in his father's house, and went off himself to the nursery.

'Let us go to my sister,' said Prince Andrey, coming back to Pierre; 'I have not seen her yet, she is in hiding now, sitting with her God's folk. Serve her right; she will be put to shame, and you will see God's folk. It's curious, upon my word.'

'What are "God's folk"?' asked Pierre.

'You shall see.'

Princess Marya certainly was disconcerted, and reddened in patches when they went in. In her snug room, with lamps before the holy picture stand, there was sitting, behind the samovar, on the sofa beside her, a young lad with a long nose and long hair, wearing a monk's cassock. In a low chair near sat a wrinkled, thin, old woman, with a meek expression on her child-like face.

'Andrey, why did you not let me know?' she said with mild reproach, standing before her pilgrims like a hen before her chickens.

'Delighted to see you. I am very glad to see you,' she said to Pierre, as he kissed her hand. She had known him as a child, and now his friendship with Andrey, his unhappy marriage, and above all, his kindly, simple face, disposed her favourably to him. She looked at him with her beautiful, luminous eyes, and seemed to say to him: 'I like you very much, but, please, don't laugh at my friends.'

After the first phrases of greeting, they sat down.

'Oh, and Ivanushka's here,' said Prince Andrey with a smile, indicating the young pilgrim.

'Andryusha!' said Princess Marya imploringly.

'You must know, it is a woman,' said Andrey to Pierre in French.

'Andrey, for heaven's sake!' repeated Princess Marya.

It was plain that Prince Andrey's ironical tone to the pilgrims, and Princess Marya's helpless championship of them, were their habitual, long-established attitudes on the subject.

'Why, my dear girl,' said Prince Andrey, 'you ought to be obliged to me, on the contrary, for explaining your intimacy with this young man to Pierre.'

'Indeed?' said Pierre, looking with curiosity and seriousness (for which Princess Marya felt particularly grateful to him) at the face of Ivanushka, who, seeing that he was the subject under discussion, looked at all of them with his crafty eyes.

Princess Marya had not the slightest need to feel embarrassed on her friends' account. They were quite at their ease. The old woman cast down her eyes, but stole sidelong glances at the newcomers, and turning her cup upside down in the saucer, and laying a nibbled lump of sugar beside it, sat calmly without stirring in her chair, waiting to be offered another cup. Ivanushka, sipping out of the saucer, peeped from under his brows with his sly, feminine eyes at the young men.

'Where have you been, in Kiev?' Prince Andrey asked the old woman.

'I have, good sir,' answered the old woman, who was conversationally disposed; 'just at the Holy Birth I was deemed worthy to be a partaker in holy, heavenly mysteries from the saints. And now, good sir, from Kolyazin a great blessing has been revealed.'

'And Ivanushka was with you?'

'I go alone by myself, benefactor,' said Ivanushka, trying to speak in a bass voice. 'It was only at Yuhnovo I joined Pelageyushka . . .'

Pelageyushka interrupted her companion; she was evidently anxious to tell of what she had seen. 'In Kolyazin, good sir, great is the blessing revealed.'

'What, new relics?' asked Prince Andrey.

'Hush, Andrey,' said Princess Marya. 'Don't tell us about it, Pelageyushka.'

'Not . . . nay, ma'am, why not tell him? I like him. He's a good gentleman, chosen of God, he's my benefactor; he gave me ten roubles,

I remember. When I was in Kiev, Kiryusha, the crazy pilgrim, tells me—verily a man of God, winter and summer he goes barefoot—why are you not going to your right place, says he; go to Kolyazin, there a wonder-working ikon, a holy Mother of God has been revealed. On these words I said good-bye to the holy folk and off I went . . .'

All were silent, only the pilgrim woman talked on in her measured voice, drawing her breath regularly. 'I came, good sir, and folks say to me: a great blessing has been vouchsafed, drops of myrrh trickle from the cheeks of the Holy Mother of God . . .'

'Come, that will do, that will do; you shall tell me later,' said Princess Marya, flushing.

'Let me ask her a question,' said Pierre. 'Did you see it yourself?' he asked.

'To be sure, good sir, I myself was found worthy. Such a brightness overspread the face, like the light of heaven, and from the Holy Mother's cheeks drops like this and like this . . .'

'Why, but it must be a trick,' said Pierre naïvely, after listening attentively to the old woman.

'Oh, sir, what a thing to say!' said Pelageyushka with horror, turning to Princess Marya for support.

'They impose upon the people,' he repeated.

'Lord Jesus Christ!' said the pilgrim woman, crossing herself. 'Oh, don't speak so, sir. There was a general did not believe like that, said "the monks cheat," and as he said it, he was struck blind. And he dreamed a dream, the holy mother of Petchersky comes to him and says: "Believe in me and I will heal thee." And so he kept beseeching them: "Take me to her, take me to her." It's the holy truth I'm telling you, I've seen it myself. They carried him, blind as he was, to her; he went up, fell down, and said: "Heal me! I will give thee," says he, "what the Tsar bestowed on me." I saw myself—a sort of star carved in it. Well—he regained his sight! It's a sin to speak so. God will punish you,' she said admonishingly to Pierre.

'How? Was the star in the holy image?' asked Pierre.

'And didn't they make the holy mother a general?' said Prince Andrey, smiling.

Pelageyushka turned suddenly pale and flung up her hands.

'Sir, sir, it's a sin of you, you've a son!' she said, suddenly turning from white to dark red. 'Sir, for what you have said, God forgive you.' She crossed herself. 'Lord, forgive him. Lady, what's this? . . .' she turned to Princess Marya. She got up, and almost crying began gathering up her wallet. Plainly she was both frightened and ashamed at having accepted bounty in a house where they could say such things, and sorry that she must henceforth deprive herself of the bounty of that house.

'What did you want to do this for?' said Princess Marya. 'Why did you come to me? . . .'

'No, I was joking really, Pelageyushka,' said Pierre. '*Princess, ma parole, je n'ai pas voulu l'offenser.* I said it, meaning nothing. Don't think of it, I was joking,' he said, smiling timidly and trying to smoothe over his crime. 'It was all my fault; but he didn't mean it, he was joking.'

Pelageyushka remained mistrustful, but Pierre's face wore a look of such genuine penitence, and Prince Andrey looked so mildly from Pelageyushka to Pierre, that she was gradually reassured.

XIV

THE pilgrim woman was appeased, and being drawn into conversation again, told them a long story again of Father Amfilohey, who was of so holy a life that his hands smelt of incense, and how some monks of her acquaintance had, on her last pilgrimage to Kiev, given her the keys of the catacombs, and how taking with her some dry bread she had spent two days and nights in the catacombs with the saints. 'I pray a bit in one, chant a hymn, and go into another. I fall asleep, again I go and kiss the holy relics; and such peace, ma'am, such blessedness, that one has no wish to come out into God's world again.'

Pierre listened to her attentively and seriously. Prince Andrey went out of the room. And leaving God's folk to finish their tea, Princess Marya followed him with Pierre to the drawing-room. 'You are very kind,' she said to him.

'Ah, I really didn't mean to hurt her feelings; I so well understand those feelings, and prize them so highly.'

Princess Marya looked mutely at him, and smiled affectionately.

'I have known you a long time, you see, and I love you like a brother,' she said. 'How do you think Andrey is looking?' she asked hurriedly, not letting him have time to say anything in reply to her affectionate words. 'He makes me very uneasy. His health was better in the winter, but last spring the wound reopened, and the doctor says he ought to go away for proper treatment. And I feel afraid for him morally. He has not a character like us women, to suffer and find relief for sorrow in tears. He keeps it all within him. Today he is lively and in good spirits. But that's the effect of your being with him; he is not often like this. If only you could persuade him to go abroad. He needs activity, and this quiet, regular life is bad for him. Others don't notice it, but I see it.'

Towards ten o'clock the footmen rushed to the steps, hearing the bells of the old prince's carriage approaching. Prince Andrey and Pierre, too, went out on to the steps.

'Who's that?' asked the old prince, as he got out of the carriage and saw Pierre.

'Ah! very glad! kiss me!' he said, on learning who the young stranger was.

The old prince was in a good humour and very cordial to Pierre.

Before supper, Prince Andrey, on coming back into his father's study, found the old prince in hot dispute with Pierre. The latter was maintaining that a time would come when there would be no more war. The old prince was making fun of him, but with good humour.

'Let off blood from men's veins and fill them up with water, then there'll be no more war. Old women's nonsense, old women's nonsense,' he was saying, but still he slapped Pierre affectionately on the shoulder, and went up to the table where Prince Andrey, evidently not caring to take part in the conversation, was looking through the papers the old prince had brought from the town. The old prince went up to him and began to talk of business.

'The marshal, a Count Rostov, hasn't sent half his contingent. Came to the town and thought fit to invite me to dinner—a pretty dinner I gave him! ... And here, look at this.... Well, my boy,' said the old prince to his son, clapping Pierre on the shoulder, 'your friend is a capital fellow; I like him! He warms me up. Other people will talk sense and one doesn't care to listen, and he talks nonsense, but it does an old man like me good. There, run along,' he said; 'maybe I'll come and sit with you at your supper. We'll have another dispute. Make friends with my dunce, Princess Marya,' he shouted to Pierre from the door.

It was only now on his visit to Bleak Hills that Pierre appreciated fully all the charm of his friendship with Prince Andrey. The charm was not so manifest in his relations with his friend himself as in his relations with all his family and household. Though he had hardly known them, Pierre felt at once like an old friend both with the harsh old prince and the gentle, timid Princess Marya. They all liked him. Not only Princess Marya, who had been won by his kindliness with the pilgrims, looked at him with her most radiant expression, little Prince Nikolay, as the old prince called the year-old baby, smiled at Pierre and went to him. Mihail Ivanitch and Mademoiselle Bourienne looked at him with smiles when he talked to the old prince.

The old prince came in to supper; it was obviously on Pierre's account. He was extremely warm with him both days of his stay at Bleak Hills, and asked him to come and stay with him again.

When Pierre had gone, and all the members of the family were met together, they began to criticise him, as people always do after a new guest has left, and as rarely happens, all said nothing but good of him.

XV

ON returning this time from his leave, Rostov for the first time felt and recognised how strong was the tie that bound him to Denisov and all his regiment.

When Rostov reached the regiment, he experienced a sensation akin to what he had felt on reaching his home at Moscow. When he caught sight of the first hussar in the unbuttoned uniform of his regiment, when he recognised red-haired Dementyev, and saw the picket ropes of the chestnut horses, when Lavrushka gleefully shouted to his master, 'The count has come!' and Denisov, who had been asleep on his bed, ran all dishevelled out of the mud-hut, and embraced him, and the officers gathered around to welcome the newcomer—Rostov felt the same sensation as when his mother had embraced him, and his father and sisters, and the tears of joy that rose in his throat prevented his speaking. The regiment was a home, too, and a home as unchangeably dear and precious as the parental home.

After reporting himself to his colonel, being assigned to his own squadron, and serving on orderly duty and going for forage, after entering into all the little interests of the regiment, and feeling himself deprived of liberty and nailed down within one narrow, unchangeable framework, Rostov had the same feeling of peace and of moral support and the same sense of being at home here, and in his proper place, as he had once felt under his father's roof. Here was none of all that confusion of the free world, where he did not know his proper place, and made mistakes in exercising free choice. There was no Sonya, with whom one ought or ought not to have a clear understanding. There was no possibility of going to one place or to another. There were not twenty-four hours every day which could be used in so many different ways. There were not those innumerable masses of people of whom no one was nearer or further from one. There were none of those vague and undefined money relations with his father; no memories of his awful loss to Dolohov. Here in the regiment everything was clear and simple. The whole world was divided into two unequal parts: one, our Pavlograd regiment, and the other—all the remainder. And with all that great remainder one had no concern. In the regiment everything was well known: this man was a lieutenant, that one a captain; this was a good fellow and that one was not; but most of all, every one was a comrade. The canteen-keeper would give him credit, his pay would come every four months. There was no need of thought or of choice; one had only to do nothing that was considered low in the Pavlograd regiment, and when occasion came, to do what was clear and distinct, defined and commanded; and all would be well.

On becoming subject again to the definite regulations of regimental life, Rostov had a sense of pleasure and relief, such as a weary man feels in lying down to rest. The regimental life was the greater relief to Rostov on this campaign, because after his loss to Dolohov (for which, in spite of his family's efforts to console him, he could not forgive himself), he had resolved not to serve as before, but to atone for his fault by good conduct, and by being a thoroughly good soldier and officer, that is a good man, a task so difficult in the *world*, but so possible in the regiment.

Rostov had determined to repay his gambling debt to his parents in the course of five years. He had been sent ten thousand a year; now he had made up his mind to take only two thousand, and to leave the remainder to repay the debt to his parents.

After continual retreats, advances, and engagements at Pultusk and Preussisch-Eylau, our army was concentrated about Bartenstein. They were waiting for the arrival of the Tsar and the beginning of a new campaign.

The Pavlograd regiment, belonging to that part of the army which had been in the campaign of 1805, had stayed behind in Russia to make up its full complement of men, and did not arrive in time for the first actions of the campaign. It took no part in the battles of Pultusk and of Preussisch-Eylau, and joining the army in the field, in the second half of the campaign, was attached to Platov's detachment.

Platov's detachment was acting independently of the main army. Several times the Pavlograd hussars had taken part in skirmishes with the enemy, had captured prisoners, and on one occasion had even carried off the carriages of Marshal Oudinot. In April the Pavlograd hussars had for several weeks been encamped near an utterly ruined, empty German village, and had not stirred from that spot.

It was thawing, muddy, and cold, the ice had broken upon the river, the roads had become impassable; for several days there had been neither provender for the horses nor provisions for the men. Seeing that the transport of provisions was impossible, the soldiers dispersed about the abandoned and deserted villages to try and find potatoes, but very few were to be found even of these.

Everything had been eaten up, and all the inhabitants of the district had fled; those that remained were worse than beggars, and there was nothing to be taken from them; indeed, the soldiers, although little given to compassion, often gave their last ration to them.

The Pavlograd regiment had only lost two men wounded in action, but had lost almost half its men from hunger and disease. In the hospitals they died so invariably, that soldiers sick with fever or the swelling that came from bad food, preferred to remain on duty, to drag their feeble limbs in the ranks, rather than to go to the hospitals. As spring came on, the soldiers found a plant growing out of the ground, like asparagus, which for some reason they called Mary's sweet-root, and they wandered about the fields and meadows seeking this Mary's sweet-root (which was very bitter). They dug it up with their swords and ate it, in spite of all prohibition of this noxious root being eaten. In the spring a new disease broke out among the soldiers, with swelling of the hands, legs, and face, which the doctors attributed to eating this root. But in spite of the prohibition, the soldiers of Denisov's squadron in particular ate a great deal of the Mary's sweet-root, because they had been for a fortnight eking out the last biscuits, giving out only half a pound a man, and the potatoes in the last lot of stores were sprouting and rotten.

The horses, too, had for the last fortnight been fed on the thatched roofs of the houses; they were hideously thin, and still covered with their shaggy, winter coats, which were coming off in tufts.

In spite of their destitute condition, the soldiers and officers went on living exactly as they always did. Just as always, though now with pale and swollen faces and torn uniforms, the hussars were drawn up for calling over, went out to collect forage, cleaned down their horses, and rubbed up their arms, dragged in straw from the thatched roofs in place of fodder, and assembled for dinner round the cauldrons, from which they rose up hungry, making jokes over their vile food and their hunger. Just as ever, in their spare time off duty the soldiers lighted camp-fires, and warmed themselves naked before them, smoked, picked out, and baked the sprouting, rotten potatoes, and told and heard either stories of Potyomkin's and Suvorov's campaigns or popular legends of cunning Alyoshka, and of the priests' workman, Mikolka.

The officers lived as usual in twos and threes in the roofless, broken-down houses. The senior officers were busily engaged in trying to get hold of straw and potatoes, and the means of sustenance for the soldiers generally, while the younger ones spent their time as they always did, some over cards (money was plentiful, though there was nothing to eat), others over more innocent games, a sort of quoits and skittles. Of the general cause of the campaign little was said, partly because nothing certain was known, partly because there was a vague feeling that the war was not going well.

Rostov lived as before with Denisov, and the bond of friendship between them had become still closer since their furlough. Denisov never spoke of any of Rostov's family, but from the tender affection the senior officer showed his junior, Rostov felt that the older hussar's luckless passion for Natasha had something to do with the strengthening of their friendship. There was no doubt that Denisov tried to take care of Rostov, and to expose him as rarely as possible to danger, and after action it was with unmistakable joy that he saw him return safe and sound. On one of his foraging expeditions in a deserted and ruined village to which he had come in search of provisions, Rostov found an old Pole and his daughter with a tiny baby. They were without clothes or food; they had not the strength to go away on foot, and had no means of getting driven away. Rostov brought them to his camp, installed them in his own quarters, and maintained them for several weeks till the old man was better. One of Rostov's comrades, talking of women, began to rally him on the subject, declaring that he was the slyest fellow of the lot, and that he ought to be ashamed not to have introduced his comrades, too, to the pretty Polish woman he had rescued. Rostov took the jest as an insult, and firing up, said such unpleasant things to the officer, that Denisov had much ado to prevent a duel. When the officer had gone away, and Denisov, who knew nothing himself of Rostov's relations with the Polish woman, began to scold him for his hastiness, Rostov said to him: 'Say what you like.... She was like a sister to me, and I can't tell you how sick it made me ... because ... well, just because ...'

Denisov slapped him on the shoulder, and fell to walking rapidly up and down the room not looking at Rostov, which was what he always did at moments of emotional excitement. 'What a jolly lot of fools all you Rostovs are,' he said, and Rostov saw tears in Denisov's eyes.

XVI

In April the army was excited by the news of the arrival of the Tsar. Rostov did not succeed in being present at the review the Tsar held at Bartenstein; the Pavlograd hussars were at the advance posts, a long way in front of Bartenstein.

They were bivouacking. Denisov and Rostov were living in a mud hut dug out by the soldiers for them, and roofed with branches and turf. The hut was made after a pattern that had just come into fashion among the soldiers. A trench was dug out an ell and a half in breadth, two ells in depth, and three and half in length. At one end of the trench steps were scooped out, and these formed the entrance and the approach. The trench itself was the room, and in it the lucky officers, such as the captain, had a plank lying on piles at the further end away from the steps—this was the table. On both sides of the trench the earth had been thrown up, and these mounds made the two beds and the sofa. The roof was so constructed that one could stand upright in the middle, and on the beds it was possible to sit, if one moved up close to the table. Denisov, who always fared luxuriously, because the soldiers of his squadron were fond of him, had a board nailed up in the front part of the roof, and in the board a broken but cemented window pane. When it was very cold, they used to bring red-hot embers from the soldiers' camp-fires in a bent sheet of iron and set them near the steps (in the drawing-room, as Denisov called that part of the hut), and this made it so warm that the officers, of whom there were always a number with Denisov and Rostov, used to sit with nothing but their shirts on.

In April Rostov had been on duty. At eight o'clock in the morning, on coming home after a sleepless night, he sent for hot embers, changed his rain-soaked underclothes, said his prayers, drank some tea, warmed himself, put things tidy in his corner and on the table, and with a wind-beaten, heated face, and with only his shirt on, lay down on his back, folding his hands behind his head. He was engaged in agreeable meditations, reflecting that he would be sure to be promoted for the last reconnoitring expedition, and was expecting Denisov to come in. He wanted to talk to him.

Behind the hut he heard the resounding roar of Denisov, unmistakably irritated. Rostov moved to the window to see to whom he was speaking, and saw the quartermaster, Toptcheenko.

'I told you not to let them stuff themselves with that root—Mary's what do you call it!' Denisov was roaring. 'Why, I saw it myself, Lazartchuk was pulling it up in the field.'

'I did give the order, your honour; they won't heed it,' answered the quartermaster.

Rostov lay down again on his bed, and thought contentedly, 'Let him see to things now; he's fussing about while I have done my work, and I am lying here—it's splendid!' Through the wall he could hear now some one besides the quartermaster speaking. Lavrushka, Denisov's smart rogue of a valet, was telling him something about some transports, biscuits and oxen, he had seen, while on the look-out for provisions.

Again he heard Denisov's shout from further away, and the words: 'Saddle! second platoon!'

'Where are they off to?' thought Rostov.

Five minutes later Denisov came into the hut, clambered with muddy feet on the bed, angrily lighted his pipe, scattered about all his belongings, put on his riding-whip and sword, and was going out of the hut. In reply to Rostov's question, where was he going? he answered angrily and vaguely that he had business to see after.

'God be my judge, then, and our gracious Emperor!' said Denisov, as he went out. Outside the hut Rostov heard the hoofs of several horses splashing through the mud. Rostov did not even trouble himself to find out where Denisov was going. Getting warm through in his corner, he fell asleep, and it was only towards evening that he came out of the hut. Denisov had not yet come back. The weather had cleared; near the next hut two officers were playing quoits, with a laugh sticking big radishes for pegs in the soft muddy earth. Rostov joined them. In the middle of a game the officers saw transport waggons driving up to them, some fifteen hussars on lean horses rode behind them. The transport waggons, escorted by the hussars, drove up to the picket ropes, and a crowd of hussars surrounded them.

'There, look! Denisov was always fretting about it,' said Rostov; 'here are provisions come at last.'

'High time, too!' said the officers. 'Won't the soldiers be pleased!'

A little behind the hussars rode Denisov, accompanied by two infantry officers, with whom he was in conversation. Rostov went to meet them.

'I warn you, captain,' one of the officers was saying, a thin, little man, visibly wrathful.

'Well, I have told you, I won't give them up,' answered Denisov.

'You will have to answer for it, captain. It's mutiny—carrying off transports from your own army! Our men have had no food for two days.'

'Mine have had nothing for a fortnight,' answered Denisov.

'It's brigandage; you will answer for it, sir!' repeated the infantry officer, raising his voice.

'But why do you keep pestering me? Eh?' roared Denisov, suddenly getting furious. 'It's I will have to answer for it, and not you; and you'd better not cry out till you're hurt. Be off!' he shouted at the officers.

'All right!' the little officer responded, not the least intimidated, and not moving away. 'It's robbery, so I tell you. . . .'

'Go to the devil, quick march, while you're safe and sound.' And Denisov moved towards the officer.

'All right, all right,' said the officer threateningly; and he turned his horse and trotted away, swaying in the saddle.

'A dog astride a fence, a dog astride a fence to the life!' Denisov called after him—the bitterest insult a cavalry man can pay an infantry man on horseback; and riding up to Rostov he broke into a guffaw.

'Carried off the transports, carried them off from the infantry by force!' he said. 'Why, am I to let the men die of hunger?'

The stores carried off by the hussars had been intended for an infantry regiment, but learning from Lavrushka that the transport was unescorted, Denisov and his hussars had carried off the stores by force. Biscuits were dealt out freely to the soldiers; they even shared them with the other squadrons.

Next day the colonel sent for Denisov, and putting his fingers held apart before his eyes, he said to him: 'I look at the matter like this; see, I know nothing, and will take no steps; but I advise you to ride over to the staff, and there, in the commissariat department, to smooth things over, and if possible give a receipt for so much stores. If not, and a claim is entered for the infantry regiments, there will be a fuss, and it may end unpleasantly.'

Denisov went straight from the colonel to the staff with a sincere desire to follow his advice.

In the evening he came back to his hut in a condition such as Rostov had never seen his friend in before. Denisov could not speak, and was gasping for breath. When Rostov asked him what was wrong with him, he could only in a faint and husky voice utter incoherent oaths and threats.

Alarmed at Denisov's condition, Rostov suggested he should undress, drink some water, and send for the doctor.

'Me to be court-martialled for brigandage—oh! some more water! —Let them court-martial me! I will, I always will, beat blacklegs, and I'll tell the Emperor.—Ice,' he kept saying.

The regimental doctor said it was necessary to bleed him. A deep saucer of black blood was drawn from Denisov's hairy arm, and only then did he recover himself sufficiently to relate what had happened.

'I got there,' Denisov said. '"Well, where are your chief's quarters," I asked. They showed me. "Will you please to wait?" "I have come on business, and I have come over thirty versts, I haven't time to wait; announce me." Very good; but the over-thief appears; he, too, thought fit to lecture me. "This is robbery!" says he. "The robber," said I, "is not the man who takes the stores to feed his soldiers, but the man who takes them to fill his pockets." "Will you please to be silent?" Very good. "Give a receipt," says he, "to the commissioner, but the affair will be reported at headquarters." I go before the commissioner. I go in. Sitting at the table ... Who? No, think of it! ... Who is it that's starving us to death?' roared Denisov, bringing the fist of his lanced arm down so violently that the table almost fell over, and the glasses jumped on it. 'Telyanin! ... "What, it's you that's starving us to death?" said I, and I gave him one on the snout, and well it went home, and then another, so ... "Ah! ... you so-and-so ..." and I gave him a thrashing. But I did have a bit of fun, though, I can say that,' cried Denisov, his white teeth showing in a smile of malignant glee under his black moustaches. 'I should have killed him, if they hadn't pulled me off.'

'But why are you shouting; keep quiet,' said Rostov; 'it's bleeding again. Stay, it must be bound up.'

Denisov was bandaged up and put to bed. Next day he waked up calm and in good spirits.

But at midday the adjutant of the regiment came with a grave and gloomy fact to the hut shared by Denisov and Rostov, and regretfully showed them a formal communication to Major Denisov from the colonel, in which inquiries were made about the incidents of the previous day. The adjutant informed them that the affair seemed likely to take a very disastrous turn; that a court-martial was to be held; and that with the strictness now prevailing as regards pillaging and breach of discipline, it would be a lucky chance if it ended in being degraded to the ranks.

The case, as presented by the offended parties, was that Major Denisov, after carrying off the transports, had without any provocation come in a drunken condition to the chief commissioner of the commissariat, had called him a thief, threatened to beat him; and, when he was led out, had rushed into the office, attacked two officials, and sprained the arm of one of them.

In response to further inquiries from Rostov, Denisov said, laughing, that it did seem certainly as though some other fellow had been mixed up in it, but that it was all stuff and nonsense; that he would never dream of being afraid of courts of any sort, and that if the scoundrels dared to pick a quarrel with him, he would give them an answer they wouldn't soon forget.

Denisov spoke in this careless way of the whole affair. But Rostov knew him too well not to detect that in his heart (though he hid it from others) he was afraid of a court-martial, and was worrying over the matter, which was obviously certain to have disastrous consequences. Documents began to come every day, and notices from the court, and

Denisov received a summons to put his squadron under the command of the officer next in seniority, and on the first of May to appear before the staff of the division for an investigation into the row in the commissariat office. On the previous day Platov undertook a reconnaissance of the enemy with two regiments of Cossacks and two squadrons of hussars. Denisov, with his usual swaggering gallantry, rode in the front of the line. One of the bullets fired by the French sharpshooters struck him in the fleshy upper part of the leg. Possibly at any other time Denisov would not have left the regiment for so slight a wound, but now he took advantage of it to excuse himself from appearing before the staff, and went into the hospital.

XVII

In the month of June was fought the battle of Friedland, in which the Pavlograd hussars did not take part. It was followed by a truce. Rostov, who sorely felt his friend's absence, and had had no news of him since he left, was uneasy about his wound and the course his difficulties might be taking, and he took advantage of the truce to get leave to visit Denisov at the hospital.

The hospital was in a little Prussian town, which had twice been sacked by Russian and French troops. In the summer weather, when the country looked so pleasant, this little town presented a strikingly melancholy contrast, with its broken roofs and fences, its foul streets and ragged inhabitants, and the sick and drunken soldiers wandering about it.

The hospital was a stone house with remnants of fence torn up in the yard, and window frames and panes partly broken. Several soldiers bandaged up, and with pale and swollen faces, were walking or sitting in the sunshine in the yard.

As soon as Rostov went in at the door, he was conscious of the stench of hospital and putrefying flesh all about him. On the stairs he met a Russian army doctor with a cigar in his mouth. He was followed by a Russian trained assistant.

'I can't be everywhere at once,' the doctor was saying; 'come in the evening to Makar Alexyevitch's, I shall be there.' The assistant asked some further question. 'Oh! do as you think best! What difference will it make?'

The doctor caught sight of Rostov mounting the stairs.

'What are you here for, your honour?' said the doctor. 'What are you here for? Couldn't you meet with a bullet that you want to pick up typhus? This is a pest-house, my good sir.'

'How so?' asked Rostov.

'Typhus, sir. It's death to any one to go in. It's only we two, Makeev and I' (he pointed to the assistant) 'who are still afoot here. Five of us, doctors, have died here already. As soon as a new one comes, he's done for in a week,' said the doctor with evident satisfaction. 'They have sent for Prussian doctors, but our allies aren't fond of the job.'

Rostov explained that he wanted to see Major Denisov of the hussars, who was lying wounded here.

'I don't know, can't tell you, my good sir. Only think, I have three hospitals to look after alone—over four hundred patients. It's a good thing the Prussian charitable ladies send us coffee and lint—two pounds a month—or we should be lost.' He laughed. 'Four hundred, sir; and they keep sending me in fresh cases. It is four hundred, isn't it? Eh?' He turned to the assistant.

The assistant looked worried. He was unmistakably in a hurry for the talkative doctor to be gone, and was waiting with vexation.

'Major Denisov,' repeated Rostov; 'he was wounded at Moliten.'

'I believe he's dead. Eh, Makeev?' the doctor queried of the assistant carelessly.

The assistant did not, however, confirm the doctor's words.

'Is he a long, red-haired man?' asked the doctor.

Rostov described Denisov's appearance.

'He was here, he was,' the doctor declared, with a sort of glee. 'He must be dead, but still I'll see. I have lists. Have you got them, Makeev?'

'The lists are at Makar Alexyevitch's,' said the assistant. 'But go to the officers' ward, there you'll see for yourself,' he added, turning to Rostov.

'Ah, you'd better not, sir!' said the doctor, 'or you may have to stay here yourself.' But Rostov bowed himself away from the doctor, and asked the assistant to show him the way.

'Don't blame me afterwards, mind!' the doctor shouted up from the stairs below.

Rostov and the assistant went into the corridor. The hospital stench was so strong in that dark corridor that Rostov held his nose, and was obliged to pause to recover his energy to go on. A door was opened on the right, and there limped out on crutches a thin yellow man with bare feet, and nothing on but his underlinen. Leaning against the doorpost, he gazed with glittering, anxious eyes at the persons approaching. Rostov glanced in at the door and saw that the sick and wounded were lying there on the floor, on straw and on overcoats.

'Can one go in and look?' asked Rostov.

'What is there to look at?' said the assistant. But just because the assistant was obviously disinclined to let him go in, Rostov went into the soldiers' ward. The stench, to which he had grown used a little in the corridor, was stronger here. Here the stench was different; it was more intense; and one could smell that it was from here that it came. In the long room, brightly lighted by the sun in the big window, lay the sick and wounded in two rows with their heads to the wall, leaving a passage down the middle. The greater number of them were unconscious, and took no notice of the entrance of outsiders. Those who were conscious got up or raised their thin, yellow faces, and all gazed intently at Rostov, with the same expression of hope of help, of reproach, and envy of another man's health. Rostov went into the middle of the room, glanced in at the open doors of adjoining rooms, and on both sides saw the same thing. He stood still, looking round him speechless. He had never expected to see anything like this. Just before him lay right across the empty space down the middle, on the bare floor, a sick man, probably a Cossack, for his hair was cut round in basin shape. This Cossack lay on his back, his huge arms and legs outstretched. His face was of a purple red, his eyes were quite sunk in his head so that only the whites could be seen, and on his legs and on his hands, which were still red, the veins stood out like cords. He was knocking his head against the floor, and he uttered some word and kept repeating it. Rostov listened to what he was saying, and distinguished the word he kept repeating. That word was 'drink—drink—drink!' Rostov looked about for some one who could lay the sick man in his place and give him water.

'Who looks after the patients here?' he asked the assistant. At that moment a commissariat soldier, a hospital orderly, came in from the adjoining room, and, marching in drill step, drew himself up before him.

'Good day, your honour!' bawled this soldier, rolling his eyes at Rostov, and obviously mistaking him for some one in authority.

'Take him away, give him water,' said Rostov, indicating the Cossack.

'Certainly, your honour, the soldier replied complacently, rolling his eyes more strenuously than ever, and drawing himself up, but not budging to do so.

'No, there's no doing anything here,' thought Rostov, dropping his eyes; and he wanted to get away, but he was aware of a significant look bent upon him from the right side, and he looked round at it. Almost in the corner there was, sitting on a military overcoat, an old soldier with a stern yellow face, thin as a skeleton's, and an unshaved grey beard. He was looking persistently at Rostov. The man next the old soldier was whispering something to him, pointing to Rostov. Rostov saw the old man wanted to ask him something. He went closer and saw that the old man had only one leg bent under him, the other had been cut off above the knee. On the other side of the old man, at some distance from him, there lay with head thrown back the motionless figure of a young soldier with a waxen pallor on his snub-nosed and still freckled face, and eyes sunken under the lids. Rostov looked at the snub-nosed soldier and a shiver ran down his back.

'Why, that one seems to be . . .' he said to the assistant.

'We've begged and begged, your honour,' said the old soldier with a quiver in his lower jaw. 'He died early in the morning. We're men, too, not dogs. . . .'

'I'll see to it directly; they shall take him, they shall take him away,' said the assistant hurriedly. 'Come, your honour.'

'Let us go, let us go,' said Rostov hastily; and dropping his eyes and shrinking together, trying to pass unnoticed through the lines of those reproachful and envious eyes fastened upon him, he went out of the room.

XVIII

THE assistant walked along the corridor and led Rostov to the officers' wards, three rooms with doors opening between them. In these rooms there were bedsteads; the officers were sitting and lying upon them. Some were walking about the room in hospital dressing-gowns. The first person who met Rostov in the officers' ward was a thin little man who had lost one arm. He was walking about the first room in a nightcap and hospital dressing-gown, with a short pipe between his teeth. Rostov, looking intently at him, tried to recall where he had seen him.

'See where it was God's will for us to meet again,' said the little man. 'Tushin, Tushin, do you remember I brought you along after Schöngraben? They have sliced a bit off me, see, . . .' said he smiling, and showing the empty sleeve of his dressing-gown. 'Is it Vassily Dmitryevitch Denisov you are looking for—a fellow-lodger here?' he said, hearing who it was Rostov wanted. 'Here, here,' and he led him into the next room, from which there came the sound of several men laughing.

'How can they live in this place even, much less laugh?' thought Rostov, still aware of that corpse-like smell that had been so overpowering in the soldiers' ward, and still seeing around him those envious eyes following him on both sides, and the face of that young soldier with the sunken eyes.

Denisov, covered up to his head with the quilt, was asleep in bed though it was twelve o'clock in the day.

'Ah, Rostov! How are you, how are you?' he shouted, still in the same voice as in the regiment. But Rostov noticed with grief, behind this habitual briskness and swagger, some new, sinister, smothered feeling that peeped out in the words and intonations and the expression of the face of Denisov.

His wound, trifling as it was, had still not healed, though six weeks had passed since he was wounded. His face had the same swollen pallor as all the faces in the hospital. But that was not what struck Rostov: what struck him was that Denisov did not seem pleased to see him, and his smile was forced. Denisov asked him nothing either of the regiment or of the general progress of the war. When Rostov talked of it, Denisov did not listen.

Rostov even noticed that Denisov disliked all reference to the regiment, and to that other free life going on outside the hospital walls. He seemed to be trying to forget that old life, and to be interested only in his quarrel with the commissariat officials. In reply to Rostov's inquiry as to how this matter was going, he promptly drew from under his pillow a communication he had received from the commissioner, and a rough copy of his answer. He grew more eager as he began to read his answer, and specially called Rostov's attention to the biting sarcasm with which he addressed his foes. Denisov's companions in the hospital, who had gathered round Rostov, as a person newly come from the world of freedom outside, gradually began to move away as soon as Denisov began reading his answer. From their faces Rostov surmised that all these gentlemen had more than once heard the whole story, and had had time to be bored with it. Only his nearest neighbour, a stout Uhlan, sat on his pallet-bed, scowling gloomily and smoking a pipe, and little one-armed Tushin still listened, shaking his head disapprovingly. In the middle of the reading the Uhlan interrupted Denisov.

'What I say is,' he said, turning to Rostov, 'he ought simply to petition the Emperor for pardon. Just now, they say, there will be great rewards given and they will surely pardon.'

'Me petition the Emperor!' said Denisov in a voice into which he tried to throw his old energy and fire, but which sounded like the expression of impotent irritability. 'What for? If I had been a robber, I'd beg for mercy; why, I'm being called up for trying to show up robbers. Let them try me, I'm not afraid of any one; I have served my Tsar and my country honestly, and I'm not a thief! And degrade me to the ranks and . . . Listen, I tell them straight out, see, I write to them, "If I had been a thief of government property . . ."'

'It's neatly put, no question about it,' said Tushin. 'But that's not the point, Vassily Dmitritch,' he too turned to Rostov, 'one must submit, and Vassily Dmitritch here won't do it. The auditor told you, you know, that it looks serious for you.'

'Well, let it be serious,' said Denisov.

'The auditor wrote a petition for you,' Tushin went on, 'and you ought to sign it and despatch it by this gentleman. No doubt he' (he indicated Rostov) 'has influence on the staff too. You won't find a better opportunity.'

'But I have said I won't go cringing and fawning,' Denisov interrupted, and he went on reading his answer.

Rostov did not dare to try and persuade Denisov, though he felt instinctively that the course proposed by Tushin and the other officers was the safest. He would have felt happy if he could have been of assistance to Denisov, but he knew his stubborn will and his straightforward, hasty temper.

When the reading of Denisov's biting replies, which lasted over an hour, was over, Rostov said nothing, and in the most dejected frame of mind spent the rest of the day in the society of Denisov's companions, who had again gathered about him. He told them what he knew, and listened to the stories told by others. Denisov maintained a gloomy silence the whole evening.

Late in the evening, when Rostov was about to leave, he asked Denisov if he had no commission for him.

'Yes, wait a bit,' said Denisov. He looked round at the officers, and taking his papers from under his pillow, he went to the window where there was an inkstand, and sat down to write.

'It seems it's no good knocking one's head against a stone wall,' said he, coming from the window and giving Rostov a large envelope. It was the petition addressed to the Emperor that had been drawn up by the auditor. In it Denisov, making no reference to the shortcoming of the commissariat department, simply begged for mercy. 'Give it, it seems . . .' He did not finish, and smiled a forced and sickly smile.

XIX

AFTER going back to the regiment and reporting to the colonel the position of Denisov's affairs, Rostov rode to Tilsit with the letter to the Emperor.

On the 13th of June the French and Russian Emperors met at Tilsit. Boris Drubetskoy had asked the personage of high rank on whom he was in attendance to include him in the suite destined to be staying at Tilsit.

'I should like to see the great man,' he said, meaning Napoleon, whom he had hitherto, like every one else, always spoken of as Bonaparte.

'You are speaking of Buonaparte?' the general said to him, smiling.

Boris looked inquiringly at his general, and immediately saw that this was a playful test.

'I am speaking, prince, of the Emperor Napoleon,' he replied. With a smile the general clapped him on the shoulder.

'You will get on,' said he, and he took him with him. Boris was among the few present at Niemen on the day of the meeting of the Emperors. He saw the raft with the royal monograms, saw Napoleon's progress through the French guards along the further bank, saw the pensive face of the Emperor Alexander as he sat silent in the inn on the bank of the Niemen waiting for Napoleon's arrival. He saw both the Emperors get into boats, and Napoleon reaching the raft first, walk rapidly forward, and meeting Alexander, give him his hand; then both the Emperors disappeared into a pavilion. Ever since he had entered these higher spheres, Boris had made it his habit to keep an attentive watch on what was passing round him, and to note it all down. During the meeting of the Emperors at Tilsit, he asked the names of the persons accompanying Napoleon, inquired about the uniforms they were wearing, and listened carefully to the utterances of persons of consequence. When the Emperors went into the pavilion, he looked at his watch, and did not forget to look at it again when Alexander came out. The interview had lasted an hour and fifty-three minutes; he noted this down that evening among other facts, which he felt were of historical importance. As the Emperors' suite were few in number, to be present at Tilsit at the meeting of the Emperors was a matter of great consequence for a man who valued success in the service, and Boris, when he succeeded in obtaining this privilege, felt that his position was henceforth perfectly secure. He was not simply known, he had become an observed and familiar figure. On two occasions he had been sent with commissions to the Emperor himself, so that the Emperor knew him personally, and all the court no longer held aloof from him, as they had done at first, considering him a new man, and would even have noticed his absence with surprise if he had been away.

Boris was lodging with another adjutant, the Polish count, Zhilinsky. Zhilinsky, a Pole educated in Paris, was a wealthy man, devotedly attached to the French, and almost every day of their stay in Tilsit, French officers of the Guards and of the French head staff were dining and breakfasting with Zhilinsky and Boris.

On the 24th of June Zhilinsky, with whom Boris shared quarters, was giving a supper to his French acquaintances. At this supper there were present one of Napoleon's adjutants—the guest of honour—several officers of the French Guards, and a young lad of an aristocratic old French family, a page of Napoleon's. On the same evening Rostov, taking advantage of the darkness to pass through unrecognised, came to Tilsit in civilian dress, and went to the quarters of Zhilinsky and Boris.

Rostov, like the whole army indeed, was far from having passed through that revolution of feeling in regard to Napoleon and the French —transforming them from foes into friends—that had taken place at headquarters and in Boris. In the army every one was still feeling the same mingled hatred, fear, and contempt for Bonaparte and the French. Only recently Rostov had argued with an officer of Platov's Cossacks the question whether if Napoleon were taken prisoner he was to be treated as an emperor or as a criminal. Only a little while previously Rostov had met a wounded French colonel on the road, and had maintained to him with heat that there could be no peace concluded between a legitimate emperor and the criminal Bonaparte. Consequently it struck Rostov as strange to see French officers in Boris's quarters wearing the uniforms at which he was used to looking with very different eyes from the line of pickets. As soon as he caught sight of a French officer, that feeling of war, of hostility, which he always experienced at the sight of the enemy, came upon him at once. He stood still on the threshold and asked in Russian whether Drubetsoy lived there. Boris, hearing a strange voice in the passage, went out to meet him. For the first time when he recognised Rostov, his face betrayed his annoyance.

'Ah, that's you, very glad, very glad to see you,' he said, however, smiling and moving towards him. But Rostov had detected his first impulse.

'I have come at a bad time, it seems,' said he; 'I shouldn't have come, but it's on a matter of importance,' he said coldly. . . .

'No, I was only surprised at your getting away from the regiment. I will be with you in a moment,' he said in reply to a voice calling him.

'I see I have come at a bad time,' repeated Rostov.

The expression of annoyance had by now vanished from Boris's face; evidently having reflected and made up his mind how to act, he took him by both hands with marked composure and led him into the next room. Boris's eyes, gazing serenely and unflinchingly at Rostov, seemed as it were veiled by something, as though a sort of screen—the blue spectacles of conventional life—had been put over them. So it seemed to Rostov.

'Oh, pease, don't talk nonsense, as if you could come at a wrong time,' said Boris. Boris led him into a room where supper was laid, introduced him to his guests, mentioning his name, and explaining that he was not a civilian, but an officer in the hussars, and his old friend. 'Count Zhilinsky, Count N. N., Captain S. S.,' he said, naming his guests. Rostov looked frowning at the Frenchmen, bowed reluctantly, and was mute.

Zhilinsky was obviously not pleased to receive this unknown Russian outsider into his circle, and said nothing to Rostov. Boris appeared not to notice the constraint produced by the newcomer, and with the same amiable composure and the same veiled look in his eyes with which he had welcomed Rostov, he endeavoured to enliven the conversation. With characteristic French courtesy one of the French officers turned to Rostov, as he sat in stubborn silence, and said to him that he had probably come to Tilsit to see the Emperor.

'No, I came on business,' was Rostov's short reply. Rostov had been out of humour from the moment when he detected the dissatisfaction on the face of Boris, and as is always the case with persons who are ill-humoured, it seemed to him that every one looked at him with hostile eyes, and that he was in every one's way. And in fact he was in every one's way, and he was the only person left out of the general conversation, as it sprang up again. And what is he sitting on here for? was the question asked by the eyes of the guests turned upon him. He got up and went up to Boris.

'I'm in your way, though,' he said to him in an undertone; 'let us have a talk about my business, and I'll go away.'

'Oh, no, not the least,' said Boris. 'But if you are tired, come to my room and lie down and rest.'

'Well, really . . .'

They went into the little room where Boris slept. Rostov, without sitting down, began speaking at once with irritation—as though Boris were in some way to blame in the matter. He told him of Denisov's scrape, asking whether he would and could through his general intercede with the Emperor in Denisov's favour, and through him present the letter. When they were alone together, Rostov was for the first time distinctly aware that he felt an awkwardness in looking Boris in the face. Boris crossing one leg over the other, and stroking the slender fingers of his right hand with his left, listened to Rostov, as a general listens to a report presented by a subordinate, at one time looking away, at the next looking Rostov straight in the face with the same veiled look in his eyes. Every time he did so, Rostov felt ill at ease, and dropped his eyes.

'I have heard of affairs of the sort, and I know that the Emperor is very severe in such cases. I think it had better not be taken before his majesty. To my mind, it would be better to apply directly to the commander of the corps.... But generally speaking, I believe...'

'Then you don't care to do anything, so say so!' Rostov almost shouted, not looking Boris in the face.

Boris smiled.

'On the contrary, I will do what I can, only I just imagine...'

At that moment they heard the voice of Zhilinsky at the door, calling Boris.

'Well, go along, go, go...' said Rostov, and refusing supper and remaining alone in the little room, he walked up and down for a long while, listening to the light-hearted French chatter in the next room.

XX

ROSTOV had arrived at Tilsit on the day least suitable for interceding in Denisov's behalf. It was out of the question for him to go himself to the general in attendance, since he was wearing civilian dress, and had come to Tilsit without permission to do so, and Boris, even had he been willing, could not have done so on the day following Rostov's arrival. On that day, the 27th of June, the preliminaries of peace were signed. The Emperors exchanged orders: Alexander received the Legion of Honour, and Napoleon the Order of St. Andrey of the first degree, and that day had been fixed for the dinner to be given by a battalion of French guards to the Preobrazhensky battalion. The Emperors were to be present at this banquet. Rostov felt so uncomfortable and ill at ease with Boris, that when the latter peeped in at him after supper he pretended to be asleep, and the next day he left early in the morning to avoid seeing him. In a frock coat and round hat, Nikolay strolled about the town, staring at the French and their uniforms, examining the streets and the houses where the Russian and the French Emperors were staying. In the market-place he saw tables set out and preparations for the banquet; in the streets he saw draperies hung across with flags of the Russian and French colours, and huge monograms of A and N. In the windows of the houses, too, there were flags and monograms.

'Boris doesn't care to help me, and I don't care to apply to him.

That question's closed,' thought Nikolay; 'everything's over between us, but I'm not going away from here without having done all I can for Denisov, and, above all, getting the letter given to the Emperor. To the Emperor? . . . He is here!' thought Rostov, who had unconsciously gone back to the house occupied by Alexander.

Saddle horses were standing at the entrance, and the suite were riding up, evidently getting ready for the Emperor to come out.

'Any minute I may see him,' thought Rostov. 'If only I could give him the letter directly, and tell him all . . . could they really arrest me for my frock coat? Impossible. He would understand on which side the truth lay. He understands everything, he knows everything. Who can be juster and more magnanimous than he? Besides, even if they were to arrest me for being here, what would it matter?' he thought, looking at an officer who was going into the house. 'Why, people go in, I see. Oh! it's all nonsense. I'll go and give the letter to the Emperor myself; so much the worse for Drubetskoy who has driven me to it.' And all at once, with a decision he would never have expected of himself, Rostov, fingering the letter in his pocket, went straight into the house where the Emperor was staying.

'No, this time I won't miss my opportunity as I did after Austerlitz,' he thought, expecting every minute to meet the Emperor, and feeling a rush of blood to the heart at the idea. 'I will fall at his feet and will beseech him. He will lift me up, hear me out, and thank me too. "I am happy when I can do good, but to cancel injustice is the greatest happiness,"' Rostov fancied the Emperor would say to him. And he passed up the stairs regardless of the inquisitive eyes that were turned upon him. The broad staircase led straight upwards from the entry; on the right was a closed door. Below, under the stairs, was a door to the rooms on the ground floor.

'Whom are you looking for?' some one asked him.

'To give a letter, a petition, to his majesty,' said Nikolay, with a quiver in his voice.

'A petition—to the officer on duty, this way; please' (he was motioned to the door below). 'Only it won't receive attention.'

Hearing this indifferent voice, Rostov felt panic-stricken at what he was doing; the idea that he might meet the Emperor at any minute was so fascinating and consequently so terrible, that he was ready to fly; but an attendant meeting him opened the door to the officer's room for him, and Rostov went in.

A short, stout man of about thirty in white breeches, high boots, and in a batiste shirt, apparently only just put on, was standing in this room. A valet was buttoning behind him some fine-looking, new, silk-embroidered braces, which for some reason attracted Rostov's notice. The stout man was conversing with some one in the adjoining room.

'A good figure and in her first bloom,' he was saying, but seeing Rostov he broke off and frowned.

'What do you want? A petition? ...'

'What is it?' asked some one in the next room.

'Another petition,' answered the man in the braces.

'Tell him to come later. He'll be coming out directly; we must go.'

'Later, later, tomorrow. It's too late....'

Rostov turned away and would have gone out, but the man in the braces stopped him.

'From whom is it? Who are you?'

'From Major Denisov,' answered Rostov.

'Who are you—an officer?'

'A lieutenant, Count Rostov.'

'What audacity! Send it through the proper channel. And go along with you, go. ...' And he began putting on the uniform the valet handed him.

Rostov went out into the hall again, and noticed that by this time there were a great many officers and generals in full dress, and he had to pass through their midst.

Cursing his temerity, ready to faint at the thought that he might any minute meet the Emperor and be put to shame before him and placed under arrest, fully aware by now of all the indecorum of his action, and regretting it, Rostov was making his way out of the house with downcast eyes, through the crowd of the gorgeously dressed suite, when a familiar voice called to him, and a hand detained him.

'Well, sir, what are you doing here in a frock coat?' asked the bass voice.

It was a cavalry general who had won the Emperor's special favour during this campaign, and had formerly been in command of the division in which Rostov was serving.

Rostov began in dismay to try and excuse himself, but seeing the good-naturedly jocose face of the general, he moved on one side, and in an excited voice told him of the whole affair, begging him to intercede for Denisov, whom the general knew.

The general on hearing Rostov's story shook his head gravely. 'I'm sorry, very sorry for the gallant fellow; give me the letter.'

Rostov had scarcely time to give him the letter and tell him all about Denisov's scrape, when the clank of rapid footsteps with spurs was heard on the stairs, and the general left his side and moved up to the steps. The gentlemen of the Emperor's suite ran downstairs and went to their horses. The postillion, the same one who had been at Austerlitz, led up the Emperor's horse, and on the stairs was heard a light footstep, which Rostov knew at once. Forgetting the danger of being recognised, Rostov moved right up to the esteps together with some curious persons from the town; and again after two years he saw the features he adored: the same face, the same glance, the same walk, the same combination of majesty and mildness.... And the feeling of enthusiasm and devotion to the Emperor rose up again in Rostov's heart with all its old force. The Emperor wore the uniform of the Preobrazhensky regiment, white elkskin breeches and high boots, and a star which Rostov did not recognise (it was the star of the Legion of Honour). He came out on the steps, holding his hat under his arm, and putting on his glove. He stopped, looking round and seeming to shed brightness around him with his glance. To some one of the generals he said a few words. He recognised, too, the former commander of Rostov's division, smiled to him, and summoned him to him.

All the suite stood back, and Rostov saw the general talking at some length to the Emperor.

The Emperor said a few words to him, and took a step towards his horse. Again the crowd of the suite and the street gazers, among whom was Rostov, moved up closer to the Emperor. Standing still with his hand on the saddle, the Emperor turned to the cavalry general and said aloud with the obvious intention of being heard by all: 'I cannot, general, and I cannot because the law is mightier than I am,' and he put his foot in the stirrup. The general bent his head respectfully; the Emperor took his seat and galloped up the street. Rostov, wild with enthusiasm, ran after him with the crowd.

XXI

In the public square towards which the Tsar rode there stood, facing each other, the battalion of the Preobrazhensky regiment on the right, and the battalion of the French guards in bearskin caps on the left.

While the Emperor was riding up to one flank of the battalions, who presented arms, another crowd of horsemen was galloping up to the opposite flank, and at the head of them Rostov recognised Napoleon. That figure could be no one else. He galloped up, wearing a little hat, the ribbon of St. Andrey across his shoulder, and a blue uniform open over a white vest. He was riding a grey Arab horse of extremely fine breed, with a crimson, gold-embroidered saddle-cloth. Riding up to Alexander, he raised his hat, and at that movement Rostov, with his cavalryman's eye, could not help noticing that Napoleon had a bad and uncertain seat on horseback. The battalions shouted hurrah, and *vive l'Empereur!* Napoleon said something to Alexander. Both emperors dismounted from their horses and took each other by the hands. Napoleon's face wore an unpleasantly hypocritical smile. Alexander was saying something to him with a cordial expression.

In spite of the kicking of the horses of the French gendarmes, who were keeping back the crowd, Rostov watched every movement of the Emperor Alexander and of Bonaparte, and never took his eyes off them. What struck him as something unexpected and strange was that Alexander behaved as though Bonaparte were his equal, and that Bonaparte in his manner to the Russian Tsar seemed perfectly at ease, as though this equal and intimate relation with a monarch were something natural and customary with him.

Alexander and Napoleon, with a long tail of suite, moved towards the right flank of the Preobrazhensky battalion, close up to the crowd which was standing there. The crowd found itself unexpectedly so close to the emperors, that Rostov, who stood in the front part of it, began to be afraid he might be recognised.

'Sire, I ask your permission to give the Legion of Honour to the bravest of your soldiers,' said a harsh, precise voice, fully articulating every letter.

It was little Bonaparte speaking, looking up straight into Alexander's eyes. Alexander listened attentively to what was said to him, and bending his head smiled amiably.

'To him who bore himself most valiantly in this last war,' added Napoleon, emphasising each syllable, and with an assurance and composure, revolting to Rostov, scanning the rows of Russian soldiers drawn up before him, all presenting arms, and all gazing immovably at the face of their own emperor.

'Will your Majesty allow me to ask the opinion of the colonel?' said Alexander, and he took a few hurried steps towards Prince Kozlovsky, the commander of the battalion. Bonaparte was meanwhile taking the glove off his little white hand, and, tearing it, he threw it away. An adjutant, rushing hurriedly forward from behind, picked it up. 'Give it to whom?' the Emperor Alexander asked of Kozlovsky in Russian, in a low voice.

'As your Majesty commands.'

The Emperor frowned, with a look of displeasure, and, looking round, said: 'Well, we must give him an answer.'

Kozlovsky scanned the ranks with a resolute air, taking in Rostov, too, in that glance.

'Won't it be me!' thought Rostov.

'Lazarev!' the colonel called with a scowling face; and Lazarev, the soldier who was the best shot in firing at the range, stepped smartly forward.

'Where are you off to? Stand still!' voices whispered to Lazarev, who did not know where he was to go. Lazarev stopped short, with a sidelong scared look at his colonel, and his face quivered, as one so often sees in soldiers called up in front of the ranks.

Napoleon gave a slight backward turn of his head, and a slight motion of his little fat hand, as though seeking something with it. The members of his suite, who guessed the same second what was wanted, were all in a bustle; they whispered together, passing something from one to another, and a page—the same one Rostov had seen the previous evening at Boris's quarters—ran forward, and respectfully bowing over the outstretched hand and not keeping it one instant waiting, put in it an order on a red ribbon. Napoleon, without looking at it, pressed two fingers together; the order was between them. Napoleon approached Lazarev, who stood rolling his eyes, and still gazing obstinately at his own emperor only. Napoleon looked round at the Emperor Alexander, as though to show that what he was doing now he was doing for the sake of his ally. The little white hand, with the order in it, just touched the button of the soldier Lazarev. It was as though Napoleon knew that it was enough for his, Napoleon's, hand to deign to touch the soldier's breast, for that soldier to be happy, rewarded, and distinguished from every one in the world. Napoleon merely laid the cross on Lazarev's breast. The cross did, in fact, stick on.

Officious hands, Russian and French, were instantaneously ready to support it, to fasten it to his uniform.

Lazarev looked darkly at the little man with white hands who was doing something to him, and still standing rigidly, presenting arms, he looked again straight into Alexander's face, as though he were asking him: 'Was he to go on standing there, or was it his pleasure for him to go now, or perhaps to do something else? But no order was given him, and he remained for a good while still in the same rigid position.

The emperors mounted their horses and rode away. The Preobrazhensky battalion broke up, and, mingling with the French guards, sat down to the tables prepared for them.

Lazarev was put in the place of honour. French and Russian officers embraced him, congratulated him, and shook hands with him. Crowds of officers and common people flocked up simply to look at Lazarev. There was a continual hum of laughter and French and Russian chatter round the tables in the square. Two officers with flushed faces passed by Rostov, looking cheerful and happy.

'What do you say to the banquet, my boy? All served on silver,' one was saying. 'Seen Lazarev?'

'Yes.'

'They say the Preobrazhenskies are to give them a dinner tomorrow.'

'I say, what luck for Lazarev! Twelve hundred francs pension for life.'

'Here's a cap, lads!' cried a Preobrazhensky soldier, putting on a French soldier's fur cap.

'It's awfully nice, first-rate!'

'Have you heard the watchword?' said an officer of the guards to another. 'The day before yesterday it was "*Napoléon, France, bravoure*"; today it's "*Alexandre, Russie, grandeur*." One day our Emperor gives it, and next day Napoleon. Tomorrow the Emperor is to send the St George to the bravest of the French guards. Can't be helped! Must respond in the same way.'

Boris, with his comrade Zhilinsky, had come too to look at the banquet. On his way back Boris noticed Rostov, who was standing at the corner of a house. 'Rostov! good day; we haven't seen each other,' he said, and could not refrain from asking him what was the matter, so strangely gloomy and troubled was the face of Rostov.

'Nothing, nothing,' answered Rostov.

'Are you coming in?'

'Yes.'

Rostov stood a long while in the corner, looking at the fête from a distance. His brain was seething in an agonising confusion, which he could not work out to any conclusion. Horrible doubts were stirring in his soul. He thought of Denisov with his changed expression, his submission, and all the hospital with torn-off legs and arms, with the filth and disease. So vividly he recalled that hospital smell of corpse that he looked round to ascertain where the stench came from. Then he thought of that self-satisfied Bonaparte, with his white hands—treated now with cordiality and respect by the Emperor Alexander. For what, then, had those legs and arms been torn off, those men been killed? Then he thought of Lazarev rewarded, and Denisov punished and unpardoned. He caught himself in such strange reflections that he was terrified at them.

Hunger and the savoury smell of the Preobrazhensky dinner roused him from this mood; he must get something to eat before going away. He went to an hotel which he had seen in the morning. In the hotel he found such a crowd of people, and of officers who had come, as he had, in civilian dress, that he had difficulty in getting dinner. Two officers of his own division joined him at table. The conversation naturally turned on the peace. The two officers, Rostov's comrades, like the greater part of the army, were not satisfied with the peace concluded after Friedland. They said that had they kept on a little longer it would have meant Napoleon's downfall; that his troops had neither provisions nor ammunition. Nikolay ate in silence, and drank heavily. He finished two bottles of wine by himself. The inward ferment working within him still fretted him, and found no solution. He dreaded giving himself up to his thoughts, and could not get away from them. All of a sudden, on one of the officers saying that it was humiliating to look at the French, Rostov began shouting with a violence that was quite unprovoked, and consequently greatly astounded the officers.

'And how can you judge what would be best!' he shouted, with his face suddenly suffused with a rush of blood. 'How can you judge of the action of the Emperor? What right have we to criticise him? We cannot comprehend the aims or the actions of the Emperor!'

'But I didn't say a word about the Emperor,' the officer said in justification of himself, unable to put any other interpretation on Rostov's violence than that he was drunk.

But Rostov did not heed him.

'We are not diplomatic clerks, we are soldiers, and nothing more,' he went on. 'Command us to die—then we die. And if we are punished, it follows we're in fault; it's not for us to judge. If it's his Majesty the Emperor's pleasure to recognise Bonaparte as emperor, and to conclude an alliance with him, then it must be the right thing. If we were once to begin criticising and reasoning about everything, nothing would be left holy to us. In that way we shall be saying there is no God, nothing,' cried Nikolay, bringing his fist down on the table. His remarks seemed utterly irrelevant to his companions, but followed quite consistently from the train of his own ideas. 'It's our business to do our duty, to hack them to pieces, and not to think; that's all about it,' he shouted.

'And to drink,' put in one of the officers, who had no desire to quarrel.

'Yes, and to drink,' assented Nikolay. 'Hi, you there! Another bottle!' he roared.

PART VI

I

IN THE YEAR 1808 the Emperor Alexander visited Erfurt for another interview with the Emperor Napoleon; and in the highest Petersburg society a great deal was said of the great significance of this meeting.

In 1809 the amity between the two sovereigns of the world, as Napoleon and Alexander used to be called, had become so close that when Napoleon declared war that year with Austria, a Russian corps crossed the frontier to co-operate with their old enemy Bonaparte against their old ally, the Austrian emperor; so close that in the highest society there was talk of a possible marriage between Napoleon and one of the sisters of the Emperor Alexander. But, apart from foreign policy, the attention of Russian society was at that time drawn with special interest to the internal changes taking place in all departments of the government.

Life meanwhile, the actual life of men with their real interests of health and sickness, labour and rest, with their interests of thought, science, poetry, music, love, affection, hatred, passion, went its way, as always, independently, apart from the political amity or enmity of Napoleon Bonaparte, and apart from all possible reforms.

Prince Andrey had spent two years without a break in the country. All those projects which Pierre had attempted on his estates, and changing continually from one enterprise to another, had never carried out to any real result—all those projects had been carried out by Prince Andrey without display to any one and without any perceptible exertion. He possessed in the highest degree the quality Pierre lacked, that practical tenacity which, without fuss or any great effort on his part, set things in working order.

On one estate of his, three hundred serfs were transformed into free cultivators (it was one of the first examples in Russia), in others forced labour was replaced by payment of rent. On Bogutcharovo a trained midwife had been engaged at his expense to assist the peasant-women in childbirth, and a priest, at a fixed salary, was teaching the children of the peasants and house servants to read and write.

Half his time Prince Andrey spent at Bleak Hills with his father and his son, who was still in the nursery. The other half he passed at his Bogutcharovo retreat, as his father called his estate. In spite of the indifference to all the external events of the world that he had shown to Pierre, he studiously followed them, received many books, and, to his own surprise, when people coming fresh from Petersburg, the very vortex of life, visited him or his father, he noticed that those people, in knowledge of all that was passing in home and foreign politics, were far behind him, though he had never left the country.

Besides looking after his estates, and much general reading of the most varied kind, Prince Andrey was busily engaged at this time upon a critical survey of our two late disastrous campaigns and the composition of a proposal for reforms in our army rules and regulations.

In the spring of 1809 Prince Andrey set off to visit the Ryazan estates, the heritage of his son, whose trustee he was.

Warmed by the spring sunshine he sat in the carriage, looking at the first grass, the first birch leaves and the first flecks of white spring clouds floating over the bright blue of the sky. He was thinking of nothing, but looking about him, lighthearted and thoughtless.

They crossed the ford where he had talked with Pierre a year before. They drove through a muddy village, by threshing floors, and patches of green corn; downhill by a drift of snow still lying near the bridge, uphill along a clay road hollowed out by the rain, by strips of stubble-field, with copse turning green here and there; and drove at last into a birch forest that lay on both sides of the road. In the forest it was almost hot, the wind could not be felt. The birches, all studded with sticky, green leaves, did not stir, and lilac-coloured flowers and the first grass lifted the last year's leaves and peeped out green from under them. Tiny fir-trees, dotted here and there among the birches, brought a jarring reminder of winter with their coarse, unchanging green. The horses neighed as they entered the forest and were visibly heated.

Pyotr the footman said something to the coachman; the coachman assented. But apparently the coachman's sympathy was not enough for Pyotr. He turned round on the box to his master.

'Your excellency, how soft it is!' he said, smiling respectfully.

'Eh?'

'It is soft, your excellency.'

'What does he mean?' wondered Prince Andrey. 'Oh, the weather, most likely,' he thought, looking from side to side. 'And, indeed, everything's green already ... how soon! And the birch and the wild cherry and the alder beginning to come out. ... But I haven't noticed the oak. Yes, here he is, the oak!'

At the edge of the wood stood an oak. Probably ten times the age of the birch-trees that formed the bulk of the forest, it was ten times the thickness and twice the height of any birch-tree. It was a huge oak, double a man's span, with branches broken off, long ago it seemed, and with bark torn off, and seared with old scars. With its huge, uncouth, gnarled arms and fingers sprawling unsymmetrically, it stood an aged, angry, and scornful monster among the smiling birches. Only the few dead-looking, evergreen firs dotted about the forest, and this oak, refused to yield to the spell of spring, and would see neither spring nor sunshine.

'Spring and love and happiness!' that oak seemed to say. 'Are you not sick of that ever-same, stupid, and meaningless cheat? Always the same, and always a cheat! There is no spring, nor sunshine, nor happiness. See yonder stand the cramped, dead fir-trees, ever the same, and here I have flung my torn and broken fingers wherever they have grown out of my back or my sides. As they have grown, so I stand, and I put no faith in your hopes and deceptions.'

Prince Andrey looked round several times at that oak as though he expected something from it. There were flowers and grass under the oak too, but still it stood, scowling, rigid, weird and grim, among them.

'Yes, he's right, a thousand times right, the old oak,' thought Prince Andrey. 'Others, young creatures, may be caught anew by that deception, but we know life—our life is over!' A whole fresh train of ideas, hopeless, but mournfully sweet, stirred up in Prince Andrey's soul in connection with that oak. During this journey he thought over his whole life as it were anew, and came to the same hopeless but calming conclusion, that it was not for him to begin anything fresh, that he must live his life, content to do no harm, dreading nothing and desiring nothing.

II

PRINCE ANDREY'S duties as trustee of his son's Ryazan estates necessitated an interview with the marshal of the district. This marshal was Count Ilya Andreivitch Rostov, and in the middle of May Prince Andrey went to see him.

It was by now the hot period of spring. The forest was already in full leaf. It was dusty, and so hot that at the sight of water one longed to bathe.

Prince Andrey drove along the avenue leading to the Rostovs' house at Otradnoe, depressed and absorbed in considering what questions he must ask the marshal about his business. Behind some trees on the right he heard merry girlish cries, and caught sight of a party of girls running across the avenue along which his coach was driving. In front of all the rest there ran towards the coach a black-haired, very slender, strangely slender, black-eyed girl in a yellow cotton gown. On her head was a white pocket-handkerchief, from under which strayed locks of her loose hair. The girl was shouting something, but perceiving a stranger, she ran back laughing, without glancing at him.

Prince Andrey for some reason felt a sudden pang. The day was so lovely, the sun so bright, everything around him so gay, and that slim and pretty girl knew nothing of his existence, and cared to know nothing, and was content and happy in her own life—foolish doubtless—but gay and happy and remote from him. What was she so glad about? What was she thinking of? Not of army regulations; not of the organisation of the Ryazan rent-paying peasants. 'What is she thinking about, and why is she so happy?' Prince Andrey could not help wondering with interest.

Count Ilya Andreivitch was living in the year 1809 at Otradnoe, exactly as he had always done in previous years; that is to say, entertaining almost the whole province with hunts, theatricals, dinner parties and concerts. He was delighted to see Prince Andrey, as he always was to see any new guest, and almost forced him to stay the night.

Prince Andrey spent a tedious day, entertained by his elderly host and hostess and the more honoured among the guests, of whom the count's house was full in honour of an approaching name-day. Several times in the course of it, Bolkonsky glanced at Natasha, continually laughing and full of gaiety among the younger members of the company, and asked himself each time, 'What is she thinking of? What is she so glad about?'

In the evening, alone in a new place, he was for a long while unable to sleep. He read for a time, then put out his candle, and afterwards lighted it again. It was hot in the bedroom with the shutters closed on the inside. He felt irritated with this foolish old gentleman (so he mentally called Count Rostov) who had detained him, declaring that the necessary deeds had not yet come from the town, and he was vexed with himself for staying.

Prince Andrey got up and went to the window to open it. As soon as he opened the shutter, the moonlight broke into the room as though it had been waiting a long while outside on the watch for this chance. He opened the window. The night was fresh and bright and still. Just in front of the window stood a row of pollard-trees, black on one side, silvery bright on the other. Under the trees were rank, moist, bushy, growing plants of some kind, with leaves and stems touched here and there with silver. Further away, beyond the black trees, was the roof of something glistening with dew; to the right was a great, leafy tree, with its trunk and branches brilliantly white, and above it the moon, almost full, in a clear, almost starless, spring sky. Prince Andrey leaned his elbow on the window, and his eyes rested on that sky.

His room was on the second story; there were people in the room over his head, and awake too. He heard girls' chatter overhead.

'Only this once more,' said a girlish voice, which Prince Andrey recognised at once.

'But when are you coming to bed?' answered another voice.

'I'm not coming; I can't sleep; what's the use? Come, for the last time....'

Two feminine voices sang a musical phrase, the finale of some song.

'Oh, it's exquisite! Well, now go to sleep, and there's an end of it.'

'You go to sleep, but I can't,' responded the first voice, coming nearer to the window. She was evidently leaning right out of the window, for he could hear the rustle of her garments and even her breathing. All was hushed and stonily still, like the moon and its lights and shadows. Prince Andrey dared not stir for fear of betraying his unintentional presence.

'Sonya! Sonya!' he heard the first voice again. 'Oh, how can you sleep! Do look how exquisite! Oh, how exquisite! Do wake up, Sonya!' she said, almost with tears in her voice. 'Do you know such an exquisite night has never, never been before.'

Sonya made some reluctant reply.

'No, do look what a moon!... Oh, how lovely it is! Do come here. Darling, precious, do come here. There, do you see? One has only to squat on one's heels like this—see—and to hold one's knees—as tight, as tight as one can—give a great spring and one would fly away.... Like this—see!'

'Mind, you'll fall.'

He heard sounds of a scuffle and Sonya's voice in a tone of vexation: 'Why, it's past one o'clock.'

'Oh, you only spoil it all for me. Well, go to bed then, go along.'

All was hushed again; but Prince Andrey knew she was still sitting there. He heard at times a soft rustle, and at times a sigh.

'O my God! my God! what does it mean?' she cried suddenly. 'To bed then, if it must be so!' and she closed the window with a slam.

'And nothing to do with my existence!' thought Prince Andrey while he had been listening to her talk, for some reason hoping and dreading she might say something about him. 'And she again! As though it were on purpose!' he thought. All at once there stirred within his soul such a wholly unexpected medley of youthful hopes and ideas, running counter to the whole tenor of his life, that he made haste to fall asleep, feeling incapable of seeing clearly into his own state of mind.

III

NEXT day Prince Andrey took leave of the count alone and set off on his way home, without waiting for the ladies to appear.

It was the beginning of June when Prince Andrey, on his return journey, drove again into the birch forest, in which the old, gnarled oak had made upon him so strange and memorable an impression. The ringing of the bells did not carry so far now in the forest as six weeks before. Everything was fully out, thick, and shut in. And the young firs, dotted about the forest, did not break the general beauty, but, subdued to the same character as the rest, were softly green with their feathery bunches of young needles.

The whole day had been hot; a storm was gathering, but only a small rain-cloud had sprinkled the dust of the road and the sappy leaves. The left side of the forest was dark, lying in shadow. The right side, glistening with raindrops, gleamed in the sunlight, faintly undulating in the wind. Everything was in flower, the nightingales twittered and carolled, now close, now far away.

'Yes, it was here, in this forest, I saw that oak, with whom I was in sympathy,' thought Prince Andrey. 'But where is he?' he thought again as he gazed at the left side of the road, and, all unaware and unrecognising, he was admiring the very oak he was seeking. The old oak, utterly transformed draped in a tent of sappy dark green, basked faintly, undulating in the rays of the evening sun. Of the knotted fingers, the gnarled excrescences, the aged grief and mistrust—nothing was to be seen. Through the rough, century-old bark, where there were no twigs, leaves had burst out so sappy, so young, that it was hard to believe that aged creature had borne them.

'Yes, that is the same tree,' thought Prince Andrey, and all at once there came upon him an irrational, spring feeling of joy and of renewal. All the best moments of his life rose to his memory at once. Austerlitz, with that lofty sky, and the dead, reproachful face of his wife, and Pierre on the ferry, and the girl, thrilled by the beauty of the night, and that night and moon—it all rushed at once into his mind.

'No, life is not over at thirty-one,' Prince Andrey decided all at once, finally and absolutely. 'It's not enough for me to know all there is in me, every one must know it too; Pierre and that girl, who wanted to fly away into the sky; every one must know me so that my life may not be spent only on myself; they must not live so apart from my life, it must be reflected in all of them and they must all share my life with me!'

On getting home after his journey, Prince Andrey made up his mind to go to Petersburg in the autumn, and began inventing all sorts of reasons for this decision. A whole chain of sensible, logical reasons, making it essential for him to visit Petersburg, and even to re-enter the service, was at every moment ready at his disposal. He could not indeed comprehend now how he could ever have doubted of the necessity of taking an active share in life, just as a month before he could not have understood how the idea of leaving the country could ever occur to him. It seemed clear to him that all his experience of life would be wasted and come to naught, if he did not apply it in practice and take an active part in life again. He could not understand indeed how on a basis of such poor arguments it could have seemed so incontestable to him that he would be lowering himself, if after the lessons he had received from life, he were to put faith again in the possibility of being useful and in the possibility of happiness and of love. Reason now gave its whole support to the other side. After his journey to Ryazan, Prince Andrey began to weary of life in the country; his former pursuits ceased to interest him, and often sitting alone in his study, he got up, went to the looking-glass and gazed a long while at his own face. Then he turned away to the portrait of Liza, who, with her curls tied up *à la grecque*, looked gaily and tenderly out of the gold frame at him. She did not now say those terrible words to him; she looked curiously and merrily at him. And, clasping his hands behind him, Prince Andrey would walk a long while up and down his room, frowning and smiling by turns, as he brooded over those irrational ideas, that could not be put into words, and were secret as a crime—the ideas connected with Pierre, with glory, with the girl at the window, with the oak, with woman's beauty, and love, which had changed the whole current of his life. And if any one came into his room at such moments, he would be particularly short, severely decided and disagreeably logical.

'*Mon cher*,' Princess Marya would say coming in at such a moment, 'Nikolushka cannot go out for a walk today; it is very cold.'

'If it were hot,' Prince Andrey would answer his sister with peculiar dryness on such occasions, 'then he would go out with only his smock on; but as it is cold, you must put him on the warm clothes that have been designed for that object. That's what follows from its being cold, and not staying at home when the child needs fresh air,' he would say, with an exaggerated logicality, as it were punishing some one for that secret, illogical element working within him.

On such occasions Princess Marya thought what a chilling effect so much intellectual work had upon men.

IV

PRINCE ANDREY arrived in Petersburg in the August of 1809. It was the period when the young Speransky was at the zenith of his fame and his reforms were being carried out with the utmost vigour. In that very month the Tsar was thrown out of his carriage, hurt his foot, and was laid up for three weeks at Peterhof, seeing Speransky every day and no one else. At that period there were in preparation the two famous decrees that so convulsed society, abolishing the bestowal of grades by court favour and establishing examinations for obtaining the ranks of collegiate assessors and state councillors. But besides these reforms, a whole political constitution was under discussion destined to transform the whole legal administrative and financial system of government from the Privy Council to the district tribunals. At this time the vague, liberal ideals with which the Emperor Alexander had ascended the throne were taking shape and being carried into practice. Those ideals he had striven to realise with the aid of Tchartorizhsky, Novosiltsev, Kotchubey, and Stroganov, whom he used himself to call in fun his *comité du salut publique.* Now all were replaced by Speransky on the civil side and Araktcheev on the military.

Soon after his arrival, Prince Andrey, as a kammerherr, presented himself at court and at a levée. The Tsar, meeting him on two occasions, did not deign to bestow a single word upon him. Prince Andrey had fancied even before then that he was antipathetic to the Tsar; that the Tsar disliked his face and his whole personality. In the cold, repellent glance with which the Tsar looked at him, Prince Andrey found further confirmation of this supposition. Courtiers explained the Tsar's slight to Prince Andrey by saying that his majesty was displeased at Bolkonsky's having retired from active service since 1805.

'I know myself that one has no control over one's likes and dislikes,' thought Prince Andrey, 'and so it is of no use to think of presenting my note on army reform in person to the Tsar, but the thing will speak for itself.' He sent word about his note to an old field-marshal, a friend of his father's. The field-marshal fixed an hour to see him, received him cordially, and promised to lay it before the Tsar. A few days later, Prince Andrey received notice that he was to call upon the minister of war, Count Araktcheev.

At nine o'clock in the morning on the day appointed, Prince Andrey entered Count Araktcheev's reception-room.

Prince Andrey did not know Araktcheev personally and had never seen him, but all that he knew about him had inspired him with little respect for the man.

'He is the minister of war, a person the Tsar trusts, and no one need have any concern with his personal qualities; he has been commissioned to look at my note, consequently he is the only person who can get it adopted,' thought Prince Andrey, as he waited among many persons of importance and unimportance in Count Araktcheev's ante-room.

During the years of his service—for the most part as an adjutant—Prince Andrey had seen the ante-rooms of many great personages, and the various characteristic types of such ante-rooms were very readily recognised by him. Count Araktcheev's ante-room had quite a special character. The faces of the persons of no consequence who were awaiting their turns for an audience with Count Araktcheev betrayed a feeling of humiliation and servility; the faces of those of superior rank all wore an expression of general discomfort, concealed under a mask of ease and ridicule, of themselves and their position and the person they were waiting to see. Some of them walked up and down plunged in thought; others were laughing and whispering together, and Prince Andrey caught the nickname *Sila Andreitch* (Sila meaning Force or Violence), and the words 'the governor'll give it you,' referring to Count Araktcheev. One general (a person of great consequence), unmistakably chagrined at being kept waiting so long, sat with crossed legs, disdainfully smiling to himself.

But as soon as the door opened, all faces instantly betrayed one feeling only—terror.

Prince Andrey asked the adjutant on duty to mention his name again, but he received a sarcastic stare, and was told his turn would come in due course. After several persons had been let in and let out of the minister's room by the adjutant, an officer was admitted at the dreadful door, whose abject and panic-stricken face had struck Prince Andrey. The officer's audience lasted a long while. Suddenly the roar of a harsh voice was heard through the door, and the officer, with a white face and trembling lips, came out, and clutching at his head, crossed the ante-room. After that, Prince Andrey was conducted to the door, and the adjutant in a whisper said: 'To the right, at the window.'

Prince Andrey went into a plain, neat study, and saw at the table a man of forty with a long waist, with a long, closely-cropped head, deep wrinkles, scowling brows over brown-green, dull eyes, and a red, overhanging nose. Araktcheev turned his head towards him, without looking at him.

'What is it you are petitioning for?' asked Araktcheev.

'There is nothing that I am . . . petitioning for, your excellency,' Prince Andrey pronounced softly. Araktcheev's eyes turned to him.

'Sit down,' said Araktcheev. 'Prince Bolkonsky?'

'I have no petition to make, but his Majesty the Tsar has graciously sent to your excellency a note submitted by me——'

'Be so good as to see, my dear sir; I have read your note,' Araktcheev interrupted, uttering only the first words civilly, again looking away from him, and relapsing more and more into a tone of grumbling contempt. 'Is it new army regulations you propose? There are regulations in plenty; no one will carry out the old ones. Nowadays every one's drawing up regulations; it's easier writing than doing.'

'I have come by the desire of his Majesty the Tsar to learn from your excellency how you propose to deal with my project,' said Prince Andrey courteously.

'I have proposed a resolution in regard to your note, and have forwarded it to the committee. I do *not* approve,' said Araktcheev, getting up and taking a paper out of the writing-table. 'Here.' He gave it to Prince Andrey. Right across the note had been scrawled, without punctuation or capital letters and with words misspelt: 'Superficially compiled seeing that it's drawn up in imitation of the French army regulations and needlessly departing from the standing orders.'

'To what committee has the note been referred?' asked Prince Andrey.

'To the Committee on Army Regulations, and I have proposed your honour being enrolled among its members. Only without salary.'

Prince Andrey smiled.

'I am not seeking a salary.'

'A member without salary,' repeated Araktcheev. 'I wish you good day. Hey! call! who's the next?' he shouted, as he bowed to Prince Andrey.

V

WHILE awaiting the announcement of his name having been put on the committee, Prince Andrey looked up old acquaintances, especially among those persons whom he knew to be in power, and so able to be of use to him. He experienced now in Petersburg a sensation akin to what he had known on the eve of a battle, when he was fretted by restless curiosity and irresistibly attracted to those higher spheres, where the future was in preparation, that future on which hung the fate of millions. From the angry irritability of the elder generation, from the curiosity of the uninitiated and the reserve of the initiated, from the hurry and anxious absorption of every one, from the multiplicity of committees and commissions—he was learning of new ones every day —he felt that now, in the year 1809, there was in preparation here in Petersburg some vast political contest, and the commander-in-chief in it was a mysterious personage whom he did not know, but imagined to be a man of genius—Speransky.

And this movement of reform, of which he knew vaguely, and Speransky, the moving spirit of it, began to interest him so keenly that his proposed reform of the army regulations very soon fell into a subordinate position in his mind.

Prince Andrey happened to be most favourably placed for obtaining a good reception in the highest and most various circles of the Petersburg society of that day. The reforming party welcomed him warmly, and sought him out, in the first place, because he had the reputation of being clever and very well read, and secondly because he had already gained the reputation of being a liberal by the emancipation of his serfs. The party of the dissatisfied older generation welcomed him simply as the son of his father, and reckoned upon his sympathy in their disapproval of the reforms. The feminine world, *society*, received him cordially because he was a wealthy match of high rank, and a person almost new, encircled by a halo of romance from his narrow escape from death and the tragic loss of his young wife. Moreover the general verdict of all who had known him previously was that he had greatly changed for the better during the last five years, had grown softer and more manly; that he had lost his old affectation, pride, and sarcastic irony, and had gained the serenity that comes with years. People talked of him, were interested in him, and eager to see him.

The day after his interview with Count Araktcheev, Prince Andrey was at a soirée at Count Kotchubey's. He described to the latter his interview with *Sila Andreitch*. (This was the name by which Kotchubey spoke of Araktcheev with that vague note of jeering in his voice which Prince Andrey had noticed in the ante-room of the minister of war.)

'*Mon cher*, even in this affair you can't do without Mihail Mihalovitch. He has a hand in everything. I'll speak to him. He promised to come in the evening . . .'

'But what has Speransky to do with the army regulations?' asked Prince Andrey.

Kotchubey shook his head, smiling, as though wondering at Bolkonsky's simplicity.

'We were talking to him about you the other day,' Kotchubey continued; 'about your free cultivators...'

'Yes, so it was you, prince, who freed your serfs?' said an old gentleman of Catherine's court, turning disdainfully to Bolkonsky.

'The little estate brought me no income as it was,' answered Bolkonsky, trying to minimise what he had done to the old gentleman, to avoid irritating him needlessly.

'You are afraid of being late,' said the old gentleman, looking at Kotchubey.

'There's one thing I don't understand,' pursued the old gentleman. 'Who is to till the land if they are set free? It's easy to pass laws, but hard work to govern. It's just the same as now; I ask you, count, who will preside over the courts when all have to pass examinations?'

'Those who pass the examinations, I suppose,' answered Kotchubey, crossing his legs and looking about him.

'Here I have Pryanitchnikov in my department, a capital man, a priceless man, but he is sixty; how is he to go in for examinations?...'

'Yes, that's a difficult question, considering that education is so restricted, but...'

Count Kotchubey did not finish his sentence; he got up, and taking Prince Andrey by the arm, went to meet a tall, bald, fair-haired man of forty, who had just come in. He had a large, open forehead, and his long face was of a strange, exceptional whiteness; he wore a blue frockcoat and had a cross at his neck and a star on the left side of his breast. It was Speransky. Prince Andrey recognised him at once, and that thrill passed through him that comes at the great moments of one's life. Whether it was a thrill of respect, of envy, of anticipation, he did not know. Speransky's whole figure had a peculiar character by which he could be distinguished immediately. Never in any one of the circles in which Prince Andrey had moved had he seen such calm and self-confidence as was manifest in this man's heavy and ungainly movements. Never in any one had he seen a glance so resolute, and yet so soft, as now in those half-closed and moist-looking eyes; never had he seen such firmness as in that smile that meant nothing. Never had he heard a voice so delicate, smooth, and soft; but what struck him most of all was the tender whiteness of the face, and still more the hands, which were rather broad, but extremely plump, soft, and white. Such whiteness and softness Prince Andrey had seen only in the faces of soldiers who had been a long while in hospital.

This was Speransky, the secretary of state, the Tsar's confidential adviser, who had accompanied him to Erfurt, and there had more than once seen and talked with Napoleon. Speransky's eyes did not shift from one face to another, as one's eyes unconsciously do on first coming into a large company, and he was in no hurry to speak. He spoke slowly, with conviction that he would be listened to, and looked only at the person to whom he was speaking. Prince Andrey watched every word and gesture of Speransky's with peculiar intentness. As is often the case with men, particularly with those who criticise their fellows severely, Prince Andrey on meeting a new person, especially one like Speransky, whom he knew by reputation, had always a hope of finding in him a full perfection of human qualities.

Speransky said to Kotchubey that he was sorry that he had not been able to come earlier, because he had been detained at the palace. He did not say that the Tsar had kept him. And this affectation of modesty did not escape Prince Andrey. When Kotchubey mentioned Prince Andrey's name to him, Speransky slowly transferred his eyes to Bolkonsky, with the same smile on his face, and gazed for a moment at him in silence.

'I am very glad to make your acquaintance; I have heard of you, as every one has,' said he.

Kotchubey said a few words about the reception Araktcheev had given Bolkonsky. Speransky's smile broadened.

'The chairman of the Committee of Army Regulations is a friend of mine—M. Magnitsky,' he said, articulating fully every word and every syllable, 'and, if you wish it, I can make you acquainted with him.' (He paused at the full stop.) 'I expect that you would meet with sympathy in him and a desire to assist in anything reasonable.'

A circle formed at once round Speransky, and the same old gentleman, who had talked of his clerk, Pryanitchnikov, addressed a question to Speransky.

Taking no part in the conversation, Prince Andrey watched every gesture of Speransky—this man, only a little time before an insignificant divinity student, who now held in his hands—those plump white hands—the fate of Russia, as Bolkonsky thought. Prince Andrey was struck by the extraordinary contemptuous composure with which Speransky answered the old gentleman. He seemed to drop him his condescending words from an immeasurable height above him. When the old gentleman began talking too loud, Speransky smiled and said that he could not judge of the advantage or disadvantage of what the Tsar saw fit to command.

After talking for a little while in the general circle, Speransky got up, and going to Prince Andrey, drew him away to the other end of the room. It was evident that he thought it well to interest himself in Bolkonsky.

'I have not had time for a word with you, prince, in the engrossing conversation into which I was dragged by that excellent old gentleman,' he said, with a smile of bland contempt, by which he seemed to take for granted that Prince Andrey and himself were at one in recognising the insignificance of the people with whom he had just been talking. This flattered Prince Andrey. 'I have known you for a long while: first from your action with your serfs, the first instance of the kind among us, an example which one would desire to find many following; and, secondly, from your being one of those kammerherrs who have not considered themselves wronged by the new decree in regard to promotion by court favour, that has provoked so much criticism and censure.'

'Yes,' said Prince Andrey, 'my father did not care for me to take advantage of that privilege; I began the service from the lower grades.'

'Your father, a man of the older generation, is undoubtedly above the level of our contemporaries, who condemn this measure, though it is simply an act of natural justice.'

'I imagine there is some basis though even for that condemnation,' said Prince Andrey, trying to resist the influence of Speransky, of which he began to be aware. He disliked agreeing with him in everything; he tried to oppose him. Prince Andrey, who usually spoke so well and so readily, felt a difficulty even in expressing himself as he talked with Speransky. He was too much occupied in observing the personality of the celebrated man.

'In the interests of personal ambition perhaps,' Speransky slowly put in his word.

'And to some extent in the interests of the state,' said Prince Andrey.

'How do you mean? . . .' said Speransky slowly, dropping his eyes.

'I am an admirer of Montesquieu,' said Prince Andrey. 'And his theory that the principle of monarchies is honour seems to me incontestable. Certain rights and privileges of the nobility appear to me to be means of maintaining that sentiment.'

The smile vanished from Speransky's white face, and his countenance gained greatly by its absence. Probably Prince Andrey's idea seemed to him an interesting one.

'If you look at the question from that point of view,' he began, pronouncing French with obvious difficulty, and speaking even more deliberately than he had done when speaking Russian, but still with perfect composure. He said that honour, *l'honneur*, cannot be supported by privileges prejudicial to the working of the government service; that honour, *l'honneur*, is either a negative concept of avoidance of reprehensible actions or a certain source of emulation in obtaining the commendation and rewards in which it finds expression.

His arguments were condensed, simple, and clear. 'The institution that best maintains that honour, the source of emulation, is an institution akin to the Legion of Honour of the great Emperor Napoleon, which does not detract from but conduces to the successful working of the government service, and not a class or court privilege.'

'I do not dispute that, but there is no denying that the court privileges did attain the same object,' said Prince Andrey. 'Every courtier thought himself bound to do credit to his position.'

'But you did not care to profit by it, prince,' said Speransky, showing with a smile that he wished to conclude with civility an argument embarrassing for his companion. 'If you will do me the honour to call on Wednesday, then I shall have seen Magnitsky, and shall have something to tell you that may interest you, and besides I shall have the pleasure of more conversation with you.' Closing his eyes, he bowed, and trying to escape unnoticed, he went out of the drawing-room without saying good-bye, *à la française.*

VI

During the first part of his stay in Petersburg, Prince Andrey found all the habits of thought he had formed in his solitary life completely obscured by the trifling cares which engrossed him in Petersburg.

In the evening on returning home he noted down in his memorandum-book four or five unavoidable visits or appointments for fixed hours. The mechanism of life, the arrangement of his day, so as to be in time everywhere, absorbed the greater part of his vital energy. He did nothing, thought of nothing even, and had no time to think, but only talked, and talked successfully, of what he had had time to think about in the past in the country.

He sometimes noticed with dissatisfaction that it happened to him to repeat the same remarks on the same day to different audiences. But he was so busy for whole days together that he had no time to reflect that he was thinking of nothing. Just as at their first meeting at Kotchubey's, Speransky had a long and confidential talk with Prince Andrey on Wednesday at his own home, where he received Bolkonsky alone and made a great impression on him.

Prince Andrey regarded the immense mass of men as contemptible and worthless creatures, and he had such a longing to find in some other man the living pattern of that perfection after which he strove himself, that he was ready to believe that in Speransky he had found this ideal of a perfectly rational and virtuous man. Had Speransky belonged to the same world as Prince Andrey, had he been of the same breeding and moral traditions, Bolkonsky would soon have detected the weak, human, unheroic sides of his character; but this logical turn of mind was strange to him and inspired him with the more respect from his not fully understanding it. Besides this, Speransky, either because he appreciated Prince Andrey's abilities or because he thought it as well to secure his adherence, showed off his calm, impartial sagacity before Prince Andrey, and flattered him with that delicate flattery that goes hand in hand with conceit, and consists in a tacit assumption that one's companion and oneself are the only people capable of understanding all the folly of the rest of the world and the sagacity and profundity of their own ideas.

In the course of their long conversation on Wednesday evening Speransky said more than once: 'Among *us* everything that is out of the common rut of tradition is looked at,' . . . or with a smile: 'But *we* want the wolves to be well fed and the sheep to be unhurt.' . . . or: '*They* can't grasp that' . . . and always with an expression that said: 'We, you and I, we understand what *they* are and who *we* are.'

This first long conversation with Speransky only strengthened the feeling with which Prince Andrey had seen him for the first time. He saw in him a man of vast intellect and sober, accurate judgment, who had attained power by energy and persistence, and was using it for the good of Russia only. In Prince Andrey's eyes Speransky was precisely the man—finding a rational explanation for all the phenomena of life, recognising as of importance only what was rational and capable of applying the standard of reason to everything—that he would have liked to be himself. Everything took a form so simple, so clear in Speransky's exposition of it that Prince Andrey could not help agreeing with him on every subject. If he argued and raised objections it was simply with the express object of being independent and not being entirely swayed by Speransky's ideas. Everything was right, everything was as it should be, yet one thing disconcerted Prince Andrey. That was the cold, mirror-like eye of Speransky, which seemed to refuse all admittance to his soul, and his flabby, white hand, at which Prince Andrey instinctively looked, as one usually does look at the hands of men who have power. That mirror-like eye and that flabby hand vaguely irritated Prince Andrey. He was disagreeably struck too by the excessive contempt for other people that he observed in Speransky, and by the variety of the lines of argument he employed in support of his views. He made use of every possible weapon of thought, except analogy, and his transitions from one line of defence to another seemed to Prince Andrey too violent. At one time he took his stand as a practical man and found fault with idealists, then he took a satirical line and jeered sarcastically at his opponents, then maintained a strictly logical position, or flew off into the domain of metaphysics. (This last resource was one he was particularly fond of using in argument.) He raised the question into the loftiest region of metaphysics, passed to definitions of space, of time, and of thought, and carrying off arguments to confute his opponent, descended again to the plane of the original discussion. What impressed Prince Andrey as the leading characteristic of Speransky's mind was his unhesitating, unmovable faith in the power and authority of the reason. It was plain that Speransky's brain could never admit the idea—so common with Prince Andrey—that one can never after all express all one thinks. It had never occurred to him to doubt whether all he thought and all he believed might not be meaningless nonsense. And that peculiarity of Speransky's mind was what attracted Prince Andrey most.

During the first period of his acquaintance with Speransky, Prince Andrey had a passionate and enthusiastic admiration for him, akin to what he had once felt for Bonaparte. The very fact that Speransky was the son of a priest, which enabled many foolish persons to regard him with vulgar contempt, as a member of a despised class, made Prince Andrey peculiarly delicate in dealing with his own feeling for Speransky, and unconsciously strengthened it in him.

On that first evening that Bolkonsky spent with him, they talked of the commission for the revision of the legal code; and Speransky described ironically to Prince Andrey how the commission had been sitting for one hundred and fifty years, had cost millions, and had done nothing, and how Rosenkampf had pasted lables on all the various legislative codes.

'And that's all the state has got for the millions it has spent!' said he. 'We want to give new judicial powers to the Senate, and we have no laws. That's why it is a sin for men like you, prince, not to be in the government.'

Prince Andrey observed that some education in jurisprudence was necessary for such work, and that he had none.

'But no one has, so what would you have? It's a *circulus viciosus*, which one must force some way out of.'

Within a week Prince Andrey was a member of the committee for the reconstruction of the army regulations, and—a thing he would never have expected—he was also chairman of a section of the commission for the revision of the legal code. At Speransky's request he took the first part of the civil code under revision; and with the help of the

Napoleonic Code and the Code of Justinian he worked at the revision of the section Personal Rights.

VII

Two years before, at the beginning of 1808, Pierre had returned to Petersburg from his visits to his estates, and by no design of his own had taken a leading position among the freemasons in Petersburg. He organised dining and funeral lodges, enrolled new members, took an active part in the formation of different lodges, and the acquisition of authentic acts. He spent his money on the construction of temples, and, to the best of his powers, made up the arrears of alms, a matter in which the majority of members were niggardly and irregular. At his own expense, almost unaided, he maintained the poorhouse built by the order in Petersburg.

Meanwhile his life ran on in the old way, yielding to the same temptations and the same laxity. He liked a good dinner and he liked strong drink; and, though he thought it immoral and degrading to yield to them, he was unable to resist the temptations of the bachelor society in which he moved.

Yet even in the whirl of his active work and his dissipations, Pierre began, after the lapse of a year, to feel more and more as though the ground of freemasonry on which he had taken his stand was slipping away under his feet the more firmly he tried to rest on it. At the same time he felt that the further the ground slipped from under his feet, the more close was his bondage to the order. When he had entered the brotherhood he had felt like a man who confidently puts his foot down on the smooth surface of a bog. Having put one foot down, he had sunk in, and to convince himself of the firmness of the ground on which he stood, he had put the other foot down on it too, and had sunk in further, had stuck in the mud, and now was against his own will struggling knee-deep in the bog.

Osip Alexyevitch was not in Petersburg. (He had withdrawn from all participation in the affairs of the Petersburg lodge, and now never left Moscow.) All the brothers who were members of the lodge were people Pierre knew in daily life, and it was difficult for him to see in them simply brothers in freemasonry, and not Prince B., nor Ivan Vasilyevitch, D., whom he knew in private life mostly as persons of weak and worthless character. Under their masonic aprons and emblems he could not help seeing the uniforms and the decorations they were striving after in mundane life. Often after collecting the alms and reckoning up twenty to thirty roubles promised—and for the most part left owing—from some ten members, of whom half were as well-off as Pierre himself, he thought of the masonic vow by which every brother promised to give up all his belongings for his neighbour; and doubts stirred in his soul, from which he tried to escape.

He divided all the brothers he knew into four classes. In the first class he reckoned brothers who took no active interest in the affairs of the lodges nor in the service of humanity, but were occupied exclusively with the scientific secrets of the order, with questions relating to the threefold designation of God, or the three first elements of things—sulphur, mercury, and salt—or the significance of the square and all the figures of the Temple of Solomon. Pierre respected this class of masons, to which the elder brothers principally belonged—in it Pierre reckoned Osip Alexyevitch—but he did not share their interests. His heart was not in the mystic side of freemasonry.

In the second class Pierre included himself, and brothers like himself, wavering, seeking, and not yet finding in freemasonry a straight and fully understood path for themselves, but still hoping to find it.

In the third class he reckoned brothers—they formed the majority—who saw in freemasonry nothing but an external form and ceremonial, and valued the strict performance of that external form without troubling themselves about its import or significance. Such were Villarsky, and the Grand Master of the lodge indeed.

The fourth class, too, included a great number of the brothers especially among those who had entered the brotherhood of late. These were men who, as far as Pierre could observe, had no belief in anything, nor desire of anything, but had entered the brotherhood simply for the sake of getting into touch with the wealthy young men, powerful through their connections or their rank, who were numerous in the lodge.

Pierre began to feel dissatisfied with what he was doing. Freemasonry, at least as he knew it here, seemed to him sometimes to rest simply upon formal observances. He never dreamed of doubting of freemasonry itself, but began to suspect that Russian freemasonry had got on to a false track, and was deviating from its original course. And so towards the end of the year Pierre went abroad to devote himself to the higher mysteries of the order.

It was in the summer of 1809 that Pierre returned to Petersburg. From the correspondence that passed between freemasons in Russia and abroad, it was known that Bezuhov had succeeded in gaining the confidence of many persons in high positions abroad; that he had been initiated into many mysteries, had been raised to a higher grade, and was bringing back with him much that would conduce to the progress of freemasonry in Russia. The Petersburg freemasons all came to see him, tried to ingratiate themselves with him, and all fancied that he had something in reserve that he was preparing for them.

A solemn assembly of the lodge of the second order was arranged, at which Pierre promised to communicate the message he had to give the Petersburg brothers from the highest leaders of the order abroad. The assembly was a full one. After the usual ceremonies Pierre got up and began to speak.

'Dear brothers,' he began, blushing and hesitating, with a written speech in his hand, 'it is not enough to guard our secrets in the seclusion of the lodge,—what is needed is to act . . . to act. . . . We are falling into slumber, and we need to act.'

Pierre opened his manuscript and began to read.

'For the propagation of the pure truth and the attainment of virtue,' he read, 'we must purify men from prejudice, diffuse principles in harmony with the spirit of the times, undertake the education of the younger generation, ally ourselves by indissoluble ties with the most enlightened men, boldly, and at the same time prudently, overcome superstition, infidelity, and folly, and form of those devoted to us men linked together by a common aim and possessed of power and authority.

'For the attainment of this aim we must secure to virtue the preponderance over vice; we must strive that the honest man may obtain his eternal reward even in this world. But in those great projects we are very gravely hindered by existing political institutions. What is to be done in the existing state of affairs? Are we to welcome revolutions, to overthrow everything, to repel violence by violence? . . . No, we are very far from that. Every reform by violence is to be deprecated, because it does little to correct the evil while men remain as they are, and because wisdom has no need of violence.

'The whole plan of our order should be founded on the training of men of character and virtue, bound together by unity of conviction and aim,—the aim of suppressing vice and folly everywhere by every means, and protecting talent and virtue, raising deserving persons out of the dust and enrolling them in our brotherhood. Only then will our order obtain the power insensibly to tie the hands of the promoters of disorder, and to control them without their being aware of it. In a word, we want to found a form of government holding universal sway, which should be diffused over the whole world without encroaching on civil obligations; under which all other governments could continue in their ordinary course and do all, except what hinders the great aim of our order, that is, the triumph of virtue over vice. This aim is that of Christianity itself. It has taught men to be holy and good, and for their own profit to follow the precept and example of better and wiser men.

'In times when all was plunged in darkness, exhortation alone was of course enough; the novelty of truth gave it peculiar force, but nowadays far more powerful means are necessary for us. Now a man guided by his senses needs to find in virtue a charm palpable to the senses. The passions cannot be uprooted; we must only attempt to direct them to a noble object, and so every one should be able to find satisfaction for his passions within the bounds of virtue, and our order should provide means to that end. As soon as we have a certain number of capable men in every state, each of them training again two others, and all keeping in close co-operation, then everything will be possible for our order, which has already done much in secret for the good of humanity.'

This speech did not merely make a great impression, it produced a thrill of excitement in the lodge. The majority of the brothers, seeing in this speech dangerous projects of 'illuminism,' to Pierre's surprise received it coldly. The Grand Master began to raise objections to it; Pierre began to expound his own views with greater and greater heat. It was long since there had been so stormy a meeting. The lodge split up into parties; one party opposed Pierre, accusing him of 'illuminism'; the other supported him. Pierre was for the first time at this meeting impressed by the endless multiplicity of men's minds, which leads to no truth being ever seen by two persons alike.

Even those among the members who seemed to be on his side interpreted him in their own way, with limitations and variations, to which he could not agree. What Pierre chiefly desired was always to transmit his thought to another exactly as he conceived it himself.

At the conclusion of the sitting, the Grand Master spoke with ill-will and irony to Bezuhov of his hasty temper; and observed that it was not love of virtue alone, but a passion for strife, that had guided him in the discussion.

Pierre made him no reply, but briefly inquired whether his proposal would be accepted. He was told that it would not be; and without waiting for the usual formalities, he left the lodge and went home.

VIII

AGAIN Pierre was overtaken by that despondency he so dreaded. For three days after the delivery of his speech at the lodge he lay on a sofa at home, seeing no one, and going nowhere.

At this time he received a letter from his wife who besought him to see her, wrote of her unhappiness on his account, and her desire to devote her whole life to him.

At the end of the letter she informed him that in a day or two she would arrive in Petersburg from abroad.

The letter was followed up by one of the freemasons whom Pierre respected least bursting in upon his solitude. Turning the conversation upon Pierre's matrimonial affairs, he gave him, by way of brotherly counsel, his opinion that his severity to his wife was wrong, and that Pierre was departing from the first principles of freemasonry in not forgiving the penitent. At the same time his mother-in-law, Prince Vassily's wife, sent to him, beseeching him to visit her, if only for a few minutes, to discuss a matter of great importance. Pierre saw there was a conspiracy against him, that they meant to reconcile him with his wife, and he did not even dislike this in the mood in which he then was. Nothing mattered to him; Pierre regarded nothing in life as a matter of great consequence, and under the influence of the despondency which had taken possession of him, he attached no significance either to his own freedom or to having his own way by punishing his wife.

'No one is right, no one is to blame, and so she, too, is not to blame,' he thought. If Pierre did not at once give his consent to being reunited to his wife, it was simply because in the despondent state into which he had lapsed, he was incapable of taking any line of action. Had his wife come to him, he could not now have driven her away. Could it matter, beside the questions that were absorbing Pierre, whether he lived with his wife or not?

Without answering either his wife or his mother-in-law, Pierre at once set off late in the evening, and drove to Moscow to see Osip Alexyevitch.

This is what Pierre wrote in his diary:

'*Moscow, November* 17.—I have only just come from seeing my benefactor, and I hasten to note down all I have been feeling. Osip Alexyevitch lives in poverty, and has been for three years past suffering from a painful disease of the bladder. No one has ever heard from him a groan or a word of complaint. From morning till late at night, except at the times when he partakes of the very plainest food, he is working at science. He received me graciously, and made me sit down on the bed on which he was lying. I made him the sign of the Knights of the East and of Jerusalem; he responded with the same, and asked me with a gentle smile what I had learned and gained in the Prussian and Scottish lodges. I told him everything as best I could, repeating to him the principles of action I had proposed in our Petersburg lodge, and telling him of the unfavourable reception given me, and the rupture between me and the brothers. Osip Alexyevitch, after some silent thought, laid all his own view of the subject before me, which immediately threw light on all the past and all the course that lies before me. He surprised me by asking whether I remembered the threefold aim of the order—(1) the preservation and study of the holy mystery; (2) the purification and reformation of self for its reception; and (3) the improvement of the human race through striving for such purification. Which, he asked, was the first and greatest of those three aims? Undoubtedly self-reformation and self-purification. It is only towards that aim that we can always strive independently of all circumstances. But at the same time it is just that aim which requires of us the greatest effort, and therefore, led astray by pride, we let that aim drop, and either strive to penetrate to the mystery which we are unworthy in our impurity to receive, or seek after the reformation of the human race, while we are ourselves setting an example of vice and abomination. "Illuminism" is not a pure doctrine precisely because it is seduced by worldly activity and puffed up with pride. On this ground Osip Alexyevitch censured my speech and all I am doing. At the bottom of my heart I agreed with him. Talking of my domestic affairs, he said to me: "The first duty of a mason, as I have told you, is the perfection of himself. But often we imagine that by removing all the difficulties of our life, we may better attain this aim. It is quite the contrary, sir," he said to me: "it is only in the midst of the cares of the world that we can reach the three great aims—(1) self-knowledge, for a man can know himself only by comparison; (2) greater perfection, which can only be obtained by conflict; and (3) the attainment of the chief virtue—love of death. Only the corruptions of life can show us all its vanity, and strengthen our innate love for death, or rather regeneration into new life." These words were the more remarkable as Osip Alexyevitch, in spite of his grievous physical sufferings, is never weary of life, though he loves death, for which he does not, in spite of all the purity and loftiness of his inner man, yet feel himself prepared. Then my benefactor explained to me fully the significance of the great square of creation, and pointed out that the third and the seventh number are the basis of everything. He counselled me not to withdraw from co-operation with the Petersburg brothers, and while undertaking duties only of the second order in the lodge, to endeavour to draw the brothers away from the seductions of pride, and to turn them into the true path of self-knowledge and self-perfection. Moreover, for myself personally, he advised me first of all to keep a watch over myself, and with that aim he gave me a manuscript-book, the one in which I am writing now, and am to note down all my actions in the future.'

'*Petersburg, November* 23.—I am reconciled with my wife. My mother-in-law came to me in tears, and said that Ellen was here, and that she besought me to hear her; that she was innocent, that she was miserable at my desertion of her, and a great deal more. I knew that if I once let myself see her, I should not be able to refuse to accede to her wishes. In my uncertainty, I did not know to whose help and advice to have recourse. If my benefactor had been here, he would have told me what to do. I retired to my own room, read over the letters of Osip Alexyevitch, recalled my conversations with him, and from all that I reached the conclusion that I ought not to refuse a suppliant, and ought to hold out a helping hand to every one, and, above all, to a person so closely connected with me, and that I must bear my cross. But if I forgive her for the sake of doing right, at least let my reunion with her have a spiritual end only. So I decided, and so I wrote to Osip Alexyevitch. I said to my wife that I begged her to forget all the past, that I begged her to forgive whatever wrong I might have done her, and that I had nothing to forgive her. It was a joy to me to tell her that. May she never know how painful it was to me to see her again! I have installed myself in the upper rooms in this great house, and I am conscious of a happy feeling of beginning anew.'

IX

AT that time, as always indeed, the exalted society that met at court and at the great balls was split up into several circles, each of which had its special tone. The largest among them was the French circle—supporting the Napoleonic alliance—the circle of Count Rumyantsev and Caulaincourt. In this circle Ellen took a leading position, as soon as she had established herself in her husband's house in Petersburg. She received the members of the French embassy, and a great number of people, noted for their wit and their politeness, and belonging to that political section.

Ellen had been at Erfurt at the time of the famous meeting of the emperors; and had there formed close ties with all the notable figures in Europe belonging to the Napoleonic circle. In Erfurt she had been brilliantly successful. Napoleon himself, seeing her at the theatre, had asked who she was, and admired her beauty. Her triumphs in the character of a beautiful and elegant woman did not surprise Pierre, for with years she had become even more beautiful than before. But what did surprise him was that during the last two years his wife had succeeded in gaining a reputation as 'a charming woman, as witty as she is beautiful,' as was said of her. The distinguished Prince de Ligne wrote her letters of eight pages. Bilibin treasured up his *mots* to utter them for the first time before Countess Bezuhov. To be received in Countess Bezuhov's salon was looked upon as a certificate of intellect. Young men read up subjects before one of Ellen's soirées, so as to be able to talk of something in her salon, and secretaries of the embassy, and even ambassadors, confided diplomatic secrets to her, so that Ellen was in a way a power. It was with a strange feeling of perplexity and alarm that Pierre, who knew she was very stupid, sometimes at her dinners and soirées listened to conversation about politics, poetry, and philosophy. At these soirées he experienced a sensation such as a conjurer must feel who expects every moment that his trick will be discovered. But either because stupidity was just what was needed for the successful management of such a salon, or because those who were deceived took pleasure in the deception, the cheat was not discovered, and the reputation 'of a charming woman' clung so persistently to Elena Vassilyevna Bezuhov, that she could utter the vulgarest and stupidest speeches, and every one was just as enthusiastic over every word, and eagerly found in it a profound meaning of which she did not dream herself.

Pierre was exactly the husband needed by this brilliant society woman. He was that absent-minded, eccentric, grand seigneur of a husband, who got in nobody's way and far from spoiling the general impression of the highest tone in her drawing-room, formed by his contrast with his wife's elegance and tact an advantageous foil to her. Pierre's continual concentration on immaterial interests during the last two years, and his genuine contempt for everything else, gave him in his wife's circle, which did not interest him, that tone of unconcern, indifference, and benevolence towards all alike, which cannot be acquired artificially, and for that reason commands involuntary respect. He entered his wife's drawing-room as though it were a theatre, was acquainted with every one, equally affable to all, and to all equally indifferent. Sometimes he took part in conversation on some subject that interested him, and then, without any consideration whether the 'gentlemen of the embassy' were present or not, he mumbled out his opinions, which were by no means always in harmony with the received catchwords of the time. But the public estimate of the eccentric husband of 'the most distinguished woman in Petersburg' was now so well established that no one took his sallies seriously.

Among the numerous young men, who were daily to be seen in Ellen's house, Boris Drubetskoy, who had by now achieved marked success in the service, was, after Ellen's return from Erfurt, the most intimate friend of the Bezuhov household. Ellen used to call him '*mon page*,' and treated him like a child. Her smile for him was the same smile she bestowed on all, but it was sometimes distasteful to Pierre to see that smile. Boris behaved to Pierre with a marked, dignified, and mournful respectfulness. This shade of respectfulness too disturbed Pierre. He had suffered so much three years before from the mortification caused him by his wife, that now he secured himself from all possibility of similar mortification; in the first place, by being his wife's husband only in name, and secondly, by not allowing himself to suspect anything. 'No, now she has become a blue-stocking, she has renounced for ever her former errors,' he said to himself. 'There has never been an instance of a blue-stocking giving way to tender passions,' he repeated to himself; a maxim he had picked up somewhere and implicitly believed. But, strange to say, the presence of Boris in his wife's drawing-room (and he was almost always there) had a physical effect on Pierre; it seemed to make all his limbs contract, and destroyed the unconsciousness and freedom of his movement.

'Such a strange antipathy,' thought Pierre; 'and at one time I really liked him very much.'

In the eyes of the world, Pierre was a great lord, the rather blind and absurd husband of a distinguished wife; a clever eccentric, who did nothing but who was no trouble to any one, a good-natured capital fellow. In Pierre's soul all this while a complex and laborious processs of inner development was going on that revealed much to him and led him to many spiritual doubts and joys.

X

HE kept up his diary and this was what he was writing in it at that time:

'*November* 24.—I got up at eight o'clock, read the Scriptures, then went to my duties' (Pierre by the advice of Osip Alexyevitch was serving on one of the government committees), 'came back to dinner, dined alone (the countess had a lot of guests whom I did not care for), ate and drank with moderation, and after dinner copied out passages for the brothers. In the evening I went down to the countess, and told a ridiculous story about B., and only bethought myself that I ought not to have done so, when every one was laughing loudly at it.

'I went to bed with a calm and happy spirit. Great Lord, help me to walk in Thy paths: (1) to flee anger by gentleness and deliberation; (2) to flee lust by self-restraint and loathing, (3) to escape from the turmoil of the world without cutting myself off from (*a*) the duties of my political work, (*b*) the cares of my household, (*c*) relations with my friends, and (*d*) the management of my finances.'

'*November* 27.—I got up late and lay a long while in bed after I was awake, giving way to sloth. My God, help me and strengthen me that I may walk in Thy ways. Read the Scriptures, but without proper feeling. Brother Urusov came: talked of the cares of this world. He told me of the Tsar's new projects. I was beginning to criticise them, but remembered my principles and the words of my benefactor, that a true mason ought to be zealous in working for the state, when his aid is required, but should look on quietly at what he is not called upon to assist in. My tongue is my enemy. Brothers G. V. and O. visited me; there was a conversation preliminary to the reception of a new brother. They lay upon me the duty of rhetor. I feel weak and unworthy. Then there was talk of the interpretation of the seven pillars and steps of the Temple, of the seven sciences, the seven virtues, the seven vices, the seven gifts of the Holy Spirit. Brother O. was very eloquent. In the evening the reception took place. The new decoration of the building added a good deal to the magnificence of the spectacle. Boris Drubetskoy was admitted. I had proposed him, and I was the rhetor. A strange feeling troubled me all the time I was with him in the dark temple. I detected in myself a feeling of hatred, which I studiously strove to overcome. And I could sincerely have desired to save him from evil and to lead him into the way of truth, but evil thoughts of him never left me. The thought came to me that his object in entering the brotherhood was simply to gain the intimacy and favour of men in our lodge. Apart from the fact that he several times asked me whether N. or S. were not members of our lodge (a question I could not answer), he is incapable, so far as my observation goes, of feeling a reverence for our holy order, and is too much occupied, and too well satisfied with the outer man, to care much for the improvement of the spiritual man. I had no grounds for doubting of him, but he seemed to me insincere; and all the time I stood face to face with him in the dark temple I kept fancying he was smiling contemptuously at my words, and I should have liked really to stab his bare chest with the sword I held pointed at it. I could not be eloquent, and could not sincerely communicate my doubts to the brothers and the Grand Master. O Great Architect of Nature, help me to find the true path that leads out of the labyrinth of falsehood!'

After this three pages of the diary were left blank, and then had been written:

'I had a long and instructive conversation with brother V., who advised me not to abandon brother A. Much was revealed to me, unworthy as I am. Adonai is the name of the creator of worlds. Elohim is the name of the ruler of all. The third name, the name unutterable, has the significance of the All. Talks with brother V. strengthen and refresh me and confirm me in the path of virtue. In his presence there is no room for doubt. I see clearly the distinction between the poor doctrine of mundane science and our sacred, all-embracing teaching. Human sciences dissect everything to understand it, and destroy everything to analyse it. In the sacred science of our order all is one, all is known for its combination and life. The trinity—the three elements of things—are sulphur, mercury, and salt. Sulphur is of an oily and fiery nature; in its combination with salt by its fiery quality it arouses a craving in it, by means of which it attracts mercury, fastens upon it, holds it, and in combination with it forms various substances. Mercury is the unsubstantial, floating, spiritual essence—Christ, the Holy Ghost, Him.'

'*December* 3.—I waked up late, read the Scripture, but was unmoved by it. Afterwards I went down and walked up and down the big hall. I tried to meditate; but instead of that my imagination brought before me an incident which occurred four years ago. Dolohov, meeting me after my duel in Moscow, said to me that he hoped I was now enjoying complete mental peace in spite of my wife's absence. At the time I made him no answer. Now I recalled all the details of that interview, and in my mind made him the most vindictive and biting retorts. I recovered myself and drove away that idea, only when I had caught myself in a passion of anger; but I did not repent of it sufficiently. Afterwards Boris Drubetskoy came and began describing various incidents. The moment he came in I felt amazed at his visit and said something horrid to him. He retorted. I got hot, and said a great deal to him that was disagreeable and even rude. He did not reply, and I checked myself only when it was too late. My God, I cannot get on with him at all. It is myself too that is to blame for it. I set myself above him, and so I become far inferior to him, for he is lenient to my rudeness, while I nourish a contempt for him. My God, grant me that in his presence I may see more clearly my own vileness and act so that it may be profitable to him too. After dinner I went to sleep, and just as I was falling asleep, I distinctly heard a voice saying in my left ear: "Thy day."

'I dreamed I was walking along in the dark and was all of a sudden surrounded by dogs, but I went on undismayed; all at once one small dog seized me by the thigh with its teeth and would not let go. I tried to strangle it with my hands. And as soon as I tore it off, another, a bigger one, began to bite me. I lifted it up, and the more I lifted it up, the bigger and heavier it became. And suddenly brother A. came up, and taking me by the arm, led me away with him and brought me into a building, to enter which we had to pass over a narrow plank. I stepped on it, and the plank bent and gave way, and I began clambering on the fence, which I just managed to get hold of with my hands. After great efforts I dragged my body up, so that my legs were hanging over on one side and my body on the other. I looked round and saw brother A. standing on the fence and pointing out to me a great avenue and garden, and in the garden a great and beautiful building. I waked up. Lord, Great Architect of Nature, help me to tear away these dogs—my evil passions and especially the last—that unites in itself the violence of all the former ones, and aid me to enter that temple of virtue, of which I was vouchsafed a vision in my sleep.'

'*December 7.*—I dreamed that Osip Alexyevitch was sitting in my house, and I was very glad to see him and eager to entertain him. But in my dream I kept chattering away incessantly with other people, and all at once I bethought myself that this could not be to his liking and I wanted to come close to him and to embrace him. But as soon as I approached him, I saw that his face was transformed, and had grown young, and he said something to me softly, some doctrine of our order, but so softly that I could not catch it. Then we all seemed to go out of the room, and something strange happened. We were sitting or lying on the floor. He was telling me something. But in my dream I longed to show him my devotional feeling, and, not listening to his words, I began picturing to myself the state of my own inner man, and the grace of God sanctifying me. And tears came into my eyes, and I was glad that he noticed it. But he glanced at me with vexation, and jumped up, breaking off his conversation with me. I was abashed and asked him whether what he had been saying did not concern me. But he made no reply, but gave me a friendly look, and then all of a sudden we found ourselves in my bedroom, where stood a big double bed. He lay down on the edge of it, and I seemed to be filled with a desire to embrace him and to lie down too. And in my dream he asked me "Tell me the truth, what is your chief temptation? Do you know it? I believe that you do know it." Abashed at this question, I answered that sloth was my besetting temptation. He shook his head incredulously. And even more abashed, I told him that though I was living here with my wife, I was not living with her as a husband. To this he replied that I had no right to deprive my wife of my embraces, and gave me to understand that this was my duty. But I answered that I should be ashamed of it, and suddenly everything vanished. And I waked up, and in my mind there was the text of scripture: "And the life was the light of man, and the light shineth in the darkness, and the darkness comprehendeth it not."

'The face of Osip Alexyevitch had been youthful and bright-looking. That day I received a letter from my benefactor, in which he wrote to me of my conjugal duties.

'*December* 9.—I had a dream from which I waked up with a throbbing heart. I dreamed I was in Moscow in my own house, in the big divan-room, and Osip Alexyevitch came out of the drawing-room. I dreamed that I knew at once that the process of regeneration had begun in him, and I rushed to meet him. I kissed his face and his hands, while he said: "Do you notice that my face is different?" I looked at him, still holding him in my arms, and I dreamed that I saw that his face was young, but he had no hair on his head and his features were quite different. And I dreamed that I said to him: "I should have recognised you if I had met you by chance"; and thought as I said it, "Am I telling the truth?" And all at once I saw him lying like a dead body; then he gradually came to himself again and went with me into the big study, holding a big folio book of manuscript. And I dreamed I said: "I wrote that." And he answered me by an inclination of the head. I opened the book, and on all the pages were fine drawings. And in my dream I knew that these pictures depicted the soul's love adventures with its beloved. And I saw a beautiful presentment of a maiden in transparent garments and with a transparent body flying up to the clouds. And I seemed to know that this maiden was nothing else but the figure of the Song of Songs. And in my dream, as I looked at these pictures, I felt I was doing wrong and could not tear myself away from them. Lord, help me! My God, if Thy forsaking me is Thy doing, then Thy will be done; but if I am myself the cause, teach me what I am to do. I perish from my vileness as though Thou wast utterly forsaking me.'

XI

THE Rostovs' pecuniary position had not improved during the two years they had spent in the country. Although Nikolay Rostov had kept firmly to his resolution, and was still living in a modest way in an obscure regiment, spending comparatively little, the manner of life at Otradnoe, and still more Mitenka's management of affairs, were such that debts went on unchecked, growing bigger every year. The sole resource that presented itself to the old count as the obvious thing to do was to enter the government service, and he had come to Petersburg to seek a post, and at the same time, as he said, to let his poor wenches enjoy themselves for the last time.

Soon after the Rostovs' arrival in Petersburg, Berg made Vera an offer, and his offer was accepted. Although in Moscow the Rostovs belonged to the best society—themselves unaware of the fact, and never troubling themselves to consider what society they belonged to—yet in Petersburg their position was an uncertain and indefinite one. In Petersburg they were provincials; and were not visited by the very people who in Moscow had dined at the Rostovs' expense without their inquiring to what society they belonged.

The Rostovs kept open house in Petersburg, just as they used to do in Moscow; and at their suppers people of the most diverse sorts could be seen together—country neighbours, old and not well-to-do country gentlemen with their daughters, and the old maid-of-honour, Madame Peronsky, Pierre Bezuhov, and the son of their district postmaster, who was in an office in Petersburg. Of the men who were constantly at the Rostovs' house in Petersburg, the most intimate friends of the family were very soon Boris, Pierre, who had been met in the street by the old count and dragged home by him, and Berg, who spent whole days with the Rostovs, and paid the elder of the young countesses, Vera, every attention a young man can pay who intends to make a proposal.

Not in vain had Berg shown everybody his right hand that had been wounded at Austerlitz, and the sword quite unnecessarily held in his left. He had related this episode to everybody so persistently and with such an air of importance, that every one had come to believe in the utility and merit of the feat, and Berg had received two decorations for Austerlitz.

In the war in Finland, too, he had succeeded in distinguishing himself. He had picked up a fragment of a grenade, by which an adjutant had been killed close to the commander-in-chief, and had carried this fragment to his commander. Again, as after Austerlitz, he talked to every one at such length and with such persistency about this incident that people ended by believing that this, too, was something that ought to have been done, and Berg received two decorations for the Finnish war too. In 1809 he was a captain in the guards with decorations on his breast, and was filling some particularly profitable posts in Petersburg.

Though there were some sceptics who smiled when Berg's merits were mentioned before them, it could not be denied that Berg was a gallant officer, punctual in the discharge of his duties, in excellent repute with the authorities, and a conscientious young man with a brilliant career before him and a secure position, indeed, in society.

Four years before, on meeting a German comrade in the *parterre* of a Moscow theatre, Berg had pointed out to him Vera Rostov, and said to him in German, 'That girl will be my wife.' From that moment he had made up his mind to marry her. Now in Petersburg, after duly considering the Rostovs' position and his own, he decided that the time had come and made his offer.

Berg's proposal was received at first with a hesitation by no means flattering for him. It seemed a strange idea at first that the son of an obscure Livonian gentleman should propose for the hand of a Countess Rostov. But Berg's leading characteristic was an egoism so naïve and good-natured that the Rostovs unconsciously began to think that it must be a good thing since he was himself so firmly convinced that it would be a good thing, and indeed a very good thing. The Rostovs were, moreover, seriously embarrassed in their pecuniary affairs, a fact of which the suitor could not but be aware; and what was the chief consideration, Vera was now four-and-twenty, and had been brought out everywhere; and, in spite of the fact that she was undeniably good-looking and sensible, no one had hitherto made her an offer. The offer was accepted.

'You see,' Berg said to a comrade, whom he called his friend—only because he knew all people do have friends—'you see, I have taken everything into consideration, and I should not have got married if I had not thought it well over, or if it had been unsuitable in any way. But at present my papa and mamma are well provided for, I have secured them the lease of that place in the Ostsee district, and I can live in Petersburg with my pay and her fortune and my careful habits. We can get along nicely. I'm not marrying for money, I consider that ungentlemanly, but the wife ought to bring her share and the husband his. I have my position in the service; she has connections and some small means. That's worth something nowadays, isn't it? And what's the chief consideration, she's a handsome, estimable girl, and she loves me. . . .'

Berg blushed and smiled.

'And I love her because she has a character that is reasonable and very nice. Her sister now—though they are of the same family—is utterly different, and her character is disagreeable, and she has none of that intelligence, but something you know . . . I don't like. . . . But my betrothed. . . . You must come and see us; come to . . .' Berg went on; he was going to say 'to dinner,' but on second thoughts he said 'to tea,' and putting out his tongue he blew a little ring of tobacco smoke that embodied for him all his dreams of happiness.

The first feeling of hesitation aroused in the parents by Berg's proposal had been followed by the festivity and rejoicing in the family usual on such occasions, but the rejoicing was apparent and not genuine. A certain embarrassment and shamefacedness could be detected in the feelings of the relations in regard to this marriage. It was as though their conscience smote them for not having been very fond of Vera and of being so ready now to get her off their hands. The old count was more disconcerted over it than any one. He would most likely have been unable to say what made him feel so, but his financial difficulties were at the root of the matter. He absolutely did not know what he had, how much his debts amounted to, and what he would be in a position to give for Vera's dowry. Each of his daughters had at their birth been assigned a portion, consisting of an estate with three hundred serfs on it. But one of those estates had by now been sold, and the other had been mortgaged, and the interest was so much in arrears that it would have to be sold, so that to give this estate was impossible. There was no money either.

Berg had been betrothed more than a month, and it was only a week before the date fixed for the wedding, but the count was still unable to come to a decision on the subject of the dowry, and had not spoken of it to his wife. At one time the count thought of making over the Ryazan estate to Vera then he thought of selling his forest, then of borrowing money on a note of hand.

A few days before the wedding, Berg went early in the morning into the count's study, and with an agreeable smile, respectfully invited his father-in-law to let him know what fortune would be given with the Countess Vera. The count was so much disconcerted by this long-foreseen inquiry that, without thinking, he said the first thing that came into his head.

'I like your being businesslike about it, I like it; you will be quite satisfied . . .'

And clapping Berg on the shoulder, he got up, intending to cut short the conversation. But Berg, smiling blandly, announced that if he were not to know for certain what would be given with Vera, and to receive at least part of the dowry in advance, he would be obliged to break off the marriage. 'Because, you must consider, count, if I were to allow myself to marry now without having a definite security for the maintenance of my wife I should be acting like a scoundrel . . .'

The conversation ended by the count, in his anxiety to be generous and to avoid further requests, saying that he would give him a note of hand for eighty thousand. Berg smiled gently, kissed the count on the shoulder, and said that he was very grateful, but could not make his arrangements in his new life without receiving thirty thousand in ready money. 'Twenty thousand at least, count,' he added, 'and then a note of hand simply for sixty thousand.'

'Yes, yes, very good,' said the count hurriedly. 'Only excuse me, my dear boy, I'll give you twenty thousand and the note of hand for eighty thousand as well. That's all right, kiss me.'

XII

NATASHA was sixteen, and it was the year 1809, that year to which she had reckoned up on her fingers with Boris, after she had kissed him four years before. Since then she had not once seen him. When Boris was mentioned she would speak quite freely of it before Sonya and her mother, treating it as a settled thing that all that had passed between them was childish nonsense, not worth talking of and long ago forgotten. But in the most secret recesses of her soul the question whether her engagement to Boris were really a mere jest or a solemn binding promise worried her.

Ever since Boris had left Moscow in 1805 to go into the army he had not once seen the Rostovs. Several times he had been in Moscow, and in travelling had passed not far from Otradnoe, but he had not once been at the Rostovs'.

It had sometimes occurred to Natasha that he did not want to see her, and her surmises had been confirmed by the mournful tone in which he was referred to by her elders.

'Old friends are soon forgotten nowadays,' the countess would say after Boris had been mentioned.

Anna Mihalovna had taken in these latter days to seeing less of the Rostovs. There was a marked dignity, too, in her manner with them, and she spoke on every occasion with thankfulness and enthusiasm of her son's great abilities and brilliant career. When the Rostovs arrived in Petersburg Boris came to call on them.

It was not without emotion that he came to see them. His reminiscences of Natasha were Boris's most poetic memories. But at the same time he came to call on them firmly resolved to make her and her relations feel that the childish vows between Natasha and him could have no binding force for her or for him. He had a brilliant position in society, thanks to his intimacy with Countess Bezuhov; a brilliant position in the service, thanks to the protection of a great person whose confidence he had completely won; and he was beginning to make plans for marrying one of the richest heiresses in Petersburg, plans which might very easily be realised. When Boris went into the Rostovs' drawing-room, Natasha was in her own room. On hearing of his arrival she almost ran with a flushed face into the drawing-room, radiant with a smile that was more than cordial.

Boris had thought of Natasha as the little girl he had known four years before in a short frock, with black eyes glancing under her curls, and a desperate, childish giggle; and so, when a quite different Natasha came in, he was taken aback and his face expressed surprise and admiration. His expression delighted Natasha.

'Well, would you know your mischievous little playmate?' said the countess. Boris kissed Natasha's hand, and said he was surprised at the change in her.

'How pretty you have grown!'

'I should hope so!' was the answer in Natasha's laughing eyes.

'And does papa look older?' she asked.

Natasha sat still, taking no part in the talk between Boris and her mother. Silently and minutely she scrutinised the young man who had been her suitor in her childhood. He felt oppressed by that persistent, friendly gaze, and glanced once or twice at her.

The uniform, the spurs, the tie, the way Boris had brushed his hair,— it was all fashionable and *comme il faut*. That Natasha noticed at once. He sat a little sideways on a lone chair beside the countess, with his right hand smacking the exquisitely clean and perfectly fitting glove on his left. He talked with a peculiar, refined compression of the lips about the divisions of the best society in Petersburg; with faint irony referred to old days in Moscow and old Moscow acquaintances. Not unintentionally, as Natasha felt, he mentioned some of the highest aristocracy, alluded to the ambassador's ball, at which he had been present, and to invitations from N. N. and from S. S.

Natasha sat the whole time without speaking, looking up from under her brows at him. Her eyes made Boris more and more uneasy and embarrassed. He looked round more frequently at Natasha, and broke off in his sentences. After staying no more than ten minutes he got up and took leave. Still the same curious, challenging, and rather ironical eyes gazed at him. After his first visit, Boris said to himself that Natasha was as attractive to him as she had been in the past, but that he must not give way to this feeling, because to marry her—a girl almost without fortune—would be the ruin of his career, and to renew their old relations without any intention of marriage would be dishonourable. Boris resolved to avoid meeting Natasha; but in spite of this resolution he came a few days later, and began to come often, and to spend whole days at the Rostovs'. He fancied that it was essential for him to have a frank explanation with Natasha, to tell her that all the past must be forgotten, that in spite of everything . . . she could not be his wife, that he had no means, and that they would never consent to her marrying him. But he always failed to do so, and felt an awkwardness in approaching the subject. Every day he became more and more entangled. Natasha—so her mother and Sonya judged—seemed to be in love with Boris, as in the past. She sang him her favourite songs, showed him her album, made him write in it, would not let him refer to the past, making him feel how delightful she considered the present; and every day he went home in a whirl without having said what he meant to say, not knowing what he was doing, why he had come, and how it would end. Boris gave up visiting Ellen, received reproachful notes every day from her, and still spent whole days together at the Rostovs'.

XIII

ONE evening the old countess in her bed-jacket, without her false curls, and with only one poor wisp of hair peeping out from under her white cotton nightcap, was bowing down on the carpet, sighing and moaning as she repeated her evening prayers. Her door creaked, and Natasha, also in a bed-jacket, ran in, bare-legged, with her feet in slippers, and her hair in curl papers. The countess looked round and frowned. She was repeating her last prayer. 'Can it be this couch will be my bier?' Her devotional mood was dispelled. Natasha, flushed and eager, stopped suddenly short in her rapid movement as she saw her mother at her prayers. She half-sat down and unconsciously put out her tongue at herself. Seeing that her mother was still praying, she ran on tiptoe to the bed; and rapidly slipping one little foot against the other, pushed off her slippers and sprang on to that couch which the countess in her prayer feared might become her bier. That couch was a high feather-bed, with five pillows, each smaller than the one below. Natasha skipped in, sank into the feather-bed, rolled over towards the side, and begun snuggling up under the quilt, tucking herself up, bending her knees up to her chin, kicking out and giving a faintly audible giggle as she alternately hid her face under the quilt and peeped out at her mother. The countess had finished her prayers, and was approaching her bed with a stern face, but seeing that Natasha was playing bo-peep with her she smiled her good-natured, weak smile.

'Come, come, come!' said the mother.

'Mamma, may I speak; yes?' said Natasha. 'Come, under the chin, one, and now another, and enough.' And she clutched at her mother's neck and kissed her favourite place on her chin. In Natasha's behaviour to her mother there was a superficial roughness of manner, but she had a natural tact and knack of doing things, so that, however she snatched her mother in her arms, she always managed so that she was not hurt, not uncomfortable, nor displeased by it.

'Well, what is it tonight?' said her mother, settling herself in the pillows and waiting for Natasha, who had already rolled over twice, to lie down by her side under the bedclothes, to put out her arms and assume a serious expression.

These visits of Natasha to her mother at night before the count came home from the club were one of the greatest pleasures both of mother and daughter.

'What is it tonight? And I want to talk to you . . .' Natasha put her hand on her mother's lips.

'About Boris . . . I know,' she said seriously; 'that's what I have come about. Don't say it; I know. No, do say it!' She took her hand away. 'Say it, mamma! He's nice, eh?'

'Natasha, you are sixteen! At your age I was married. You say Boris is nice. He is very nice, and I love him like a son! But what do you want? . . . What are you thinking about? You have quite turned his head, I can see that . . .'

As she said this, the countess looked round at her daughter. Natasha was lying, looking steadily straight before her at one of the mahogany sphinxes carved on a corner of the bedstead, so that the countess could only see her daughter's face in profile. Her face impressed the countess by its strikingly serious and concentrated expression.

Natasha was listening and considering.

'Well, so what then?' she said.

'You have completely turned his head, and what for? What do you want of him? You know you can't marry him.'

'Why not?' said Natasha, with no change in her attitude.

'Because he's so young, because he's poor, because he's a relation . . . because you don't care for him yourself.'

'How do you know that?'

'I know. It's not right, my darling.'

'But if I want to . . .' said Natasha.

'Leave off talking nonsense,' said the countess.

'But if I want to . . .'

'Natasha, I am serious . . .

Natasha did not let her finish; she drew the countess's large hand to her, and kissed it on the upper side, and then on the palm, then turned it over again and began kissing it on the knuckle of the top joint of the finger, then on the space between the knuckles, then on a knuckle again, whispering; 'January, February, March, April, May.'

'Speak, mamma; why are you silent? Speak,' she said, looking round at her mother, who was gazing tenderly at her daughter, and apparently in gazing at her had forgotten all she meant to say.

'This won't do, my dear. It's not every one who will understand your childish feelings for one another, and seeing him on such intimate terms with you may prejudice you in the eyes of other young men who visit us, and what is of more consequence, it's making him wretched for nothing. He had very likely found a match that would suit him, some wealthy girl, and now he's half-crazy.'

'Half-crazy?' repeated Natasha.

'I'll tell you what happened in my own case. I had a cousin ...'

'I know—Kirilla Matveitch; but he's old.'

'He was not always old. But I tell you what, Natasha, I'll speak to Boris. He mustn't come so often ...'

'Why mustn't he, if he wants to?'

'Because I know it can't come to anything.'

'How do you know? No, mamma, don't speak to him. What nonsense!' said Natasha, in the tone of a man being robbed of his property. 'Well, I won't marry him, so let him come, if he enjoys it and I enjoy it.' Natasha looked at her mother, smiling. 'Not to be married, but—just so,' she repeated.

'How so, my dear?'

'Oh, just *so*. I see it's very necessary I shouldn't marry him, but ... just *so*.'

'Just so, just so,' repeated the countess, and, shaking all over, she went off into a good-natured, unexpected elderly laugh.

'Don't laugh, stop,' cried Natasha; 'you're shaking all the bed. You're awfully like me, just such another giggler ... Stop ...' She snatched both the countess's hands, kissed one knuckle of the little finger, for June, and went on kissing—July, August—on the other hand. 'Mamma, is he very much in love? What do you think? Were men as much in love with you? And he's very nice, very, very nice! Only not quite to my liking—he's so narrow, somehow, like a clock on the wall. ... Don't you understand? ... Narrow, you know, grey, light-coloured ...'

'What nonsense you talk!' said the countess.

Natasha went on:

'Don't you really understand? Nikolenka would understand ... Bezuhov now—he's blue, dark blue and red, and he's quadrangular.'

'You're flirting with him, too,' said the countess, laughing.

'No, he's a freemason, I have heard. He's jolly, dark blue and red; how am I to explain to you ...'

'Little countess,' they heard the count's voice through the door.

'you're not asleep?' Natasha skipped up, snatched up her slippers, and ran barefoot to her own room. For a long while she could not go to sleep. She kept musing on no one's being able to understand all she understood and all that was in her.

'Sonya?' she wondered, looking at her friend asleep, curled up like a kitten with her great mass of hair. 'No, how could she! She's virtuous. She's in love with Nikolenka and doesn't care to know anything more. Mamma, even she doesn't understand. It's wonderful how clever I am and how . . . she is charming,' she went on, speaking of herself in the third person, and fancying that it was some very clever, the very cleverest and finest of men, who was saying it of her . . . 'There is everything, everything in her,' this man continued, 'extraordinarily clever, charming and then pretty, extraordinarily pretty, graceful. She swims, rides capitally, and a voice!—a marvellous voice, one may say!' She hummed her favourite musical phrase from an opera of Cherubini, flung herself into bed, laughed with delight at the thought that she would soon be asleep, called to Dunyasha to blow out the candle; and before Dunyasha had left her room she had already passed into another still happier world of dreams, where everything was as easy and as beautiful as in reality, and was only better because it was all different.

Next day the countess sent for Boris, and talked to him, and from that day he gave up visiting at the Rostovs'.

XIV

ON the 31st of December, on the eve of the new year 1810, a ball was given by a grand personage who had been a star of the court of Catherine. The Tsar and the diplomatic corps were to be present at this ball.

The well-known mansion of this grandee in the English Embankment was illuminated by innumerable lights. The police were standing at the lighted entry, laid with red baize; and not merely policemen, but a police commander was at the entrance, and dozens of officers of the police. Carriages kept driving away, and fresh ones kept driving up, with grooms in red livery and grooms in plumed hats. From the carriages emerged men wearing uniforms, stars, and ribbons; while ladies in satin and ermine stepped carefully out on the carriage steps, that were let down with a bang, and then walked hurriedly and noiselessly over the baize of the entry.

Almost every time a new carriage drove up, a whisper ran through the crowd and hats were taken off. 'The Emperor? . . . No, a minister . . . prince . . . ambassador . . . Don't you see the plumes? . . .' was audible in the crowd. One person, better dressed than the rest, seemed to know every one, and mentioned by name all the most celebrated personages of the day.

A third of the guests had already arrived at this ball, while the Rostovs, who were to be present at it, were still engaged in hurried preparations.

Many had been the discussions and the preparations for that ball in the Rostov family; many the fears that an invitation might not arrive, that the dresses would not be ready, and that everything would not be arranged as it ought to be.

The Rostovs were to be accompanied by Marya Ignatyevna Peronsky, a friend and relation of the countess, a thin and yellow maid-of-honour of the old court, who was acting as a guide to the provincial Rostovs in the higher circles of Petersburg society.

At ten o'clock the Rostovs were to drive to Tavritchesky Garden to call for the maid-of-honour. Meantime it was five minutes to ten, and the young ladies were not yet dressed.

Natasha was going to her first great ball. She had got up at eight o'clock that morning, and had spent the whole day in feverish agitation and activity. All her energies had since morning been directed to the one aim of getting herself, her mother, and Sonya as well dressed as possible. Sonya and her mother put themselves entirely in her hands. The countess was to wear a dark red velvet dress; the two girls white tulle dresses over pink silk slips, and roses on their bodices. They were to wear their hair *à la grecque*.

All the essentials were ready. Feet, arms, necks, and ears had been washed, scented, and powdered with peculiar care in readiness for the ball. Openwork silk stockings and white satin shoes with ribbons had been put on. The hairdressing was almost accomplished. Sonya was finishing dressing, so was the countess; but Natasha, who had been busily looking after every one, was behindhand. She was still sitting before the looking-glass with a *peignoir* thrown over her thin shoulders. Sonya, already dressed, stood in the middle of the room, and was trying to fasten in a last ribbon, hurting her little finger as she pressed the pin with a scrooping sound into the silk.

'Not like that, Sonya, not like that!' said Natasha, turning her head, and clutching her hair in both hands, as the maid arranging it was not quick enough in letting it go. 'The ribbon mustn't go like that; come here.' Sonya squatted down. Natasha pinned the ribbon in her own way.

'Really, miss, you mustn't do so,' said the maid, holding Natasha's hair.

'Oh, my goodness! Afterwards! There, that's right, Sonya.'

'Will you soon be ready?' they heard the countess's voice. 'It will be ten in a minute.'

'Immediately, immediately.... And are you ready, mamma?'

'Only my cap to fasten on.'

'Don't do it without me,' shouted Natasha; 'you don't know how to!'

'But it's ten o'clock already.'

It had been arranged to be at the ball at half-past ten, and Natasha still had to dress, and they had to drive to Tavritchesky Garden.

When her coiffure was finished, Natasha, in her mother's dressing-jacket and a short petticoat under which her dancing-shoes could be seen, ran up to Sonya, looked her over, and then ran to her mother. Turning her head round, she pinned on her cap, and hurriedly kissing her grey hair, ran back to the maids who were shortening her skirt.

All attention was now centred on Natasha's skirt, which was too long. Two maids were running it up round the edge, hurriedly biting off the threads. A third one, with pins in her teeth and lips, was running from the countess to Sonya; a fourth was holding up the whole tulle dress in her arms.

'Mavrushka, quicker, darling!'

'Give me that thimble, miss.'

'Will you be quick?' said the count from outside the door, coming in. 'Here are your smelling-salts. Madame Peronsky must be tired of waiting.'

'Ready, miss,' said the maid, lifting up the shortened tulle skirt on two fingers, blowing something off it, and giving it a shake to show her appreciation of the transparency and purity of what she had in her hands.

Natasha began putting on the dress.

'In a minute, in a minute, don't come in, papa,' she shouted to her father at the door, from under the tulle of the dress that concealed all her face. Sonya slammed the door. A minute later the count was admitted. He was wearing a blue frockcoat, stockings, and dancing-shoes, and was perfumed and pomaded.

'Ah, papa, how nice you look, lovely!' said Natasha, standing in the middle of the room, stroking out the folds of her tulle.

'If you please, miss, if you please . . .' said a maid, pulling up the skirt and turning the pins from one corner of her mouth to the other with her tongue.

'Say what you like!' cried Sonya, with despair in her voice, as she gazed at Natasha's skirt, 'say what you like!—it's too long still!'

Natasha walked a little further off to look at herself in the pierglass. The skirt was too long.

'My goodness, madam, it's not a bit too long,' said Mavrushka, creeping along the floor on her knees after her young lady.

'Well, if it's long, we'll tack it up, in one minute, we'll tack it up,' said Dunyasha, a resolute character. And taking a needle out of the kerchief on her bosom she set to work again on the floor.

At that moment the countess in her cap and velvet gown walked shyly with soft steps into the room.

'Oo-oo! my beauty!' cried the count. 'She looks nicer than any of you!' ... He would have embraced her, but, flushing, she drew back to avoid being crumpled.

'Mamma, the cap should be more on one side,' said Natasha. 'I'll pin it fresh,' and she darted forward. The maids turning up her skirt, not prepared for her hasty movement, tore off a piece of the tulle.

'Oh, mercy! What was that? Really it's not my fault...'

'It's all right, I'll run it up, it won't show,' said Dunyasha.

'My beauty, my queen!' said the old nurse coming in at the doorway. 'And Sonyushka, too; ah the beauties!...'

At a quarter past ten they were at last seated in their carriage and driving off. But they still had to drive to Tavritchesky Garden.

Madame Peronsky was ready and waiting. In spite of her age and ugliness, just the same process had been going on with her as with the Rostovs, not with flurry, for with her it was a matter of routine. Her elderly and unprepossessing person had been also washed and scented and powdered; she had washed as carefully behind her ears, and like the Rostovs' nurse, her old maid had enthusiastically admired her mistress's attire, when she came into the drawing-room in her yellow gown adorned with her badge of a maid-of-honour. Madame Peronsky praised the Rostovs' costumes, and they praised her attire and her taste. Then, careful of their coiffures and their dresses, at eleven o'clock they settled themselves in the carriages and drove off.

XV

NATASHA had not had a free moment all that day, and had not once had time to think of what lay before her.

In the damp, chill air, in the closeness and half dark of the swaying carriage, she pictured to herself for the first time what was in store for her there, at the ball, in the brightly lighted halls—music, flowers, dancing, the Tsar, all the brilliant young people of Petersburg. The prospect before her was so splendid that she could not even believe that it would come to pass: so incongruous it seemed with the chilliness, darkness, and closeness of the carriage. She could only grasp all that awaited her when, walking over the red cloth, she went into the vestibule, took off her cloak, and walked beside Sonya in front of her mother between the flowers up the lighted staircase. Only then she remembered how she must behave at a ball, and tried to assume the majestic manner that she considered indispensable for a girl at a ball. But luckily she felt that there was a mist before her eyes; she could see nothing clearly, her pulse beat a hundred times a minute, and the blood throbbed at her heart. She was unable to assume the manner that would have made her absurd; and moved on, thrilling with excitement, and trying with all her might simply to conceal it. And it was just in this mood that she looked her best. In front and behind them walked guests dressed in similar ball-dresses and conversing in similarly subdued tones. The looking-glasses on the staircases reflected ladies in white, blue, and pink dresses, with diamonds and pearls on their bare arms and necks.

Natasha looked into the looking-glasses and could not distinguish herself from the rest. All was mingled into one brilliant procession. At the entrance into the first room, the regular hum of voices, footsteps, greetings, deafened Natasha; the light and brilliance dazzled her still more. The host and hostess who had been already standing at the door for half an hour, saying exactly the same words to every guest on arrival, *Charmé de vous voir*, gave the same greeting to the Rostovs and Madame Peronsky. The two young girls in their white dresses, with roses alike in their black hair, made curtsies just alike, but unconsciously the hostess's eyes rested longer on the slender figure of Natasha. She looked at her, and smiled at her a smile that was something more than the smile of welcome she had for all. Looking at her, the hostess was reminded perhaps of her golden days of girlhood, gone never to return, of her own first ball. The host too followed Natasha with his eyes, and asked the count which of the girls was his daughter.

'Charming!' he said, kissing his own finger-tips.

In the ballroom, guests stood crowding about the entry in expectation of the Tsar. The countess took up her position in the front row of this crowd. Natasha heard and felt that several voices were asking who she was, that many pairs of eyes were fixed on her. She knew that she was making a good impression on those who noticed her, and this observation calmed her somewhat.

'There are some like ourselves, and some not as good,' she thought.

Madame Peronsky was pointing out to the countess the most distinguished persons at the ball.

'That is the Dutch ambassador, do you see, the greyhaired man,' Madame Peronsky was saying, indicating an old man with a profusion of silver-grey curls, who was surrounded by ladies laughing at some story he was telling. 'And here she comes, the queen of Petersburg society, Countess Bezuhov,' she said, pointing to Ellen who had just come in.

'How lovely! She's quite equal to Marya Antonovna. Look how attentive all the men are to her, young and old alike. She's both lovely and clever. . . . They say Prince So-and-So is wild about her. And you see these two, though they are not good-looking, they are even more run after.'

She pointed out a lady who was crossing the room accompanied by a very ugly daughter.

'That's the heiress of a million,' said Madame Peronsky. 'And, look, here come her suitors. . . . That's Countess Bezuhov's brother, Anatole Kuragin,' she said, pointing to a handsome officer in the Horse Guards, who passed by them looking from the height of his lifted head over the ladies to something beyond them. 'He is handsome, isn't he? They say he is to be married to that heiress. And your cousin, Drubetskoy, is very attentive to her too. They say she has millions. Oh, that's the French ambassador himself,' she said in answer to the countess's inquiry as to the identity of Caulaincourt. 'Just look, he's like some monarch. But yet they're nice, the French are very nice. No people more charming in society. Ah, here she is! Yes, still lovelier than any one, our Marya Antonovna! And how simply dressed! Exquisite!'

'And that stout fellow in spectacles is a universal freemason,' said Madame Peronsky, indicating Bezuhov. 'Set him beside his wife: he's a motley fool!'

Swinging his stout frame, Pierre slouched through the crowd, nodding to right and to left, as casually and good-naturedly as though he were walking through a crowd in a market. He made his way through the crowd unmistakably looking for some one.

Natasha looked with joy at the familiar face of Pierre, the motley fool, as Madame Peronsky called him, and knew that it was they, and she in particular, of whom Pierre was in search in the crowd. Pierre had promised her to be at the ball and to find her partners. But before reaching them, Pierre came to a standstill beside a very handsome, dark man of medium height in a white uniform, who was standing in a window talking to a tall man wearing stars and a ribbon.

Natasha at once recognised the handsome young man in the white uniform; it was Bolkonsky, who seemed to her to have grown much younger, happier, and better looking.

'There's some one else we know, Bolkonsky, do you see, mamma?' said Natasha, pointing out Prince Andrey. 'Do you remember he stayed a night at home, at Otradnoe?'

'Oh, do you know him?' said Madame Peronsky. 'I can't bear him. Every one is crazy over him. And his conceit! it's beyond all bounds! He takes after his worthy papa! And he's hand in glove now with Speransky, making out some sort of plans for reform. Just look how he behaves with ladies! She's speaking to him, and he has turned his back on her,' she said, pointing to him. 'I would soon send him about his business if he were to treat me like those ladies.'

XVI

THERE was a sudden stir, the crowd began talking, rushed forward, then moved apart again, and down the space left open through it, the Tsar walked to the strains of the band, which struck up at once. Behind him walked the host and hostess. The Tsar walked in rapidly, bowing to right and to left, as though trying to hurry over the first moments of greeting. The musicians played the polonaise in vogue at the time on account of the words set to it. The words began: 'Alexander, Elisaveta, our hearts ye ravish quite.' The Tsar went into the drawing-room, the crowd made a dash for the door; several persons ran hurriedly to the door and back with excited faces. The crowd made another rush back, away from the drawing-room door at which the Tsar appeared in conversation with the hostess. A young man, looking distraught, pounced down on the ladies and begged them to move aside. Several, with faces that betrayed a total oblivion of all the rules of decorum, squeezed forward, to the destruction of their dresses. The men began approaching the ladies, and couples were formed for the polonaise.

There was a general movement of retreat, and the Tsar, smiling, came out at the drawing-room door, leading out the lady of the house, and not keeping time to the music. He was followed by the host with Marya Antonovna Narishkin; then came ambassadors, ministers, and various generals, whose names Madame Peronsky never tired of recitting. More than half the ladies had partners, and were taking part or preparing to take part, in the polonaise.

Natasha felt that she would be left with her mother and Sonya in that minority of the ladies who were crowded back against the wall, and not invited to dance the polonaise. She stood, her thin arms hanging at her sides, and her scarcely outlined bosom heaving regularly. She held her breath, and gazed before her with shining frightened eyes, with an expression of equal readiness for the utmost bliss or the utmost misery. She took no interest in the Tsar, nor in all the great people Madame Peronsky was pointing out; her mind was filled by one thought: 'Is it possible no one will come up to me? Is it possible that I shall not dance among the foremost? Is it possible I shall not be noticed by all these men, who now don't even seem to see me, but if they look at me, look with an expression as though they would say: "Ah! that's not she, so it's no use looking"? No, it cannot be!' she thought. 'They must know how I long to dance, how well I dance, and how they would enjoy dancing with me.'

The strains of the polonaise, which had already lasted some time, were beginning to sound like a melancholy reminiscence in the ears of Natasha. She wanted to cry. Madame Peronsky had left them. The count was at the other end of the ballroom, the countess, Sonya, and she stood in that crowd of strangers as lonely as in a forest, of no interest, of no use to any one. Prince Andrey with a lady passed close by them, obviously not recognising them. The handsome Anatole said something smiling to the lady on his arm, and he glanced at Natasha's face as one looks at a wall. Boris passed by them twice, and each time turned away. Berg and his wife, who were not dancing, came towards them.

This family meeting here, in a ballroom, seemed a humiliating thing to Natasha, as though there were nowhere else for family talk but here at a ball. She did not listen, and did not look at Vera, who said something to her about her own green dress.

At last the Tsar stood still beside the last of his partners (he had danced with three), the music ceased. An anxious-looking adjutant ran up to the Rostovs, begging them to move a little further back, though they were already close to the wall, and from the orchestra came the circumspect, precise, seductively, stately rhythm of the waltz. The Tsar glanced with a smile down the ballroom. A moment passed; no one had yet begun. An adjutant, who was a steward, went up to Countess Bezuhov and asked her to dance. Smiling, she raised her hand and laid it on the adjutant's shoulder without looking at him. The adjutant-steward, a master of his art, grasped his partner firmly, and with confident deliberation and smoothness broke with her into the first gallop round the edge of the circle, then at the corner of the ballroom caught his partner's left hand, turned her; and through the quickening strains of the music nothing could be heard but the regular jingle of the spurs on the adjutant's rapid, practised feet, and at every third beat the swish of his partner's flying velvet skirt as she whirled round.

Natasha looked at them, and was ready to cry that it was not she dancing that first round of the waltz.

Prince Andrey, in his white uniform of a cavalry colonel wearing white stockings and dancing-shoes, stood looking eager and lively, in the front of the ring not far from the Rostovs. Baron Firhoff was talking to him of the proposed first sitting of the State Council to be held next day. From his intimacy with Speransky, and the part he was taking in the labours of the legislative commission, Prince Andrey was in a position to give authoritative information in regard to that sitting, about which the most diverse rumours were current. But he did not hear what Firhoff was saying to him, and looked from the Tsar to the gentlemen preparing to dance, who had not yet stepped out into the ring.

Prince Andrey was watching these gentlemen, who were timid in the presence of the Tsar, and the ladies, who were dying to be asked to dance.

Pierre went up to Prince Andrey and took him by the arm.

'You always dance. Here is my protégée, the younger Rostov girl, ask her,' he said.

'Where?' asked Bolkonsky. 'I beg your pardon,' he said, turning to the baron, 'we will finish this conversation in another place, but at a ball one must dance.' He went forward in the direction indicated by Pierre. Natasha's despairing tremulous face broke upon Prince Andrey. He recognised her, guessed her feelings, saw that it was her debut, remembered what she had said at the window, and with an expression of pleasure on his face he approached Countess Rostov.

'Permit me to introduce you to my daughter,' said the countess, reddening.

'I have the pleasure of her acquaintance already, if the countess remembers me,' said Prince Andrey, with a low and courteous bow, which seemed a direct contradiction to Madame Peronsky's remarks about his rudeness. He went up to Natasha, and raised his hand to put it round her waist before he had fully uttered the invitation to dance. He proposed a waltz to her. The tremulous expression of Natasha's face, ready for despair or for ecstasy, brightened at once into a happy, grateful, childlike smile.

'I have been a long while waiting for you,' that alarmed and happy young girl seemed to say to him in the smile that peeped out through the starting tears as she raised her hand to Prince Andrey's shoulder. They were the second couple that walked forward into the ring.

Prince Andrey was one of the best dancers of his day. Natasha danced exquisitely. Her little feet in their satin dancing-shoes peformed their task lightly and independently of her, and her face beamed with a rapture of happiness.

Her bare neck and arms were thin, and not beautiful compared with Ellen's shoulders. Her shoulders were thin, her bosom undefined, her arms were slender. But Ellen was, as it were, covered with the hard varnish of those thousands of eyes that had scanned her person, while Natasha seemed like a young girl stripped for the first time, who would have been greatly ashamed if she had not been assured by every one that it must be so.

Prince Andrey loved dancing. He was anxious to escape as quickly as he could from the political and intellectual conversations into which every one tried to draw him, and anxious too to break through that burdensome barrier of constraint arising from the presence of the Tsar; so he made haste to dance, and chose Natasha for a partner because Pierre pointed her out to him, and because she was the first pretty girl who caught his eyes. But he had no sooner put his arm round that slender, supple waist, and felt her stirring so close to him, and smiling so close to him, than the intoxication of her beauty flew to his head. He felt full of life and youth again as, drawing a deep breath, he brought her to a standstill and began to watch the other couples.

XVII

AFTER Prince Andrey, Boris came up to ask Natasha to dance, and he was followed by the dancing adjutant who had opened the ball, and many other young men. Natasha, flushed and happy, passed on her superfluous partners to Sonya, and never ceased dancing all the evening. She noticed nothing and saw nothing of what was absorbing every one else at that ball. She did not notice that the Tsar talked a long time with the French ambassador, that his manner was particularly gracious to a certain lady, that Prince So-and-So and Mr. So-and-So had said and done this and that, that Ellen's success had been brilliant, and that So-and-So had paid her marked attention. She did not even see the Tsar, and was only aware that he was gone from noticing that the ball became livelier after his departure.

In one of the most enjoyable cotillions before supper, Prince Andrey danced again with Natasha. He reminded her of how he had first seen her in the avenue at Otradnoe, and how she could not sleep on that moonlight night, and told her how he had unwittingly listened to her. Natasha blushed at these recollections, and tried as it were to excuse herself, as though there were something to be ashamed of in the emotion to which Prince Andrey had unwittingly played the eavesdropper.

Like all men who have grown up in society, Prince Andrey liked meeting any thing not of the conventional society stamp. And such was Natasha with her wonder, her delight, her shyness, and even her mistakes in talking French. His manner was particularly tender and circumspect as he talked to her. Sitting beside her, and talking of the simplest and most trifling subjects, Prince Andrey admired the radiant brilliance of her eyes and her smile, that had no concern with what was said but was due simply to her own happiness. When Natasha was chosen again, and she had got up with a smile and was dancing, Prince Andrey particularly admired her shy grace. In the middle of the cotillion, Natasha went back to her place, breathless at the end of a figure. Another partner again chose her. She was tired and panting, and evidently she thought for an instant of refusing, but immediately she put her hand on her partner's shoulder and was off again gaily, smiling to Prince Andrey.

'I should have been glad to rest and sit by you. I'm tired; but you see how they keep asking me, and I'm glad of it, and I'm happy, and I love every one, and you and I understand all about it,' and more, much more was said in that smile. When her partner left her side, Natasha flew across the room to choose two ladies for the figure.

'If she goes first to her cousin and then to another lady, she will be my wife,' Prince Andrey—greatly to his own surprise—caught himself saying mentally, as he watched her. She did go first to her cousin.

'What nonsense does sometimes come into one's mind!' thought Prince Andrey, 'but one thing's certain, that girl is so charming, so original, that she won't be dancing here a month before she will be married.... She's a rare thing here,' he thought, as Natasha settled beside him, sticking in the rose that was falling out of her bodice.

At the end of the cotillion, the old count in his blue frock-coat went up to the young people who had been dancing. He invited Prince Andrey to come and see them, and asked his daughter whether she were enjoying herself. Natasha did not at once answer, she only smiled a smile that said reproachfully: 'How can you ask such a question?'

'Enjoying myself as I never have before in my life!' she said, and Prince Andrey noticed how her thin arms were swiftly raised as though to embrace her father, and dropped again at once. Natasha was happy as she had never been in her life. She was at that highest pitch of happiness, when one becomes completely good and kind, and disbelieves in the very possibility of evil, unhappiness, and sorrow.

At that ball Pierre for the first time felt humiliated by the position his wife took in the highest court circle. He was sullen and absent-minded. There was a broad furrow right across his forehead, as he stood in a window, staring over his spectacles and seeing no one. Natasha passed close by him on her way to supper. Pierre's gloomy, unhappy face struck her. She stopped, facing him. She longed to come to his aid, to bestow on him some of her own overflowing happiness. 'How delightful it is, count,' she said; 'isn't it?'

Pierre smiled an absent-minded smile, obviously not grasping what was said to him. 'Yes, I'm very glad,' he said.

'How can people be discontented at anything!' thought Natasha. 'Especially any one as nice as Bezuhov.'

In Natasha's eyes all the people at the ball were particularly kind, sweet, good people, loving one another; none were capable of wronging one another, and so all must be happy.

XVIII

NEXT day when Prince Andrey thought of the ball it did not occupy his mind for long. 'Yes, it was a very successful ball. And besides . . . yes, the younger Rostov is very charming. There's something fresh in her, original, unlike Petersburg.' That was all he thought about the previous day's ball, and after his morning tea he set to work.

But from fatigue and want of sleep he was not very well disposed for work, and could get nothing done. He was continually criticising his own work—a habit common with him—and was glad when he heard a visitor arrive.

The visitor was Bitsky, a man who was a member of various committees and of all the societies in Petersburg. He was a passionate adherent of the new ideas and of Speransky, and the busiest purveyor of news in Petersburg, one of those men who choose their opinions like their clothes—according to the fashion—but for that very reason seem the most vehement partisans. Scarcely waiting to remove his hat, he ran fussily up to Prince Andrey, and at once began talking. He had just learned particulars of the sitting of the State Council of that morning, opened by the Tsar, and began enthusiastically upon the subject. The Tsar's speech had been, he said, an extraordinary one. It had been a speech such as are only delivered by constitutional monarchs. 'The Emperor directly asserted that the Council and the Senate are the estates of the realm; he said that government should be founded, not on arbitrary authority, but on a *secure basis*. The Emperor said that the fiscal system must be reconstituted and the accounts must be public,' Bitsky announced, laying stress on certain words, and opening his eyes significantly. 'Yes, today's sitting marks an epoch, the greatest epoch in our history,' he concluded.

Prince Andrey heard his account of the opening of the State Council, to which he had been looking forward with such eagerness, and to which he had attached so much consequence, and was amazed that now, when it had come to pass, this event, far from affecting him, struck him as less than insignificant. With quiet irony he listened to Bitsky's enthusiastic description. The idea in his mind was of the simplest. 'What is it to me and Bitsky,' he thought, 'what is it to us, whatever the Emperor is pleased to say in the Council? Can all that make me any happier or better?'

And this simple reflection suddenly destroyed all Prince Andrey's former interest in the reforms that were being made. That day Prince Andrey was to dine with Speransky, 'with only a few friends,' as the host had said in inviting him. That dinner, in the intimate home circle of the man who had so fascinated him, had seemed very attractive to Prince Andrey, especially as he had not hitherto seen Speransky in his home surroundings. But now he had no wish to go to it.

At the hour fixed, however, Prince Andrey was entering the small house in Tavritchesky Garden. The little house, which was Speransky's property, was distinguished by an extraordinary cleanliness, suggestive of the cleanliness of a convent. In the parqueted dining-room, Prince Andrey, who was a little late, found all that circle of Speransky's intimate friends already gathered together at five o'clock. There were no ladies present, except Speransky's little daughter (with a long face like her father's) and her governess. The guests were Gervais, Magnitsky and Stolypin. From the vestibule Prince Andrey had caught the sound of loud voices and a ringing, staccato laugh—a laugh such as one hears on the stage. Some one—it sounded like Speransky—was giving vent to a staccato 'ha ... ha ... ha ...' Prince Andrey had never before heard Speransky laugh, and this shrill, ringing laugh from the great statesman made a strange impression on him.

Prince Andrey went into the dining-room. The whole party were standing between the two windows at a little table laid with *hors d'œuvres*. Speransky was standing at the table with a mirthful countenance, wearing a grey frockcoat, with a star, and the white waistcoat and high white stock, in which he had been at the famous sitting of the State Council. His guests formed a ring round him. Turning towards him Magnitsky was relating an anecdote. Speransky listened, laughing beforehand at what Magnitsky was going to say. Just as Prince Andrey walked into the room, Magnitsky's words were again drowned in laughter. Stolypin gave vent to a bass guffaw as he munched a piece of bread and cheese. Gervais softly hissed a chuckle, and Speransky laughed his shrill, stacatto laugh.

Speransky, still laughing, gave Prince Andrey his soft, white hand. 'Very glad to see you, prince,' he said. 'One minute . . .' he turned to Magnitsky, whose tale he was interrupting. 'We have made a compact today; this is a holiday dinner, and not one word about business.' And he turned again to the story-teller, and again he laughed.

With a sense of wondering and melancholy disillusion, Prince Andrey heard his laughter and looked at Speransky laughing. It was not Speransky, but some other man, it seemed to Prince Andrey. All that had seemed mysterious and attractive in Speransky suddenly seemed to Prince Andrey obvious and unattractive.

At dinner the conversation never paused for a moment, and consisted of something like the contents of a jest-book. Magnitsky had hardly finished his anecdote when another gentleman expressed his readiness to relate something even more amusing. The anecdotes for the most part related, if not to the service itself, to persons prominent in the service. It was as though in this circle the utter insignificance of these prominent persons was so completely accepted that the only attitude possible towards them was one of good-humoured hilarity. Speransky told them how at the council that morning a deaf statesman, on being asked his opinion, replied that he was of the same opinion. Gervais described a whole episode of the revision, only remarkable for the imbecility of all concerned in it. Stolypin, stammering, took up the conversation and began talking of the abuses of the old order of things, with a warmth that threatened to give the conversation a serious turn. Magnitsky began to make fun of Stolypin's earnestness. Gervais put in his joke, and the conversation resumed its former lively tone. It was obvious that after his labours Speransky liked to rest and be amused in the circle of his friends; and all his friends understood his tastes, and were trying to amuse him and themselves. But this kind of gaiety seemed to Prince Andrey tiresome and anything but gay. Speransky's high voice struck him unpleasantly, and his continual laugh in its high-pitched, falsetto note was for some reason an offence to Prince Andrey's feelings. Prince Andrey did not laugh, and was afraid he would be felt uncongenial by this party. But no one noticed his lack of sympathy with the general merriment. All of them appeared to be greatly enjoying themselves.

Several times he tried to enter into the conversation, but every time the word was snatched out of his mouth, like a cork out of water, and he could not bandy jokes with them. There was nothing wrong or unseemly in what they said; it was all witty, and might have been amusing, but something—that very something that makes the zest of gaiety—was wanting, and they did not even know of its existence.

After dinner Speransky's daughter and her governess rose from the table. Speransky patted his daughter with his white hand, and kissed her. And that gesture, too, seemed to Prince Andrey unnatural.

The men sat on over their port, after the English fashion. A conversation sprang up about Napoleon's doings in Spain, of which all were united in approving, while Prince Andrey attacked them. But in the middle of this discussion Speransky, obviously wishing to change the subject, began with a smile telling an anecdote, which had no connection with it. For several instants every one was silent.

As they sat at table, Speransky, corking up a bottle of wine and saying, 'Nowadays good wine doesn't go a-begging!' gave it to the servant and got up. All rose, and talking, just as noisily, went into the drawing-room. Speransky was handed two envelopes brought by a special courier. He took them and went into his study. As soon as he had gone, there was a lull in the general gaiety, and the guests began conversing sensibly in low tones together.

'Well, now for the recitation!' said Speransky, coming out of his study. 'A marvellous talent!' he said to Prince Andrey. Magnitsky at once threw himself into an attitude, and began to recite comic French verses, a skit he had composed on various well-known persons. Several times he was interrupted by applause. At the conclusion of the recitation Prince Andrey went up to Speransky to say good-bye.

'Why so early?' said Speransky.

'I promised to be at a *soirée*....'

They said no more. Prince Andrey looked at those mirror-like, impenetrable eyes, so close to his, and he felt it ludicrous that he should have expected anything from Speransky, and from all his own work connected with him, and marvelled how he could have ascribed any value to what Speransky was doing. That punctual, mirthless laugh was ringing in Prince Andrey's ears long after he had left Speransky's.

On reaching home Prince Andrey began looking at his life in Petersburg during the last four months, as though it were something new. He thought of the efforts he had made, and the people he had tried to see, and the history of his project of army reform, which had been accepted for consideration, and had been shelved because another scheme, a very poor one, had already been worked out and presented to the Tsar. He thought of the sittings of the committee, of which Berg was a member. He thought of the conscientious and prolonged deliberations that took place at those sittings on every point relating to the formalities of the sittings themselves, and the studious brevity with which anything relating to the reality of their duties was touched on in passing. He thought of his work on the legislative reforms, of his careful translation of the Roman and French codes into Russian, and he felt ashamed of himself. Then he vividly imagined Bogutcharovo, his pursuits in the country, his expedition to Ryazan; he thought of his peasants, of Dron the village elder; and applying the section on Personal Rights, which he had divided into paragraphs, to them, he marvelled how he could have so long busied himself on work so idle.

XIX

THE next day Prince Andrey paid calls on various people whom he had not visited before, and among them on the Rostovs, with whom he had renewed his acquaintance at the ball. Apart from considerations of politeness, which necessitated a call on the Rostovs, Prince Andrey wanted to see at home that original, eager girl, who had left such a pleasant recollection with him.

Natasha was one of the first to meet him. She was in a blue everyday dress, in which she struck Prince Andrey as looking prettier than in her ball-dress. She and all the family received Prince Andrey like an old friend, simply and cordially. All the family, which Prince Andrey had once criticised so severely, now seemed to him to consist of excellent, simple, kindly people. The hospitality and good-nature of the old count, particularly striking and attractive in Petersburg, was such that Prince Andrey could not refuse to stay to dinner. 'Yes, these are good-natured, capital people,' thought Bolkonsky. 'Of course they have no conception what a treasure they possess in Natasha; but they are good people, who make the best possible background for the strikingly poetical figure of that charming girl, so full of life!'

Prince Andrey was conscious in Natasha of a special world, utterly remote from him, brimful of joys unknown to him, that strange world, which even in the avenue at Otradnoe, and on that moonlight night at the window had tantalised him. Now that no longer tantalised him, it seemed no longer an alien world; but he himself was stepping into it, and finding new pleasures in it.

After dinner Natasha went to the clavichord, at Prince Andrey's request, and began singing. Prince Andrey stood at the window talking to the ladies, and listened to her. In the middle of a phrase, Prince Andrey ceased speaking, and felt suddenly a lump in his throat from tears, the possibility of which he had not dreamed of in himself. He looked at Natasha singing, and something new and blissful stirred in his soul. He was happy, and at the same time he was sad. He certainly had nothing to weep about, but he was ready to weep. For what? For his past love? For the little princess? For his lost illusions? ... For his hopes for the future? ... Yes, and no. The chief thing which made him ready to weep was a sudden, vivid sense of the fearful contrast between something infinitely great and illimitable existing in him, and something limited and material, which he himself was, and even she was. This contrast made his heart ache, and rejoiced him while she was singing.

As soon as Natasha had finished singing, she went up to him, and asked how he liked her voice. She asked this, and was abashed after saying it, conscious that she ought not to have asked such a question. He smiled, looking at her, and said he liked her singing, as he liked everything she did.

It was late in the evening when Prince Andrey left the Rostovs. He went to bed from the habit of going to bed, but soon saw that he could not sleep. He lighted a candle and sat up in bed; then got up, then lay down again, not in the least wearied by his sleeplessness: he felt a new joy in his soul, as though he had come out of a stuffy room into the open daylight. It never even occurred to him that he was in love with this little Rostov girl. He was not thinking about her. He only pictured her to himself, and the whole of life rose before him in a new light as he did so. 'Why do I struggle? Why am I troubled in this narrow, cramped routine, when life, all life, with all its joys, lies open before me?' he said to himself. And for the first time for a very long while, he began making happy plans for the future. He made up his mind that he ought to look after his son's education, to find a tutor, and entrust the child to him. Then he ought to retire from the army, and go abroad, see England, Switzerland, Italy. 'I must take advantage of my liberty, while I feel so much youth and strength in me,' he told himself. 'Pierre was right in saying that one must believe in the possibility of happiness, in order to be happy, and now I do believe in it. Let us leave the dead to bury the dead; but while one is living, one must live and be happy,' he thought.

XX

ONE morning Colonel Adolphe Berg, whom Pierre knew just as he knew every one in Moscow and Petersburg, called upon him. He was wearing a brand-new uniform, and had his powdered locks standing up over his forehead, as worn by the Tsar Alexander Pavlovitch.

'I have just been calling on the countess, your spouse, and to my misfortune, my request could not be granted. I hope I shall be more fortunate with you, count,' he said, smiling.

'What is it you desire, colonel? I am at your disposal.'

'I am by now, count, quite settled in my new quarters,' Berg informed him, with perfect conviction that to hear this fact could not but be agreeable; 'and so I was desirous of giving a little *soirée* for my friends and my spouse. (He smiled still more blandly.) I meant to ask the countess and you to do me the honour to come to us for a cup of tea, and . . . to supper.'

Only the Countess Elena Vassilyevna, who considered it beneath her to associate with nobodies like the Bergs, could have had the cruelty to refuse such an invitation. Berg explained so clearly why he wanted to gather together a small and select company at his new rooms, and why it would be agreeable to him to do so; and why he would grudge spending money on cards, or anything else harmful; but was ready for the sake of good society to incur expense, that Pierre could not refuse, and promised to come.

'Only not late, count, if I may venture to beg. Ten minutes to eight, I venture to beg. We will make up a party for boston. Our general is coming; he is very kind to me. We will have a little supper, count, so I shall esteem it an honour.'

Contrary to his usual habit (he was almost always late) Pierre arrived at the Bergs not at ten minutes to eight, but at a quarter to eight.

The Bergs had made all necessary preparations for their little party, and were quite ready to receive their guests.

Berg and his wife were sitting in a new, clean, light study, furnished with little busts and pictures and new furniture. Berg, with his new uniform closely buttoned up, sat beside his wife, and was explaining to her that one always could and ought to cultivate the acquaintance of people above one—for only then is there anything agreeable in acquaintances. 'You pick up something, you can put in a word for something. Look at me now, how I used to manage in the lower grades (Berg reckoned his life not by years but by promotions). My comrades are nothing still, while I'm a lieutenant-colonel. I have the happiness of being your husband' (he got up and kissed Vera's hand, but on the way turned back the corner of the rug, which was rucked up). 'And how did I obtain all this? Chiefly by knowing how to select my acquaintances. It goes without saying, of course, that one has to be conscientious and punctual in the discharge of one's duties.'

Berg smiled with a sense of his own superiority over a mere weak woman, and paused, reflecting that this charming wife of his was, after all, a weak woman, who could never attain all that constituted a man's dignity,—*ein Mann zu sein*. Vera smiled, too, at the same time with a sense of her superiority over her conscientious, excellent husband, who yet, like all men, according to Vera's ideas of them, took such a mistaken view of life. Berg, judging from his wife, considered all women weak and foolish. Vera, judging from her husband only, and generalising from her observation of him, supposed that all men ascribed common-sense to none but themselves, and at the same time had no understanding for anything, and were conceited and egoistic.

Berg got up, and cautiously embracing his wife so as not to crush the lace bertha, for which he had paid a round sum, he kissed her just on her lips.

'There's only one thing: we mustn't have children too soon,' he said, by a connection of ideas of which he was himself unconscious.

'Yes,' answered Vera, 'I don't at all desire that. We must live for society.'

'Princess Yusupov was wearing one just like that,' said Berg, pointing with a happy and good-humoured smile to the bertha.

At that moment they were informed that Count Bezuhov had arrived. Both the young couple exchanged glances of self-satisfaction, each mentally claiming the credit of this visit.

'See what comes of knowing how to make acquaintances,' thought Berg. 'See what comes of behaving properly!'

'But, please, when I am entertaining guests,' said Vera, 'don't you interrupt me, because I know with what to entertain each of them, and what to say in the company of different people.'

Berg, too, smiled.

'Oh, but sometimes men must have their masculine conversation,' he said.

Pierre was shown into the little drawing-room, in which it was impossible to sit down without disturbing the symmetry, tidiness and order; and consequently it was quite comprehensible, and not strange, that Berg should magnanimously offer to disturb the symmetry of the armchair or of the sofa for an honoured guest, and apparently finding himself in miserable indecision in the matter, should leave his guest to solve the question of selection. Pierre destroyed the symmetry, moved out a chair for himself, and Berg and Vera promptly began their *soirée*, interrupting each other in their efforts to entertain their guest.

Vera, deciding in her own mind that Pierre ought to be entertained with conversation about the French Embassy, promptly embarked upon that subject. Berg, deciding that masculine conversation was what was required, interrupted his wife's remarks by reference to the question of war with Austria, and made an unconscious jump from that general subject to personal considerations upon the proposal made him to take part in the Austrian campaign, and the reasons which had led him to decline it. Although the conversation was extremely disconnected, and Vera resented the intervention of the masculine element, both the young people felt with satisfaction that although only one guest was present, the *soirée* had begun very well, and that their *soirée* was as like every other *soirée* as two drops of water,—with the same conversation and tea and lighted candles.

The next to arrive was Boris, an old comrade of Berg's. There was a certain shade of patronage and condescension in his manner to Berg and Vera. After Boris came the colonel and his lady, then the general himself, then the Rostovs, and the *soirée* now began to be exactly, incontestably, like all other *soirées*. Berg and Vera could hardly repress their smiles of glee at the sight of all this movement in their drawing-room, at the sound of the disconnected chatter, and the rustle of skirts and of curtsies. Everything was precisely as everybody always has it; especially so was the general, who admired their rooms, clapped Berg on the shoulder, and with paternal authority insisted on arranging the table for boston. The general sat by Count Ilya Andreivitch, as the guest next in precedence to himself. The elderly guests were together, the younger people together, the hostess at the tea-table, on which there were cakes in the silver cake-basket exactly like the cakes at the Panins' *soirée*. Everything was precisely like what everybody else had.

XXI

PIERRE, as one of the most honoured guests, was obliged to sit down to boston with the old count, the general, and the colonel. As he sat at the boston-table he happened to be directly facing Natasha, and he was struck by the curious change that had come over her since the day of the ball. Natasha was silent, and not only was she not so pretty as she had been at the ball, she would have been positively plain but for the look of gentle indifference to everything in her face.

'What is wrong with her?' Pierre wondered, glancing at her. She was sitting by her sister at the tea-table; she gave reluctant answers to Boris at her side and did not look at him. After playing all of one suit and taking five tricks to his partner's satisfaction, Pierre, having caught the sound of greetings and the steps of some one entering while he took his tricks, glanced at her again.

'Why, what has happened to her?' he said to himself in still greater wonder.

Prince Andrey was standing before her, saying something to her with an expression of guarded tenderness on his face. She, lifting her head, was looking at him, flushing crimson, and visibly trying to control her breathing, which came in panting gasps. And the vivid glow of some inner fire that had been quenched before was alight in her again. She was utterly transformed. From a plain girl she was once more the beautiful creature she had been at the ball.

Prince Andrey went up to Pierre, and Pierre noticed a new youthful expression in his friend's face. Several times Pierre changed his seat during the play, sitting sometimes with his back to Natasha, sometimes facing her, and during all the six rubbers he was observing her and his friend.

'Something very serious is happening between them,' thought Pierre, and a feeling at once of gladness and of bitterness made him agitated and forgetful of the game.

After six rubbers the general got up, saying it was of no use playing like that, and Pierre was at liberty. Natasha, at one side of the room, was talking to Sonya and Boris. Vera, with a subtle smile, was saying something to Prince Andrey. Pierre went up to his friend, and, asking whether they were talking secrets, sat down beside them. Vera, noticing Prince Andrey's attention to Natasha, felt that at a *soiree*, at a real *soiree*, it was absolutely necessary there should be delicate allusions to the tender passion, and seizing an opportunity when Prince Andrey was alone, began a conversation with him upon the emotions generally, and her sister in particular. She felt that, with a guest so intellectual as she considered Prince Andrey, she must put all her diplomatic tact into the task before her. When Pierre went up to them he noticed that Vera was in full flow of self-complacent talk, while Prince Andrey seemed embarrassed—a thing that rarely happened to him.

'What do you think?' Vera was saying with a subtle smile. 'You, prince, have so much penetration and see into people's characters at once. What do you think about Natalie? Is she capable of constancy in her attachments? Is she capable, like other women' (Vera meant herself) 'of loving a man once for all and remaining faithful to him for ever? That's what I regard as true love! What do you think, prince?'

'I know your sister too little,' answered Prince Andrey, with a sarcastic smile, under which he tried to conceal his embarrassment, 'to decide a question so delicate; and, besides, I have noticed that the less attractive a woman is, the more constant she is apt to be,' he added, and he looked at Pierre, who at that moment joined them.

'Yes, that is true, prince. In these days,' pursued Vera (talking of 'these days,' as persons of limited intellect as a rule love to do, supposing they have discovered and estimated the peculiarities of the times, and that human characteristics do change with the times), 'in these days a girl has so much liberty that the pleasure of being paid attention often stifles these feelings in her. And Natalie, it must be confessed, is very susceptible on that side.'

This going back to Natasha again made Prince Andrey contract his brows disagreeably. He tried to get up, but Vera persisted with a still more subtle smile.

'Nobody, I imagine, has been so much run after as she has,' Vera went on; 'but no one, until quite of late, has ever made a serious impression on her. Of course, you know, count,' she turned to Pierre, 'even our charming cousin, Boris, who, *entre nous*, was very, very far gone in the region of the tender passion . . .' She intended an allusion to the map of love then in fashion.

Prince Andrey scowled, and was mute.

'But, of course, you are a friend of Boris's?' Vera said to him.

'Yes, I know him. . . .'

'He has probably told you of his childish love for Natasha?'

'Oh, was there a childish love between them?' asked Prince Andrey, with a sudden, unexpected flush on his face.

'Yes. You know between cousins the close intimacy often leads to love. Cousinhood is a dangerous neighbourhood. Isn't it?'

'Oh, not a doubt of it,' said Prince Andrey, and with sudden and unnatural liveliness, he began joking with Pierre about the necessity of his being careful with his cousins at Moscow, ladies of fifty, and in the middle of these jesting remarks he got up, and taking Pierre's arm, drew him aside.

'Well, what is it?' said Pierre, who had been watching in wonder his friend's excitement, and noticed the glance he turned upon Natasha as he got up.

'I must, I must talk to you,' said Prince Andrey. 'You know that pair of women's gloves' (he referred to the masonic gloves given to a newly initiated brother to be entrusted to the woman he loved). 'I . . . but no, I will talk to you later on. . . .' And with a strange light in his eyes and a restlessness in his movements, Prince Andrey approached Natasha and sat down beside her. Pierre saw that Prince Andrey asked her some question, and she answered him, flushing hotly.

But at that moment Berge approached Pierre, and insisted upon his taking part in an argument between the general and the colonel on affairs in Spain.

Berg was satisfied and happy. The smile of glee never left his face. The *soirée* was a great success, and exactly like other *soirées* he had seen. Everything was precisely similar: the ladies' refined conversation, and the cards, and after the cards the general raising his voice and the samovar and the tea cakes; but one thing was still lacking, which he had always seen at *soirées*, and wished to imitate. There was still wanting the usual loud conversation between the gentlemen and discussion about some serious intellectual question. The general had started that conversation, and Berg drew Pierre into it.

XXII

NEXT day Prince Andrey went to dine at the Rostovs', as Count Ilya Andreitch had invited him, and spent the whole day with them.

Every one in the house perceived on whose account Prince Andrey came, and he openly tried to be all day long with Natasha.

Not only in the soul of Natasha—scared, but happy and enthusiastic—in the whole household, too, there was a feeling of awe, of something of great gravity being bound to happen. With sorrowful and sternly serious eyes the countess looked at Prince Andrey as he talked to Natasha, and shyly and self-consciously tried to begin some insignificant talk with him as soon as he looked round at her. Sonya was afraid to leave Natasha, and afraid of being in their way if she stayed with them. Natasha turned pale in a panic of expectation every time she was left for a moment alone with him. Prince Andrey's timidity impressed her. She felt that he wanted to tell her something, but could not bring himself up to the point.

When Prince Andrey had gone away in the evening, the countess went up to Natasha and whispered:

'Well?'

'Mamma, for God's sake, don't ask me anything just now. This one can't talk of,' said Natasha.

But in spite of this answer, Natasha lay a long while in her mother's bed that night, her eyes fixed before her, excited and scared by turns. She told her how he had praised her, how he had said he was going abroad, how he had asked where they were going to spend the summer, and how he had asked her about Boris.

'But anything like this, like this . . . I have never felt before!' she said. 'Only I'm afraid with him, I'm always afraid with him. What does that mean? Does it mean that it's the real thing? Mamma, are you asleep?'

'No, my darling. I'm afraid of him myself,' answered her mother. 'Go to bed.'

'Anyhow, I shouldn't go to sleep. How stupid sleep is! Mamma, mamma, nothing like this have I ever felt before,' she said, with wonder and terror at the feeling she recognised in herself. 'And could we ever have dreamed! . . .'

It seemed to Natasha that she had fallen in love with Prince Andrey the first time she saw him at Otradnoe. She was as it were terrified at this strange, unexpected happiness that the man she had chosen even then (she was firmly convinced that she had done so)—that very man should meet them again now and be apparently not indifferent to her.

'And it seems as though it all happened on purpose—his coming to Petersburg just while we are here. And our meeting at that ball. It was all fate. It's clear that it is fate, that it has all led up to this. Even then, as soon as I saw him, I felt something quite different.'

'What has he said to you? What are those verses? Read them . . .' said the mother thoughtfully, referring to the verses Prince Andrey had written in Natasha's album.

'Mamma, does it matter his being a widower?'

'Hush, Natasha. Pray to God. Marriages are made in heaven,' she said, quoting the French proverb.

'Mamma, darling, how I love you! how happy I am!' cried Natasha, shedding tears of excitement and happiness and hugging her mother.

At that very time Prince Andrey was telling Pierre of his love for Natasha and of his fixed determination to marry her.

That evening the Countess Elena Vassilyevna gave a reception; the French ambassador was there, and a royal prince who had become a very frequent visitor at the countess's of late, and many brilliant ladies and gentlemen. Pierre came down to it, wandered through the rooms and impressed all the guests by his look of concentrated preoccupation and gloom.

Pierre had been feeling one of his attacks of nervous depression coming upon him ever since the day of the ball, and had been making desperate efforts to struggle against it. Since his wife's intrigue with the royal prince, Pierre had been to his surprise appointed a kammer-herr, and ever since he had felt a sense of weariness and shame in court society, and his old ideas of the vanity of all things human began to come back oftener and oftener. The feeling he had lately noticed between his protégée Natasha and Prince Andrey had aggravated his gloom by the contrast between his own position and his friend's. He tried equally to avoid thinking of his wife and also of Natasha and Prince Andrey. Again everything seemed to him insignificant in comparison with eternity; again the question rose before him: 'What for?' And for days and nights together he forced himself to work at masonic labours, hoping to keep off the evil spirit. Pierre had come out of the countess's apartments at midnight, and was sitting in a shabby dressing-gown at the table in his own low-pitched, smoke-blackened room upstairs, copying out long transactions of the Scottish freemasons, when some one came into his room. It was Prince Andrey.

'Oh, it's you,' said Pierre, with a preoccupied and dissatisfied air. 'I'm at work, you see,' he added, pointing to the manuscript book with that look of escaping from the ills of life with which unhappy people look at their work.

Prince Andrey stood before Pierre with a radiant, ecstatic face, full of new life, and with the egoism of happiness smiled at him without noticing his gloomy face.

'Well, my dear boy,' he said, 'I wanted to tell you yesterday, and I have come to do so today. I have never felt anything like it. I am in love.'

Pierre suddenly heaved a heavy sigh, and dumped down his heavy person on the sofa beside Prince Andrey.

'With Natasha Rostov, yes?' he said.

'Yes, yes, who else could it be? I would never have believed it, but the feeling is too strong for me. Yesterday I was in torment, in agony, but I would not exchange that agony even for anything in the world. I have never lived till now, but I cannot live without her. But can she love me? ... I'm too old for her.... Why don't you speak? ...'

'I? I? What did I tell you?' said Pierre, suddenly getting up and walking about the room. 'I always thought so.... That girl is a treasure ... She's a very rare sort of girl.... My dear fellow, don't, I entreat you, be too wise, don't doubt, marry, marry, marry! ... And I am sure no man was ever happier than you will be.'

'But she?'

'She loves you.'

'Don't talk nonsense, ...' said Prince Andrey, smiling and looking into Pierre's face.

'She loves you, I know it,' Pierre cried angrily.

'No; do listen,' said Prince Andrey, taking hold of him by the arm and stopping him. 'Do you know the state I am in? I must talk about it to some one.'

'Well, well, talk away, I'm very glad,' said Pierre, and his face did really change, the line of care in his brow was smoothed away, and he listened gladly to Prince Andrey. His friend seemed, and was indeed, an utterly different, new man. What had become of his ennui, his contempt of life, his disillusionment? Pierre was the only person to whom he could have brought himself to speak quite openly; but to him he did reveal all that was in his heart. Readily and boldly he made plans reaching far into the future; said he could not sacrifice his own happiness to the caprices of his father; declared that he would force his father to agree to the marriage and like her, or dispense with his consent altogether; then he marvelled at the feeling which had taken possession of him, as something strange, and apart, independent of himself.

'I should never have believed it, if any one had told me I could love like this,' said Prince Andrey. 'It is utterly different from the feeling I once had. The whole world is split into two halves for me: one—she, and there all is happiness, hope, and light; the other half—all where she is not, there all is dejection and darkness....'

'Darkness and gloom,' repeated Pierre; 'yes, yes, I understand that.'

'I can't help loving the light; that's not my fault; and I am very happy. Do you understand me? I know you are glad for me.'

'Yes, yes,' Pierre assented, looking at his friend with eyes full of tenderness and sadness. The brighter the picture of Prince Andrey's fate before his mind, the darker seemed his own.

XXIII

To get married his father's consent was wanted, and to obtain this Prince Andrey set off to see his father.

The father received his son's communication with external composure, but with inward wrath. He could not comprehend how any one could want to alter his life, to introduce any new element into it, when life was for him so near its end. 'If they would only let me live my life out as I want to, and then do as they like,' the old man said to himself. With his son, however, he made use of that diplomacy to which he always had resort in cases of gravity. Assuming a calm tone, he went into the whole question judicially.

In the first place, the marriage was not a brilliant one from the point of view of birth, fortune, or distinction. Secondly, Prince Andrey was not in his first youth, and was delicate in health (the old man laid special stress on this), and the girl was very young. Thirdly, there was his son, whom it would be a pity to entrust to a mere girl. 'Fourthly, and finally,' said the father, looking ironically at his son, 'I beg you to defer the matter for a year; go abroad, and get well; find a German, as you want to do so, for Prince Nikolay, and then, if your love, your passion, your obstinacy—what you choose—are so great, then get married. And that's my last word on the subject; you know, the last . . .' the old prince concluded, in a tone that showed that nothing would compel him to alter his decision.

Prince Andrey saw clearly that the old man hoped that either his feeling or that of his betrothed would not stand the test of a year, or that he, the old prince, would die himself in the course of it, and he decided to act in accordance with his father's wish; to make an offer and to defer the marriage for a year.

Three weeks after his last visit to the Rostovs, Prince Andrey returned to Petersburg.

The day after her conversation with her mother, Natasha spent the whole day expecting Bolkonsky, but he did not come. The next day, and the third, it was just the same. Pierre too stayed away, and Natasha, not knowing Prince Andrey had gone away to see his father, did not know how to interpret his absence.

So passed the three weeks. Natasha would not go out anywhere, and wandered like a shadow about the house, idle and listless, wept at night in secret, and did not go in to her mother in the evenings. She was continually flushing and very irritable. It seemed to her that every one knew of her disappointment, was laughing at her, and pitying her. In spite of all the intensity of her inward grief, the wound to her vanity aggravated her misery.

She came in to the countess one day, tried to say something, and all at once burst into tears. Her tears were the tears of an offended child, who does not know why it is being punished. The countess tried to comfort Natasha. At first she listened to her mother's words, but suddenly she interrupted her:

'Stop, mamma, I don't think of him or want to think of him! Why, he kept coming, and he has left off, and he has left off . . .' Her voice quivered, she almost began to cry, but recovered herself, and went on calmly:

'And I don't want to be married at all. And I'm afraid of him; I have quite, quite got over it now . . .'

The day after this conversation, Natasha put on the old dress she specially associated with the fun she had often had when wearing it in the mornings, and began from early morning to take up her old manner of life, which she had given up ever since the ball. After morning tea, she went into the big hall, which she particularly liked on account of the loud resonance in it, and began singing her sol-fa exercises. When she had finished the first exercise she stood still in the middle of the room and repeated a single musical phrase which particularly pleased her. She listened with delight, as though it were new to her, to the charm of these notes ringing out, filling the empty space of the great room and dying slowly away, and she felt all at once cheerful. 'Why think so much about it; things are nice even as it is,' she said to herself; and she began walking up and down the room, not putting her feet simply down on the resounding parquet, but at each step bending her foot from the heel to the toe (she had on some new shoes she particularly liked), and listening to the regular tap of the heel and creak of the toe with the same pleasure with which she had listened to the sound of her own voice. Passing by the looking-glass, she glanced into it. 'Yes, that's me!' the expression of her face seemed to say at the sight of herself. 'Well, and very nice too. And I need nobody.'

A footman would have come in to clear away something in the room, but she would not let him come in. She shut the door after him, and continued her promenade about the room. She had come back that morning to her favourite mood of loving herself and being ecstatic over herself. 'What a charming creature that Natasha is!' she said again of herself, speaking as some third person, a generic, masculine person.

'Pretty, a voice, young, and she's in nobody's way, only leave her in peace.' But, however much she might be left in peace, she could not now be at peace, and she felt that immediately.

In the vestibule the hall-door opened; some one was asking, 'At home?' and steps were audible. Natasha was looking at herself in the glass, but she did not see herself. She heard sounds in the vestibule. When she saw herself, her face was pale. It was *he*. She knew it for certain, though she herself caught the sound of his voice at the opened door.

Natasha, pale and panic-stricken, flew into the drawing-room.

'Mamma, Bolkonsky has come,' she said. 'Mamma, this is awful, unbearable! ... I don't want ... to be tortured! What am I to do?'

The countess had not time to answer her before Prince Andrey with a troubled and serious face walked into the drawing-room. As soon as he saw Natasha his face beamed with delight. He kissed the countess's hand and Natasha's, and sat down beside the sofa.

'It's a long while since we have had the pleasure ...' the countess was beginning, but Prince Andrey cut her short, answering her implied question, and obviously in haste to say what he had to say.

'I have not been to see you all this time because I have been to see my father; I had to talk over a very important matter with him. I only returned last night,' he said, glancing at Natasha .'I want to have a talk with you countess,' he added, after a moment's silence.

The countess dropped her eyes, sighing heavily.

'I am at your disposal,' she brought out.

Natasha knew she ought to go, but she was unable to do so: something seemed gripping her throat, and, regardless of civility, she stared straight at Prince Andrey with wide-open eyes.

'At once? . . . This minute? . . . No, it cannot be!' she was thinking.

He glanced at her again, and that glance convinced her that she was not mistaken. Yes, at once, this very minute her fate was to be decided.

'Run away, Natasha; I will call you,' the countess whispered.

With frightened and imploring eyes Natasha glanced at Prince Andrey and at her mother, and went out.

'I have come, countess, to ask you for your daughter's hand,' said Prince Andrey.

The countess's face flushed hotly, but she said nothing.

'Your offer . . .' the countess began at last, sedately. He sat silent, looking into her face. 'Your offer' . . . (she hesitated in confusion) 'is agreeable to us, and . . . I accept your offer; I am glad of it. And my husband . . . I hope . . . but it must rest with herself . . .'

'I will speak to her, when I have received your consent. . . . Do you give it me?' said Prince Andrey.

'Yes,' said the countess, and she held out her hand to him, and with mingled feelings of aversion and tenderness she pressed her lips to his forehead as he bent to kiss her hand. Her wish was to love him as a son; but she felt that he was a man alien to her, and that she was afraid of him.

'I am sure my husband will consent,' said the countess; 'but your father . . .'

'My father, whom I have informed of my plans, has made it an express condition that the marriage should not take place for a year. That, too, I meant to speak of to you,' said Prince Andrey.

'It is true that Natasha is very young, but—so long as that?'

'It could not be helped,' said Prince Andrey with a sigh.

'I will send her to you,' said the countess, and she went out of the room.

'Lord, have mercy upon us!' she kept repeating as she looked for her daughter.

Sonya told her that Natasha was in her bedroom. She was sitting on her bed, with a pale face and dry eyes; she was gazing at the holy picture, and murmuring something to herself, as she rapidly crossed herself. Seeing her mother, she leaped up and flew towards her.

'Well, mamma, . . . well?'

'Go, go to him. He asks your hand,' said the countess, coldly it seemed to Natasha. . . . Yes . . . go . . .' the mother murmured mournfully and reproachfully with a deep sigh as her daughter ran off.

Natasha could not have said how she reached the drawing-room. As she entered the door and caught sight of him, she stopped short: 'Is it possible that this stranger has now become *everything* to me?' she asked herself, and instantly answered: 'Yes, everything: he alone is dearer to me now than everything in the world.' Prince Andrey approached her with downcast eyes.

'I have loved you from the first minute I saw you. Can I hope?'

He glanced at her and was struck by the serious, impassioned look in her face. Her face seemed to say: 'Why ask? Why doubt of what you cannot but know? Why talk when no words can express what one feels?'

She came nearer to him and stopped. He took her hand and kissed it.

'Do you love me?'

'Yes, yes,' said Natasha, almost angrily it seemed. She drew a deep sigh, and another, her breathing came more and more quickly, and she burst into sobs.

'What is it? What's the matter?'

'Oh, I am so happy,' she answered, smiling through her tears. She bent over closer to him, thought a second, as though wondering whether it were possible, and then kissed him.

Prince Andrey held her hands, looked into her eyes and could find no trace of his former love for her in his heart. Some sudden reaction seemed to have taken place in his soul; there was none of the poetic and mysterious charm of desire left in it; instead of that there was pity for her feminine and childish weakness, terror at her devotion and trustfulness, an irksome, yet sweet, sense of duty, binding him to her for ever. The actual feeling, though not so joyous and poetical as the former feeling, was more serious and deeper.

'Did your mamma tell you that it cannot be for a year?' said Prince Andrey, still gazing into her eyes.

'Can this be I, the baby-girl (as every one used to call me)?' Natasha was thinking. 'Can I really be from this minute a *wife*, on a level with this unknown, charming, intellectual man, who is looked up to even by my father? Can it be true? Can it be true that now there can be no more playing with life, that now I am grown up, that now a responsibility is laid upon me for every word and action? Oh, what did he ask me?'

'No,' she answered, but she had not understood his question.

'Forgive me,' said Prince Andrey, 'but you are so young, and I have had so much experience of life. I am afraid for you. You don't know yourself.'

Natasha listened with concentrated attention, trying to take in the meaning of his words; but she did not understand them.

'Hard as that year will be to me, delaying my happiness,' continued Prince Andrey, 'in that time you will be sure of yourself. I beg you to make me happy in a year, but you are free; our engagement shall be kept a secret, and if you should find out that you do not love me, or if you should come to love . . .' said Prince Andrey with a forced smile.

'Why do you say that?' Natasha interrupted. 'You know that from the very day when you first came to Otradnoe, I have loved you,' she said, firmly persuaded that she was speaking the truth.

'In a year you will learn to know yourself. . . .'

'A who-ole year!' cried Natasha suddenly, only now grasping that their marriage was to be deferred for a year. 'But why a year? . . . Why a year? . . .'

Prince Andrey began to explain to her the reasons for this delay. Natasha did not hear him.

'And can't it be helped?' she asked. Prince Andrey made no reply, but his face expressed the impossibility of altering this decision.

'That's awful! Oh, it's awful, awful!' Natasha cried suddenly, and she broke into sobs again. 'I shall die if I have to wait a year; it's impossible, it's awful.' She glanced at her lover's face and saw the look of sympathetic pain and perplexity on it.

'No, no, I'll do anything,' she said, suddenly checking her tears; 'I'm so happy!'

Her father and mother came into the room and gave the betrothed couple their blessing. From that day Prince Andrey began to visit the Rostovs as Natasha's affianced lover.

XXIV

THERE was no formal betrothal and no announcement was made of the engagement of Bolkonsky and Natasha; Prince Andrey insisted upon that. He said that since he was responsible for the delay of their marriage, he ought to bear the whole burden of it. He said that he was bound for ever by his word, but he did not want to bind Natasha and would leave her perfect freedom. If in another six months she were to feel that she did not love him, she would have a perfect right to refuse him. It need hardly be said that neither Natasha nor her parents would hear of this possibility; but Prince Andrey insisted on having his own way. Prince Andrey came every day to the Rostovs', but he did not behave as though he were engaged to her; he addressed her formally and kissed only her hand. From the day of his proposal Prince Andrey's relations with Natasha had become quite different from what had existed between them before: their relations were simple and intimate. It seemed as though till then they had not known each other. Both loved to recall how they had regarded one another when they were *nothing* to each other. Now they both felt utterly different creatures— then affected, now simple and sincere. At first there had been a feeling of awkwardness in the family in regard to Prince Andrey. He seemed a man from another world, and Natasha used for a long while to try and make her people understand Prince Andrey, and declared to every one with pride that he only seemed to be so different, that he was really like every one else, and that she was not afraid of him and no one need be. After a few days, the rest of the family got accustomed to seeing him, and went on without constraint with their usual manner of life, in which he took part. He knew how to talk to the count about the management of his estates, to the countess and Natasha about dress, and to Sonya about her album and embroidery. Sometimes the Rostovs among themselves, and in Prince Andrey's presence, expressed their wonder at the way it had all happened, and at the events that obviously betokened that it was to be: Prince Andrey's coming to Otradnoe, and their coming to Petersburg, and the resemblance between Natasha and Prince Andrey, which the old nurse had remarked on Prince Andrey's first visit, and the meeting in 1805 between Andrey and Nikolay, and many other incidents betokening that it was to be, were observed by the family.

The house was full of that poetic atmosphere of dullness and silence, which always accompanies the presence of an engaged couple. Often as they all sat together every one was silent. Sometimes the others got up and went away, and the engaged pair were still as mute when they were left alone. Rarely they spoke of their future life together. Prince Andrey felt frightened and ashamed to speak of it. Natasha shared the feeling, as she did all his feelings, which she never failed to divine. Once Natasha began questioning him about his son.

Prince Andrey blushed—a thing frequent with him at that time, which Natasha particularly liked to see—and said that his son would not live with them.

'Why not?' said Natasha, taking fright.

'I cannot take him from his grandfather and then...'

'How I should have loved him!' said Natasha, at once divining his thought; 'but I know you want to avoid any pretext for our being blamed.'

The old count sometimes came up to Prince Andrey, kissed him and asked his advice about some question relating to Petya's education or Nikolay's position. The old countess sighed as she looked at them. Sonya was afraid every instant of being in their way, and was always trying to find excuses for leaving them alone, even when they had no wish to be alone. When Prince Andrey talked—he described things very well—Natasha listened to him with pride. When she talked, she noticed with joy and dread that he watched her with an intent and scrutinising look. She asked herself in perplexity: 'What is it he seeks in me? What is it he is probing for with that look? What if I haven't in me what he is searching for in that look?' Sometimes she fell into the mood of wild gaiety characteristic of her, and then she particularly loved to see and hear how Prince Andrey laughed. He rarely laughed, but when he did laugh he abandoned himself utterly to his mirth, and she always felt herself drawn closer to him by this laughter. Natasha would have been perfectly happy if the thought of the separation before her, coming closer and closer, had not terrified her. He too turned pale and cold at the mere thought of it.

On the day before he was to leave Petersburg, Prince Andrey brought with him Pierre, who had not been at the Rostovs' since the day of the ball. Pierre seemed absent-minded and embarrassed. He talked chiefly to the countess. Natasha was sitting at the chess-board with Sonya, and invited Prince Andrey to join them. He went to them.

'You have known Bezuhov a long while, haven't you?' he asked. 'Do you like him?'

'Yes; he's very nice, but very absurd.'

And she began, as people always did when speaking of Pierre, to tell anecdotes of his absent-mindedness, anecdotes which were made up, indeed, about him.

'You know, I have confided our secret to him,' said Prince Andrey. 'I have known him from childhood. He has a heart of gold. I beg you, Natalie,' he said, with sudden seriousness, 'I am going away; God knows what may happen. You may change... Oh, I know I ought not to speak of that. Only one thing—if anything were to happen to you, while I am away...'

'What could happen?'

'If any trouble were to come,' pursued Prince Andrey. 'I beg you,

Mademoiselle Sophie, if any thing were to happen, to go to him and no one else for advice and help. He is a most absent-minded and eccentric person, but he has the truest heart.'

Neither her father, nor her mother, neither Sonya nor Prince Andrey could have foreseen the effect of the parting on Natasha. She wandered about the house all that day, flushed, excited, and tearless, busying herself about the most trivial matters as though she had no notion of what was before her. She did not weep even at the moment when he kissed her hand for the last time.

'Don't go away!' was all she said, in a voice that made him wonder whether he ought not really to remain, and that he remembered long after. When he had gone, she still did not weep; but for several days she sat in her room, not crying, but taking no interest in anything, and only saying from time to time: 'Oh, why did he go?' But a fortnight after his departure, she surprised those around her equally by recovering from her state of spiritual sickness, and became herself again, only with a change in her moral physiognomy, such as one sees in the faces of children after a long illness.

XXV

THE health and character of Prince Nikolay Andreitch Bolkonsky had, during that year, after his son had left him, grown considerably feebler. He became more irritable than ever, and it was Princess Marya who as a rule bore the brunt of his outbursts of causeless fury. He seemed studiously to seek out all the tender spots in her consciousness so as to inflict on her the cruellest wounds possible. Princess Marya had two passions and consequently two joys: her nephew, Nikolushka, and religion; and both were favourite subjects for the old prince's attacks and jeers. Whatever was being spoken of, he would bring the conversation round to the superstitiousness of old maids, or the petting and spoiling of children. 'You want to make him' (Nikolushka) 'just such another old maid as you are yourself. Prince Andrey wants a son and not an old maid,' he would say. Or addressing Mademoiselle Bourienne he would ask her, before Princess Marya, how she liked our village priests and holy pictures, and make jests about them....

He was constantly wounding Princess Marya's feelings, but his daughter needed no effort to forgive him. Could he be to blame in anything he did to her, could her father, who as she knew in spite of it all, loved her, be unjust? And indeed what is justice? Princess Marya never gave a thought to that proud word, 'justice.' All the complex laws of humanity were summed up for her in one clear and simple law—the law of love and self-sacrifice, laid down by Him who had in His love suffered for humanity, though He was God Himself. What had she to do with the justice or injustice of other people? All she had to do was to suffer and to love: and that she did.

In the winter Prince Andrey had come to Bleak Hills, had been gay, gentle, and affectionate, as Princess Marya had not seen him for years. She felt that something had happened to him, but he said nothing to his sister of his love. Before his departure, Prince Andrey had a long conversation with his father, and Princess Marya noticed that they were ill pleased with each other at parting.

Soon after Prince Andrey had gone, Princess Marya wrote from Bleak Hills to her friend in Petersburg, Julie Karagin, whom Princess Marya had dreamed—as girls always do dream—of marrying to her brother. She was at this time in mourning for the death of a brother, who had been killed in Turkey.

'Sorrow, it seems, is our common lot, my sweet and tender friend Julie.

'Your loss is so terrible that I can only explain it to myself, as a special sign of the grace of God, who in His love for you would chasten you and your incomparable mother.

'Ah, my dear, religion, and religion alone can—I don't say comfort us—but save us from despair. Religion alone can interpret to us what, without its aid, man cannot comprehend: to what end, for what cause, good, elevated beings who are able to find happiness in life, not injuring others, but indispensable to their happiness, are called away to God, while the wicked, the useless, injuring others and a burden to themselves and others, are left living. The first death which I have seen, and which I shall never forget—the death of my dear little sister-in-law—made on me just the same impression. Just as you question destiny, and ask why your noble brother had to die, so did I wonder what reason there was for that angel Liza to die—who had never done the slightest harm to any one, never even had a thought in her heart that was not kind. And yet—do you know, dear friend—five years have passed since then, and even I, with my poor intelligence, begin now to understand clearly why it was needful she should die, and in what way that death was but an expression of the boundless grace of the Creator, all of whose acts, though for the most part we comprehend them not, are but manifestations of His infinite love for His creature. Perhaps, I often think, she was of too angelic an innocence to have the force to perform all a mother's duties. As a young wife, she was irreproachable; possibly she could not have been equally so as a mother. As it is, not only has she left us, and particularly Prince Andrey, the purest memories and regrets, but there she is in all likelihood receiving a place for which I dare not hope for myself. But not to speak of her alone, that early and terrible death has had the most blessed influence on me and on my brother, in spite of all our grief. At the time, at the moment of our loss, I could not have entertained such thoughts; at that time I should have dismissed them in horror, but now it seems clear and incontestable. I write all this to you, dear friend, simply to convince you of the Gospel truth, which has become a principle of life for me: not one hair of our head falls without His will. And the guiding principle of His will is only His infinite love for us, and so whatever may befall us, all is for our good.

'You ask whether we shall spend next winter in Moscow. In spite of all my desire to see you, I do not expect and do not wish to do so. And you will be surprised to hear that Bonaparte is responsible for this! I will tell you why: my father's health is noticeably weaker; he cannot endure contradiction and is easily irritated. This irritability is, as you are aware, most readily aroused on political subjects. He cannot endure the idea that Bonaparte is treating on equal terms with all the sovereigns of Europe, especially our own, the grandson of the great Catherine! As you know, I take absolutely no interest in politics, but from my father and his conversations with Mihail Ivanovitch, I know all that goes on in the world, and have heard of all the honours conferred on Bonaparte. It seems that Bleak Hills is now the only spot on the terrestrial globe where he is not recognised as a great man—still less as Emperor of France. And my father cannot tolerate this state of things. It seems to me that my father shows a disinclination for the visit to Moscow, chiefly owing to his political views and his foreseeing the difficulties likely to arise from his habit of expressing his opinions freely, with no regard for any one. All that he would gain from medical treatment in Moscow, he would lose from the inevitable discussions upon Bonaparte. In any case the matter will very soon be settled.

'Our home life goes on in its way, except for the absence of my brother Andrey. As I wrote to you before, he has greatly changed of late. It is only of late, during this year that he seems to have quite recovered from the shock of his loss. He has become again just as I knew him as a child, good-natured, affectionate, with a heart such as I know in no one else. He feels now, it seems to me, that life is not over for him. But, together with this moral change, he has become very weak physically. He is thinner than ever and more nervous. I feel anxious about him and glad that he is taking this tour abroad, which the doctors prescribed long ago. I hope that it will cure him. You write to me that he is spoken of in Petersburg as one of the most capable, cultivated, and intellectual young men. Forgive me for the pride of family—I never doubted it. The good he did here to every one—from his peasants to the local nobility—is incalculable. When he went to Petersburg he was received as he deserved. I wonder at the way reports fly from Petersburg to Moscow, and especially such groundless ones as the rumour you wrote to me about, of my brother's supposed engagement to the little Rostov girl. I don't imagine that Andrey will ever marry any one at all, and certainly not her. And I will tell you why. In the first place, I know that though he rarely speaks of his late wife, the grief of his loss has penetrated too deeply into his heart for him ever to be ready to give her a successor, and our little angel a stepmother. Secondly, because, as far as I can ascertain, that girl is not one of the kind of women who could attract my brother Andrey. I do not believe that Andrey has chosen her for his wife; and I will frankly confess, I should not wish for such a thing. But how I have been running on; I am finishing my second sheet. Farewell, my sweet friend; and may God keep you in His holy and mighty care. My dear companion, Mademoiselle Bourienne, sends you kisses.

MARIE.'

XXVI

IN the middle of the summer Princess Marya, to her surprise, received a letter from Prince Andrey, who was in Switzerland. In it he told her strange and surprising news. He informed his sister of his engagement to the younger Rostov. His whole letter was full of loving enthusiasm for his betrothed, and tender and confiding affection for his sister. He wrote that he had never loved as he loved now, and that it was only now that he saw all the value and meaning of life. He begged his sister to forgive him for having said nothing of his plans to her on his last visit to Bleak Hills, though he had spoken of it to his father. He had said nothing to her for fear Princess Marya would beg her father to give his consent, and, without attaining her object, would irritate her father and draw all the weight of his displeasure upon herself. The matter was not, however, then, he wrote to her, so completely settled as now. 'At that time our father insisted on a delay of a year, and now *six months*, half of the period specified, is over, and I remain firmer than ever in my resolution. If it were not for the doctors keeping me here at the waters I should be back in Russia myself; but, as it is, I must put off my return for another three months. You know me and my relations with our father. I want nothing from him. I have been, and always shall be, independent; but to act in opposition to his will, to incur his anger when he has perhaps not long left to be with us, would destroy half my happiness. I am writing a letter to him now, and I beg you to choose a favourable moment to give him the letter, and to let me know how he looks at the whole matter, and if there is any hope of his agreeing to shorten the year by three months.'

After long hesitations, doubts and prayers, Princess Marya gave the letter to her father. The next day the old prince said to her calmly:

'Write to your brother to wait till I'm dead.... He won't have long to wait. I shall soon set him free.'

The princess tried to make some reply, but her father would not let her speak, and went on, getting louder and louder. 'Let him marry, let him marry, the dear fellow.... A nice connection!... Clever people, eh? Rich, eh?. Oh yes, a fine stepmother for Nikolushka she'll make! You write to him he can marry her tomorrow. Nikolushka shall have her for a stepmother, and I'll marry little Bourienne!... Ha, ha, ha, and so he shall have a stepmother too! Only there's one thing, I won't have any more women-folk about my house; he may marry and go and live by himself. Perhaps you'll go and live with him too?' He turned to Princess Marya: 'You're welcome to, and good luck to you!'

After this outburst the prince did not once allude to the subject again. But his repressed anger at his son's poor-spirited behaviour found a vent in his treatment of his daughter. He now added to his former subjects for jeering and annoying her a new one—allusions to a stepmother and gallantries to Mademoiselle Bourienne.

'Why shouldn't I marry her?' he would say to his daughter. 'A capital princess she will make!' And latterly, to her perplexity and amazement, Princess Marya began to notice that her father was really beginning to attach himself more and more closely to the Frenchwoman. Princess Marya wrote to Prince Andrey and told him how their father had taken the letter, but comforted her brother with hopes that he would become reconciled to the idea.

Nikolushka and his education, her brother Andrey and religion, were Princess Marya's joys and consolations. But apart from those, since every one must have personal hopes, Princess Marya cherished, in the deepest secrecy of her heart, a hidden dream and hope that was the source of the chief comfort in her life. This comforting dream and hope was given her by 'God's folk'—the crazy prophets and the pilgrims, who visited her without the prince's knowledge. The longer Princess Marya lived, the more experience and observation she had of life, the more she wondered at the shortsightedness of men, who seek here on earth for enjoyment, toil, suffer, strive and do each other harm to attain that impossible, visionary, and sinful happiness. Prince Andrey had loved a wife; she died; that was not enough for him, he wanted to bind his happiness to another woman. Her father did not want that, because he coveted a more distinguished or a wealthier match for Andrey. And they were all striving, and suffering, and in torment, and sullying their souls, their eternal souls, to attain a bliss the duration of which was but a moment. Not only do we know that for ourselves. Christ, the Son of God, came down upon earth and told us that this life is but for a moment, is but a probation; yet we still cling to it and think to find happiness in it. 'How is it no one has realised that?' Princess Marya wondered. 'No one but these despised people of God who, with wallets over their shoulders, come to me by the backstairs, afraid of the prince catching sight of them, and not from fear of ill-usage, but from fear of tempting him to sin. To leave home and country, give up all thoughts of worldly blessings, and clinging to nothing, to wander from place to place in a home-spun smock under a different name, doing people no harm, but praying for them, praying equally for those who drive them away and those who succour them: higher than that truth and that life there is no truth and no life!'

There was one pilgrim-woman, Fedosyushka, a quiet, little woman of about fifty, marked by smallpox, who had been wandering for over thirty years barefooted and wearing chains. Princess Marya was particularly fond of her. One day when sitting in a dark room, by the light only of the lamp before the holy picture, Fedosyushka told her about her life. Princess Marya felt all at once so strongly that Fedosyushka was the one person who had found the right way of life, that she resolved to go on a pilgrimage herself. When Fedosyushka had gone to bed Princess Marya pondered a long while over it, and at last made up her mind that—however strange it might be—she must go on a pilgrimage. She confided her intention to no one but a monk, Father Akinfy, and this priest approved of her project. On the pretence of getting presents for pilgrim women, Princess Marya had prepared for herself the complete outfit of a pilgrim—a smock, plaited shoes, a full-skirted coat, and a black kerchief. Often she went to her secret wardrobe, where she kept them, and stood in uncertainty whether the time to carry out her plan had come or not.

Often as she listened to the pilgrims' tales, their simple phrases—that had become mechanical to them, but were to her ears full of the deepest significance—worked upon her till she was several times ready to throw up everything and run away from home. In imagination she already saw herself with Fedosyushka in a coarse smock, trudging along the dusty road with her wallet and her staff, going on her pilgrimage, free from envy, free from earthly love, free from all desires, from one saint to another; and at last thither where there is neither sorrow nor sighing, but everlasting joy and blessedness.

'I shall come to one place, I shall pray there, and before I have time to grow used to it, to love it, I shall go on further. And I shall go on till my legs give way under me and I lie down and die somewhere, and reach at last that quiet, eternal haven, where is neither sorrow nor sighing! . . .' thought Princess Marya.

But then at the sight of her father, and still more of little Nikolushka, she wavered in her resolution, wept in secret, and felt that she was a sinner, that she loved her father and her nephew more than God.

PART VII

I

THE BIBLICAL tradition tells us that the absence of work—idleness—was a condition of the first man's blessedness before the Fall. The love of idleness has remained the same in fallen man; but the curse still lies heavy upon man, and not only because in the sweat of our brow we must eat bread, but because from our moral qualities we are unable to be idle and at peace. A secret voice tells us that we must be to blame for being idle. If a man could find a state in which while being idle he could feel himself to be of use and to be doing his duty, he would have attained to one side of primitive blessedness. And such a state of obligatory and irreproachable idleness is enjoyed by a whole class—the military class. It is in that obligatory and irreproachable idleness that the chief attraction of military service has always consisted, and will always consist.

Nikolay Rostov was enjoying this blessed privilege to the full, as after the year 1807 he remained in the Pavlograd regiment, in command of the squadron that had been Denisov's.

Rostov had become a bluff, good-natured fellow, who would have been thought rather bad form by his old acquaintances in Moscow, though he was loved and respected by his comrades, his subordinates, and his superior officers, and was well content with his life. Of late—in the year 1809—he had found more and more frequently in letters from home complaints on the part of his mother that their pecuniary position was going from bad to worse, and that it was high time for him to come home, to gladden and comfort the hearts of his old parents.

As he read those letters, Nikolay felt a pang of dread at their wanting to drag him out of the surroundings in which, by fencing himself off from all the complexities of existence, he was living so quietly and peacefully. He felt that sooner or later he would have to plunge again into that whirlpool of life, with many difficulties and business to attend to, with the steward's accounts, with quarrels and intrigues, with ties, with society, with Sonya's love and his promise to her. All that was terribly difficult and complicated; and he answered his mother's letters with cold letters in French on the classic model, beginning '*Ma chere maman*,' and ending: '*Votre obéissant fils*,' saying nothing of any intention of coming home. In 1810 he received letters from home in which he was told of Natasha's engagement to Bolkonsky, and of the marriage being deferred for a year, because the old prince would not consent to it. This letter chagrined and mortified Nikolay. In the first place, he was sorry to be losing from home Natasha, whom he cared more for than all the rest of the family. Secondly, from his hussar point of view, he regretted not having been at home at the time, as he would have shown this Bolkonsky that it was by no means such an honour to be connected with him, and that if he cared for Natasha he could get on just as well without his crazy old father's consent. For a moment he hesitated whether to ask for leave, so as to see Natasha engaged, but then the manœuvres were just coming on, and thoughts of Sonya, of complications, recurred to him, and again he put it off. But in the spring of the same year he got a letter from his mother, written without his father's knowledge, and that letter decided him. She wrote that if Nikolay did not come and look after things, their whole estate would have to be sold by auction, and they would all be beggars. The count was so weak, put such entire confidence in Mitenka, and was so good-natured, and every one took advantage of him, so that things were going from bad to worse. 'I beseech you, for God's sake, to come at once, if you don't want to make me and all your family miserable,' wrote the countess.

That letter produced an effect on Nikolay. He had that common sense of mediocrity which showed him what was his duty.

His duty now was, if not to retire from the army, at least to go home on leave. Why he had to go, he could not have said; but, after his after-dinner nap, he ordered his grey mare to be saddled, a terribly vicious beast that he had not ridden for a long while.

He returned home with his horse in a lather, and told Lavrushka—he had kept on Denisov's old valet—and the comrades who dropped in that evening, that he had applied for leave and was going home. It was strange and difficult for him to believe that he was going away without hearing from the staff whether he had been promoted to be a captain or had received the St. Anne for the last manœuvres (a matter of the greatest interest to him). It was strange to him to think of going away like this without having sold Count Goluhovsky his three roan horses, over which the Polish count was haggling with him. Rostov had taken a bet that he would get two thousand for them. It seemed inconceivable that without him the ball could take place which the hussars were to give in honour of their favourite Polish belle, Madame Pshazdetsky, to outdo the Uhlans, who had given a ball to their favourite belle, Madame Borzhozovsky. Yet he knew he must leave this world, where all was well and all was clear, to go where all was nonsensical and complicated. A week later his leave came. His comrades—not only in the regiment, but throughout the whole brigade—gave Rostov a dinner that cost a subscription of fifteen roubles a head. Two bands of musicians played, two choruses sang; Rostov danced the *trepak* with Major Bazov; the drunken officers tossed him in the air, hugged him, dropped him; the soldiers of the third squadron tossed him once more, and shouted hurrah! Then they put Rostov in a sledge and escorted him as far as the first posting-station on his way.

For the first half of the journey, from Krementchug to Kiev, all Rostov's thoughts—as is apt to be the case with travellers—turned to what he had left behind—to his squadron. But after being jolted over the first half of the journey, he had begun to forget his three roans and his quartermaster, Dozhoyveyky, and was beginning to wonder uneasily what he should find on reaching Otradnoe. The nearer he got, the more intense, far more intense, were his thoughts of home (as though moral feeling were subject to the law of acceleration in inverse ratio with the square of the distance). At the station nearest to Otradnoe he gave the sledge-driver a tip of three roubles, and ran breathless up the steps of his home, like a boy.

After the excitement of the first meeting, and the strange feeling of disappointment after his expectations—the feeling that 'it's just the same; why was I in such a hurry?'—Nikolay began to settle down in his old world of home. His father and mother were just the same, only a little older. All that was new in them was a certain uneasiness and at times a difference of opinion, which he had never seen between them before, and soon learned to be due to the difficulties of their position.

Sonya was now nearly twenty. She would grow no prettier now; there was no promise in her of more to come; but what she had was enough. She was brimming over with love and happiness as soon as Nikolay came home, and this girl's faithful, steadfast love for him gladdened his heart. Petya and Natasha surprised Nikolay more than all the rest. Petya was a big, handsome lad of thirteen, whose voice was already cracking; he was full of gaiety and clever pranks. Nikolay did not get over his wonder at Natasha for a long while, and laughed as he looked at her.

'You're utterly different,' he told her.

'How? Uglier?'

'No, quite the contrary; but what dignity! A real princess!' he whispered to her.

'Yes, yes, yes,' cried Natasha gleefully.

Natasha told him all the story of Prince Andrey's love-making, of his visit to Otradnoe, and showed him his last letter.

'Well, are you glad?' asked Natasha. 'I'm so at peace and happy now.'

'Very glad,' answered Nikolay. 'He's a splendid fellow. Are you very much in love, then?'

'How shall I say?' answered Natasha. 'I was in love with Boris, with our teacher, with Denisov, but this is utterly different. I feel calm, settled. I know there is no one better than he in the world, and so I am calm now and content. It's utterly different from anything before...'

Nikolay expressed his dissatisfaction at the marriage being put off for a year. But Natasha fell on him with exasperation, proving to him that no other course was possible, that it would be a horrid thing to enter a family against the father's will, and that she would not consent to it herself.

'You don't understand at all, at all,' she kept saying.

Nikolay paused a moment, and then said he agreed with her.

Her brother often wondered as he looked at her. It seemed quite incredible that she was a girl in love and parted from her betrothed lover. She was even-tempered, serene, and quite as light-hearted as ever. This made Nikolay wonder, and look on the engagement to Bolkonsky rather sceptically. He could not believe that her fate was by now sealed, especially as he had never seen her with Prince Andrey. It still seemed to him that there was something not real in this proposed marriage.

'Why this delay? Why were they not formally betrothed?' he thought.

Once in talking to his mother about his sister, he found to his surprise, and partly to his satisfaction, that at the bottom of her heart his mother sometimes regarded the marriage as sceptically as he did.

'Here, you see, he writes,' she said, showing her son a letter from Prince Andrey with that latent feeling of grudge which mothers always have in regard to their daughter's happiness in marriage, 'he writes that he won't be coming before December. What can it be that keeps him? Illness, no doubt! His health is very weak. Don't tell Natasha. Don't make a mistake, because she seems in good spirits, it's the last she has of her girlhood, and I know how she is when she gets his letters. Still, God grant, all may be well yet,' she always concluded: 'he's a splendid fellow.'

II

IN the early part of his time at home Nikolay was serious and even dull. He was worried by the necessity of meddling in the stupid business matters which his mother had sent for him to look after. To be rid of this burden as soon as possible, on the third day after his return, he marched angrily off, making no reply to inquiries where he was going, with scowling brows entered Mitenka's lodge, and demanded from him an *account* in full. What he meant by an account in full, Nikolay knew even less than the panic-stricken and bewildered Mitenka. The conversation and Mitenka's accounts did not last long. The village elder, the deputy, and the village clerk, waiting in the entry of the lodge, heard with awe and delight at first the booming and snapping of the young count's voice in a constantly ascending scale, then terrible words of abuse, flung one after another.

'Robber! Ungrateful brute! . . . I'll thrash the dog! . . . not papa to deal with . . . plundering us . . .' and so on.

Then, with no less awe and delight, these persons saw the young count, with a red face and bloodshot eyes, dragging Mitenka out by the collar, kicking him with great dexterity at every appropriate moment between his words, and shouting:

'Away with you! Never let me set eyes on you, blackguard!'

Mitenka flew head first down six steps and ran to the shrubbery. This shrubbery was well known as a haven of refuge for delinquents at Otradnoe. Mitenka had, on coming home drunk from the town, himself hidden in the shrubbery, and many of the residents of Otradnoe had been indebted to the saving power of the shrubbery when anxious to conceal themselves from Mitenka.

Mitenka's wife and sister-in-law, with frightened faces, peeped into the passage from the door of their room, where was a bright samovar boiling, and the bailiff's high bedstead stood under a quilted patchwork coverlet.

The young count walked by, treading resolutely and breathing hard, taking no notice of them, and went into the house.

The countess heard at once through her maids of what had been happening in the lodge, and on one side was comforted by the reflection that now their position would be sure to improve, though on the other hand she was uneasy as to the effect of the scene on her son. She went several times on tiptoe to his door, and listened as he lighted one pipe after another.

The next day the old count drew his son on one side, and, with a timid smile, said to him, 'But you know, my dear boy, you had no reason to be so angry. Mitenka has told me all about it.'

'I knew,' thought Nikolay, 'that I should never make head or tail of anything in this crazy world.'

'You were angry at his not having put down these seven hundred and eight roubles. But you see they were carried forward by double entry, and you didn't look at the next page.'

'Papa, he's a blackguard and a thief, I am certain. And what I have done, I have done. But if you don't wish it, I will say nothing to him.'

'No, my dear boy!' (The old count was confused. He was conscious that he had mismanaged his wife's estate and had wronged his children, but he had no notion how to rectify the position.) 'No, I beg you to go into things. I am old. I . . .'

'No, papa, forgive me if I have done what you dislike. I know less about it than you do.'

'Damn them all, these peasants, and money matters and double entries,' he thought. 'I used once to understand scoring cards, but book-keeping by double entry is quite beyond me,' he said to himself, and from that time he did not meddle further with the management of the family affairs. But one day the countess called her son into her room, told him that she had a promissory-note from Anna Mihalovna for two thousand roubles, and asked Nikolay what he thought it best to do about it.

'Well,' answered Nikolay, 'you say that it rests with me. I don't like Anna Mihalovna, and I don't like Boris, but they were our friends, and they were poor. So that's what I would do!' and he tore up the note, and by so doing made the countess sob with tears of joy. After this, young Rostov took no further part in business of any sort, but devoted himself with passionate interest to everything to do with the chase, which was kept up on a great scale on the old count's estate.

III

WINTRY weather was already setting in, the morning frosts hardened the earth drenched by the autumn rains. Already the grass was full of tufts, and stood out bright green against the patches of brown winter cornland trodden by the cattle, and the pale yellow stubble of the summer cornfields, and the reddish strips of buckwheat. The uplands and copses, which at the end of August had still been green islands among the black fields ploughed ready for winter corn, and the stubble had become golden and lurid red islands in a sea of bright green autumn crops. The grey hare had already half-changed its coat, the foxes' cubs were beginning to leave their parents, and the young wolves were bigger than dogs. It was the best time of the year for the chase. The dogs of an ardent young sportsman like Rostov were only just coming into fit state for hunting, so that at a common council of the huntsmen it was decided to give the dogs three days' rest, and on the 16th of September to go off on a hunting expedition, beginning with Dubravy, where there was a litter of wolves that had never been hunted.

Such was the position of affairs on the 14th of September.

All that day the dogs were kept at home. It was keen and frosty weather, but towards evening the sky clouded over and it began to thaw. On the morning of the 15th of September when young Rostov in his dressing-gown looked out of window he saw a morning which was all the heart could desire for hunting. It looked as though the sky were melting, and without the slightest wind, sinking down upon the earth. The only movement in the air was the soft downward motion of microscopic drops of moisture or mist. The bare twigs in the garden were hung with transparent drops which dripped on to the freshly fallen leaves. The earth in the kitchen-garden had a gleaming, wet, black look like the centre of a poppy, and at a short distance away it melted off into the damp, dim veil of fog.

Nikolay went out on to the wet and muddy steps. There was a smell of decaying leaves and dogs. The broad-backed, black and tan bitch Milka, with her big, prominent, black eyes, caught sight of her master, got up, stretched out her hind-legs, lay down like a hare, then suddenly jumped up and licked him right on his nose and moustache. Another harrier, catching sight of his master from the bright coloured path, arched its back, darted headlong to the steps, and, lifting its tail, rubbed itself against Nikolay's legs.

'O, hoy!' He heard at that moment the inimitable hunting halloo which unites the deepest bass and the shrillest tenor notes. And round the corner came the huntsman and whipper-in, Danilo, a grey, wrinkled man, with his hair cropped round in the Ukrainian fashion. He held a bent whip in his hand, and his face had that expression of independence and scorn for everything in the world, which is only to be seen in huntsmen. He took off his Circassian cap to his master and looked scornfully at him. That scorn was not offensive to his master. Nikolay knew that this Danilo, disdainful of all, and superior to everything, was still his man and his huntsman.

'Danilo,' said Nikolay, at the sight of this hunting weather, those dogs, and the huntsman, feeling shyly that he was being carried away by that irresistible sporting passion in which a man forgets all his previous intentions, like a man in love at the sight of his mistress.

'What is your bidding, your excellency?' asked a bass voice, fit for a head deacon, and hoarse from hallooing, and a pair of flashing black eyes glanced up from under their brows at the silent young master. 'Surely you can't resist it?' those two eyes seemed to be asking.

'It's a good day, eh? Just right for riding and hunting, eh?' said Nikolay, scratching Milka behind the ears.

Danilo winked and made no reply.

'I sent Uvarka out to listen at daybreak,' his bass boomed out after a moment's silence. 'He brought word *she's moved* into the Otradnoe enclosure; there was howling there.' ('She's moved' meant that the mother wolf, of whom both knew, had moved with her cubs into the Otradnoe copse, which was a small hunting preserve about two versts away.)

'Shouldn't we go, eh?' said Nikolay. 'Come to me with Uvarka.'

'As you desire.'

'Then put off feeding them.'

'Yes, sir!'

Five minutes later Danilo and Uvarka were standing in Nikolay's big study. Although Danilo was not tall, to see him in a room gave one an impression such as one has on seeing a horse or bear standing on the floor among the furniture and surroundings of human life. Danilo felt this himself, and as usual he kept close to the door and tried to speak more softly, and not to move for fear of causing some breakage in the master's apartments. He did his utmost to get everything said quickly so as to get as soon as might be out into the open again, from under a ceiling out under the sky.

After making inquiries and extracting from Danilo an admission that the dogs were fit (Danilo himself was longing to go), Nikolay told them to have the horses saddled. But just as Danilo was about to go, Natasha, wrapped in a big shawl of her old nurse's, ran into the room, not yet dressed, and her hair in disorder. Petya ran in with her.

'Are you going?' said Natasha. 'I knew you would! Sonya said you weren't going. I knew that on such a day you couldn't help going!'

'Yes, we're going,' Nikolay answered reluctantly. As he meant to attempt serious hunting he did not want to take Natasha and Petya. 'We are going, but only wolf-hunting; it will be dull for you.'

'You know that it's the greatest of my pleasures,' said Natasha. 'It's too bad—he's going himself, has ordered the horses out and not a word to us.'

'No hindrance bars a Russian's path!' declaimed Petya; 'let's go!'

'But you mustn't, you know; mamma said you were not to,' said Nikolay to Natasha.

'No, I'm going, I must go,' said Natasha stoutly. 'Danilo, bid them saddle my horse, and tell Mihailo to come with my leash,' she said to the huntsman.

Simply to be in a room seemed irksome and unfitting to Danilo, but to have anything to do with a young lady he felt to be utterly impossible. He cast down his eyes and made haste to get away, making as though it were no affair of his, and trying to avoid accidentally doing some hurt to the young lady.

IV

THE old count, whose hunting establishment had always been kept up on a large scale, had now handed it all over to his son's care, but on that day, the 15th September, being in excellent spirits he prepared to join the expedition. Within an hour the whole party was before the porch. When Natasha and Petya said something to Nikolay he walked by them with a stern and serious air, betokening that he had no time to waste on trifles. He looked over everything to do with the hunt, sent a pack of hounds and huntsmen on ahead to cut off the wolf from behind, got on his chestnut Don horse, and whistling to the dogs of his leash, he set off across the threshing-floor to the field leading to the Otradnoe preserve. The old count's horse, a sorrel gelding, with a white mane and tail, called Viflyanka, was led by the count's groom; he was himself to drive straight in a light gig to the spot fixed for him to stand.

Fifty-four hounds were led out under the charge of six whippers-in and grooms. Of huntsmen, properly speaking, there were taking part in the hunt eight men besides the members of the family, and more than forty greyhounds ran behind them, so that with the hounds in leashes there were about a hundred and thirty dogs and twenty persons on horseback.

Every dog knew its master and its call. Every man in the hunt knew his task, his place, and the part assigned him. As soon as they had passed beyond the fence, they all moved without noise or talk, lengthening out along the road and the field to the Otradnoe forest.

The horses stepped over the field as over a soft carpet, splashing now and then into pools as they crossed the road. The foggy sky still seemed falling imperceptibly and regularly down on the earth; the air was still and warm, and there was no sound but now and then the whistle of a huntsman, the snort of a horse, the clack of a whip, or the whine of a dog who had dropped out of his place. When they had gone a verst, five more horsemen accompanied by dogs appeared out of the mist to meet the Rostovs. The foremost of them was a fresh, handsome old man with large, grey moustaches.

'Good day, uncle,' said Nikolay as the old man rode up to him.

'All's well and march! ... I was sure of it,' began the man addressed as uncle. He was not really the Rostov's uncle, but a distant relative, who had a small property in their neighbourhood.

'I was sure you couldn't resist it, and a good thing you have come out. All's well and quick march.' (This was the uncle's favourite saying.) 'You had better attack the preserve at once, for my Girtchik brought me word that the Ilagins are out with their hounds at Korniky; they'll snatch the litter right under your noses.'

'That's where I'm going. Shall we join the packs?' asked Nikolay.

The hounds were joined into one pack, and the uncle and Nikolay rode on side by side.

Natasha, muffled up in a shawl which did not hide her eager face and shining eyes, galloped up to them, accompanied by Petya, who kept beside her, and Mihailo, the huntsman and groom, who had been told to look after her. Petya was laughing and switching and pulling his horse. Natasha sat her raven Arabtchick with grace and confidence and controlled him with an easy and steady hand.

The uncle looked with disapproval at Petya and Natasha. He did not like a mixture of frivolity with the serious business of the hunt.

'Good-day, uncle; we're coming to the hunt too!' shouted Petya.

'Good-day, good-day, and mind you don't ride down the dogs,' said the uncle sternly.

'Nikolenka, what a delightful dog Trunila is! he knew me,' said Natasha of her favourite dog.

'In the first place, Trunila's not a dog, but a wolf-hound,' thought Nikolay. He glanced at his sister trying to make her feel the distance that lay between them at that moment. Natasha understood it.

'Don't imagine we shall get in anybody's way, uncle,' said Natasha. 'We'll stay in our right place and not stir from it.'

'And you'll do well, little countess,' said the uncle. 'Only don't fall off your horse,' he added, 'or you'd never get on again—all's well, quick march!'

The Otradnoe preserve came into sight, an oasis of greenness, two hundred and fifty yards away. Rostov, settling finally with the uncle from what point to set the dogs on, pointed out to Natasha the place where she was to stand, a place where there was no chance of anything running out, and went round to close in from behind above the ravine.

'Now, nephew, you're on the track of an old wolf,' said the uncle; 'mind he doesn't give you the slip.'

'That's as it happens,' answered Rostov. 'Karay, hey!' he shouted, replying to the uncle's warning by this call to his dog. Karay was an old, misshapen, muddy-coloured hound, famous for attacking an old wolf unaided. All took their places.

The old count, who knew his son's ardour in the hunt, hurried to avoid being late, and the whippers-in had hardly reached the place when Count Ilya Andreitch, with a cheerful face, and flushed and quivering cheeks, drove up with his pair of raven horses, over the green field to the place left for him. Straightening his fur coat and putting on his hunting appurtenances, he mounted his sleek, well-fed, quiet, good-humoured Viflyanka, who was turning grey like himself. The horses with the gig were sent back. Count Ilya Andreitch, though he was at heart no sportsman, knew well all the rules of sport. He rode into the edge of the thicket of bushes, behind which he was standing, picked up the reins, settled himself at his ease in the saddle, and, feeling that he was ready, looked about him smiling.

Near him stood his valet, Semyon Tchekmar, a veteran horseman, though now heavy in the saddle. Tchekmar held on a leash three wolf-hounds of a special breed, spirited hounds, though they too had grown fat like their master and his horse. Two other keen old dogs were lying beside them not in a leash. A hundred paces further in the edge of the copse stood another groom of the count's, Mitka, a reckless rider and passionate sportsman. The count had followed the old custom of drinking before hunting a silver goblet of spiced brandy; he had had a slight lunch and after that half a bottle of his favourite bordeaux.

Count Ilya Andreitch was rather flushed from the wine and the drive; his eyes, covered by moisture, were particularly bright, and sitting in the saddle wrapped up in his fur coat, he looked like a baby taken out for a drive.

After seeing after his duties, Tchekmar, with his thin face and sunken cheeks, looked towards his master, with whom he had lived on the best of terms for thirty years. Perceiving that he was in a genial humour, he anticipated a pleasant chat. A third person rode circumspectly—he had no doubt been cautioned—out of the wood, and stood still behind the count. This personage was a grey-bearded old man, wearing a woman's gown and a high, peaked cap. It was the buffoon, Nastasya Ivanovna.

'Well, Nastasya Ivanovna,' whispered the count, winking at him, 'you only scare off the game, and Danilo will give it you.'

'I wasn't born yesterday,' said Nastasya Ivanovna.

'Sh!' hissed the count, and he turned to Semyon. 'Have you seen Natalya Ilyinitchna?' he asked Semyon. 'Where is she?'

'Her honour's with Pyotr Ilyitch, behind the high grass at Zharvry,' answered Semyon, smiling. 'Though she is a lady, she has a great love for the chase.'

'And you wonder at her riding, Semyon, ... eh?' said the count, 'for a man even it wouldn't be amiss!'

'Who wouldn't wonder! So daring, so smart!'

'And where's Nikolasha? Above the Lyadovsky upland, eh?' the count asked, still in a whisper.

'Yes, sir. His honour knows where he had best stand. He knows the ins and outs of hunting, so that Danilo and I are sometimes quite astonished at him,' said Semyon, who knew how to please his master.

'He's a good, clever sportsman, eh? And what do you say to his riding, eh?'

'A perfect picture he is! How he drove the fox out of the Zavarzinsky thicket the other day. He galloped down from the ravine, it was a sight—the horse worth a thousand roubles, and the rider beyond all price. Yes, you would have to look a long while to find his match!'

'To look a long while ...' repeated the count, obviously regretting that Semyon's praises had come to so speedy a termination. 'A long while,' he said, turning back the skirt of his coat and looking for his snuff-box.

'The other day they were coming out from Mass in all their glory, Mihail Sidoritch ...' Semyon stopped short, hearing distinctly in the still air the rush of the hounds, with not more than two or three dogs giving tongue. With his head on one side, he listened, shaking a warning finger at his master. 'They're on the scent of the litter ...' he whispered; 'they have gone straight toward Lyadovsky upland.'

The count, with the smile still lingering on his face, looked straight before him along the path, and did not take a pinch from the snuff-box he held in his hand. The hounds' cry was followed by the bass note of the hunting cry for a wolf sounded on Danilo's horn. The pack joined the first three dogs, and the voices of the hounds could be heard in full cry with the peculiar note which serves to betoken that they are after a wolf. The whippers-in were not now hallooing, but urging on the hounds with cries of 'Loo! loo! loo!' and above all the voices rose the voice of Danilo, passing from a deep note to piercing shrillness. Danilo's voice seemed to fill the whole forest, to pierce beyond it, and echo far away in the open country.

After listening for a few seconds in silence, the count and his groom felt certain that the hounds had divided into two packs: one, the larger, was going off into the distance, in particularly hot cry; the other part of the pack was moving along the forest past the count, and it was with this pack that Danilo's voice was heard urging the dogs on. The sounds from both packs melted into unison and broke apart again, but both were getting further away. Semyon sighed and stooped down to straighten the leash, in which a young dog had caught his leg. The count too sighed, and noticing the snuff-box in his hand, he opened it and took a pinch.

'Back!' cried Semyon to the dog, which had poked out beyond the bushes. The count started, and dropped the snuff-box. Nastasya Ivanovna got off his horse and began picking it up.

The count and Semyon watched him. All of a sudden, as so often happens, the sound of the hunt was in an instant close at hand, as though the baying dogs and Danilo's cries were just upon them.

The count looked round, and on the right he saw Mitka, who was staring at the count with eyes starting out of his head. Lifting his cap, he pointed in front to the other side.

'Look out!' he shouted in a voice that showed the words had long been fretting him to be uttered. And letting go the dogs, he galloped towards the count.

The count and Semyon galloped out of the bushes, and on their left they saw a wolf. With a soft, rolling gait it moved at a slow amble further to their left into the very thicket in which they had been standing. The angry dogs whined, and pulling themselves free from the leash, flew by the horses' hoofs after the wolf.

The wolf paused in his flight; awkwardly, like a man with a quinsy, he turned his heavy-browed head towards the dogs, and still with the same soft, rolling gait gave one bound and a second, and, waving its tail, disappeared into the bushes. At the same instant, with a cry like a wail, there sprang desperately out of the thicket opposite one hound, then a second and a third, and all the pack flew across the open ground towards the very spot where the wolf had vanished. The bushes were parted behind the dogs, and Danilo's brown horse, dark with sweat, emerged from them. On its long back Danilo sat perched up and swaying forward. He had no cap on his grey hair, that fluttered in disorder above his red, perspiring face.

'Loo! loo! loo! . . .' he was shouting. When he caught sight of the count, there was a flash like lightning in his eyes.

'B——!' he shouted, using a brutally coarse term of abuse, and menacing the count with his lifted whip. 'Let the wolf slip! . . . sportsmen indeed!' And as though scorning to waste more words on the confused and frightened count, he lashed the moist and heavy sides of his brown gelding with all the fury that had been ready for the count, and flew off after the dogs. The count stood like a man who has been thrashed, looking about him and trying to smile and call for Semyon to sympathise with his plight. But Semyon was not there; he had galloped round to cut the wolf off from the forest. The greyhounds, too, were running to and fro on both sides. But the wolf got off into the bushes, and not one of the party succeeded in coming across him.

V

NIKOLAY ROSTOV was standing meanwhile at his post, waiting for the wolf. He was aware of what must be taking place within the copse from the rush of the pack coming closer and going further away, from the cries of the dogs, whose notes were familiar to him, from the nearness, and then greater remoteness, and sudden raising of the voices of the huntsmen. He knew that there were both young and also old wolves in the enclosure. He knew the hounds had divided into two packs, that in one place they were close on the wolf, and that something had gone wrong. Ever second he expected the wolf on his side. He made a thousand different suppositions of how and at what spot the wolf would run out, and how he would set upon it. Hope was succeeded by despair. Several times he prayed to God that the wolf would rush out upon him. He prayed with that feeling of passion and compunction with which men pray in moments of intense emotion due to trivial causes. 'Why, what is it to Thee,' he said to God, 'to do this for me? I know Thou art great and that it's a sin to pray to Thee about this, but for God's sake do make the old wolf come out upon me, and make Karay fix his teeth in his throat and finish him before the eyes of "uncle," who is looking this way.' A thousand times over in that half-hour, with intent, strained, and uneasy eyes Rostov scanned the thickets at the edge of the copse, with two scraggy oaks standing up above the undergrowth of aspen, and the ravine with its overhanging bank, and 'uncle's' cap peeping out from behind a bush on the right. 'No, that happiness is not to be,' thought Rostov, 'yet what would it cost Him! It's not to be! I'm always unlucky, at cards, in war, and everything.' Austerlitz and Dolohov flashed in distinct but rapid succession through his imagination. 'Only once in my life to kill an old wolf; I ask for nothing beyond!' he thought, straining eyes and ears, looking from left to right, and back again, and listening to the slightest fluctuations in the sounds of the dogs. He looked again to the right, and saw something running across the open ground towards him. 'No, it can't be!' thought

Rostov, taking a deep breath, as a man does at the coming of what he has long been hoping for. The greatest piece of luck had come to him, and so simply, without noise, or flourish, or display to signalise it. Rostov could not believe his eyes, and this uncertainty lasted more than a second. The wolf was running forward; he leaped clumsily over a rut that lay across his path.

It was an old wolf with a grey back and full, reddish belly. He was running without haste, plainly feeling secure of being unseen. Rostov held his breath and looked round at the dogs. They were lying and standing about, not seeing the wolf and quite unaware of him. Old Karay had his head turned round, and was angrily searching for a flea, snapping his yellow teeth on his haunches. 'Loo! loo! loo!' Rostov whispered, pouting out his lips. The dogs leaped up, jingling the iron rings of the leashes, and pricked up their ears. Karay scratched his hind-leg and got up, pricking up his ears and wagging his tail, on which there were hanging matted locks of his coat.

'Loose them? or not loose them?' Nikolay said to himself as the wolf moved away from the copse towards him. All at once the whole physiognomy of the wolf was transformed. He started, seeing—probably for the first time—human eyes fixed upon him; and, turning his head a little towards Rostov, stood still, in doubt whether to go back or forward. 'Ay! Never mind, forward! . . .' the wolf seemed to be saying to himself, and he pushed on ahead, without looking round, softly and not rapidly, with an easy but resolute movement. 'Loo! loo! . . .' Nikolay cried in a voice not his own, and of its own accord his gallant horse galloped at break-neck pace downhill, and leaped over the watercourse to cut off the wolf's retreat; the hounds dashed on even more swiftly, overtaking it.

Nikolay did not hear his own cry; he had no consciousness of galloping; he saw neither the dogs nor the ground over which he galloped. He saw nothing but the wolf, which, quickening its pace, was bounding in the same direction across the glade. Foremost of the hounds was the black and tan, broad-backed bitch, Milka, and she was getting close upon him. But the wolf turned a sidelong glance upon her, and instead of flying at him, as she always had done, Milka suddenly stopped short, her fore-legs held stiffly before her and her tail in the air.

'Loo! loo! loo!' shouted Nikolay.

The red hound, Lyubima, darted forward from behind Milka, dashed headlong at the wolf, and got hold of him by the hind leg, but in the same second bounded away on the other side in terror. The wolf crouched, gnashed its teeth, rose again, and bounded forward, followed at a couple of yards' distance by all the dogs: they did not try to get closer.

'He'll get away! No, it's impossible!' thought Nikolay, still shouting in a husky voice.

'Karay! Loo! loo! . . .' he kept shouting, looking for the old hound, who was his one hope now.

Karay, straining his old muscles to the utmost, and watching the wolf intently, was bounding clumsily away from the beast, to cut across his path in front of him. But it was plain from the swiftness of the wolf's course and the slowness of the hounds that Karay was out in his reckoning. Nikolay saw the copse not far now ahead of him. If once the wolf reached it, he would escape to a certainty. But in front dogs and men came into sight, dashing almost straight towards the wolf. There was still hope. A long, young hound, not one of the Rostovs'—Nikolay did not recognise him—flew from in front straight at the wolf, and almost knocked him over. The wolf got up again with a surprising rapidity and flew at the young hound; his teeth clacked, and the hound, covered with blood from a gash in his side, thrust its head in the earth, squealing shrilly.

'Karay! old man!' Nikolay wailed.

The old dog, with the tufts of matted hair, quivering on his haunches, had succeeded, thanks to the delay, in cutting across the wolf's line of advance, and was now five paces in front of him. The wolf stole a glance at Karay, as though aware of his danger, and tucking his tail further between his legs, he quickened his pace. But then—Nikolay could only see that something was happening with Karay—the hound had dashed instantly at the wolf and had rolled in a struggling heap with him into the watercourse before them.

The moment when Nikolay saw the dogs struggling with the wolf in the watercourse, saw the wolf's grey coat under them, his outstretched hind-leg, his head gasping in terror, and his ears turned back (Karay had him by the throat)—the moment when Nikolay saw all this was the happiest moment of his life. He had already grasped the pommel of his saddle to dismount and stab the wolf, when suddenly the beast's head was thrust up above the mass of dogs, then his fore-legs were on the bank of the watercourse. The wolf clacked his teeth (Karay had not hold of his throat now), leaped with his hind-legs out of the hollow, and with his tail between his legs, pushed forward, getting away from the dogs again. Karay, his hair starting up, had difficulty in getting out of the watercourse; he seemed to be bruised or wounded.

'My God, why is this!' Nikolay shouted in despair. The uncle's huntsman galloped across the line of the wolf's advance from the other side, and again his hounds stopped the wolf, again he was hemmed in.

Nikolay, his groom, the uncle, and his huntsman pranced about the beast with shouts and cries of 'loo,' every minute on the point of dismounting when the wolf crouched back, and dashing forward again every time the wolf shook himself free and moved towards the copse, where his safety lay.

At the beginning of this onset Danilo, hearing the hunters' cries, had darted out of the copse. He saw that Karay had hold of the wolf and checked his horse, supposing the deed was done. But seeing that the hunters did not dismount from their horses, and that the wolf was shaking himself free, and again making his escape, Danilo galloped his own horse, not towards the wolf, but in a straight line towards the copse, to cut him off, as Karay had done. Thanks to this manœuvre, he bore straight down on the wolf when the uncle's dogs had a second time fallen behind him.

Danilo galloped up in silence, holding a drawn dagger in his left hand, and thrashing the heaving sides of his chestnut horse with his riding whip, as though it were a flail.

Nikolay neither saw nor heard Danilo till his panting chestnut darted close by him, and he heard the sound of a falling body and saw Danilo lying in the midst of the dogs on the wolf's back, trying to get him by the ears. It was obvious to the dogs, to the hunters, and to the wolf that all was over now. The beast, its ears drawn back in terror, tried to get up, but the dogs clung to him. Danilo, as he got up, stumbled, and as though sinking down to rest, rolled with all his weight on the wolf, and snatched him by the ears. Nikolay would have stabbed him, but Danilo whispered: 'Don't; we will string him up!' and shifting his position he put his foot on the wolf's neck. They put a stick in the wolf's jaws, fastened it, as it were bridling him with a leash, and tied his legs. Danilo swung the wolf twice from side to side. With happy, exhausted faces they tied the great wolf alive on a horse, that started and snorted in alarm at it; and with all the dogs trooping after and whining at the wolf, they brought it to the place where all were to meet. The wolf hounds had captured two cubs, and the greyhounds three. The party met together to show their booty and tell their stories, and every one went to look at the big old wolf, which with its heavy-browed head hanging downwards and the stick in its teeth, gazed with its great, glassy eyes at the crowd of dogs and men around it. When they touched him, his fastened legs quivered and he looked wildly and yet simply at all of them. Count Ilya Andreitch too went up and touched the wolf.

'Oh, what a great beast!' he said. 'He's an old one, eh?' he asked Danilo, who was standing near him.

'That he is, your excellency,' answered Danilo, hurriedly taking off his cap.

The count remembered the wolf he had let slip and Danilo's outburst. 'You have a hot temper though, my man,' said the count.

Danilo said nothing, but he shyly smiled a smile of childlike sweetness and amiability.

VI

THE old count went home. Natasha and Petya promised to follow immediately. The hunting party went on further as it was still early. In the middle of the day they set the hounds into a ravine covered with thickly growing young copse. Nikolay, standing on the stubble land above, could see all his party.

Facing Nikolay on the opposite side was a field of green corn, and there stood his huntsman, alone in a hollow behind a nut bush. As soon as they loosed the hounds, Nikolay heard a hound he knew—Voltorn—give tongue at intervals; other hounds joined him, pausing now and then, and taking up the cry again. A moment later he heard from the ravine the cry that they were on the scent of a fox, and all the pack joining together made for the opening towards the green corn away from Nikolay.

He saw the whippers-in in their red caps galloping along the edge of the overgrown ravine; he could see the dogs even, and was every instant expecting the fox to come into sight on the farther side among the green corn.

The huntsman standing in the hollow started off and let his dogs go, and Nikolay saw the red, uncouth-looking fox hurrying along close to the ground, with its bushy tail, through the green corn. The dogs bore down on it. And now they were getting close, and now the fox was beginning to wind in circles between them, making the circles more and more rapidly, and sweeping its bushy brush around it, when all of a sudden a strange white dog flew down upon it, and was followed by a black one, and everything was confusion, and the dogs formed a star-shaped figure round it, scarcely moving, with their heads together, and their tails out. Two huntsmen galloped down to the dogs; one in a red cap, the other, a stranger, in a green coat.

'What's the meaning of it?' wondered Nikolay. 'Where did that huntsman spring from? That's not uncle's man.'

The huntsmen got the fox, and remained a long while standing on foot there, without hanging the fox on the saddle.

He could see the horses with their snaffles jutting up standing close by the huntsmen, and the dogs lying down. The huntsmen were waving their arms and doing something with the fox. A horn was sounded—the signal agreed upon in case of a dispute.

'That's Ilagin's huntsman getting up a row of some sort with our Ivan,' said Nikolay's groom.

Nikolay sent the groom to call his sister and Petya to come to him, and rode at a walking pace towards the spot where the whippers-in were getting the hounds together. Several of the party galloped to the scene of the squabble.

Nikolay dismounted, and, with Natasha and Petya, who had ridden up, he stood by the hounds waiting to hear how the difficulty was settled. The huntsman who had been quarrelling came riding out of the bushes with the fox on the crupper, and rode towards his young master. He took off his cap a long way off, and tried as he came up to speak respectfully. But he was pale and gasping for breath, and his face was wrathful. One of his eyes was blackened, but he was probably not aware of it.

'What was the matter over there?' asked Nikolay.

'Why, he was going to kill the fox right under our hounds' noses! And my bitch it was—the mouse-coloured one—that had got hold of it. You can go and have me up for it! Snatching hold of the fox! I gave him one with the fox. Here it is on my saddle. Is it a taste of this you want?' said the huntsman, pointing to his hunting-knife and apparently imagining that he was still talking to his enemy.

Nikolay did not waste words on the man, but asking his sister and Petya to wait for him, rode over to where the hounds and the men of the enemy, Ilagin, were gathered together.

The victorious huntsman rode off to join his fellows, and there, the centre of a sympathetic and inquisitive crowd, he recounted his exploit.

The point was that Ilagin, with whom the Rostovs had some quarrel and were engaged in a lawsuit, was hunting over places that by old custom belonged to the Rostovs, and now, as though of design, had sent his men to the ravine where the Rostovs were, and had allowed his man to snatch a fox under a stranger's dogs.

Nikolay had never seen Ilagin, but he had heard of the quarrelsomeness and obstinacy of their neighbour; and rushing, as he always did, to an extreme in his judgments and feelings, he cordially detested him, and looked upon him as his bitterest foe. Excited and angry, he rode up to him now, grasping his whip in his hand, fully prepared to take the most energetic and desperate measures in dealing with the enemy.

He had scarcely ridden beyond the ridge of the copse when he saw a stout gentleman in a beaver cap riding towards him on a handsome raven horse, accompanied by two grooms.

Instead of an enemy Nikolay found in Ilagin a courteous gentleman of imposing appearance, who was particularly anxious to make the young count's acquaintance. Ilagin took off his beaver cap as he approached Rostov, and said that he greatly regretted what had occurred, that he would have the man punished, that he begged the count to let them be better acquainted, and offered him the use of his preserves for hunting.

Natasha had ridden up not far behind her brother, in some excitement, fearing he might do something awful. Seeing that the opponents were exchanging affable greetings, she rode up to them. Ilagin lifted his beaver cap higher than ever to Natasha, and, smiling agreeably, said that the countess was indeed a Diana both in her passion for the chase and her beauty, of which he had heard so much.

Ilagin, to efface the impression of his huntsman's crime, insisted on Rostov coming to his upland a verst away, which he preserved for his own shooting, and described as teeming with hares. Nikolay agreed, and the whole party, its numbers now doubled, moved on. They had to ride through the fields to get there. The huntsmen moved in line, and the gentry rode together. The uncle, Rostov, and Ilagin glanced stealthily at each other's dogs, trying not to be observed by the others, and looking uneasily for rivals likely to excel their own dogs.

Rostov was particularly struck by the beauty of a small thoroughbred, slender, black and tan bitch of Ilagin's, with muscles like steel, a delicate nose, and prominent black eyes. He had heard of the sporting qualities of Ilagin's dogs, and in that handsome bitch he saw a rival of his Milka's.

In the middle of a sedate conversation about the crops of the year, started by Ilagin, Nikolay pointed out the black and tan bitch.

'You have a fine bitch there!' he said, in a careless tone. 'Is she clever?'

'That one? Yes, she's a good beast—she can catch a hare,' Ilagin said indifferently of his black and tan Yerza, a bitch for whom he had a year before given a neighbour three families of house-serfs. 'So they don't brag of their thrashing, count,' he went on, taking up their previous conversation. And feeling it only polite to repay the young count's compliment, Ilagin scanned his dogs, and pitched on Milka, whose broad back caught his eye.

'That's a good black and tan you have there—a fine one!' he said.

'Yes, she's all right, she can run,' answered Nikolay. 'Oh, if only a good big hare would run into the field, I would show you what she's like!' he thought, and turning to his groom, he said he would give a rouble to any one who would unearth a hare.

'I can't understand,' Ilagin went on, 'how it is other sportsmen are so envious over game and dogs. I will tell you for myself, count. I enjoy hunting, as you know; the chase in such company . . . what could be more delightful' (he doffed his beaver cap again to Natasha); 'but this reckoning up of the skins one has carried off—I don't care about that.'

'Oh no!'

'Nor could I be chagrined at my dog's being outdone by another man's—all I care about is the chase itself, eh, count? And so I consider . . .'

'Oh, . . . ho . . . ho,' sounded at that moment in a prolonged call from one of the grooms. He was standing on a knoll in the stubble with his whip held up, and he called once more, 'O . . . ho . . . aho!' (This call, and the lifted whip, meant that he saw a hare squatting before him.)

'Ah, he has started a hare, I fancy,' said Ilagin carelessly. 'Well, let us course it, count!'

'Yes, we must . . . but what do you say, together?' answered Nikolay, looking intently at Yerza and the uncle's red Rugay, the two rivals against whom he had never before had a chance of pitting his dogs. 'What if they outdo my Milka from the first?' he thought, riding by the uncle and Ilagin towards the hare.

'Is it full-grown?' asked Ilagin, going up to the groom who had started it, and looking about him with some excitement, as he whistled to his Yerza. . . . 'And you, Mihail Nikanoritch?' he said to the uncle.

The uncle rode on, looking sullen.

'What's the use of my competing with you? Why, your dogs—you have paid a village for each of them; they're worth thousands. You try yours against each other, and I'll look on!'

'Rugay! Hey, hey,' he shouted. 'Rugayushka!' he added, involuntarily expressing his tenderness, and the hope he put in the red dog by this affectionate diminutive. Natasha saw and felt the emotion concealed by the two elderly men and by her brother, and was herself excited by it. The groom on the knoll was standing with his whip lifted; the gentlemen rode up to him at a walking pace; the pack were on the rim of the horizon, moving away from the hare; the rest of the hunting party too were riding away. Everything was done slowly and deliberately.

'Which way is its head?' asked Nikolay, after riding a hundred paces towards the groom. But before the groom had time to answer, the hare, who had been sniffing in the ground the frost coming next morning, leapt up from its squatting posture. The pack of hounds on leashes flew baying downhill after the hare; the harriers, who were not on leash, rushed from all sides towards the hounds or after the hare. The whippers-in, who had been moving so deliberately, galloped over the country getting the dogs together, with shouts of 'stop!' while the huntsmen directed their course with shouts of 'o ... o ... ahoy!' Nikolay, Natasha, and the uncle and Ilagin, who had been hitherto so composed, flew ahead, reckless of how or where they went, seeing nothing but the dogs and the hare, and afraid of nothing but losing sight for an instant of the course. The hare turned out to be a fleet and strong one. When he jumped up he did not at once race off, but cocked up his ears, listening to the shouts and tramp of hoofs that came from all sides at once. He took a dozen bounds not very swiftly, letting the dogs gain on him, but at last choosing his direction, and grasping his danger, he put his ears back, and dashed off at full speed. He had been crouching in the stubble, but the green field was in front of him, and there it was marshy ground. The two dogs of the groom who had started him were the nearest and the first to be on the scent after him. But they had not got near him, when Ilagin's black and tan Yerza flew ahead of them, got within a yard, pounced on him with fearful swiftness, aiming at the hare's tail, and rolled over, thinking she had hold of him. The hare arched his back, and bounded off more nimbly than ever. The broad-backed, black and tan Milka flew ahead of Yerza, and began rapidly gaining on the hare.

'Milashka! little mother!' Nikolay shouted triumphantly. Milka seemed on the point of pouncing on the hare, but she overtook him and flew beyond. The hare doubled back. Again the graceful Yerza dashed at him, and kept close to the hare's tail, as though measuring the distance, so as not to miss getting hold of the hare, by the haunch this time.

'Yerzinka, little sister!' wailed Ilagin, in a voice unlike his own. Yerza did not heed his appeals. At the very moment when she seemed about to seize the hare, he doubled and darted away to the ditch between the stubble and the green field. Again Yerza and Milka, running side by side, like a pair of horses, flew after the hare; the hare was better off in the ditch, the dogs could not gain on him so quickly.

'Rugay! Rugayushka! Forward—quick march,' another voice shouted this time. And Rugay, the uncle's red, broad-shouldered dog, stretching out and curving his back, caught up the two foremost dogs, pushed ahead of them, flung himself with complete self-abandonment right on the hare, turned him out of the ditch into the green field, flung himself still more viciously on him once more, sinking up to his knees in the swampy ground, and all that could be seen was the dog rolling over with the hare, covering his back with mud. The dogs formed a star-shaped figure round him. A moment later all the party pulled their horses up round the crowding dogs. The uncle alone dismounted in a rapture of delight, and cutting off the feet, shaking the hare for the blood to drip off, he looked about him, his eyes restless with excitement, and his hands and legs moving nervously. He went on talking, regardless of what or to whom he spoke. 'That's something like, quick march ... there's a dog for you ... he outstripped them all ... if they cost a thousand or they cost a rouble ... forward, quick march, and no mistake!' he kept saying, panting and looking wrathfully about him, as though he were abusing some one, as though they had all been his enemies, had insulted him, and he had only now at last succeeded in paying them out. 'So much for your thousand rouble dogs—forward, quick march! Rugay, here's the foot,' he said, dropping the dog the hare's muddy foot, which he had just cut off; 'you've deserved it—forward, quick march!'

'She wore herself out—ran it down three times all alone,' Nikolay was saying, listening to no one, and heedless whether he were heard or not.

'To be sure, cutting in sideways like that!' Ilagin's groom was saying.

'Why, when it had been missed like that, and once down, any yard-dog could catch it of course,' said Ilagin, at the same moment, red and breathless from the gallop and the excitement. At the same time Natasha, without taking breath, gave vent to her delight and excitement in a shriek so shrill that it set every one's ears tingling. In that shriek she expressed just what the others were expressing by talking all at once. And her shriek was so strange that she must have been ashamed of that wild scream, and the others must have been surprised at it at any other time. The uncle himself twisted up the hare, flung him neatly and smartly across his horse's back, seeming to reproach them all by this gesture, and with an air of not caring to speak to any one, he mounted his bay and rode away. All but he, dispirited and disappointed, rode on, and it was some time before they could recover their previous affectation of indifference. For a long time after they stared at the red dog, Rugay, who with his round back spattered with mud, and clinking the rings of his leash, walked with the serene air of a conqueror behind the uncle's horse.

'I'm like all the rest till it's a question of coursing a hare; but then you had better look out!' was what Nikolay fancied the dog's air expressed.

When the uncle rode up to Nikolay a good deal later, and addressed a remark to him, he felt flattered at the uncle's deigning to speak to him after what had happened.

VII

WHEN Ilagin took leave of them in the evening, Nikolay found himself so great a distance from home that he accepted the uncle's invitation to stop hunting and to stay the night at the uncle's little place, Mihailovka.

'And if you all come to me—forward, quick march!' said the uncle, 'it would be even better; you see, the weather's damp, you could rest, and the little countess could be driven back in a trap.' The invitation was accepted; a huntsman was sent to Otradnoe for a trap, and Nikolay, Natasha, and Petya rode to the uncle's house.

Five men servants—little and big—ran out on to the front steps to meet their master. Dozens of women, old and big and little, popped out at the back entrance to have a look at the huntsmen as they arrived. The presence of Natasha—a woman, a lady, on horseback—excited the curiosity of the uncle's house-serfs to such a pitch that many of them went up to her, stared her in the face, and, unrestrained by her presence, made remarks about her, as though she were some prodigy on show, not a human being, and not capable of hearing and understanding what was said about her.

'Arinka, look-ée, she sits sideways! Sits on so, while her skirt flies about.... And look at the little horn!'

'Sakes alive! and the knife too....'

'A regular Tatar woman!'

'How do you manage not to tumble off?' said the forwardest of them, addressing Natasha boldly.

The uncle got off his horse at the steps of his little wooden house, which was shut in by an overgrown garden. Looking from one to another of his household, he shouted peremptorily to those who were not wanted to retire, and for the others to do all that was needed for the reception of his guests.

They all ran off in different directions. The uncle helped Natasha to dismount, and gave her his arm up the shaky, plank steps.

Inside, the house, with boarded, unplastered walls, was not very clean; there was nothing to show that the chief aim of the persons living in it was the removal of every spot, yet there were not signs of neglect. There was a smell of fresh apples in the entry, and the walls were hung with foxskins and wolfskins.

The uncle led his guests through the vestibule into a little hall with a folding-table and red chairs, then into a drawing-room with a round birchwood table and a sofa, and then into his study, with a ragged sofa, a threadbare carpet, and portraits of Suvorov, of his father and mother, and of himself in military uniform. The study smelt strongly of tobacco and dogs. In the study the uncle asked his guests to sit down and make themselves at home, and he left them. Rugay came in, his back still covered with mud, and lay on the sofa, cleaning himself with his tongue and his teeth. There was a corridor leading from the study, and in it they could see a screen with ragged curtains. Behind the screen they heard feminine laughter and whispering. Natasha, Nikolay, and Petya took off their wraps and sat down on the sofa. Petya leaned on his arm and fell asleep at once; Natasha and Nikolay sat without speaking. Their faces were burning; they were very hungry and very cheerful. They looked at one another—now that the hunt was over and they were indoors, Nikolay did not feel called upon to show his masculine superiority over his sister. Natasha winked at her brother; and they could neither of them restrain themselves long, and broke into a ringing laugh before they had time to invent a pretext for their mirth.

After a brief interval, the uncle came in wearing a Cossack coat, blue breeches, and little top-boots. And this very costume, at which Natasha had looked with surprise and amusement when the uncle wore it at Otradnoe, seemed to her now the right costume here, and in no way inferior to frockcoats or ordinary jackets. The uncle, too, was in good spirits; far from feeling mortified at the laughter of the brother and sister (he was incapable of imagining that they could be laughing at his mode of life), he joined in their causeless mirth himself.

'Well, this young countess here—forward, quick march!—I have never seen her like!' he said, giving a long pipe to Rostov, while with a practised motion of three fingers he filled another—a short broken one—for himself.

'She's been in the saddle all day—something for a man to boast of —and she's just as fresh as if nothing had happened!'

Soon the door was opened obviously, from the sound, by a barefoot servant-girl, and a stout, red-cheeked, handsome woman of about forty, with a double chin and full red lips, walked in, with a big tray in her hands. With hospitable dignity and cordiality in her eyes and in every gesture, she looked round at the guests, and with a genial smile bowed to them respectfully.

In spite of her exceptional stoutness, which made her hold her head flung back, while her bosom and all her portly person was thrust forward, this woman (the uncle's housekeeper) stepped with extreme lightness. She went to the table, put the tray down, and deftly with her plump, white hands set the bottles and dishes on the table. When she had finished this task she went away, standing for a moment in the doorway with a smile on her face. 'Here I am—I am *she*! Now do you understand the uncle?' her appearance had said to Rostov. Who could fail to understand? Not Nikolay only, but even Natasha understood the uncle now and the significance of his knitted brows, and the happy, complacent smile, which puckered his lips as Anisya Fyodorovna came in. On the tray there were liqueurs, herb-brandy, mushrooms, biscuits of rye flour made with buttermilk, honey in the comb, foaming mead made from honey, apples, nuts raw and nuts baked, and nuts preserved in honey. Then Anisya Fyodorovna brought in preserves made with honey and with sugar, and ham and a chicken that had just been roasted.

All these delicacies were of Anisya Fyodorovna's preparing, cooking or preserving. All seemed to smell and taste, as it were, of Anisya Fyodorovna. All seemed to recall her buxomness, cleanliness, whiteness, and cordial smile.

'A little of this, please, little countess,' she kept saying, as she handed Natasha first one thing, then another. Natasha ate of everything, and it seemed to her that such buttermilk biscuits, such delicious preserves, such nuts in honey, such a chicken, she had never seen nor tasted anywhere. Anisya Fyodorovna withdrew. Rostov and the uncle, as they sipped cherry brandy after supper, talked of hunts past and to come, of Rugay, and Ilagin's dogs. Natasha sat upright on the sofa, listening with sparkling eyes. She tried several times to waken Petya, and make him eat something, but he made incoherent replies, evidently in his sleep. Natasha felt so gay, so well content in these new surroundings, that her only fear was that the trap would come too soon for her. After a silence had chanced to fall upon them, as almost always happens when any one receives friends for the first time in his own house, the uncle said, in response to the thought in his guests' minds:

'Yes, so you see how I am finishing my days.... One dies—forward, quick march!—nothing is left. So why sin!'

The uncle's face was full of significance and even beauty as he said this. Rostov could not help recalling as he spoke all the good things he had heard said by his father and the neighbours about him. Through the whole district the uncle had the reputation of being a most generous and disinterested eccentric. He was asked to abitrate in family quarrels; he was chosen executor; secrets were entrusted to him; he was elected a justice, and asked to fill other similar posts; but he had always persisted in refusing all public appointments, spending the autumn and spring in the fields on his bay horse, the winter sitting at home, and the summer lying in his overgrown garden.

'Why don't you enter the service, uncle?'

'I have been in the service, but I flung it up. I'm not fit for it. I can't make anything of it. That's your affair. I haven't the wit for it. The chase, now, is a very different matter; there it's all forward and quick march! Open the door there!' he shouted. 'Why have you shut it?' A door at the end of the corridor (which word the uncle always pronounced *collidor*, like a peasant) led to the huntsmen's room, as the sitting-room for the huntsmen was called. There was a rapid patter of bare feet, and an unseen hand opened the door into the huntsmen's room. They could then hear distinctly from the corridor the sounds of the balalaika, unmistakably played by a masterhand. Natasha had been for some time listening, and now she went out into the corridor to hear the music more clearly.

'That's Mitka, my coachman . . . I bought him a good balalaika; I'm fond of it,' said the uncle. It was his custom to get Mitka to play the balalaika in the men's room when he came home from the chase. He was fond of hearing that instrument.

'How well he plays! It's really very nice,' said Nikolay, with a certain unconscious superciliousness in his tone, as though he were ashamed to admit he liked this music.

'Very nice?' Natasha said reproachfully, feeling the tone in which her brother had spoken. 'It's not nice, but splendid, really!' Just as the uncle's mushrooms and honey and liqueurs had seemed to her the most delicious in the world, this playing struck her at that moment as the very acme of musical expression.

'More, more, please,' said Natasha in the doorway, as soon as the balalaika ceased. Mitka tuned up and began again gallantly twanging away at 'My Lady,' with shakes and flourishes. The uncle sat listening with his head on one side, and a slight smile. The air of 'My Lady' was repeated a hundred times over. Several times the balalaika was tuned up and the same notes were thrummed again, but the audience did not weary of it, and still longed to hear it again and again. Anisya Fyodorovna came in and stood with her portly person leaning against the doorpost.

'You are pleased to listen!' she said to Natasha, with a smile extraordinarily like the uncle's smile. 'He does play nicely,' she said.

'That part he never plays right,' the uncle said suddenly with a vigorous gesture. 'It ought to be taken more at a run—forward, quick march! . . . to be played lightly.'

'Why, can you do it?' asked Natasha.

The uncle smiled, and did not answer.

'Just you look, Anisyushka, whether the strings are all right on the guitar, eh? It's a long while since I have handled it. I had quite given it up!'

Anisya Fyodorovna went very readily with her light step to do her master's bidding, and brought him his guitar. Without looking at any one the uncle blew the dust off it, tapped on the case with his bony fingers, tuned it, and settled himself in a low chair. Arching his left elbow with a rather theatrical gesture, he held the guitar above the finger-board, and winking at Anisya Fyodorovna, he played, not the first notes of 'My Lady,' but a single pure musical chord, and then smoothly, quietly, but confidently began playing in very slow time the well-known song, 'As along the high road.' The air of the song thrilled in Nikolay's and Natasha's hearts in time, in tune with it, with the same sober gaiety—the same gaiety as was manifest in the whole personality of Anisya Fyodorovna. Anisya Fyodorovna flushed, and hiding her face in her kerchief, went laughing out of the room. The uncle still went on playing the song carefully, correctly, and vigorously, gazing with a transformed, inspired face at the spot where Anisya Fyodorovna had stood. Laughter came gradually into his face on one side under his grey moustache, and it grew stronger as the song went on, as the time quickened, and breaks came after a flourish.

'Splendid, splendid, uncle! Again, again!' cried Natasha, as soon as he had finished. She jumped up from her place and kissed and hugged the uncle. 'Nikolenka, Nikolenka!' she said, looking round at her brother as though to ask, 'What do you say to it?'

Nikolay, too, was much pleased by the uncle's playing. He played the song a second time. The smiling face of Anisya Fyodorovna appeared again in the doorway and other faces behind her.... 'For the water from the well, a maiden calls to him to stay!' played the uncle. He made another dexterous flourish and broke off, twitching his shoulders.

'Oh, oh, uncle darling!' wailed Natasha, in a voice as imploring as though her life depended on it. The uncle got up, and there seemed to be two men in him at that moment—one smiled seriously at the antics of the merry player, while the merry player naïvely and carefully executed the steps preliminary to the dance.

'Come, little niece!' cried the uncle, waving to Natasha the hand that had struck the last chord.

Natasha flung off the shawl that had been wrapped round her, ran forward facing the uncle, and setting her arms akimbo, made the movements of her shoulder and waist.

Where, how, when had this young countess, educated by a French émigrée, sucked in with the Russian air she breathed the spirit of that dance? Where had she picked up these movements which the *pas de châle* would, one might have thought, long ago have eradicated? But the spirit, the motions were those inimitable, unteachable, Russian gestures the uncle had hoped for from her. As soon as she stood up, and smiled that triumphant, proud smile of sly gaiety, the dread that had come on Nikolay and all the spectators at the first moment, the dread that she would not dance it well, was at an end and they were already admiring her.

She danced the dance well, so well indeed, so perfectly, that Anisya Fyodorovna, who handed her at once the kerchief she needed in the dance, had tears in her eyes, though she laughed as she watched that slender, graceful little countess, reared in silk and velvet, belonging to another world than hers, who was yet able to understand all that was in Anisya and her father and her mother and her aunt and every Russian soul.

'Well done, little countess—forward, quick march!' cried the uncle, laughing gleefully as he finished the dance. 'Ah, that's a niece to be proud of! She only wants a fine fellow picked out now for her husband, —and then, forward, quick march!'

'One has been picked out already,' said Nikolay, smiling.

'Oh!' said the uncle in surprise, looking inquiringly at Natasha. Natasha nodded her head with a happy smile.

'And such an one!' she said. But as soon as she said it a different, new series of ideas and feelings rose up within her. 'What was the meaning of Nikolay's smile when he said: "One has been picked out already?" Was he glad of it, or not glad? He seemed to think my Bolkonsky would not approve, would not understand our gaiety now. No, he would quite understand it. Where is he now?' Natasha wondered, and her face became serious at once. But that lasted only one second. 'I mustn't think, I mustn't dare to think about that,' she said to herself; and smiling, she sat down again near the uncle, begging him to play them something more.

The uncle played another song and waltz. Then, after a pause, he cleared his throat and began to sing his favourite hunting song:

> 'When there falls at evening glow
> The first flakes of winter snow.' . . .

The uncle sang, as peasants sing, in full and naïve conviction that in a song the whole value rests in the words, that the tune comes of itself, and that a tune apart is nothing, that the tune is only for the sake of the verse. And this gave the uncle's unselfconscious singing a peculiar charm, like the song of birds. Natasha was in ecstasies over the uncle's singing. She made up her mind not to learn the harp any longer, but to play only on the guitar. She asked the uncle for the guitar and at once struck the chords of the song.

At ten o'clock there arrived the wagonette, a trap, and three men on horseback, who had been sent to look for Natasha and Petya. The count and countess did not know where they were and were very anxious, said one of the men.

Petya was carried out and laid in the wagonette as though he had been a corpse. Natasha and Nikolay got into the trap. The uncle wrapped Natasha up, and said good-bye to her with quite a new tenderness. He accompanied them on foot as far as the ridge which they had to ride round, fording the stream, and bade his huntsmen ride in front with lanterns.

'Farewell, dear little niece!' they heard called in the darkness by his voice, not the one Natasha had been familiar with before, but the voice that had sung 'When fall at evening glow.'

There were red lights in the village they drove through and a cheerful smell of smoke.

'What a darling that uncle is!' said Natasha as they drove out into the highroad.

'Yes,' said Nikolay. 'You're not cold?'

'No, I'm very comfortable; very. I am so happy,' said Natasha, positively perplexed at her own wellbeing. They were silent for a long while.

The night was dark and damp. They could not see the horses, but could only hear them splashing through the unseen mud.

What was passing in that childlike, responsive soul, that so eagerly caught and made its own all the varied impressions of life? How were they all stored away in her heart? But she was very happy. They were getting near home when she suddenly hummed the air of 'When falls at evening glow,' which she had been trying to get all the way, and had only just succeeded in catching.

'Have you caught it?' said Nikolay.

'What are you thinking of just now, Nikolay?' asked Natasha. They were fond of asking each other that question.

'I?' said Nikolay, trying to recall. 'Well, you see, at first I was thinking that Rugay, the red dog, is like the uncle, and that if he were a man he would keep uncle always in the house with him, if not for racing, for music he'd keep him anyway. How jolly uncle is! Isn't he? Well, and you?'

'I? Wait a minute; wait a minute! Oh, I was thinking at first that here we are driving and supposing that we are going home, but God knows where we are going in this darkness, and all of a sudden we shall arrive and see we are not at Otradnoe but in fairyland. And then I thought, too ... no; nothing more.'

'I know, of course, you thought of *him*,' said Nikolay, smiling, as Natasha could tell by his voice.

'No,' Natasha answered, though she really had been thinking at the same time of Prince Andrey and how he would like the uncle. 'And I keep repeating, too, all the way I keep repeating: how nicely Anisyushka walked; how nicely ...' said Natasha. And Nikolay heard her musical, causeless, happy laugh.

'And do you know?' she said suddenly. 'I know I shall never be as happy, as peaceful as I am now ...'

'What nonsense, idiocy, rubbish!' said Nikolay, and he thought: 'What a darling this Natasha of mine is! I have never had, and never shall have, another friend like her. Why should she be married? I could drive like this with her for ever!'

'What a darling this Nikolay of mine is!' Natasha was thinking.

'Ah! Still a light in the drawing-room,' she said, pointing to the windows of their house gleaming attractively in the wet, velvety darkness of the night.

VIII

COUNT ILYA ANDREITCH had given up being a marshal of nobility, because that position involved too heavy an expenditure. But his difficulties were not removed by that. Often Natasha and Nikolay knew of uneasy, private consultations between their parents, and heard talk of selling the sumptuous ancestral house of the Rostovs and the estate near Moscow. When the count was no longer marshal it was not necessary to entertain on such a large scale, and they led a quieter life at Otradnoe than in former years. But the immense house and the lodges were still full of people; more than twenty persons still sat down to table with them. These were all their own people, time-honoured inmates of their household, almost members of the family, or persons who must, it seemed, inevitably live in the count's house. Such were Dimmler, the music-master, and his wife; Vogel the dancing-master, with his family; an old Madame Byelov, and many others besides; Petya's tutors, the girls' old governess, and persons who simply found it better or more profitable to live at the count's than in a house of their own. They did not entertain so many guests as before, but they still lived in that manner, apart from which the count and countess could not have conceived of life at all. There was still the same hunting establishment, increased indeed by Nikolay. There were still the same fifty horses and fifteen grooms in the stables; the same costly presents on name-days, and ceremonial dinners to the whole neighbourhood. There were still the count's games of whist and boston, at which, letting every one see his cards, he allowed himself to be plundered every day of hundreds by his neighbours, who looked upon the privilege of making up a rubber with Count Ilya Andreitch as a profitable investment.

The count went into his affairs as though walking into a huge net, trying not to believe that he was entangled, and at every step getting more and more entangled, and feeling too feeble either to tear the nets that held him fast, or with care and patience to set about disentangling them. The countess with her loving heart felt that her children were being ruined, that the count was not to blame, that he could not help being what he was, that he was distressed himself (though he tried to conceal it) at the consciousness of his own and his children's ruin, and was seeking means to improve their position. To her feminine mind only one way of doing so occurred—that was, to marry Nikolay to a wealthy heiress. She felt that this was their last hope, and that if Nikolay were to refuse the match she had found for him she must bid farewell for ever to all chance of improving their position. This match was Julie Karagin, the daughter of excellent and virtuous parents, known to the Rostovs from childhood, and now left a wealthy heiress by the death of her last surviving brother.

The countess wrote directly to Madame Karagin in Moscow, suggesting to her the marriage of her daughter to her own son, and received a favourable reply from her. Madame Karagin replied that she was quite ready for her part to consent to the match, but everything must depend on her daughter's inclinations. Madame Karagin invited Nikolay to come to Moscow. Several times the countess, with tears in her eyes, had told her son that now that both her daughters were settled, her only wish was to see him married. She said that she could rest quietly in her grave if this were settled. Then she would say that she had an excellent girl in her eye, and would try and get from him his views on matrimony.

On other occasions she praised Julie and advised Nikolay to go to Moscow for the holidays to amuse himself a little. Nikolay guessed what his mother's hints were aiming at, and on one such occasion he forced her to complete frankness. She told him plainly that all hope of improving their position rested now on his marrying Julie Karagin.

'What, if I loved a girl with no fortune would you really desire me, mamma, to sacrifice my feeling and my honour for the sake of money?'

he asked his mother, with no notion of the cruelty of his question, but simply wishing to show his noble sentiments.

'No; you misunderstand me,' said his mother, not knowing how to retrieve her mistake. 'You misunderstand me, Nikolenka. It is your happiness I wish for,' she added, and she felt she was speaking falsely, that she was blundering. She burst into tears.

'Mamma, don't cry, and only tell me that you wish it, and you know that I would give my whole life, everything for your peace of mind,' said Nikolay; 'I will sacrifice everything for you, even my feelings.'

But the countess did not want the question put like that; she did not want to receive sacrifices from her son, she would have liked to sacrifice herself to him.

'No; you don't understand me, don't let us talk of it,' she said, wiping away her tears.

'Yes, perhaps I really do love a poor girl,' Nikolay said to himself; 'what, am I to sacrifice my feeling and my honour for fortune? I wonder how mamma could say such a thing. Because Sonya is poor I must not love her,' he thought; 'I must not respond to her faithful, devoted love. And it is certain I should be happier with her than with any doll of a Julie. To sacrifice my feelings for the welfare of my family I can always do,' he said to himself, 'but I can't control my feelings. If I love Sonya, that feeling is more than anything and above anything for me.'

Nikolay did not go to Moscow, the countess did not renew her conversations with him about matrimony, and with grief, and sometimes with exasperation, saw symptoms of a growing attachment between her son and the portionless Sonya. She blamed herself for it, yet could not refrain from scolding and upbraiding Sonya, often reproving her without cause and addressing her as 'my good girl.' What irritated the kind-hearted countess more than anything was that this poor, dark-eyed niece was so meek, so good, so devoutly grateful to her benefactors, and so truly, so constantly, and so unselfishly in love with Nikolay that it was impossible to find any fault with her.

Nikolay went on spending his term of leave with his parents. From Prince Andrey a fourth letter had been received from Rome. In it he wrote that he would long ago have been on his way back to Russia, but that in the warm climate his wound had suddenly re-opened, which would compel him to defer his return till the beginning of the new year. Natasha was as much in love with her betrothed, as untroubled in her love, and as ready to throw herself into all the pleasures of life as ever. But towards the end of the fourth month of their separation she began to suffer from fits of depression, against which she was unable to contend. She felt sorry for herself, sorry that all this time should be wasted and be of no use to any one, while she felt such capacity for loving and being loved.

Life was not gay in the Rostovs' household.

IX

CHRISTMAS came, and except for the High Mass, the solemn and wearisome congratulations of neighbours and house-serfs, and the new gowns donned by every one, nothing special happened to mark the holidays, though the still weather with twenty degrees of frost, the dazzling sunshine by day and the bright, starlit sky at night seemed to call for some special celebration of the season.

On the third day of Christmas week, after dinner, all the members of the household had separated and gone to their respective rooms. It was the dullest time of the day. Nikolay, who had been calling on neighbours in the morning, was asleep in the divan-room. The old count was resting in his own room. In the drawing-room Sonya was sitting at a round table copying a design for embroidery. The countess was playing patience. Nastasya Ivanovna, the buffoon, with a dejected countenance, was sitting in the window with two old ladies. Natasha came into the room, went up to Sonya, looked at what she was doing, then went up to her mother and stood there mutely.

'Why are you wandering about like an unquiet spirit?' said her mother. 'What do you want?'

'I want *him* . . . I want *him* at once, this minute,' said Natasha, with a gleam in her eyes and no smile on her lips. The countess raised her head and looked intently at her daughter.

'Don't look at me, mamma; don't look at me like that; I shall cry in a minute.'

'Sit down; come and sit by me,' said the countess.

'Mamma, I want *him*. Why should I be wasting time like this, mamma?' . . . Her voice broke, tears gushed into her eyes, and to hide them, she turned quickly and went out of the room. She went into the divan-room, stood there, thought a moment and went to the maids' room. There an old maid-servant was scolding a young girl who had run in breathless from the cold outside.

'Give over playing,' said the old woman; 'there is a time for everything.'

'Let her off, Kondratyevna,' said Natasha. 'Run along, Mavrusha, run along.'

And after releasing Mavrusha, Natasha crossed the big hall and went to the vestibule. An old footman and two young ones were playing cards. They broke off and rose at the entrance of their young mistress. 'What am I to do with them?' Natasha wondered.

'Yes, Nikita, go out, please . . . Where am I to send him? . . . Yes, go to the yard and bring me a cock, please; and you, Misha, bring me some oats.'

'Just a few oats, if you please?' said Misha, with cheerful readiness.

'Run along; make haste,' the old man urged him.

'Fyodor, you get me some chalk.'

As she passed the buffet she ordered the samovar, though it was not the right time for it.

The buffet-waiter, Foka, was the most ill-tempered person in the house. Natasha liked to try her power over him. He did not believe in her order, and went to inquire if it were really wanted.

'Ah, you're a nice young lady!' said Foka, pretending to frown at Natasha.

No one in the house sent people on errands and gave the servants so much work as Natasha. She could not see people without wanting to send them for something. She seemed to be trying to see whether one of them would not be cross or sulky with her; but no one's orders were so readily obeyed by the servants as Natasha's. 'What am I to do? Where am I to go?' Natasha wondered, strolling slowly along the corridor.

'Nastasya Ivanovna, what will my children be?' she asked the buffoon, who came towards her in his woman's jacket.

'Fleas, and dragon-flies, and grasshoppers,' answered the buffoon.

'My God! my God! always the same. Oh, where am I to go? What am I to do with myself?' And she ran rapidly upstairs, tapping with her shoes, to see Vogel and his wife, who had rooms on the top floor. The two governesses were sitting with the Vogels and on the table were plates of raisins, walnuts, and almonds. The governesses were discussing the question which was the cheaper town to live in, Moscow or Odessa. Natasha sat down, listened to their talk with a serious and dreamy face, and got up. 'The island Madagascar,' she said. 'Māda-gascar,' she repeated, articulating each syllable distinctly; and making no reply to Madame Schoss's inquiry into her meaning, she went out of the room.

Petya, her brother, was upstairs too. He was engaged with his tutor making fireworks to let off that night.

'Petya! Petka!' she shouted to him, 'carry me downstairs.' Petya ran to her and offered her his back, and he pranced along with her. 'No, enough. The island Madagascar,' she repeated, and jumping off his back she went downstairs.

Having as it were reviewed her kingdom, tried her power, and made sure that all were submissive, but yet that she was dull, Natasha went into the big hall, took up the guitar, and sat down with it in a dark corner behind a bookcase. She began fingering the strings in the bass, picking out a phrase she recalled from an opera she had heard in Petersburg with Prince Andrey. For other listeners the sounds that came from her guitar would have had no sort of meaning, but these sounds called up in her imagination a whole series of reminiscences. She sat behind the bookcase with her eyes fixed on a streak of light that fell from the crack in the pantry door, and listened to herself and recalled the past. She was in the mood for brooding over memories.

Sonya crossed the hall, and went into the pantry with a glass in her hand. Natasha glanced at her through the crack in the pantry door, and it seemed to her that she remembered the light falling through the crack in the pantry door, and Sonya passing with the glass in just the same way. 'Yes, and it was exactly the same in every detail,' thought Natasha.

'Sonya, what is this?' called Natasha, twanging the thick cord with her fingers.

'Oh, are you there?' said Sonya starting, and she came up and listened. 'I don't know. A storm?' she said timidly, afraid of being wrong.

'Why, she started in just the same way, and came up and smiled the same timid smile when it all happened before,' thought Natasha; 'and just in the same way, too. . . . I thought there was something wanting in her.'

'No, it's the chorus from the "Water Carrier," listen.' And Natasha hummed the air of the chorus, so that Sonya might catch it. 'Where were you going?' asked Natasha.

'To change the water in my glass. I am just finishing colouring the design.'

'You always find something to do, but I can't, you know,' said Natasha. 'And where's Nikolenka?'

'I think he's asleep.'

'Sonya, do go and wake him,' said Natasha. 'Tell him I want him to sing with me.'

She sat a little longer, pondering on what was the meaning of its all having happened before, and not solving that question, and not in the least chagrined at being unable to do so, she passed again in her imagination to the time when she was with him, and he gazed at her with eyes of love.

'Oh, if he would come quickly! I'm so afraid it will never come!

And worst of all, I'm getting older, that's the thing. There won't be in me what there is in me now. Perhaps he is coming today, will be here immediately. Perhaps he has come, and is sitting there in the drawing-room. Perhaps he did come yesterday, and I have forgotten.' She got up, put down her guitar, and went into the parlour. All their domestic circle, tutors, governesses, and guests were sitting at the tea-table. The servants were standing round the table. But Prince Andrey was not here, and the same old life was still going on.

'Here she is,' said the count, seeing Natasha coming in. 'Come, sit by me.' But Natasha stayed by her mother, looking about her as though seeking for something.

'Mamma!' she said. 'Give me *him*, give me him, mamma, quickly, quickly,' and again she could hardly suppress her sobs. She sat down to the table and listened to the talk of the elders and Nikolay, who had come in to tea. 'My God, my God, the same people, the same talk, papa holding his cup, and blowing it just the same as always,' thought Natasha, feeling with horror an aversion rising up in her for all her family, because they were always the same.

After tea Nikolay, Sonya, and Natasha went into the divan-room to their favourite corner, where their most intimate talks always began.

X

'DOES it happen to you,' said Natasha to her brother, when they were settled in the divan-room, 'to feel that nothing will ever happen—nothing; that all that is good is past? And it's not exactly a bored feeling, but melancholy?'

'I should think so!' said he. 'It has sometimes happened to me that when everything's all right, and every one's cheerful, it suddenly strikes one that one's sick of it all, and all must die. Once in the regiment when I did not go to some merrymaking, and there the music was playing . . . and I felt all at once so dreary . . .'

'Oh, I know that feeling; I know it, I know it,' Natasha assented; 'even when I was quite little, I used to have that feeling. Do you remember, once I was punished for eating some plums, and you were all dancing, and I sat in the schoolroom sobbing. I shall never forget it; I felt sad and sorry for every one, sorry for myself, and for every—every one. And what was the chief point, I wasn't to blame,' said Natasha; 'do you remember?'

'I remember,' said Nikolay. 'I remember that I came to you afterwards, and I longed to comfort you, but you know, I felt ashamed to.

Awfully funny we used to be. I had a wooden doll then, and I wanted to give it you. Do you remember?'

'And do you remember,' said Natasha, with a pensive smile, 'how long, long ago, when we were quite little, uncle called us into the study in the old house, and it was dark; we went in, and all at once there stood . . .'

'A negro,' Nikolay finished her sentence with a smile of delight; 'of course, I remember. To this day I don't know whether there really was a negro, or whether we dreamed it, or were told about it.'

'He was grey-headed, do you remember, and had white teeth; he stood and looked at us . . .'

'Do you remember, Sonya?' asked Nikolay.

'Yes, yes, I do remember something too,' Sonya answered timidly.

'You know I have often asked both papa and mamma about that negro,' said Natasha. 'They say there never was a negro at all. But you remember him!'

'Of course, I do. I remember his teeth, as if it were today.'

'How strange it is, as though it were a dream. I like that.'

'And do you remember how we were rolling eggs in the big hall, and all of a sudden two old women came in, and began whirling round on the carpet. Did that happen or not? Do you remember what fun it was?'

'Yes. And do you remember how papa, in a blue coat, fired a gun off on the steps.'

Smiling with enjoyment, they went through their reminiscences; not the melancholy memories of old age, but the romantic memories of youth, those impressions of the remotest past in which dreamland melts into reality. They laughed with quiet pleasure.

Sonya was, as always, left behind by them, though their past had been spent together.

Sonya did not remember much of what they recalled, and what she did remember, did not rouse the same romantic feeling in her. She was simply enjoying their pleasure, and trying to share it.

She could only enter into it fully when they recalled Sonya's first arrival. Sonya described how she had been afraid of Nikolay, because he had cording on his jacket, and the nurse had told her that they would tie her up in cording too.

'And I remember, I was told you were found under a cabbage,' said Natasha; 'and I remember I didn't dare to disbelieve it then, though I knew it was untrue, and I felt so uncomfortable.'

During this conversation a maid popped her head in at a door leading into the divan-room.

'Miss, they've brought you a cock,' she said in a whisper.

'I don't want it, Polya; tell them to take it away,' said Natasha.

In the middle of their talk in the divan-room, Dimmler came into the room, and went up to the harp that stood in the corner. He took off the cloth-case, and the harp gave a jarring sound. 'Edward Karlitch, do, please, play my favourite nocturne of M. Field,' said the voice of the old countess from the drawing-room.

Dimmler struck a chord, and turning to Natasha, Nikolay, and Sonya, he said:

'How quiet you young people are!'

'Yes, we're talking philosophy,' said Natasha, looking round for a minute, and going on with the conversation. They were talking now about dreams.

Dimmler began to play. Natasha went noiselessly on tiptoe to the table, took the candle, carried it away, and going back, sat quietly in her place. It was dark in the room, especially where they were sitting on the sofa, but the silver light of the full moon shone in at the big windows and lay on the floor.

'Do you know, I think,' said Natasha, in a whisper, moving up to Nikolay and Sonya, when Dimmler had finished, and still sat, faintly twanging the strings, in evident uncertainty whether to leave off playing or begin something new, 'that one goes on remembering, and remembering, and remembering; one remembers till one recalls what happened before one was in this world....'

'That's metempsychosis,' said Sonya, who had been good at lessons, and remembered all she had learned. 'The Egyptians used to believe that our souls had been in animals, and would go into animals again.'

'No, do you know, I don't believe that we were once in animals,' said Natasha, still in the same whisper, though the music was over; 'but I know for certain that we were once angels somewhere beyond, and we have been here, and that's why we remember everything....'

'May I join you?' said Dimmler, coming up quietly, and he sat down by them.

'If we had been angels, why should we have fallen lower?' said Nikolay. 'No, that can't be!'

'Not lower ... who told you we were lower? ... This is how I know I have existed before,' Natasha replied, with conviction: 'The soul is immortal, you know ... so, if I am to live for ever, I have lived before too, I have lived for all eternity.'

'Yes, but it's hard for us to conceive of eternity,' said Dimmler, who had joined the young people, with a mildly condescending smile, but now talked as quietly and seriously as they did.

'Why is it hard to conceive of eternity?' said Natasha. 'There will be today, and there will be tomorrow, and there will be for ever, and yesterday has been, and the day before....'

'Natasha! now it's your turn. Sing me something,' called the voice of the countess. 'Why are you sitting there so quietly, like conspirators?'

'Mamma, I don't want to a bit!' said Natasha, but she got up as she said it.

None of them, not even Dimmler, who was not young, wanted to break off the conversation, and come out of the corner of the divan-room; but Natasha stood up, and Nikolay sat down to the clavichord. Standing, as she always did, in the middle of the room, and choosing the place where the resonance was greatest, Natasha began singing her mother's favourite song.

She had said she did not want to sing, but it was long since she had sung, and long before she sang again as she sang that evening. Count Ilya Andreitch listened to her singing from his study, where he was talking to Mitenka, and like a schoolboy in haste to finish his lesson and run out to play, he blundered in his orders to the steward, and at last paused, and Mitenka stood silent and smiling before him, listening too. Nikolay never took his eyes off his sister, and drew his breath when she did. Sonya, as she listened, thought of the vast difference between her and her friend, and how impossible it was for her to be in ever so slight a degree fascinating like her cousin. The old countess sat with a blissful, but mournful smile, and tears in her eyes, and now and then she shook her head. She, too, was thinking of Natasha and of her own youth, and of how there was something terrible and unnatural in Natasha's marrying Prince Andrey.

Dimmler, sitting by the countess, listened with closed eyes. 'No, countess,' he said, at last, 'that's a European talent; she has no need of teaching: that softness, tenderness, strength...'

'Ah, I'm afraid for her, I'm afraid,' said the countess, not remembering with whom she was speaking. Her motherly instinct told her that there was too much of something in Natasha, and that it would prevent her being happy.

Natasha had not finished singing, when fourteen-year-old Petya ran in great excitement into the room to announce the arrival of the mummers.

Natasha stopped abruptly.

'Idiot!' she screamed at her brother. She ran to a chair, sank into it, and broke into such violent sobbing that it was a long while before she could stop.

'It's nothing, mamma, it's nothing really, it's all right; Petya startled me,' she said, trying to smile; but the tears still flowed, and the sobs still choked her.

The mummers—house-serfs dressed up as bears, Turks, tavern-keepers, and ladies—awe-inspiring or comic figures, at first huddled shyly together in the vestibule, bringing in with them the freshness of the cold outside, and a feeling of gaiety. Then, hiding behind one another, they crowded together in the big hall; and at first with constraint, but afterwards with more liveliness and unanimity, they started singing songs, and performing dances, and songs with dancing, and playing Christmas games. The countess after identifying them, and laughing at their costumes, went away to the drawing-room. Count Ilya Andreitch sat with a beaming smile in the big hall, praising their performances. The young people had disappeared.

Half an hour later there appeared in the hall among the other mummers an old lady in a crinoline—this was Nikolay. Petya was a Turkish lady, Dimmler was a clown, Natasha a hussar, and Sonya a Circassian with eyebrows and moustaches smudged with burnt cork.

After those of the household who were not dressed up had expressed condescending wonder and approval, and had failed to recognise them, the young people began to think their costumes so good that they must display them to someone else.

Nikolay, who wanted to drive them all in his sledge, as the road was in capital condition, proposed to drive to their so-called uncle's, taking about a dozen of the house-serfs in their mummer-dress with them.

'No; why should you disturb the old fellow?' said the countess. 'Besides you wouldn't have room to turn round there. If you must go, let it be to the Melyukovs'.'

Madame Melyukov was a widow with a family of children of various ages, and a number of tutors and governesses living in her house, four versts from the Rostovs.

'That's a good idea, my love,' the old count assented, beginning to be aroused. 'Only let me dress up and I'll go with you. I'll make Pashette open her eyes.'

But the countess would not agree to the count's going; for several days he had had a bad leg. It was decided that the count must not go, but that if Luisa Ivanovna (Madame Schoss) would go with them, the young ladies might go to Madame Melyukov's. Sonya, usually so shy and reticent, was more urgent than any in persuading Luisa Ivanovna not to refuse.

Sonya's disguise was the best of all. Her moustaches and eyebrows were extraordinarily becoming to her. Every one told her she looked very pretty, and she was in a mood of eager energy unlike her. Some inner voice told her that now or never her fate would be sealed, and in her masculine attire she seemed quite another person. Luisa Ivanovna consented to go; and half an hour later four sledges with bells drove up to the steps, their runners crunching, with a clanging sound, over the frozen snow.

Natasha was foremost in setting the note tone of holiday gaiety; and that gaiety, reflected from one to another, grew wilder and wilder, and reached its climax when they all went out into the frost, and talking, and calling to one another, laughing and shouting, got into the sledges.

Two of the sledges were the common household sledges; the third was the old count's, with a trotting horse from Orlov's famous stud; the fourth, Nikolay's own, with his own short, shaggy, raven horse in the shafts. Nikolay, in his old lady's crinoline and a hussar's cloak belted over it, stood up in the middle of the sledge picking up the reins. It was so light that he could see the metal discs of the harness shining in the moonlight, and the eyes of the horses looking round in alarm at the noise made by the party under the portico of the approach.

Sonya, Natasha, Madame Schoss, and two maids got into Nikolay's sledge. In the count's sledge were Dimmler with his wife and Petya; the other mummers were seated in the other two sledges.

'You go on ahead, Zahar!' shouted Nikolay to his father's coachman, so as to have a chance of overtaking him on the road.

The count's sledge with Dimmler and the others of his party started forward, its runners creaking as though they were frozen to the snow, and the deep-toned bell clanging. The trace-horses pressed close to the shafts and sticking in the snow kicked it up, hard and glittering as sugar.

Nikolay followed the first sledge: behind him he heard the noise and crunch of the other two. At first they drove at a slow trot along the narrow road. As they drove by the garden, the shadows of the leafless trees often lay right across the road and hid the bright moonlight. But as soon as they were out of their grounds, the snowy plain, glittering like diamond with bluish lights in it, lay stretched out on all sides, all motionless and bathed in moonlight. Now and again a hole gave the first sledge a jolt; the next was jolted in just the same way, and the next, and the sledges followed one another, rudely breaking the iron-bound stillness.

'A hare's track, a lot of tracks!' Natasha's voice rang out in the frost-bound air.

'How light it is, Nikolenka,' said the voice of Sonya.

Nikolay looked round at Sonya, and bent down to look at her face closer. It was a quite new, charming face with black moustaches, and eyebrows that peeped up at him from the sable fur—so close yet so distant—in the moonlight.

'That used to be Sonya,' thought Nikolay. He looked closer at her and smiled.

'What is it, Nikolenka?'

'Nothing,' he said, and turned to his horses again.

As they came out on the trodden highroad, polished by sledge runners, and all cut up by the tracks of spiked horseshoes—visible in the snow in the moonlight—the horses of their own accord tugged at the reins and quickened their pace. The left trace-horse, arching his head, pulled in jerks at his traces. The shaft-horse swayed to and fro, pricking up his ears as though to ask: 'Are we to begin or is it too soon?' Zahar's sledge could be distinctly seen, black against the white snow, a long way ahead now, and its deep-toned bell seemed to be getting further away. They could hear shouts and laughter and talk from his sledge.

'Now then, my darlings!' shouted Nikolay, pulling a rein on one side, and moving his whip hand. It was only from the wind seeming to blow more freely in their faces, and from the tugging of the pulling trace-horses, quickening their trot, that they saw how fast the sledge was flying along. Nikolay looked behind. The other sledges, with crunching runners, with shouts, and cracking of whips, were hurrying after them. Their shaft-horse was moving vigorously under the yoke, with no sign of slackening, and every token of being ready to go faster and faster if required.

Nikolay overtook the first sledge. They drove down a hill, and into a wide, trodden road by a meadow near a river.

'Where are we?' Nikolay wondered. 'Possibly Kosoy Meadow, I suppose. But no; this is something new I never saw before. This is not the Kosoy Meadow nor Demkin hill. It's something—there's no knowing what. It's something new and fairy-like. Well, come what may!' And shouting to his horses, he began to drive by the first sledge. Zahar pulled up his horses and turned his face, which was white with hoar frost to the eyebrows.

Nikolay let his horses go; Zahar, stretching his hands forward, urged his on. 'Come, hold on, master,' said he.

The sledges dashed along side by side, even more swiftly, and the horses' hoofs flew up and down more and more quickly. Nikolay began to get ahead. Zahar, still keeping his hands stretched forward, raised one hand with the reins.

'Nonsense, master,' he shouted. Nikolay put his three horses into a gallop and outstripped Zahar. The horses scattered the fine dry snow in their faces; close by they heard the ringing of the bells and the horses' legs moving rapidly out of step, and they saw the shadows of the sledge behind. From different sides came the crunch of runners over the snow, and the shrieks of girls. Stopping his horses again, Nikolay looked round him. All around him lay still the same enchanted plain, bathed in moonlight, with stars scattered over its surface.

'Zahar's shouting that I'm to turn to the left, but why to the left?' thought Nikolay. 'Are we really going to the Melyukovs'; is this really Melyukovka? God knows where we are going, and God knows what is going to become of us—and very strange and nice it is what is happening to us.' He looked round in the sledge.

'Look, his moustache and his eyelashes are all white,' said one of the strange, pretty, unfamiliar figures sitting by him, with fine moustaches and eyebrows.

'I believe that was Natasha,' thought Nikolay; 'and that was Madame Schoss; but perhaps it's not so; and that Circassian with the moustaches I don't know, but I love her.'

'Aren't you cold?' he asked them. They laughed and did not answer. Dimmler from the sledge behind shouted, probably something funny, but they could not make out what he said.

'Yes, yes,' voices answered, laughing.

But now came a sort of enchanted forest with shifting, black shadows, and the glitter of diamonds, and a flight of marble steps, and silver roofs of enchanted buildings, and the shrill whine of some beasts. 'And if it really is Melyukovka, then it's stranger than ever that after driving, God knows where, we should come to Melyukovka,' thought Nikolay.

It certainly was Melyukovka, and footmen and maidservants were running out with lights and beaming faces.

'Who is it?' was asked from the entrance.

'The mummers from the count's; I can see by the horses,' answered voices.

XI

PELAGEA DANILOVNA MELYUKOV, a broad-shouldered, energetic woman, in spectacles and a loose house dress, was sitting in her drawing-room, surrounded by her daughters, and doing her utmost to keep them amused. They were quietly occupied in dropping melted wax into water and watching the shadows of the shapes it assumed, when they heard the noise of steps in the vestibule, and the voices of people arriving.

The hussars, fine ladies, witches, clowns, and bears, coughing and rubbing the hoar-frost off their faces, came into the hall, where they were hurriedly lighting candles. The clown—Dimmler—and the old lady—Nikolay—opened the dance. Surrounded by the shrieking children, the mummers hid their faces, and disguising their voices, bowed to their hostess and dispersed about the room.

'Oh, there's no recognising them. And Natasha! See what she looks like! Really, she reminds me of some one. How good Edward Karlitch is! I didn't know him. And how he dances! Oh, my goodness, and here's a Circassian too, upon my word; how it suits Sonyushka! And who's this? Well, you have brought us some fun! Take away the tables, Nikita, Vanya. And we were sitting so quiet and dull!'

'Ha—ha—he! . . . The hussar, the hussar! Just like a boy; and the legs! . . . I can't look at him, . . .' voices cried.

Natasha, the favourite of the young Melyukovs, disappeared with them into rooms at the back of the house, and burnt cork and various dressing-gowns and masculine garments were sent for and taken from the footman by bare, girlish arms through the crack of the half-open door. In ten minutes all the younger members of the Melyukov family reappeared in fancy dresses too.

Pelagea Danilovna, busily giving orders for clearing the room for the guests and preparing for their entertainment, walked about among the mummers in her spectacles, with a suppressed smile, looking close at them and not recognising any one. She not only failed to recognise the Rostovs and Dimmler, but did not even know her own daughters, or identify the masculine dressing-gowns and uniform in which they were disguised.

'And who is this?' she kept saying, addressing her governess and gazing into the face of her own daughter disguised as a Tatar of Kazan. 'One of the Rostovs, I fancy. And you, my hussar, what regiment are you in, pray?' she asked Natasha. 'Give the Turk a preserved fruit,' she said to the footman carrying round refreshments; 'that's not forbidden by his law.'

Sometimes, looking at the strange and ludicrous capers cut by the dancers, who, having made up their minds once for all that no one recognised them, were quite free from shyness, Pelagea Danilovna hid her face in her handkerchief, and all her portly person shook with irrepressible, good-natured, elderly laughter.

'My Sashinette, my Sashinette!' she said.

After Russian dances and songs in chorus, Pelagea Danilovna made all the party, servants and gentry alike, join in one large circle. They brought in a string, a ring, and a silver rouble, and began playing games.

An hour later all the fancy dresses were crumpled and untidy. The corked moustaches and eyebrows were wearing off the heated, perspiring, and merry faces. Pelagea Danilovna began to recognise the mummers. She was enthusiastic over the cleverness of the dresses and the way they suited them, especially the young ladies, and thanked them all for giving them such good fun. The guests were invited into the drawing-room for supper, while the servants were regaled in the hall.

'Oh, trying one's fate in the bath-house, that's awful!' was said at the supper-table by an old maiden lady who lived with the Melyukovs.

'Why so?' asked the eldest daughter of the Melyukovs.

'Well, you won't go and try. It needs courage ...'

'I'll go,' said Sonya.

'Tell us what happened to the young lady,' said the second girl.

'Well, it was like this,' said the old maid. 'The young lady went out; she took a cock, two knives and forks, and everything proper, and sat down. She sat a little while, and all of a sudden she hears some one coming,—a sledge with bells driving up. She hears him coming. He walks in, precisely in the shape of a man, like an officer, and sat down beside her at the place laid for him.'

'Ah! ah ...' screamed Natasha, rolling her eyes with horror.

'But what did he do? Did he talk like a man?'

'Yes, like a man. Everything as it should be, and began to try and win her over, and she should have kept him in talk till the cock crew; but she got frightened,—simply took fright, and hid her face in her hands. And he caught her up. Luckily the maids ran in that minute ...'

'Come, why are you scaring them?' said Pelagea Danilovna.

'Why, mamma, you tried your fate yourself ...' said her daughter.

'And how do they try fate in a granary?' asked Sonya.

'Why, at a time like this they go to the granary and listen. And according to what you hear,—if there's a knocking and a tapping, it's bad; but if there's a sound of sifting corn, it is good. But sometimes it happens ..'

'Mamma, tell us what happened to you in the granary?'

Pelagea Danilovna smiled.

'Why, I have forgotten ...' she said. 'I know none of you will go.'

'No. I'll go. Pelagea Danilovna, do let me, and I'll go,' said Sonya.

'Oh, well, if you're not afraid.'

'Luisa Ivanovna, may I?' asked Sonya.

Whether they were playing at the ring and string game, or the rouble game, or talking as now, Nikolay did not leave Sonya's side, and looked at her with quite new eyes. It seemed to him as though today, for the first time, he had, thanks to that corked moustache, seen her fully as she was. Sonya certainly was that evening gay, lively, and pretty, as Natasha had never seen her before.

'So, this is what she is, and what a fool I have been!' he kept thinking, looking at her sparkling eyes, at the happy, ecstatic smile dimpling her cheeks under the moustache. He had never seen that smile before.

'I'm not afraid of anything,' said Sonya. 'May I go at once?' She got up. They told Sonya where the granary was; how she was to stand quite silent and listen, and they gave her a cloak. She threw it over her head and glanced at Nikolay.

'How exquisite that girl is!' he thought. 'And what have I been thinking about all this time?'

Sonya went out into the corridor to go to the granary. Nikolay hastily went out to the front porch, saying he was too hot. It certainly was stuffy indoors from the crowd of people.

Outside there was the same still frost, the same moonlight, only even brighter than before. The light was so bright, and there were so many stars sparkling in the snow, that the sky did not attract the eye, and the real stars were hardly noticeable. The sky was all blackness and dreariness, the earth all brightness.

'I'm a fool; a fool! What have I been waiting for all this time?' thought Nikolay; and running out into the porch he went round the corner of the house along the path leading to the back door. He knew Sonya would come that way. Halfway there was a pile of logs of wood, seven feet long. It was covered with snow and cast a shadow. Across it and on one side of it there fell on the snow and the path a network of shadows from the bare old lime-trees. The wall and roof of the granary glittered in the moonlight, as though hewn out of some precious stone. There was the sound of the snapping of wood in the garden, and all was perfect stillness again. The lungs seemed breathing in, not air, but a sort of ever-youthful power and joy.

From the maidservants' entrance came the tap of feet on the steps; there was a ringing crunch on the last step where the snow was heaped, and the voice of the old maid said:

'Straight on, along this path, miss. Only don't look round!'

'I'm not afraid,' answered Sonya's voice, and Sonya's little feet in their dancing-shoes came with a ringing, crunching sound along the path towards Nikolay.

Sonya was muffled up in the cloak. She was two paces away when she saw him. She saw him, too, not as she knew him, and as she was always a little afraid of him. He was in a woman's dress, with tousled hair, and a blissful smile that was new to Sonya. She ran quickly to him.

'Quite different, and still the same,' thought Nikolay, looking at her face, all lighted up by the moon. He slipped his hands under the cloak that covered her head, embraced her, drew her to him, and kissed the lips that wore a moustache and smelt of burnt cork. Sonya kissed him full on the lips, and putting out her little hands held them against his cheeks on both sides.

'Sonya! . . . Nikolenka! . . .' was all they said. They ran to the granary and went back to the house, each at their separate door.

XII

WHEN they were all driving back from Pelagea Danilovna's, Natasha, who always saw and noticed everything, managed a change of places, so that Luisa Ivanovna and she got into the sledge with Dimmler, while Sonya was with Nikolay and the maids.

Nikolay drove smoothly along the way back, making no effort now to get in front. He kept gazing in the fantastic moonlight at Sonya, and seeking, in the continually shifting light behind those eyebrows and moustaches, his own Sonya, the old Sonya, and the Sonya of today, from whom he had resolved now never to be parted. He watched her intently, and when he recognised the old Sonya and the new Sonya, and recalled, as he smelt it, that smell of burnt cork that mingled with the thrill of the kiss, he drew in a deep breath of the frosty air, and as he saw the earth flying by them, and the sky shining above, he felt himself again in fairyland.

'Sonya, is it well with *thee*?' he asked her now and then.

'Yes,' answered Sonya. 'And *thee*?'

Half-way home, Nikolay let the coachman hold the horses, ran for a moment to Natasha's sledge, and stood on the edge of it.

'Natasha,' he whispered in French, 'do you know I have made up my mind about Sonya?'

'Have you told her?' asked Natasha, beaming all over at once with pleasure.

'Ah, how strange you look with that moustache and those eyebrows, Natasha! Are you glad?'

'I'm so glad; so glad! I was beginning to get cross with you. I never told you so, but you have not been treating her nicely. Such a heart as she has, Nikolenka. I am so glad! I'm horrid sometimes; but I felt ashamed of being happy without Sonya,' Natasha went on. 'Now, I'm so glad; there, run back to her.'

'No; wait a moment. Oh, how funny you look!' said Nikolay, still gazing intently at her; and in his sister, too, finding something new, extraordinary, and tenderly bewitching that he had never seen in her before. 'Natasha, isn't it fairylike? Eh?'

'Yes,' she answered, 'you have done quite rightly.'

'If I had seen her before as she is now,' Nikolay was thinking, 'I should have asked her long ago what to do, and should have done anything she told me, and it would have been all right.'

'So you're glad,' he said, 'and I have done right?'

'Oh, quite right! I had a quarrel with mamma about it a little while ago. Mamma said she was trying to catch you. How could she say such a thing! I almost stormed at mamma. I will never let any one say or think any harm of her, for there's nothing but good in her.'

'So it's all right?' said Nikolay, once more gazing intently at his sister's expression to find out whether that were the truth. Then he jumped off the sledge and ran, his boots crunching over the snow, to his sledge. The same happy, smiling Circassian, with a moustache and sparkling eyes, peeping from under the sable hood, was still sitting there, and that Circassian was Sonya, and that Sonya was for certain now his happy and loving future wife.

On reaching home, the young ladies told the countess how they had spent the time at the Melyukovs', and then went to their room. They changed their dresses, but without washing off their moustaches, sat for a long while talking of their happiness. They talked of how they would live when they were married, how their husbands would be friends, and they would be happy. Looking-glasses were standing on Natasha's table, set there earlier in the evening by Dunyasha, and arranged in the traditional way for looking into the future.

'Only when will that be? I'm so afraid it never will be. . . . It would be too happy!' said Natasha, getting up and going to the looking-glasses.

'Sit down, Natasha, perhaps you will see him,' said Sonya.

Natasha lighted the candles and sat down. 'I do see some one with a moustache,' said Natasha, seeing her own face.

'You mustn't laugh, miss,' said Dunyasha.

With the assistance of Sonya and the maid, Natasha got the mirrors into the correct position. Her face took a serious expression, and she was silent. For a long while she went on sitting, watching the series of retreating candles reflected in the looking-glasses, and expecting (in accordance with the tales she had heard) at one minute to see a coffin, at the next to see *him*, Prince Andrey, in the furthest, dimmest, indistinct square. But ready as she was to accept the slightest blur as the form of a man or of a coffin, she saw nothing. She began to blink, and moved away from the looking-glass.

'Why is it other people see things and I never see anything?' she said. 'Come, you sit down, Sonya; today you really must. Only look for me ... I feel so full of dread today!'

Sonya sat down to the looking-glass, got the correct position, and began looking.

'You will see, Sonya Alexandrovna will be sure to see something,' whispered Dunyasha, 'you always laugh.'

Sonya heard these words, and heard Natasha say in a whisper: 'Yes, I know she'll see something; she saw something last year too.' For three minutes all were mute.

'Sure to!' whispered Natasha, and did not finish. ... All at once Sonya drew back from the glass she was holding and put her hand over her eyes. 'O Natasha!' she said. 'Seen something? Seen something? What did you see?' cried Natasha, supporting the looking-glass. Sonya had seen nothing. She was just meaning to blink and to get up, when she heard Natasha's voice say: 'Sure to!' ... She did not want to deceive either Dunyasha or Natasha, and was weary of sitting there. She did not know herself how and why that exclamation had broken from her as she covered her eyes.

'Did you see him?' asked Natasha, clutching her by the hand.

'Yes. Wait a bit. ... I ... did see him,' Sonya could not help saying, not yet sure whether by *him* Natasha meant Nikolay or Andrey. 'Why not say I saw something? Other people see things! And who can tell whether I have or have not?' flashed through Sonya's mind.

'Yes, I saw him,' she said.

'How was it? How? Standing or lying down?'

'No, I saw ... At first there was nothing; then I saw him lying down.'

'Andrey lying down? Is he ill?' Natasha asked, fixing eyes of terror on her friend.

'No, on the contrary—on the contrary, his face was cheerful, and he turned to me'; and at the moment she was saying this, it seemed to herself that she really had seen what she described.

'Well, and then, Sonya?'...'

'Then I couldn't make out more; something blue and red....'

'Sonya, when will he come back? When shall I see him? My God! I feel so frightened for him, and for me, and frightened for everything ...' cried Natasha; and answering not a word to Sonya's attempts to comfort her, she got into bed, and long after the candle had been put out she lay with wide-open eyes motionless on the bed, staring into the frosty moonlight through the frozen window-panes.

XIII

SOON after the Christmas fêtes were over, Nikolay spoke to his mother of his love for Sonya, and his immovable resolution to marry her. The countess had long before observed what was passing between Sonya and Nikolay, and was expecting this announcement. She listened to his words without comment, and then told her son that he could marry whom he chose, but that neither she nor his father would give their blessing to such a marriage. For the first time in his life Nikolay felt that his mother was displeased with him, that in spite of all her love for him she would not give way to him. Coldly, without looking at her son, she sent for her husband; and when he came in, the countess would have briefly and coldly, in Nikolay's presence, told him her son's intention, but she could not control herself, burst into tears of anger, and went out of the room. The old count began irresolutely persuading and entreating Nikolay to give up his intention. Nikolay replied he could not be false to his word, and his father, sighing and visibly embarrassed, quickly cut short the conversation and went in to the countess. In all difficulties with his son, the old count could never lose his sense of guiltiness to him for having wasted their fortunes, and so he could not feel angry with his son for refusing to marry an heiress and choosing the portionless Sonya. He only felt more keenly that if their fortune had not been squandered, no better wife could have been desired for Nikolay than Sonya; and that he, with his Mitenka and his invincible bad habits, was alone to blame for their fortune having been squandered. The father and mother did not speak of the subject again with their son; but a few days later the countess sent for Sonya to her room, and with a cruelty that surprised them both, the countess upbraided her niece for alluring her son and for ingratitude. Sonya, with downcast eyes, listened in silence to the countess's cruel words, and did not understand what was expected of her. She was ready to sacrifice everything for her benefactors. The idea of self-sacrifice was her favourite idea. But in this case she could not see whom and what she ought to sacrifice. She could not help loving the countess and all the Rostov family, but neither could she help loving Nikolay and knowing that his happiness depended on that love. She was silent and dejected; she made no reply. Nikolay could not, so he fancied, endure this position any longer, and he went in to his mother to have it out with her. Nikolay first besought his mother to forgive him and Sonya and to agree to their marriage; then threatened his mother that if Sonya were persecuted he would at once marry her in secret. The countess, with a coldness her son had never seen before, replied that he was of full age, that Prince Andrey was marrying without his father's consent, and that he could do the same, but that she would never receive that *intriguing creature* as her daughter.

Stung to fury by the words '*intriguing creature,*' Nikolay, raising his voice, told his mother that he had never expected her to try and force him to sell his feelings, and that since it was so, then for the last time he . . . But he had not time to utter the fatal word, which his mother seemed, from her expression, to be awaiting in terror, and which would, perhaps, have remained a cruel memory between them for ever. He had not time to finish, because Natasha, who had been listening at the door, ran into the room with a pale and set face.

'Nikolenka, you are talking nonsense; hush, hush, hush! I tell you hush!' . . . she almost screamed to overpower his voice.

'Mamma, darling, it's not at all so . . . My sweet, poor darling,' she said, turning to her mother, who gazed in terror at her son, feeling herself on the edge of an abyss; but in the obstinacy and heat of the conflict unwilling and unable to give in. 'Nikolenka, I'll explain to you; you go away—listen, mamma, darling,' she said to her mother.

Her words were incoherent, but they attained the effect at which she was aiming.

The countess, with a deep sob, hid her face on her daughter's bosom, while Nikolay got up, clutched at his head, and went out of the room.

Natasha set to work to bring about a reconciliation, and succeeded so far that Nikolay received a promise from his mother that Sonya should not be worried, and himself made a promise that he would take no step without his parents' knowledge.

Firmly resolved to settle things in his regiment, to retire, come home, and marry Sonya, Nikolay at the beginning of January went back to his regiment, sad and serious at being on bad terms with his parents, but, as it seemed to him, passionately in love.

After Nikolay's departure, it was more depressing than ever in the Rostovs' house. The countess fell ill from the emotional strain she had passed through.

Sonya was depressed at parting from Nikolay, and still more at the hostile tone the countess could not help adopting towards her. The count was more worried than ever by the difficulties of his position, which called for some decisive action. It was necessary to sell the Moscow house and the estate near Moscow, and to do so it was necessary to go to Moscow. But the countess's illness forced them to put off going from day to day. Natasha, who had at first borne the separation from her betrothed so easily and even cheerfully, grew now more impatient and overstrung every day. The thought that her best time, that might have been spent in loving him, was being wasted like this for no object, continually fretted her. Prince Andrey's letters generally angered her. It mortified her to think that while she was simply living in the thought of him, he was living a real life, seeing new places and new people who were interesting to him. The more interesting his letters were, the more they vexed her. Her letters to him, far from giving her comfort, were looked upon by her as a wearisome and artificial duty. She could not write, because she could not attain to expressing truly in a letter a thousandth part of what she habitually expressed in voice and smile and eyes. She wrote him formal letters, all on one pattern. She did not attach the smallest importance to them herself, and the countess corrected the mistakes in spelling in the rough copy of them. The countess's health still did not mend, but the visit to Moscow could be deferred no longer. The trousseau had to be got, the house had to be sold, and Prince Andrey was to arrive first in Moscow, where his father was spending the winter, and Natasha believed that he had already arrived there. The countess was left in the country, and towards the end of January the count took Sonya and Natasha with him to Moscow.

PART VIII

I

AFTER PRINCE ANDREY'S engagement to Natasha, Pierre suddenly, for no apparent reason, felt it impossible to go on living in the same way as before. Firm as his belief was in the truths revealed to him by his benefactor, the old freemason, and happy as he had been at first in the task of perfecting his inner spiritual self, to which he had devoted himself with such ardour, yet after Prince Andrey's engagement to Natasha, and the death of Osip Alexyevitch, the news of which reached him almost simultaneously, the whole zest of his religious life seemed to have suddenly vanished. Nothing but the skeleton of life remained: his house with his brilliant wife, now basking in the favours of a very grand personage indeed, the society of all Petersburg, and his service at court with its tedious formalities. And that life suddenly filled Pierre with unexpected loathing. He gave up keeping his diary, avoided the society of brother-masons, took to visiting the club again and to drinking a great deal; associated once more with gay bachelor companions, and began to lead a life so dissipated that Countess Elena Vassilyevna thought it necessary to make severe observations to him on the subject. Pierre felt that she was right; and to avoid compromising his wife, he went away to Moscow.

In Moscow, as soon as he entered his huge house with the faded and fading princesses, his cousins, and the immense retinue of servants, as soon as, driving through the town, he saw the Iversky chapel with the lights of innumerable candles before the golden setting of the Madonna, the square of the Kremlin with its untrodden snow, the sledge-drivers, and the hovels of Sivtsev Vrazhok; saw the old Moscow gentlemen quietly going on with their daily round, without hurry or desire of change; saw the old Moscow ladies, the Moscow balls, and the English Club—he felt himself at home, in a quiet haven of rest. In Moscow he felt comfortable, warm, at home, and snugly dirty, as in an old dressing-gown.

All Moscow society, from the old ladies to the children, welcomed Pierre back like a long-expected guest, whose place was always ready for him, and had never been filled up. For the Moscow world, Pierre was the most delightful, kind-hearted, intellectual, good-humoured, and generous eccentric, and a heedless and genial Russian gentleman of the good old school. His purse was always empty, because it was always open to every one.

Benefit-entertainments, poor pictures and statues, benevolent societies, gypsy choruses, schools, subscription dinners, drinking parties, the masons, churches, and books—no one and nothing ever met with a refusal, and had it not been for two friends, who had borrowed large sums of money from Pierre and constituted themselves guardians of a sort over him, he would have parted with everything. Not a dinner, not a *soirée* took place at the club without him.

As soon as he was lolling in his place on the sofa, after a couple of bottles of margot, he was surrounded by a circle of friends, and arguments, disputes, and jokes sprang up round him. Where there were quarrels, his kindly smile and casually uttered jokes were enough to reconcile the antagonists. The masonic dining lodges were dull and dreary when he was absent.

When after a bachelor supper, with a weak and good-natured smile, he yielded to the entreaties of the festive party that he would drive off with them to share their revels, there were shouts of delight and triumph. At balls he danced if there were a lack of partners. Girls and young married ladies liked him, because he paid no special attention to any one, but was equally amiable to all, especially after supper. 'He is charming; he is of no sex,' they used to say of him.

Pierre was just a kammerherr, retired to end his days in Moscow, like hundreds of others. How horrified he would have been if, seven years before, when he had just come home from abroad, any one had told him that there was no need for him to look about him and rack his brains, that the track had long ago been trodden, marked out from all eternity for him, and that, struggle as he would, he would be just such another as all men in his position. He could not have believed it then! Had he not longed with his whole heart to establish a republic in Russia; then to be himself a Napoleon; then to be a philosopher; and then a great strategist and the conqueror of Napoleon? Had he not passionately desired and believed in the regeneration of the sinful race of man and the schooling of himself to the highest point of perfect virtue? Had he not founded schools and hospitals and liberated his serfs?

But instead of all that, here he was the wealthy husband of a faithless wife, a retired kammerherr, fond of dining and drinking, fond, too, as he unbuttoned his waistcoat after dinner, of indulging in a little abuse of the government, a member of the Moscow English Club, and a universal favourite in Moscow society. For a long while he could not reconcile himself to the idea that he was precisely the retired Moscow kammerherr, the very type he had so profoundly scorned seven years before.

Sometimes he consoled himself by the reflection that it did not count, that he was only temporarily leading this life. But later on he was horrified by another reflection, that numbers of other men, with the same idea of its being temporary, had entered that life and that club with all their teeth and a thick head of hair, only to leave it when they were toothless and bald.

In moments of pride, when he was reviewing his position, it seemed to him that he was quite different, distinguished in some way from the retired kammerherrs he had looked upon with contempt in the past; that they were vulgar and stupid, at ease and satisfied with their position, 'while I am even now still dissatisfied; I still long to do something for humanity,' he would assure himself in moments of pride. 'But possibly all of them too, my fellows, struggled just as I do, tried after something new, sought a path in life for themselves, and have been brought to the same point as I have by the force of surroundings, of society, of family, that elemental force against which man is powerless,' he said to himself in moments of modesty. And after spending some time in Moscow he no longer scorned his companions in destiny, but began even to love them, respect them, and pity them like himself.

Pierre no longer suffered from moments of despair, melancholy, and loathing for life as he had done. But the same malady that had manifested itself in acute attacks in former days was driven inwards and never now left him for an instant. 'What for? What's the use? What is it is going on in the world?' he asked himself in perplexity several times a day, instinctively beginning to sound the hidden significance in the phenomena of life. But knowing by experience that there was no answer to these questions, he made haste to try and turn away from them, took up a book, or hurried off to the club, or to Apollon Nikolaevitch's to chat over the scandals of the town.

'Elena Vassilyevna, who has never cared for anything but her own body, and is one of the stupidest women in the world,' Pierre thought, 'is regarded by people as the acme of wit and refinement, and is the object of their homage. Napoleon Bonaparte was despised by every one while he was really great, and since he became a pitiful buffoon the Emperor Francis seeks to offer him his daughter in an illegal marriage. The Spaniards, through their Catholic Church, return thanks to God for their victory over the French on the 14th of June, and the French, through the same Catholic Church, return thanks to God for their victory over the Spaniards on the same 14th of June. My masonic brothers swear in blood that they are ready to sacrifice all for their neighbour, but they don't give as much as one rouble to the collections for the poor, and they intrigue between Astraea and the manna-seekers, and are in a ferment about the authentic Scottish rug, and an act, of which the man who wrote it did not know the meaning and no one has any need. We all profess the Christian law of forgiveness of sins and love for one's neighbour—the law, in honour of which we have raised forty times forty churches in Moscow—but yesterday we knouted to death a deserter; and the minister of that same law of love and forgiveness, the priest, gave the soldier the cross to kiss before his punishment.'

Such were Pierre's reflections, and all this universal deception recognised by all, used as he was to seeing it, was always astounding him, as though it were something new. 'I understand this deceit and tangle of cross-purposes,' he thought, 'but how am I to tell them all I understand? I have tried and always found that they understood it as I did, at the bottom of their hearts, but were only trying not to see it. So I suppose it must be so! But me—what refuge is there for me?' thought Pierre.

He suffered from an unlucky faculty—common to many men, especially Russians—the faculty of seeing and believing in the possibility of good and truth, and at the same time seeing too clearly the evil and falsity of life to be capable of taking a serious part in it. Every sphere of activity was in his eyes connected with evil and deception. Whatever he tried to be, whatever he took up, evil and falsity drove him back again and cut him off from every field of energy. And meanwhile he had to live, he had to be occupied. It was too awful to lie under the burden of those insoluble problems of life, and he abandoned himself to the first distraction that offered, simply to forget them. He visited every possible society, drank a great deal, went in for buying pictures, building, and above all reading.

He read and re-read everything he came across. On getting home he would take up a book, even while his valets were undressing him, and read himself to sleep; and from sleep turned at once to gossip in the drawing-rooms and the club; from gossip to carousals and women; from dissipation back again to gossip, reading, and wine. Wine was more and more becoming a physical necessity to him, and at the same time a moral necessity. Although the doctors told him that in view of his corpulence wine was injurious to him, he drank a very great deal. He never felt quite content except when he had, almost unconsciously, lifted several glasses of wine to his big mouth. Then he felt agreeably warm all over his body, amiably disposed towards all his fellows, and mentally ready to respond superficially to every idea, without going too deeply into it. It was only after drinking a bottle or two of wine that he felt vaguely that the terrible tangled skein of life which had terrified him so before was not so terrible as he had fancied. With a buzzing in his head, chatting, listening to talk or reading after dinner and supper, he invariably saw that tangled skein on some one of its sides. It was only under the influence of wine that he said to himself: 'Never mind. I'll disentangle it all; here I have a solution all ready. But now's not the time. I'll go into all that later on!' But that *later on* never came.

In the morning, before breakfast, all the old questions looked as insoluble and fearful as ever, and Pierre hurriedly snatched up a book and rejoiced when any one came in to see him.

Sometimes Pierre remembered what he had been told of soldiers under fire in ambuscade when they have nothing to do, how they try hard to find occupation so as to bear their danger more easily. And Pierre pictured all men as such soldiers trying to find a refuge from life: some in ambition, some in cards, some in framing laws, some in women, some in playthings, some in horses, some in politics, some in sport, some in wine, some in the government service. 'Nothing is trivial, nothing is important, everything is the same; only to escape from it as best one can,' thought Pierre. 'Only not to see *it*, that terrible *it*.'

II

AT the beginning of the winter Prince Nikolay Andreitch Bolkonsky and his daughter moved to Moscow. His past, his intellect and originality, and still more the falling off at about that time of the popular enthusiasm for the rule of the Tsar Alexander and the anti-French and patriotic sentiments then prevailing at Moscow, all contributed to make Prince Nikolay Andreitch at once an object of peculiar veneration and the centre of the Moscow opposition to the government.

The prince had greatly aged during that year. He had begun to show unmistakable signs of failing powers, sudden attacks of drowsiness, and forgetfulness of events nearest in time, and exact memory of remote incidents, and a childlike vanity in playing the part of leader of the Moscow opposition. But in spite of that, when the old man came into the drawing-room in the evenings to tea, in his wig and fur coat, and on being incited to do so by some one, began uttering abrupt observations on the past, or still more abrupt and harsh criticisms on the present—he aroused the same feeling of esteem and reverence in all his guests. For visitors, that old-fashioned house, with its huge mirrors, pre-revolutionary furniture, and powdered lackeys, and the stern and shrewd old man, himself a relic of a past age, with the gentle daughter and the pretty Frenchwoman, both so reverently devoted to him, made a stately and agreeable spectacle. But those visitors did not reflect that, apart from the couple of hours during which they saw the household, there were twenty-two hours of the day and night during which the secret, private life of the house went on its accustomed way.

That inner life had become very hard for Princess Marya of late in Moscow. She was deprived in Moscow of her two greatest pleasures—talks with God's folk and the solitude which had refreshed her spirit at Bleak Hills, and she had none of the advantages and pleasures of town life. She did not go into society; every one knew that her father would not allow her to go anywhere without him, and owing to his failing health he could go nowhere himself. She was not even invited now to dinner-parties or balls. Princess Marya had laid aside all hopes of marriage. She saw the coldness and hostility with which the old prince received and dismissed the young men, possible suitors, who sometimes appeared at the house. Friends, Princess Marya now had none; during this stay in Moscow she had lost all faith in the two friends who had been nearest to her. Mademoiselle Bourienne, with whom she had never been able to be perfectly open, she now regarded with dislike, and for certain reasons kept at a distance. Julie, with whom Princess Marya had kept up an unbroken correspondence for five years, was in Moscow. When Princess Marya renewed her personal relations with her, she felt her former friend to be utterly alien to her. Julie, who had become, by the death of her brothers, one of the wealthiest heiresses in Moscow, was at that time engrossed in a giddy whirl of fashionable amusements. She was surrounded by young men, whom she believed to have become suddenly appreciative of her qualities. Julie was at that stage when a young lady is somewhat past her first youth in society and feels that her last chance of marrying has come, and that now or never her fate must be decided. With a mournful smile Princess Marya reflected every Thursday that she had now no one to write to, seeing that Julie was here and saw her every week, though her friend's actual presence gave her no sort of pleasure. Like the old French *emigre*, who declined to marry the lady with whom he had for so many years spent his evenings, she regretted that Julie was here and she had no one to write to. In Moscow Princess Marya had no one to speak to, no one to confide her sorrows to, and many fresh sorrows fell to her lot about this time. The time for Prince Andrey's return and marriage was approaching, and his commission to her to prepare her father's mind was so far from being successfully carried out that the whole thing seemed hopeless; and any reference to the young Countess Rostov infuriated the old prince, who was for the most part out of humour at all times now. Another trouble that weighed on Princess Marya of late was due to the lessons she gave to her six-year-old nephew. In her relations with little Nikolay she recognised to her consternation symptoms of her father's irritable character in herself. However often she told herself that she must not let herself lose her temper, when teaching her nephew, almost every time she sat down with a pointer showing him the French alphabet, she so longed to hasten, to make easy the process of transferring her knowledge to the child, who was by now always afraid his auntie would be angry the next moment, that at the slightest inattention she was quivering in nervous haste and vexation, she raised her voice and sometimes pulled him by his little hand and stood him in the corner. When she had stood him in the corner she would begin to cry herself over her evil, wicked nature, and little Nikolay, his sobs vying with hers, would come unbidden out of the corner to pull her wet hands from her face and try to comfort her. But the greatest, far the greatest of the princess's burdens was her father's irascibility, which was invariably directed against his daughter, and had of late reached the point of cruelty. Had he forced her to spend the night bowing to the ground, had he beaten her, or made her carry in wood and water, it would never have entered her head that her position was a hard one. But this loving despot—most cruel of all because he loved, and for that very reason tortured himself and her—knew not only how to mortify and humiliate her, but, of set purpose, to prove to her that she was always to blame in everything. Of late he had taken a new departure, which caused Princess Marya more misery than anything—that was his closer and closer intimacy with Mademoiselle Bourienne. The idea, that had occurred to him in jest at the first moment of receiving the news of his son's intentions, that if Andrey got married he, too, would marry Mademoiselle Bourienne, obviously pleased him, and he had of late—simply, as Princess Marya fancied, to annoy her—persisted in being particularly gracious to Mademoiselle Bourienne and manifesting his dissatisfaction with his daughter by demonstrations of love for the Frenchwoman.

One day in Princess Marya's presence (it seemed to her that her father did it on purpose because she was there) the old prince kissed Mademoiselle Bourienne's hand, and drawing her to him embraced her affectionately. Princess Marya flushed hotly and ran out of the room. A few minutes later, Mademoiselle Bourienne went into Princess Marya's, smiling and making some cheerful remarks in her agreeable voice. Princess Marya hastily wiped away her tears, with resolute steps went up to the Frenchwoman, and obviously unconscious of what she was doing, with wrathful haste and breaks in her voice she began screaming at her:

'It's loathsome, vile, inhuman to take advantage of feebleness . . .' She could not go on. 'Go out of my room,' she cried, and broke into sobs.

The next day the old prince did not say a word to his daughter, but she noticed that at dinner he gave orders for the dishes to be handed to Mademoiselle Bourienne first. When towards the end of dinner, the footman from habit handed the coffee, beginning with the princess, the old prince flew into a sudden frenzy of rage, flung his cane at Filipp, and immediately gave orders for him to be sent for a soldier.

'He won't obey . . . twice I told him! . . . and he didn't obey. She's the first person in this house, she's my best friend,' screamed the old prince. 'And if you allow yourself,' he shouted in a fury, for the first time addressing Princess Marya, 'ever again, as you dared yesterday . . . to forget yourself in her presence, I'll show you who is master in this house. Away! don't let me set eyes on you! Beg her pardon!'

Princess Marya begged Amalia Yevgenyevna's pardon and also her father's, both for herself and the footman Filipp, who implored her intervention.

At such moments the feeling that prevailed in Princess Marya's soul was akin to the pride of sacrifice. And all of a sudden at such moments, that father whom she was judging would look for his spectacles, fumbling by them and not seeing them, or would forget what had just happened, or would take a tottering step with his weak legs, and look round to see whether any one had noticed his feebleness, or what was worst of all, at dinner when there were no guests to excite him, he would suddenly fall asleep, letting his napkin drop and his shaking head sink over his plate. 'He is old and feeble, and I dare not judge him!' she thought, revolted by herself.

III

IN the year 1811 there was living in Moscow a French doctor called Metivier, who was rapidly coming into fashion. He was a very tall, handsome man, polite as only a Frenchman is, and was said by every one in Moscow to be an extraordinarily clever doctor. He was received in the very best houses, not merely as a doctor, but as an equal.

Prince Nikolay Andreitch had always ridiculed medicine, but of late he had by Mademoiselle Bourienne's advice allowed this doctor to see him, and had become accustomed to his visits. Metivier used to see the old prince twice a week.

On St. Nikolay's day, the name-day of the old prince, all Moscow was driving up to the approach of his house, but he gave orders for no one to be admitted to see him. Only a few guests, of whom he gave a list to Princess Marya, were to be invited to dinner.

Metivier, who arrived in the morning with his felicitations, thought himself as the old prince's doctor entitled to *forcer la consigne*, as he told Princess Marya, and went in to the prince. It so happened that on that morning of his name-day the old prince was in one of his very worst tempers. He had spent the whole morning wandering about the house, finding fault with every one, and affecting not to understand what was said to him and to be misunderstood by everybody. Princess Marya knew that mood well from the subdued and fretful grumbling, which usually found vent in a violent outburst of fury, and as though facing a cocked and loaded gun, she went all the morning in expectation of an explosion. The morning passed off fairly well, till the doctor's arrival. After admitting the doctor, Princess Marya sat down with a book in the drawing-room near the door, where she could hear all that passed in the prince's study.

At first she heard Metivier's voice alone, then her father's voice, then both voices began talking at once. The door flew open, and in the doorway she saw the handsome, terrified figure of Metivier with his shock of black hair, and the old prince in a skull-cap and dressing-gown, his face hideous with rage and his eyes lowered.

'You don't understand,' screamed the old prince, 'but I do! French spy, slave of Bonaparte, spy, out of my house—away, I tell you!' And he slammed the door. Metivier, shrugging his shoulders, went up to Mademoiselle Bourienne, who ran out of the next room at the noise.

'The prince is not quite well, bile and rush of blood to the head. Calm yourself, I will look in tomorrow,' said Metivier; and putting his fingers to his lips he hurried off.

Through the door could be heard steps shuffling in slippers and shouts: 'Spies, traitors, traitors everywhere! Not a minute of peace in my own house!'

After Metivier's departure the old prince sent for his daughter, and the whole fury of his passion spent itself on her. She was to blame for the spy's having been admitted to see him. Had not he told her, told her to make a list, and that those not on the list were on no account to be admitted? Why then had that scoundrel been shown up? She was to blame for everything. With her he could not have a minute of peace, could not die in peace, he told her.

'No, madam, we must part, we must part, I tell you! I can put up with no more,' he said, and went out of the room. And as though afraid she might find some comfort, he turned back and trying to assume an air of calmness, he added: 'And don't imagine that I have said this in a moment of temper; no, I'm quite calm and I have thought it well over, and it shall be so—you shall go away, and find some place for yourself! . . .' But he could not restrain himself, and with the vindictive fury which can only exist where a man loves, obviously in anguish, he shook his fists and screamed at her: 'Ah! if some fool would marry her!' He slammed the door, sent for Mademoiselle Bourienne, and subsided into his study.

At two o'clock the six persons he had selected arrived to dinner. Those guests—the celebrated Count Rastoptchin, Prince Lopuhin and his nephew, General Tchatrov, an old comrade of the prince's in the field, and of the younger generation Pierre and Boris Drubetskoy were awaiting him in the drawing-room. Boris, who had come on leave to Moscow shortly before, had been anxious to be presented to Prince Nikolay Andreitch, and had succeeded in so far ingratiating himself in his favour, that the old prince made in his case an exception from his usual rule of excluding all young unmarried men from his house.

The prince did not receive what is called 'society,' but his house was the centre of a little circle into which—though it was not talked of much in the town—it was more flattering to be admitted than anywhere else. Boris had grasped that fact a week previously, when he heard Rastoptchin tell the commander-in-chief of Moscow, who had invited him to dine on St. Nikolay's day, that he could not accept the invitation.

'On that day I always go to pay my devotions to the relics of Prince Nikolay Andreitch.'

'Oh yes, yes . . .' assented the commander-in-chief. 'How is he? . . .'

The little party assembled before dinner in the old-fashioned lofty drawing-room, with its old furniture, was like the solemn meeting of some legal council board.

All sat silent, or if they spoke, spoke in subdued tones. Prince Nikolay Andreitch came in, serious and taciturn. Princess Marya seemed meeker and more timid than usual. The guests showed no inclination to address their conversation to her, for they saw that she had no thought for what they were saying. Count Rastoptchin maintained the conversation alone, relating the latest news of the town and the political world. Lopuhin and the old general took part in the conversation at rare intervals. Prince Nikolay Andreitch listened like a presiding judge receiving a report submitted to him, only testifying by his silence, or from time to time by a brief word, that he was taking cognizance of the facts laid before him.

The tone of the conversation was based on the assumption that no one approved of what was being done in the political world. Incidents were related obviously confirming the view that everything was going from bad to worse. But in every story that was told, and in every criticism that was offered, what was striking was the way that the speaker checked himself, or was chekced, every time the line was reached where a criticism might have reference to the person of the Tsar himself.

At dinner the conversation turned on the last political news, Napoleon's seizure of the possessions of the Duke of Oldenburg, and the Russian note, hostile to Napoleon, which had been despatched to all the European courts.

'Bonaparte treats all Europe as a pirate does a captured vessel,' said Rastoptchin, repeating a phrase he had uttered several times before. 'One only marvels at the long-suffering or the blindness of the ruling sovereigns. Now it's the Pope's turn, and Bonaparte doesn't scruple to try and depose the head of the Catholic Church, and no one says a word. Our Emperor alone has protested against the seizure of the possessions of the Duke of Oldenburg. And even . . .' Count Rastoptchin broke off, feeling that he was on the very border line beyond which criticism was impossible.

'Other domains have been offered him instead of the duchy of Oldenburg,' said the old prince. 'He shifts the dukes about, as I might move my serfs from Bleak Hills to Bogutcharovo and the Ryazan estates.'

'The Duke of Oldenburg supports his misfortune with admirable force of character and resignation,' said Boris, putting his word respectfully. He said this because on his journey from Petersburg he had had the honour of being presented to the duke. The old prince looked at the young man as though he would have liked to say something in reply, but changed his mind, considering him too young.

'I have read our protest about the Oldenburg affair, and I was surprised at how badly composed the note was,' said Count Rastoptchin in the casual tone of a man criticising something with which he is very familiar.

Pierre looked at Rastoptchin in naïve wonder, unable to understand why he should be troubled by the defective composition of the note.

'Does it matter how the note is worded, count,' he said, 'if the meaning is forcible?'

'My dear fellow, with our five hundred thousand troops, it should be easy to have a good style,' said Count Rastoptchin.

Pierre perceived the point of Count Rastoptchin's dissatisfaction with the wording of the note.

'I should have thought there were scribblers enough to write it,' said the old prince. 'Up in Petersburg they do nothing but write—not notes only, but new laws they keep writing. My Andryusha up there has written a whole volume of new laws for Russia. Nowadays they're always at it!' And he laughed an unnatural laugh.

The conversation paused for a moment; the old general cleared his throat to draw attention.

'Did you hear of the last incident at the review in Petersburg? Didn't the new French ambassadors expose themselves!'

'Eh? Yes, I did hear something; he said something awkward in the presence of his majesty.'

'His majesty drew his attention to the grenadier division and the parade march,' pursued the general; 'and it seems the ambassador took no notice and had the insolence to say "We in France," says he, "don't pay attention to such trivial matters." The emperor did not vouchsafe him a reply. At the review that followed the emperor, they say, did not once deign to address him.'

Every one was silent; upon this fact which related to the Tsar personally, no criticism could be offered.

'Impudent rogues!' said the old prince. 'Do you know Metivier? I turned him out of the house today. He was here, he was allowed to come in, in spite of my begging no one should be admitted,' said the old prince, glancing angrily at his daughter. And he told them his whole conversation with the French doctor and his reasons for believing Metivier to be a spy. Though his reasons were very insufficient and obscure, no one raised an objection.

After the meat, champagne was handed round. The guests rose from their places to congratulate the old prince. Princess Marya too went up to him. He glanced at her with a cold, spiteful glance, and offered her his shaven, wrinkled cheek. The whole expression of his face told her that their morning's conversation was not forgotten, that his resolution still held good, and that it was only owing to the presence of their visitors that he did not tell her so now.

When they went into the drawing-room to coffee, the old men sat together.

Prince Nikolay Andreitch grew more animated, and began to express his views on the impending war. He said that our wars with Bonaparte would be unsuccessful so long as we sought alliances with the Germans and went meddling in European affairs, into which we had been drawn by the Peace of Tilsit. We had no business to fight for Austria or against Austria. Our political interests all lay in the East, and as regards Bonaparte, the one thing was an armed force on the frontier, and a firm policy, and he would never again dare to cross the Russian frontier, as he had done in 1807.

'And how should we, prince, fight against the French!' said Count Rastoptchin. 'Can we arm ourselves against our teachers and divinities? Look at our young men, look at our ladies. Our gods are the French, and Paris—our Paradise.'

He began talking more loudly, obviously with the intention of being heard by every one.

'Our fashions are French, our ideas are French, our feelings are French! You have sent Metivier about his business because he's a Frenchman and a scoundrel, but our ladies are crawling on their hands and knees after him. Yesterday I was at an evening party, and out of five ladies three were Catholics and had a papal indulgence for embroidering on Sundays. And they sitting all but naked, like the signboards of some public bath-house, if you'll excuse my saying so. Ah, when one looks at our young people, prince, one would like to take Peter the Great's old cudgel out of the museum, and break a few ribs in the good old Russian style, to knock the nonsense out of them!'

All were silent. The old prince looked at Rastoptchin with a smile on his face and shook his head approvingly.

'Well, good-bye, your excellency; don't you be ill,' said Rastoptchin, getting up with the brisk movements characteristic of him, and holding out his hand to the old prince.

'Good-bye, my dear fellow. Your talk is a music I'm always glad to listen to!' said the old prince, keeping hold of his hand and offering him his cheek for a kiss. The others, too, got up when Rastoptchin did.

IV

PRINCESS MARYA, sitting in the drawing-room, and hearing the old men's talk and criticisms, did not understand a word of what she was hearing. She thought of nothing but whether all their guests were noticing her father's hostile attitude to her. She did not even notice the marked attention and amiability shown her during the whole of dinner by Drubetskoy, who was that day paying them his third visit.

Princess Marya turned with an absent-minded, questioning glance to Pierre, who, with a smile on his face, came up to her, hat in hand, the last of the guests, after the prince had gone out, and they were left alone together in the drawing-room.

'Can I stay a little longer?' he said, dropping his bulky person into a low chair beside Princess Marya.

'Oh yes,' she said. 'You noticed nothing?' her eyes asked.

Pierre was in an agreeable, after-dinner mood. He looked straight before him and smiled softly. 'Have you known that young man long, princess?' he said.

'Which one?'

'Drubetskoy.'

'No, not long . . . .'

'Well, do you like him?'

'Yes; he's a very agreeable young man. Why do you ask me?' said Princess Marya, still thinking of her conversation in the morning with her father.

'Because I have observed, that when a young man comes from Petersburg to Moscow on leave, it is invariably with the object of marrying an heiress.'

'Have you observed that?' said Princess Marya.

'Yes,' Pierre went on with a smile, 'and that young man now manages matters so that wherever there are wealthy heiresses—there he is to be found. I can read him like a book. He is hesitating now which to attack, you or Mademoiselle Julie Karagin. He is very attentive to her.'

'Does he visit them?'

'Yes, very often. And do you know the new-fashioned method of courting?' said Pierre, smiling good-humouredly, and obviously feeling in that light-hearted mood of good-natured irony, for which he had so often reproached himself in his diary.

'No,' said Princess Marya.

'To please the Moscow girls nowadays one has to be melancholy. He is very melancholy with Mademoiselle Karagin,' said Pierre.

'Really!' said Princess Marya, looking at the kindly face of Pierre, and thinking all the time of her own trouble. 'It would ease my heart,' she was thinking, 'if I could make up my mind to confide all I am feeling to some one. And it is just Pierre I should like to tell it all to. He is so kind and generous. It would ease my heart. He would give me advice.'

'Would you marry him?' asked Pierre.

'O my God, count! there are moments when I would marry any one'—to her own surprise Princess Marya said, with tears in her voice.

'Ah! how bitter it is to love some one near to one and to feel,' she went on in a shaking voice, 'that you can do nothing for him, but cause him sorrow, and when you know you cannot alter it. There's only one thing —to go away, and where am I to go?'

'What is wrong? what is the matter with you, princess?'

But Princess Marya, without explaining further, burst into tears.

'I don't know what is the matter with me today. Don't take any notice of me, forget what I said to you.'

All Pierre's gaiety had vanished. He questioned the princess anxiously, begged her to speak out, to confide her trouble to him. But she would only repeat that she begged him to forget what she had said, that she did not remember what she had said, and that she had no trouble except the one he knew—her anxiety lest Prince Andrey's marriage should cause a breach between him and his father.

'Have you heard anything of the Rostovs?' she asked to change the subject. 'I was told they would soon be here. I expect Andrey, too, every day. I should have liked them to see each other here.'

'And how does he look at the matter now?' asked Pierre, meaning by *he* the old prince. Princess Marya shook her head.

'But it can't be helped. There are only a few months left now before the year is over. And it can't go on like this. I should only have liked to spare my brother the first minutes. I could have wished they were coming sooner. I hope to get to know her well. . . . You have known them a long while,' said Princess Marya. 'Tell me the whole truth, speaking quite seriously. What sort of a girl is she, and how do you like her? But the whole truth, because, you see, Andrey is risking so much in doing this against our father's will, that I should like to know . . .'

A vague instinct told Pierre that these pleas and repeated requests to him to tell her the *whole truth* betrayed Princess Marya's ill-will towards her future sister-in-law, that she wanted Pierre not to approve of Prince Andrey's choice; but Pierre said what he felt rather than what he thought. 'I don't know how to answer your question,' said he, blushing though he could not have said why himself. 'I really don't know what kind of girl she is. I can't analyse her. She's fascinating; and why she is, I don't know; that's all that one can say about her.'

Princess Marya sighed, and her face expressed: 'Yes; that's what I expected and feared.'

'Is she clever?' asked Princess Marya. Pierre thought a moment.

'I suppose not,' he said. 'Yes, though. She does not think it worth while to be clever. . . . Yes, no; she is fascinating, and nothing more.'

Princess Marya again shook her head disapprovingly.

'Ah, I do so want to like her! You tell her so if you see her before I do.'

'I have heard that they will be here in a few days,' said Pierre.

Princess Marya told Pierre her plan of getting to know her future sister-in-law as soon as the Rostovs arrived, and trying to get the old prince accustomed to her.

V

BORIS had not succeeded in marrying a wealthy heiress in Petersburg, and it was with that object that he had come to Moscow. In Moscow Boris found himself hesitating between two of the wealthiest heiresses,—Julie and Princess Marya. Though Princess Marya, in spite of her plainness, seemed to him anyway more attractive than Julie, he felt vaguely awkward in paying court to the former. In his latest conversation with her, on the old prince's name-day, she had met all his attempts to talk of the emotions with irrelevant replies, and had obviously not heard what he was saying.

Julie, on the contrary, received his attentions eagerly, though she showed it in a peculiar fashion of her own.

Julie was seven-and-twenty. By the death of her two brothers she had become extremely wealthy. She had by now become decidedly plain. But she believed herself to be not merely as pretty as ever, but actually far more attractive than she had ever been. She was confirmed in this delusion by having become a very wealthy heiress, and also by the fact that as she grew older her society involved less risk for men; and they could behave with more freedom in their intercourse with her, and could profit by her suppers, her *soirées*, and the lively society that gathered about her, without incurring any obligations to her. A man who would have been afraid of going ten years before to a house where there was a young girl of seventeen, for fear of compromising her and binding himself, would now boldly visit her every day, and treat her not as a marriageable girl, but as an acquaintance of no sex.

The Karagins' house was that winter one of the most agreeable and hospitable houses in Moscow. In addition to the dinner-parties and *soirées*, to which guests came by invitation, there were every day large informal gatherings at the Karagins', principally of men, who had supper there at midnight and stayed on till three o'clock in the morning. Julie did not miss a single ball, entertainment, or theatre. Her dresses were always of the most fashionable. But in spite of that, Julie appeared to have lost all illusions, told every one that she had no faith in love or friendship, or any of the joys of life, and looked for consolation only to the *realm beyond*. She had adopted the tone of a girl who has suffered a great disappointment, a girl who has lost her lover or been cruelly deceived by him. Though nothing of the kind had ever happened to her, she was looked upon as having been disappointed in that way, and she did in fact believe herself that she had suffered a great deal in her life. This melancholy neither hindered her from enjoying herself nor hindered young men from spending their time very agreeably in her society. Every guest who visited at the house paid his tribute to the melancholy temper of the hostess, and then proceeded to enjoy himself in society gossip, dancing, intellectual games, or *bouts rimés* which were in fashion at the Karagins'. A few young men only, among them Boris, entered more deeply into Julie's melancholy, and with these young men she had more prolonged and secluded conversations on the nothingness of all things earthly, and to them she opened her albums, full of mournful sketches, sentences, and verses.

Julie was particularly gracious to Boris. She deplored his early disillusionment with life, offered him those consolations of friendship she was so well able to offer, having herself suffered so cruelly in life, and opened her album to him. Boris sketched two trees in her album, and wrote under them: 'Rustic trees, your gloomy branches shed darkness and melancholy upon me.'

In another place he sketched a tomb and inscribed below it:

> 'Death is helpful, and death is tranquil,
> Ah, there is no other refuge from sorrow!'

Julie said that couplet was exquisite.

'There is something so ravishing in the smile of melancholy,' she said to Boris, repeating word for word a passage copied from a book. 'It is a ray of light in the shadow, a blend between grief and despair, which shows consolation possible.'

Upon that Boris wrote her the following verses in French:

> 'Poisonous nourishment of a soul too sensitive,
> Thou, without whom happiness would be impossible to me,
> Tender melancholy, ah, come and console me,
> Come, calm the torments of my gloomy retreat,
> And mingle a secret sweetness with the tears I feel flowing.'

Julie played to Boris the most mournful nocturnes on the harp. Boris read aloud to her the romance of *Poor Liza,* and more than once broke down in reading it from the emotion that choked his utterance. When they met in general society Julie and Boris gazed at one another as though they were the only people existing in the world, disillusioned and comprehending each other.

Anna Mihalovna, who often visited the Karagins, took a hand at cards with the mother, and meanwhile collected trustworthy information as to the portion that Julie would receive on her marriage (her dowry was to consist of two estates in the Penza province and forests in the Nizhnigorod province). With tender emotion and deep resignation to the will of Providence, Anna Mihalovna looked on at the refined sadness that united her son to the wealthy Julie.

'Still as charming and as melancholy as ever, my sweet Julie,' she would say to the daughter. 'Boris says he finds spiritual refreshment in your house. He has suffered such cruel disillusionment, and he is so sensitive,' she would say to the mother.

'Ah, my dear, how attached I have grown to Julie lately,' she would say to her son, 'I can't tell you. But, indeed, who could help loving her! A creature not of this earth! Ah, Boris! Boris!' She paused for a moment. 'And how I feel for her mother,' she would go on. 'She showed me today the letters and accounts from Penza (they have an immense estate there), and she, poor thing, with no one to help her. They do take such advantage of her!'

Boris heard his mother with a faintly perceptible smile. He laughed blandly at her simple-hearted wiles, but he listened to her and sometimes questioned her carefully about the Penza and Nizhnigorod estates.

Julie had long been expecting an offer from her melancholy adorer, and was fully prepared to accept it. But a sort of secret feeling of repulsion for her, for her passionate desire to be married, for her affectation, and a feeling of hooror at renouncing all possibility of real love made Boris still delay. The term of his leave was drawing to a close. Whole days at a time, and every day he spent at the Karagins'; and each day Boris resolved, as he thought things over, that he would make an offer on the morrow. But in Julie's presence, as he watched her red face and her chin, almost always sprinkled with powder, her moist eyes, and the expression of her countenance, which betokened a continual readiness to pass at once from melancholy to the unnatural ecstasies of conjugal love, Boris could not utter the decisive word, although in imagination he had long regarded himself as the owner of the Penza and Nizhnigorod estates, and had disposed of the expenditure of their several revenues. Julie saw the hesitation of Boris, and the idea did sometimes occur to her that she was distasteful to him. But feminine self-flattery promptly afforded her comfort, and she assured herself that it was love that made him retiring. Her melancholy was, however, beginning to pass into irritability, and not long before the end of Boris's leave she adopted a decisive plan of action. Just before the expiration of Boris's leave there appeared in Moscow, and—it need hardly be said—also in the drawing-room of the Kuragins', no less a person than Anatole Kuragin, and Julie, abruptly abandoning her melancholy, became exceedingly lively and cordial to Kuragin.

'My dear,' said Anna Mihalovna to her son, 'I know from a trustworthy source that Prince Vassily is sending his son to Moscow to marry him to Julie. I am so fond of Julie that I should be most sorry for her. What do you think about it, my dear?' said Anna Mihalovna.

Boris was mortified at the idea of being unsuccessful, of having wasted all that month of tedious, melancholy courtship of Julie, and of seeing all the revenues of those Penza estates—which he had mentally assigned to the various purposes for which he needed them—pass into other hands, especially into the hands of that fool Anatole. He drove off to the Karagins with the firm determination to make an offer. Julie met him with a gay and careless face, casually mentioned how much she had enjoyed the ball of the previous evening, and asked him when he was leaving. Although Boris had come with the intention of speaking of his love, and was therefore resolved to take a tender tone, he began to speak irritably of the fickleness of woman; saying that women could so easily pass from sadness to joy, and their state of mind depended entirely on what sort of man happened to be paying them attention. Julie was offended, and said that that was quite true, indeed, that a woman wanted variety, and that always the same thing would bore any one.

'Then I would advise you . . .' Boris was beginning, meaning to say something cutting; but at that instant the mortifying reflection occurred to him that he might leave Moscow without having attained his object, and having wasted his efforts in vain (an experience he had never had yet). He stopped short in the middle of a sentence, dropped his eyes, to avoid seeing her disagreeably exasperated and irresolute face, and said, 'But it was not to quarrel with you that I have come here. On the contrary . . .' He glanced at her to make sure whether he could go on. All irritation had instantly vanished from her face, and her uneasy and imploring eyes were fastened upon him in greedy expectation.

'I can always manage so as to see very little of her,' thought Boris. 'And the thing's been begun and must be finished!' He flushed crimson, raised his eyes to her face, and said to her, 'You know my feeling for you!' There was no need to say more. Julie's countenance beamed with triumph and self-satisfaction; but she forced Boris to say everything that is usually said on such occasions, to say that he loved her, and had never loved any woman more than her. She knew that for her Penza estates and her Nizhnigorod forests she could demand that, and she got all she demanded.

The young engaged couple, with no further allusions to trees that enfolded them in gloom and melancholy, made plans for a brilliant establishment in Petersburg, paid visits, and made every preparation for a splendid wedding.

VI

Count Ilya Andreitch Rostov arrived in Moscow towards the end of January with Natasha and Sonya. The countess was still unwell, and unable to travel, but they could not put off coming till she recovered, for Prince Andrey was expected in Moscow every day. They had, besides, to order the trousseau, to sell the estate in the suburbs of Moscow, and to take advantage of old Prince Bolkonsky's presence in Moscow to present his future daughter-in-law to him. The Rostovs' house in Moscow had not been heated all the winter; and as they were coming only for a short time, and the countess was not with them, Count Ilya Andreitch made up his mind to stay with Marya Dmitryevna Ahrosimov, who had long been pressing her hospitality upon the count.

Late in the evening the four loaded sledges of the Rostovs drove into the courtyard of Marya Dmitryevna in Old Equerrys' Place. Marya Dmitryevna lived alone. She had by now married off her daughter. Her sons were all in the service.

She still held herself as erect; still gave every one her opinions in the same loud, outspoken, decided fashion; and her whole bearing seemed a reproof to other people for every sort of weakness, passion, and temptation, of which she would not admit the bare possibility. In the early morning, in a house-jacket, she looked after the management of her household. Then she drove on saints' days to Mass, and from Mass to the gaols and prisons; and of what she did there, she never spoke to any one.

On ordinary days she dressed and received petitioners of various classes, of whom some sought her aid every day. Then she had dinner, an abundant and appetising meal, at which some three or four guests were always present. After dinner she played a game of boston; and at night had the newspapers and new books read aloud to her while she knitted. It was only as a rare exception that she went out in the evening; if she did so, it was only to visit the most important people in the town.

She had not gone to bed when the Rostovs arrived, and the door in the vestibule squeaked on the block, as the Rostovs and their servants came in from the cold outside. Marya Dmitryevna stood in the doorway of the hall, with her spectacles slipping down on her nose, and her head flung back, looking with a stern and irate face at the newcomers. It might have been supposed that she was irritated at their arrival, and would pack them off again at once, had she not at the very time been giving careful instructions to her servants where to install her guests and their belongings.

'The count's things? Bring them here,' she said, pointing to the trunks, and not bestowing a greeting on any one. 'The young ladies, this way to the left. Well, what are we pottering about for?' she called to her maids. 'Warm the samovar! She's plumper, prettier,' she pronounced of Natasha, flushed from the frosty air, as she drew her closer by her hood. 'Foo! she is cold! You make haste and get your wraps off,' she shouted to the count, who would have kissed her hand. 'You're frozen, I warrant. Rum for the tea! Sonyushka, *bonjour*,' she said to Sonya, indicating by this French phrase the slightly contemptuous affectionateness of her attitude to Sonya.

When they had all taken off their outdoor things, set themselves straight after the journey, and come in to tea, Marya Dmitryevna kissed them all in due course.

'Heartily glad you have come, and are staying with me,' she said. 'It's long been time you were here,' she said, with a significant glance at Natasha.... 'The old fellow's here, and his son's expected from day to day. You must, you must make their acquaintance. Oh, well, we shall talk of that later on,' she added, with a glance at Sonya, showing that she did not care to talk of it before her. 'Now, listen,' she turned to the count, 'what do you want to do tomorrow? Whom will you send for? Shinshin?'—she crooked one finger. 'The tearful Anna Mihalovna—two. She's here with her son. The son's to be married too! Then Bezuhov. He's here, too, with his wife. He ran away from her, and she has come trotting after him. He dined with me last Wednesday. Well, and I'll take them'—she indicated the young ladies—'tomorrow to Iversky chapel, and then we shall go to Aubert-Chalmey. You'll be getting everything now, I expect! Don't judge by me—the sleeves nowadays are like this! The other day the young princess, Irina Vassilyevna, came to see me, just as though she had put two barrels on her arms, a dreadful fright. Every day there's a new fashion. And what sort of business is it you have come for yourself?' she said severely, addressing the count.

'Everything has come together,' answered the count. 'There's the girl's rags to buy; and now there's a purchaser turned up for the Moscow estate and the house. If you'll graciously permit it, I'll choose an opportunity and drive over to Maryinskoe for a day, leaving my girls on your hands.'

'Very good, very good, they'll be safe enough with me. I'm as safe as the Mortgage Bank. I'll take them where they must go, and scold them and pet them too,' said Marya Dmitryevna, putting her big hand on the cheek of her favourite and goddaughter Natasha.

Next morning Marya Dmitryevna bore the young ladies off to Iversky chapel and to Madame Aubert-Chalmey, who was so frightened of Marya Dmitryevna that she always sold her dresses at a loss simply to get rid of her as soon as possible. Marya Dmitryevna ordered almost the whole trousseau. On their return, she sent every one out of the room but Natasha, and called her favourite to sit beside her armchair.

'Well, now we can have a chat. I congratulate you on your betrothed. A fine fellow you have hooked! I'm glad of it for your sake, and I have known him since he was that high'—she held her hand a yard from the floor. Natasha flushed joyfully. 'I like him and all his family. Now, listen! You know, of course, that old Prince Nikolay was very much against his son's marrying. He's a whimsical old fellow! Of course, Prince Andrey is not a child, he can get on without him, but to enter a family against the father's will is not a nice thing to do. One wants peace and love in a family. You're a clever girl, you'll know how to manage things. You must use your wits and your kind heart. And every thing will come right.'

Natasha was silent, not as Marya Dmitryevna supposed from shyness. In reality Natasha disliked any one's interfering in what touched her love for Prince Andrey, which seemed to her something so apart from all human affairs, that no one, as she imagined, could understand it. She loved Prince Andrey, and only him, and knew only him; he loved her, and was to arrive in a day or two and carry her off. She did not care about anything else.

'I have known him a long while, do you see; and Masha, your sister-in-law, I love. Sisters-in-law are said to be mischief-makers, but she—well, she wouldn't hurt a fly. She has begged me to bring you two together. You must go to see her tomorrow with your father, and be as nice as possible; you are younger than she is. By the time your young man comes back, you'll be friends with his sister and his father, and they will have learned to love you. Yes or no? It will be better so, eh?'

'Oh yes!' Natasha responded reluctantly.

VII

NEXT day, by the advice of Marya Dmitryevna, Count Ilya Andreitch went with Natasha to call on Prince Nikolay Andreitch. The count prepared for the visit by no means in a cheerful spirit: in his heart he was afraid. Count Ilya Andreitch had a vivid recollection of his last interview with the old prince at the time of the levying of the militia, when, in reply to his invitation to dinner, he had had to listen to a heated reprimand for furnishing less than the required number of men. Natasha in her best dress was, on the contrary, in the most cheerful frame of mind. 'They can't help liking me,' she thought; 'every one always does like me. And I'm so ready to do anything they please for them, so ready to love them—him for being his father, and her for being his sister—they can have no reason for not loving me!'

They drove to the gloomy old house in Vosdvizhenka, and went into the vestibule.

'Well now, with God's blessing,' said the count, half in jest, half in earnest. But Natasha noticed that her father was in a nervous fidget as he went into the entry, and asked timidly and softly whether the prince and the princess were at home. After their arrival had been announced, there was some perturbation visible among the prince's servants. The footman, who was running to announce them, was stopped by another footman in the big hall, and they whispered together. A maid-servant ran into the hall, and hurriedly said something, mentioning the princess. At last one old footman came out with a wrathful air, and announced to the Rostovs that the prince was not receiving, but the princess begged them to walk up. The first person to meet the visitors was Mademoiselle Bourienne. She greeted the father and daughter with marked courtesy, and conducted them to the princess's apartment. The princess, with a frightened and agitated face, flushed in patches, ran in, treading heavily, to meet her visitors, doing her best to seem cordial and at ease. From the first glance Princess Marya disliked Natasha. She thought her too fashionably dressed, too frivolously gay and vain. Princess Marya had no idea that before she had seen her future sister-in-law she had been unfavourably disposed to her, through unconscious envy of her beauty, her youth, and her happiness, and through jealousy of her brother's love for her. Apart from this insuperable feeling of antipathy to her, Princess Marya was at that moment agitated by the fact that on the Rostovs having been announced the old prince had shouted that he didn't want to see them, that Princess Marya could see them if she chose, but they were not to be allowed in to see him. Princess Marya resolved to see the Rostovs, but she was every instant in dread of some freak on the part of the old prince, as he had appeared greatly excited by the arrival of the Rostovs.

'Well, here I have brought you my songstress, princess,' said the count, bowing and scraping, while he looked round uneasily as though he were afraid the old prince might come in. 'How glad I am that you should make friends. . . . Sorry, very sorry, the prince is still unwell'; and uttering a few more stock phrases, he got up. 'If you'll allow me, princess, to leave you my Natasha for a quarter of an hour, I will drive round—only a few steps from here—to Dogs' Square to see Anna Semyonovna, and then come back for her.'

Count Ilya Andreitch bethought himself of this diplomatic stratagem to give the future sisters-in-law greater freedom to express their feelings to one another (so he told his daughter afterwards), but also to avoid the possibility of meeting the prince, of whom he was afraid. He did not tell his daughter this; but Natasha perceived this dread and uneasiness of her father's, and felt mortified by it. She blushed for her father, felt still angrier at having blushed, and glanced at the princess with a bold, challenging air, meant to express that she was not afraid of any one. The princess told the count that she would be delighted, and only begged him to stay a little longer at Anna Semyonovna's, and Ilya Andreitch departed.

In spite of the uneasy glances flung at her by Princess Marya, who wanted to talk to Natasha by herself, Mademoiselle Bourienne would not leave the room, and persisted in keeping up a conversation about Moscow entertainments and theatres. Natasha felt offended by the delay in the entry, by her father's nervousness, and by the constrained manner of the princess, who seemed to her to be making a favour of receiving her. And then everything displeased her. She did not like Princess Marya. She seemed to her very ugly, affected, and frigid. Natasha suddenly, as it were, shrank into herself, and unconsciously assumed a nonchalant air, which repelled Princess Marya more and more. After five minutes of irksome and constrained conversation, they heard the sound of slippered feet approaching rapidly. Princess Marya's face expressed terror: the door of the room opened, and the prince came in, in a white night-cap and dressing-gown.

'Ah, madam,' he began, 'madam, countess, . . . Countess Rostov . . . if I'm not mistaken . . . I beg you to excuse me, to excuse me . . . I didn't know, madam. As God's above, I didn't know that you were deigning to visit us, and came in to my daughter in this costume. I beg you to excuse me . . . as God's above, I didn't know,' he repeated so unnaturally, with emphasis on the word 'God,' and so unpleasantly, that Princess Marya rose to her feet with her eyes on the ground, not daring to look either at her father or at Natasha. Natasha, getting up and curtseying, did not know either what she was to do. Only Mademoiselle Bourienne smiled agreeably.

'I beg you to excuse me, I beg you to excuse me! As God's above, I didn't know,' muttered the old man, and looking Natasha over from head to foot, he went out.

Mademoiselle Bourienne was the first to recover herself after this apparition, and began talking about the prince's ill-health. Natasha and Princess Marya gazed dumbly at one another, and the longer they gazed dumbly at one another without saying what they wanted to say, the more unfavourably each felt disposed to the other.

When the count returned, Natasha showed a discourteous relief at seeing him, and made haste to get away. At that moment she almost hated that stiff, oldish princess, who could put her in such an awkward position, and spend half an hour with her without saying a word about Prince Andrey. 'I couldn't be the first to speak of him before that Frenchwoman,' thought Natasha. Princess Marya meanwhile was tortured by the very same feeling. She knew what she had to say to Natasha, but she could not do it, both because Mademoiselle Bourienne prevented her, and because—she did not know herself why—it was difficult for her to begin to speak of the marriage. The count was already going out of the room when Princess Marya moved rapidly up to Natasha, took her hand, and, with a heavy sigh, said: 'Wait a moment, I want . . .' Natasha's expression as she looked at Princess Marya was ironical, though she did not know why.

'Dear Natalie,' said Princess Marya, 'do believe how glad I am that my brother has found such happiness . . .' She paused, feeling she was telling a lie. Natasha noticed the pause, and guessed the reason of it.

'I imagine, princess, that it is not now suitable to speak of that,' said Natasha, with external dignity and coldness, though she felt the tears rising in her throat.

'What have I said, what have I done?' she thought as soon as she had gone out of the room.

They had to wait a long while for Natasha to come to dinner that day. She was sitting in her room, crying like a child, choking, and sobbing. Sonya stood over her, and kept kissing her on the head.

'Natasha, what is it?' she kept saying. 'Why need you mind about them? It will pass, Natasha.'

'No, if only you knew how insulting it was . . . as though I . . .'

'Don't talk of it, Natasha; it's not your fault, you see, so what does it matter to you! Kiss me,' said Sonya.

Natasha raised her head, and kissing her friend on the lips, pressed her wet face against her.

'I can't say; I don't know. It's no one's fault,' said Natasha: 'it's my fault. But it's awfully painful. Oh, why doesn't he come? ...'

She went down to dinner with red eyes. Marya Dmitryevna, who had heard how the old prince had received the Rostovs, pretended not to notice Natasha's troubled face, and kept up a loud, jesting conversation at table with the count and the other guests.

VIII

THAT evening the Rostovs went to the opera, for which Marya Dmitryevna had obtained them a box.

Natasha had no wish to go, but it was impossible to refuse after Marya Dmitryevna's kindness, especially as it had been arranged expressly for her. When she was dressed and waiting for her father in the big hall, she looked at herself in the big looking-glass, and saw that she was looking pretty, very pretty. She felt even sadder, but it was a sweet and tender sadness.

'My God, if he were only here, I wouldn't have any stupid shyness of something as I used to, but in quite a new way, simply, I would embrace him, press close to him, force him to look at me with those scrutinising, inquisitive eyes, with which he used so often to look at me, and then I would make him laugh, as he used to laugh then; and his eyes—how I see those eyes!' thought Natasha. 'And what does it matter to me about his father and sister; I love no one but him, him, him, with that face and those eyes, with his smile, manly, and yet childlike. . . . No, better not think of him, not think, forget, utterly forget him for the time. I can't bear this suspense; I shall sob in a minute,' and she turned away from the looking-glass, making an effort not to weep. 'And how can Sonya love Nikolenka so quietly, so calmly, and wait so long and so patiently!' she wondered, looking at Sonya, who came in, dressed for the theatre with a fan in her hand. 'No, she's utterly different. I can't.'

Natasha at that moment felt so softened and moved that to love and know that she was loved was not enough for her: she wanted now, now at once to embrace the man she loved, and to speak and hear from him the words of love, of which her heart was full. When she was in the carriage sitting beside her father and pensively watching the lights of the street lamps flitting by the frozen window, she felt even sadder and more in love, and forgot with whom and where she was going. The Rostovs' carriage fell into the line of carriages, and drove up to the theatre, its wheels crunching slowly over the snow. Natasha and Sonya skipped hurriedly out holding up their dresses; the count stepped out supported by the footmen, and all three walked to the corridor for the boxes in the stream of ladies and gentlemen going in and people selling programmes. They could hear the music already through the closed doors.

'Natasha, your hair . . .' whispered Sonya. The box-opener deferentially and hurriedly slipped before the ladies and opened the door of the box. The music became more distinctly audible at the door, and they saw the brightly lighted rows of boxes, with the bare arms and shoulders of the ladies, and the stalls below, noisy, and gay with uniforms. A lady entering the next box looked round at Natasha with an envious, feminine glance. The curtain had not yet risen and they were playing the overture. Natasha smoothing down her skirt went in with Sonya, and sat down, looking round at the brightly lighted tiers of boxes facing them. The sensation she had not experienced for a long while—that hundreds of eyes were looking at her bare arms and neck—suddenly came upon her both pleasantly and unpleasantly, calling up a whole swarm of memories, desires, and emotions connected with that sensation.

The two strikingly pretty girls, Natasha and Sonya, with Count Ilya Andreitch, who had not been seen for a long while in Moscow, attracted general attention. Moreover, every one had heard vaguely of Natasha's engagement to Prince Andrey, knew that the Rostovs had been living in the country ever since, and looked with curiosity at the girl who was to make one of the best matches in Russia.

Natasha had, so every one told her, grown prettier in the country; and that evening, owing to her excited condition, she was particularly pretty. She made a striking impression of fulness of life and beauty, together with indifference to everything around her. Her black eyes gazed at the crowd, seeking out no one, while her slender arm, bare to above the elbow, leaned on the velvet edge of the box, and her hand, holding the programme, clasped and unclasped in time to the music with obvious unconsciousness.

'Look, there's Alenina,' said Sonya, 'with her mother, isn't it?'

'Heavens, Mihail Kirillitch is really stouter than ever,' said the old count.

'Look! our Anna Mihalovna in such a cap!'

'The Karagins, Julie, and Boris with them. One can see at once they are engaged.'

'Drubetskoy has made his offer! To be sure, I heard so today,' said Shinshin, coming into the Rostovs' box.

Natasha looked in the direction her father was looking in and saw Julie with diamonds on her thick, red neck (Natasha knew it was powdered), sitting with a blissful face beside her mother.

Behind them could be seen the handsome, well-brushed head of Boris, with a smile inclining his ear towards Julie's mouth. He looked from under his brows at the Rostovs, and said something, smiling, to his betrothed.

'They are talking about us, about me and himself!' thought Natasha. 'And he is, most likely, soothing his fiancée's jealousy of me; they needn't worry themselves! If only they knew how little they matter to me, any one of them.'

Behind the engaged couple sat Anna Mihalovna in a green cap, with a face happy, in honour of the festive occasion, and devoutly resigned to the will of God. Their box was full of that atmosphere of an engaged couple—which Natasha knew so well and liked so much. She turned away; and suddenly all that had been humiliating in her morning visit came back to her mind.

'What right has he not to want to receive me into his family? Ah, better not think about it, not think till he comes back!' she said to herself, and began to look about at the faces, known and unknown, in the stalls.

In the front of the stalls, in the very centre, leaning back against the rail stood Dolohov, in a Persian dress, with his huge shock of curly hair combed upwards. He stood in the most conspicuous place in the theatre, well aware that he was attracting the attention of the whole audience, and as much at his ease as though he had been alone in his room. The most brilliant young men in Moscow were all thronging about him, and he was obviously the leading figure among them.

Count Ilya Andreitch, laughing, nudged the blushing Sonya, pointing out her former admirer.

'Did you recognise him?' he asked. 'And where has he dropped from?' said he, turning to Shinshin. 'I thought he had disappeared somewhere?'

'He did disappear,' answered Shinshin. 'He was in the Caucasus, and he ran away from there, and they say he has been acting as minister to some reigning prince in Persia, and there killed the Shah's brother. Well, all the Moscow ladies are wild about him! "Dolohov the Persian," that's what does it! Nowadays there's nothing can be done without Dolohov; they do homage to him, invite you to meet him, as if he were a sturgeon,' said Shinshin. 'Dolohov and Anatole Kuragin have taken all the ladies' hearts by storm.'

A tall, handsome woman with a mass of hair and very naked, plump, white arms and shoulders, and a double row of big pearls round her throat, walked into the next box, and was a long while settling into her place and rustling her thick silk gown.

Natasha unconsciously examined that neck and the shoulders, the pearls, the coiffure of this lady, and admired the beauty of the shoulders and the pearls. While Natasha was scrutinising her a second time, the lady looked round, and meeting the eyes of Count Ilya Andreitch, she nodded and smiled to him. It was the Countess Bezuhov, Pierre's wife. The count, who knew every one in society, bent over and entered into conversation with her.

'Have you been here long?' he began. 'I'm coming; I'm coming to kiss your hand. I have come to town on business and brought my girls with me. They say Semyonovna's acting is superb,' the count went on. 'Count Pyotr Kirillovitch never forgot us. Is he here?'

'Yes, he meant to come,' said Ellen, looking intently at Natasha.

Count Ilya Andreitch sat down again in his place.

'Handsome, isn't she?' he whispered to Natasha.

'Exquisite!' said Natasha. 'One might well fall in love with her!'

At that moment they heard the last chords of the overture, and the tapping of the conductor's stick. Late comers hurried to their seats in the stalls, and the curtain rose.

As soon as the curtain rose, a hush fell on the boxes and stalls, and all the men, old and young, in their frockcoats or uniforms, all the women with precious stones on their bare flesh concentrated all their attention with eager curiosity on the stage. Natasha too began to look at it.

IX

THE stage consisted of a boarded floor in the middle, with painted cardboard representing trees at the sides, and linen stretched over boards at the back. In the middle of the stage there were sitting maidens in red bodices and white skirts. An excessively stout woman in a white silk dress was sitting apart on a low bench with green cardboard fixed on the back of it. They were all singing something. When they had finished their song, the woman in white moved towards the prompter's box, and a man, with his stout legs encased in silk tights, with a plume and a dagger, went up to her and began singing and waving his arms.

The man in the tights sang alone, then she sang alone. Then both paused, while the music played, and the man fumbled with the hand of the woman in white, obviously waiting for the bar at which he was to begin singing with her. They sang a duet, and every one in the theatre began clapping and shouting, while the man and woman on the stage, supposed to represent lovers, began bowing with smiles and gesticulations.

After the country, and in her serious mood, Natasha felt it all grotesque and extraordinary. She could not follow the opera; she could not even listen to the music; she saw nothing but painted cardboard and strangely dressed-up men and women, talking, singing, and moving strangely about in the bright light. She knew what it all was meant to represent; but it was all so grotesquely false and unnatural that she felt alternately ashamed and amused at the actors. She looked about her at the faces of the spectators, seeking in them signs of the same irony and bewilderment that she was feeling herself. But all the faces were watching what was passing on the stage, and expressed nothing but an affected—so Natasha thought—rapture. 'I suppose it is meant to be like this!' thought Natasha. She looked alternately at the rows of pomaded masculine heads in the stalls, and at the naked women in the boxes, especially at her next neighbour Ellen, who, quite undressed, sat gazing intently, with a quiet and serene smile, at the stage, and basking in the bright light that flooded the theatre, and the warm air, heated by the crowd. Natasha began gradually to pass into a state of intoxication she had not experienced for a long while. She lost all sense of what she was and where she was and what was going on before her eyes. She gazed and dreamed, and the strangest ideas flashed unexpectedly and disconnectedly into her mind. At one moment the idea occurred to her to leap over the footlights and sing that air the actress was singing; then she felt inclined to hook her fan into an old gentleman sitting near her, or to bend over to Ellen and tickle her.

At a moment when there was a lull on the stage before the beginning of a song, the door opening to the stalls creaked on the side nearest the Rostovs' box, and there was the sound of a man's footsteps. 'Here he is, Kuragin!' whispered Shinshin. Countess Bezuhov turned smiling to the newcomer. Natasha looked in the direction of the Countess Bezuhov's eyes, and saw an exceedingly handsome adjutant coming towards their box with a confident, but yet courteous, bearing. It was Anatole Kuragin, whom she had seen long before, and noticed at the Petersburg ball. He was now wearing an adjutant's uniform, with one epaulette and a shoulder knot. He walked with a jaunty strut, which would have been ridiculous if he had not been so handsome, and if his good-looking face had not expressed such simple-hearted satisfaction and good spirits. Although the performance was going on he walked lightly, without haste, along the carpeted corridor, holding his scented, handsome head high, and accompanied by a slight clank of spurs and sword. Glancing at Natasha, he went up to his sister, laid his hand in a close-fitting glove on the edge of her box, nodded his head at her, and, bending down, asked her a question, with a motion towards Natasha.

'Very, very charming!' he said, obviously speaking of Natasha. She did not exactly hear the words, but divined them from the movement of his lips. Then he went on to the front row and sat down beside Dolohov, giving a friendly and careless nudge with his elbow to the man whom other people treated with such punctilio. With a merry wink, he smiled at him, and leaned with his foot against the footlights.

'How like the brother is to his sister!' said the count. 'And how handsome they both are!'

Shinshin began telling the count in an undertone some story of an intrigue of Kuragin's in Moscow, to which Natasha listened, simply because he had said of her 'very charming.'

The first act was over; every one stood up in the stalls, changed places, and began going out and coming in.

Boris came to the Rostovs' box, received their congratulations very simply, and lifting his eyebrows with an absent-minded smile, gave Natasha and Sonya his fiancée's message, begging them to come to her wedding, and went away. Natasha, with a gay and coquettish smile, talked to him and congratulated him on his approaching marriage— the very Boris she had once been in love with. In the condition of emotional intoxication in which she found herself everything seemed simple and natural.

Ellen sat in her nakedness close by her, and smiled on all alike, and just such a smile Natasha bestowed on Boris.

Ellen's box was filled and surrounded on the side of the stalls by the most distinguished and intellectual men, who seemed vying with one another in their desire to show every one that they knew her.

All through that entr'acte Kuragin stood with Dolohov in front of the footlights staring at the Rostovs' box. Natasha knew he was talking about her, and that afforded her satisfaction. She even turned so that he could see her profile from what she believed to be the most becoming angle. Before the beginning of the second act she observed in the stalls the figure of Pierre, whom the Rostovs had not seen since their arrival. His face looked sad, and he had grown stouter since Natasha had seen him last. He walked up to the front rows, not noticing any one. Anatole went up to him, and began saying something to him, with a look and a gesture towards the Rostovs' box. Pierre looked pleased at seeing Natasha, and walked hurriedly along the rows of stalls towards their box. Leaning on his elbow, he talked smiling to Natasha for a long while,

While she was talking to Pierre, Natasha heard a man's voice speaking in Countess Bezuhov's box, and something told her it was Kuragin. She looked round and met his eyes. He looked her straight in the eyes, almost smiling, with a look of such warmth and admiration that it seemed strange to be so near him, to look at him like that, to be so certain that he admired her, and not to be acquainted with him.

In the second act there was scenery representing monuments, and a hole in the drop at the back that represented the moon, and shades were put over the footlights, and trumpets and bassoons began playing, and a number of people came in on the right and on the left wearing black cloaks. These people began waving their arms, and in their hands they had something of the nature of a dagger. Then some more people ran in and began dragging away the woman who had been in white but who was now in a blue dress. They did not drag her away at once; they spent a long while singing with her; but finally they did drag her away, and behind the scenes they struck something metallic three times, and then all knelt down and began singing a prayer. All these performances were interrupted several times by the enthusiastic shouts of the spectators.

During the act, every time Natasha glanced towards the stalls, she saw Anatole Kuragin, with one arm flung across the back of his chair, staring at her. It pleased her to see that he was so captivated by her, and it never entered her head that there could be anything amiss in it.

When the second act was over, Countess Bezuhov got up, turned towards the Rostovs' box (the whole of her bosom was completely exposed), with her gloved little finger beckoned the old count to her, and taking no notice of the men who were thronging about her box, began with an amiable smile talking to him.

'Oh, do make me acquainted with your charming daughters,' she said. 'All the town is singing their praises, and I don't know them.'

Natasha got up and curtseyed to the magnificent countess. Natasha was so delighted at the praise from this brilliant beauty that she blushed with pleasure.

'I quite want to become a Moscow resident myself,' said Ellen. 'What a shame of you to bury such pearls in the country!'

Countess Bezuhov had some right to her reputation of being a fascinating woman. She could say what she did not think, especially what was flattering, with perfect simplicity and naturalness.

'No, dear count, you must let me help to entertain your daughters, though I'm not here now for very long, nor you either. But I'll do my best to amuse them. I have heard a great deal about you in Petersburg, and wanted to know you,' she said to Natasha, with her unvarying beautiful smile. 'I have heard of you, too, from my page, Drubetskoy—you have heard he is to be married—and from my husband's friend, Bolkonsky, Prince Andrey Bolkonsky,' she said, with peculiar emphasis, by which she meant to signify that she knew in what relation he stood to Natasha. She asked that one of the young ladies might be allowed to sit through the rest of the performance in her box that they might become better acquainted, and Natasha moved into it.

In the third act the scene was a palace in which a great many candles were burning, and pictures were hanging on the walls, representing knights with beards. In the middle stood a man and a woman, probably meant for a king and a queen. The king waved his right hand, and, obviously nervous, sang something very badly, and sat down on a crimson throne. The actress, who had been in white at first and then in blue, was now in nothing but a smock, and had let her hair down. She was standing near the throne, singing something very mournful, addressed to the queen. But the king waved his hand sternly, and from the sides there came in men and women with bare legs who began dancing all together. Then the violins played very shrilly and merrily: one of the actresses, with thick, bare legs and thin arms, leaving the rest, went to the side to set straight her bodice, then walked into the middle of the stage and began skipping into the air and kicking one leg very rapidly with the other. Every one in the stalls clapped their hands and roared 'bravo!' Then one man stood alone at one corner of the stage. The cymbals and trumpets struck up more loudly in the orchestra, and this man began leaping very high in the air and rapidly waving his legs. (This was Duport, who earned sixty thousand a year by this accomplishment.) Every one in the boxes and in the stalls began clapping and shouting with all their might, and the man stood still and began smiling and bowing in all directions. Then other men and women with bare legs danced; then again the king shouted something to music, and they all began singing. But suddenly a storm came on, chromatic scales and chords with the diminishing sevenths could be heard in the orchestra, and they all ran off, dragging one of the performers again behind the scenes, and the curtain dropped. Again a fearful uproar of applause arose among the spectators, and all began screaming with rapturous faces:

'Duport! Duport! Duport!'

Natasha did not now feel this strange. She looked about her with pleasure, smiling joyfully.

'Isn't Duport admirable?' said Ellen, turning to her.

'Oh yes,' answered Natasha.

X

In the entr'acte there was a current of chill air in Ellen's box, the door was opened, and Anatole walked in, bending and trying not to brush against any one.

'Allow me to introduce my brother,' said Ellen, her eyes shifting uneasily from Natasha to Anatole. Natasha turned her pretty little head towards the handsome adjutant and smiled over her bare shoulder. Anatole, who was as handsome on a closer view as he was from a distance, sat down beside her, and said he had long wished to have this pleasure, ever since the Narishkins' ball, at which he had had the pleasure he had not forgotten of seeing her. Kuragin was far more sensible and straightforward with women than he was in men's society. He talked boldly and simply, and Natasha was strangely and agreeably impressed by finding nothing so formidable in this man, of whom such stories were told, but, on the contrary, seeing on his face the most innocent, merry, and simple-hearted smile.

Kuragin asked her what she thought of the performance, and told her that at the last performance Semyonova had fallen down while she was acting.

'And do you know, countess,' said he, suddenly addressing her as though she were an old friend, 'we are getting up a costume ball; you ought to take part in it: it will be great fun. They are all assembling at the Karagins'. Please, do come, really now, eh?' he said. As he said this he never took his smiling eyes off the face, the neck, the bare arms of Natasha. Natasha knew beyond all doubt that he was fascinated by her. That pleased her, yet she felt for some reason constrained and oppressed in his presence. When she was not looking at him she felt that he was looking at her shoulders, and she could not help trying to catch his eyes that he might rather look in her face. But as she looked into his eyes, she felt with horror that, between him and her, there was not that barrier of modest reserve she had always been conscious of between herself and other men. In five minutes she felt—she did not know how—that she had come fearfully close to this man. When she turned away, she felt afraid he might take her from behind by her bare arm and kiss her on the neck. They talked of the simplest things, and she felt that they were close as she had never been with any man. Natasha looked round at Ellen and at her father, as though to ask them what was the meaning of it. But Ellen was absorbed in talking to a general and did not respond to her glance, and her father's eyes said nothing to her but what they always said: 'Enjoying yourself? Well, I'm glad then.'

In one of the moments of awkward silence, during which Anatole gazed calmly and persistently at her, Natasha, to break the silence, asked him how he liked Moscow. Natasha asked this question and blushed as she did so; she was feeling all the while that there she was doing something improper in talking to him. Anatole smiled as though to encourage her.

'At first I didn't like it much, for what is it makes one like a town? It's the pretty women, isn't it? Well, but now I like it awfully,' he said, with a meaning look at her. 'You'll come to the fancy dress ball, countess? Do come,' he said, and putting his hand out to her bouquet he said, dropping his voice, 'You will be the prettiest. Come, dear countess, and as a pledge give me this flower.'

Natasha did not understand what he was saying, nor did he himself; but she felt that in his uncomprehended words there was some improper intention. She did not know what to say, and turned away as though she had not heard what he said. But as soon as she turned away she felt that he was here behind her, so close to her.

'What is he feeling now? Is he confused? Is he angry? Must I set it right?' she wondered. She could not refrain from looking round. She glanced straight into his eyes, and his nearness and confidence, and the simple-hearted warmth of his smile vanquished her. She smiled exactly as he did, looking straight into his eyes. And again, she felt with horror that no barrier lay between him and her.

The curtain rose again. Anatole walked out of the box, serene and good-humoured. Natasha went back to her father's box, completely under the spell of the world in which she found herself. All that passed before her eyes now seemed to her perfectly natural. But on the other hand all previous thoughts of her betrothed, of Princess Marya, of her life in the country, did not once recur to her mind, as though all that belonged to the remote past.

In the fourth act there was some sort of devil who sang, waving his arms till the boards were moved away under him and he sank down into the opening. That was all Natasha saw of the fourth act; she felt harassed and excited; and the cause of that excitement was Kuragin, whom she could not help watching. As they came out of the theatre Anatole came up to them, called their carriage and helped them into it. As he assisted Natasha he pressed her arm above the elbow. Natasha, flushed and excited, looked round at him. He gazed at her with flashing eyes and a tender smile.

It was only on getting home that Natasha could form any clear idea of what had happened. All at once, remembering Prince Andrey, she was horrified, and at tea, to which they all sat down after the theatre, she groaned aloud, and flushing crimson ran out of the room. 'My God! I am ruined!' she said to herself. 'How could I sink to such a depth?' she thought. For a long while she sat, with her flushed face hidden in her hands, trying to get a clear idea of what had happened and unable to grasp either what had happened or what she was feeling. Everything seemed to her dark, obscure, and dreadful. In that immense, lighted hall, where Duport had jumped about to music with his bare legs on the damp boards in his short jacket with tinsel, and young girls and old men, and that Ellen, proudly and serenely smiling in her nakedness, had enthusiastically roared 'bravo'; there, in the wake of that Ellen, all had been clear and simple. But now, alone by herself, it was past comprehending. 'What does it mean? What is that terror I felt with him? What is the meaning of those gnawings of conscience I am feeling now?' she thought.

To no one but to her mother at night in bed Natasha could have talked of what she was feeling. Sonya she knew, with her strict and single-minded view of things, would either have failed to understand at all, or would have been horrified at the avowal. Natasha all by herself had to try and solve the riddle that tormented her.

'Am I spoilt for Prince Andrey's love or not?' she asked herself, and with reassuring mockery she answered herself: 'What a fool I am to ask such a thing! What has happened to me? Nothing. I have done nothing; I did nothing to lead him on. No one will ever know, and I shall never see him again,' she told herself. 'So it's plain that nothing has happened, that there's nothing to regret, that Prince Andrey can love me *still*. But why *still*? O my God, my God, why isn't he here!' Natasha felt comforted for a moment; but again some instinct told her that though that was all true, and though nothing had happened, yet some instinct told her that all the old purity of her love for Prince Andrey was lost. And again, in her imagination, she went over all her conversation with Kuragin, and saw again the face, the gestures, and the tender smile of that handsome, daring man at the moment when he had pressed her arm.

XI

ANATOLE KURAGIN was staying in Moscow because his father had sent him away from Petersburg, where he had been spending twenty thousand a year in hard cash and running up bills for as much more, and his creditors had been dunning his father. The father informed his son that for the last time he would pay half his debts; but only on condition that he would go away to Moscow, where his father had, by much exertion, secured a post for him as adjutant to the commander-in-chief, and would try finally to make a good match there. He suggested to him either Princess Marya or Julie Karagin.

Anatole consented, and went away to Moscow, where he stayed with Pierre. Pierre at first was by no means pleased to receive Anatole, but after a while he got used to his presence; sometimes accompanied him on his carousals, and by way of loans gave him money.

As Shinshin had with truth said of him, Anatole had won the hearts of all the Moscow ladies, especially by the nonchalance with which he treated them and the preference he openly showed for gypsy girls and actresses, with the most prominent of whom, Mademoiselle George, he was said to have an intrigue. He never missed a single drinking party at Danilov's, or any other Moscow festivity, spent whole nights drinking, outdoing all the rest, and was at every soirée and ball in the best society. There were rumours of several intrigues of his with Moscow ladies, and at balls he flirted with a few of them. But he fought shy of unmarried ladies, especially the wealthy hieresses, who were most of them plain. He had a good reason for this, of which no one knew but his most intimate friends: he had been for the last two years married. Two years previously, while his regiment had been stationed in Poland, a Polish landowner, by no means well-to-do, had forced Anatole to marry his daughter.

Anatole had very shortly afterwards abandoned his wife, and in consideration of a sum of money, which he agreed to send his father-in-law, he was allowed by the latter to pass as a bachelor unmolested.

Anatole was very well satisfied with his position, with himself, and with other people. He was instinctively and thoroughly convinced that he could not possibly live except just in the way he did live, and that he had never in his life done anything base. He was incapable of considering either how his actions might be judged by others, or what might be the result of this or that action on his part. He was convinced that just as the duck is created so that it must always live in the water, so he was created by God such that he must spend thirty thousand a year, and always take a good position in society. He had such perfect faith in this that looking at him, others too were persuaded of it, and refused him neither the exalted position in society nor the money, which he borrowed right and left, obviously with no notion of repaying it.

He was not a gambler, at least he never greatly cared about winning money at cards. He was not vain. He did not care a straw what people thought of him. Still less could he have been reproached with ambition. Several times he had, to his father's irritation, spoiled his best chances of a career and he laughed at distinctions of all kinds. He was not stingy, and never refused any one who asked him for anything. What he loved was dissipation and women; and as, according to his ideas, there was nothing dishonourable in these tastes, and as he was incapable of considering the effect on others of the gratification of his tastes, he believed himself in his heart to be an irreproachable man, felt a genuine contempt for scoundrels and mean persons, and with an untroubled conscience held his head high. Rakes, those masculine Magdalens, have a secret feeling of their own guiltlessness, just as have women Magdalens, founded on the same hope of forgiveness. 'All will be forgiven her, because she loved much; and all will be forgiven him, because he has enjoyed himself much.'

Dolohov had that year reappeared in Moscow after his exile and his Persian adventures. He spent his time in luxury, gambling and dissipation; renewed his friendship with his old Petersburg comrade Kuragin, and made use of him for his own objects.

Anatole sincerely liked Dolohov for his cleverness and daring. Dolohov, for whom Anatole's name and rank and connections were of use in ensnaring wealthy young men into his society for gambling purposes, made use of Kuragin without letting him feel it, and was amused by him too. Apart from interested motives, for which he needed Anatole, the process itself of controlling another man's will was an enjoyment, a habit, and a necessity for Dolohov.

Natasha had made a great impression on Kuragin. At supper, after the theatre, he analysed to Dolohov, with the manner of a connoisseur, the points of her arms, her shoulders, her foot, and her hair, and announced his intention of getting up a flirtation with her. What might come of such a flirtation—Anatole was incapable of considering, and had no notion, as he never had a notion of what would come of any of his actions.

'She's pretty, my lad, but she's not for us,' Dolohov said to him.

'I'll tell my sister to ask her to dinner,' said Anatole. 'Eh?'

'You'd better wait till she's married ...'

'You know I adore little girls,' said Anatole; 'they're all confusion in a minute.'

'You've come to grief once already over a "little girl,"' said Dolohov, who knew of Anatole's marriage. 'Beware!'

'Well, one can't do it twice! Eh?' said Anatole, laughing good-humouredly.

XII

THE next day the Rostovs did not go anywhere, and no one came to see them. Marya Dmitryevna had a discussion with Natasha's father, which she kept secret from her. Natasha guessed they were talking of the old prince and making some plan, and she felt worried and humiliated by it. Every minute she expected Prince Andrey, and twice that day she sent a man to Vosdvizhenka to inquire whether he had not arrived. He had not arrived. She felt more dreary now than during the first days in Moscow. To her impatience and pining for him there were now added the unpleasant recollections of her interview with Princess Marya and the old prince, and a vague dread and restlessness, of which she did not know the cause. She was continually fancying either that he would never come or that something would happen to her before he came. She could not brood calmly for long hours over his image by herself as she had done before. As soon as she began to think of him, her memory of him was mingled with the recollection of the old prince and Princess Marya, and of the theatre and of Kuragin. Again the question presented itself whether she had not been to blame, whether she had not broken her faith to Prince Andrey, and again she found herself going over in the minutest detail every word, every gesture, every shade in the play of expression on the face of that man, who had known how to awaken in her a terrible feeling that was beyond her comprehension. In the eyes of those about her, Natasha seemed livelier than usual, but she was far from being as serene and happy as before.

On Sunday morning Marya Dmitryevna invited her guests to go to Mass to her parish church of Uspenya on Mogiltse.

'I don't like those fashionable churches,' she said, obviously priding herself on her independence of thought. 'God is the same everywhere. Our parish priest is an excellent man, and conducts the service in a suitable way, so that is all as it should be, and his deacon too. Is there something holier about it when there are concerts in the choir? I don't like it; it's simply self-indulgence!'

Marya Dmitryevna liked Sundays, and knew how to keep them as holidays. Her house was always all scrubbed out and cleaned on Saturday; neither she nor her servants did any work, and every one wore holiday-dress and went to service. There were additional dishes at the mistress's dinner, and the servants had vodka and roast goose or a sucking-pig at theirs. But in nothing in the whole house was the holiday so marked as in the broad, severe face of Marya Dmitryevna, which on that day wore a never-varying expression of solemnity.

When after service they were drinking coffee in the drawing-room, where the covers had been removed from the furniture, the servant announced that the carriage was ready, and Marya Dmitryevna, dressed in her best shawl in which she paid calls, rose with a stern air, and announced that she was going to call on Prince Nikolay Andreitch Bolkonsky to ask for an explanation of his conduct about Natasha. After Marya Dmitryevna had gone, a dressmaker waited upon the Rostovs from Madame Chalmey, and Natasha, very glad of a diversion, went into a room adjoining the drawing-room, and shutting the door between, began trying on her new dresses. Just as she had put on a bodice basted together, with the sleeves not yet tacked in, and was turning her head to look at the fit of the back in the looking-glass, she caught the sound of her father's voice in the drawing-room in eager conversation with another voice, a woman's voice, which made her flush red. It was the voice of Ellen. Before Natasha had time to take off the bodice she was trying on, the door opened, and Countess Bezuhov walked into the room, wearing a dark heliotrope velvet gown with a high collar, and beaming with a good-natured and friendly smile.

'O my enchantress!' she said to the blushing Natasha. 'Charming! No, this is really beyond anything, count,' she said to Count Ilya Andreitch, who had followed her in. 'How can you be in Moscow, and go nowhere? No, I won't let you off! This evening we have Mademoiselle George giving a recitation, and a few people are coming; and if you don't bring your lovely girls, who are much prettier than Mademoiselle George, I give up knowing you! My husband's not here, he has gone away to Tver, or I should have sent him for you. You must come, you positively must, before nine o'clock.'

She nodded to the dressmaker, who knew her, and was curtseying respectfully, and seated herself in a low chair beside the looking-glass, draping the folds of her velvet gown picturesquely about her. She kept up a flow of good-humoured and light-hearted chatter, and repeatedly expressed her enthusiastic admiration of Natasha's beauty. She looked through her dresses and admired them, spoke with admiration, too, of a new dress of her own 'of metallic gas,' which she had received from Paris, and advised Natasha to have one like it.

'But anything suits you, my charmer!' she declared. The smile of pleasure never left Natasha's face. She felt happy, and as it were blossoming out under the praises of this charming Countess Bezuhov, who had seemed to her before a lady so unapproachable and dignified, and was now being so kind to her. Natasha's spirits rose, and she felt almost in love with this handsome and good-natured woman. Ellen, for her part, was genuine in her admiration of Natasha, and in her desire to make her enjoy herself. Anatole had begged her to throw him with Natasha, and it was with that object she had come to the Rostovs'. The idea of throwing her brother and Natasha together amused her.

Although Ellen had once owed Natasha a grudge for carrying off Boris from her in Petersburg, she thought no more of that now, and with all her heart wished Natasha nothing but good. As she was leaving the Rostovs', she drew her protegee aside.

'My brother was dining with me yesterday—we half died with laughing at him—he won't eat, and does nothing but sigh for you, my charmer! He is madly, madly in love with you, my dear.'

Natasha flushed crimson on hearing those words.

'How she blushes, how she blushes, my pretty!' Ellen went on. 'You must be sure to come. If you do love some one, it is not a reason to cloister yourself. Even if you are betrothed, I am sure your betrothed would have preferred you to go into society rather than to languish in ennui.'

'So then she knows I am engaged. So then they with her husband, with Pierre, with that good Pierre, talked and laughed about it. So that it means nothing.'

And again under Ellen's influence what had struck her before as terrible seemed to her simple and natural. 'And she, such a *grand dame*, is so kind, and obviously she likes me with all her heart,' thought Natasha, gazing at Ellen with wide-open, wondering eyes.

Marya Dmitryevna came back to dinner silent and serious, having evidently been defeated by the old prince. She was too much agitated by the conflict she had been through to be able to describe the interview. To the count's inquiries, she replied that everything had been all right and she would tell him about it next day. On hearing of the visit of Countess Bezuhov and the invitation for the evening, Marya Dmitryevna said:

'I don't care to associate with Countess Bezuhov and I don't advise you to, but still, since you have promised, better go. It will divert your mind,' she added, addressing Natasha.

XIII

COUNT ILYA ANDREITCH took his two girls to the Countess Bezuhov's. There were a good many people assembled there. But Natasha hardly knew any of the persons present. Count Ilya Andreitch observed with dissatisfaction that almost all the company consisted of men or of ladies notorious for the freedom of their behaviour. Mademoiselle George was standing in one corner of the room, surrounded by young men. There were several Frenchmen present, and among them Metivier, who had been a constant visitor at Countess Bezuhov's ever since her arrival in Moscow. Count Ilya Andreitch made up his mind not to take a hand at cards, not to leave his daughter's side, and to get away as soon as Mademoiselle George's performance was over.

Anatole was at the door, unmistakably on the look-out for the Rostovs. At once greeting the count, he went up to Natasha and followed her in. As soon as Natasha saw him, the same feeling came upon her as at the theatre—the feeling of gratified vanity at his admiration of her, and terror at the absence of any moral barrier between them.

Ellen gave Natasha a delighted welcome, and was loud in her admiration of her loveliness and her dress. Soon after their arrival, Mademoiselle George went out of the room to change her dress. In the drawing-room chairs were being set in rows and people began to sit down. Anatole moved a chair for Natasha, and would have sat down by her, but the count, who was keeping his eye on Natasha, took the seat beside her. Anatole sat down behind.

Mademoiselle George, with bare, fat, dimpled arms, and a red scarf flung over one shoulder, came into the empty space left for her between the chairs and threw herself into an unnatural pose. An enthusiastic whisper was audible.

Mademoiselle George scanned her audience with stern and gloomy eyes, and began reciting French verses, describing her guilty love for her son. In places she raised her voice, in places she dropped to a whisper solemnly lifting her head; in places she broke off and hissed with rolling eyes.

'Exquisite, divine, marvellous!' was heard on all sides. Natasha gazed at the fat actress; but she heard nothing, saw nothing and understood nothing of what was passing before her. She felt nothing, but that she was borne away again irrevocably into that strange and senseless world so remote from her old world, a world in which there was no knowing what was good and what was bad, what was sensible and what was senseless. Behind her was sitting Anatole; and conscious of his nearness, she was in frightened expectation of something.

After the first monologue all the company rose and surrounded Mademoiselle George, expressing their admiration.

'How handsome she is!' said Natasha to her father, as he got up with the rest and moved through the crowd to the actress.

'I don't think so, looking at you,' said Anatole, following Natasha. He said this at a moment when no one but she could hear him. 'You are charming ... from the moment I first saw you, I have not ceased ...'

'Come along, come along, Natasha!' said the count, turning back for his daughter. 'How pretty she is!'

Natasha saying nothing went up to her father, and gazed at him with eyes of inquiring wonder.

After several recitations in different styles, Mademoiselle George went away, and Countess Bezuhov invited all the company to the great hall.

The count would have taken leave, but Ellen besought him not to spoil her improvised ball. The Rostovs stayed on. Anatole asked Natasha for a waltz, and during the waltz, squeezing her waist and her hand, he told her she was bewitching and that he loved her. During the Ecossaise, which she danced again with Kuragin, when they were left alone Anatole said nothing to her, he simply looked at her. Natasha was in doubt whether she had not dreamed what he said to her during the waltz. At the end of the first figure he pressed her hand again. Natasha lifted her frightened eyes to his face, but there was an expression of such assurance and warmth in his fond look and smile that she could not as she looked at him say what she had to say to him. She dropped her eyes.

'Don't say such things to me. I am betrothed, and I love another man . . .' she articulated rapidly. She glanced at him. Anatole was neither disconcerted nor mortified at what she had said.

'Don't talk to me of that. What is that to me,' he said; 'I tell you I am mad, mad with love for you. Is it my fault that you are fascinating? . . . It's for us to begin.'

Natasha, eager and agitated, looked about her with wide-open, frightened eyes, and seemed to be enjoying herself more than usual. She scarcely grasped anything that happened that evening. They danced the Ecossaise and 'Grandfather'. Her father suggested their going, and she begged him to stay longer. Wherever she was, and with whomsoever she was speaking, she felt his eyes upon her. Then she remembered that she had asked her father's permission to go into a dressing-room to rearrange her dress, that Ellen had followed her, had talked to her, laughing, of her brother's passion, and that in the little divan-room she had been met again by Anatole; that Ellen had somehow vanished, they were left alone, and Anatole taking her by the hand, had said in a tender voice:

'I can't come to see you, but is it possible that I shall never see you! I love you madly. Can I never . . . ?' and barring her way, he brought his face close to hers.

His large, shining, masculine eyes were so close to her eyes, that she could see nothing but those eyes.

'Natalie?' his voice whispered interrogatively, and her hands were squeezed till it hurt. 'Natalie?'

'I don't understand; I have nothing to say,' was the answer in her eyes.

Burning lips were pressed to her lips, and at the same instant she felt herself set free again, and caught the sound of Ellen's steps and rustling gown in the room again. Natasha looked round towards Ellen; then, red and trembling, she glanced at him with alarmed inquiry, and moved towards the door.

'One word, just one word, for God's sake,' Anatole was saying. She stopped. She so wanted him to say that word, that would have explained to her what had happened and to which she could have found an answer.

'Natalie, one word... one..,' he kept repeating, plainly not knowing what to say, and he repeated it till Ellen reached them.

Ellen went back with Natasha to the drawing-room. The Rostovs went away without staying to supper.

When she got home, Natasha did not sleep all night. She was tortured by the insoluble question, Which did she love, Anatole or Prince Andrey? Prince Andrey, she did love—she remembered clearly how great her love was for him. But she loved Anatole too, of that there was no doubt. 'Else could all that have happened?' she thought. 'If after that I could answer with a smile to his smile at parting, if I could sink to that, it means that I fell in love with him from the first minute. So he must be kind, noble, and good, and I could not help loving him. What am I to do, if I love him and the other too?' she said to herself, and was unable to find an answer to those terrible questions.

XIV

T H E morning came with daily cares and bustle. Every one got up and began to move about and to talk; dressmakers came again; again Marya Dmitryevna went out and they were summoned to tea. Natasha kept uneasily looking round at every one with wide-open eyes, as though she wanted to intercept every glance turned upon her. She did her utmost to seem exactly as usual.

After luncheon—it was always her best time—Marya Dmitryevna seated herself in her own armchair and drew Natasha and the old count to her.

'Well, my friends, I have thought the whole matter over now, and I'll tell you my advice,' she began. 'Yesterday, as you know, I was at Prince

Bolkonsky's; well I had a talk with him . . . He thought fit to scream at me. But there's no screaming me down! I had it all out with him.'

'Well, but what does he mean?' asked the count.

'He's crazy . . . he won't hear of it, and there's no more to be said. As it is we have given this poor girl worry enough,' said Marya Dmitryevna. 'And my advice to you is, to make an end of it and go home to Otradnoe . . . and there to wait.'

'Oh no!' cried Natasha.

'Yes, to go home,' said Marya Dmitryevna, 'and to wait there. If your betrothed comes here now, there'll be no escaping a quarrel; but alone here he'll have it all out with the old man, and then come on to you.'

Count Ilya Andreitch approved of this suggestion, and at once saw all the sound sense of it. If the old man were to come round, then it would be better to visit him at Moscow or Bleak Hills, later on; if not, then the wedding, against his will, could only take place at Otradnoe.

'And that's perfectly true,' said he. 'I regret indeed that I ever went to see him and took her too,' said the count.

'No, why regret it? Being here, you could do no less than show him respect. If he wouldn't receive it, that's his affair,' said Marya Dmitryevna, searching for something in her reticule. 'And now the trousseau's ready, what have you to wait for? What is not ready, I'll send after you. Though I'm sorry to lose you, still the best thing is for you to go, and God be with you.' Finding what she was looking for in her reticule, she handed it to Natasha. It was a letter from Princess Marya. 'She writes to you. How worried she is, poor thing! She is afraid you might think she does not like you.'

'Well, she doesn't like me,' said Natasha.

'Nonsense, don't say so,' cried Marya Dmitryevna.

'I won't take any one's word for that, I know she doesn't like me,' said Natasha boldly as she took the letter, and there was a look of cold and angry resolution in her face, that made Marya Dmitryevna look at her more closely and frown.

'Don't you answer me like that, my good girl,' she said. 'If I say so, it's the truth. Write an answer to her.'

Natasha made no reply, and went to her own room to read Princess Marya's letter.

Princess Marya wrote that she was in despair at the misunderstanding that had arisen between them. Whatever her father's feelings might be, wrote Princess Marya, she begged Natasha to believe that she could not fail to love her, as the girl chosen by her brother, for whose happiness she was ready to make any sacrifice.

'Do not believe, though,' she wrote, 'that my father is ill-disposed to you. He is an old man and an invalid, for whom one must make excuses. But he is good-hearted and generous, and will come to love the woman who makes his son happy.' Princess Marya begged Natasha, too, to fix a time when she might see her again.

After reading the letter, Natasha sat down to the writing-table to answer it. 'Dear princess,' she began, writing rapidly and mechanically in French, and there she stopped. What more could she write after what had happened the day before? 'Yes, yes, all that had happened, and now everything was different,' she thought, sitting before the letter she had begun. 'Must I refuse him? Must I really? That's awful! . . .' And to avoid these horrible thoughts, she went in to Sonya, and began looking through embroidery designs with her.

After dinner Natasha went to her own room and took up Princess Marya's letter again. 'Can everything be over?' she thought. 'Can all this have happened so quickly and have destroyed all that went before?' She recalled in all its past strength her love for Prince Andrey, and at the same time she felt that she loved Kuragin. She vividly pictured herself the wife of Prince Andrey, of her happiness with him, called up the picture she had so often dwelt on in her imagination, and at the same time, all aglow with emotion, she recalled every detail of her interview the previous evening with Anatole.

'Why could not that be as well?' she wondered sometimes in complete bewilderment. 'It's only so that I could be perfectly happy; as it is, I have to choose, and without either of them I can't be happy. There's one thing,' she thought, 'to tell Prince Andrey what has happened; to hide it from him—are equally impossible. But with *him* nothing is spoilt. But can I part for ever from the happiness of Prince Andrey's love, which I have been living on for so long?'

'Madam,' whispered a maid, coming into the room with a mysterious air, 'a man told me to give you this.' The girl gave her a letter. 'Only for Christ's sake . . .' said the girl, as Natasha, without thinking, mechanically broke the seal and began reading a love-letter from Anatole, of which she did not understand a word, but understood only that it was a letter from him, from the man whom she loved. 'Yes, she loved him; otherwise, how could what had happened have happened? How could a love-letter from him be in her hand?'

With trembling hands Natasha held that passionate love-letter, composed for Anatole by Dolohov, and as she read it, she found in it echoes of all that it seemed to her she was feeling herself.

'Since yesterday evening my fate is sealed: to be loved by you or to die. There is nothing else left for me,' the letter began. Then he wrote that he knew her relations would never give her to him, to Anatole; that there were secret reasons for that which he could only reveal to her alone; but that if she loved him, she had but to utter the word *Yes*, and no human force could hinder their happiness. Love would conquer all. He could capture her and bear her away to the ends of the earth.

'Yes, yes, I love him!' thought Natasha, reading the letter over for the twentieth time, and finding some special deep meaning in every word.

That evening Marya Dmitryevna was going to the Arharovs, and proposed taking the young ladies with her. Natasha pleaded a headache and stayed at home.

XV

ON returning late in the evening, Sonya went into Natasha's room, and to her surprise found her not undressed asleep on the sofa. On the table near her Anatole's letter lay open. Sonya picked up the letter and began to read it.

She read it, and looked at Natasha asleep, seeking in her face some explanation of what she had read and not finding it. Her face was quiet, gentle, and happy. Clutching at her own chest to keep herself from choking, Sonya, pale and shaking with horror and emotion, sat down in a low chair and burst into tears.

'How was it I saw nothing? How can it have gone so far? Can she have ceased loving Prince Andrey? And how could she have let this Kuragin go as far as this? He's a deceiver and a villain, that's clear. What will Nikolenka—dear, noble Nikolenka—do when he hears of it? So that was the meaning of her excited, determined, unnatural face the day before yesterday, and yesterday and today,' thought Sonya. 'But it's impossible that she can care for him! Most likely she opened the letter not knowing from whom it was. Most likely she feels insulted by it. She's not capable of doing such a thing!'

Sonya dried her tears and went up to Natasha, carefully scrutinising her face again.

'Natasha!' she said, hardly audibly.

Natasha waked up and saw Sonya.

'Ah, you have come back?'

And with the decision and tenderness common at the moment of awakening she embraced her friend. But noticing embarrassment in Sonya's face, her face too expressed embarrassment and suspicion.

'Sonya, you have read the letter?' she said.

'Yes,' said Sonya softly.

Natasha smiled ecstatically.

'No, Sonya, I can't help it!' she said. 'I can't keep it secret from you any longer. You know we love each other! . . . Sonya, darling, he writes . . . Sonya . . .'

Sonya gazed with wide-open eyes at Natasha, as though unable to believe her ears.

'But Bolkonsky?' she said.

'Oh Sonya, oh, if you could only know how happy I am!' said Natasha. 'You don't know what love . . .'

'But, Natasha, you can't mean that all *that* is over?'

Natasha looked with her big, wide eyes at Sonya as though not understanding her question.

'Are you breaking it off with Prince Andrey then?' said Sonya.

'Oh, you don't understand; don't talk nonsense; listen,' said Natasha, with momentary annoyance.

'No, I can't believe it,' repeated Sonya. 'I don't understand it. What, for a whole year you have been loving one man, and all at once . . . Why, you have only seen him three times. Natasha, I can't believe you, you're joking. In three days to forget everything, and like this . . .'

'Three days,' said Natasha. 'It seems to me as though I had loved him for a hundred years. It seems to me that I have never loved any one before him. You can't understand that. Sonya, stay, sit here.' Natasha hugged and kissed her. 'I have been told of its happening, and no doubt you have heard of it too, but it's only now that I have felt such love. It's not what I have felt before. As soon as I saw him, I felt that he was my sovereign and I was his slave, and that I could not help loving him. Yes, his slave! Whatever he bids me, I shall do. You don't understand that. What am I to do? What am I to do, Sonya?' said Natasha, with a blissful and frightened face.

'But only think what you are doing,' said Sonya. 'I can't leave it like this. These secret letters . . . How could you let him go so far as that?' she said, with a horror and aversion she could with difficulty conceal.

'I have told you,' answered Natasha, 'that I have no will. How is it you don't understand that? I love him!'

'Then I can't let it go on like this. I shall tell about it,' cried Sonya, with a burst of tears.

'What . . . for God's sake . . . If you tell, you are my enemy,' said Natasha. 'You want to make me miserable, and you want us to be separated . . .'

On seeing Natasha's alarm, Sonya wept tears of shame and pity for her friend.

'But what has passed between you?' she asked. 'What has he said to you? Why doesn't he come to the house?'

Natasha made no answer to her question.

'For God's sake, Sonya, don't tell any one; don't torture me,' Natasha implored her. 'Remember that it doesn't do to meddle in such matters. I have told you . . .'

'But why this secrecy? Why doesn't he come to the house?' Sonya persisted. 'Why doesn't he ask for your hand straight out? Prince Andrey, you know, gave you complete liberty, if it really is so; but I can't believe in it. Natasha, have you thought what the *secret reasons* can be?'

Natasha looked with wondering eyes at Sonya. Evidently it was the first time that question had presented itself to her, and she did not know how to answer it.

'What the reasons are, I don't know. But there must be reasons!'

Sonya sighed and shook her head distrustfully.

'If there were reasons . . .' she was beginning. But Natasha, divining her doubts, interrupted her in dismay.

'Sonya, you mustn't doubt of him; you mustn't, you mustn't! Do you understand?' she cried.

'Does he love you?'

'Does he love me?' repeated Natasha, with a smile of compassion for her friend's dullness of comprehension. 'Why, you have read his letter, haven't you? You have seen him.'

'But if he is a dishonourable man?'

'*He!* . . . a dishonourable man? If only you knew!' said Natasha.

'If he is an honourable man, he ought either to explain his intentions, or to give up seeing you; and if you won't do that, I will do it. I'll write to him. I'll tell papa,' said Sonya resolutely.

'But I can't live without him!' cried Natasha.

'Natasha, I don't understand you. And what are you saying. Think of your father, of Nikolenka.'

'I don't care for any one, I don't love any one but him. How dare you say he's dishonourable! Don't you know that I love him?' cried Natasha. 'Sonya, go away; I don't want to quarrel with you; go away, for God's sake, go away; you see how wretched I am,' cried Natasha angrily, in a voice of repressed irritation and despair. Sonya burst into sobs and ran out of the room.

Natasha went to the table, and without a moment's reflection wrote that answer to Princess Marya, which she had been unable to write all the morning. In her letter she told Princess Marya briefly that all misunderstandings between them were at an end, as taking advantage of the generosity of Prince Andrey, who had at parting given her full liberty, she begged her to forget everything and forgive her if she had been in fault in any way, but she could not be his wife. It all seemed to her so easy, so simple, and so clear at that moment.

The Rostovs were to return to the country on Friday, but on Wednesday the count went with the intending purchaser to his estate near Moscow.

On the day the count left, Sonya and Natasha were invited to a big dinner-party at Julie Karagin's, and Marya Dmitryevna took them. At that dinner Natasha met Anatole again, and Sonya noticed that Natasha said something to him, trying not to be overheard, and was all through the dinner more excited than before. When they got home, Natasha was the first to enter upon the conversation with Sonya that her friend was expecting.

'Well, Sonya, you said all sorts of silly things about him,' Natasha began in a meek voice, the voice in which children speak when they want to be praised for being good. 'I have had it all out with him today.'

'Well, what did he say? Come, what did he say? Natasha, I'm so glad you're not angry with me. Tell me everything, all the truth. What did he say?'

Natasha sank into thought.

'Oh Sonya, if you knew him as I do! He said . . . He asked me what promise I had given Bolkonsky. He was so glad that I was free to refuse him.'

Sonya sighed dejectedly.

'But you haven't refused Bolkonsky, have you?' she said.

'Oh, perhaps I have refused him! Perhaps it's all at an end with Bolkonsky. Why do you think so ill of me?'

'I don't think anything, only I don't understand this. . . .'

'Wait a little, Sonya, you will understand it all. You will see the sort of man he is. Don't think ill of me, or of him.'

'I don't think ill of any one; I like every one and am sorry for every one. But what am I to do?'

Sonya would not let herself be won over by the affectionate tone Natasha took with her. The softer and the more ingratiating Natasha's face became, the more serious and stern became the face of Sonya.

'Natasha,' she said, 'you asked me not to speak to you, and I haven't spoken; now you have begun yourself. Natasha, I don't trust him. Why this secrecy?'

'Again, again!' interrupted Natasha.

'Natasha, I am afraid for you.'

'What is there to be afraid of?'

'I am afraid you will be ruined,' said Sonya resolutely, herself horrified at what she was saying.

Natasha's face expressed anger again.

'Then I will be ruined, I will; I'll hasten to my ruin. It's not your business. It's not you, but I, will suffer for it. Leave me alone, leave me alone. I hate you!'

'Natasha!' Sonya appealed to her in dismay.

'I hate you, I hate you! And you're my enemy for ever!'

Natasha ran out of the room.

Natasha avoided Sonya and did not speak to her again. With the same expression of agitated wonder and guilt she wandered about the rooms, taking up first one occupation and then another, and throwing them aside again at once.

Hard as it was for Sonya, she kept watch over her friend and never let her out of her sight.

On the day before that fixed for the count's return, Sonya noticed that Natasha sat all the morning at the drawing-room window, as though expecting something, and that she made a sign to an officer who passed by, whom Sonya took to be Anatole.

Sonya began watching her friend even more attentively, and she noticed that all dinner-time and in the evening Natasha was in a strange and unnatural state, unlike herself. She made irrelevant replies to questions asked her, began sentences and did not finish them, and laughed at everything.

After tea Sonya saw the maid timidly waiting for her to pass at Natasha's door. She let her go in, and listening at the door, found out that another letter had been given her. And all at once it was clear to Sonya that Natasha had some dreadful plan for that evening. Sonya knocked at her door. Natasha would not let her in.

'She is going to run away with him!' thought Sonya. 'She is capable of anything. There was something particularly piteous and determined in her face today. She cried as she said good-bye to uncle,' Sonya remembered. 'Yes, it's certain, she's going to run away with him; but what am I to do?' wondered Sonya, recalling now all the signs that so clearly betokened some dreadful resolution on Natasha's part. 'The count is not here. What am I to do? Write to Kuragin, demanding an explanation from him? But who is to make him answer? Write to Pierre, as Prince Andrey asked me to do in case of trouble? . . . But perhaps she really has refused Bolkonsky (she sent off a letter to Princess Marya yesterday). Uncle is not here.'

To tell Marya Dmitryevna, who had such faith in Natasha, seemed to Sonya a fearful step to take.

'But one way or another,' thought Sonya, standing in the dark corridor, 'now or never the time has come for me to show that I am mindful of all the benefits I have received from their family and that I love Nikolay. No, if I have to go three nights together without sleep; I won't leave this corridor, and I will prevent her passing by force, and not let disgrace come upon their family,' she thought.

XVI

ANATOLE had lately moved into Dolohov's quarters. The plan for the abduction of Natasha Rostov had been all planned out and prepared several days before by Dolohov, and on the day when Sonya had listened at Natasha's door and resolved to protect her, that plan was to be put into execution. Natasha had promised to come out to Kuragin at the back entrance at ten o'clock in the evening. Kuragin was to get her into a sledge that was to be all ready with three horses in it, and to drive her off sixty versts from Moscow to the village of Kamenka, where an unfrocked priest was in readiness to perform a marriage ceremony over them. At Kamenka a relay of horses was to be in readiness, which was to take them as far as the Warsaw road, and thence they were to hasten abroad by means of post-horses.

Anatole had a passport and an order for post-horses and ten thousand roubles borrowed from his sister, and ten thousand more raised by the assistance of Dolohov.

The two witnesses of the mock marriage ceremony—Hvostikov, once a petty official, a man of whom Dolohov made use at cards, and Makarin, a retired hussar, a weak and good-natured man, whose devotion to Kuragin was unbounded—were sitting over their tea in the outer room.

In Dolohov's big study, decorated from the walls to the ceiling with Persian rugs, bearskins, and weapons, Dolohov was sitting in a travelling tunic and high boots in front of an open bureau on which lay accounts and bundles of bank notes. Anatole, in an unbuttoned uniform, was walking to and fro from the room where the witnesses were sitting through the study into a room behind, where his French valet with some other servants was packing up the last of his belongings. Dolohov was reckoning up money and noting down sums.

'Well,' he said, 'you will have to give Hvostikov two thousand.'

'Well, give it him then,' said Anatole.

'Makarka now' (their name for Makarin), 'he would go through fire and water for you with nothing to gain by it. Well, here then, our accounts are finished,' said Dolohov, showing him the paper. 'That's all right?'

'Yes, of course, it's all right,' said Anatole, evidently not attending to Dolohov, and looking straight before him with a smile that never left his face.

Dolohov shut the bureau with a slam, and turned to Anatole with an ironical smile.

'But I say, you drop it all; there's still time!' he said.

'Idiot!' said Anatole. 'Leave off talking rubbish. If only you knew. . . . Devil only knows what this means to me!'

'You'd really better drop it,' said Dolohov. 'I'm speaking in earnest. It's no joking matter this scheme of yours.'

'Why, teasing again, again? Go to the devil! Eh. . . .' said Anatole, frowning. 'Really, I'm in no humour for your stupid jokes.' And he went out of the room.

Dolohov smiled a contemptuous and supercilious smile when Anatole had gone.

'Wait a bit,' he called after Anatole. 'I'm not joking. I'm in earnest. Come here, come here!'

Anatole came back into the room, and trying to concentrate his attention, looked at Dolohov, obviously obeying him unwillingly.

'Listen to me. I'm speaking to you for the last time. What should I want to joke with you for? Have I ever thwarted you? Who was it arranged it all for you? Who found your priest? Who took your passport? Who got you your money? It has all been my doing.'

'Well, and thank you for it. Do you suppose I'm not grateful?' Anatole sighed and embraced Dolohov.

'I have helped you; but still I ought to tell you the truth: it's a dangerous business, and if you come to think of it, it's stupid. Come, you carry her off, well and good. Do you suppose they'll let it rest? It will come out that you are married. Why, they will have you up on a criminal charge, you know . . .'

'Oh, nonsense, nonsense!' said Anatole, frowning again. 'Why, didn't I explain to you? Eh?' And Anatole, with that peculiar partiality (common in persons of dull brain), for any conclusion to which they have been led by their own mental processes, repeated the argument he had repeated a hundred times over to Dolohov already. 'Why, I explained it; I settled that. If this marriage is invalid,' he said, crooking his finger, 'then it follows I'm not answerable for it. Well, and if it is valid, it won't matter. No one will ever know of it abroad, so, you see, it's all right, isn't it? And don't talk to me; don't talk to me; don't talk to me!'

'Really, you drop it. You'll get yourself into a mess...'

'You go to the devil!' said Anatole, and clutching at his hair he went off into the next room, but at once returning he sat with his legs up on an armchair close to Dolohov and facing him. 'Devil only knows what's the matter with me! Eh? See how it beats.' He took Dolohov's hand and put it on his heart. 'Ah, what a foot, my dear boy, what a glance! A goddess!' he said in French. 'Eh?'

Dolohov, with a cold smile and a gleam in his handsome, impudent eyes, looked at him, obviously disposed to get a little more amusement out of him.

'Well, your money will be gone, what then?'

'What then? Eh?' repeated Anatole, with genuine perplexity at the thought of the future. 'What then? I don't know what then ... Come, why talk nonsense?' He looked at his watch. 'It's time!'

Anatole went into the back room.

'Well, will you soon have done? You're dawdling there,' he shouted at the servants.

Dolohov put away the money; and calling a servant to give him orders about getting something to eat and drink before the journey, he went into the room where Hvostikov and Makarin were sitting.

Anatole lay down on the sofa in the study, and, propped on his elbows, smiled pensively and murmured something fervently to himself.

'Come and have something to eat. Here, have a drink!' Dolohov shouted to him from the other room.

'I don't want to,' answered Anatole, still smiling.

'Come, Balaga is here.'

Anatole got up, and went into the dining-room. Balaga was a well-known driver, who had known Dolohov and Anatole for the last six years, and driven them in his three-horse sledges. More than once, when Anatole's regiment had been stationed at Tver, he had driven him out of Tver in the evening, reached Moscow by dawn, and driven him back the next night. More than once he had driven Dolohov safe away when he was being pursued. Many a time he had driven them about the town with gypsies and 'gay ladies,' as he called them. More than one horse had he ruined in driving them. More than once he had driven over people and upset vehicles in Moscow, and always his 'gentlemen,' as he called them, had got him out of trouble. Many a time had they beaten him, many a time made him drunk with champagne and madeira, a wine he loved, and more than one exploit he knew of each of them, which would long ago have sent any ordinary man to Siberia. They often called Balaga in to their carousals, made him drink and dance with the gypsies, and many a thousand roubles of their money had passed through his hands. In their service, twenty times a year, he risked his life and his skin, and wore out more horses than they repaid him for in money. But he liked them, liked their furious driving, eighteen versts an hour, liked upsetting coachmen, and running down people on foot in Moscow, and always flew full gallop along the Moscow streets. He liked to hear behind him the wild shout of drunken voices, 'Get on; get on!' when it was impossible to drive faster; liked to give a lash on the neck to a passing peasant who was already hastening out of his way more dead than alive. 'Real gentlemen!' he thought.

Anatole and Dolohov liked Balaga, too, for his spirited driving, and because he liked the same things that they liked. With other people Balaga drove hard bargains; he would take as much as twenty-five roubles for a two hours' drive, and rarely drove himself, generally sending one of his young men. But with his own gentlemen, as he called them, he always drove himself, and never asked for anything for the job.

Only after learning through their valets when money was plentiful, he would turn up once every few months in the morning; and sober, and bowing low, would ask them to help him out of his difficulties. The gentlemen always made him sit down.

'Please, help me out of a scrape, Fyodor Ivanovitch, or your excellency,' he would say. 'I'm quite run out of horses; lend me what you can to go to the fair.'

And whenever they were flush of money Anatole and Dolohov would give him a thousand or two.

Balaga was a flaxen-headed, squat, snub-nosed peasant of seven and twenty, with a red face and a particularly red, thick neck, little sparkling eyes, and a little beard. He wore a fine blue silk-lined full coat, put on over a fur pelisse.

He crossed himself, facing the opposite corner, and went up to Dolohov, holding out his black, little hand.

'Respects to Fyodor Ivanovitch!' said he, bowing.

'Good-day to you, brother. Well, here he comes!'

'Good-morning, your excellency!' he said to Anatole as he came in, and to him, too, he held out his hand.

'I say, Balaga,' said Anatole, laying his hands on his shoulders, 'do you care for me or not? Eh? Now's the time to do me good service. ... What sort of horses have you come with? Eh?'

'As the messenger bade me; your favourite beasts,' said Balaga.

'Come, Balaga, do you hear? You may kill all three of them; only get there in three hours. Eh?'

'If I kill them, how are we to get there?' said Balaga, winking.

'None of your jokes now. I'll smash your face in!' cried Anatole suddenly, rolling his eyes.

'Jokes!' said the driver, laughing. 'Do I grudge anything for my gentlemen? As fast as ever the horses can gallop we shall get there.'

'Ah!' said Anatole. 'Well, sit down.'

'Come, sit down,' said Dolohov.

'Oh, I'll stand, Fyodor Ivanovitch.'

'Sit down; nonsense! have a drink,' said Anatole, and he poured him out a big glass of madeira. The driver's eyes sparkled at the sight of the wine. Refusing it at first for manners' sake, he tossed it off, and wiped his mouth with a red silk handkerchief that lay in his cap.

'Well, and when are we to start, your excellency?'

'Oh! . . .' Anatole looked at his watch. 'We must set off at once. Now mind, Balaga. Eh? You'll get there in time?'

'To be sure, if we've luck in getting off. Why shouldn't we do it in the time?' said Balaga. 'We got you to Tver, and got there in seven hours. You remember, I bet, your excellency!'

'Do you know, I once drove from Tver at Christmas time,' said Anatole, with a smile at the recollection, addressing Makarin, who was gazing admiringly at him. 'Would you believe it, Makarka, one could hardly breathe we flew so fast. We drove into a train of wagons and rode over two of them! Eh?'

'They were horses, too,' Balaga went on. 'I'd put two young horses in the traces with the bay in the shafts'—he turned to Dolohov—'and, would you believe me, Fyodor Ivanovitch, sixty versts those beasts galloped. There was no holding them, for my hands were numb; it was a frost. I flung down the reins. "You hold them yourself, your excellency," said I, and I rolled up inside the sledge. No need of driving them. Why, we couldn't hold them in when we got there. In three hours the devils brought us. Only the left one died of it.'

XVII

ANATOLE went out of the room, and a few minutes later he came back wearing a fur pelisse, girt with a silver belt, and a sable cap, jauntily stuck on one side, and very becoming to his handsome face. Looking at himself in the looking-glass, and then standing before Dolohov in the same attitude he had taken before the looking-glass, he took a glass of wine.

'Well, Fedya, farewell; thanks for everything, and farewell,' said

Anatole. 'Come, comrades, friends . . .'—he grew pensive—'of my youth . . farewell,' he turned to Makarin and the others.

Although they were all going with him, Anatole evidently wanted to make a touching and solemn ceremony of this address to his comrades. He spoke in a loud, deliberate voice, squaring his chest and swinging one leg.

'All take glasses; you, too, Balaga. Well, lads, friends of my youth, we have had jolly sprees together. Eh? Now, when shall we meet again? I'm going abroad! We've had a good time, and farewell, lads. Here's to our health! Hurrah! . . .' he said, tossing off his glass, and flinging it on the floor.

'To your health!' said Balaga. He, too, emptied his glass and wiped his lips with his handkerchief.

Makarin embraced Anatole with tears in his eyes.

'Ah, prince, how it grieves my heart to part from you,' he said.

'Start! start!' shouted Anatole.

Balaga was going out of the room.

'No; stay,' said Anatole. 'Shut the door; we must sit down. Like this.' They shut the door and all sat down.

'Well, now, quick march, lads!' said Anatole, getting up.

The valet, Joseph, gave Anatole his knapsack and sword, and they all went out into the vestibule.

'But where's a fur cloak?' said Dolohov. 'Hey, Ignatka! Run in to Matryona Matveyevna, and ask her for the sable cloak. I've heard what elopements are like,' said Dolohov, winking. 'She'll come skipping out more dead than alive just in the things she had on indoors; the slightest delay and then there are tears, and dear papa and dear mamma, and she's frozen in a minute and for going back again—you wrap her up in a cloak at once and carry her to the sledge.'

The valet brought a woman's fox-lined pelisse.

'Fool, I told you the sable. Hey, Matryoshka, the sable,' he shouted, so that his voice rang out through the rooms.

A handsome, thin, and pale gypsy woman, with shining black eyes and curly black hair, with a bluish shade in it, ran out, wearing a red shawl and holding a sable cloak on her arm.

'Here, I don't grudge it; take it,' she said, in visible fear of her lord, and regretful at losing the cloak.

Dolohov, making her no answer, took the cloak, flung it about Matryosha, and wrapped her up in it.

'That's the way,' said Dolohov. 'And then this is the way,' he said, and he turned the collar up round her head, leaving it only a little open before the face. 'And then this is the way, do you see?' and he moved

Anatole's head forward to meet the open space left by the collar, from which Matryosha's flashing smile peeped out.

'Well, good-bye, Matryosha,' said Anatole, kissing her. 'Ah, all my fun here is over! Give my love to Styoshka. There, good-bye! Good-bye, Matryosha; wish me happiness.'

'God grant you great happiness, prince,' said Matryosha, with her gypsy accent.

At the steps stood two three-horse sledges; two stalwart young drivers were holding them. Balaga took his seat in the foremost, and holding his elbows high, began deliberately arranging the reins in his hands. Anatole and Dolohov got in with him. Makarin, Hvostikov, and the valet got in to the other sledge.

'Ready, eh?' queried Balaga. 'Off!' he shouted, twisting the reins round his hands, and the sledge flew at break-neck pace along the Nikitsky Boulevard.

'Tprroo! Hi! . . . Tproo!' Balaga and the young driver on the box were continually shouting.

In Arbatsky Square the sledge came into collision with a carriage; there was a crash and shouts, and the sledge flew off along Arbaty. Turning twice along Podnovinsky, Balaga began to pull up, and turning back, stopped the horses at the Old Equerrys' crossing.

A smart young driver jumped down to hold the horses by the bridle; Anatole and Dolohov walked along the pavement. On reaching the gates, Dolohov whistled. The whistle was answered, and a maid-servant ran out.

'Come into the courtyard, or you'll be seen; she is coming in a minute,' she said.

Dolohov stayed at the gate. Anatole followed the maid into the courtyard, turned a corner, and ran up the steps.

He was met by Gavrilo, Marya Dmitryevna's huge groom.

'Walk this way to the mistress,' said the groom in his bass, blocking up the doorway.

'What mistress? And who are you?' Anatole asked in a breathless whisper.

'Walk in; my orders are to show you in.'

'Kuragin! back!' shouted Dolohov. 'Treachery, back!'

Dolohov, at the little back gate where he had stopped, was struggling with the porter, who was trying to shut the gate after Anatole as he ran in. With a desperate effort Dolohov shoved away the porter, and clutching at Anatole, pulled him through the gate, and ran back with him to the sledge.

XVIII

Marya Dmitryevna coming upon Sonya weeping in the corridor had forced her to confess everything. Snatching up Natasha's letter and reading it, Marya Dmitryevna went in to Natasha, with the letter in her hand.

'Vile girl, shameless hussy!' she said to her. 'I won't hear a word!' Pushing aside Natasha, who gazed at her with amazed but tearless eyes, she locked her into the room, and giving orders to her gate porter to admit the persons who would be coming that evening, but not to allow them to pass out again, and giving her grooms orders to show those persons up to her, she seated herself in the drawing-room awaiting the abductors.

When Gavrilo came to announce to Marya Dmitryevna that the persons who had come had run away, she got up frowning, and clasping her hands behind her, walked a long while up and down through her rooms, pondering what she was to do. At midnight she walked towards Natasha's room, feeling the key in her pocket. Sonya was sitting sobbing in the corridor. 'Marya Dmitryevna, do, for God's sake, let me go in to her!' she said.

Marya Dmitryevna, making her no reply, opened the door and went in. 'Hateful, disgusting, in my house, the nasty hussy, only I'm sorry for her father!' Marya Dmitryevna was thinking, trying to allay her wrath. 'Hard as it may be, I will forbid any one to speak of it, and will conceal it from the count.' Marya Dmitryevna walked with resolute steps into the room.

Natasha was lying on the sofa; she had her head hidden in her hands and did not stir. She was lying in exactly the same position in which Marya Dmitryevna had left her.

'You're a nice girl, a very nice girl!' said Marya Dmitryevna. 'Encouraging meetings with lovers in my house! There's no use in humbugging. You listen when I speak to you.' Marya Dmitryevna touched her on the arm. 'You listen when I speak. You've disgraced yourself like the lowest wench. I don't know what I couldn't do to you, but I feel for your father. I will hide it from him.'

Natasha did not change her position, only her whole body began to writhe with noiseless, convulsive sobs, which choked her. Marya Dmitryevna looked round at Sonya, and sat down on the edge of the sofa beside Natasha.

'It's lucky for him that he escaped me; but I'll get hold of him,' she said in her coarse voice. 'Do you hear what I say, eh?' She put her big hand under Natasha's face, and turned it towards her. Both Marya Dmitryevna and Sonya were surprised when they saw Natasha's face. Her eyes were glittering and dry; her lips tightly compressed; her cheeks looked sunken.

'Let me be . . . what do I . . . I shall die . . .' she articulated, with angry effort, tore herself away from Marya Dmitryevna, and fell back into the same attitude again.

'Natalya! . . .' said Marya Dmitryevna. 'I wish for your good. Lie still; come, lie still like that then, I won't touch you, and listen. . . . I'm not going to tell you how wrongly you have acted. You know that yourself. But now your father's coming back tomorrow. What am I to tell him? Eh?'

Again Natasha's body heaved with sobs.

'Well, he will hear of it, your brother, your betrothed!'

'I have no betrothed; I have refused him,' cried Natasha.

'That makes no difference,' pursued Marya Dmitryevna. 'Well, they hear of it. Do you suppose they will let the matter rest? Suppose he—your father, I know him—if he challenges him to a duel, will that be all right? Eh?'

'Oh, let me be; why did you hinder everything! Why? why? who asked you to?' cried Natasha, getting up from the sofa, and looking vindictively at Marya Dmitryevna.

'But what was it you wanted?' screamed Marya Dmitryevna, getting hot again. 'Why, you weren't shut up, were you? Who hindered his coming to the house? Why carry you off, like some gypsy wench? . . . If he had carried you off, do you suppose they wouldn't have caught him? Your father, or brother, or betrothed? He's a wretch, a scoundrel, that's what he is!'

'He's better than any of you,' cried Natasha, getting up. 'If you hadn't meddled. . . . O my God, what does it mean? Sonya, why did you? Go away! . . .' And she sobbed with a despair with which people only bewail a trouble they feel that they have brought on themselves.

Marya Dmitryevna was beginning to speak again; but Natasha cried, 'Go away, go away, you all hate me and despise me!' And she flung herself again on the sofa.

Marya Dmitryevna went on for some time longer lecturing Natasha, and urging on her that it must all be kept from the count, that no one would know anything of it if Natasha would only undertake to forget it all, and not to show a sign to any one of anything having happened. Natasha made no answer. She did not sob any more, but she was taken with shivering fits and trembling. Marya Dmitryevna put a pillow under her head, laid two quilts over her, and brought her some lime-flower water with her own hands; but Natasha made no response when she spoke to her.

'Well, let her sleep,' said Marya Dmitryevna, as she went out of the room, supposing her to be asleep. But Natasha was not asleep; her wide-open eyes gazed straight before her out of her pale face. All that night Natasha did not sleep, and did not weep, and said not a word to Sonya, who got up several times and went in to her.

Next day, at lunch time, as he had promised, Count Ilya Andreitch arrived from his estate in the environs. He was in very good spirits: he had come to terms with the purchaser, and there was nothing now to detain him in Moscow away from his countess, for whom he was pining. Marya Dmitryevna met him, and told him that Natasha had been very unwell on the previous day, that they had sent for a doctor, and that now she was better. Natasha did not leave her room that morning. With tightly shut, parched lips, and dry, staring eyes, she sat at the window, uneasily watching the passers-by along the street, and hurriedly looking round at any one who entered her room. She was obviously expecting news of him, expecting that he would come himself or would write to her.

When the count went in to her, she turned uneasily at the sound of his manly tread, and her face resumed its previous cold and even vindictive expression. She did not even get up to meet him.

'What is it, my angel; are you ill?' asked the count.

Natasha was silent a moment.

'Yes, I am ill,' she answered.

In answer to the count's inquiries why she was depressed and whether anything had happened with her betrothed, she assured him that nothing had, and begged him not to be uneasy. Marya Dmitryevna confirmed Natasha's assurances that nothing had happened. From the pretence of illness, from his daughter's agitated state, and the troubled faces of Sonya and Marya Dmitryevna, the count saw clearly that something had happened in his absence. But it was so terrible to him to believe that anything disgraceful had happened to his beloved daughter, and he so prized his own cheerful serenity, that he avoided inquiries and tried to assure himself that it was nothing very out of the way, and only grieved that her indisposition would delay their return to the country.

XIX

FROM the day of his wife's arrival in Moscow, Pierre had been intending to go away somewhere else, simply not to be with her. Soon after the Rostovs' arrival in Moscow, the impression made upon him by Natasha had impelled him to hasten in carrying out his intention. He went to Tver to see the widow of Osip Alexyevitch, who had long before promised to give him papers of the deceased's.

When Pierre came back to Moscow, he was handed a letter from Marya Dmitryevna, who summoned him to her on a matter of great importance, concerning Andrey Bolkonsky and his betrothed. Pierre had been avoiding Natasha. It seemed to him that he had for her a feeling stronger than a married man should have for a girl betrothed to his friend. And some fate was continually throwing him into her company.

'What has happened? And what do they want with me?' he thought as he dressed to go to Marya Dmitryevna's. 'If only Prince Andrey would make haste home and marry her,' thought Pierre on the way to the house.

In the Tverskoy Boulevard some one shouted his name.

'Pierre! Been back long?' a familiar voice called to him. Pierre raised his head. Anatole, with his everlasting companion Makarin, dashed by in a sledge with a pair of grey trotting-horses, who were kicking up the snow on to the forepart of the sledge. Anatole was sitting in the classic pose of military dandies, the lower part of his face muffled in his beaver collar, and his head bent a little forward. His face was fresh and rosy; his hat, with its white plume, was stuck on one side, showing his curled, pomaded hair, sprinkled with fine snow.

'Indeed, he is the real philosopher!' thought Pierre. 'He sees nothing beyond the present moment of pleasure; nothing worries him, and so he is always cheerful, satisfied, and serene. What would I not give to be just like him!' Pierre mused with envy.

In Marya Dmitryevna's entrance-hall the footman, as he took off Pierre's fur coat, told him that his mistress begged him to come to her in her bedroom.

As he opened the door into the reception-room, Pierre caught sight of Natasha, sitting at the window with a thin, pale, and ill-tempered face. She looked round at him, frowned, and with an expression of frigid dignity walked out of the room.

'What has happened?' asked Pierre, going in to Marya Dmitryevna.

'Fine doings,' answered Marya Dmitryevna. 'Fifty-eight years I have lived in the world—never have I seen anything so disgraceful.' And exacting from Pierre his word of honour not to say a word about all he was to hear, Marya Dmitryevna informed him that Natasha had broken off her engagement without the knowledge of her parents; that the cause of her doing so was Anatole Kuragin, with whom Pierre's wife had thrown her, and with whom Natasha had attempted to elope in her father's absence in order to be secretly married to him.

Pierre, with hunched shoulders and open mouth, listened to what Marya Dmitryevna was saying, hardly able to believe his ears. That Prince Andrey's fiancée, so passionately loved by him, Natasha Rostov, hitherto so charming, should give up Bolkonsky for that fool Anatole, who was married already (Pierre knew the secret of his marriage), and be so much in love with him as to consent to elope with him—that Pierre could not conceive and could not comprehend. He could not reconcile the sweet impression he had in his soul of Natasha, whom he had known from childhood, with this new conception of her baseness, folly, and cruelty. He thought of his wife. 'They are all alike,' he said to himself, reflecting he was not the only man whose unhappy fate it was to be bound to a low woman. But still he felt ready to weep with sorrow for Prince Andrey, with sorrow for his pride. And the more he felt for his friend, the greater was the contempt and even aversion with which he thought of Natasha, who had just passed him with such an expression of rigid dignity. He could not know that Natasha's heart was filled with despair, shame, and humiliation, and that it was not her fault that her face accidentally expressed dignity and severity.

'What! get married?' cried Pierre at Marya Dmitryevna's words. 'He can't get married; he is married.'

'Worse and worse,' said Marya Dmitryevna. 'He's a nice youth. A perfect scoundrel. And she's expecting him; she's been expecting him these two days. We must tell her; at least she will leave off expecting him.'

After learning from Pierre the details of Anatole's marriage, and pouring out her wrath against him in abusive epithets, Marya Dmitryevna informed Pierre of her object in sending for him. Marya Dmitryevna was afraid that the count or Bolkonsky, who might arrive any moment, might hear of the affair, though she intended to conceal it from them, and might challenge Kuragin, and she therefore begged Pierre to bid his brother-in-law from her to leave Moscow and not to dare to show himself in her presence. Pierre promised to do as she desired him, only then grasping the danger menacing the old count, and Nikolay, and Prince Andrey. After briefly and precisely explaining to him her wishes, she let him go to the drawing-room.

'Mind, the count knows nothing of it. You behave as though you know nothing,' she said to him. 'And I'll go and tell her it's no use for her to expect him! And stay to dinner, if you care to,' Marya Dmitryevna called after Pierre.

Pierre met the old count. He seemed upset and anxious. That morning Natasha had told him that she had broken off her engagement to Bolkonsky.

'I'm in trouble, in trouble, my dear fellow,' he said to Pierre, 'with those girls without the mother. I do regret now that I came. I will be open with you. Have you heard she has broken off her engagement without a word to any one. I never did, I'll admit, feel very much pleased at the marriage. He's an excellent man, of course, but still there could be no happiness against a father's will, and Natasha will never want for suitors. Still it had been going on so long, and then such a step, without her father's or her mother's knowledge! And now she's ill, and God knows what it is. It's a bad thing, count, a bad thing to have a daughter away from her mother. . . .' Pierre saw the count was greatly troubled, and tried to change the conversation to some other subject, but the count went back again to his troubles.

Sonya came into the drawing-room with an agitated face.

'Natasha is not very well; she is in her room and would like to see you. Marya Dmitryevna is with her and she asks you to come too.'

'Why, yes, you're such a great friend of Bolkonsky's; no doubt she wants to send him some message,' said the count. 'Ah, my God, my God! How happy it all was!' And clutching at his sparse locks, the count went out of the room.

Marya Dmitryevna had told Natasha that Anatole was married. Natasha would not believe her, and insisted on the statement being confirmed by Pierre himself. Sonya told Pierre this as she led him across the corridor to Natasha's room.

Natasha, pale and stern, was sitting beside Marya Dmitryevna, and she met Pierre at the door with eyes of feverish brilliance and inquiry. She did not smile nor nod to him. She simply looked hard at him, and that look asked him simply: was he a friend or an enemy like the rest, as regards Anatole? Pierre in himself had evidently no existence for her.

'He knows everything,' said Marya Dmitryevna, addressing Natasha. 'Let him tell you whether I have spoken the truth.'

As a hunted, wounded beast looks at the approaching dogs and hunters, Natasha looked from one to the other.

'Natalya Ilyinitchna,' Pierre began, dropping his eyes and conscious of a feeling of pity for her and loathing for the operation he had to perform, 'whether it is true or not cannot affect you since . . .'

'Then it is not true that he is married?'
'No; it is true.'
'Has he been married long?' she asked. 'On your word of honour?'
Pierre told her so on his word of honour.
'Is he still here?' she asked rapidly.
'Yes, I have just seen him.'
She was obviously incapable of speaking; she made a sign with her hands for them to leave her alone.

XX

PIERRE did not stay to dinner, but went away at once on leaving Natasha's room. He drove about the town looking for Anatole Kuragin, at the very thought of whom the blood rushed to his heart, and he felt a difficulty in breathing. On the ice-hills, at the gypsies', at Somoneno he was not to be found. Pierre drove to the club. In the club everything was going on just as usual: the members who had come in to dinner were sitting in groups; they greeted Pierre, and talked of the news of the town. The footman, after greeting him, told him, as he knew his friends and his habits, that there was a place left for him in the little dining-room, that Prince Mihail Zaharitch was in the library, and that Pavel Timofeitch had not come in yet. One of Pierre's acquaintances asked him in the middle of a conversation about the weather, whether he had heard of Kuragin's elopement with Natalie Rostov, of which every one was talking in the town; was it true? Pierre said, laughing, that it was all nonsense, for he had just come from the Rostovs'. He asked every one about Anatole; one man told him he had not come in yet; another said he was to dine there that day. It was strange to Pierre to look at that calm, indifferent crowd of people, who knew nothing of what was passing in his soul. He walked about the hall, waited till every one had come in, and still seeing nothing of Anatole, he did not dine, but drove home.

Anatole was dining that day with Dolohov, and consulting with him how to achieve the exploit that had miscarried. It seemed to him essential to see Natasha. In the evening he went to his sister's, to discuss with her means for arranging their meeting. When Pierre, after vainly driving about all Moscow, returned home, his valet told him that Prince Anatole Vassilyevitch was with the countess. The drawing-room of the countess was full of guests.

Pierre did not bestow a greeting on his wife, whom he had not seen since his return (she was more hateful to him than ever at that moment); he walked into the drawing-room, and seeing Anatole, went straight up to him.

'Ah, Pierre,' said the countess, going up to her husband, 'you don't know what a plight our poor Anatole is in . . .' She stopped short, seeing in her husband's bowed head, in his glittering eyes, in his resolute tread, that terrible look of rage and power, which she knew and had experienced in her own case after the duel with Dolohov.

'Wherever you are, there is vice and wickedness,' said Pierre to his wife. 'Anatole, come along, I want a word with you,' he said in French. Anatole looked round at his sister, and got up obediently, prepared to follow Pierre.

Pierre took him by the arm, drew him to him, and walked out of the room.

'If you allow yourself in my drawing-room . . .' Ellen whispered; but Pierre walked out of the room, without answering her.

Anatole followed him, with his usual jaunty swagger. But his face betrayed uneasiness. Going into his own room, Pierre shut the door, and addressed Anatole without looking at him. 'Did you promise Countess Rostov to marry her? Did you try to elope with her?'

'My dear fellow,' answered Anatole, in French (as was the whole conversation), 'I don't consider myself bound to answer questions put to me in that tone.'

Pierre's face, which had been pale before, was distorted by fury. With his big hand he clutched Anatole by the collar of his uniform, and proceeded to shake him from side to side, till Anatole's face showed a sufficient degree of terror.

'When I say I *want* a word with you . . .' Pierre repeated.

'Well, what? this is stupid. Eh?' said Anatole, feeling a button of his collar that had been torn off with the cloth.

'You're a scoundrel and a blackguard; and I don't know what prevents me from permitting myself the pleasure of braining you with this, see,' said Pierre, expressing himself so artificially, because he was speaking French. He took up a heavy paper-weight, and lifted it in a menacing way, but at once hurriedly put it down in its place.

'Did you promise to marry her?'

'I, I, . . . I . . . didn't think . . . I never promised, though, because . . .'

Pierre interrupted him.

'Have you any of her letters? Have you any letters?' Pierre repeated, advancing upon Anatole. Anatole glanced at him, and at once thrust his hand in his pocket, and took out a pocket-book.

Pierre took the letter he gave him, and pushing away a table that stood in the way, he plumped down on the sofa.

'I won't be violent, don't be afraid,' said Pierre, in response to a gesture of alarm from Anatole. 'Letters—one,' said Pierre, as though repeating a lesson to himself. 'Two'—after a moment's silence he went on, getting up again and beginning to walk about—'tomorrow you are to leave Moscow.'

'But how can I . . .?'

'Three'—Pierre went on, not heeding him—'you are never to say a word of what has passed between you and the young countess. That I know I can't prevent your doing; but if you have a spark of conscience . . .' Pierre walked several times up and down the room. Anatole sat at the table, scowling and biting his lips.

'You surely must understand that, apart from your own pleasure, there's the happiness, the peace of other people; that you are ruining a whole life, simply because you want to amuse yourself. Amuse yourself with women like my wife—with them you're within your rights, they know what it is you want of them. They are armed against you by the same experience of vice; but to promise a girl to marry her . . . to deceive, to steal . . . Surely you must see that it's as base as attacking an old man or a child! . . .'

Pierre paused and glanced at Anatole, more with inquiry now than with wrath.

'I don't know about that. Eh?' said Anatole, growing bolder as Pierre gained control over his rage. 'I don't know about that, and I don't want to,' he said, looking away from Pierre, and speaking with a slight quiver of his lower jaw, 'but you have said words to me, base and all that sort of thing, which as a man of honour I can't allow any one to do.'

Pierre looked at him in amazement, not able to understand what it was he wanted.

'Though it has been only *tête-à-tête*,' Anatole went on, 'still I can't . . .'

'What, do you want satisfaction?' said Pierre sarcastically.

'At any rate you might take back your words. Eh? If you want me to do as you wish. Eh?'

'I'll take them back, I'll take them back,' said Pierre, 'and beg you to forgive me.' Pierre could not help glancing at the loose button. 'And here's money too, if you want some for your journey.'

Anatole smiled.

The expression of that base and cringing smile, that he knew so well in his wife, infuriated Pierre. 'Oh, you vile, heartless tribe!' he cried, and walked out of the room.

Next day Anatole left for Petersburg.

XXI

PIERRE drove to Marya Dmitryevna's to report to her the execution of her commands, as to Kuragin's banishment from Moscow. The whole house was in excitement and alarm. Natasha was very ill; and as Marya Dmitryevna told him in secret, she had on the night after she had been told Anatole was married, taken arsenic, which she had procured by stealth. After swallowing a little, she had been so frightened that she waked Sonya, and told her what she had done. Antidotes had been given in time, and now she was out of danger; but she was still so weak, that they could not dream of moving her to the country, and the countess had been sent for. Pierre saw the count in great trouble, and Sonya in tears, but he could not see Natasha.

That day Pierre dined at the club, and heard on every side gossip about the attempted abduction of the young Countess Rostov, and persistently denied the story, assuring every one that the only foundation for it was that his brother-in-law had made the young lady an offer and had been refused. It seemed to Pierre that it was part of his duty to conceal the whole affair, and to save the young countess's reputation.

He was looking forward with terror to Prince Andrey's return, and drove round every day to ask for news of him from the old prince.

Prince Nikolay Andreitch heard all the rumours current in the town through Mademoiselle Bourienne; and he had read the note to Princess Marya, in which Natasha had broken off her engagement. He seemed in better spirits than usual, and looked forward with impatience to seeing his son.

A few days after Anatole's departure, Pierre received a note from Prince Andrey to inform him that he had arrived, and to beg him to go and see him.

The first minute of Prince Andrey's arrival in Moscow, he was handed by his father Natasha's note to Princess Marya, in which she broke off her engagement (the note had been stolen from Princess Marya, and given to the old prince by Mademoiselle Bourienne). He heard from his father's lips the story of Natasha's elopement, with additions.

Prince Andrey had arrived in the evening; Pierre came to see him the following morning. Pierre had expected to find Prince Andrey almost in the same state as Natasha, and he was therefore surprised when as he entered the drawing-room he heard the sound of Prince Andrey's voice in the study, loudly and eagerly discussing some Petersburg intrigue. The old prince and some other voice interrupted him from time to time. Princess Marya came out to meet Pierre. She sighed, turning her eyes towards the door of the room, where Prince Andrey was, plainly intending to express her sympathy with his sorrow; but Pierre saw by Princess Marya's face that she was glad both at what had happened and at the way her brother had taken the news of his fiancée's treachery.

'He said he had expected it,' she said. 'I know his pride will not allow him to express his feelings; but any way, he has borne it better, far better, than I had expected. It seems it was to be so ...'

'But is it all really at an end?' said Pierre.

Princess Marya looked at him with surprise. She could not understand how one could ask such a question. Pierre went into the study. Prince Andrey was very much changed, and visibly much more robust, but there was a new horizontal line between his brows. He was in civilian dress, and standing facing his father and Prince Meshtchersky, he was hotly arguing, making vigorous gesticulations.

The subject was Speransky, of whose sudden dismissal and supposed treason news had just reached Moscow.

'Now he' (Speranksy) 'will be criticised and condemned by all who were enthusiastic about him a month ago,' Prince Andrey was saying, 'and were incapable of understanding his aims. It's very easy to condemn a man when he's out of favour, and to throw upon him the blame of all the mistakes of other people. But I maintain that if anything of value has been done in the present reign, it has been done by him—by him alone ...' He stopped, seeing Pierre. His face quivered, and at once assumed a vindictive expression. 'And posterity will do him justice,' he finished, and at once turned to Pierre. 'Well, how are you, still getting stouter?' he said eagerly, but the new line was still more deeply furrowed on his forehead. 'Yes, I'm very well,' he answered to Pierre's question, and he smiled. It was clear to Pierre that his smile meant, 'I am well, but my health is of no use to any one now.'

After saying a few words to Pierre of the awful road from the frontiers of Poland, of people he had met in Switzerland who knew Pierre, and of M. Dessalle, whom he had brought back from Switzerland as a tutor for his son, Prince Andrey warmly took part again in the conversation about Speransky, which had been kept up between the two old gentlemen.

'If there had been treason, and there were proofs of his secret relations with Napoleon, they would have made them public,' he said, with heat and haste. 'I don't and I didn't like Speransky personally, but I do like justice.'

Pierre recognised now in his friend that desire he knew only too well, for excitement and discussion of something apart from himself, simply in order to stifle thoughts that were too painful and too near his heart.

When Prince Meshtchersky had gone, Prince Andrey took Pierre's arm, and asked him to come to the room that had been assigned him. In that room there was a folding bedstead and open trunks and boxes. Prince Andrey went up to one of them and took out a case. Out of the case he took a packet of letters. He did all this in silence, and very rapidly. He stood up again and cleared his throat. His face was frowning, and his lips set.

'Forgive me, if I'm troubling you . . .' Pierre saw that Prince Andrey was going to speak of Natasha, and his broad face showed sympathy and pity. That expression in Pierre's face exasperated Prince Andrey. He went on resolutely, clearly, and disagreeably: 'I have received a refusal from Countess Rostov, and rumours have reached me of your brother-in-law's seeking her hand, or something of the kind. Is that true?'

'Both true and untrue,' began Pierre; but Prince Andrey cut him short.

'Here are her letters and her portrait,' he said. He took the packet from the table and gave it to Pierre.

'Give that to the countess . . . if you will see her.'

'She is very ill,' said Pierre.

'So she's still here?' said Prince Andrey. 'And Prince Kuragin?' he asked quickly.

'He has been gone a long while. She has been at death's door.'

'I am very sorry to hear of her illness,' said Prince Andrey. He laughed a cold, malignant, unpleasant laugh like his father's.

'But M. Kuragin, then, did not deign to bestow his hand on Countess Rostov?' said Prince Andrey. He snorted several times.

'He could not have married her, because he is married,' said Pierre.

Prince Andrey laughed unpleasantly, again recalling his father.

'And where is he now, your brother-in-law, may I ask?' he said.

'He went to Peter . . . but, really, I don't know,' said Pierre.

'Well, that's no matter,' said Prince Andrey. 'Tell Countess Rostov from me that she was and is perfectly free, and that I wish her all prosperity.'

Pierre took the packet. Prince Andrey, as though reflecting whether he had not something more to say, or waiting for Pierre to say something, looked at him with a fixed gaze.

'Listen. Do you remember our discussion in Petersburg?' said Pierre. 'Do you remember about———?'

'I remember,' Prince Andrey answered hurriedly. 'I said that a fallen woman should be forgiven, but I did not say I could forgive one. I can't.'

'How can you compare it? . . .' said Pierre.

Prince Andrey cut him short. He cried harshly: 'Yes, ask her hand again, be magnanimous, and all that sort of thing? . . . Oh, that's all very noble, but I'm not equal to following in that gentleman's tracks. If you care to remain my friend, never speak to me of that . . . of all this business. Well, good-bye. So you'll give that? . . .'

Pierre left him, and went in to the old prince and Princess Marya.

The old man seemed livelier than usual. Princess Marya was the same as usual, but behind her sympathy for her brother, Pierre detected her relief that her brother's marriage was broken off. Looking at them, Pierre felt what a contempt and dislike they all had for the Rostovs; felt that it would be impossible in their presence even to mention the name of the girl who could give up Prince Andrey for any one in the world.

At dinner they talked of the coming war, of which there could now be no doubt in the near future. Prince Andrey talked incessantly, and argued first with his father, and then with Dessalle, the Swiss tutor. He seemed more eager than usual, with that eagerness of which Pierre knew so well the inner cause.

XXII

THAT evening Pierre went to the Rostovs' to fulfil Prince Andrey's commission. Natasha was in bed, the count was at the club, and Pierre, after giving the letters to Sonya, went in to see Marya Dmitryevna, who was interested to know how Prince Andrey had taken the news. Ten minutes later, Sonya came in to Marya Dmitryevna.

'Natasha insists on seeing Count Pyotr Kirillitch,' she said.

'Why, are we to take him up to her, eh? Why, you are all in a muddle there,' said Marya Dmitryevna.

'No, she has dressed and gone into the drawing-room,' said Sonya.

Marya Dmitryevna could only shrug her shoulders. 'When will the countess come, she has quite worn me out? You mind now, don't tell her everything,' she said to Pierre. 'One hasn't the heart to scold her, she's so piteous, poor thing.'

Natasha was standing in the middle of the drawing-room, looking thinner, and with a pale, set face (not at all overcome with shame, as Pierre had expected to see her). When Pierre appeared in the doorway, she made a hurried movement, evidently in uncertainty whether to go to meet him, or to wait for him to come to her.

Pierre went hurriedly towards her. He thought she would give him her hand as usual. But coming near him she stopped, breathing hard, and letting her hands hang lifelessly, exactly in the same pose in which she used to stand in the middle of the room to sing, but with an utterly different expression.

'Pyotr Kirillitch,' she began, speaking quickly, 'Prince Bolkonsky was your friend—he is your friend,' she corrected herself. (It seemed to her that everything was in the past, and now all was changed.) 'He told me to apply to you . . .'

Pierre choked dumbly as he looked at her. Till then he had in his heart blamed her, and tried to despise her; but now he felt so sorry for her, that there was no room in his heart for blame.

'He is here now, tell him . . . to for . . . to forgive me.' She stopped short and breathed even more quickly, but she did not weep.

'Yes . . . I will tell him,' said Pierre; 'but . . .' He did not know what to say.

Natasha was evidently dismayed at the idea that might have occurred to Pierre.

'No, I know that everything is over,' she said hurriedly. 'No, that can never be. I'm only wretched at the wrong I have done him. Only tell him that I beg him to forgive, to forgive, forgive me for everything . . .' Her whole body was heaving; she sat down on a chair.

A feeling of pity he had never known before flooded Pierre's heart.

'I will tell him, I will tell him everything once more,' said Pierre; 'but . . . I should like to know one thing . . .'

'To know what?' Natasha's eyes asked.

'I should like to know, did you love . . .' Pierre did not know what to call Anatole, and flushed at the thought of him—'did you love that bad man?'

'Don't call him bad, said Natasha. 'But I don't . . . know, I don't know . . .' She began crying again, and Pierre was more than ever overwhelmed with pity, tenderness, and love. He felt the tears trickling under his spectacles, and hoped they would not be noticed.

'We won't talk any more of it, my dear,' he said. It seemed suddenly so strange to Natasha to hear the gentle, tender, sympathetic voice in which he spoke. 'We won't talk of it, my dear, I'll tell him everything. But one thing I beg you, look on me as your friend; and if you want help, advice, or simply want to open your heart to some one—not now, but when things are clearer in your heart—think of me.' He took her hand and kissed it. 'I shall be happy, if I am able . . .' Pierre was confused.

'Don't speak to me like that; I'm not worth it!' cried Natasha, and she would have left the room, but Pierre held her hand. He knew there was something more he must say to her. But when he said it, he was surprised at his own words.

'Hush, hush, your whole life lies before you,' he said to her.

'Before me! No! All is over for me,' she said, with shame and self-humiliation.

'All over?' he repeated. 'If I were not myself, but the handsomest, cleverest, best man in the world, and if I were free I would be on my knees this minute to beg for your hand and your love.'

For the first time for many days Natasha wept with tears of gratitude and softened feeling, and glancing at Pierre, she went out of the room.

Pierre followed her, almost running into the vestibule, and restraining the tears of tenderness and happiness that made a lump in his throat. He flung on his fur coat, unable to find the armholes, and got into his sledge.

'Now where, your excellency?' asked the coachman.

'Where?' Pierre asked himself. 'Where can I go now? Not to the club or to pay calls.' All men seemed to him so pitiful, so poor in comparison with the feeling of tenderness and love in his heart, in comparison with that softened, grateful glance she had turned upon him that last minute through her tears.

'Home,' said Pierre, throwing open the bearskin coat over his broad, joyously breathing chest in spite of ten degrees of frost.

It was clear and frosty. Over the dirty, half-dark streets, over the black roofs was a dark, starlit sky. It was only looking at the sky that Pierre forgot the mortifying meanness of all things earthly in comparison with the height his soul had risen to. As he drove into Arbatsky Square, the immense expanse of dark, starlit sky lay open before Pierre's eyes. Almost in the centre of it above the Prechistensky Boulevard, surrounded on all sides by stars, but distinguished from all by its nearness to the earth, its white light and long, upturned tail, shone the huge, brilliant comet of 1812; the comet which betokened, it was said, all manner of horrors and the end of the world. But in Pierre's heart that bright comet, with its long, luminous tail, aroused no feeling of dread. On the contrary, his eyes wet with tears, Pierre looked joyously at this bright comet, which seemed as though after flying with inconceivable swiftness through infinite space in a parabola, it had suddenly, like an arrow piercing the earth, stuck fast at one chosen spot in the black sky, and stayed there, vigorously tossing up its tail, shining and playing with its white light among the countless other twinkling stars. It seemed to Pierre that it was in full harmony with what was in his softened and emboldened heart, that had gained vigour to blossom into a new life.